The
Later India
Novels
Part B

The Collected Novels of P. C. Wren
Volume 5B

Fiction Titles by P. C. Wren

Dew and Mildew. 1912
Father Gregory. 1913
The Snake and Sword. 1914.
Driftwood Spars. 1916
The Wages of Virtue. 1916
The Young Stagers. 1917
Stepsons of France. 1917
Cupid in Africa. 1920
Beau Geste. 1924
Beau Sabreur. 1926
Beau Ideal. 1928
Good Gestes. 1929
Soldiers of Misfortune. 1929
The Mammon of Righteousness. 1930 (U.S. title:
      Mammon)
Mysterious Waye. 1930
Sowing Glory. 1931
Valiant Dust. 1932
Flawed Blades. 1933
Action and Passion. 1933
Port o' Missing Men. 1934
Beggars' Horses. 1934 (U.S. title: The Dark Woman)
Sinbad the Soldier. 1935
Explosion. 1935
Spanish Maine. 1935 (U.S. title: The Desert Heritage)
Bubble Reputation. 1936 (U.S. title: The Cortenay
      Treasure)
Fort in the Jungle. 1936
The Man of a Ghost. 1937 (U.S. title: The Spur of Pride)
Worth Wile. 1937 (U.S. title: To the Hilt)
Cardboard Castle. 1938
Rough Shooting. 1938
Paper Prison. 1939 (U.S. Title: The Man the Devil
      Didn't Want)
The Disappearance of General Jason. 1940
Two Feet From Heaven. 1940
The Uniform of Glory. 1941
Odd—But Even So. 1941

The Later India Novels

Part B

by

Percival Christopher Wren

THE MAN OF A GHOST
WORTH WILE

Edited

by

John L. Espley

Riner Publishing Company
Culpeper Virginia
2019

ISBN
9780999074954

The text of *The Man of a Ghost* will be in the Public Domain as of 1 January 2033 since it was originally published in 1937

The text of *Worth Wile* will be in the Public Domain as of 1 January 2033 since it was originally published in 1937

Contents

PREFACE

The Later India Novels Part A and *The Later India Novels Part B* by Percival Christopher Wren are the fifth of a multi-volume series, *The Collected Novels of P. C. Wren.* The purpose of publishing this series is to make the novels written by P. C. Wren more available to the reading public. His novel, *Beau Geste*, is usually recognized by most of the book dealers I have met over the years, but his other works are not so easily remembered.

I have been collecting P. C. Wren for over fifty years, and have been working on a comprehensive bibliography for almost as long. The text of the twenty-eight novels was easily obtained from copies in my own collection. For that collection, I certainly need to thank the hundreds of used book dealers I have purchased items from, and I need to thank some by name: Steven Temple, David Mason, Walt Barrie and, especially, the late Denis McDonnell for the advice and help they have provided over the years.

Mr. John Venmore and Mr. Philip Fairweather, both descendants of the late Mr. Richard Alan Graham-Smith, Wren's stepson and the executor of Wren's estate, have both been very helpful in providing information about Wren.

As it has been over seventy years since the death of P. C. Wren (November 21, 1941), Wren's works have passed into the public domain in the United Kingdom. In the United States, fourteen of the twenty-eight novels are still under copyright. Thanks to information provided by Messrs. Venmore and Fairweather, the heirs to Wren's literary estate, Mr. Danny Adekoya Campbell and Mr. Christopher Oladipo Graham-Smith, were located and permission has been granted to reprint Wren's works.

I also need to acknowledge the help and guidance of my family members: my daughter and son-in-law,

Dawn and Andrew; my son and daughter-in-law, Jared and Claudia; and my long-suffering wife, Cathy. Thank you.

In conclusion, I need to thank Percival Christopher Wren for the many years of great enjoyment that his stories have provided. I know that Wren is not a literary or critical success, but, for me, he is one of the great storytellers of the early twentieth century.

John L. Espley
Culpeper, Virginia
June 14, 2019

INTRODUCTION

Percival Christopher Wren is best known as a novelist, publishing twenty-eight novels from 1912 to 1941, the most famous being *Beau Geste* (1924). Wren also published seven short story collections; *Stepsons of France* (1917), *The Young Stagers* (1917), *Good Gestes* (1929), *Flawed Blades* (1933), *Port o' Missing Men* (1934), *Rough Shooting* (1938), and *Odd—But Even So* (1941), containing a total of 116 stories. There were also two omnibus collections, *Stories of the Foreign Legion* (1947) and *Dead Men's Boots* (1949), containing stories selected from *Stepsons of France*, *Good Gestes, Flawed Blades*, and *Port o' Missing Men*. All 116 short stories can be found in the five volume collection, *The Collected Short Stories of Percival Christopher Wren.*[1]

Wren was a man of mystery in that the majority of biographical statements about him seem to be more fiction than fact. A typical biography places his birth in Devon in 1885, his education at Oxford, and his career as that of world traveler, hunter, journalist, tramp, British cavalry trooper, legionnaire in the French Foreign Legion, assistant director of education in Bombay, and a Justice of the Peace. Most of the above biography, however, is false or has not been verified.

Wren was born Percy Wren on November 1, 1875 in Deptford, a district of South London on the banks of the Thames. He did attend Oxford University, graduating in 1898 with a 3rd class honours in History leading to a Bachelor of Arts degree. He attained his "M.A." in 1901. In those days, a person acquired a "M.A." after a certain number of years (three in Wren's case) and upon payment of a fee.

After leaving Oxford, he married Alice Lucie

---

[1] For further information on *The Collected Short Stories of Percival Christopher Wren* see rinerpublishing.wordpress.com

Shovelier in December 1899 with whom he had a daughter, Estelle Lenore Wren, born in February 1901, and a son, Percival Rupert Christopher Wren, born in February 1904. Percy worked as a teacher at various commercial schools until 1903, when he and his family left England for India.

From 1903 to approximately 1919, Wren was employed as an educator by the Indian Educational Service (I.E.S.). During that time he published a number of educational textbooks, some of which are still in use in Indian schools today. It was during this period that he started using the name Percival C. and Percival Christopher on the textbooks.

From 1905 to 1915, he also served in the Volunteer Corps (Sind and Poona) in India (see the novel *Driftwood Spars*, which contains a description of a Volunteer Corps), and was appointed a Captain in the Indian Army Reserve of Officers, the 101st Grenadiers of the Indian Infantry, in November 1914. He probably saw action in the East African campaign of World War I (see the novel *Cupid in Africa*, which takes place in East Africa during the War), and resigned from the Indian Army Reserve of Officers in November 1915.[2]

Wren's first novel, *Dew and Mildew*, was published by Longmans, Green in 1912. His first novel of the French Foreign Legion, *The Wages of Virtue*, was written in 1913 and published by John Murray in 1916. One of the many questions about Wren is whether he did serve in the French Foreign Legion. Given the chronology of his documented biography it is difficult to see where he had time to actually serve in the Legion.[3] Wren himself always maintained that he

---

[2] Most of the biographical information about Wren has been obtained through certificates, documents, and original research at the British Library, Bodleian Library, and the India Office papers. Further information on Wren and his works was obtained during a three week research visit in September 2018 at the John Murray Archives in the National Library of Scotland. Detailed documentation and sources will be cited in the biographical essay to be included in the forthcoming publication, *An Annotated Bibliography of Percival Christopher Wren*.

[3] After examining just over half of the available files at the John Murray Archives, it is evident that Wren was consistent about serving in the Legion. The only available time though would have been between 1891, when Wren was fifteen and 1894 when he entered Oxford, shortly before he was nineteen.

had served and his stepson, Richard Alan Graham-Smith, who died in 2006, "strongly maintained that Wren had indeed served in the French Foreign Legion and was always quick to refute those who said otherwise."[4]

*   *   *   *   *   *   *

The series, *The Collected Novels of P. C. Wren*, is intended to include all twenty-eight novels in seven thematic omnibus volumes. The number of physical volumes will be fourteen, with each thematic volume divided into Part A and Part B. The individual titles will not be in Wren's original publication order, but will instead have a connecting theme such as characters or locale. The seven volumes are:[5]

> v. 1 - The Geste Novels
>> Part A:
>>> Beau Geste
>>> Beau Sabreur
>> Part B:
>>> Beau Ideal
>>> Spanish Maine
> v. 2 - The Sinbad Novels
>> Part A:
>>> Action and Passion
>>> Sinbad the Soldier
>> Part B:
>>> Fort in the Jungle
>>> The Disappearance of General Jason
> v. 3 - The Foreign Legion Novels
>> Part A:
>>> The Wages of Virtue
>>> Sowing Glory
>> Part B:
>>> The Uniform of Glory
>>> Paper Prison

---

[4] wikipedia.org/wiki/P._C._Wren
[5] The order of volumes four through seven has been modified since the publication of volume two.

*   *   *   *   *   *   *

Volume Five of *The Collected Novels of P. C. Wren*, *The Later India Novels*, contains four novels located primarily in India that Wren published later in his career: *Beggars' Horses*, *Explosion*, *The Man of a Ghost*, and *Worth Wile*. All four novels are loosely connected in that characters in *Beggars' Horses* and *Explosion* appear or are mentioned in *The Man of a Ghost* and *Worth Wile*.

---

[6] Previous to May 2019 volume seven's title was "The Other Novels".

*　　*　　*　　*　　*　　*　　*

The Later India Novels Part B

The Later India Novels Part B contains two novels,
The Man of a Ghost and *Worth Wile*, that could be
considered just one long novel since *Worth Wile* is a
direct sequel to *The Man of a Ghost*. Both novels are
concerned with the story of Richard Wendover and are
typical adventure novels of the "Northwest Frontier" of
British India, which were very popular in the early
twentieth century in both book and film productions.

The Man of a Ghost begins in East Africa during
World War I where Wendover is the commanding officer
of a small outpost on a remote river. The only other
surviving officer is the medical doctor, Breckinge, an
Eurasian, who dislikes Wendover immensely for a perceived prejudice against mixed races. Breckinge, in
collusion with the senior native officers, drugs Wendover and, when a relief force arrives, the Colonel finds
Wendover in an apparent drunken state: while on duty!
Wendover is subsequently court-martialed and dishon-
orably discharged. In disgrace, Wendover wanders over
East Africa with his former orderly, Shere Khan, a
Pathan. Wendover fakes his death and, eventually, he
and Shere Khan make their way to the mountains of
the Northwest Frontier and Afghanistan.

While on a Secret Service trip in the mountains, a
friend of Wendover's, Ganesh Hazelrigg from *Beggars'
Horses*, discovers Wendover is still alive. Hazelrigg has
never believed that Wendover was guilty and sets out
to prove it. At the conclusion of the novel, Hazelrigg,
Wendover, and Shere Khan are in a British fort under
siege from Pathan raiders. The regular British officers
in the fort are all dead except for the medical doctor,
Breckinge, who is negotiating with the leader of the
Pathans to surrender the fort and abandon the sick
and wounded. Hazelrigg and Wendover prevent the
surrender and compel Breckinge to sign a confession
about Wendover's drug-induced coma in Africa. At the
end, Breckinge saves Wendover's life and Wendover

refuses to use the confession.

Worth Wile is the conclusion to the story of Richard Wendover. The book starts out seemingly unrelated to *The Man of a Ghost* with the story of a military airplane raid that crashes in the mountains of the Northwest Frontier. A young airman, John Vere-Vaughan, survives the crash and is taken prisoner by the Pathans who are undecided as to whether to kill him or hold him for ransom. This story comprises the first quarter of the book. The novel then continues with a flashback to when Wendover was a young boy and introduces his best friend, Sybil Ffoulkes. Sybil is one of Wren's typical girls, an all-around "tom-boy" who is in love with the hero, similar to Isabel in the "Beau" novels, Lucille in *The Snake and the Sword*, and Margaret in *Soldiers of Misfortune* and *Valiant Dust*. The tale continues by summarizing Wendover's story from *The Man of a Ghost*, but provides more information on a villain only briefly mentioned in that book: Prince (and Commissar) Bailitzin who was a rival for Sybil's hand. With the rise of the Soviet Union, Bailitzin becomes a Russian secret service agent and is involved in capturing and torturing Wendover, believing him to be a British secret service agent. With the help of Shere Khan, Wendover eventually escapes and vows revenge on Bailitzin.

Wendover becomes aware of a plot to use the captured airman, Vere-Vaughan, as a ruse for a gang of Pathan outlaws to capture a British fort. Vere-Vaughan is unaware of the plot and thinks the Pathans are only interested in the ransom for returning him. Wendover is unsuccessful in rescuing Vere-Vaughan, but a native soldier in the fort recognizes the outlaws and they are captured. Vere-Vaughan is accused of being a traitor and a coward. Wendover is able to tell the British officials in Peshawar that Vere-Vaughan was merely a dupe, but only after Wendover is restored to his proper station and office. In the meantime, Sybil has come out to the frontier town of Peshawar on Hazelrigg's advice to try to rescue Wendover. After the reinstatement of Wendover and Vere-

Introduction

Vaughan, a tragic series of events occur where Wend-over has to break Shere Khan out of jail and flee back to the mountains.

The Man of a Ghost and *Worth Wile* were written and published late in Wren's career, but they are both of the type of book that Wren is best known for: adventure stories. The books are notable for their relevance to today's headlines about conflict in the mountains of Afghanistan and western Pakistan. For example, the plan, in *Worth Wile*, to infiltrate the British fort with seemingly friendly Pathans, and the occurrence of attacks on Western soldiers by "friendly" forces in the Afghanistan of today. Also, Wren's writing about the life and thinking of Pathans does not seem that much different from what is read in accounts written today.

The manuscript for *The Man of a Ghost* was sent to Wren's publisher in early January 1936, and a few days later Sir John Murray wrote he "can honestly say that I have never enjoyed a story of yours more." The contract between Wren and John Murray for a first edition printing of *The Man of a Ghost* of 10,000 copies with a twenty-five percent royalty was signed in the middle of January.[7] It was not until later that year in October that Houghton Mifflin wrote to John Murray, saying that they liked the book "very much", but wanted to change the title from *The Man of a Ghost* to *The Spur of Pride*. Due to a lack of coordination between Houghton Mifflin and Wren's foreign agent, Curtis Brown, and to the annoyance of John Murray and Wren, the usual simultaneous publication between the English and American editions of Wren's books was not done. *The Spur of Pride* was published by Houghton Mifflin on 5 January 1937 and *The Man of a Ghost* was published on 16 February 1937.[8]

Worth Wile, submitted on 26 January 1937 and, according to Wren written under difficult and disheartening conditions due to illness, was still "better

---

[7] John Murray Archive, National Library of Scotland (cited hereafter as JMA), file Acc. 13328/16 CU18, dates of 6, 9, and 14 January 1936.
[8] JMA, file Acc. 13328/16 CU18, dates of 23 and 30 October 1936, and 13 and 15 January 1937.

than *The Man of a Ghost*. There is more to it, and I think it will have a wide appeal to the feminine public."[9] Again, Houghton Mifflin wanted to change the title of *Worth Wile*, but Wren was not happy with the new title, *To the Hilt*. Wren wrote that "*To the Hilt* is common place, childish and obviously the product of a thoroughly second-rate mind: I would enter a mild protest against them, save for the fact that presumably they know their business and the sort of title that is calculated to appeal to the American reader. And if we did adopt *To the Hilt*, it is more probable the film producer would choose a third and worse one!"[10]

John Murray originally wanted *Worth Wile* to be published sometime in October 1937, but Houghton Mifflin wanted an earlier publication date in August 1937. The compromise was that *Worth Wile* was published on 6 September 1937 by John Murray and as *To the Hilt* on 7 September 1937 by Houghton Mifflin.[11]

In addition to the usual differences between British and American spelling and punctuation, there are significant differences in the length (word count) in the British and American editions of both novels. *The Spur of Pride* (the Houghton Mifflin title) is approximately fourteen percent less than *The Man of a Ghost*. *To the Hilt* (the Houghton Mifflin title) is approximately twenty-four percent less than *Worth Wile*.[12]

Wren was always anxious to get his books produced as motion pictures, and *The Man of a Ghost* and *Worth Wile* were no exceptions. *The Man of a Ghost* was close to actually being made into a film, but the project eventually failed. As early as November 1936 there is correspondence regarding "the film people" wanting permission to use no more than 3,500 words for publicity either in print form or on the radio. A contract was signed with Loew's Inc. on 22 December

---

[9] JMA, file Acc. 12927/279 F53, dates of 26 January and 16 February 1937.
[10] JMA, file Acc. 12927/279 F53, date of 13 May 1937.
[11] JMA, file Acc. 12927/279 F53, dates of 1, 8, 10, and 13 July 1937.
[12] The actual word count in the digital files for *The Man of Ghost* is 93,655 words, and for *The Spur of Pride*, is 80,699 words, for a difference of 12,956 words. The word count for *Worth Wile* is 122,895 words, and for *To the Hilt*, it is 93,813 words, for a difference of 29,082 words.

1936 (Loew's Inc. being the parent company to Metro-Goldwyn-Mayer Studios (MGM) at that time).[13] In February 1937 Wren wrote that he had heard that Adoph Zuker and Paramount intend to beat their previous *Beau Geste* record with the 1939 *Beau Geste* film, and that MGM intends to beat them with *The Man of a Ghost* (*The Spur of Pride*), and that both films (*Beau Geste* and *The Spur of Pride*) are already cast and under way.[14] Louella O. Parsons, a popular Hollywood gossip/news columnist, wrote that Clark Gable and Robert Taylor wanted to do a picture together, and that MGM had purchased rights to *The Spur of Pride*, but that the film "won't be filmed, however, until next fall or winter."[15] No documented evidence has been seen to explain why the film was never produced, but *Gone with the Wind* with Clark Gable was issued the same year as Paramount's 1939 *Beau Geste*.[16]

The dedication in *The Man of a Ghost*, "To Negley Farson with the hope that *The Way of the Transgressor* may be long", is slightly different in the Houghton Mifflin edition, which ends with "may long be continued," instead of "may be long."

There is no dedication in the American edition of *Worth Wile*, but the English edition has "To Dr. Maurice Campbell, physician to Guy's Hospital London". In a copy of a first edition of *Worth Wile*, inscribed by Wren to Dr. Campbell, was inserted two typed letters from Wren to Campbell and a small handwritten note (presumably written by Campbell). The first letter, dated 18 November 1936, is Wren thanking Dr. Campbell "[. . .] for the tremendous care and attention you gave me; and also for your patience and courtesy in explaining everything to my wife." The letter concludes with Wren stating that he is sending a few of his books to Campbell. The second, longer, letter, dated 19 July 1937, has some information about Wren's condition, at

---

[13] JMA, file Acc. 13328/16 CU18, dates of 19 November and 22 December 1936.
[14] JMA, file Acc. 12927/279 F53, date of 16 February 1937.
[15] Parsons, Louella O. "Tie This—Gable, Taylor in Same Picture", in various newspapers, including *The San Antonio Light*, 20 February 1937.
[16] Further research on this topic of the film *The Spur of Pride* is required.

least as he perceived it. "My heart stood up to the prolonged acute pain splendidly, and it seems almost normal now, inasmuch as I go for days and nights without being conscious of it. The diabetes is quite in abeyance, and now that the kidney pain-and-illness has gone, I have only colitis left to comfort me." The handwritten, unsigned, note states: "Only one patient, P. C. Wren, dedicated a book to me and unfortunately it was not as good as *Beau Geste*. He thought there must be something the matter with his heart because when he sat at his desk no ideas would flow for a new book. Considering the number he had written it was not surprising but it was not easy to explain. I saw him many times over several years."

The *Man of a Ghost* was reprinted in 1952 in a paperback series, Cherry Tree Books, and again in 1973 by Remploy. *Worth Wile* has not been reprinted until this edition by the Riner Publishing Company.

*   *   *   *   *   *   *

The original spelling, punctuation, and grammar of the British editions, except for obvious errors, has been preserved as found in the latest editions/printings of the stories during Wren's lifetime (1875-1941). The footnotes, in the novels, are also as found in the original source material.

THE MAN OF A GHOST

TO

NEGLEY FARSON

<small>WITH THE HOPE THAT</small>

THE WAY OF THE TRANSGRESSOR

<small>MAY BE LONG</small>

PROLOGUE

There is a haunted bungalow at Napierpur, in India, the scene of a tragedy in Mutiny or pre-Mutiny days.

On the night before the return of Captain Thorburn of Napier's Horse, they were talking about it, as it happened, at Mess, the latest-joined subaltern (an amateur of the occult) being curious and interested.

The Senior Subaltern, a profound believer, was laughed to scorn by his Squadron-Leader, a sceptic and a cynic, who believed in what he saw, and then only when strictly sober.

And, as the discussion developed, there emerged as usual the three attitudes, that of the unbelievers, that of the believers, and that of the open-minded unconvinced. But definitely the sceptics prevailed, mightily, and with contempt.

It was thus a curious coincidence, that on his return next day, Captain Thorburn—tall and slim, fair, with pale-blue eyes and a pointed inquisitive nose above a little upturned wiry moustache which in nowise concealed the firm lips of a well-cut mouth, least imaginative and most matter-of-fact of men—should announce that he had seen a ghost.

He had gone on shooting-leave, had travelled by train to Karachi, and thence by native bunder-boat along the Mekran coast to a mountainous spot where ibex were sometimes to be found. But Fortune had not favoured the brave *shikari*.

"Well, Thorburn, see any ibex?" enquired Colonel Warre, commanding Napier's Horse, tall, grey, grim and saturnine, greeting Captain Thorburn at lunch next day.

"No, Sir. Saw nothing at all . . . except a ghost," was the reply.

"A ghost? What, in the Talar Mountains?"

"No, Sir. Near a caravanserai at Godoz, on the

Gulf."

"*Ghost!*" snapped Major Sampson, thick-set, short, rubicund and endowed with a liver. "Ghost—in a caravanserai. Ghost of a man, d'ye mean?"

"Yes," replied Thorburn, "in a manner of speaking."

"Or perhaps it was really the man of a ghost," he added, smiling.

"What the devil *are* you talking about?" enquired Major Sampson.

"A ghost . . . The ghost of a man," replied Thorburn, in his quiet and serious way.

"What man?"

"Richard Wendover."

"What!" ejaculated the Colonel. "Good God! You don't mean to say . . ."

"I do, Sir. He was the man of this ghost, I'll swear."

"You've been dreaming—or drinking," growled the Major. "No wonder you didn't see any ibex . . . *Richard Wendover!* What next? . . ."

"Tell us," requested the Colonel.

"Well, I had made the *naukhada* of my bunder-boat put in several times between Karachi and Godoz; places like the mouth of the Hingol River, Ormara, Basul River, Pasni, and such, and had tried to get *khabar*[17] of ibex. I had no luck, and decided to get a bit farther inland. My *shikari* made a camel-*bandobast*,[18] and I made a chukka round, overland, and struck the coast near Godoz, where the boat was waiting for me. A few miles outside Godoz there is an old caravanserai and, near it, I found a biggish camp and camel-market, with all sorts of *budmashes*[19] loafing around; Afghans, Baluchis, Ghilzais, Afridis, Mahsuds, Mohmands and assorted Pathan ruffians, a very tough crowd who might quite well have been with one of the Powindah gun-running gangs.

"As my little caravan rode by this camp, I noticed that the camel-guards, loafing about, eyed me without enthusiasm or affection, quite definitely."

---

[17] *News.*

[18] *Arrangement.*

[19] *Scoundrels, rogues.*

"Probably thought you were a Secret Service man on this anti-gun-running stunt," observed the Colonel.

"That's what I thought, and didn't linger, but pushed straight on towards Godoz. And just beyond this camp, in a very narrow pass, between precipices, I met a couple of Pathans on the track leading to it. One of those two Pathans was the ghost I have mentioned."

"The ghost of Richard Wendover!" mused the Colonel, nodding his head slowly.

"Are you absolutely certain?" asked a guest of the Napier's Horse Mess, a Major Hazelrigg, known as "Ganesh the Elephant God," who appeared deeply interested. "*Really* Richard Wendover?"

Major Sampson emitted a loud and somewhat unpleasant noise which was either a snort of derision, a laugh of contempt, or a combination of the two.

"Why, the feller was killed in Africa," he said. "They found his body. That chap building the Tabundi Railway buried him, didn't he?"

"This was Richard Wendover—or his ghost," repeated Captain Thorburn.

"In point of fact, you really saw a Pathan who faintly resembled Wendover—or you thought you did," growled Major Sampson. "And as you didn't see any ibex, you come back and tell us you saw the ghost of a man, eh?"

"Or the man of a ghost," murmured Ganesh Hazelrigg softly. "The live man of a poor dead ghost, eh?"

"It was the ghost of Richard Wendover, then," smiled Thorburn.

"Resemblance as strong as all that, was it?" observed the Colonel.

"And stronger," replied Thorburn quietly. "I spoke to the—ghost.

"'*Salaam-un-alaik,*' said I, and the ghost's companion promptly replied:

"'*Alaik-us-salaam.*'

"'*May you never be tired,*' said I correctly, in my best Pushtu, and,

"'*May you never be poor,*' duly countered the ghost's companion, as the Pathan always does. But never a

5

word spake the ghost—whom I had addressed personally, directly and pointedly—which struck me as
curious; or rather, as not at all curious, but as entirely
bearing out my belief, fantastic as that was.

"And before they could dismount on the narrow
path where there was no room to pass mounted, I leant
across to him, to it, to the ghost, and said quietly, in
English:

"'*I know your face.*'

"And,

"'*Congratulations*,' replied the ghost unpleasantly in
purest English and with a bitter sort of sneer. '*So nice
for you.*'

"And the man of that ghost was undoubtedly
Richard Wendover, for in that sentence I recognized his
voice and knew it as well as I knew his face.

"'*And I know your name*,' I added.

"'*So do I*,' said the ghost.

"'*It is . . .*' I began.

"'*Gul Mahommed*,' he interrupted.

"'*I see*,' said I.

"'*I'm glad you do*,' said he, and added, '*I suppose
you haven't a train to catch, or anything?*'

"As the nearest train was a few hundred miles
away, I hadn't; but I took the hint, and yet I hated
going off and leaving him like that.

"'*Look here, is there anything I can do for you—er—
Gul Mahommed?*' I said.

"'*Yes*,' replied the ghost. '*You can push on.*'

"'*In fact*,' said I, '*you'd prefer that I should* 'wend
over' *the hill there, eh?*'

"And with an impish grin that I knew, oh, so well,
and the short laugh of a man who has forgotten how to
laugh, Wendover nodded."

"And of course that clinched it, eh?" mused Ganesh
Hazelrigg. "Yes, I think you did see—a ghost."

"I know I did, Sir . . . And the man of that ghost was
Richard Wendover who once was one of Us," replied
Captain Thorburn.

Major Sampson snorted; the Colonel pursed

judgmatic lips as he wrinkled thoughtful considering brows; and Major Ganesh Hazelrigg made careful note that his beloved friend, Richard Wendover, long believed to be dead, was alive, was in Mekran, was apparently engaged in gun-running, and was probably on his way to Afghanistan or the North-West Frontier—the wrong side of it.

PART I

CHAPTER I

Captain Richard Wendover was almost worried.

A more imaginative man, one more nervous and highly strung, would have been quite worried. For he and his men were in parlous state and, for the first time in his life, he was in a military position that he felt he did not understand, a situation that filled him with doubt. For he was not absolutely certain of the loyalty of his colleague, a man upon whom he should have been able to depend for all possible assistance, for frank companionship, for stout support, and for ungrudging and unstinted effort.

Nor had he the fullest trust in every one of the native officers and men under his command.

A most unsatisfactory and indeed disturbing state of affairs—for the general situation was already sufficiently bad, without this particular difficulty and unusual danger from within.

However, the facts that the Fort was surrounded by an extremely active, watchful and aggressive enemy; that communication with its base was completely cut off; that food, supplies and ammunition were running very low, troubled him not at all—and the other was only a matter of suspicion, albeit strong suspicion, rapidly growing.

Deep in the heart of the African jungle stood this little *boma*, with its garrison of a company of sepoys; its wide surrounding trench and high loop-holed stockade—a wall of earth, two feet thick, between stout high hurdles of plaited pliant branches—enclosing rude grass-thatched *bandas*, huts which served the purposes of Officer's quarters, store-houses, cookhouse, hospital and combined Orderly-Room and Officers' Mess.

Apart from these *bandas*, and near the stockade walls, long communal dwelling-places of wattle-and-

11

daub, thatched with plaited palm-leaf, provided rude shelter for the sepoys.

Not an attractive spot; scarcely a home from home; and everyone in it had been in it far too long.

So thought Captain Richard Wendover as he yawned, stretched himself, struck a match and glanced at his wrist-watch.

Yes, he thought so. Two minutes to five. Curious how he always woke just before the *reveille* bugle. Funny thing that. But there were fellows who said that if you bumped your head five times on the pillow before you went to sleep, and said, "I will wake at five," you would infallibly do so.

He had never tried that, and he had no need to do so; for, regularly as the clock, he woke just in time to yawn, stretch, look at his watch and wait a minute or so for *reveille*.

Punctually the bugle blew. Good old Shere Khan. He was no bugler himself, but he'd damn' well see that a bugle was blown by somebody, and to the minute. Priceless chap. Pity he wasn't Subedar-Major.

But on the other hand, he certainly saw and heard more, and was probably far more useful as a sepoy orderly. Besides, he really hadn't the brains for a Native Officer's job and, happily, was entirely devoid of ambition.

No, Shere Khan would scarcely do as *naik* or *havildar*, much less as *jemadar* or *subedar*.

And yet there was no man as valuable in the outpost, and he would sooner have parted with any Native Officer or non-commissioned officer, than with Shere Khan. Sooner have parted with Breckinge. Very much sooner.

Cruel hard luck that poor dear old Hunter-Ward had been killed, and Alec Breckinge—hadn't. He had been a tower of strength, Hunter-Ward, even when malaria and dysentery had left him without any strength of his own. His cheerfulness alone had been worth anything. Priceless. And a lot of the men had been very fond of him indeed, and would have listened to him instead of to Breckinge.

Yes, a tower of strength—and Breckinge a source of weakness. Damn Breckinge. He'd twist his tail for him, the first time he got a chance and a reason. That was where the fellow was so infernally clever. There was nothing to take hold of, and you can't twist a tail until you can take hold of it.

Richard Wendover grinned.

As the mournful notes of *reveille* rang out on the still, dank air of the hot dark morning, Wendover arose from his camp-bed, and dressed for the day by putting on his helmet. As he had lain down for a brief rest at three o'clock, in boots, putties, khaki cotton shirt and shorts, there was nothing else to put on.

Stepping out of his *banda*, the rickety hut built of saplings, interlaced branches, reeds, grass and palm-leaves, Captain Richard Wendover ran an experienced and observant eye over the too-familiar scene, with its two intersecting "streets" of porter-built huts; its Officers' Mess in the central square, consisting of four posts and a roof of trellis and grass, with a floor of mud, and its furniture of a table made with four stumps and some packing-case boards, and native frame-and-string beds for chairs.

How he wished Shere Khan would not keep Hunter-Ward's place at the uneven roughly-nailed table, with the stencil-marks yet upon its packing-case boards. Was it just force of habit, or superstition, that made him pull up a seat to the side where the poor chap had always sat?

Would there be any tea this morning?

He knew that the small store was running very low, but, each day, forbore to ask whether there would be any to-morrow.

Having no tea would be worse than having no whisky. Far worse. Tea was a necessity. In the morning, anyhow.

Whisky at night. Just as necessary, really, when one was whacked to the wide, and too tired, or anxious, to sleep.

It would come as a real blow when Shere Khan told him there was no more tea, although daily he expected

13

it. A genuine hardship. How could one begin the day in a place like this, without a big basin of tea, hot and strong and sweet?

Suppose there were none this morning, just when he was feeling rather more sleep-starved, shaky, giddy and sick than usual. One must keep one's sense of proportion, of course, but at the moment, he wasn't quite sure which of the three troubles was the worst— the death of Hunter-Ward whom he really loved; the certainty that Breckinge and some of the men were disloyal; or the fact that the end of the stock of tea was in sight.

Love; loyalty; and tea.

Suppose there were none to-day! Well, he'd have to drink his water ration. It was the colour of tea, any- how, what with mud, stewed leaf-mould and general assorted filth . . .

No. Good. Here came Shere Khan with the metal teapot which had once been enamelled white, a con- densed-milk tin and a mug.

Lacking a tray, but knowing what was fitting, he bore these things upon a piece of wood which had once formed the side of a box.

The teapot contained good strong Sergeant-Major's tea; the condensed-milk tin, some brown sugar; and the mug, yet another piece of wood useful for stirring and other purposes.

"I think we'll put that in the sugar-basin," smiled Wendover, sticking the wood upright in the sugar, "and call it a spoon."

Sepoy Shere Khan, who spoke little English but apparently understood everything that was said to him in that language, grinned cheerfully, his saturnine and forbidding countenance, with its blue-black beard, heavy black moustache, and thick beetling black eye- brows, changing and lighting up as does a dark and stormy sky when through a rift the sun beams brightly.

The distance from the top of his high-piled *puggri*, wound about his tall conical *kullah* cap, to the soles of his heavy ammunition boots must have been over seven feet; for, bare-headed and bare-footed, Shere Khan was six feet and six inches in height; a man of tremendous shoulder-breadth, barrel-like chest, mighty girth of arm and thigh; a magnificent specimen of the Pathan race, great and hard of thew and sinew and, like so many of his compatriots, loyal to the core and faithful unto death, when once loyalty and fidelity had been won and given.

This was a man.

As they stood in speech, the two, Officer and Sepoy, were not unlike, for both were tall and broad beyond the ordinary, and the Englishman, naturally sallow, and tanned by the sun, was also of dark complexion, his hair, moustache and eyebrows being black and the iris of his eyes dark brown.

Had the two exchanged clothing, the Englishman donning the Pathan's head-gear and tunic, and the Pathan shaving off his beard, the difference would not have been very great.

"What about the *Daktar-Sahib*?" asked Wendover, raising his eyebrows in assumed surprise.

The Pathan grunted and observed that there was very little tea.

"Fetch another cup," directed Wendover, and smiled to himself when, a minute later, the other mug was brought by the filthy black-faced nondescript who called himself a cook. If there was nothing that Shere Khan would not do for Captain Richard Wendover, there was nothing that he would do for Lieutenant Alec Breckinge.

No, thought Wendover, Shere Khan had taken Breckinge's measure all right, and regarded him in very much the same way as he himself did.

And here he came with his jaunty swagger and false smile.

§2

Lieutenant Alec Breckinge, of the Indian Medical Service, was also of dark complexion, but with a darkness due not, as in the case of Richard Wendover, to exposure. He was wont to blame the sun, but would have been more accurate had he accused his mother and grandmother instead. For, although he was, as he would inform you at the very earliest opportunity, the grandson of a British General, he was also the grandson of an Indian sweeper-woman of caste so low as to have no caste, to be an outcaste—an Untouchable, in fact.

Untouchable by an Indian, that is to say. For General Sir Percy Vereker Breckinge, K.C.M.G., K.C.S.I., had found her quite otherwise. And, in the spacious manner of his day and kind, had temporarily promoted her to a place in that part of his unwieldy and ever-expanding household known to irreverent subordinates as his harem.

Not a few of the remarkable soldiers who served John Company lived more in the style of Indian Rajahs than of English gentlemen, and, when gathered to their fathers, or returned to their native land, left behind them quite a considerable number of sons who inherited their father's name and nothing else from that side of the family, save perhaps a strain or streak of the more stalwart virtues and a skin lighter than that of the pure-bred Indian.

From their low-caste mothers, these unfortunates were apt to inherit vices additional to those of the fathers; and, inevitably, from the twain inherited the cruel curse of the half-caste, the Eurasian.

It was not General Sir Percy Vereker Breckinge's habit to treat his half-breed dusky sons as he did his white ones. For the latter, Home and the Public School; for the former, anything they could get on the strength of their name, generally a very small and subordinate position in some such Government Department as that of the Revenue, Gaol, Public Works, Salt and Abkari, or the Police.

And into the Indian Police went General Sir Percy Vereker Breckinge's son, Vereker, who was this Lieutenant Alec Breckinge's father, in the grade of European Constable. And from that grade, by virtue of his perfect knowledge of the country, the people, and the language; his undoubted ability and courage; his distinguished name; and a certain unscrupulousness of method, he rose steadily to gazetted rank, and, eventually, to the grade and position of Superintendent of Police.

Unfortunately, while yet a constable, young, ardent and impetuous, he married a woman who, whatever her claims to virtue and to beauty, possessed not the most modest share of European blood, her father being an excellent da Costa and her mother an admirable da Silva, both late of Goa, and of pure low-caste Indian descent.

However, Mr. Vereker Breckinge, Superintendent of Police, did better for his son, Alec, than his father had done for him; gave him the best education that he could afford; enabled him to qualify as a doctor, and lived to see him commissioned as Lieutenant in the admirable and excellent Indian Medical Service, which, though consisting of English gentlemen as to some ninety-five per cent of its personnel, is open, in theory, to any British subject who can qualify for admission to its exclusive ranks.

And yet, in this success, Mr. Vereker Breckinge was happier than Alec Breckinge, his successful son.

True, to Alec Breckinge, it was delightful to wear, upon occasion, the distinguished uniform of the Indian Medical Service, with helmet, sword and gold braid; delightful to have military rank, and to know that one would rise, through the grades of Captain and Major, to Colonel; and might, with good luck and hard work, become Surgeon-General of a Presidency.

It gave one, and most particularly one who was a Eurasian, a heart-warming and soul-satisfying sense of established place and position, rank and social security.

But, unfortunately, it did not give one a white skin; and that of Alec Breckinge was definitely dark; far darker than that of his Eurasian father or his Goanese-Indian mother; a throw-back, indeed, to the tribe of his low-caste sweeper grandmother.

And the darkness of his countenance darkened the

outlook, and, indeed, the whole life, of Lieutenant Alec Breckinge of the I.M.S. For, on the subject of colour, he was extremely sensitive; always on the look out for slights, snubs and differentiations. And every real or imagined slight, every fancied or intended snub, every illusory or actual differentiation between him and brother officers of British birth and origin, became an insult, each insult deliberate, intentional and cruel.

Nor, unfortunately, was there utter lack of grounds for complaint; complete absence of reasons for hurt, for indignation, and for injured pride. There is undeniably a colour-feeling among European society in India, a prejudice against mixed blood; a colour-bar exists and a strong and clear demarcation line is drawn. One of the most unpleasant and wounding allegations that can be made by one alleged European concerning another, is that he or she has "a touch of the tar-brush."

This does not deny for one moment that there exists a very warm regard, appreciation and admiration on the part of very many Europeans for very many Indians; but the Indian and the European move, socially, in water-tight compartments; belonging not to each other's Clubs, exchanging practically no hospitality; and the fault, if fault it be, lies with both sides.

But while the European and the Indian may entertain strong mutual regard, neither has, generally speaking, any kindness for the offspring of both.

Lieutenant Alec Breckinge then, though far more often wrong than right, was occasionally not mistaken in thinking that certain social invitations failed to reach him which would have reached him but for his complexion, and which did reach his European colleagues; and that many a Mamma who would have looked without fear and with favour upon the association of her daughter with other members of his Service, was not at all anxious that Lieutenant Alec Breckinge should become friendly with the young lady.

This is a hard and cruel state of affairs maintained by people who are neither hard nor cruel, but who naturally and justly, from the intimate social and especially the matrimonial points of view, prefer Europeans to half-castes, and white faces to dark.

So the path of Lieutenant Alec Breckinge was not strewn with roses, and on such roses as he did discover on Life's way, he invariably expected to find, and sometimes did find, a sharp and cruel thorn.

Unlike his father, Mr. Vereker Breckinge, bluff and hardy of spirit, thick-skinned and tough of temperament, suffering nothing from the slings and arrows of outrageous snobs, Lieutenant Breckinge was morbidly sensitive, thin-skinned to the point of nakedness, against the pin-pricks of hurt, and the cold cutting winds of neglect. Easily wounded, he had a great capacity for suffering, and was a living example of the truth that the ills from which we suffer most are those which never happen to us.

In point of fact, had Breckinge been a little less self-centred, morbid and defensive, he could have got along very comfortably indeed under the protection of his uniform and the ægis of the magnificent Service to which he belonged.

But he who incorrigibly seeks trouble, of whatever kind, invariably finds it; and there is no more successful search than that for slights, snubs and petty insult.

Little wonder was it that Lieutenant Breckinge grew more and more bitter, and that the abrupt and unhappy termination of his first love-affair turned increasing bitterness, moroseness and malcontent to a mental condition that was extremely unwholesome. His inferiority-complex and his eternal preoccupation with the subject of his colour, developed into a persecution mania, the accompaniment and corollary of which was an acute dislike of the class to which he wished to belong, and a virulent hatred of those members of it whom he believed to despise him.

First and foremost of these was Captain Richard Wendover who, quite innocently and unintentionally, had done him what he considered to be an unforgivable and deadly wrong, and offered him what he imagined to be a mortal insult.

Paradoxically and pathetically enough, it was the fact that the members of the Madrutta Gymkana and the Madrutta Club—far from despising and snubbing him, had admitted him to both these exclusive societies—that led to his undoing. Had he not become a member of the Gymkana he would never have met Annabel Leighton, never have played tennis with her, never have had an opportunity of going for morning rides with her, and never have fallen in love with her. He would have had no opportunity to cultivate and pay his court to her mother, a sprightly matron who, freely admitting that all flesh is grass, was something of a female Nebuchadnezzar, a grass widow when possible, and much addicted to frolicking in green pastures beside still and deep waters.

Had he not been a member of the Madrutta Club, it is improbable that he would have met Annabel's father, Mr. John Leighton, Merchant, Chairman of the Madrutta Chamber of Commerce and President of the Municipality.

Nor would Breckinge have been able to return the Leighton hospitality by giving tea-parties on the Club lawn, and inviting Annabel and her mother thereunto.

Both ladies, in their respective ways, found Breckinge attractive, for he was undeniably handsome in his dark and saturnine way. Mrs. Leighton thought the smouldering passionate fire of his large lucent eyes intriguing; the smile of his weak shapely mouth, with the small, perfect and pearly teeth, beneath the little curling black moustache, attractive; the expression of his olive-tinted melancholy face romantic, yea, Byronic.

But whereas Mrs. Leighton thought his eyes lovely, his mouth almost kissable, his small well-formed filbert-nailed hands attractive and his whole person and personality what she called exotically and subtly provocative, Annabel, less susceptible and less tolerant, found the young man merely agreeable, useful and tolerable, and that only up to a point.

She declared that, at times, he rather gave her the creeps, and that anyway the said smouldering and passionate eyes were apt to be a lot too warm and the said small and well-formed hands a lot too cold—and clammy.

And these views she communicated to Mrs. Leighton long before Captain Richard Wendover, seconded from his Regiment, came to Madrutta on special duty.

Had Breckinge known this, it is doubtful whether he would have hated Wendover less, or ceased to persuade himself that, intentionally and wilfully, he had "come between" him and the girl he adored, deliberately ruined his romance, and wantonly wrecked his life.

Certainly he would not have hated him less had he realized that Wendover acted as he did, not only with complete indifference to the existing situation, but in utter ignorance both of it and of Breckinge's state of mind.

No, it was another injustice to the Eurasian; another cruel insult and bitter injury to the poor half-caste, on the part both of Wendover and of Annabel Leighton.

Until Wendover came he was good enough for the girl, worthy to dance and ride and play tennis with her. Now he was only good enough for the mother, the whole of Annabel's thoughts being occupied with the newcomer. She had no time now for Alec Breckinge.

And why? Simply by reason of the colour of his face. Purely a matter of pigmentation. For did not Alec Breckinge dance, ride and play tennis as well as Wendover did? Were not his manners as good, his Service and position as good? Was he not as handsome, or a good deal more so?

It was a shame, a cruel, wicked, burning shame, and he'd . . . he'd . . .

What he did do was to sink yet deeper into the slough of despond and bitterness and hatred from which his hitherto-hopeful love had begun to raise him up; to wallow with more abandon in the muck of the bazaar; and to turn ever more frequently to the solace of that Daughter of Delight, Azizun. She, at least, admired him and found no fault with his colour, his kin or his cash. Yes, Azizun knew a gentleman when she saw one, could appreciate an ardent wooer, and could find great uses for one who had one foot in the great world and the other in the half-world—and who was, incidentally, a doctor.

And Captain Richard Wendover, with whom Breckinge came into frequent official and social contact, was undoubtedly casual, and had an undeniably off-hand manner—a manner that could be construed as rude by anyone desiring to do so, and which was, by the rest of his friends, regarded as bluff and cheery, a facet and an indication of that blunt and matter-of-fact character which to them was part of his undeniable charm.

So little indeed did Richard Wendover realize the terrible injury done to the young dark-faced doctor whom he did not dislike, and for whom he was rather sorry, that he would have been utterly amazed had he been informed that the latter's pleasant smile, ingratiating manner and boisterous camaraderie, hid a sense of wrong and outrage, a fierce hatred, and a burning desire for vengeance of some sort; something terrible, a vengeance adequate, if that were possible, to the wrong that had provoked it.

Nevertheless, it was with no feeling of particular satisfaction that, a year or so after his transfer from Napierpur to Madrutta, Captain Richard Wendover found himself in the same African outpost with Lieutenant Breckinge, and dependent upon him for the medical care of his company of sepoys; for social intercourse during the brief hours of relaxation; and for general support in his dealings with these down-country Indians whom Breckinge understood far better than did Wendover. For he, hitherto, had dealt only with the upstanding, outspoken Pathan and Punjabi Mahommedan, whose general outlook, mentality and characteristics were not very remarkably different from his own.

Things had not been so bad while Hunter-Ward, his second-in-command, was alive; but from the day that he fell, recklessly exposing himself in defence of the side of the Fort for which he was responsible, Wend-over had been increasingly aware of Breckinge's utter inadequacy as a doctor, as a companion, and as a colleague.

While the Mess had consisted of the three of them, talk had been free, natural and easy, though Breckinge had contributed but little to it; and, thanks to Hunter-Ward's indefatigable ubiquity as second-in-command, Wendover had not quite realized all Breckinge's grave shortcomings.

He realized now that Hunter-Ward, doing as usual all he could to spare his Commanding Officer unnecessary bother and worry, must have kept Breckinge up to his work, handled him, used him and driven him, getting the best out of him, without appeal to Wendover.

Moreover, Hunter-Ward, who had spent all his service with this down-country battalion, ever since he left his British Regiment, knew the characters and idiosyncrasies of these sepoys and could manage them with the minimum of friction and maximum of result.

True, Hunter-Ward had from time to time admitted that he neither liked nor trusted the Subedar-Major, and that he felt that somebody had made a very big and bad mistake in ever promoting him beyond the rank of *havildar*; but he had contrived to get on with the man all right, and to prevent his surly and difficult temper from exhibiting itself too plainly.

Personally, Wendover detested the fellow, believed in him even less than Hunter-Ward had done, and had neither the desire nor the patience to manage him as Hunter-Ward, subtle and supple diplomatist, had succeeded in doing. An iron hand within his velvet glove Hunter-Ward had had, but when he considered it advisable, he had worn an extremely thick one.

In dealing with sepoys, Wendover preferred to use the iron hand, with no glove at all. In absolute justice, in easy pleasantness where desirable, and in warm friendship where possible, he believed; but for the type of sepoy or Native Officer of whom careful and tactful handling was necessary, he had no use whatever.

And Wendover's methods, conduct, and character had been thoroughly understood and entirely approved by the up-country stalwarts, chiefly mountaineers, born fighting men, raiders and rievers, who had formed his Squadron, the leaving of which he would have deeply regretted but for the fact that he was on active service.

And, thank God, he had been able to bring Shere Khan from the Regiment with him.

With these men it was different. They, though fellow-Indians of the men of the Punjab and Frontier Regiments, were as different from them as are Greeks from Prussians or Portuguese from Scotsmen—and they did not like the officer in temporary command of them.

Certain habits and customs which they had always hitherto regarded as rights, were to him abominations, anathema; and, for the first time in their sepoy service, prohibited.

While Hunter-Ward lived, the outpost, isolated like a ship alone on a wide sea, was a not-unhappy ship. After his death, with the Captain in constant and intimate contact with all ranks, it was not a happy ship.

There was an unpleasant spirit abroad.

Not for one moment was it to be described as a mutinous spirit; but a sullen, unwilling, and unfriendly one it was, the attitude of the Subedar-Major being as disagreeable as he dared to make it, and that of his brother and his cousin, one of whom was Subedar and the other, one of the two Jemadars, very similar to it.

Naturally this spirit was reflected by the non-commissioned officers and men; there being cliques among them in which it was better than the company-average, others in which it was worse.

And what troubled and deeply offended Wendover was the obvious fact that Lieutenant Alec Breckinge was hand-in-glove with the least loyal, cheerful, and willing elements in the garrison; his particular crony being the Subedar-Major with whom Wendover needed but a fair opportunity and excuse to deal rigorously, even though such action precipitated the trouble that he feared.

Breckinge.

Rotten bad luck that it should be he of all people, and not the usual type of I.M.S. officer, who would have been indefatigable in his care of the men, invaluable as a companion, and priceless as a colleague and a pillar of moral support.

Yes, he would probably have been almost as good as a regular combatant officer, from that point of view —another pair of ears and eyes, and a connecting-file, a lightning-conductor, interpreter, and general liaison-officer between Wendover and these difficult people with whose wretched whims and fancies and requirements and idiosyncrasies he had neither time nor inclination to deal single-handed.

Well, there it was. And as people had always said when he'd defended, not so much Breckinge himself as the fact of Breckinge in gazetted rank, you can't make a silk purse out of a sow's ear, nor, conversely, a good pig-skin one out of a piece of silk.

Poor Breckinge couldn't help being what he was— sins of the fathers and all that—but the fact remained that, valuable and admirable a metal as lead may be in its proper uses, you cannot make a blade with it; or, if you do, you cannot blame it for not being a steel one.

The trouble with this type of people was that, even where the paternal ancestor was a man of breeding, back-bone and character—as in Breckinge's case—the mother was almost invariably of the lowest caste, generally of almost the lowest human type. And that was bound to tell, breed being breed—whether in human beings or animals.

Of course there were numerous cases of splendid brave brilliant men whose fathers had been European and mothers Asiatic—but their mothers had been women of birth, education and character, who had married their white husbands on equal terms—and had produced sons endowed with the virtues of both races. Notably had this been the case when British Officers had married Afghan or North Indian Mussulman ladies of high rank. But Breckinge—with his sweeper grandmother and low-class Goanese mother. What could one expect?

And there were certain things for which one couldn't blame Breckinge. Nevertheless, you could expect loyalty, and the giving of the best that was in him.

If the fellow were half-English, half-Indian, he needn't exhibit the whole Indian side in the circumstances; needn't hob-nob with the sullen and difficult Subedar-Major (who was probably seditious and would be mutinous if he dared), instead of consorting frankly and freely with his European Commanding Officer who had given him every encouragement to do so.

Far from doing that, he quite definitely avoided him, and moreover, except at meal-times—to call them meals—seemed to contrive to keep out of his way, out of his sight, in fact.

Breckinge. Eurasian.

And here he came with his jaunty swagger and false smile.

CHAPTER II

"Good morning, old chap," smiled Breckinge with uneasy familiarity, showing the perfect pearly teeth of which he was justly proud.

"Morning."

"How are you feeling?"

"Ill."

"Oh, bad luck! What's the matter?"

Wendover raised eyebrows of surprise, and refrained from reply. What would be the matter, in this fever-ridden jungle-hole, but malaria, with a trifle of dysentery and a touch of jaundice and a little weakness due to these things and to starvation? All very well for a native-bred acclimatized doctor, who treated himself prophylactically and was in charge of medical comforts.

"Have you got any calomel?" he asked.

"Oh, yes."

"I'll have some, then. And some quinine. Send them over to my *banda*."

"Right-o, Wendover," replied Breckinge airily; and, seating himself on a *charpai*,[20] poured out a cup of tea, liberally sweetened it, and enquired:

"No more condensed milk?"

"No, and precious little of anything else . . . I suppose you've still got plenty of it for the dysentery cases?"

"Er—no. Hardly any left."

"Good Lord! You must have been using it pretty freely."

He had, for it was a comestible of which he was particularly fond, whether in tea, coffee or cocoa; or with boiling water and rum, whisky, gin or brandy. In fact, from childhood's days he had been addicted to the consuming of it neat, straight from the tin.

---

[20] *Native bed-frame.*

Wendover glanced at his watch, pulled the end of a lanyard from the breast-pocket of his shirt, and blew a blast upon the whistle that hung at the end of it.

The note was taken up in other parts of the Fort, and shouts of "*Stand to!*" resounded.

Wendover rose to his feet as a tall bearded Indian officer approached, halted, saluted and said in Hindustani:

"*Stand to, Sahib. Sub tyar hai.*"[21]

As Wendover returned the native officer's salute, Shere Khan appeared, bearing his tunic and cross-belt. These Wendover donned, that he might be reasonably correctly dressed for the morning inspection of the Stand-to parade.

"Come round with me," he said somewhat curtly to Breckinge, who was lounging off in the direction of his *banda*.

Followed by Breckinge, the Subedar-Major, the Subedar and the Jemadar-Adjutant, Wendover made the round, first of the deep outside trench that enclosed the *boma* and was now occupied by half the force, and then of the Fort wall itself, at each loophole of which stood a sepoy sighting his rifle in the direction of the jungle. Here and there, he inspected a rifle, and the contents of a water-bottle.

Thereafter, he visited the hospital, a loathsome pit dug some two feet into the ground and covered by tent-canvas slung across a ridge-pole supported above the hole by posts planted in the ground at the ends of the pit.

"How many sick this morning?" he enquired of Lieutenant Breckinge.

"Oh, about twenty-five," was the reply.

Having visited the cook-house, the sepoys' sleeping-quarters and the store-rooms, he inspected the water-tank and the ammunition store, and then ordered the native officers, with the exception of the Subedar-Major, to return to their posts, dismiss their men, and carry on with the routine of the day. The Subedar-Major he bade accompany him to the Officers' Mess

---

[21] *Everything is ready.*

banda, intimating to Breckinge that he wished to see him there also, in ten minutes' time.

"Now then, Subedar-Major," said he, when the two men were alone. "There are one or two things I want to speak to you about, and I didn't wish to find fault with you in front of your subordinates. Are you satisfied with the condition of the trenches?"

"*Han*,[22] Sahib," replied the scowling Subedar-Major promptly.

"Oh, you are, are you? Well, I'm not. Nor would you be, if you knew your job and were fit for it."

"What is wrong with them, Sahib?" enquired the native officer, affecting a look of bewilderment.

"I'll tell you to-morrow morning—and in a way you won't like—if you haven't found out by then, and put it right.

"Next thing—the condition of the rifles is not satisfactory. Three of the seven rifles I inspected had not been properly cleaned."

"Sahib, I can't . . ."

"Oh, can't you? Then it won't take me long to find someone who can. Next thing—haven't I told you once, already, to see that every man's water-bottle is full, always? There's not to be a water-bottle in this Fort that isn't full, ever."

"Sahib, I . . ."

"Next thing," interrupted Wendover. "Haven't I told you more than once that all the small canvas water-tanks are always to be full, as well as the water-bottles; and that all water is to be taken from the big tank? I will see that that is kept full; and you are to see that the *chagals* are. How do we know when we may be entirely cut off from the river? Don't let me have to tell you again.

"Next thing—why wasn't Sepoy Dhondoo Lakhsman on parade?"

The Subedar-Major, who had been studying his feet, looked up sharply.

"Sick, Sahib," he replied. What a *shaitan* was this Wendover Sahib! Fancy missing one man like that.

---

[22] *Yes.*

In point of fact, Dhondoo Lakhsman, by reason of his very prematurely grey beard, one side of which was almost white, the other iron-grey, was a man whose absence any observant officer would have noticed.

"Sick? Then why wasn't he in hospital?"

What a *shaitan* he was! Fancy noting that the man was not in hospital.

"I gave him permission to lie down in his hut."

"Did you? Then why wasn't he doing it? There was nobody in the sleeping-quarters his Section occupies. Where was he?"

The Subedar-Major shuffled uncomfortably.

"I don't know, Sahib."

"You don't know? Oh! And you don't know why the trenches are littered and untidy; why half the rifles haven't been cleaned since yesterday morning; why all the water-bottles are not filled, nor why the *chagals* are empty? What *do* you know? I'll tell you something you'll know very soon, Subedar-Major Ganga Charan, and that will be that you are under arrest. Go and fetch Sepoy Dhondoo Lakhsman here immediately."

The Subedar-Major stood, half-turned away, and hung irresolute.

"Go on," snarled Wendover, "you heard what I said. Go and fetch him yourself."

Knowing Indians as he did, he was certain that there was something behind this, something fishy.

Yes, undoubtedly he had stumbled on something. They had taken a chance on his not noticing Sepoy Dhondoo Lakhsman's absence from parade and hospital. There was nowhere else where he could be, for daily patrols had not yet been sent out, nor day pickets and sentries posted. Besides, had the man been on any sort of fatigue or duty, the Subedar-Major would have said so instantly.

Lieutenant Breckinge approached.

"You wanted to speak to me?" he said.

"I do. And as, at the moment, this *banda* is functioning as Orderly-Room and not as Officers' Mess, you will say 'Sir' when you speak to me."

Lieutenant Breckinge's weakly pleasant face became strongly unpleasant as he scowled and glanced downward.

"Now then," continued Wendover. "When I asked you this morning how many sick there were, you said '*About twenty-five.*' If you answer me like that again, I shall have something to say to you in front of the men. What do you mean by '*about*'? Is that what you have been in the habit of telling Mr. Hunter-Ward hitherto? When I've done with you, go straight and make me out a proper Sick Statement, a nominal roll, with each man's trouble against his name, and a very brief estimate of his condition.

"Next thing. What are you doing about flies? They are getting worse every day. Hardly push my way through them this morning; and they are worst round the Hospital. What are you doing about it?"

"Flies?" expostulated Breckinge. "What can I do about flies?"

"Good Lord above us, man, are you asking *me*? Aren't you supposed to be a doctor? Do I have to teach you the rudiments of sanitation? How do people deal with flies—people with any knowledge and ability; any initiative and attention to duty? . . . Did you ever hear of burying hospital waste and rubbish; ever hear of muslin, netting, chloride of lime; any . . ."

"I haven't any of those things," protested Breckinge.

"No. And why not? You made out the requisitions, didn't you? Didn't you think any further ahead than quinine, calomel, iodoform and bandages?

"And medical comforts," he added unpleasantly. "Anyhow, you let me find fewer flies under that awning, and round your hospital premises generally, when I inspect them to-morrow.

"Next thing. How many times did you visit the hospital last night? Personally, I visited it twice myself, and found no orderly, and nobody in charge. What I did find was one or two men just about dying of thirst. When did you hold a sick-parade last? When did you see that any drinking-water was boiled? When did you issue a quinine ration? When did you inspect trenches, sleeping-quarters, latrines and cooking-places—from the hygienic point of view? When did you do anything except hob-nob familiarly with the Subedar-Major and his gang?"

"Look here, Wendover," began the enraged Breckinge.

"*What* did you say?" interrupted Wendover softly. "Did I hear you say '*Look here*'? Did I hear you call me *Wendover*? I'll mention again, and for the last time, that, at the present moment, these four posts and that alleged roof are my Orderly-Room, and that you are up before your Commanding Officer for reprimand and admonition, by reason of gross dereliction of duty. Now then, begin again, and instead of saying '*Look here, Wendover*,' say '*Excuse me, Sir*,' if you wish to offer excuses, which doubtless you do."

"I wasn't going to make excuses. I was going to protest."

"Oh? Against what?"

"Your accusing me of hob-nobbing with the men."

"I didn't accuse you of hob-nobbing with the men. *Qui s'excuse s'accuse.* I said the Subedar-Major and his gang. And you know as well as I do who they are. Subedar Gopal Mangal, who is his brother; Jemadar Ganpat Mahadeo, who is his cousin; and Havildar Ramrao Dalkesar, who is his cousin or brother-in-law or something of the sort; and the whole of the Section who are his nephews or sons-in-law or cousins of his grandfather's brother's niece's daughter's husband's uncles or aunts or something. If you spent less time with them, and more with your sick, it would be better for all concerned, including yourself and your prospects of promotion. Understand me?"

Lieutenant Breckinge looked down at the ground, his hands clenching and unclenching. Raising his eyes, he darted a glance of venomous hatred at his superior officer.

Wendover rose to his feet and resumed his helmet.

"Well now," he said in a pleasanter and kindlier voice, "I've said my say, and I hope I shan't have to talk to you like this again. We've all been here a damn sight too long, and we are up against it—but we are all in the same boat. We must pull together. All right Breckinge. Carry on."

And without a word, Breckinge turned on his heel to depart. As he did so, an idea occurred to Wendover.

"Oh, by the way," he said, still speaking as comrade to comrade rather than as Commanding Officer to offending subordinate as he had been doing, "where's Sepoy Dhondoo Lakhsman?"

Definitely Breckinge started, and Wendover noted the fact.

Hullo, what was this? So Breckinge knew something about the mystery of the missing sepoy.

"How should I know . . . Sir?" he asked.

Then why should he look surprised, almost startled, not to say apprehensive? Obviously he knew something.

"True. How should you? That's where I miss poor Hunter-Ward."

"Well, there's no man of that name in hospital, nor did he come to me and report sick."

"And beyond that you know nothing and care less, eh, although you and I are the only two . . . European . . . officers here."

Wendover could have bitten his tongue for the pause before the word 'European.' But it had been absolutely involuntary. He had been about to say 'English,' but how could he, with that dark and sullen, that lowering and absolutely Indian, face glowering at him?

To Breckinge it was an intentional and studied insult—and the last straw.

"*European? European?*" he screamed, his eyes blazing, his lips retracted. "Why can't you . . . ?"

"That's enough," interrupted Wendover in his quiet compelling voice. "That'll do. Pull yourself together. Go and make out that Sick Statement and let me have it as soon as possible."

And as the Subedar-Major approached, he turned his back on the infuriated doctor who departed, trembling with rage, speechless and angry, almost foaming at the mouth.

"Well?" enquired Wendover of the Subedar-Major.

"Sahib, the man cannot be found," announced the latter.

Wendover eyed him in cold astonishment.

"Are you insane, or do you think I am? What do you mean—cannot be found? Is this Bombay or an outpost, fifty yards by fifty square?"

The Native Officer shuffled uncomfortably beneath his superior's hard and penetrating gaze.

"Look here, what is this *banao*?[23] What's the game? Answer me at once and speak the truth."

"I cannot find him anywhere, Sahib," mumbled the man.

With heavy frown and concentrated stare, Wendover remained silent, well aware that nothing is more disconcerting to the Indian of uneasy conscience, or an easy one, for that matter.

The tense silence grew unbearable—to the Subedar-Major.

"Havildar Ramrao Dalkesar thinks he must have deserted."

"What! In the middle of Africa, and not knowing a word of any language spoken between here and Mombasa? An accomplished thinker, isn't he?"

The man shrugged shoulders and threw out hands of protest, in affected helplessness.

"What do I know?" he growled.

"That's what I intend to find out," was the quiet reply.

"Shere Khan!" he called, and the huge orderly came striding. "Go and find the Jemadar-Adjutant Sahib. Give him my salaams and tell him I want to speak to him here."

A minute later Jemadar Ganpat Mahadeo approached the wall-less mess *banda*, halted, saluted and stood at attention.

"Where are Sepoy Dhondoo Lakhsman's rifle and accoutrements?"

"Sahib, he is . . ."

"Where are Sepoy Dhondoo Lakhsman's rifle and

---

[23] *Lie, concocted story.*

accoutrements? I asked," repeated Wendover, in his cold quiet voice, now somewhat hard and menacing.

Evidently the man had expected the question, "Where is Sepoy Dhondoo Lakhsman?" and had his answer ready.

"Sahib, they have not been . . . they were . . ."

Silence.

"Well?"

"Sahib, I do not know."

"You do know. You were just going to tell me, and you thought better of it."

Jemadar Ganpat Mahadeo glanced at Subedar-Major Ganga Charan.

"Shere Khan, go and tell Havildar Ramrao Dalkesar to come here at once."

Suddenly Wendover shot a question at the Jemadar-Adjutant.

"What did the Doctor Sahib say when he knew about it?"

The man glanced around him shifty-eyed, anywhere but at Wendover's face, moistened his lips, and then darted a quick look at the Subedar-Major.

"Well, speak up!"

"Sahib, he said nothing."

"H'm! In what language did he say it?"

For a moment the Jemadar's eyes met Wendover's.

"So you told him, did you, and he 'said nothing.' What was it you told him?"

The Jemadar glanced at the Subedar-Major. This was a question for him to answer.

"No, you needn't look at the Subedar-Major," observed Wendover, "and you needn't answer. I have just had a long talk with the Doctor Sahib about it, and I wanted to see whether you'd speak the truth."

That was the only way to get anything out of these people. Play their own game, distasteful as it might be. Damn Breckinge—once again—for putting him in the position of having to take this line at all. If only he had been a white man—in both senses of the term!

Shepherded by the gigantic Shere Khan, the sepoy Sergeant approached, saluted, and stood outside the *banda.*

"Where are Sepoy Dhondoo Lakhsman's rifle and kit?" asked Wendover, briefly returning the salute. "The Subedar-Major Sahib and the Jemadar Sahib say that you . . ."

Wendover paused to encourage the protest that he knew would almost instantly break forth.

"Sahib, it was not my fault! They have not been recovered. They are lost. It was not my fault. I know nothing."

"What steps did you take to recover them?" asked Wendover quickly.

What the devil was this? It looked as though he was going to find foothold in this morass of lies and deceit.

"Sahib, the river is swift and strong and the water deep. What could we do?"

And suddenly Wendover saw daylight. Saw also a tragic little scene as clearly as though the drama had been enacted before his eyes. . . .

A tiny entrenched stockaded picket-post on the other side of the treacherous swiftly-flowing Ubele River; the sound of the Retreat bugle blown in the Fort at sunset; a local *shenzi*,[24] hired or intimidated for the purpose, waiting to pull the long keel-less, narrow and terribly unstable, one-man dug-out across, with its precariously-balanced cargo of a clumsy sepoy in full marching order, with rifle and kit.

Slowly, painfully, anxiously, the dug-out, at an ever-increasing angle, the rope almost torn from the negro ferryman's grasp, is pulled across, and the sepoy thankfully scrambles up the bank. The brawny naked negro who has been paying out a rope attached to the other end of the dug-out, now hauls it back to the opposite bank, and another sepoy, unhandy and awkward, laden like a beast of burden and encumbered with his rifle, unhappily crawls into it, while the clumsy hollowed tree-trunk, its roughly-shaped sides but an inch above the swirling water, rocks, with the exasperating devilishness of something as sentient as malicious, to every movement of the nervous occupant.

---

[24] *Savage; jungle native; uncivilized negro.*

At length it is reasonably still and steady, and the passage perilous begins, the rope at the bow taut, the rope at the stern trailing loose, for the least tightening of that, to help prevent the canoe from being carried down with the stream, would cause a surge of water instantly to flow over the side and swamp the crazy craft.

After two or three of his men have crossed safely, the Native Officer ventures, satisfied that the rope is dependable and that the ferryman has got his eye in.

The Native Officer, unencumbered by pack, haversack, ground-sheet, water-bottle, bandolier, entrenching-tool, bayonet and rifle, or any other impedimenta, makes a quicker, easier and safer crossing.

The black Hercules on the other side pulls the empty dug-out back, and another sepoy, Dhondoo Lakhsman this time, his eyes, his whole expression, showing the fear that bemuses and weakens him, steps into the bobbing unstable travesty of a boat, while the negro desperately clutches its sides.

Like a bullock boarding a racing-skiff, Sepoy Dhondoo Lakhsman clatters into the dug-out, seizes its sides and kneels down.

Had the fool but lain down, he might have been saved.

With a cluck of his tongue, the *shenzi* lets go and picks up the trailing tow-rope while his opposite number hauls mightily. For a minute all goes well; and then, by reason of some change of position, some clumsy movement on the part of Sepoy Dhondoo Lakhsman, there is a lurch, a swirl, a splash, a shout, as the dugout rolls over, half-fills and rights itself, and the laden sepoy disappears beneath the surface of the swirling muddy river.

Not the strongest swimmer in the stillest and most buoyant water could have swum any distance, weighted and hampered as was this unfortunate.

Not the strongest swimmer, though he were naked, could have swum against, or across, that current, or done anything but keep his head above water as he was swirled downward to the rapids and waterfall,

37

where he would be dashed to pieces.

Wendover saw it all, the more clearly by reason of the fact that it was against this very contingency that he had issued stringent instructions.

"Dismiss," said he to Havildar Ramrao Dalkesar.

"You may go," he added, addressing the Jemadar-Adjutant, ere he turned upon the Subedar-Major, the whites of whose eyes now seemed larger, more notice-able than hitherto they had been.

"So that's it, is it?" he said, his voice quieter than ever, and yet more cutting, more sinister and men-acing. "You know nothing, do you? Then I'll tell you something. You flatly and flagrantly and impudently disobeyed my most clear, definite and emphatic orders that the river was only to be crossed by the secret upstream bridge!

"Why did I have the tree-trunk-and-rope bridge made for crossing the river? For amusement, do you suppose? Why did I absolutely prohibit the crossing of the Ubele River by dug-out canoe, except in a case of the greatest emergency, such as an attack?

"Simply because I knew that precisely this would happen, if sepoys used that dug-out canoe.

"And whatever my reasons were, what are you here for, except to carry out my orders?"

Again the Subedar-Major looked at the ground and shifted uneasily from one foot to the other.

"Well?"

The man maintained a sullen silence.

"Now then, repeat to me the orders I gave you about the relief of the river-picket. Go on, get on with it. I've something better to do than . . ."

"Sir, you are knowing well what you . . ."

"Don't you talk English to me! Tell me what your orders were."

Silence.

What could he do with the fellow? What he would have liked to do would have been to knock him down, for his present sulky half-veiled insolence, and for the gross dereliction of duty, nay, the flat disobedience of orders, which had led to the death of a sepoy—not to mention the undermining of authority and lessening of the bonds of discipline by reason of the fact that every man in the outpost knew what the orders were.

What could he do, if the man refused to answer him, beyond putting him under open arrest and telling him what would happen to him if, and when, the outpost was relieved, the Company rejoined its Battalion, and he could accuse him to his Colonel and demand a Court-Martial.

How could he put him under close arrest here, when his services were so badly needed that he should have been indispensable; when his subordinates were not only in sympathy but hand-in-glove with him; when his influence with most of the men was all-powerful; and when, in point of practical detail, there was nowhere to confine him and no facilities or personnel for holding a proper Field General Court-Martial?

But he'd get the beggar. He'd get him all right. And meanwhile he'd show him who commanded Ubele Fort; and whether Captain Richard Wendover's orders were going to be disobeyed with impunity.

Meanwhile, if the brute would not repeat the orders, he'd better make him commit himself. Ordeal by question.

"Well, first of all, why did I put that picket beyond the river?"

"To command the path leading down to it," growled the Subedar-Major.

"Yes. The only jungle-path in hundreds of square miles leading down to a place where there is a ford in the dry season. Sited where the path makes a right-angle in impenetrable jungle.

"And what were the orders in case of a large enemy party being seen by the sentry posted at the farthest point within sight of the picket?"

"Alarm to be given by volley-firing."

"Yes. And then?"

"Sentry group to retreat, one by one, crossing by means of the dug-out canoe."

"Yes?"

"Havildar or *naik* in charge to retreat along the river-bank, and cross by the rope-and-pole bridge."

"Yes?"

"They and the bridge-sentry were then to pull it across to this side."

"Yes? And except in case of emergency what were the standing orders? How was the sentry-group *always* to leave the picket?"

"March along the river-bank and cross by the bridge."

"Yes, *always*! And what were *your* orders about the picket?"

"Personally to see it relieved every night."

"Yes. Exactly. I ordered you, as senior Native Officer, and now Second-in-Command here, to see that those orders were carried out. Actually to visit the picket yourself every evening at Retreat. To see that it was evacuated in the way I directed; and that the men crossed by the bridge and in no other way. Also to see that the night picket was mounted on this side of the bridge; that nobody ever crossed by boat, and that the dug-out, the only craft in this part of the world, was always kept on this side.

"Those were the orders, weren't they?"

"*Han*, Sahib."

"And the fact that you carried them out until last night—so far as I know—shows that you understood them. Now then. Did you go yourself every night?"

And before the man could reply, Wendover answered his own question.

"No, you know you didn't. You sent Jemadar Rama Narayen or Jemadar Ganpat Mahadeo instead. You yourself went last night—and were too lazy to march a couple of miles, weren't you?"

The man shot an angry glare at Wendover, and began a protest.

"Too lazy. Too lacking in sense of duty, discipline and efficiency."

"Sahib, I . . ."

"Keep what you have to say for a Court-Martial. You are utterly unfit for your rank; unreliable and untrustworthy; a dishonest shirker. Through your laziness, misconduct, disobedience, a good man has been lost, and the garrison weakened, when every rifle counts. You are a disgrace to your Regiment."

The Native Officer's eyes blazed.

"And as soon as this post is relieved and we return to Headquarters, I'll have you put under arrest, and you shall stand your trial for causing the death of one of your men through deliberate disobedience and defiance of orders.

"*Shere Khan!*" he called, "give my salaams to the Doctor Sahib, and ask him to come and speak to me again here."

The Subedar-Major and Breckinge should have no opportunity for collusion until he had had another talk with the latter.

As Breckinge approached the Mess *banda*, Wendover again told the Subedar-Major that he might go. As he did so, the man cast a long and meaning look at Breckinge while they passed each other.

"I've been hearing things!" said Wendover, in a very significant tone of voice, as soon as the Native Officer was out of ear-shot; and awaited Breckinge's reply.

Receiving none, he continued:

"Tell me, Breckinge; why on earth did you want to pretend you knew nothing about what had happened to Sepoy Dhondoo Lakhsman?"

"I didn't say I knew nothing about it."

"I'm not talking about what you said, I'm talking about pretending. You deliberately gave me to understand that you didn't know what had happened to him."

"It's not my fault if you misunderstand what . . ."

"Don't talk rubbish. And don't wriggle and twist. Why can't you be straightforward? I distinctly remember saying to you '*Where's Sepoy Dhondoo Lakhsman?*' and your replying '*How should I know?*' What's that but giving me to understand that you didn't know what had happened to him?"

"It was no part of my duty to . . ."

"Look here, suppose you think less about what's

'part' of your duty and make *everything* your duty. Everything that will help, I mean. I know you are not a combatant Officer, and I am not going to ask you to use a rifle or take command of part of the defence if we are attacked again—though there are men in your service who would not need asking . . . But what I do say is—that you surely might do everything else in your power to assist in the defence of this post. That's what you are here for, isn't it?"

"I'm a doctor . . ."

"Yes," interrupted Wendover, "although at times one would not think it. You are a doctor, and you are here to assist in the defence of this post, primarily by looking after the health of the men. But I don't know that it is laid down in Regulations that you are forbidden to do everything in your power to help in other ways. Why didn't you tell me that Sepoy Dhondoo Lakhsman had been drowned?"

"It was no part of my duty to come and report to you that . . ."

"No part of your duty to come and report to me that one of the men was dead? Supposing for one moment that it were not, is it 'part of your duty' to pretend you know nothing about it when I ask you?"

"It was Subedar-Major Ganga Charan's business, not mine. I didn't wish to get him into trouble by . . ."

"Look here. Is your first duty to Subedar-Major Ganga Charan or to me? Even supposing your delicate conscience and high sense of duty prevented you even mentioning it, much less reporting it, why should you deny knowing anything about it?"

"I didn't deny it, I . . ."

"Oh, for God's sake, don't start that prevarication again. What sort of a reply is '*How should I know?*' but a negative? Now then, tell me all you know about it."

"The Subedar-Major can do that better than . . ."

"Don't I make myself clear? I ordered you to tell me all that you know about it."

"I only know what I was told."

"And so do I. And so will the Court-Martial. For the third and, I hope for your sake, last time—will you tell me what you know about the death of Sepoy Dhondoo Lakhsman."

"The Subedar-Major went to relieve the rifle-picket as usual . . ."

"Yes, 'as usual'!" prompted Wendover with a sarcastic inflection in his voice.

". . . and on this occasion, for some reason, gave orders for the sentry-group to cross by means of the dug-out canoe."

"Yes, in spite of strict and explicit orders that this was never to be done."

"Possibly he thought the manœuvre ought to be practised."

"And possibly, having walked a mile, he was too world-weary to walk back again. However, go on."

"And the last man coming over was upset and drowned."

"And you didn't think it worth mentioning to me. But you *did* think your knowledge of the matter worth denying."

To this Breckinge made no reply.

"Very interesting. Now, what is even more interesting is this. The Subedar-Major, whose duty it was, as you rightly say, immediately to report the matter to me, failed to do so. Not only that, but when, to his great surprise, I missed that particular sepoy, he went one better than you did. He didn't say *'How do I know?'* He didn't even say that he didn't know. He actually said the man was sick! When I asked why he wasn't in hospital, he said he had given him permission to lie down on his ground-sheet. When I pointed out that there was nobody lying down in his Section's sleeping-quarters, he said that, that being so, he didn't know where he was!"

"Well, I am not responsible for what he said to you," growled Breckinge insolently.

"No, but the interesting point, the point I'm getting at, is what he said to you, or rather, why he should have said it to *you*. You pretended to be very upset, just now, because I accused you of hob-nobbing with him and his crew. But doesn't it look as though that is

43

just about the state of affairs—since you know all about this matter, whereas I am told nothing at all? Why should *you* know all about it? Queer, isn't it?"

To this Breckinge made no reply beyond a sullen scowl.

"It will all sound a bit queer at the Court-Martial, won't it?" continued Wendover. "For I will certainly make no secret of the fact that there was something uncommonly like collusion between you and him to conceal a piece of absolutely criminal disobedience, indiscipline, and . . ."

"It was no business of mine. The orders he gave to the picket were nothing to do with . . ."

"And the reporting of the death of one of my men was nothing to do with you either, eh? The concealing of the fact was a part of your duty, eh? It was quite in order for you to reply '*How do I know?*' when I asked you the definite question. Well, we'll see what the Court-Martial thinks about it."

"I don't see that I . . . I don't think I . . ."

"No. Well, you'd better do a bit of pretty hard thinking. You'd better try to think up something to explain away what looks uncommonly like being an accessory; conspiring with a Native Officer to hide both the fact and the cause of the death of one of the men in your medical charge; being in collusion with a Native Officer deliberately to deceive me with a suggestion that a man had deserted with his kit, an excellent man whose death . . ."

A sentry shouted and fired his rifle.

Instantly Wendover pulled the whistle from his pocket and blew a long blast as he ran from the *banda* shouting "*Stand to!*" at the top of his voice. Whistles were loudly blown in all directions, and the cry of "*Stand to!*" repeated.

Snatching rifles and bandoliers, sepoys rushed from cooking-fires, washing-troughs and sleeping-quarters, to man the loop-holes.

For the whole of that day the outpost was besieged, a steady fire being maintained upon its walls from

44

hidden riflemen posted behind tree-trunks and in tree-tops; and for the whole of the following night Wendover patrolled its walls and trenches, visiting sentries, and doing all that courage, ability and devotion could, to strengthen and hearten its defence.

At dawn, the enemy again attacked the post from all four sides; but after a heavy fusillade, to which the garrison replied with vigour and effect, drew off, and a great peace fell upon the brooding jungle and exhausted Fort.

After doing all he could, and taking every precaution of which he could think, Wendover retired to his hut, ate a small portion of a stew of tough and disgusting bully beef which he decided had been left over, and returned to store, after the Boer War, treated himself to a stiff whisky-and-sparklet, and having given Shere Khan strict orders to wake him in a couple of hours' time, lay down for long over-due and much-needed sleep.

CHAPTER III

One morning a week later, the distant sound of gun-fire roused the hopes and revived the drooping spirits of the garrison of the Ubele outpost. And the same evening the *shenzis* who haunted the ford and owned the dug-out canoe informed a Swahili stretcher-bearer, formerly an askari of the King's African Rifles, that there had been a battle in which the latter had been victorious.

In the amazing way in which news does travel by *lokali*[25] and other means through the African jungle, further rumour reached the Ubele outpost. It was said that there were movements both to the North and South, and that relief would soon arrive.

What did arrive, next day, was a messenger announcing that a convoy and reinforcements had been despatched; that it would arrive the following morning; that it would be quickly followed by a strong column; that the Ubele post would be relieved; and that the survivors of its present garrison would be evacuated to the Base for rest and recuperation.

This message, typed on a small sheet of paper, was brought by a negro runner, a bold and intelligent fellow, one Marbrouk bin Suliman, who had been gun-boy to more than one mighty hunter in piping times of peace, and hoped to be so again when the war was o'er.

Having been bidden, by the Intelligence Officer who employed him, to carry it carefully and see that it arrived safely, he had cut himself a coconut, hacked off its thick green rind, bored a hole in its shell, poured out the milk, rolled the message up till it resembled a cigarette, poked it through the hole and closed the aperture with clay. Should any inquisitive and interfering person stop him on his hundred-mile journey,

---

[25] *Message-drums.*

46

he would be a humble *shenzi*, devoid of all possessions save a coconut, his poor provision for the morrow.

Having reached Ubele outpost and advanced cautiously into the open with his hands above his head, the one bearing the coconut and the other the branch of a tree in token of peaceful intent—an olive-branch, in fact—he was challenged by the sentry over the narrow and tortuous entrance to the *boma*, and bidden to halt.

In reply to the sepoy's *"Harlt! Who com dar?"* Marbrouk bin Suliman replied in Swahili and then in Mission School English, to the effect that he had a message for the *Bwana Macouba*.

The sentry called the Havildar of the Guard, in whose presence Marbrouk smashed the coconut and extracted the slightly damp but undamaged paper.

This the Havildar immediately sent to Wendover's *banda*, at the entrance of which the huge Pathan orderly, Shere Khan, formerly a *sowar* in Napier's Horse, squatted on his heels, cleaning and oiling his Sahib's clean and oily revolver.

"Get to Hell out of this, pig; for the Presence sleepeth," said he in Pushtu to the Hindu sepoy who carried the paper. His meaning was abundantly clear to the Hindustani-speaking sepoy.

Returning to the guard-hut, the man informed the Havildar that the Presence slept.

"Then take it to the Doctor Sahib," ordered the Havildar, anxious only for the avoidance of responsibility.

And to Breckinge the sepoy carried the message.

Twice and thrice Breckinge read it; thought awhile; stared before him for a minute, saying nothing; moistened his lips; smiled; and, taking an indelible pencil from his pocket, wrote on the back of the paper:

"Received, noted, and returned. A. Breckinge, Lt. I.M.S.," adding the word Ubele and the date.

"Look you," said he to the sepoy, "give this to the messenger, tell him to run quickly back and give it to the Colonel Sahib. Or perhaps you'd better bring him here to me."

47

And to Lieutenant Breckinge the sepoy brought Marbrouk bin Suliman, to whom, in very halting Swahili, in Hindustani and pidgin-English, Breckinge made it clear that the answer was as important as the message itself, and must, without fail and without loss of time, be taken back to the Base Camp. Particularly was the messenger to note that, should he meet a force on the way from the base to Ubele, the answer was to be shewn to the *Bwana* in command, before being taken on to the Base Camp.

"Very good, *Bwana*. I am running all the way," replied Marbrouk bin Suliman, saluting and showing magnificent teeth in a broad grin. And, turning upon his heel, he started forthwith upon his hundred-mile return journey.

Alec Breckinge, having sat awhile in thought, arose and went in search of Subedar-Major Ganga Charan. With this worthy he collogued for an hour; propounded to him a great, glowing and splendid idea; and with him came to what they considered a most satisfactory understanding, agreement and arrangement.

§2

Colonel Maldon was puzzled.

Obviously the messenger, bearing a book[26] wedged into a cleft stick, had come from Ubele; and the message was genuine. There could be no doubt that the man was speaking the simple truth when he said he had taken this 'book' to Ubele inside a coconut, as he did not know whether the way was clear and safe; that it had been read and signed by a black-faced *Bwana* who had told him to return with it and show it to the *Bwana* commanding any troops he might meet coming from Butindi to Ubele.

But why hadn't Wendover signed it?

And if he had been killed, why hadn't Breckinge mentioned the fact? There was plenty of room for him to have written a few words on the subject.

All very curious.

---

[26] *All letters are known as 'books' to the natives of East Africa.*

Again he questioned Marbrouk bin Suliman, but received no enlightenment. The man had evidently been challenged by a sentry, taken to the guard-hut, kept there until he had been sent for by Breckinge; and he had been told by Breckinge to return with the answer that he had written on the back.

Had he seen no other *Bwana*; no—er—white-faced *Bwana*?

No, only the black-faced *Bwana* who had written the 'book'.

From what the man said, Ubele outpost was obviously all right.

But apparently Lieutenant Breckinge, I.M.S., was in command.

And it was undoubtedly queer that he had not, at any rate, jotted down after his name,

"*For Captain Wendover, wounded,*" or sick, or something of that sort.

Presumably, if Wendover had been killed, Breckinge would have signed himself as,

"*Acting O.C. Ubele,*" if he didn't choose to state the fact in plain English that Wendover was dead. Perhaps he had some funny idea that the message might fall into enemy hands, and that there was no need to give them the information.

But that was absurd, as the messenger who had at that moment reached Ubele had just come unmolested through unoccupied country with the news of the advance and the information that the way between Butindi and Ubele was clear.

Well, he'd know soon enough, for they'd reach the place at dawn, as promised; and no doubt Wendover would come out with a patrol, and meet the relieving force.

And of course, Wendover might have been out on a patrol when the messenger reached Ubele; and this fellow Breckinge might have taken it upon him to sign the chit and return it without waiting for Wendover to come back—especially if he were out on a whole day's reconnaissance.

That wasn't likely, though.

No, Wendover would have sent out an officer's patrol under a Subedar.

Queer.

Next morning, according to plan and schedule, the relieving force, under Colonel Maldon, reached Ubele.

And as, riding the mule—to the use of which for a charger, the ravages of the *tsetse* fly had reduced him —Colonel Maldon, at the head of a long snake-like column, debouched from the jungle into the clearing, he noted that it was not Captain Richard Wendover, typical British Officer, who was coming forth to meet him, but a swarthy-faced man, dark as an Indian, whose tunic, donned for the occasion, bore the black tabs of the Indian Medical Service.

"Good morning. Where's Wendover?" he asked dismounting from his mule and returning the Medical, Officer's salute. "Not wounded, I hope?"

Breckinge looked uncomfortable and glanced away.

"Not been killed?"

"Oh, no, Sir. No."

"Sick?"

Again Breckinge looked away from Colonel Maldon's face, in apparent embarrassment.

"Damn it all, man!" snapped the Colonel. "Can't you answer a plain question? Where's Captain Wendover?"

There was a moment's silence; and as the Colonel opened his mouth for the utterance of one of the remarkable ejaculations and tirades for which he was famous,

"He's lying down," said Breckinge.

"Lying down? Lying down? What the devil do you mean? Is he ill?"

"No, Sir. He's not ill."

"What then?"

"He's . . . asleep."

"*Asleep!* At ten o'clock in the morning! But wasn't he expecting me? Didn't he get my message? I sent a man on, a couple of hours ago."

"Yes, Sir. We had the information yesterday, saying you'd arrive this morning; and your own messenger arrived just after *reveille* this morning."

"Well?"

"Captain Wendover was asleep when the messenger arrived yesterday. And he was still asleep this morning."

Colonel Maldon did then utter one of his private personal and peculiar ejaculations.

"But confound it all," he added, "he isn't a Damned Dormouse, is he? Not a Blasted Bee hibernating, is he?"

Breckinge remained silent.

"I say! He hasn't got sleeping sickness, has he?" enquired Colonel Maldon, with real concern in his voice. "No, you said he wasn't sick," he added.

"No, Sir, he's not sick."

"What then?"

"You'd better come and have a look at him, Sir."

By this time, Colonel Maldon and Breckinge had passed the arms-presenting guard and entered the *boma*.

"This way, Sir," said Breckinge, and led the Colonel to Wendover's doorless *banda*.

Colonel Maldon looked inside the hut.

On a folding canvas camp-bed, furnished with a dirty khaki sheet and khaki-covered pillow, lay Captain Richard Wendover, breathing stertorously. Beside him was an almost-empty uncorked whisky-bottle, some of the contents of which had run over his clothing and the frowsy bed.

On the small folding camp-table, beside the bed, stood another whisky-bottle, empty; and on the mud floor beside it, lay a tin mug.

A squalid and unpleasant sight.

To the fastidious eye of Colonel Maldon, military martinet, a most disgusting scene; incredible; an unshaven tousled officer in crumpled filthy clothing on a whisky-sodden bed, snoring open-mouthed.

Drunk.

A man among whose many virtues patience was not the most prominent, the Colonel seized Wendover's arm and shook him violently, pulled him into a sitting position, bawled loud and lurid exhortations in his ear, and then let him fall back limp, inert and senseless on the filthy bed.

For a long minute he stared at the unconscious officer, his face expressive of mingled contempt, disgust and sorrow.

"Good God!" he breathed. "Drunk as David's sow!" and retired from the stinking hut.

So that was it.

"How long has he been like this?" he asked.

"On this occasion, Sir? Oh, about twenty-four hours," replied Breckinge.

"Let your men dismiss; and bring me the Subedar-Major and the other native officers," ordered Colonel Maldon.

CHAPTER IV

At the Court-Martial—consisting of Lieutenant-Colonel Matheson of The King's African Rifles; Major Bonnington, R.E.; Major Hawley of the R.F.A.; Captain Marvin and Captain Brace of the Twentieth Bombay Infantry—Lieutenant Breckinge did his painful duty with evident reluctance. Nevertheless it was most utterly damning—and completely unshakeable under cross-examination.

Captain Wendover had kept strict personal charge of the ration whisky. Before the death of Lieutenant Hunter-Ward, things had not been so bad. This officer had acted as Quarter-Master, and all stores, including ration whisky, had been in his charge.

And although there had always been a bottle of whisky in Captain Wendover's *banda*, it could not be said that the latter had ever been patently the worse for drink. Not what a liberal-minded reasonable man-of-the-world would call really drunk. He had drunk whisky at dinner, to call it such, in the Mess *banda*; and as Captain Wendover, Lieutenant Hunter-Ward and Lieutenant Breckinge had sat round the table after mess, Captain Wendover had continued to drink whisky. Lieutenant Hunter-Ward had always confined himself to one whisky-and-sparklet at dinner.

Lieutenant Breckinge himself was a teetotaller.

When, on various occasions, witness had had reason to go to Captain Wendover's *banda* during the night, there had always been a whisky-bottle and a mug on the table beside his camp-bed. He had rather gathered the impression that Captain Wendover drank it neat. At night-time, that is to say. Probably it helped him to sleep. He had never seen the sparklet-syphon in his *banda*.

No, up to that time witness had never seen him what might be called really intoxicated; completely drunk.

Of that he was quite sure.

But after the death of Lieutenant Hunter-Ward, Captain Wendover had himself taken charge of stores and acted as Quarter-Master—possibly because there was no other European combatant Officer, and he did not trust his Native Officers. Though why this should have been the case, witness did not know.

It was from then onward that things had got so bad, and had rapidly gone from bad to worse.

Undoubtedly Captain Wendover drank alone in his *banda*, drank continually, drank to excess, was always more or less drunk, and at night quite definitely so.

It had made things very difficult for Lieutenant Breckinge, to whom the Native Officers, from time to time, had appealed for assistance and advice, in spite of the fact that he was not a combatant Officer. He had done his best; had tried to shield Captain Wendover; to explain away his misconduct; and to foster the belief that his incredible behaviour was due to illness, fever, heat-stroke—that sort of thing.

In point of fact, witness had had a very bad time indeed; and, even early in the morning, Captain Wendover would be quite irresponsible; labouring under delusions; violent-tempered; as intemperate in speech as in habits; and most insulting.

Twice witness had gone to prisoner's *banda* at night and had found it quite impossible to wake him up. Nor, to a doctor, did it need the evidence of the empty whisky-bottle, still clutched in Captain Wendover's hand, to show the reason for this.

In fact, the questions, both of the prosecuting and defending officers, merely served to bear out the plain, clear, and simple statement of Colonel Maldon as to the state of affairs he had discovered on reaching the Ubele outpost.

The reluctance of Subedar-Major Ganga Charan was not quite so apparent.

That there should be a Court-Martial, Captain Richard Wendover had promised, and a Court-Martial indeed there was! But not upon the excellent Subedar-

Major Ganga Charan. Oh, no! Far otherwise had the Gods of Ind ordained.

What a truly colossal jest! And gloriously subtle as it was colossal. Rightly indeed had the Subedar-Major had his caste-mark painted on his forehead by the holiest of Brahmins, a grain of rice securely adhering in the middle of it.

A Court-Martial indeed! And on the tyrannical, over-bearing, fault-finding, *zubberdusti* Sahib who had threatened to Court-Martial and break him; *him*, Subedar-Major Ganga Charan.

Here was *zulm* rightly punished!

Yes, he swore under cross-examination; all had indeed been as the Doctor Sahib had stated in evidence. And worse. Many times, when the Subedar-Major had gone to the Captain Sahib to make report, he had found him *matwala*, violent, noisy, abusive; not only unwilling to listen to a word the Subedar-Major had to say, but quite unable to understand it when he did say it. *Bé-hosh anr bé-ukl* with *sherab*; drunk with whisky.

It was a dreadful pity, for at other times, when sober, he had been a very good officer, and it had been a pleasure to be under his kind control, though of course it wasn't like being under one's own proper officer, whom one knew, and who always treated one correctly.

Young Captain Brace, just promoted, and so the junior officer of the Court-Martial, was much impressed by the reluctant evidence of this dignified Native Officer, in whom a strong sense of duty seemed to struggle with the desire to say as little as possible that would be damaging to the accused.

Captain Brace found the whole business extremely painful; and, while pitying Captain Wendover in his terrible plight, could scarcely repress the indignation that he felt against a responsible British Officer who could put himself in such a position that the evidence of Indian officers and sepoys had to be taken concerning his conduct.

However, pity was all very well; but it was a shameful and disgraceful thing, utterly unpardonable, that a British Officer should be found blind drunk when in command of a post.

Bad enough at any time, but bad beyond words in time of war and in the presence of Indian troops, not to mention the presence of the enemy. For the post had been under fire not many hours before, and might have been again, at any moment. A nice thing if the place had been attacked while its Commanding Officer lay on his bed in his hut, blind to the world.

He didn't wish to be priggish, narrow-minded or censorious, but . . .

Personally, he wasn't a teetotaller, but . . .

And, of course, it must have been drink, though the man most certainly did not look a drunkard, nor even an habitual user of alcohol in fairish moderation. Could it possibly be something else? One of those sad cases of the use of some such muck as hashish or opium? Well, if so, that was as bad as drink or worse. Yes, much worse. More cold-blooded and deliberate. Or could it have been an attempt at suicide with some sort of sleeping-draught? A case like that of the wounded doctor whom he had seen . . . But why should Wendover commit suicide when relief was at hand? Out of his mind with strain and anxiety? No— not that sort of chap at all.

Awful tragedy. And the evidence left no possibility of doubt. This Subedar-Major evidently hated the way he had been let down—and who should blame him?

Yes, Subedar-Major Ganga Charan made a very good impression upon him, and by no means an unfavourable one upon the other members of the Court-Martial, though the President, Colonel Matheson, seemed disposed to question him at some length.

Nor did the evidence of Subedar Gopal Mangal materially differ from that of his brother-in-law, the Subedar-Major.

It would, indeed, have been remarkable if it had done so, in view of the fact that the two officers understood each other (and the position) very thoroughly, and had spent no little time in discussing the matter together—and again with Jemadar Rama Narayen, who was the Subedar-Major's cousin, and Jemadar Ganpat Mahadeo, who was the cousin of Jemadar Rama Narayen.

Jemadar Rama Narayen, it appeared, had also found Captain Wendover a good and kindly officer, save when—well—when he was 'under the influence,' so to speak; when he had the bottle of *sherab* at his elbow. Then was he indeed filled with the spirit of *zubberdust* and *zulm*; harsh, oppressive, and insulting; very *sakht*, and quite unjust. At other times also, when he had been drinking, he was without sense or understanding; stupid, and liable to give absurd and impossible orders; and, to respectful questions, absurd and impossible answers.

Upon Captain Brace, Jemadar Rama Narayen also made a very favourable impression, heightening his indignation against the wretched drunkard, who seemed to have done his best to lower the whole standard of prestige of the British Officer, in the eyes of those grave, responsible and experienced men.

Subedar Gopal Mangal, brother of the Subedar-Major, questioned by the prosecution, also gave chapter and verse, instance and example, of extremely peculiar behaviour on the part of Captain Wendover. He had received shameful and face-blackening abuse from him; and had been witness of painful and somewhat disgraceful scenes in which his superior officers had been involved with the Captain Sahib.

Jemadar Ganpat Mahadeo gave evidence of how, once, the Captain Sahib had threatened to strike him, and had appeared to be about to do so. On cross-examination it was elicited from this witness that on the occasion to which he referred, the Captain Sahib had shouted at him, clenched his fist and shaken it in his face.

This painful event had been witnessed by Havildar Ramrao Dalkesar. Most clearly he remembered it. Who could forget such a thing? He had thought at the time that the Captain Sahib had gone mad, so red was his face, so thick his utterance; but when he had gone off with uncertain and staggering gait, the Havildar had been forced reluctantly to modify his opinion.

Nor, unfortunately, was the evidence of certain sepoys different from that of their officers, or to be in anywise shaken by the cross-examination of the officer in charge of the defence.

Perhaps the testimony of the nondescript creature who cooked—or failed to cook—food for the Captain Sahib, was not regarded as being of much value, though he swore upon the Koran that it was that gentleman's habit to call him most evil names; to assault him violently in the rear every time he turned his back to leave his presence; and daily to threaten to seat him firmly on his own cooking-fire. He had gone in terror of the officer when that cruel and terrible man was under the influence of the Forbidden Drink. When quite sober he had been no worse than the other *Bwanas* who had employed deponent.

In point of fact, the sole witness who might have been of any help to the officer detailed for the defence, was the accused's orderly, Shere Khan; and more than one member of the Court listened to his testimony with a hidden smile. Such was the vehemence and truculence of this witness, that with a glance at Major Bonnington, the President murmured "Save us from our friends." For Shere Khan, ere he could be checked and sharply reprimanded, declared that the Doctor Sahib was a black-faced liar, and the Hindoo Native Officers and sepoys were pigs—and worse than pigs— for they were simply Hindoos.

When reduced to glowering silence and bidden by the President to answer the questions that were put to him and refrain from offending the ears of the Court with a statement of his outrageous opinions, he did so with a superfluity of zeal.

According to Shere Khan, the Captain Sahib never drank whisky at all. Shere Khan had never seen a whisky-bottle in the Captain Sahib's *banda*. He had never come into the *banda* and found the Captain Sahib asleep. In reply to the Judge Advocate's question as to whether he had ever found the accused sleeping so soundly that he had been unable to wake him, he was not content with denying this, but added a statement of his firm belief that the Captain Sahib never slept at all. Anyhow, he had never seen him sleeping.

When cross-examined on the subject of the accused Officer's threatening, abusive, and insulting speech when addressing witnesses, he roundly swore that nothing of the sort had ever taken place in his presence or hearing. And this in spite of the fact that Lieutenant Breckinge and Subedar-Major Ganga Charan stated that he had been present on one particularly and peculiarly painful occasion, and had, moreover, actually been the messenger who had fetched them from their respective posts to the Mess *banda* where Captain Wendover awaited them, and where the incident took place.

And then as to the allegation of Sepoy Arjun Atmaran that he had been sent by the Havildar of the Guard to the Captain Sahib's *banda* with the chit brought by the Swahili messenger. Sepoy Arjun Atmaran testified that Orderly Shere Khan had been seated in front of the *banda*, and, with curses and foul insults, had bade him begone because the Captain Sahib was asleep and could not be awakened.

"*Must* not be awakened, or *could* not be awakened?" enquired the Prosecuting Counsel.

"Could not," replied the sepoy emphatically.

And the point was elaborated.

"Are you quite sure that Orderly Shere Khan said,

"'*Go away, for the Captain Sahib cannot be awakened. It is an order'?*" asked the Prosecuting Officer.

"It is the truth. I am quite sure," replied Sepoy Arjun Atmaran. "Orderly Shere Khan said,

"'*Begone, pig of a Hindoo. It is useless to wait here, for I cannot awaken the Captain Sahib. No one could awaken him. Nothing could awaken him.'*"

Nor did Shere Khan at this point improve matters at all by shooting a most sinister and baleful glare at Sepoy Arjun Atmaran, and, in a softly sibilant but clearly audible voice, promising to disembowel him at an early date.

It cannot be said that Captain Richard Wendover made a particularly good impression upon the President or any member of the Court-Martial, in spite of the fact that each of his judges was, consciously or unconsciously, prejudiced in his favour by reason of his record, appearance, and conduct of the defence of the Fort up to the time of the death of Lieutenant Hunter-Ward—when it really seemed that he had relinquished control and command of the post to Lieutenant Breckinge and the Subedar-Major Ganga Charan.

Certainly his manner before the Court bore out, to some extent, the charge of truculence; for, short of a display of ill-manners, ill-breeding, indiscipline and contempt of court, he showed signs, to say the least of it, of short temper, frayed nerves and a lack of reverence, if not respect, for the majesty of the Law as embodied in his present judges.

His answers were brief and given with an impatience that was just not contemptuous; his attitude being one of,

"Good Lord above us, are you mad, or do you think I am? Are you drunk, that you think I was? What are you talking about; and why the devil are you talking such nonsense? Of course I drank whisky in reasonable moderation—like you do. Yes, of course I had a drink before I lay down, and of course I did not drink two bottles, neat. Why don't you ask a real fool question while you are about it?"

Without using those words, he contrived to give that tone to his defence, and to imply that the four Officers before him, or before whom he was, ought to have something better to do, especially in time of war, than to sit there pestering him with futile, puerile and idiotic questions.

Under cross-examination he became very definitely restive, put a very patent curb on what was very obvious anger, and contrived to show that such respect as he had for the Court was not respect for any individual member of it—inasmuch as they had forfeited his regard by their incredible credulity and stupidity.

To the question,

"What's the last thing you remember before going to sleep on the Thursday night?"

"Yawning," he replied.

"That's not a proper answer," rapped the President, whose patience was being rapidly exhausted by the prisoner's unpleasant and unrepentant manner. "Not a proper answer at all."

"It's the truth, anyway. Last thing I can remember is—yawning."

"Well," resumed the Prosecuting Officer, "we'll go back a little further. What's the last thing you remember before yawning?"

"Scratching myself."

"Indeed! And before that?"

"I couldn't be absolutely certain as to the order in which the events occurred, but I think that, before doing that, I had another drink of whisky."

"I've no doubt you did. . . . Did you pour it out into a mug or drink out of the bottle?"

"Neither."

"What d'you mean—'neither'?"

"What I say. It was already poured out."

"Oh. You mean you had another drink of what was already in the mug."

"Obviously."

"And how many times did you re-fill the mug?"

"None."

"None?"

"What do you mean—'none'?" interrupted the President of the Court.

"I mean that I had not re-filled the mug at all."

"Well, what else *do* you mean, if you mean anything?"

"I mean that I finished the drink that was in the mug."

"But you've just said you took another drink."

Wendover sighed with a somewhat ostentatiously

weary patience.

"I did. I took another drink at the whisky-and-water already in the mug."

Frowning, Colonel Matheson tapped the papers in front of him with the end of his pen.

"And you really mean to tell the Court," resumed the Prosecuting Officer, "that that one drink made you so absolutely drunk and incapable that Colonel Maldon was quite unable to wake you?"

"I don't mean to tell the Court anything of the sort. I have told the Court that I had one drink."

"Then how do you account for being found drunk?"

"I don't account for it. And I don't admit that I was drunk."

"In the face of all the evidence to the contrary—and part of it expert medical evidence?"

"Particularly in the face of the latter," was the reply; an answer which moved Colonel Matheson once again to remark that the accused was not doing himself or his cause any good at all by taking that sort of line.

". . . And how do you account for the fact that you never received Colonel Maldon's message?"

"Simply because it was never brought to me."

"And why was it not brought to you?"

"Because I was asleep; and because, knowing that I had had hardly any sleep for some time, my orderly refused to allow me to be awakened."

"Had you given any such instructions?"

"No."

"Doesn't it seem a little curious that your orderly should have taken it upon him, on this particular occasion, to do what you had not told him to do, and what he had never done before?"

"Curious? No. Very sensible, in the circumstances."

"H'm. . . . You deny that your orderly failed to give you the message because he was *unable* to wake you?"

"Totally."

"How do you know he didn't try to wake you?"

"Because he says he didn't."

"He's incapable of a lie, eh? Like all Indians. Like all Pathans."

"And like all the rest of us," growled Wendover, and again received the sharp admonition of the Court.

"You wish us to understand that, like George Washington also, he could not tell a lie, eh?" resumed the prosecution.

"Understand what you like. I said nothing of the sort. In point of fact, he's a remarkably good liar. But as it happens, he tells me the truth."

"And is he telling us the truth?"

"Absolutely—in saying he did not try to wake me."

"And once again, how do you know that?"

"Once again—because he told me so."

"Ah! . . . Now, would it surprise you to learn that, being informed that you were asleep, Lieutenant Breckinge came and endeavoured to wake you himself?"

"It would. Very much indeed."

"What is there surprising about his coming to try to awaken you, so that you could receive the message?"

"Nothing. Nothing whatever. What would be surprising would be the fact of his *failing* to do it."

"Yes," agreed prosecuting Counsel significantly. "It was truly surprising."

And Lieutenant Breckinge, being recalled and cross-questioned, testified again that, feeling it his duty to attempt to bring the message to the notice of his superior officer, he had tried every means known, both to lay experience and to science, of awakening a sleeper and arousing a—drunkard. And had tried in vain.

On being further cross-questioned by the defence as to why the orderly, Shere Khan, was in total ignorance of the Doctor's visit to the accused's *banda*, Breckinge quite frankly admitted that it might not be by reason of the orderly's perjury. It was quite possible that the orderly had not seen the Doctor enter the *banda*. To be quite honest, he himself couldn't remember whether the orderly had been sitting outside the *banda* (as Sepoy Arjun Atmaran had found him) or not; but it was quite possible that he had gone away for some reason. Anyhow, the fact remained . . .

And in the minds of the members of the Court it had remained.

Why *should* a doctor swear, upon oath, that he had gone to try to arouse an officer, and had been unable to do so, if such were not the case?

No, it cannot be said that the accused made a favourable impression upon his judges, five plain, honourable, simple men; men who would infinitely have preferred to find the accused Not Guilty; men anxious only to do their duty; but at the same time anxiously hopeful that it might be the pleasant duty of acquitting a brother officer of a shameful charge.

Nevertheless, had one of them been a doctor, and that doctor a man of wide experience, keen powers of observation and of sympathetic understanding, there would have been at least one member of the Court-Martial who would not have written down the accused as merely truculent and resentful almost to the point of insolence.

To such a man, the undeniable "queerness" of the accused would have suggested an explanation which did not occur to any layman present at the trial, save only—and very briefly—to Captain Brace.

A doctor there was, but he was not a judge.

He was a witness, and for the Prosecution.

Not for him was it to draw attention to the condition of the pupils of the accused's eyes; the state of his skin; his breathing; his manner (most unusual in Wendover) of alternating excitement and lethargy, a period of irritability followed by one of apparent indifference, weariness and boredom.

To him, the reason for the accused's appearance and conduct was known; and to the judges he had no intention of making it known.

And as he sat and watched the man whom he considered to be his mortal enemy, no smile of satisfaction marred the extremely correct expression of his countenance while he offered himself double felicitation—as a scientist and as a man of affairs.

The Man of a Ghost

As a man of affairs, he had given an enemy a lesson and a well-deserved punishment; to himself a neat revenge and a well-earned gratification.

As a man of science, genuinely interested in toxicology, he had evidently effected the perfect quantitative combination of morphine, *datura* and the little-known—indeed, to Europeans unknown—native drug which the African *shenzis* call *tafu*, and which has very remarkable properties.

Yes, any good doctor present at the Court-Martial would have known that there was something mentally and physically—and temporarily—wrong with the accused; and he might have saved him.

Lieutenant Breckinge knew exactly what was wrong, and that nobody but Lieutenant Breckinge could save him.

Young Captain Brace, an imaginative and very conscientious man, was sorely worried. As junior officer of the Court-Martial he would be the first called upon to pronounce judgment, in accordance with the salutary rule which orders this procedure, by reason of the fact that the opinion of junior officers would probably be swayed by that of their experienced seniors.

Having carefully studied King's Regulations, he was aware that an officer found guilty by Field General Court-Martial, was liable to the penalties of death, penal servitude for life, a term of imprisonment, cashiering, dismissal from the Service, reduction in seniority, reprimand, or fine by stoppage of pay.

Clearly there could be no question as to the verdict. Most obviously Captain Richard Wendover was guilty, and the prolongation of the trial scarcely necessary, in view of the fact that Colonel Maldon had himself found him drunk and incapable while in command of a post in time of war.

What would the punishment be, provided the verdict were 'Guilty'—as it must be?

Death!

For that to be the sentence, all members of the Court-Martial must concur. They must be unanimous in their condemnation of him to death; and then the finding of the Court must be confirmed by superior authority, presumably the General Officer Commanding at Headquarters. And after that, he believed the proceedings of the Court-Martial would have to be reviewed by the Judge-Advocate-General, who could agree to, or refuse, the confirmation of the General. But probably the death sentence would be considered unnecessarily harsh and severe.

Penal servitude or imprisonment?

A dreadful thought. On the other hand, it was a very dreadful thing that an Officer of the King, in time of war, should do such a thing, set such an example.

Yes, the sentence might well be one of imprisonment, seeing that the offence had been committed on active service. Probably much would depend on the view taken by the General; and, whatever he and the Judge-Advocate-General thought about it, there was still the right of appeal, either to the Army Council or through the Army Council to the King.

Well, it might be a wise provision that the junior officer must speak first; but he could wish the authorities had not been quite so wise. He would greatly have preferred to hear what Colonel Matheson, Major Bonnington, Major Hawley and Captain Marvin had to say, before he was called on to open his mouth.

The sentence of the Court, confirmed by the General Officer Commanding, and reviewed without objection by the Judge-Advocate-General, was that Captain Richard Wendover, for behaving in a scandalous manner unbecoming an officer and a gentleman, be cashiered. In other words, dismissed with ignominy from the King's Service, not only forfeiting his commission, but being permanently disqualified from ever serving the State in any capacity whatsoever.

It was generally considered that Captain Wendover had been very lucky, treated very leniently; and that his previous good service had been given every consideration and been allowed to weigh very heavily in his favour.

But few of his friends and acquaintances heard with regret, some months later, that Richard Wendover was dead; and perhaps those who loved him best regarded this as best.

Richard Wendover was dead—and better dead.

PART II

CHAPTER I

Major Robinson, R.E., in charge of the construction of the Morovo section of the railway that was being built from Navoi to Tabundi, was having trouble again at rail-head; trouble between his Hindu and Mohammedan labour forces—masons, navvies and coolies—and trouble between himself and the unruly and turbulent Pathan gangs who called themselves *karygars*, *mymars* and *barkays*—artisans, skilled workmen, builders, carpenters and masons worth fifty rupees a month, and who were nothing of the sort, being mere brawny unskilled labourers, plain coolies worth something more like ten rupees.

Outspokenly, these sturdy rogues called Major Robinson a skinflint, a hard-faced robber who ground the faces of the poor; while Major Robinson, equally outspoken, called them what they were, impostors, liars and humbugs.

This would have been all very well had these gangs of Afridis, Mahsuds, Mohmands, Zakka Khel, Ghilzais, Shinwaris and assorted tribesmen from the North-West Frontier of India, been Hindus or even British subjects. Since they were nobody's subjects, and each man not only considered himself, but knew himself, to be as good a man as Major Robinson, and perhaps a good deal better, awkward crises were apt to arise; and it was then that Major Robinson and Mr. Angus Mackenzie, his Superintendent of Works, wished that the nearest body of armed Military Police or Company of the King's African Rifles was not quite so far away.

But for the turbulent Pathans, trouble among the thousands of Indian coolies working on the line would have been easily settled and almost negligible.

As it was, the two Britons knew that they went not only in danger of their lives, but, what was much more important, in grave danger of a more or less protracted hold-up of the work that had to be completed by a given date, a day which seemed to approach with greater speed than that with which the railway approached its destination.

The Pathans were a curse, and, but for the fact that any one of them could do the unskilled work of two Hindus, they would never have been engaged and imported, by labour-contractors, from Peshawar to Mombasa, to be despatched to the great railway construction work.

And having engaged them and brought them to Africa, there was no dismissing them, apart from any question of contract, for they would not have accepted dismissal; and had not their pay been forthcoming promptly, there would have been a riot, loot, destruction and murder.

So that it was not with great enthusiasm that Major Robinson interviewed two Pathans brought to him by the *jemadar maistri* in charge of a gang of navvies.

It appeared that the two men had, in the amazing way of the wandering Pathan, strolled up from the coast, and had applied for work. However, inasmuch as they were a pair of fine upstanding men, whose faces he rather liked, and who seemed to have no unduly exalted ideas of their powers, importance and value as workmen, he agreed to the *jemadar maistri* engaging them.

As Major Robinson turned away with a curt, "You may go," the applicant calling himself Shere Khan, and who had spoken for the two of them, observed casually, and speaking not only as man to man but as equal to equal,

"Oh, by the way, we found a dead Sahib three days ago."

"*What?* Where?" enquired Robinson.

"Oh, over there," replied the Pathan, pointing to the north. "In the bush, out on the plains, three days ago. Undoubtedly a Sahib—or part of one."

"What do you mean?"

"A lion had had him. These are his boots that I am wearing."

"The man's boots, I mean. Not the lion's," he added with a chuckle.

What nameless tragedy was this? Some adventurous wandering trader, professional hunter, missionary, cold-weather big-game sportsman, planter out on a shooting-trip, or what?

"But were there no 'boys' anywhere near? No camp?"

"No; nobody."

"What did you do with his rifle?"

"Hadn't got one."

"I don't believe it."

"No?"

"What did you do with the body?"

"Buried it."

"Oh? What with?"

"Well, not to say buried it, perhaps," replied the Pathan. "Piled stones on it, you know, and put a *boma* of thorn-branches round the cairn."

"H'm. How was the body dressed?"

"Rags and blood, mostly. He had only had a shirt, shorts, puttees and boots, like yourself."

"Oh. No rifle, hunting-knife, ammunition-belt?"

"No. Nothing," grinned the Pathan.

"And you brought away nothing except the boots, eh?"

"Yes," replied the Pathan, and nodding his head in the direction of his companion, added, "He said, '*Bring the top of the collar of the shirt along*,' because it had got writing on it, and doubtless we should get a large reward," and he grinned again.

"Well, where is it?"

From beneath his own long and dirty shirt, worn outside baggy trousers fastened round the ankle, the Pathan produced a piece of soiled and blood-stained khaki which, unrolled, proved to be the collar and part of the yoke of a khaki army shirt, on the inner side of which was sewn a white tab on which was worked, in small red letters, the name of its owner:

R. WENDOVER.

"Mackenzie!" called Major Robinson as he stared at the rag. "Come and look at this."

And from his tent, pitched close by, the Superintendent of Works emerged.

"Look," said Robinson, holding out the fragment of shirt.

Mackenzie read the name and stared in amazement.

"Good God!" he whispered, "Wendover. That's the chap who was kicked out of the army, for being drunk in charge of a fort, and disappeared, isn't it?"

"That's the chap. Vanished at Nairobi when he should have been going down to Kilindini to take ship for England. Supposed to have cleared off and gone native instead of going—Home."

"Best thing he could do, too," observed Mackenzie.

"Well, these two bright lads seem to have found his body," said Robinson. "Took this off a white man's body, anyhow. Been mauled and half eaten by a lion."

"Just as likely they murdered him," opined Angus Mackenzie, who had very little love, and only grudging admiration, for Pathans.

"Quite likely," agreed Major Robinson, "but for the fact that they brought his collar here. Why should they do that if they had come across him camped in the jungle, and murdered him for his rifle and kit."

"To get a reward for 'finding' him," observed Mackenzie pawkily.

"Wouldn't put it past them. In point of fact, the chap who brought it does propose that he be rewarded. Said the other cove noticed the name on the collar, and suggested taking it to the nearest official. High sense of public duty—stimulated by hope of something out of the poor-box."

"Well, there it is," he added. "Whether the lion did him in or they did him down, it seems to put clear *Finis* to the Wendover story, doesn't it?"

"Yes, poor devil! And not even Christian burial," agreed Angus Mackenzie, a strictly pious and religious-minded man, to whom such an idea was most abhorrent.

"I suppose they want a job of work," he asked.

"Yes."

"Well, we can do with them."

"What's your name?" Major Robinson asked the man who had produced the collar.

"Shere Khan," was the reply.

"And yours?"

"Gul Mahommed," growled the other.

"Well, I'll keep this and . . ."

"What reward do I get, *Huzoor*?" asked Shere Khan.

"Reward? I don't know. A rope perhaps. We'll wait and hear what the Police have to say about it when they've found the body and discovered whether the lion killed him with a bullet or a knife. You may go."

Shere Khan and Gul Mahommed saluted airily and went, grinning broadly.

In due course, and when opportunity arose, Major Robinson reported Shere Khan's story to the District Officer, and forwarded the piece of khaki shirt bearing the name of Wendover.

Later, an officer of the Railway Police arrived at the ever-advancing rail-head and questioned the two Pathans, Shere Khan and Gul Mahommed, but was unable to shake their testimony.

Inasmuch as the scene of the tragedy was apparently fifty or sixty miles distant; was in some vague and unlocated spot on the vast rolling scrub-covered Kathedong Plains, search for the grave was, not unnaturally, fruitless. A patrol of the King's African Rifles, having business in that direction, kept a sharp lookout for a little thorn-enclosed cairn of stones that should mark a grave; and with the same degree of hope and success wherewith they would have sought a needle in a haystack.

§2

Although under some slight suspicion of murder, the two Pathans, Shere Khan and Gul Mahommed, earned the approval of their overseer, who reported them as being steady, if utterly unskilled, workers, quiet and well-behaved men, not troublesome nor truculent, and peaceful beyond the ordinary of Pathans. Indeed, the silent one, Gul Mahommed, was the sort of man who might look for promotion by reason of his unusual intelligence, industry and sense of responsibility. He would make a very good gang-leader and, in time, a *maistri* foreman-overseer of navvies. It was a great pity he had been taught no trade and was not a skilled mason.

Like his fellow-tribesman, brother or friend, he really knew nothing at all about working or dressing stone; and, having no knowledge whatever of stone-cutting, could not possibly be called a *mymar*, a mason, and be given forty or fifty rupees a month. Yet it was a pity to keep him as an ordinary coolie, because, although untaught and untrained, he undoubtedly had brain as well as brawn.

Major Robinson, who had served on the North-West Frontier of India, spoke Pushtu, and not only knew the Pathan well but liked him very well—save when he had to employ him in bulk as a labour force.

He preferred Pathan soldiers to any other, and numbered among the head-men of the Khyber country many friends whose village hospitality he had enjoyed when on survey or shooting trips. Shoot you in the front, as an uninvited and unwanted trespasser, they would . . . Stab you in the back while, or after, enjoying their hospitality they would not.

And frequently, Robinson chatted with the Pathan workmen of his construction gangs. When, through some real or fancied grievance, generally the latter, there was trouble afoot or mischief brewing, they would be unresponsive, surly and unfriendly. At other times, they would talk freely, as man to man, with quip and jest, sly reference to alleged victories of the Tribesmen over the British, and to all-too-authentic and bloody raids upon Peshawar.

As a man, they liked Major Robinson, who knew

their country and spoke their language, even though, as a paymaster, they might dislike him to the point of cutting his throat.

With Shere Khan and his friend Gul Mahommed, as two of the pleasantest and most interesting of the Pathans, Major Robinson frequently talked. Widely travelled, they knew much of India and Africa; and had, in Robinson's opinion, undoubtedly served in the Indian Army.

Of the two, Shere Khan was the more forthcoming, merry and chatty—a most genial great ruffian; Gul Mahommed the more intelligent, educated and observant. He took great interest in news of the outside world which reached Major Robinson with his somewhat irregular and infrequent mail. Two very fine specimens of a very fine race. Indeed, as Major Robinson remarked to Mr. Angus Mackenzie, two of the nicest murderers he had ever met.

He had good occasion to think so later—though he was left but little time or inclination for thinking of anything for some while—by reason of the receipt of a most amazing letter. This was written in pencil on a piece of somewhat dirty paper which had been found near, or purloined from, the hut which served as Mr. Mackenzie's Office of Works. Written in perfect English and excellent handwriting, it ran as follows:

"*Sir,*
You are most urgently advised to carry a revolver to-morrow, loaded, and to keep the flap of the holster unfastened, if you go near the Pathan construction-gangs, or if a deputation comes to your tent. Also to look out for an ambush if you go by trolley to the bridge. There is trouble brewing among the Mahsud coolies whom you have refused to pay at mason rates.
Do please take notice of this warning.
Yours very sincerely,
John Smith."

"What do you make of this, Mackenzie?" he asked his Superintendent of Works.

"Who the devil is John Smith?" was the reply.

"God knows. There's no such person about here, that I've heard of."

"Just what I was thinking," was the reply. "Smith? Smith? There's no European at rail-head or for a hundred miles, is there, except the Doctor; and as his name's Hannington, he probably doesn't spell it Smith."

"Nor write anonymous letters," agreed Robinson, "or rather, write under a *nom de plume*."

"What's the Greek contractor's name?" asked Mackenzie.

"Pericles Anastasiadi Economosodimitriadi or words to that effect; and not pronounced Smith. And if he knew that a gang was going to ambush me, he'd lend 'em a gun, I should think."

"And the hospital assistant? He's a Goanese. Da Sousa, isn't he?"

"Yes. One of the great and distinguished family of the Da Sousas of Goa."

"And that's not his handwriting?"

"No, nothing like it. Besides, he wouldn't do good by stealth and blush to find it fame. Or hide his light under a bushel of blue pills."

"No; queer, isn't it? Do any of the Sikh *maistris* write English?"

"Not this sort of English, certainly. Besides, why make a mystery of it?"

"Horrible ghastly pun," observed the unsmiling Mackenzie. "Shocking. But a *maistri* might make a mystery of it—for fear it became known that he had warned you and would share your fate for doing so."

"Well, he could tell me privately, couldn't he? Anyway, this wasn't written by a Sikh *maistri* or any other native. It's damned queer."

"Yes. Do you know what I'd do, Robinson?"

"What?"

"Precisely what the letter says."

"No particular harm in doing that, anyway—though I don't quite see what good a revolver is going to do against a hundred of 'em. And how can one 'look out for an ambush' when one's buzzing along the line on a trolley?"

"Well, as to the revolver, the fact that you were wearing it would have quite a deterrent effect on the lad deputed to knock you down when the others come crowding round. And that's how one gets killed in these shemozzles. Somebody lays you out with the haft of a pick-axe, and all the rest have a whang at you. Then it's nobody's murder, because nobody did more than kick your ribs in or bust your skull."

"You always were a cheerful cove, Mackenzie."

"Yes. And as for the ambush, you can at least keep awake and notice a little thing like a sleeper across the line, or a rock."

"Oh, well, if they are going to get me, they'll get me."

"Not a doubt of it," agreed Mackenzie, as he went off: and, like Major Robinson, forgot all about the matter.

§3

But Major Robinson was reminded of it quite soon, when making his usual inspection from rail-head to the temporary bridge beside which a permanent one was in course of construction over a wide and deep nullah.

Across the line lay not merely a sleeper or a rock, but a very respectable barricade of sleepers and big blocks of stone.

There was nothing for it but to stop.

As the coolies who, at a quick run, were pushing the trolley along the line, came to a standstill, a large band of Pathans emerged from the dense jungle on either side of the line, each man being armed with some such weapon as a stone-hammer, pick-axe, a spade or a crow-bar.

Well, here it was.

The warning had been genuine enough, and it was a pity he had not brought his revolver; not because he believed for one moment that a revolver was going to save him from a gang of some fifty Pathan *budmashes*

—than whom there are no more determined and callous ruffians in the world—but because it would have afforded him definite satisfaction to have given half a dozen of them something to remember him by—or cause to forget him, and everything else, for ever.

As he rose to his feet and stood up on the trolley platform, the trolley-coolies and the native overseer who accompanied him fled into the jungle.

"Well, why aren't you worthless, idle, loafing, blackguards at work?" he asked, standing cool and self-possessed, hands on hips, and glancing angrily from face to face.

The answer was a menacing howl of defiance as the two mobs coalesced and crowded round the trolley, brandishing crow-bars, stone-hammers and other ugly weapons.

"Now then, stop that damned row," shouted Robinson. "Who's your leader? If you've got anything to say, let him say it."

"Oh, it's you, is it, Khawas Khan," he added, as a squint-eyed scoundrel was thrust to the front. "I thought as much. What do you want?"

With regret he noted that the man was closely followed by Shere Khan, one of the two Pathans with whom he had frequently talked.

"More pay, you Son of Shaitan," shouted the man. "Fifty rupees a month, we want, you infidel pig." And spat.

"Oh, you do, do you! Well, listen," began Robinson.

If he could turn ambush-for-murder into a wrangle-for-wages and a vulgar slanging-match, he might get away with it; might save his life. Truculent and treacherous brutes as these Mahsuds were, it was improbable that they would murder him in cold blood if he could get them to listen to him, to air their grievances, and to bargain. Certainly they wouldn't if he could make them laugh.

As they hadn't rushed him and battered him to death immediately the trolley stopped, there was a chance.

"You think you are worth fifty rupees a month, do

you? How much did they pay you in Peshawar Gaol for your work when you got three months' hard labour for stealing *pice* out of a blind man's begging bowl?"

There was a loud laugh from Shere Khan.

"What? *Me?* You liar, I . . ." shouted Khawas Khan.

"Or was it for knocking a boy down and running away with his stick of sugar-cane?"

"*Me?* I . . ."

"Or was it for shooting your wife from behind a rock—because she used to beat you so?"

At this there was a general snigger.

"Oh yes, that was it. You told the Court you went in fear of your life—and went in fear of your wife. I remember."

The snigger became a roar of laughter.

"Well? What did they pay you in gaol?"

"I never . . ."

"No. Never got an *anna*, did you? And you have the damned impudence to come here and talk to me about fifty rupees, you jungly coolie. *You!* Fifty rupees! You're not worth fifty *pice*,[27] really. Not like some of these men, who *are* men."

The equivalent of "*Hear, hear!*" was heard from several members of the jostling crowd.

"Now then, talk sense, just for once in your life. Can you dress stone?"

"Yes, I can," bawled Khawas Khan.

"Well then, why don't you do it? Why have you hidden your great cleverness all this time? You shall start to-morrow. And if you do it well, you shall get fifty rupees. That good enough?"

More cries of approval from the crowd.

"Very well, that's you. Now then, anybody else here think he can dress stone? And do proper mason's work? If so, I want him. Can't get too many trained *mymars*. Fifty rupees for any man that can earn it."

"Fifty rupees for everybody," bawled a loud harsh voice.

Robinson glanced quickly in the direction of the speaker.

[27] *Farthings.*

"You, Yacoub Beg? *You?* I wouldn't insult you with it. You ought to have a hundred."

All heads turned to where Yacoub Beg towered above the rest.

"A hundred?" he said stupidly.

"Yes—across your back," was the reply.

And after the yelp of laughter that followed this bright sally had ceased, he added:

"What you want and what you'll get is a hundred *days*—Mombasa Gaol—when the Railway Police come up again. For starting a riot, you . . ."

Khawas Khan replied not in words, but, swinging a great hammer, made a rush at the trolley, only to trip and fall heavily, as Shere Khan thrust out a foot.

So that was it, was it? Shere Khan was on the side of the angels. Good man.

"*Fool,*" roared Shere Khan in a voice like that of a bellowing bull as Khawas Khan rose to his feet, "Do you want us all hanged for . . . ?"

Khawas Khan raised his hammer to smash Shere Khan's skull; but with the quickness and skill of a man who had learned bayonet-fighting, Shere Khan, holding his spade like a rifle, drove it hard at Khawas Khan's throat, the sharp edge inflicting an ugly wound, and again sending him sprawling.

With shouts of "*Kill! Kill!*" the crowd surged in upon Shere Khan, as a giant Mahsud sprang on to the trolley. Him, Robinson smote with all his strength upon the point of the jaw as he was in the act of striking, knocking him back upon those who followed and impeding the rush upon Shere Khan.

As the fellow dropped his long-handled hammer, Robinson stooped and seized it. Might as well die fighting, and he had got to do something for Shere Khan.

"*Back*, you herd of swine!" he shouted. "Drop those tools and get back to your work. Go on, you worthless sons of pigs. Back to your work—or I'll . . ."

"*Kill! Kill!*"

Not a hope. For once the master's word of command fell upon deaf ears.

Well, not such a bad death—to die fighting.

Bang! . . . Bang! . . . Bang!

And again. And again. And again.

"*The Police! The Police!*" was the cry, and—

"*Run! Run!*" shouted Shere Khan, setting the example as the fusillade from the jungle began afresh, and heading the swift and sudden flight from death.

Major Robinson heaved a great sigh of relief and wiped his brow.

A near thing.

§4

"Can't make it out at all," said Major Robinson to the District Officer, as he, the Superintendent of Railway Police, and Angus Mackenzie sat about the camp table outside his tent, a few days later. "It's a mystery. It was an absolute fusillade. That saved the situation, of course. Nevertheless, but for Shere Khan, they'd undoubtedly have done me in, before the shooting; and, but for the shooting, they'd have done us both in. And when I sent for Shere Khan that night, to pat him on the back and ask if he wasn't afraid of the others rounding on him, he had disappeared."

"And the other fellow—what did you say his name was . . ."

"Gul Mahommed."

". . . has disappeared too?" asked the Superintendent of Police.

"Yes."

"Well, I suppose they thought they had better go while the going was good, after upsetting the ringleaders' apple-cart," surmised the District Officer.

"Yes, but what I don't understand, is his not coming to me before he bolted. It isn't like a Pathan."

"No," agreed Mackenzie. "You don't catch him missing anything good. Probably hadn't time."

"By the way," observed the District Officer, "you didn't see his pal in the crowd?"

"No. I'm almost sure he wasn't in the mob. Anyhow,

he wasn't to the fore—wasn't backing-up Shere Khan."

"Well then, the idea occurs to me that it may have been he who did the shooting!" observed the District Officer thoughtfully.

"What with?" asked the Superintendent of Police.

"He certainly hadn't a rifle when he came here," said Robinson.

"No, not across his shoulder," replied the District Officer. "But weren't they the two who professed to have discovered Wendover's corpse? And whether they killed him or not, and whether it was Wendover or not, isn't it more than likely they got his rifle and ammunition if they found a white man who had been killed by a lion?"

"Or if they murdered one," murmured the District Officer.

"It may or may not have been Wendover," continued the District Officer. "Almost certainly was. And they may or may not have found him or his remains, but it is quite likely they 'found' a rifle—or a revolver."

"By Jove! You've said something," applauded Robinson. "That would account for the rapid fire—there were at least six quick shots. It accounts for the brief 'cease fire,' and then the second burst of 'rapid.' That would be quite consistent with the fellow popping off six chambers, loading quickly, and doing it again."

"But you'd have known a rifle from a revolver," observed Mackenzie.

"*You* might, 'my dear Watson,'" jeered Robinson. "Personally I was a bit too hot and bothered to analyse . . . Besides, an army revolver fired towards you at close range makes quite a noise.

"Yes, there must have been about a dozen shots," he added.

"The Wendover revolver idea is a theory, anyway," observed the Superintendent of Police. "It would account for the number and rapidity of the shots, and also for a Pathan having a pistol here."

"Yes, that's about it. It was a one-man show," agreed Robinson, "though it sounded like 'independent' from a section of K.A.R.'s."

"And taken in conjunction with the letter you got, it's an amazing business," said the District Officer.

"Still more amazing that Shere Khan and his boyfriend didn't pay you a nocturnal visit and suggest *bakshish*," observed the Superintendent of Railway Police.

"By the way," he added half apologetically, "excuse what sounds humourous, but I suppose this well-done-thou-good-and-faithful-servant Shere Khan feller isn't—Wendover himself in disguise?"

Major Robinson laughed.

"Good Lord, no. This chap's three inches taller than poor Wendover was. I met him once at the Yacht Club in Bombay. Oh—inches taller. Bigger altogether. And older. Nothing like him. No. Shere Khan's a Pathan all right."

"And the other chap, what's-his-name—Jan Mahommed?"

"Gul Mahommed? Wendover? Not he. He's a Pathan all right. I used to talk to him."

"I still think he may have done the shooting though —or why wasn't he with Shere Khan," said the District Officer. "He and Shere Khan knew what was coming and laid a proper Pathan plot to diddle their pals and get a reward for saving you. One did the patter and the other the shooting."

"And yet nobody was hit," he mused.

"No. The mob ran like hares—no doubt thinking that the artful Sahib had ambushed their ambush! . . . Still, whoever was shooting could have got somebody with his first two or three rounds."

"Aye," agreed Mackenzie, "and a great pity he didn't."

And at the same time, Shere Khan was making much the same observation to his beloved friend and former master, Captain Richard Wendover.

"You should have shot half a dozen of the swine, *Huzoor*," he said. "Especially that squint-eyed, black-faced bastard, Khawas Khan."

"Oh, no need," replied 'Gul Mahommed.' "I'd have

shot straight enough if it had been necessary."

But Shere Khan shook his head. There was only one thing to do with enemies. Otherwise, what was the good of having enemies.

§5

Richard Wendover, seated cross-legged with his friend and follower, Shere Khan, on the dirty matting of the broad balcony at the back of a native seamen's eating house in Vasco da Gama bazaar of Zanzibar, gazed unseeing across the rustling palms to the white beach and sapphire sea of the strait that divides the island from the mainland.

"*Huzoor,*"[28] said Shere Khan.

"Once again, don't call me *Huzoor*. You must get into the way of calling me Gul Mahommed," said Wendover.

"There's no one within hearing, *Huzoor*," smiled Shere Khan.

"No. Not here. But you might say it on some occasion when there is. It might lead to all sorts of trouble if you call me *Huzoor* in the presence of some-one understanding the meaning of the word."

"*Huzoor*, it is not fitting and seemly that I, your servant, should address you familiarly thus. Shall I, whose life you saved at the risk of your own; I, who have served you, ridden behind you in the ranks, been your orderly and your man, use 'thou' and 'thee' when . . ."

"Yes. Try to get it, once and for all, into your thick skull that the past is past, that I am no longer your Officer, a Sahib and an Englishman. I am a homeless dog. I am nothing. Since you refuse to leave me . . ."

"Never will I leave you, *Huzoor*. Never while I draw breath, and you will tolerate my presence," and unconsciously Shere Khan plagiarized. "Entreat me not to leave the presence of the Sahib," he said, touching his forehead with the finger-tips of hands clasped as in prayer. "Bid me to be his servant and follower. For

[28] *Sahib; master; presence.*

wheresoever he goeth there will I go; and my people shall be his people."

". . . Since you refuse to leave me, Shere Khan, and ask me to bid you not to leave me, it is possible only for you to stay with me as a friend and an equal. If you can do that, ceasing to call me *Huzoor*, and calling me friend and brother—Gul Mahommed and not *Huzoor*—we can travel together, adventure together, live together. But friends and equals we must be. And as for my people being thy people, Shere Khan, I have no people. I have finished with those that were. They have cast me out. So be it."

"I said '*Let my people be thy people*'—Gul Mahommed," smiled Shere Khan.

And looking up quickly from out the dark dream in which he brooded, Gul Mahommed gazed into the eyes of Shere Khan.

"Let thy people be my people?" he whispered. "Become a Pathan myself."

"*Huzoor*,"

"Gul Mahommed," growled Wendover.

"Air and water of this land are bad," continued Shere Khan, using the Pathan formula of objection to foreign places.

And indeed the air of all plains compares unfavourably with that of a tribesman's hills.

§6

After a long period of brooding cogitation, weeks of black misery, during which he fought bitterness and Giant Despair with the weapons of philosophy and courage, Richard Wendover came to a decision.

He would go on living, and he would live in his own way.

His announcement of his final and fixed intentions for the future filled his friend Shere Khan with extravagant joy.

Having made up his mind, he also made certain arrangements, financial and other, through the far-famed and trusted Arab pearl-merchant, broker and banker, Suleiman Zanzibari.

And now to live a really interesting life, a man's life among men, a mad life—while the hideous wound healed over and he returned to mental wholeness and, perchance, to forgetfulness and peace.

CHAPTER II

The Arab dhow made its steady way northward over a deep blue oily sea, running before a favouring breeze that kept its huge triangular lateen sail bellied from its forward-slanting mast, and put an apparently dangerous strain upon the piece of string which fastened to it the tapering yard, longer than the mast itself and almost as perpendicular.

To at least one of its crew, a surly and taciturn Pathan, Gul Mahommed, it seemed little short of a miracle that so crank a craft should not only propose to make its way from Zanzibar on the south-eastern coast of Africa to Muscat in the Persian Gulf, but should actually do so; and with a certain regularity that gave suggestion of competence, reliability, and safety; almost of infallibility.

The *naukhada* or captain, seated at the helm, a roughly rounded spar attached to the high-posted rudder, knew not when the dhow would reach Muscat, but that it would eventually reach that remarkable town he did know, such being the will of Allah.

Always it had been the will of Allah, and doubtless always it would be—but as to when, who knew or cared?

To the *naukhadas* of the East African coasting trade, the wind bloweth not whither it listeth, but where it is directed—by Allah of course—and that is invariably due south-west during six months of the year and due north-east for the other six months. Save for these two directions, it has no choice; and thus will it always blow—save when it blows not at all and there is a dead calm, dead being a sinisterly appropriate word, since such a calm is the dhow-crew's greatest danger. Few such seamen meet death by drowning; many suffer death from thirst.

No, it being the will of Allah that the blessed monsoon should blow straight and steady along the coast, then what should prevent the ship from reaching port?

So many times had the good Kassim bin Isa made the journey from the time when he was a black imp of a cabin-boy—taken to sea that there might be someone to do the cooking and receive the kicking; climb the mast; steer, and clean the pots—that, like a Devon fisherman, he could wake up in the morning, or indeed during the night or the afternoon siesta, and tell you exactly where he was—off Pemba Island, Mombasa, Malindi, Lamu, or Port Durnford in British East Africa; Kismayu, Brava, Merka, Mogadishu, Warsheik, Ras Aswad, Obbia, Ras Awath, Ras Hafun or Cape Gardafui in Italian Somaliland—and after that you had to look out that you were not run down by the great fire-ships steaming out of the Gulf of Aden—or off the Socotra Islands.

And, at any given time, he could thereafter tell you about how far you were across the Gulf of Aden—not so bad a place in which to be becalmed as, sooner or later, a passing ship would be sure to answer your signal and give you water. And having crossed the Gulf of Aden, he could tell you where you were off the coast of Arabia, the horrible Hadh-ramaut coast where, once you had passed the Bled el Engris, the country of the English who held Aden, you could hardly hope for food, water, or friendship, except, perhaps, at the Kuria Muria Islands, until you turned the Ras el Hadd, put your helm over, entered the Gulf of Oman and reached Muscat at the south-eastern end of the Persian Gulf.

So when Gul Mahommed or his friend Shere Khan asked the *naukhada*—in their horrible, if amazingly effective mixture of Pushtu, Hindustani and Swahili, with an occasional helpful word of Arabic—when they would reach Muscat, he would reply reassuringly and quite definitely:

"When Allah wills."

Gul Mahommed who, in other days and other places, had been a keen yachtsman, rather enjoyed the long sea-voyage, and was interested in this weird hundred-ton craft, with its almost fiddle-bow, the stern rising with a long slope from the water, and its single

yard of such enormous length, and its definitely mediæval Portuguese stern. Also in its attractive motley
crew of scallywags, homogeneous only in their cheerful
villainy—slavers, gun-runners, pearl-poachers, hashish-
smugglers; scoundrels all.

The *naukhada* and *neapara* were Arabs, as were
two or three of the leading gentlemen, capitalists, financiers of anything in the way of slave, rifle, pearl or
hashish business, but primarily gun-runners.

Next to them in the ethnological scale, were Negro-
Arab pearl-poachers, Swahili smugglers and a pair of
Abyssinian slavers; then three or four Somalis, *charas*
dealers; and the remainder assorted negroes hailing
from every part of the coast, from Delagoa Bay to Port
Sudan—Dervishes, Sudanese, Zanzibaris, Seedees,
and lastly the coal-black crew of Hubshis, just plain
nigger.

Watching the Captain and his Mate, the Bosun and
his men, the passengers and their servants, Gul Mahommed decided that probably the biggest scoundrel of
the lot was a French half-caste from Djbouti, Jean
Moron, who unnecessarily added European vices to the
fine assortment natural and native to those of his
African birth and breeding, unless it were the Portuguese half-caste Miguel Lobo from Mozambique, who
ran him very close.

In the *lingua franca* of the coast, this pair wrangled
incessantly, each claiming that the life of his home
town was more vicious than that of the other; the
French subject hotly defending the claims of Djbouti
against those of Mozambique, the Portuguese denying,
and protesting with weighty evidence; the twain uniting
to agree that the British police had utterly ruined Port
Said, and quarrelling once more as to whether Marseilles was or was not worse than Macao, and now the
wickedest city in the world.

Widely travelled and experienced gentlemen, who
had not only witnessed but done some remarkable
deeds.

And if this crew of police-dodging ruffians, who
went in mortal fear of the British Navy, was interesting,

how much more so, reflected Gul Mahommed, must be the history of this sinister slave-dhow, of which the hull at least was probably not less than a hundred years old. What cargoes she had carried; what crimes she had seen, as she dodged across the Red Sea or the Persian Gulf, laden with slaves or rifles, crept into little secret harbours to land rich ragged men and their cargo of priceless pearls; crept cautiously into ports where venal Customs men passed innocent bales, whether of hides or of cotton or piece-goods, that hid guilty secrets in the shape of parcels of *charas*, the deadly hashish drug.

It was clearly understood by all the company that the two big men, uncommunicative, haughty and truculent, alien in all things save that they were sons of the Prophet, calling like the others upon Allah, were interested in the gun-running business, the supplying of rifles to the Tribesmen of the mountains lying far to the north of the Persian coast.

And interested one of them undoubtedly was. The facts of the source and means of the supply, together with the problem of the best method of preventing it from meeting its great demand, had deeply interested Richard Wendover from the days when such rifles had been fired at him in the Khyber Pass. It was now his present intention to be a gun-runner and to trace the course of a rifle from producer to consumer, from shop to customer, from Muscat to Kabul and beyond.

And so to the ancient city of Muscat on the shores of the Gulf of Oman at the entrance to the Persian Gulf.

CHAPTER III

To Richard Wendover, amateur of adventure, interested from childhood in new places and fresh people, the unique town of Muscat was most intriguing, with its medley of Arabian, Persian, Indian, African, Afghan and many other peoples; its amazing combination of the tenth, the sixteenth and the twentieth centuries; its air of intrigue and mystery, and its complete difference from all other places that he had hitherto visited.

As the dhow slowly approached the land-locked harbour on the iron-bound, rocky, barren coast that reminded Wendover of that of Aden, "like a burnt-out barrack stove," the *naukhada* and his mate uttered remarkable curses, pungent, powerful and comprehensive, as the light cruiser H.M.S. *Fox* was sighted, a ship from their point of view inappropriately named, inasmuch as the dhow was all too apt and liable to be the fox, and the *Fox*, her pinnaces and boats, the huntsman and the pack of hounds that would pursue her to her undoing.

The gun-runners vied with the *naukhada*, the Mate and the Bosun in cursing the British warship, for to them she represented past and potential losses of hundreds of thousands of rupees in contraband rifles seized and cast into the ocean.

With them, in friendly rivalry, competed the slavers to whom the *Fox* had meant, or might mean, cruel loss and bitter constraint—in Aden gaol.

And to the volume of their prayers were added those of the *hashish*-smugglers and the pearl-poachers.

To be in the fashion and to maintain their rôle of anxious business men, deeply concerned in the gun-running industry, Shere Khan and Gul Mahommed lifted up deep voices, calling the particular attention and peculiar attentions of Allah to the thrice-accursed sport-spoiling Infidels.

93

Further up the harbour lay the Muscat Navy, in the shape of a gunboat called *The Sheikh*, the pride and joy of the heart of His Highness the Sultan, a valuable ship which could do almost anything but steam from its moorings, and equipped with a handsome complement of guns, useful and ornamental, that would do almost anything but fire—move up, move down, move left, move right, forward, backward; provide resting-place and support for tired naval men and seagulls; impress friend and foe alike; improve the appearance of the ship; serve as *cache* and ditty box, and in their time play many parts.

There was, among the personnel of the *Fox*, an untried and probably erroneous theory that, in the likely event of *The Sheikh* sinking, one day, at her moorings, the guns would serve yet another useful purpose—that of life-buoys, as they floated away.

As the dhow opened up the tiny cove, Wendover stared in pleased amazement at the little town basking beneath its great protecting cliffs in the shadow of the two mediaeval European castles that towered above it. Those incredible Portuguese . . .

Not long ago he had gazed in wonder at their great Fort at Mombasa; and now here, in this waterless sun-blasted corner of Arabia, were castles straight from Portugal, irresistibly reminding him of Cintra, as he tried to imagine stout Albuquerque and his men, clad in steel helmet and breast-plate, in heavy leather and thick silk, labouring, marching and fighting in that appalling heat.

As he gazed, he idly wondered how many of the scores and scores of the cannon that were visible, still glowering through their embrasures, would carry a ball from the castle to the water.

Later he visited the castles, and in the one called Fort Jellali, saw cannon of Albuquerque's own day, on which were clearly visible the Royal Arms of Portugal.

Others that interested him almost as much were British guns, one or two of them, to his surprise, bearing the Royal Crown of England and the monogram C.R. What untold tale of mighty venture, of ship-wreck or pirate capture, did those guns of the days of Charles I or Charles II tell? Guns, the roar of which great Admiral Blake might have heard; guns whose smoke might have been seen by Van Tromp himself when "'*I've a broom at the mast,*'" said he. The very gun on which Wendover laid his hand might have put a ball into more than one Barbary corsair, and into Algiers itself. Or again, the Royal Lord High Admiral and War-den of the Cinque Ports, James, Duke of York, after-wards James II, King of England, might have stood by this very gun which Wendover now touched, when James fought and beat de Ruyter . . .

Anyway, there it stood on the walls of Fort Jellali in Muscat, a gun cast in England in the seventeenth century, a gun that had crossed the seas, defending one of the Wooden Walls of England, and manned by the iron men that took those wooden ships around the world—under incredible conditions horrible to contem-plate.

Richard Wendover sighed as he turned from the gun.

His England . . .

To the *killadar*, the custodian of the Fort, by whose favour he and Shere Khan were taken over it, and who had himself actually been a Subedar in the Indian Army, he observed in Hindustani:

"Different guns to-day, Subedar Sahib."

"*Bé-shak*," smiled the old man. "They tell me that the guns on the King Emperor's ship, the *Fokkus*, will hit a target five *kos*[29] distant."

"Wah! wah!" ejaculated Gul Mahommed, duly im-pressed.

From the deck of the dhow as she crept to her anchorage, Wendover could see watch-towers that re-minded him of the Corsair watch-towers of the Medi-terranean, dotted about the tops of the low mountains surrounding the town, watch-towers which, he sur-mised, had been erected to keep ward against the

---

[29] *One kos = two miles.*

predatory Arab bands of the desert hinterland.

A few minutes before mid-day, the clumsy anchor, with its futile-looking cable of palm-fibre rope, was cast overboard a few fathoms from the blinding white walls of official buildings, go-downs, and old balconied Arab houses rising sheer from the water.

Going ashore with the other financiers of the rifle, slave, hashish and pearl businesses, Wendover found the town of Muscat as disappointing as is every port that is admirable from the sea; and reflected that the contrast between the view of a city from a ship, compared with the appearance of that city as seen from its own streets, is not unlike the difference between the front and the back of a picture.

The streets of Muscat he found to be poisonously foul, the denizens of its bazaars repulsively filthy and indeed filthily repulsive, quite the ugliest people he had yet seen in bulk, far uglier than either the original negro slaves from whom they are descended or their Arab owners.

As in no other part of Arabia or Africa with which he was familiar, here the admixture of Arab blood, instead of improving the negro strain, seemed definitely to have degraded it.

And he decided that the marked difference between the black Muscatis and the Swahilis of Africa—equally Arab-negro in origin—must be due to local in-breeding, the average Swahili, though no beauty, being a fine fellow, markedly superior in every way to the Negro, with thinner lips, finer nose, straighter hair, more dignified presence and carriage, and more nearly approximating to the Arab than to the aborigine.

Not only were the town and the people disgustingly dirty, but the whole place stank abominably, a fact only partly attributable to masses of ancient unsold and superfluous tunny and other fish rotting about the landing-places.

Having accompanied Messrs. Moron (*sous ce nom là!*) and Lobo, who by reason of the yellowish tinge of their swarthy faces assumed almost European airs of superiority, to the house of the wealthy Mekrani—the principal irons in whose many fires were fire-irons indeed—and been introduced as gentlemen from Afghanistan and the Border, deeply interested in that particular class of iron, Gul Mahommed and Shere Khan found themselves warmly welcomed, invited to regard their host's house and all in it as their own, to attend that night a rice-and-mutton feast, and only then to fatigue their noble minds with business.

A stroll round the town of Muscat was a pleasure that Wendover had no wish to repeat, though the visit to the two castles was, as has been said, deeply interesting. So was the ancient wall surrounding the town, with its two gates, Big Gate and Little Gate, the former of which opens to the mouth of a pass whence set forth, and whither arrive, all the caravans slowly and silently journeying to and from the mysterious and almost unknown interior of Arabia.

It was a new experience for Wendover, to find himself in a walled city of which the gates were locked at night, and from the summit of whose surrounding hill-tops watchmen on the towers, in powerful voices like those of Muezzins, called regularly from time to time and from one to another; the deep diapason of their mournful voices reminding the dwellers of the town that all was well—but at any moment might be far otherwise.

A mediæval touch indeed, and probably an unbroken connecting-link with mediæval times.

§2

Listening most attentively to the conversation of his associates, and asking questions in Hindustani, Swahili and Pushtu, of Yacoub Ali, the Mekrani proprietor of the establishment that was part hotel, part whole-sale-business premises, part clearing-house, part conspirators' meeting-place and part plain rifle-shop, Wendover learned that Yacoub Ali's establishment was only one of a dozen small-arms and ammunition stores and depôts; that every other shop was a gun-shop; and that the Customs House, in spite of constant and copious withdrawals, was kept full to bursting-point by the almost daily delivery of huge consignments of rifles from Europe and principally from France; that the customers were mainly Afghans, Baluchis and Pathans; while the delivery agents were the bold resourceful Arab *naukhadas* of the gun-running fleet of dhows plying between Muscat and the little ports and harbours of the opposite Persian Mekran coast.

The Ghilzais of Central Asia were perhaps the best middlemen purveyors; while notable and invaluable purchasers, local agents, retailers and depôt owners on the other side of the Gulf were the excellent Mir Barkat Khan, formerly Governor of Biyaban, and the noble Mullah Khan Mahommed of Karkindar (known to all Persia, Mekran, Baluchistan, Afghanistan and the Frontier as "The Kafila Sahib").

Better progress in the pursuit of information he made when, at Yacoub Ali's house, he was introduced to a very interesting, a literally intriguing, Armenian gentleman, a Monsieur Mamoulian, who was Muscat agent for the notable, not to say notorious, French rifle-merchants, Messrs. Goguyer et Fils, who openly, frankly, freely, without let or hindrance, *sans peur et sans reproche*, exported discarded French Army and other rifles from Marseilles to Djbouti, and imported them thence to Muscat.

The Armenian, a travelled and enlightened man, speaking, in addition to his own Armenian, Syrian Arabic, fluent French, good Turkish, good Hindustani, fair English and Persian, soon made all things abundantly clear to Gul Mahommed, new recruit to the ranks of the arms traffickers, intelligent, travelled and reputedly wealthy, a man who in addition to his own Pushtu, spoke fluent Hindustani, a little French and quite comprehensible English.

In bazaar Hindustani they came to a complete understanding, making all things abundantly clear; and it did not surprise the Armenian that, when in doubt and anxious to understand exactly, his Pathan friend resorted to English, inasmuch as that typical tribesman had, on his own confession, served in the

British Army and sojourned long in British India.

Naturally he would learn some English, reflected Monsieur Mamoulian, and understand it a great deal better than he spoke it.

To Gul Mahommed, so intelligent, travelled, and interested in affairs, he merrily explained the local situation, which was truly Gilbertian.

There, as Gul Mahommed could see, lay His Britannic Majesty's cruiser *Fox*, stationed in Muscat harbour for the sole and specific purpose of preventing the export of rifles from Muscat to the Persian coast.

There, on the quay, as Gul Mahommed could see, was the Customs House, bulging with rifles and issuing them on demand all day long.

And not only was the Customs House bursting with rifles and ammunition, but there, as he or anybody else who chose to stroll along could observe, was the whole of the Customs House quay, littered, cluttered and covered with great wooden crates, piled up one upon the other, each one filled with rifles or with the cartridges that fitted them.

And further, anyone interested was at complete liberty to go and watch dhow after dhow being loaded far above where her Plimsoll mark should be, with the said rifles and ammunition, under the very bows of the *Fox* and the noses of her personnel.

But the British being British, smiled Monsieur Mamoulian, and such wonderful sticklers for law, treaty rights, and the sanctity of agreements, they did absolutely nothing at all about it!

In Muscat harbour, that is to say.

For Muscat harbour belongs to the Sultan of Muscat, ally of Britain, friend of the Government of India and, occasionally, host of the Viceroy himself.

No, what goes on in Muscat harbour is not to be noticed by the Captain of a British cruiser, even though he be sent there on purpose to stop precisely what is going on. Anything that he is going to do must be done outside the three-mile limit of territorial waters, where no offence can be given to the tender susceptibilities of the Sultan of Muscat by the seizure of a dhow manned by people who may or may not be subjects of his, and who are engaged in carrying contraband to the enemies of Britain.

And even there, again smiled Monsieur Mamoulian, the impeccably correct British are in a difficulty, for a greater than the Sultan of Muscat then comes into the matter; no less a person than *Madame la République* of France.

For between France and Muscat there had long ago been made, with the knowledge and consent of England, a treaty permitting Muscat to be used by France as a shop and a depôt and clearing-house for her considerable and valuable arms-traffic.

Unlike the British with their microscopic army, Monsieur Mamoulian pointed out, the French have a standing army that runs into millions; so that when they shed the Chassepot and the Gras there is something more than a few hundred perfectly good guns for sale; and it is useless for Messrs. Goguyer et Fils or any other enterprising contractors to bid for fifty thousand, one hundred thousand, half a million or a whole million of good army rifles, if there is no sale for them. Let the Government guarantee the market and the *entrepreneur* will buy their guns.

"But since Britain became responsible for peace and order on the present North-West Frontier, and for the protection of the people of British India, has nothing been done about this treaty and understanding between France and Muscat?" asked Gul Mahommed.

"Oh, yes," replied Monsieur Mamoulian, "up to the time of the Tirah campaign the arms traffic had been with Persia and the Arabs of the Gulf; but when the British found that their soldiers were being shot down with French rifles, and they traced the sale of them to the Mekran and Persian coast, and across to Muscat, they got the Sultan to agree to allow British men-of-war to search dhows flying the Muscat or Persian or British flags, all of which they used to fly—especially British—the funny fellows.

"But when the British gunboat *Lapwing* began seizing the dhows of poor *naukhadas* flying the Union

Jack and taking the rifles out of the holds and the bread out of the *naukhadas'* mouths, they refused to fly the flag of such treacherous people any more; and as the British did just the same in the case of the Persian and Muscat flags, the *naukhadas*, specially permitted by the Sultan of Muscat—himself by no means uninterested in the arms business—decided to fly the flag of France.

"They did—and under this flag they were safe. Every dhow which the British overhauled thenceforth hailed from the French-protected port of Sur, or said it did, and flew the French flag.

"So there was nothing for the British Government to do but to approach the French Government and see about the abrogation of the treaty which allowed Muscat to be a gun-shop, and the amphibian inhabitants of the port of Sur to be French subjects.

"But, as the French Government very properly replied to the British Government, they had a perfect right to sell their discarded rifles to any brisk and enterprising French business men who chose to buy them, and the brisk and enterprising French business men had a perfect right to export them to the Republic's colony of French Somaliland.

"And what happened to the rifles thereafter was no business of theirs or of *Madame la République*.

"And if other brisk and enterprising business men chose to sell them to the Sultan of Muscat, that again was no business of *Madame la République*.

"And if there they were bought by Arabs, Persians, or the Mekranis—or by Eskimos, Red Indians, Hairy Anus, Australian Aborigines, the head-hunters of Borneo or the Chinese Emperor, that again was not of the faintest interest to *Madame la République*.

"Surely while a gun is a gun and a shop is a shop, a man can go into a shop and buy a gun, can't he? And the Emperor of China, the head-hunter of Borneo, the Red Indian, the Hairy Anu, the Aborigine of Australia, or the Eskimo has as much right to buy a gun as any good Briton has, *hein?*

"'*Yes, but they are being bought by our enemies, the*

tribesmen of our Indian Frontier,' said the British Government.

"'*Now isn't that just too bad!*' said the French Government. And while far too polite to offer unwanted advice, undoubtedly implied that somebody ought to keep those rascals in better order."

"And so that was the end of the matter, eh?" observed the intelligent Gul Mahommed.

"Yes, except that France, always with an eye to the main chance, offered to exchange her perfect right to sell arms to the Sultan of Muscat for, say, Nigeria, or even perhaps Ashanti, or possibly Sierra Leone—at which the British Government smiled, and sent the *Fox* to watch the arms traffic whereby her enemies are provided with rifles as good as her own.

"And there you see His Britannic Majesty's cruiser *Fox*—watching."

"But something is done about it, surely?" enquired Gul Mahommed.

"Oh, yes. Quite a lot, out at sea. Quite a lot. Every now and then she catches some poor fellow with a dhow-load of rifles and ammunition, who can't prove that Sur is his place of clearance and that he has any right to fly the French flag. Then overboard goes the lot. And on board the *Fox* goes the poor *naukhada*."

"But such dhows surely don't sail out from here under the eyes of the Captain of the *Fox*, quite openly, do they?" asked Gul Mahommed.

"Oh dear, no. While the *Fox* is here, the gun-running dhows put out from other places along the Pirate Coast; and when she gets intelligence concerning them and steams out, then away goes the Muscat fleet in seven different directions, and many of them are quite safe to reach Gwada, Tiz, Kunarak, Puzin, Rashid, Gurdim, Rapch, Hushdan, Bunji or Kuhistak."

"No, of course the ship cannot be in two places, or go in two different directions at once," agreed Gul Mahommed.

"You'd think not, but in a manner of speaking that is just what she does do, curse her," smiled Monsieur Mamoulian.

"Oh, how?"

"Why, she gets over to the Mekran coast, and then puts down about a dozen boats, and off they go independently. Each of these, with an officer and a dozen men, hangs about the places I have mentioned, and lies in wait for the poor dhow; and what can a *naukhada* and half a dozen boatmen do against these fellows with their rifles and bayonets?

"Not but what they get a bad time up the creeks sometimes," laughed Monsieur Mamoulian, "when the *shumal* is blowing, and they have to go close inshore. Sometimes they have to choose between a storm at sea and a hail of bullets from the land."

"But plenty of rifles still get across?" said Gul Mahommed.

"Oh, yes. About thirty thousand a year, what with the dhows that dodge the boat-cruisers and those that legitimately fly the French flag. Oh, yes, plenty get across, but the trade is not what it was, not by a long way."

"The British Navy ships frighten capital away, eh?" observed Gul Mahommed.

"Well, there's still plenty of capital in the business. It's the *naukhadas* that are the trouble. Not enough of them willing to take the risks."

"Do they work on a commission basis, then?"

"No, not exactly. Up till recently, the arrangement was that the financier gave the *naukhada* a lump sum in hire, and a third of what his dhow was worth, cash down, with a promise to pay the other two-thirds if the ship were captured, or sunk. But they won't do it now, in spite of enormous rates for freightage. They want the whole value of the dhow in advance, to be returned when the dhow does. But it doesn't—naturally. As soon as the *naukhada* has got the value of his ship, off he goes, of course, to Zanzibar or the Red Sea or somewhere, and is never seen in the Persian Gulf again.

"One good business man did it in Bushire, then came down here and did it again, and then sailed off for Mombasa or somewhere, with double the value of his dhow in his pocket! No, the trade isn't what it was.

And the only way the dealer can be quite sure of a *naukhada*, is to agree to his terms and then go across with him. But that's very unpleasant, of course, because then the dealer is just as liable to capture as anybody else."

"Very unpleasant," said Gul Mahommed, who hadn't the slightest desire to be captured by the British Navy in the act of gun-running, co-operating with arms-smugglers, aiding and abetting those who were engaged in supplying contraband of war to the King's enemies, active or potential, on the North-West Frontier of India. It wouldn't look well, in view of his position as a disgraced and ruined outcast.

"I want to go across with a parcel, myself," he said.

"You'd be all right if you went with Ilderim Durani, the friend of Yacoub Ali the Mekrani. He'll be taking a big consignment over soon, along with some Powindahs. If you can get a passage with him, that is. His boats are always frightfully crowded."

"Why?"

"Well, Ilderim Durani, who is a very wily man indeed, is one of the people to whom the Sultan of Muscat has sold the right to fly the French flag."

"The right?"

"Oh, yes; absolutely. Treaty right between the Sultan and the French. Certain subjects of the Sultan have as much right to fly the French flag as the *Fox* has to fly the British; and under it they are absolutely safe from molestation. If they are challenged and searched, they produce their papers, and it would be an international incident if they were in any way molested. The good Ilderim has made himself one of those 'subjects' of the Sultan by right of purchase."

"*With a great sum obtained I this freedom,*" thought Gul Mahommed.

Monsieur Mamoulian removed the mouthpiece of his hookah from his lips and laughed.

"Do you know that Ilderim Durani's father actually prosecuted the British Government when the *Lapwing* took two hundred and twenty cases of arms and ammunition off his dhow?" continued Monsieur

Mamoulian.

"He won his case, too, in the High Court of Justice at Bombay. He won his case there, but the Government of India appealed to the British House of Lords and it was reversed, on some technical ground or other. But none of the people to whom the Sultan has given—or rather sold—the right to fly the French flag has been interfered with since."

"Well, I had better go in one of his boats if I can, then," said Gul Mahommed.

"Yes. I'll speak to Yacoub Ali for you, and he will see whether Ilderim Durani can give you a passage. You will have to pay, of course, and Ilderim won't carry your rifles."

"No, I suppose not," agreed Gul Mahommed, who, in point of fact, was quite sure that Ilderim Durani would carry no rifles belonging to Gul Mahommed.

And after enjoying yet more of the conversation and the excellent coffee and tobacco of Monsieur Mamoulian, Gul Mahommed said a very friendly farewell and returned to the house of Yacoub Ali the Mekrani, where Shere Khan took his ease and gossiped with fellow Pathans who, though not of his tribe, were of his nation and knew his part of the Khyber country.

And that night the obliging Yacoub Ali introduced Shere Khan and his surly brother Gul Mahommed to Ilderim Durani, one of his most respected customers, a man known and feared from Muscat to Kabul; a friend and business associate of Persian Governors, Baluchi Sirdars, Bakhtiari Chiefs, influential Mullahs and other men of light and leading in the great gun-running industry of Arabia, Persia, Afghanistan and the North-West Frontier of India.

CHAPTER IV

On the terribly hot and extremely uncomfortable voyage from Muscat across the Gulf of Oman to the mouth of the Rapch River, a river which sometimes lacks the important element of water, Gul Mahommed realized that, but for Shere Khan, he would have been in an awkward and, indeed, highly dangerous situation.

For the extremely suspicious Afghans, Ghilzais and Pathan dealers and traders in guns were obviously somewhat puzzled by his boorish taciturnity and avoidance of confidences, or even conversation, concerning his own private business or their own, the engrossing and only subject that interested them.

Frequently, when asked a question, he would make no reply whatsoever; and from time to time, in spite of this guarded economy of speech, he displayed an ignorance somewhat surprising.

However, Shere Khan, while completely failing to make his fellow-tribesman popular or entirely satisfactory, saved the situation by tapping his forehead significantly and explaining that he had always been like that. It was his nature *to*. Always the poor Gul Mahommed had been *bé-wakuf* and *bé-ukl*, just slightly afflicted of Allah.

Oh, afflicted of Allah, was he? Poor fellow. That accounted for everything. And though not an explanation to evoke sympathy from men who knew not the meaning of the kindly word, it was sufficient to account for and excuse his undeniable queerness.

Yes, he had been like that from childhood, explained Shere Khan, and moreover had had very bad luck. It had been his deplorable *kismet* to have had concussion of the brain, possibly caused through his head having been pounded, one day when he was sleeping, by an enemy, with a heavy rock. Never much of a brain, of course, but that hadn't done it any good.

106

And this Shere Khan's listeners could well understand, they having known several such cases of head-battering, a common if unpleasant trick of one's enemies who found one sleeping by the wayside. And that would account for his apparently capricious memory and those curious lapses during which he appeared to have forgotten things that he must have known—such as the importance and position of Bampur in Persian Baluchistan, and how at one time Ilderim Durani, Mir Barkat Khan and Mullah Khan Mahommed of Karkindar, all met there with a *lashkar* of four thousand Afghans, Ghilzais, Baluchis and Pathans, and cut up five miles of the Central Persian telegraph-line and raided Chabbar and Jask, shooting-up the telegraph stations, defying the Consular guards and wrecking the property of the British and Persian Governments alike, having a rare old time, and getting a bit of their own back on them for their high-handed, tyrannical and oppressive interference with the arms trade.

Was it not a shameful thing, asked Ilderim Durani of Gul Mahommed, that harmless and innocent Ghilzais could not buy guns from His Highness the Sultan of Muscat and take them in peace and safety across the Persian Gulf and overland through Mekran and Baluchistan and Afghanistan, or through Persia, to their customers in Central Asia?

Most shameful, agreed Gul Mahommed.

It was to the Turcomans they sold their rifles; and what business was that of the British?

"What indeed?" murmured Gul Mahommed.

And what reason was there for the Persians of Kerman to butt in and make trouble? demanded Ilderim Durani.

"Obviously paid by the British to do so," observed Gul Mahommed.

Quite so. Quite so. Then there was that *budmash*, the British Consul-General in Meshed. Time somebody shoved a Khyber knife into his liver. He'd see about it himself next time he took that route to Merv for Samarcand, Bokhara, Khiva, Ferghana, Kohqand and

Tashkent.

"Good business up that way still?" asked a Baluchi trader.

Fine. You could sell all the rifles and ammunition you could possibly take up there. Those Turcomans and Usbegs could never get enough. And the profits! And then the whole lot seized and confiscated after you had nursed your camels along for a thousand miles. Heart-breaking. Allah smite their souls to lowest hell.

"What does it matter to them how many rifles go into the Turcoman country, eh, Gul Mahommed?" growled Ilderim Durani.

"Nothing," agreed Gul Mahommed. "Just *zulm*."

"No, nor into Khorasan. What does it matter to them how many rifles there are in Herat?"

"Or in Gazhni," interrupted another.

"What has Khandahar to do with them?" asked a third.

"The fact is," said Ghulam Shah Powindah, "they've never forgiven the Ghilzais."

"For what?" asked Gul Mahommed, as the speaker was addressing him more particularly.

"For *what*?" ejaculated the man in obvious surprise.

"For Maiwand, he means," put in Shere Khan quickly, with a wink at Ghulam Shah Powindah as significantly he tapped his forehead. Obviously the poor Gul Mahommed's mind was wandering again.

"Oh, yes," said the latter. "Of course it was the Ghilzais who cut them up at Maiwand."

"I should say so," replied Ghulam Shah Powindah. "The Ghilzais and nobody else. There wasn't a Durani there. No, nor a Tajic. And none of your Pathans, either. It was our Ayub Khan and his Ghilzai *lashkar* who did it, near the Helmund River, opposite my own town of Girishk. Outflanked the British army and wiped out the whole brigade, and captured all their artillery; every gun they had got."

"After they had fired all their ammunition," observed Gul Mahommed.

"Well?"

"And after Shere Ali, the Wali of Kandahar, had

treacherously deserted the British General so that he had to retreat to Khushk-i-Nakhud," he added.

"Well?"

"Why shouldn't Shere Ali betray the Infidel dogs and sons of dogs?" enquired Ilderim Durani.

"Because the British General, Burrows Sahib, had . . ." began Gul Mahommed.

"Peace! Peace!" interrupted Shere Khan. "Always must wrangle, mustn't you, Gul Mahommed, and say the opposite to everybody else."

"Don't argue with him," he added, turning to Ghulam Shah Powindah. "He's like that," and changed the subject to the more interesting one of the respective conveniences of the Western and Eastern routes through Persia and Baluchistan respectively to the Helmund Lake Road to Girishk, Kandahar and Gazhni.

And thus and similarly did Shere Khan, many a time and oft, stand between Gul Mahommed and the consequences of his ignorance or his folly.

§2

But, a few days after the dhow had reached Godoz, Shere Khan was unable to prevent an eruption of the smouldering volcanic temper of his friend and master, though no evil consequences followed. Nevertheless the incident troubled him as showing how much Gul Mahommed had to learn, both in self-control, habitude and experience, before he would be really safe in his rôle of Pathan.

For on their way from Godoz to the secret camp of the gun-runners, they encountered a British Officer. The British Officer accosted Gul Mahommed and, although Shere Khan promptly assumed the place of leader and answered the Officer in Pushtu, the latter addressed Gul Mahommed in English, and in that language the *soi-disant* Gul Mahommed replied . . .

And on the long and weary route from Godoz on the Mekran coast to Duzdab in Persia, on the gun-runners' road to Afghanistan, Shere Khan, in season and out of season, bade Richard Wendover forget himself, his past and his language, and remember his new name, new personality, and his new tongue, even to the point of thinking in Pushtu, cursing in Pushtu, yea, and even counting in that language.

CHAPTER V

Duzdab greatly interested Gul Mahommed and to a less extent, Shere Khan. A hard-baked—and as to its inhabitants, undoubtedly hard-boiled—sun-blistered, mud-coloured town consisting of thousands of houses of dried mud, surrounded by walls of dried mud and of hundreds of narrow, crooked, wandering streets and bazaars, the rutted roads of which were of dried mud, save in the rainy season when they were of wet and very deep mud.

A strange place, inexplicable in its being there in the heart of a Persian desert, a microcosm of the Middle East, a *mélange* of its people, creeds and castes. A somewhat Holy City, and quite deserving of its name of Duzdab which, being interpreted, meaneth *The Drinking-place of the Thieves* or *The Robbers' Water-Hole*, since it is something of a nest of robbers and undoubtedly a place where water of a kind is fairly easily procurable.

Nor can it be supposed that its honourable name of Robbers' Roost is due to the fact that it is a depôt on the great arms-smuggling route from the Persian Gulf to the North-West Frontier of India, inasmuch as its name is as old as Iran, as old as ancient Persia, where-as the great and profitable gun-running industry dates back no further than the invention of the grooved gun-barrel.

And thither arrived from the North the purchasers of rifles, and thither from the South come the import-ers and vendors of the admired and desired weapons, which though discarded and rejected of Europe are to the Tribesmen infinitely preferable to the home-made weapons of the Kabul gun-makers' bazaar or of the Afghan Government arsenal.

Here, from the North and East, Gul Mahommed and Shere Khan met men from all the tribes of near-by Afghanistan; Duranis, Hazaras, Kafirs, Ghilzais,

111

Usbegs, Tajics and Turcomans; men from Kabul, Khandahar, Jellalabad and Herat; men from every tribe of the North-West Frontier of India; Afridis, Mahsuds, Mohmands, Zakka Khel and their great enemies the Kuki Khel, Shinwaris, Turis, Orakzai, Khostwals, Waziris and every other kind of Pathan; as well as Baluchis, Bokharans, Mekranis, Persians, Indian Mussulmans, Hindus and Sikhs.

To Gul Mahommed it appeared that there were two lines of business which occupied the time and energies of the visitors to the lively city of Duzdab; the rifle trade and seditious intrigue; while the permanent residents flourished more or less by taking in each others' washing.

In their capacity of wandering and intelligent dervishes, Gul Mahommed and Shere Khan held converse upon Religion and other subjects, with Christians; Mussulmans, both Shiah and Sunni; Brahmins; Buddhists; Hindus of a dozen castes; Sikhs; Zoroastrians; Baha'is; Jews, Turks and Infidels. Different sorts of Christians were represented by Catholic and Protestant missionaries, Armenians, a Nestorian, a Russian and a Greek; Mussulmans of both creeds by Persians, Afghans, Pathans and Indians; Buddhism by a trio of unexplained and inexplicable Japanese and a pair of equally incredible Chinese. Each of these two groups of Far Easterners seemed to Gul Mahommed to have no concern save deep concern concerning the doings of the other.

In their capacity of wandering and intelligent lay agitators, apparently desirous of agitating anybody and everybody about anything and everything, they held converse upon politics with Anglophobe Afghans; seditious Indians; anti-monarchical Persians who abhorred the heavy hand of the Shah; intriguing Afghan refugees from the mercy of the Amir; agents of Moscow deeply interested in all who were interested in undermining the power of any neighbouring ruler, be he Shah, Amir or King-Emperor, and detesting them all equally and alike; politically-conscious Persian mullahs who foamed at the mouth as they spoke of the evil done by the godless infidel Soviet in the holy Mussulman cities which had fallen into their power, such as Samarcand, Khiva and Bokhara. Was it not notoriously true that they had turned the holiest and most ancient mosques into warehouses, stables, dance-halls, picture-palaces and worse?

A seething hot-bed of political intrigue, this town of Duzdab, most of which plotting was directed against Britain; a congeries of subversive and seditious societies, the largest and most active of which was directed against the British Raj and consisted of Hindu, Mussulman and other Indians, the most numerous of whom were Sikhs. These brave bearded and burly men were mainly artisans, excellent repairers of rifles and of disintegrating motor-cars by day; repairers of the ancient Sikh Kingdom and destroyers of the disintegrating British Empire by night.

And from them, as from the rest, Gul Mahommed learned much.

And much of what he learned he set forth on paper; and the paper, by curious and devious ways, he despatched to Peshawar, Quetta or Dera Ismail Khan, whence it was forwarded to Simla and there studied with great interest and considered with the greatest care by Colonel Ormesby of the Political Department.

This new and unknown Secret Service agent was working—and working to some purpose, by Jove—in Duzdab now, of all places on this earth—and sending invaluable information concerning not only the gun-running business but the plot-hatching industry as well.

§2

"Hullo, what's up?" said Gul Mahommed to Shere Khan, in English, the speaking of which was a foolish practice of which he had not yet completely broken himself, as, turning a corner of the street that led from their caravanserai outside Duzdab to the central market-place, they beheld a large crowd about the beautiful new gallows, lofty and commodious, a gift

113

from the Shah, commemorating his recent visit to his loyal and loving citizens of Duzdab.

Shere Khan remonstrated with him in much the words that he himself had used when rebuking Shere Khan for addressing him as *Huzoor*, a habit of which even yet he was scarcely cured.

"Seem to be hanging somebody," Gul Mahommed answered his own question.

"One Duzdabi scoundrel the less," shrugged Shere Khan indifferently. "Let's go and watch."

"I'm not really very fond of watching executions," said Gul Mahommed.

"No? I rather like them," was the reply. "Especially when it's one of these down-country scum.

"You ought to accustom yourself to watching all sorts of funny things," he added. "You'll certainly see some in Kabul and up north, whether you wish to or not."

"Sufficient unto the day is the evil thereof," paraphrased Gul Mahommed sententiously in Pushtu.

"We may have to watch each other hanging, for all we know," observed Shere Khan, whose humour was apt to be grim. "Or rather, one of us, in disguise, may have to watch the other being hanged—and without turning a hair or blinking an eyelid."

"Oh, I could do that quite easily," replied Gul Mahommed in Shere Khan's happiest vein.

"Oh, man, what's all the hanging about?" the latter asked of a passing Afghan.

"Pies," replied the honest tradesman.

"What, been making heavy pastry? Serve him right," decided Shere Khan censoriously.

"Well no, the objection was not exactly to the pastry so much," replied the Afghan, scratching industriously beneath his huge turban.

"Oh, tough mutton? Serve him right again, then. Hanging's too good for these street-corner swine. The other day I bought a *shahi*'s worth of *kaibobs* from one of them and was swindled both ways, quantity and quality. Tough meat and not enough of it. And I doubt if it was mutton."

"This fellow's wasn't," growled the Afghan. "Wasn't mutton at all."

"What then? Dog?" grinned Shere Khan.

"No. Man. And the Judge sentenced him to be hanged for dishonesty, the dirty swindler," replied the Afghan as he turned away to go about his business.

"Well, I'm damned," observed Gul Mahommed, again in English.

"I wish you would not talk English, Gul Mahommed," smiled Shere Khan. "Not that anybody in this Allah-forgotten dust-heap would know it was English, but still . . ."

"Do you think it was true?" interrupted Gul Mahommed.

"What?"

"About the human flesh."

"Why not? Is there anything a Persian wouldn't do? They really are the very best swindlers in Asia. Afghans are children to them."

"But is such a thing possible? I say—have you bought any mutton-pies at the street corner or . . . ?"

"No. I got everything from the *serai*-keeper. Ours has been mutton all right—when it wasn't goat. You can see the joints and watch them being cooked. No, I don't think I bought anything in the street except fruit and *hulwa*. Only now and again, anyway. Let's go and have a look at him. I should recognize him if I . . ."

"Yes, if that's what he has been doing—and selling. I don't at all mind watching him get what . . ." said Gul Mahommed.

"But no," he interrupted himself, "it isn't possible. Where would he get the . . . meat?"

"I'll ask," said Shere Khan.

And not only from gossips of the bazaar, but from men who had known the vendor, the purchasers, and the prosecutor, men who had been present in the Qadi's court, it was apparently only too true that the enterprising pie-man had caused quite a considerable number of the citizens of Duzdab unconsciously to become anthropophagi; cannibals.

As is apt to happen when business men quarrel,

more had been divulged than either intended, when the grave-digger employed at the latest burial-ground and the itinerant restaurateur had quarrelled over the sordid matter of prices and payments, the peculiarly filthy lucre offered by the delicatessen-merchant being less than that promised to the obliging and helpful sexton.

In spite of peremptory request that Shere Khan would not go into further detail, Gul Mahommed learned that corpses, particularly those of children, buried by day, had been exhumed by night.

"That's enough, Shere Khan," said he, as, at dinner that night, his friend, with mordant wit and ghoulish humour, told the obviously true tale that he had learned in the bazaar.

"Why didn't they hang the grave-digger, too?" asked Gul Mahommed.

"When the grave-digger heard that the police had arrested the pie-man, he took his annual holiday at once. I suppose he thought that they would consider him to be as dishonest a grave-digger as the other was a dishonest pie-man."

"*Dishonest!*" growled Gul Mahommed.

"Thoroughly," agreed Shere Khan. "It was dis-honesty, wasn't it? Have some more mutton?"

"No, thank you."

§3

And in due course, and by wanderings the tale of which would fill a book, Gul Mahommed and Shere Khan made their devious way to Kabul, the capital of Afghanistan.

CHAPTER VI

In Kabul, Gul Mahommed had long and most interesting conversations with assorted gentlemen interested in the small-arms and ammunition business, buyers and sellers of rifles who knew to a farthing the buying-price to offer and the selling-price to ask, for every kind of rifle, from a new British short .303 to a Belgian flintlock; interested also in the various kinds of ammunition pertaining to such arms of precision and lack of precision; chiefly Afghans, Ghilzais, Powindahs and every sort and kind of Pathan.

Also with others interested less in rifles and ammunition than in the objects of their use and in those who use them, chiefly Russians, Anglophobe Kabuli mullahs, seditious Sikhs, "Hindustani fanatics" or Sitana, Mussulman and Hindu seditionists, and certain notorious outlaws who had fled from Border justice to the protection of the Amir.

To Gul Mahommed and to his brother and apparent business-partner, Shere Khan, these various and extremely varied people, sooner or later, talked more or less freely, as to fellow gun-runners or fellow-seditionists and plotters, as the case might be.

To such a person as the notorious Powindah Mullah the Second, bitter enemy of the British and of anybody else whose influence might lead eventually to the enlightenment of the people and the weakening of the power of the priests, the two were political agents and emissaries interested only in the fomentation of trouble, the carrying of verbal messages too important and dangerous to be written, the representatives of those whose aim and work in life was the destruction of the British Raj.

To such people as the son of Mir Barkat Khan, once Governor of Biyaban, chief of the gun-running profiteers; or the brother of Mullah Khair Mahommed, known as the Kafila Sahib, powerful and professional importer of rifles, the two were representatives and agents of the most important gun-purchasing agency on the Border, men who knew the gun-running business from top to bottom and the salesmanship side of the industry equally well.

And thus it was that the frequent, almost regular, letters from Kabul and elsewhere which reached Colonel Ormesby of the Political Department in Simla, were remarkably interesting and extremely welcome. Before long, he came to accept every statement made therein as reliable; every forecast as extremely likely to prove accurate; and every piece of advice as worthy of his careful attention and consideration.

Using the letters to check the reports of his known-and-own Secret Service agents, he found them invaluable; and quickly came to the conclusion that where they differed from the official reports, the latter were almost invariably inaccurate. His unknown correspondent, signing himself John Smith, writing in excellent English, and occasionally using French for dispatches containing information particularly important and secret, provided him not only with first-hand accurate and early information, but with one of the puzzles of a lifetime.

Who could he be?

Why was he working as he did?

And what earthly reason could there be for his not coming to Simla or Delhi, and making himself known to Colonel Ormesby, entering the Secret Service, receiving salary, rank and appointment, and generally regularising his position?

Who and what on earth could the fellow be?

One thing he was—the most amazingly well-informed, active and acutely observant commentator upon current affairs that Colonel Ormesby had encountered.

Only he had not encountered him, and that was the pity.

§2

And from Kabul, Gul Mahommed and Shere Khan again set forth upon a journey so long, so adventurous and so interesting, that the tale only of their experiences on the long gun-runners' road from Kabul to the outer confines of the country of the Turcomans and on and on until they heard Russian speech, would fill yet another book.

And keeping ever northward and somewhat westward towards the Kazak country, they at last reached the town of Orenburg; and thence, travelling westward, came by way of the Ural River to Uralsk; and journeying on again, one day beheld from a hill-top, the waters of the Volga River; and embarking on a river-boat, came, in a great and restful peace, by way of Nikolaievskoi, by Kamishindubovka and Tchernyiyar to Astrakan; and thence by little rusty steamer down the Caspian Sea to Baku; and from Baku they journeyed, with difficulty and hardship, to Tabriz, from Tabriz to Teheran, from Teheran to Meshed, from Meshed to Herat, and so from Herat once more to Kabul.

And in every place in which they sojourned, Gul Mahommed and Shere Khan, with widely-opened ears and closely-shut mouths, heard the talk of the bazaars and *serais*, as with keen-glancing though well-veiled eyes, they strove to behold all things of interest, that it was possible for them to see.

And from every single place in which they sojourned, Gul Mahommed wrote letters to India, most of which, though not in chronological order of writing, reached Colonel Ormesby of the Intelligence Department.

And at Kabul, the day dawned for Shere Khan, as it must for every Pathan, when the nostalgia for his own hills became too strong to be longer borne.

"Let's go home, Gul Mahommed," said he, as they sat in the courtyard of the house of Ilderim the Gun-runner.

"Home? I have no home," replied Gul Mahommed.

"But I have, Friend of my Heart; and my home is thy home; my people thy people. Come there with me. We will arise and go to my father, the Khan Saheb of Khairastan, and I will say:

"'Father, in this man, my brother, thou hast another son.'"

CHAPTER VII

Clad in snowy white shirts, baggy trousers caught in at the ankle, gold-embroidered velvet waistcoats, and baggy turbans bound about their peaked conical *kullah* caps, Gul Mahommed and Shere Khan sunned themselves on a bench in a corner of the Khan of Khairastan's courtyard.

From time to time, Gul Mahommed yawned cavernously.

Shere Khan studied his beloved friend's face, sunburnt and seamed, with its thick black eyebrows, black beard and moustache, dark-brown eyes and aquiline nose, a strong and hawk-like countenance, hard and grim.

"You are all Pathan now, Gul Mahommed," he said, "and you have a home. In one year you have become a son of this House. My father the Khan would grieve if you left us. To my father you are a son, to my brothers a brother. You are a freeman of the Free Country now, a Tribesman and a Pathan."

"Not quite," smiled Gul Mahommed. "I can't sit on my heels. Not for long, or with any comfort."

"No. That's strange, isn't it? It is the most restful position there is, you know, to sit on your own heels with your arms stretched out straight and resting on your knees, the knees behind the unbending elbows, and the hands dangling."

"I prefer to lie flat."

"Much more dangerous."

"How?"

"Well, obviously your enemy can get at you better. You can't jump up so quickly; or sleep with one eye open; or shoot; or . . ."

"Shere Khan, I'm tired," interrupted Gul Mahommed.

"Well, try sitting on your heels."

"I mean I'm bored, weary, what's the word . . . I can

121

only think of *ennuyé*, which is not good Pushtu. I love this place and I love the mountains. But I have sat here over-long, and I am weary."

"Well, there are two things to cure that," said Shere Khan weightily. "Love and war."

Gul Mahommed looked up quickly. Was this fortuitous, or had Shere Khan noticed anything? Was he toying with an idea?

"And horses," he added, "and ambition. But the less said about that the better."

"Well, three then, love and war and horses," amended Shere Khan.

"Yes. It has been said before. How does it go?

"*'Four things greater than all things are*
Women and horses and power and war,'"

quoted Gul Mahommed, and translated.

"Yes? I should say love and war and then horses."

"No, you don't bother much about power up here, do you? A real democracy. You don't worry about the Captains and the Kings."

"No, we are all free men here. Each man's power is in his own right hand and right eye . . . Unless he shoots from the left shoulder," smiled Shere Khan.

"Women and horses and war," he mused. "Which of those would charm away your weariness best, Gul Mahommed, because any or all are . . ."

"You'd start a private war for my benefit, would you?"

"Why not? A word to the Khan and he'd order a raid against Dost Mahommed over the hills to the North there, or against Gazi-ud-din Haidar to the West; or you and I and a dozen or two of the young men could go off and join the Zakka Khel Afridis in their next raid against the Kuki Khel Afridis . . . I heard last night that they are fighting now, all up and down the Road— between the Zakka Khel villages and Ali Masjid, on the days when the Road is closed to the *kafilas* . . . Or the Kuki Khel would be very glad to have our help against the Zakka Khel . . . Or again, if you like, we could go to

Dadi the Brigand or Usman the Outlaw and join them in a raid on Peshawar or somewhere . . . Oh, yes, we could have some fighting if you feel like a bit of war."

"Well, I'm not going to be captured and hanged raiding Peshawar with outlaws, my son."

"We might not be."

"And we might. And I don't know that I am keen on raiding Dost Mahommed or Gazi-ud-din Haidar. I wouldn't mind joining in with the Kuki Khel next time the Zakka Khel raid them. The Zakka Khel are too fond of it. Overdo it altogether. Damned bullies. I wish we could get a machine-gun into the next Kuki Khel village that they shoot up, and give the Zakka Khel a surprise."

"Well, the Kuki Khel are silly fools, anyway," shrugged Shere Khan. "Up near the Kohat Pass there are two clans of the Kuki Khel forever fighting each other. Kill more of one another than the Zakka Khel do of them. They've both got some cannon; something like those we saw at Muscat, you remember. And the two Khans spent half their income on gunpowder. The funny thing is, there are only forty-three cannon-balls left that fit those cannon. And when one side fires one, the other side all rush off and chase the ball, so as to be able to fire it back again. They are frightfully annoyed when one gets buried in the wall of the Fort."

"What's the 'war' about?" asked Gul Mahommed, yawning again.

"Oh, the origin is forgotten, of course, but it breaks out afresh whenever one side has got most of the cannon-balls, and enough powder to fire them. Then they bang away at each other, and the Zakka Khel hear the row, and come down in the middle of it, and take both sides in flank."

"Oh well, it's their own fault then. I'm not going to risk my life fighting for fools," said Gul Mahommed.

"Well, horses then. If you won't raid, will you ride?" asked Shere Khan.

"Where to?"

"End of the world."

"The Golden Road to Samarcand again, eh?"

"And Tashkent too? And cut Bailitzin's throat? Follow the *kafila* road to that place and kill him? Then to Samarcand. And Bokhara and Khiva. Or only just Tashkent again, if you like. Anywhere."

"It's an idea. It is an idea. The Golden Road to Samarcand. Romantic. Used to attract me when I was a *butcha*.[30] No, I'd give all I've got, to meet Bailitzin just once again—but I don't think we'll show our noses near the Russian Officers' School of Oriental Languages at Tashkent again" he growled.

"Well. There's love, then, Gul Mahommed. Why not marry? It's time you saw some sons round your knees."

"Marry? Marry a Pathan girl? Who'd give a landless outlander his daughter?"

"I would. To you."

"Pity you haven't got any daughters, isn't it, Shere Khan!"

"I've got sisters."

"And you'd let one of your sisters marry me?"

"Let her? I'd tell her to, if you cast the eye of favour upon her."

"And your father, the old Khan?"

"He, too . . . I should think. He's old-fashioned, of course, and would have something to say concerning the modern girl and new-fangled ideas about marrying outside the Tribe. But he has the greatest admiration for you. Oh, yes. He'd agree. And in any case, he cannot live much longer, peace be upon him."

"It's an idea. It's an idea," said Gul Mahommed, again. "Marry a Pathan girl, eh? One of your sisters."

"Yes. It would be something to do," said Shere Khan. "Occupy your mind for a time, and then we could go riding or raiding. You could marry Zobeida or Zara or Selima; or there's Zeinub or Miriam or Leila; and what about Mumtaz—she's all right. Or Bhabi—she's a good-tempered lass. Raisha's very well-behaved, too; but if I remember rightly, she squints."

"That is a drawback," admitted Gul Mahommed.

"Yes, they say that when a woman's eyes are crooked, her nature is crooked, too, and her character

---

[30] *Small boy.*

and all that. But I don't know. Raisha's all right. Not that she gets much chance to be otherwise; but you know what I mean, a woman might never glance outside the home but still be a damned nuisance in it, nagging and so on."

"What about little Bibi Jan?" asked Gul Mahommed.

"Our Jan Begum?" laughed Shere Khan. "Ah! . . . Daughter of my mother's cousin Ali Abdullah who was hanged in Peshawar? Now that *is* a girl. Lovely as a rose and brave as a lion. She ought to have been a boy."

"So I thought, when she was at the loop-hole the other night."

"Oh, good as a man at a loop-hole.

"Yes, Jan certainly ought to have been a boy," continued Shere Khan enthusiastically. "Full of spirit; and she's got the pluck of the devil. She'd make a fine wife. But I should be sorry for the husband who beat her."

"Stick a knife in him while he slept?" smiled Gul Mahommed.

"No, while he woke. She wouldn't wait for him to go to sleep. She'd stand up to him. She'd be faithful, too, and she wouldn't scold or nag . . . Nevertheless, if she thought you were a fool, she'd tell you so. Even if you were her husband."

Shere Khan, who had Pathan cunning in full measure, and excellent powers of observation, noticed that Gul Mahommed had ceased to yawn. Power, horses, war, love. In that order, they had interested him. Ah, there he was, talking English again. He'd regret that some day, though hitherto he had never made a slip and spoken English when anyone else was present . . .

> "*Two things greater than all things are*
> *The first is love and the second war,*"

mused Gul Mahommed.

Yes, he could quite imagine himself happy with Bibi Jan. For a time, at any rate. Doubtless she would pall after a while. They would have so little in common.

Of what could they talk together? No mutual sympathies, tastes, experience, background; nothing. When passion waned, would love wax? How could it? The love that wears and lasts and grows must be based on community of taste, outlook, standards, ideas. People who live happily together must laugh together, laugh at the same things; talk, discuss, compare; must have common ground on which to roam hand-in-hand.

Oh, Lord, what sentimental tripe!

But of what, then, did Pathan husbands talk with their wives? Didn't talk with them at all, probably. Well, neither did some European husbands so far as that went. Grunted from behind the newspaper when their wives tried to start some topic of conversation. How many European husbands, a year after the honeymoon, really conversed with their wives, discussed things with them, talked over the books they had read, the plays they had seen, the places they had visited; discussed art, music, drama, philosophy, religion, politics, anything at all—except the quality of the breakfast bacon, the cost of frocks, and the size of household bills?

And probably the Pathan husband did the same— spoke to her of nothing at all except the quality of the dinner mutton, the cost of the new *sari* or bangle, and her extravagance with the *ghee*.

The honeymoon, "*Light of my life and moon of my desire that knowst no wane, I need no food save that of love which is the music of thy voice. Speak on,*" soon changes to, "*Hag, when will that mutton stew be ready? Hold your foolish tongue, and see there be more mint in the meat-balls this time.*"

Yes, to how many husbands, the world over, were their wives real companions and friends, on whichever side the fault might be? Precious few. So he need not let that worry him. Besides, since he was going to be a Pathan, live and die a Pathan, the best thing he could do would be to have a Pathan wife. He certainly would not have any other kind.

But, oh, Lord! . . . Baths . . . hair . . . odour . . .

colour . . . habits . . .

But damn it all, he was going to be a Pathan himself. It was no good half-doing it. No good clinging to the belief that he, much less his wife, must follow every British tradition, custom, convention, habit, shibboleth.

If no Pathan considered a hot bath, or a cold one either, an integral part of his daily routine, did Wendover's great-grandfather, or grandfather, for that matter? Hadn't he heard his father say that there wasn't a single bathroom in the house in which he was born? And as to the Noble Lords and Ladies of the Age of Chivalry, they probably had a bath as often as they got caught in a rain-storm.

No, there was no running h. and c. in the bed-sits of the Château Gaillard—or Whitehall Palace, for that matter. Were there any in the original Buckingham Palace?

In the old days, he had always despised and condemned those *soi-disant* Sahibs who had anything to do with native women, whether as a resident "wife" or casually. Disgusting. But he had been intolerant and perhaps self-righteous in those days. Besides, this was entirely different. Bibi Jan would be his legal, lawful and permanent wife; as much his wife as—Sybil Ffoulkes would have become.

In point of fact, it would be a very sound thing to do, for it would put the final seal on his adoption of Pathan nationality; his repudiation of his British birth.

Yes, it would undoubtedly be a sound thing to do. It is not good to live alone.

It would be a gesture to himself as well as to others, a proof to himself that he really was a Tribesman now; a free unfettered hillman; a mountaineer of the Free Land; a Pathan by choice and adoption; naturalized; permanent; for life.

And his children . . . Oh, Lord! Children. Half-castes, like, yes, like the excellent Lieutenant Breckinge. Probably Captain or Major Breckinge by now.

Yes, half-castes. On the other hand, this again would be a very, very different thing. They'd be of quite another breed from the Breckinges of this Eastern world. Very different from the sweeper-bred scum; or the Portuguese-Indian-descended Goanese servants who are excellent people, of course, in their own walk of life, but . . .

Half-castes! Still, why not? What could be a finer cross than that between good British stock and good Pathan stock, with the virtues of both? How many fine men had been the sons of British officers and Afghan ladies—men who had risen to be Generals, Governors, men all the finer and stronger for the admixture of the blood of such fighting-stock as this.

But a native girl—instead of Sybil Ffoulkes!

And, in the end, Alexander Breckinge saved him, for he decided that, on the whole, he would not add any Eurasians to the world's stock thereof, would not provide himself with a half-caste son lest he grow up to be—a Breckinge.

§2

And so Shere Khan, who loved her, himself married Bibi Jan, according to Islamic law and Pathan custom.

In the biggest room of the house of Khan Khudadad Khan Hassan Ali Khan of Khairastan, Bibi Jan and her female relatives and other members of the household, stood upon a dais behind a curtain. Shere Khan, with Gul Mahommed in close support, stood on the other side of the curtain, while behind them, but not upon the dais, stood as many of the Khan's clansmen as could crowd into the hall.

All being ready on both sides of the curtain, nothing happened, as is usual in India and the parts thereunto adjacent.

After half an hour or so of uneasy shuffling, whispering, clearing of throats and general wedding-guest anticipatory activity, sudden alarums and excursions without announced the arrival of the officiating Mullah, an aged gentleman robed in a voluminous white beard and a black garment, a gaberdine which was a sort of cassock. Receiving the salutations of the faithful and returning their blessings, he made his slow way to the dais, where he took his place beside the bridegroom.

Here he prayed aloud, and then, facing the heavy curtain, cried three times:

"Oh, Bibi Jan, kinswoman of Khan Khudadad Khan Hassan Ali Khan, do you, in the sight of Allah and this assembly gathered together, accept this man, Shere Khan, son of the great Khan Khudadad Khan Hassan Ali Khan of Khairastan, descendant of a long line of warriors, as your husband, with such dowry as he has undertaken to provide?"

And each time Bibi Jan replied "Yes" in a whisper modest and meek, but sufficiently audible withal.

And then again the Mullah, lifting up his surprisingly powerful *muezzin* voice, again asked thrice:

"Oh, Shere Khan, son of the Great Khan Khudadad Khan Hassan Ali Khan of Khairastan, descendant of a long line of warriors, do you undertake to receive this woman, Bibi Jan, daughter of Ali Abdullah, as your wife, and to provide her with such dowry as has been agreed upon?"

And each time, in a strong voice, Shere Khan replied: "Yes."

And again the Mullah prayed aloud; and then, turning to the assembly on his side of the curtain, addressed them:

"Men of the clan of the Khan of Khairastan, you are witnesses in the sight of Allah and before me, the Mullah of Khairabad, that Bibi Jan, the daughter of Ali Abdullah, is this day married to Shere Khan, the son of Khan Khudadad Khan Hassan Ali Khan of Khairastan, according to Islamic Law and the custom of the Border. Pray with me that it may be the will of Allah that they dwell together in health and happiness and prosperity for the remainder of their long lives."

And with the invocation:

"The blessings of Allah upon this man and upon this woman," he pulled aside the curtain and revealed Bibi Jan and the women.

Bibi Jan, veiled, now stood face to face with Shere Khan, who took her hand, and turning, faced the assembled tribesmen.

These, placing their hands upon the hilts of their *tulwars* or their Khyber knives, declared themselves witnesses of the ceremony, friends and protectors of the bride and bridegroom, their willing defenders in time of strife and their helpers in the hour of trouble.

They then trooped out from the house into the courtyard to join the hundreds of wedding-guests who had been unable to crowd into the hall to witness the actual ceremony, fired a ragged *feu-de-joie*, shouted, cheered and sang, and then settled down to what was to them the really serious business of the day—the wedding-feast.

With brief intervals for rest, if not refreshment, the guests feasted for the remainder of the day and most of the night.

It was a memorable marriage-breakfast, with relay after relay of huge dishes piled with boiled roast mutton and rice, with chickens, with vast mounds of pilau, consisting of saffron rice, sultanas, almonds, chopped meat, banana, pistachio nut and shredded onion; most succulent dishes of that noble delicacy, the fat tails of fat-tailed sheep; joints of roast mutton stuck full of cloves; innumerable force-meat balls flavoured with mint, and as appetizers between meat courses, puddings of cream and sweetmeat, *hulwa*, mulberries, melons, walnuts, apples and oranges and other trifles of fruit and home-made preserves and confections of sugar.

And for many a day and week and month, clansman would say to clansman:

"*Wah!* What a feast! By Allah, I was ill. Lovely."

And after the wedding, Shere Khan and Bibi Jan rode away to the fortified house with its loop-holed square of high walls and its strongly-built watch-tower that the Khan had placed at his disposal on a kind of feudal tenure, whereby he paid his father a nominal rent, a portion of the yield of the poor stony fields, and undertook to place himself and his servants at the Khan's disposal in time of war.

And, soon after, to dwell with him as friend and retainer and chief of his other retainers, came Gul Mahommed, whom Shere Khan so loved that he could not live happily away from him; whom he so loved that he would have given him the girl Bibi Jan to be his wife, though her he also loved, and had for long hoped to marry.

CHAPTER VIII

The *chowkidar*, in the watch-tower above the main gate of Khairabad Fort, challenged sharply, his quick ears having caught the sound of a rolling pebble. A high cracked wavering voice answered with a burst of what is best described as religious profanity, and a demand for the prompt opening of the wicket door of the great gate in the name of hospitality, of Allah, and of the Pir Saleh-ud-din Ali Moussa.

"And who the devil is he?" bawled the watchman into the night from whence came the high-pitched quavering cackle.

"One who'll blast the flesh from your bones, wither the hide from your flesh, and wish the hair from your hide. Aye, and smite the soul from your body and send it direct to the lowest floor of Hell."

"H'm," said the watchman. This was evidently a person to consider; and, clattering down the stair from his turret eyrie, he bade his two colleagues of the gate-guard to stand by with loaded rifles. Opening the little wicket in the guard-gate, and thrusting forth his rifle, he bade the alleged Pir approach, slowly, with raised hands—and alone.

Not particularly slowly, and without raised hands, though alone, a quaint figure of fun stepped over the high lintel of the wicket and into the light of the guard-lantern dimly burning.

"Yes, he's a Pir all right, evidently," observed the *chowkidar*, noting the man's wild eye, bird's-nest of hair, absurd whiskers, dribbling mouth and grotesque clothing.

From his fantastic lop-sided turban to his gondola *chaplis*, painted red and adorned with tufts of feathers, he was fantastically arrayed, his chief garment a cross between a short-sleeved night-shirt or a dressing-gown and a djibba or a poncho, which had evidently begun life as a quilted *rezai*, bed-cover, or eiderdown—lacking

132

the eiderdown. A couple of cross-belts, worn bandolier fashion, the one yellow and the other red, were evidently ancient flags; while about his middle were several yards of rope forming a sash, from the back of which depended the tail of a horse.

Beneath his right arm were the disintegrating remains of a *serenai* or Pathan bag-pipes which lacked nothing but the chanter, one of the drones, and a few dependable patches to make it a musical or unmusical instrument.

Beneath his other arm, was a foolish-looking wand or sceptre, adorned with dirty ribbon, tinsel and copper wire, the handle of which was nevertheless a remarkably stout staff.

Obviously a genuine Holy Man.

As the door closed behind him, the Pir raised his hand, invoked the name of Allah and of Mahommed his Prophet, and called down a blessing upon his hearers,

"Announce to the Khan that the Pir Saleh-ud-din Ali Moussa honours him with a visit," he said.

According to custom, the itinerant Holy Man was made welcome, fed full and bidden to rest and refresh himself. This he would doubtless do for the usual three days and then go upon his way in peace, having called down the blessings of Allah upon his hosts.

On being brought into the presence of the Khan and the men of his household, his brothers, half-brothers, brothers-in-law, cousins, sons, sons-in-law, adopted sons, nephews and the rest—just relatives unspecified, kinsmen, clansmen and fellow-tribesmen —the Pir was not received with any particular enthusiasm, inasmuch as, though he might be a genuine Pir of the very holiest and a man of great influence with the Prophet, he might also be nothing of the sort, a fraud, a wandering rascal who subscribed unhesitatingly to the doctrine "To walk is better than to work," and whose private slogan was "Dig I will not, and to beg I am unashamed."

Well the Khan knew that, while always showing reasonable hospitality to any wayfarer, one had to be a little careful. One would hate to be churlish to a Saint, but had no desire to be gushing to a sinner who pretended to be one. On the whole, perhaps it was better to over-do than to under-do the hospitality, as much more harm might accrue from offending a genuine Saint than over-pleasing a genuine sinner. For, while the blessing of the latter would do one no good, the curse of the former might do one infinite harm, not only here but hereafter.

And there again, one had to take a risk, for it was a by-no-means unknown thing for the cunning scout of an outlaw band to come to such a fort as the Khan's in the guise of a Pir and spy out the land, observe the strength or weakness of the garrison, take note of the number and condition of the rifles, see whether there was anything in the nature of a cannon or wall-gun, note whether the water supply lay inside or outside the fort, make a mental map of the defences, and generally perform invaluable work for the brigands who intended to make a raid.

Once or twice such a spy in the guise of a Holy Man had been recognized for what he was, and had died a most unpleasant death, *pour encourager les autres* of the bandits of the mountains.

And between the two extremes, the genuine saintly Pir and the robber spy, were numerous gradations of rogue, from the man who knew something of the Koran and had been a bit of a Mullah in his day, to the mere tramp, ignorant, lazy and worthless, who wore the weird and wonderful garb of a border fakir, as a means of getting free food, shelter and alms for the asking, not to mention absolute immunity from molestation by outlaws, brigands and robbers.

The fact that such professional fakirs had nothing to fear from robbers, speaks not so much for the religious scruples of the latter as for their knowledge that no Holy Man is worth robbing.

The old Khan took stock of the *soi-disant* Pir Saleh-ud-din Ali Moussa as he was brought into the hall where the men-folk sprawled about, relaxed, leaning against the great bolster-like cushions, tightly stuffed in their more or less white covers, that lay along the four sides of the room where the walls joined the floor; or squatting upon rugs about the Khan who occupied a small dais-like bed in the centre of the long wall opposite the door.

"*Salaam-un-alaik.* Peace be upon this house," greeted the Pir.

"*Alaik-us-salaam.* Peace be upon you," replied the Khan.

"May you be strong," wished the Pir.

"May you never be tired," hoped the Khan.

"May you have many sons," blessed the Pir.

"May you never be poor," prayed the Khan.

"Be seated," he added. "Have you been well fed?"

"Well indeed," answered the Pir, and hiccupped loudly in support of his statement and in proof of his meal.

"Whence come you, Holy One?"

"From the North," replied the Pir non-committally.

"Ah . . . And whither go you?" enquired the Khan.

"To the South," replied the Pir.

"Ah . . . And what is the news?" asked the Khan politely.

"Foolish men in Kabul plot against the life of the Amir and say that when he dies, the Border Tribes should take advantage of his death."

"How?"

"By raiding into Hindustan."

There was a stirring among the young men, many of whom literally sat up that they might take notice of the words of the Pir.

"Why?"

"Because the English cannot call upon Kabul to rebuke the Tribesmen and bid them keep the peace, lest the Amir fall upon them in the rear with an army."

"And is this good counsel?" asked the Khan blandly.

"It is bad counsel. None could be worse," replied the Pir.

"And why?"

"Because if this Amir is gathered to his fathers, a

stronger than he will take his place. The plotters are fools. They say '*Let us slay him that his brother, who is our puppet, may take his place*'. But his brother will not take his place. Or but for a brief space. A strong man, who already watches, will send the brother to join his brother, and the plotters will die a death that will make them wish they had not been born. And the Tribe that breaks the peace of the Border will find itself between the upper and the nether millstones—that strong man's army and the army of the *Farungis*."

"For a Holy Man, you interest yourself much in such matters?" observed the Khan.

"Like many Mullahs," agreed the Pir. "But unlike many Mullahs, I preach not war. I preach not that great folly whereby our young men are slain in battle, our villages burnt in punishment, our forts and watch-towers blown up in revenge, our rifles confiscated in thousands, our rupees demanded in reparation, our valleys invaded in scores by military roads. The counsel that leads to these things is bad counsel."

"By Allah, it is true," agreed the Khan, stroking his beard.

"And have you come direct from Kabul?" enquired the ancient Abdul Karim, the Khan's brother.

"I come straight from No-where and go straight No-whither," was the reply. "I wander as Allah wills, and as the Prophet, his Servant, upon whom be peace, directs my feet."

"It does not happen that the Prophet, upon whom be peace, directed your feet hither from the village of Zargun Khel, perchance?" enquired the even more ancient Islam Hamzullah, cousin and chief counsellor of the Khan, a wise and wily man.

"It does not," was the reply.

"It is well," replied Islam Hamzullah; and broke the ensuing silence by observing dreamily:

"One there was, once, long ago, who came here professing to be a Saint, and was none other than the biggest *budmash* of the band of Multan the Robber, his emissary, scout and spy, a strong and sturdy rogue. Clever he was not, but brave he was.

"Yes, he came here and enjoyed the hospitality of the Khan Saheb of that time, my uncle, on whom be peace. I was but a young man then, and foolish. Foolish no doubt; but I trapped the rogue. I had my suspicions of him from the first, for I, a wanderer, knew that I had seen his face before. I knew his voice. And I thought that I had seen, somewhere else and on someone else, a silver talisman that he wore about his neck.

"And in the night I woke him, with a knife at his throat; told him that if he moved I would thrust; told him that I recognized him . . . and he knew that he was caught, for, all about him, lay our young men sleeping, and there was no escape.

"Then I told him that long I had yearned to be a robber, to take to the hills, to live in a cave, to lead a man's life, to be such a one as the great Usman the Outlaw, or Dadai the Brigand, head of a great band of warriors, and to make for myself name and fame as a Border robber, raider and outlaw.

"If I helped him to escape, got him safe out of the Fort, would he take me to his leader and ask him to let me join the band?

"By the strong light of the full moon that fell upon his face, I could see the rascal thinking quickly as he glanced around him, thinking whether he should seize my wrist, wrest the knife from my hand, slay me and escape—and realizing that I had but to shout; that the fact of his showing fight would prove that he was but a trapped rat, a robber, a spy, and no Holy Man. I knew he was wondering whether my words were true as my eyes stared into his, knew that he was wondering whether it were his only chance and that he must take it.

"'*But what is this?*' he whispered in his fear. '*I know naught of Multan the . . .*'

"'*Who mentioned Multan?*' I jeered, pricking his throat. And he knew that he had said too much.

"And I shouted and the young men sprang from their *charpais* and seized him, and we took him before the Khan Saheb, roused from his sleep. And I denounced him as a spy of Multan the Robber, and the

137

Khan Saheb bade his son bring the holy Koran from its place beneath the green velvet cover on the window-ledge.

"And he said to the man:

"'*Swear upon the Koran, by the Ninety and Nine Sacred Names of Allah, and by the Beard of the Prophet, that you know nothing of Multan the Robber and that you are a holy Pir.*'

"And the man feared, of course, to swear upon the Koran; for though life is dear, salvation is dearer.

"'*Then,*' said the Khan Saheb, '*you are caught. You have come into my fort as a spy . . . If I give you your life, will you lead my warriors to the hiding-place of Multan the Robber, bringing us to his cave while he sleeps, that we may capture him?*'

"'*How can I?*' asked the man. '*He keeps good-watch.*'

"'*Where is his hiding-place?*' asked the Khan Saheb.

"'*Two* kos *beyond the western end of the Kohat Pass and north of it. At the back of the hill called Kuh-i-band, looking towards the Lakka Peak.*'

"'*And if I give you your life, will you lead us to within sight of it, that we, feigning to be a* kafila *of Powindah merchants, may decoy them down, to fall upon us?*'

"'*I will try,*' replied the man. '*But if Multan the Robber catches me . . .*'

"'*Fear not. He will never catch you,*' replied the Khan Saheb, '*for I have caught you.*'

"And of that spy, pretending to be a Holy Man, a saintly Pir, he made an example," concluded Islam Hamzullah.

"Serve him right. The Khan Saheb did well," asserted the Pir Saleh-ud-din Ali Moussa roundly, as the murmur of applause died away.

"What did he do to him?" he added in a voice possibly less robust.

"Basted him," giggled Islam Hamzullah.

"Yes? What with?"

"Gravy, of course," was the reply. And the assembly laughed merrily.

"Yes, you see, Multan the Robber had raided Khairabad village while the Khan Saheb was himself away from Khairastan, raiding, and there were but a few fighting men in the place, the rest being aged greybeards and the women-folk.

"And having burned down the gates and burst in, he made a slaughter—and worse.

"And this man, this spy, had been with them and not backward in evil doing. So, as I have said, of him the Khan Saheb made an example, that when Multan the Robber and his band came to know of it, as assuredly they must, they would know what to expect. Also that the Khan Saheb was a man who knew how to take his right and proper vengeance upon such grave-defiling jackals.

"So he gave his orders and next day the Holy Man spy, the Pir robber and murderer and torturer, was bidden to a mutton-feast. And the 'feast' being ready, he was brought forth from the hut in which he had been guarded all night, and he was seated upon the ground in the midst of the courtyard, his ankles being bound together and his wrists tied to his ankles.

"And there he sat with his chin upon his knees, and the Khan Saheb bade them remove his *puggri* and his shirt.

"And on either side of him a tripod of long and strong *lathis* was set up, and across them was laid a pole, the pole being some three or four feet above the head of the false Holy Man.

"And when all was ready, and the great company of tribesmen had seated themselves around the spy, bidding him to be of good cheer and of good appetite, a large cooking-pot was borne forth by two men, and hung by its short chains above the head of the spy.

"Yes. He was a brave man, though an evil dog, for he lifted up his voice, not in lamentation and prayers for mercy, but in curses upon the Khan Saheb, his sons, his relatives, his house and all his tribe.

"And in the midst of it, the Khan Saheb gave a sign, and the cook gave a pull upon a cord fastened to the chain on the opposite side of the cooking-pot. The great pot tipped over, spilling its contents—and a gallon of boiling fat poured down in a stream upon the head of the spy.

"And screaming he died."

And to the mind of one of the hearers of Hamzullah's story, came memories of another time and another place—of an Opera House and well-remembered words and music.

"*Something with boiling oil in it.*"

"Well, he never spied again, the *budmash*," observed the Pir Saleh-ud-din Ali Moussa, as he glanced at the man who had hummed a bar of the music of *The Mikado*.

"No," agreed Islam Hamzullah, "nor any other of the gang. Not in this valley. 'Twas even better than blinding him, cutting off his ears and hands, and sending him back as one does when one singes the fur from a rat, chops off his tail and sends him home to tell the rest that air and water in these parts are not good."

"Yes," agreed the Pir, "much better. Much more striking. After all, a man is liable to have that done to him anywhere, isn't he? I mean to say, a robber expects blinding and maiming and that sort of thing; but the other was a real novelty, and the story of it must have made quite an impression on Multan and his band."

"Quite. They never troubled us again, and never sent any more spies," replied Islam Hamzullah.

"Unless, of course, you are one of them," he added.

"*I?*" replied the Pir Saleh-ud-din Ali Moussa. "*I?* A spy? Do I look like one?"

"Yes," replied Islam Hamzullah.

"Well now, do I behave like one?" smiled the Pir, and rising from his cushion, strode across to where Islam Hamzullah sat upon the dais at the feet of the Khan.

"Look at that," he said, stretching forth his hand. "What do you see?"

"I see an empty hand," replied Islam Hamzullah.

Whereupon the Pir closed his hand and opened it

again. And upon its broad palm lay a shining rupee.

"*Wah, wah!*" marvelled the assembly.

"Take it," said the Holy Man, throwing it into Islam Hamzullah's lap. "And this one, too," he added, producing a second from that astonished ancient's left ear.

A silence fell upon the company as they stared wide-eyed and open-mouthed at the Holy Man.

"How often can you do that?" enquired Shere Khan, who had seen a certain amount of conjuring in his time, and was less impressionable than his untravelled kinsmen.

"Thrice," replied the Holy Man, dexterously producing a third rupee from the circumambient air, and tossing it to the speaker.

"A pity you cannot do it all day long, Pir Saheb," observed the Khan.

"As a matter of fact, I could do it all day and all night," replied the Pir Saheb, "but I have better things to do, nobler matters of which to think, higher pursuits in which to engage my time and the powers with which Allah has been pleased to endow me."

The tribesmen were impressed.

Islam Hamzullah—albeit a little uncomfortable in view of the fact that here was obviously a Holy Man of parts and power, whom he had perhaps antagonised with his sceptical demeanour—maintained a somewhat ambiguous if not hostile attitude.

"Obviously, Pir Saheb," he said, "you are what you profess to be; and auspicious is the day on which you have honoured us with your presence."

The Holy Man acknowledged the compliment.

"On the other hand, how inauspicious would be the day on which you left us," smiled Islam Hamzullah. "Could you not shed the light of your countenance upon us always, and enrich this valley with your shining presence permanently?"

Smiling, the Pir shook his head.

"I am a wanderer," he said. "It is my kismet that I must travel from place to place, exhorting the faithful and providing them with the opportunity for obeying the Koranic law that bids them give alms . . . Save only when rest is necessary can my feet be still."

"And what of a long rest?" enquired Islam Hamzullah. "The rest that is unbroken. Having travelled so far and for so long, what about eternal rest?"

The Holy Man eyed the speaker askance as, naively, the latter mused:

"We have no *Ziarat*, no holy shrine, in this valley, Pir Saheb."

"No?"

"No. And it is a matter for regret that we have here no place of pilgrimage; no sacred tomb of a Holy Man; no sanctuary inviolable by enemies, by thieves, yea, by the most shameless Allah-forgotten bandits—such as was Multan the Robber himself."

Uneasy smiles wreathed the countenances of Islam Hamzullah's hearers.

What a wag he was, and how daring. But really, he was overdoing it a bit with this Holy Man who was so obviously the genuine article.

"You know what some of the Adam Khel did in similar circumstances?" continued Islam Hamzullah.

"What?"

"Why, they felt that it was a reproach unto them that they had no *Ziarat*, no holy shrine, in their valley; so what did they do but send a deputation to the famous Sayed Yacoub Ali Achmed, Pir of Landi—known as the Pearl of Wisdom, and famous for his piety, holiness and learning—bearing gifts, and begging that he would visit their valley, give them his blessing, lighten their darkness and instruct their ignorance and accept an annual endowment from their clan.

"And the Sayed, the Holy Pir of Landi, accepted the invitation, paid the Adam Khel a visit. And never returned home.

"No, he is there still—and a noble *Ziarat* marks his resting-place."

"He died there?" asked Pir Saleh-ud-din Ali Moussa.

"Yes, by request, the same night.

"And we, we of this valley, also have no *Ziarat*," he mused.

The Pir rose to his feet.

"That shall be remedied," he said. "I will return here when old age comes upon me. I will return, and lay my bones among you; and you shall build me a *Ziarat* worthy of myself and you, worthy of your pious generosity and of my holiness. I have spoken. I would sleep."

And on the morrow the Pir Saleh-ud-din Ali Moussa, having given his blessing to the good men of Khairabad, went on his way rejoicing; a devious way that eventually took him to a house in the bazaar of the native city of Peshawar, a house belonging to one Moussafa Shah, formerly Rissaldar of the Cavalry Regiment of the Corps of Guides.

Into this house the wayfarer entered as the Pir Saleh-ud-din Ali Moussa, the wandering fakir, and from it he emerged as Major "Ganesh" Hazelrigg of the Secret Service. Thence he made his unobtrusive way to the Military Cantonment of Peshawar and to a secluded and inconspicuous little bungalow therein, whose elusive and retiring occupant, a brilliant and invaluable Secret Service agent who, unknown, unhonoured and unsung by the many, was, under the name of Tommy Dodd, admired and treasured by the few, his official colleagues, for his great knowledge, ability, courage and accomplishments.

By him Major Ganesh Hazelrigg was received without any amazement.

But with undoubted amazement he and his other visitor received the information, imparted casually by Hazelrigg, as they sat side by side in long chairs and smoked their cheroots on the verandah, that, in a far-distant village, many marches beyond the Khyber, he had seen a ghost.

"Frightened you, I expect," murmured Tommy Dodd, knowing that nothing and no one on this earth had ever really succeeded in frightening Ganesh Hazelrigg.

"A ghost!" smiled Colonel Ormesby, head of the Secret Service, who was the other visitor to the elusive and retiring occupant of the secluded and inconspicuous little bungalow.

"Shouldn't have thought that was much in your line, Ganesh. What sort of a ghost?"

"Well," mused Major Ganesh Hazelrigg, "first of all, it was a Pathan. An absolutely complete, perfect and typical Pathan. Never was a Pathan looked so much like a Pathan as this Pathan did. And then it turned into a ghost. The ghost of a man I used to know. Yes. I used to know the man of that ghost—well."

"And how did the perfect Pathan turn into—a ghost?"

"By humming in plain English."

"How do you hum—in English?" enquired Colonel Ormesby.

And Ganesh Hazelrigg hummed:

"Oh, it hummed that, did it? It's from *The Mikado*, isn't it? Yes. Yes . . . Very queer indeed . . . But then I suppose a Pathan with a musical ear might conceivably remember a bar or two of English music? Remember it well enough to reproduce it accurately, too. But I shouldn't have thought it."

"And where would a Pathan hear *The Mikado*?" asked Hazelrigg.

"Oh, well, on a gramophone record in a Peshawar bawdy-house."

"They don't have 'em there," stated the occupant of the bungalow.

"How d'you know, Tommy?" enquired Colonel Ormesby.

"Well, damn it, I ought to. I spend enough weary hours in the Abodes of Joy in Peshawar, listening to bazaar-gossip . . . No, the music you get in those places is Indian stuff, ghastly native music—*sitar*, *sarangi*, *surnai* and *banshri* and tom-toms—and the horrible nasal chanting of the eternal *Zakhmi Dil*. The only Western tunes I've ever heard on a gramophone in a *dasi*-house are the sort of foul-disgrace-to-civilization noises that are called 'music-hall songs.'"

"*And her golden hair was hanging down her back*," murmured Ormesby.

"Yes, that sort of thing," agreed Tommy.

"Oh, but damn it all, Ganesh," said Ormesby "supposing your Pathan had been a sepoy in the Indian Army—Guides; 40th Pathans; 127th or 129th Baluchis; 29th, or other, Punjabis, why shouldn't he have heard selections from *The Mikado* played by the band on Mess night? As a matter of fact, one of the most delightful things I ever remember seeing was a huge white-bearded Pathan band-master peering through enormous steel-rimmed spectacles at his music, while he conducted his band—which was actually playing Gounod's *Serenade* on the Yacht Club lawn at Bombay.

"No," he added, "I don't think that humming a stave from *The Mikado* is enough to make a man of a ghost No. Your ghost stays a man."

"Yes," smiled Ganesh, "he is a *man* all right. But the man of a ghost, nevertheless. Do you know the words of those particular bars of music?"

"No—I'm not a Pathan," grinned Tommy Dodd.

"No? Well, I'll tell you what the words are," replied Hazelrigg. "They're:

> "*It is my very humane endeavour*
> *To make, to some extent,*
> *Each evil liver a running river*
> *Of harmless merriment.*'"

"What about it?" enquired Colonel Ormesby.

"This about it, Sir. The whole company was laughing merrily at the idea of a feller being put to death, on that very spot, by having boiling oil poured over him. See? . . . And evidently the man of this ghost was reminded of *The Mikado*. He had sat many a time and oft in the stalls of *The Savoy* with his girl—or somebody else's—beside him and . . ."

"No, it won't do, Ganesh," interrupted Colonel Ormesby. "I admit it was queer. Not queer that a Pathan should be able to hum or whistle a bar or two of *The Mikado*, but that he should have made it quite so *à propos*."

"Yes, funny, wasn't it?" said Ganesh. "Quite strange. Because even if he knew English, you'd hardly expect him to know the words as well as the music of *The Mikado*, would you?"

"No, I wouldn't. But I'd still write it off as a coincidence. A really amazing coincidence, I admit. But the longer one lives and the more one sees, the less one is surprised at the truly astounding coincidences that do happen."

"Yes," yawned Ganesh. "That's a fact. It is also a fact that the ghost gave a little laugh that wasn't a Pushtu laugh at all. It was an English one."

"Oh, come, come, Ganesh."

"Well, Sir, I agree with Ganesh," put in the elusive and retiring occupant of the bungalow known to his few friends as Tommy Dodd. "It's one of the things you've got to learn when you 'go native.' You've not only got to talk the vernacular more vernacularly than the vernacularist, so to speak, but you've got to laugh in the vernacular—and cough and sneeze and hiccup in the vernacular, too."

"Yes, it *is* so," affirmed Hazelrigg. "And this chap laughed in English—just as he had hummed in English."

"Well, far be it from me to contradict you, Ganesh, when you are on your native heath," propitiated Colonel Ormesby. "Still, I wouldn't be absolutely sure that a 'typical Pathan' wasn't a Pathan because he laughed in English or hummed in English."

"Perhaps not, Sir. But just when I was being clever, and putting two and two together and making five; putting the coincidence of the applicable humming together with the English chuckle; the fellow went and made it all a waste of time by . . ."

"Scratching himself in Pushtu?" enquired Colonel

Ormesby.

"No. Murmuring under his breath: '*Something with boiling oil in it,*' in English."

"O-h-h-h! . . . O-h-h-h! . . . I see. I see. And I beg your pardon, Ganesh. Why the devil couldn't you have said so at once."

"Well, can't say everything at once."

"And that's when the Pathan turned into a ghost, eh?"

"Yes. A ghost that has been seen before, too."

"Seen before? By whom?"

"Thorburn of Napier's Horse. He saw him down on the Mekran Coast near Godoz, with a bunch of gun-runners."

"How do you know it was the same man? Or ghost?"

"Because I happened to be in the Napier's Horse Mess when Thorburn came back and was telling them about it. He said he had seen a ghost and that the man of that ghost was—*Captain Richard Wendover,* late of Napier's Horse."

Tommy Dodd emitted a long low whistle, and then shook his head.

"But no, Wendover's *dead,*" he said. "Killed in Africa. Body found by Major Robinson."

"By Gad!" exclaimed Colonel Ormesby suddenly. "*That's* it, is it? That explains a lot, whether the man is Wendover or not. Ever seen Wendover's handwriting?"

"Yes. Rather. Why?"

"Because I'm willing to make a small bet, or a big one, that your 'ghost' is the man who has, from time to time, sent me all sorts of priceless information from all sorts of places. I knew it was an Englishman, from the handwriting and the English . . . That's it. It's your ghost—whether it's Wendover or not. Must be. Yes. He must have made his way up from Godoz across Mekran and Persia to Afghanistan and Turkistan; through Bampur, Duzdab, Nasirabad, Herat, Penjdeh, Maimana, Hissar and Bokhara to Khojend, Tashkent and Khoqand; and down through Tashkurgan to Kabul, and thence to Gazni and Jellalabad. Because I got letters from the same chap from all those places and a lot of others; same handwriting and signature—John Smith. I sat up and took notice from the very first one I got—that was from Duzdab—because the writer was obviously an Englishman, a soldier, an acute and accurate observer, and very much behind the scenes—I mean, in a position to know exactly what was going on, to see beneath the surface, and to put an accurate construction on what he saw and heard.

"His information, too, has proved so consistently correct that I have come simply to accept it as gospel, and to act on it even before checking-up. And when I do check-up and find that his statements don't tally with those of my own man I am pretty sure that my own man is wrong."

"And so it proves, eh?" asked Tommy Dodd.

"Always. When I get notice from 'John Smith' that something is going to happen, it does happen. And when I receive information that something has happened, it has happened.

"By Jove, Ganesh," he added, "this is interesting. Are you quite sure that the man—of your ghost—was Wendover?"

"Quite sure," replied Ganesh Hazelrigg.

"But Wendover's dead, I tell you," repeated Tommy Dodd plaintively.

"Then I've seen his ghost, Tommy," replied Hazelrigg.

"You recognized him?" asked Colonel Ormesby.

"No, I won't say that. He's gone so marvellously Pathan, with the Mussulman-clipped moustache and beard; Pathan side-curls; hair bobbed at the back; and burnt-brown face and hands, that I shouldn't have recognized him. I shouldn't have dreamed, for a moment, that he was anything but what he looked, a typical Tribesman. He's got the face and physique, you know. Fortune favoured the poor devil, for once, there. Just the sallow complexion, the eyes and eyebrows; just the frame and physique.

"No, I couldn't have picked him out of that couple of score of Pathans if I had been told that he was among them. No, and if he walked in here, now, with any Pathan *budmash* he picked up in the Suddar Bazaar in Peshawar, you wouldn't know which of the two was the Englishman. Nor should I, if I hadn't just encountered him. If I had met him alone on a hill-path, I shouldn't have given him a second glance. Why, bless my soul, I believe I could have engaged him here in Peshawar as a body-servant, a *chowkidar* or a syce, and had him for years without ever spotting him."

"No, of course he must be perfect, to have got away with it as he has," mused Colonel Ormesby. "Absolutely perfect. And he must have been in some tight corners and had some narrow squeaks. I wonder how on earth he managed to start it all. How he got in with them."

"Yes, and with the gun-runners among whom Thorburn saw him."

"Thought he saw him . . . There's one thing, Colonel," smiled Tommy Dodd, "if he's right, the clever old Ganesh has scored once again. He has spotted this chap—Wendover or not—without being spotted himself."

"Trust Ganesh," agreed Colonel Ormesby. "Wisest old elephant on two legs."

"No, no," protested Hazelrigg. "I told you he took me in completely, and I should never have spotted him at all if he hadn't been so carried away—by the marvellously dramatic story-telling of the old bird who was spinning the yarn about the boiling mutton-fat—that he went all English for a moment, forgot where he was, and remembered his *Mikado*."

"Well, there's where you're the better man," observed Tommy Dodd. "You'd never have done that, in like circumstances."

"Oh, I don't know," replied Major Hazelrigg modestly. "I've been longer at the game than he has. One's bound to make a slip sometimes. Bound to forget for a moment, sooner or later, and lower one's guard. What's the betting that if you were sitting one night in a corner of a Bokhara caravanserai with your tummy full of mutton-stew or *pilau*, just gooping at the stars and thinking of Piccadilly or Ascot or the nicest girl you ever knew, and the lad squatting next to you in a lamb's-skin bowler hat and a poshteen coat, suddenly said '*Got a match?*'—what's the betting your hand wouldn't go to your pocket? Or if he just suddenly said '*By Gum, look up at the balcony!*' what's the betting that you wouldn't glance up at the balcony?"

"Yes, you might. Though I doubt it in your case, Ganesh. But that's different. A sudden surprise-attack like that. What I meant was that you'd never burst into song, so to speak."

"You'd think so, wouldn't you? And yet, do you know that, one particularly glorious morning, going down the Tunjind Pass, I suddenly found myself whistling at the top of my—er—whistle. In English, too. It was *John Peel*, and the connection was a marvellous lad in pink, with a pack of hounds."

"What?" jeered Tommy Dodd. "Riding to a meet. On a horse? In hunting pink with a pack of fox-hounds?"

"No," replied Ganesh. "Riding to Thibet. On a yak. In quilted pink satin. With a pack of curs."

"And before you knew it, you were whistling *John Peel, eh?*"

"I was."

"Still, you were alone and didn't give yourself away, whereas Wendover, if it were he, was in the middle of a regular *mejlis* of Tribesmen."

"Yes, but he didn't give himself away by humming an air and murmuring under his breath."

"But he did. To you."

"Yes, but I mean, he didn't—to them. No, I hand it to him. He's wonderful. And if he did hum and murmur in English, the others never noticed anything."

"I wonder if it is Wendover," mused Tommy Dodd. "I heard the most definite and detailed account of his having been killed in Africa."

"From the man who saw his corpse, I suppose?" enquired Ganesh Hazelrigg sarcastically.

"No, but from a man who knew Major Robinson, the chap who built the Tabundi railway; and this man told me that Robinson assured him that Wendover was dead. He knew it for a fact. Had proof of it."

"I'm sure he did. Absolute proof," smiled Hazelrigg. "He's alive again, nevertheless."

"Oh, yes, I remember the details now," replied Tommy Dodd. "Robinson saw his shirt, all torn and gory. He had been eaten by lions."

"May have been in a lions' den—like Daniel," said Hazelrigg.

"But he came out again," he added. "I tell you, Wendover is alive, and at the present moment he's in the Khan of Khairastan's country, and in his Khaira-bad Fort, or was, when I passed through. I saw him and recognized him, just as Thorburn did at Godoz."

"Perhaps you saw the same man whom Thorburn saw at Godoz," suggested Colonel Ormesby. "A rene-gade Englishman—not Wendover—some chap who has gone native, turned Pathan, and who is nevertheless doing what he can for his country by sending valuable secrets to the Secret Service . . . There's really no reason to suppose it is Wendover—since you admit you didn't recognize him as Wendover."

"No, I didn't exactly say that, Colonel," replied Hazelrigg. "I said I should never have recognized him, or imagined for one moment that he was other than a Pathan, if he hadn't drawn my attention to himself by humming, and then murmuring a sentence, in English. But when I realized that the man must be an English-man, I immediately remembered Thorburn's encounter with Wendover, and looked again. Considered him as a Wendover proposition, so to speak.

"And it was Wendover," he added impressively.

"Don't think me—er—over-sceptical and contuma-cious," said Colonel Ormesby. "I don't want to be irri-tating, but I do want to get to the bottom of this, and be absolutely certain. So I want to raise all the objec-tions I can, and hear you dispose of them. I'm perfectly convinced, of course, that you stumbled on a disguised Englishman—who is most certainly not one of my men, for I know exactly where they all are, and I've got nobody within hundreds of miles of the Khairastan khanate—and I absolutely accept everything except the man's identity. Now, isn't it possible that you and Thorburn saw the same man; and, inasmuch as he has the physique and make-up to play Pathan, and you admit that Wendover had the physique and make-up to play Pathan, this man must, to some slight extent, resemble Wendover. Now, may not both you and Thorburn have jumped to the wrong conclusion—that this fellow is Wendover?"

"No," replied Ganesh Hazelrigg. "No. Impossible."

"Why?"

"Because Thorburn spoke to him, and he answered in English. Thorburn told him that he knew his name and the fellow said, still in English:

"'*Yes, I know my name, too, and it is Gul Mahommed.*' And then Thorburn asked him if there was anything he could do for him, and the man answered, '*Yes, there is. You can clear out of here.*' Then Thorburn, shrugging his shoulders and saying in effect, '*Oh, well, if that's your line, stick to it,*' nevertheless had a quiet dig at him. He said, '*You want me to "wend over" the mountains, eh?*' And the Englishman laughed at Thorburn's little pun, and nodded."

"Thorburn himself told you all this, I suppose?" asked Colonel Ormesby.

"Yes. Well; in point of fact, he actually told it to his Colonel and the Second-in-Command in my presence, and we all questioned him. Thorburn knew it was Wendover; and he absolutely convinced me that, without a shadow of a doubt the man was Wendover. And mind you, he and Thorburn had been brother officers in Napier's Horse for years."

"And besides," added Hazelrigg, "I myself knew it was Wendover there in Khairabad of Khairastan. I realized it the moment I knew that he was an Englishman and remembered that Thorburn had seen Wendover in Pathan kit . . . No, I'm as sure of it as I ever was of anything in this world; and you can take it from me, Colonel, that Captain Richard Wendover, late of Napier's Horse, is, or very recently was, living as a Pathan in Khairabad."

"Well then, why the devil didn't you speak to him?"

enquired Tommy Dodd.

"Because it was more than my life was worth. And possibly his, too. I was doing my Holy Man stuff, and they were a bit sceptical as to my *bona fides*. They had been had like that before. The Holy Man business is getting a bit overcrowded, and every *budmash* who wants to live on the country sticks straws in his hair, puts on a patchwork quilt, plays the goat, and says he's a Number One Pir . . . You can bet that if I had had the ghost of a chance of a quiet word with Wendover, I'd have taken it. I couldn't bat an eyelid in his direction in the hall there, with the Khan's chief counsellor more than hinting that it wouldn't be half a bad tip to give me a job as leading man in a funeral act —bury me as a perfectly good Pir and take a chance on whether I turned up trumps as a draw for the faithful, the miracle-seeking pilgrims. In fact, he remarked that they had not got a place of pilgrimage in the whole khanate, and could do with one as a source of revenue.

"No, my own skin was my first preoccupation, and of course I didn't know whether Wendover was in the same boat, pretending to be a genuine Pathan; and I didn't want to involve him in my fall from grace, into the tomb, if they decided that I would be more useful dead than alive. And I hoped to get a chance of a word with him next day. But I didn't. I got a very straight tip instead, from a chap who I think must have been in the Indian Army, that it wouldn't be a bad idea for me to go while the going was good.

"His line was that if I were a genuine Holy Man he would acquire merit by saving my life; but that there was a party who took the view that if I wandered on I certainly should be of no further use to them, whereas if I remained under a nice white shrine I might be a lot of good, if they could spread a yarn that I had come to Khairabad on purpose to work a miracle, and had then died.

"In point of fact I had worked a few miracles, too," he added, "to prove my genuineness."

"I see," smiled Colonel Ormesby. "Over-did it, eh? Too good a chance for them to lose."

"Yes. I decided that Khairabad was a splendid place to get out of; and though I hung on as long as I dared, I didn't get another glimpse of Wendover."

"Pity. Do you think he had the slightest suspicion of you?" asked Colonel Ormesby.

"No, I don't. He had no reason to. Mind you, it never occurred to anybody, for one moment, that I wasn't a Tribesman. The only doubt was as to whether I was a genuine honest-to-Allah Pir, who was worthy of reverence—and martyrdom."

"So you put your valuable life before your very natural curiosity, and came away without settling the question," observed Colonel Ormesby.

"I came away without communicating with Wendover," was the reply. "But there is no 'question' about it, Sir. You really can take it as an indisputable fact."

"H'm," mused Colonel Ormesby, a man cautious by nature and by training. "If so, I wonder how one could get in touch with him. You didn't hear what he called himself now, of course?"

"No. Nobody addressed him by name in my presence; and naturally I wasn't going to draw attention to him by asking him his name, or enquiring from anybody else."

"And if I sent a letter addressed to *John Smith, Esq., care of the Khan of Khairastan, Khairabad*, Wendover—if it be he—would never get it, of course. Even if it reached Khairabad."

"No. Not without his giving himself away as a European, assuming that the letter reached the Khan, and Wendover was aware of the fact."

"What about going that way, Ganesh, next time you go to Afghanistan and Turkistan."

"Yes, I could do that if you like, Sir, of course. A bit out of the way—and a bit risky. They may decide next time that they will have a *ziarat* and that my sainted bones shall occupy it."

"Yes, you run enough risks in the ordinary way of business without going where you are 'wanted.'"

"Still, I could go in a different rôle, of course," observed Hazelrigg. "I could be a Powindah merchant beating up a bit of trade—rifles and ammunition or piece-goods . . . But then, of course, Wendover may not be there a few months hence."

"No."

"What made you go there, in the first place?" asked Tommy Dodd.

"Oh, I was skirting round the Lakhi Khel country, avoiding old One-eared Suleiman and his merry men; and also I had heard that the Khan of Khairastan was said to be going to join the Singing Hadji of Sufed Kot with the Abazai and the Basar Afridis at a conference on the Afghan border near Giltraza, and I wanted to see whether his young men were rampaging. There's the usual sort of silly gup about their having a shot at Giltraza Fort one fine day, and lifting the rifles and ammunition—the arms-traffic being in such a bad way now that the Gulf is practically closed.

"I've shoved all that in the Report, Colonel," he added.

"Well," mused Colonel Ormesby, "whether this chap is Wendover or not, I'd certainly give something to get in touch with him, get hold of him, and use him regularly. You see, it would double his value if I could give him instructions, and send him wherever I wanted him to go, instead of just being thankful for receiving whatever information he chooses to send me. Think what it would mean if I could plant a man like that permanently at . . .

"By the way," he interrupted himself. "What exactly is the Wendover story, and how long ago was it—if the man *is* Wendover . . ."

Ganesh Hazelrigg laughed curtly.

"He's Wendover, all right, Sir. I know it, and you can safely accept it. I wouldn't tell you so, otherwise."

"No, no, Ganesh. I'm sure you wouldn't, but . . ."

"He was cashiered for being drunk on duty, in time of war. Blind drunk, when commanding an extremely important post that was actually besieged. The relieving force found him dead drunk, and the place commanded by an I.M.S. Lieutenant. There's no possible shadow of doubt, on the evidence. And the most

155

damning of that was given by the Colonel who commanded the relief force. He found him on his bed with a couple of empty whisky bottles, dead to the world, unwakeable. The doctor himself gave medical and other evidence that was unshakeable, unquestionable. There were also the Native Officers of the garrison, and sepoys—orderlies, messengers, sentries and so forth. Some people thought he was lucky merely to be dismissed with ignominy. Overwhelming evidence and not a shadow of doubt."

"No," said Tommy Dodd. "I was on Intelligence in Mombasa at the time. Not a possibility of doubt."

"None whatever," agreed Hazelrigg. "In my mind, at any rate. Not the faintest shadow of the suspicion of a doubt that Wendover was never drunk in his life. He took his peg like we do, and was just about as likely to get drunk."

"I *knew* him," he added.

"Yes, but did you ever see him under extreme stress and strain?" asked Colonel Ormesby. "I recollect the case now. I was in England at the time. As I remember it, there had been a long siege, and they were in a bad way—half-rations, malaria, dysentery and so on. Isn't it probable that Wendover, unable to eat pantile biscuits, india-rubber bully-beef and raw coconut, lived on whisky—until it became a necessity? And then increased the dose, both in frequency and strength, still as a necessity—until he collapsed?"

"No, it isn't," replied Ganesh Hazelrigg. "Not in the case of Richard Wendover. It wouldn't begin even to sound possible to anybody who really knew him. Granted he was as ill as a man could be and keep on his feet—with no proper food and sleep, and proper dysentery and malaria instead: and granted he kept himself going with whisky. Nevertheless, he never drank too much, and I'll stake my life on it that he never went to bed with a couple of bottles of whisky, and drank himself drunk. He never even got the least bit drunk. He never even drank enough to make himself feel that he was beginning to get drunk. However ill and weak he was, he never touched whisky till evening."

"How do you know?"

"Because I know Wendover."

"H'm. He was your friend, and we know you'd always stick up for a friend, Ganesh, whatever . . ."

"I tell you, Sir, that, either I know nothing whatso-ever about my fellow-man, that I am absolutely no judge of men at all, that I'm an ignorant, unobservant, gullible fool—or else Richard Wendover never in his life drank more whisky than he could carry without showing it in the slightest degree."

Tommy Dodd leant across and patted his friend upon the shoulder.

"Quite so, Ganesh. That's all right, old bird. But look here. Have you never been so weak and tired, so down and out, that when you took a whisky and soda you said, '*Damn it, that stuff has gone straight to my head*'? Why, a man can be in such a condition that his ordinary normal sundowner, his one and only of the day, that he takes every day of his life, knocks him clean off his perch, and makes him feel as though he had had half a dozen."

"Yes, yes, my good ass," replied Ganesh Hazelrigg. "We know all about that. And I daresay that when Wendover took his evening bracer, he did say to himself, '*By Jove! that warms me up. That tickles my tummy. Blest if it isn't going to my head!*' Quite so. And the last thing he'd dream of doing would be to take another one, much less go to bed with a couple of bottles and a quart pot, and drink himself pretty nearly to death. Talk sense."

There was a brief silence while the three men pon-dered, considered.

"*Drunk!*" ejaculated Ganesh Hazelrigg. "Wendover blind drunk! I tell you he was never more drunk than we three are at this moment. I'd stake my soul on it that Wendover was found guilty of a crime that he never committed, was disgraced and cashiered and broken for something he never did. It was an abominable miscarriage of justice. A cruel tragedy. The most devilish and abominable . . ."

157

"Well then, how do you account for it, Ganesh?" Colonel Ormesby interrupted the elephantine rumblings of the man affectionately known to his friends as the Elephant God.

"I don't account for it," was the reply. "I can't. But I'm going to have a damned good shot at doing it, now that I know that Wendover really is alive, and has gone native. You see, when it happened I was in gaol . . ."

"Best place for you," murmured Tommy Dodd.

". . . in Tashkent; and when I got out, I had to go on to Hunza, and by the time I got back to India it was too late to do anything. Wendover was dead. As you say, his mangled body had been found with the name-tab sewn on to his shirt. So I wrote Wendover off. And wrote his case down as one of the saddest and darkest and most mysterious tragedies I had ever come across —which is saying something—intending some time to go into the matter. It was too late to do anything for Wendover, but I could satisfy myself, either that it was true, which I knew it wasn't, or that it was untrue, in which case I might be able to do something to . . . to . . . prove it; to clear up the mystery; and to rehabilitate the poor chap's memory. Posthumous vindication, anyhow."

"Yes," agreed Colonel Ormesby. "I can understand your wanting to try."

"And then, on my way from the Gulf, by Karachi and Quetta, to Peshawar and Afghanistan, I stayed a night with Napier's Horse, as I say, and heard Thorburn's tale of having seen Wendover's ghost at Godoz in Mekran. And though he didn't say that the disguised Englishman admitted that he was Wendover, I was quite convinced that it was he, alive and well, and that Thorburn had seen him. And now *I* have seen him, and I know that Thorburn was right.

"And I'm going to do something about it," he added.

"But what can anyone do, after all this time?" asked Colonel Ormesby. "And what can anyone do in the face of the findings of a Court-Martial? It's not as though it were a hole-and-corner affair, either; hurriedly held under a tree; with doubtful witnesses; *shenzis*, who say what they think you want them to say, and in a language that you don't understand. The trial was completely regular, very thorough, and the evidence overwhelming."

"Yes, as good a case of 'trial by one's peers' as you could have," agreed Tommy Dodd. "Not merely one judge, and he possibly prejudiced or biased, but five of them; and every one of the five only too anxious to be able to find him 'Not Guilty.'"

"And what's more, don't forget, my good chap," added Colonel Ormesby, "that there was not only unbiased and intelligent evidence, but actually expert evidence. There was a doctor there, remember."

"Yes, I remember the doctor all right," growled Ganesh Hazelrigg.

"And he had Wendover under observation, too," said Colonel Ormesby.

"Yes; and Wendover had had him under observation," was the stubborn and apparently pointless reply.

"What d'you mean?" asked Colonel Ormesby. "We all know that there is no exact definition of drunkenness, and that different people hold different opinions as to whether a man is drunk or not. When a man is run in, accused of being drunk in charge of a motorcar, the Station Sergeant says he is drunk because he can't stand against a wall with his eyes shut, or walk along a chalk line, or spell Nebuchadnezzar backwards. And the accused and his friends say that of course he wasn't drunk and that he had only had a small one, three days ago; and his excited manner was due to the rude way in which the policeman spoke to him. Then they call in a doctor, and his evidence is generally considered conclusive, one way or the other. . . . Well, here it wasn't a case of calling in a doctor to have a look at Wendover and give an opinion on his condition. The doctor had been living with him for months and knew exactly what Wendover was doing, all the time. He gave evidence, both as a colleague who had actually seen him drinking hard, and as a doctor who had seen him helplessly and hopelessly drunk."

"'Fraid it's no good, Ganesh," Tommy Dodd agreed

with Colonel Ormesby. "When you come to consider the evidence of the man who found him and the man who had lived with him. I happen to know Colonel Maldon—one of the best. An awfully good sort. He never made trouble for anybody yet, and he'd have saved Wendover if it had been humanly possible. But he had to testify that he found him blind drunk. It isn't as though there were no European witnesses. And when one of them is actually a doctor . . ."

"Did you ever meet that doctor, Tommy?" asked Ganesh.

"No."

"Well, he's not a European, except in name. Breckinge. He's as black as your boot. A Eurasian. And of a very bad type. Native Goanese blood on one side, and sweeper on the other. I do know him. Know something about him, too. And I wouldn't convict a dog on his evidence. As it happens, I stayed with Wendover down in Madrutta before he went to Africa. I was there looking for that seditionist, Ranjit Singh, who had just landed from America and who was meeting Sant Arjun Rama and Luxman Dhonde and the rest of that gang. And, poking about in the bazaar, as a one-eyed leper, I noticed Master Breckinge, whom I had seen at the Gymkana, go into a funny-place. And a night or two afterwards, poking around as a Gulf pearl-merchant, I found him in the funny-place, had a talk with him, and learned some very interesting things. Not only from him, but about him, from a Heart's Delight who occasionally turns an honest penny, on the side, by selling 'information received' to the C.I.D. or the Secret Service. A very knowledgable wench and a most useful young woman."

"Yes, when I heard about Wendover's case and the details of the Court-Martial, I remembered the good Breckinge," he added.

"Led a double life in Madrutta, did he?" asked Tommy Dodd.

"Yes. Quadruple one, too. He had some queer hobbies and diversions. Very much of a blackguard. And it is on him I fix my hopes."

"What of?" asked Colonel Ormesby.

"Learning the truth about Wendover."

"Don't you think he told the truth about Wendover at the Court-Martial? The truth, the whole truth and nothing but the truth?" asked Tommy Dodd.

"I think he told the truth and nothing but the truth. But I am perfectly certain he didn't tell the whole truth," was the reply.

"And what about Colonel Maldon?" asked Colonel Ormesby.

"He, of course, told the truth," admitted Ganesh, "the truth, the whole truth, and nothing but the truth —as he saw it."

"And as he saw Wendover," observed Tommy Dodd. "Dead drunk."

"No one ever saw him drunk any more than they ever saw him dead," replied Hazelrigg stubbornly. "And I'm going to prove it. If I were free, I'd set about it now. Anyhow, I'll devote my next leave to it. Yes, I'll see Wendover if I can, on my way North; and speak to him, too, if it is possible. I'll go as an Afghan merchant with a red-dyed beard; or as a horse-coper; and try to chum up with him as though he were a Pathan and I had taken a fancy to him. Get him to go out for a ride with me, or guide me somewhere, and then give him the surprise of his life."

"Suppose he denies that he is Wendover?"

"He won't, when I've talked to him," was the confident reply.

"And when I've learned all he can tell me," he continued, "I'll find Breckinge and give him a surprise, too."

"What will you do?" asked Colonel Ormesby.

"Well, I haven't thought it out yet, but something on the lines of *All is discovered and your one chance is to make a clean breast of it* sort of idea."

Tommy Dodd laughed.

"You are an unscrupulous devil, Ganesh," he said.

"Regular Bad Man," agreed Colonel Ormesby.

"Or perhaps take a blackmailing line," smiled Ganesh, "if the *Fly immediately, for they are on your track* gambit doesn't work. Or perhaps put one of our Heart's Delights on to him, to make him drunk and get him boasting. He's the sort of chap who'd talk when he was in liquor, especially if a woman got him bragging of how he had done-down the wicked enemies who had triumphed over him."

"Was Wendover his enemy?" asked Colonel Ormesby.

"Wendover was the sort of man who'd be bound to make an enemy of a subordinate of the Breckinge type. He'd be everything that Wendover hated, and Wendover would be everything that Breckinge hated. Knowing them both, I'm perfectly certain that Wendover and Breckinge couldn't be shut up together in a besieged post without bad trouble. Wendover's attitude would be one of contemptuous dislike, and Breckinge's one of resentful hatred."

"Got it all cut and dried, old son, haven't you?" smiled Tommy Dodd.

"Yes, pretty well," asserted Ganesh. "Knowing the position and the men, I can see what happened . . . Look here, damn it all, Tommy, don't *you* know anybody who couldn't possibly, under any conceivable circumstances, go and get blind drunk when men's lives depended on him; when the defence of a very important fort depended on him; and possibly the success of a whole campaign. Don't you?"

"Well, yes, of course I do," admitted Tommy Dodd.

"And don't you, Colonel?"

"Yes, certainly," admitted Colonel Ormesby. "In point of fact, I think I could begin with myself," he smiled.

"Of course you could, Sir."

"Well, believe me," continued Hazelrigg, "Richard Wendover could no more do that than you could do it yourself. Can you imagine such people as, say, General Gordon doing it during the last days of Khartoum. Could you imagine Lord Roberts having done it? Or Sir George White at Ladysmith? Or Baden-Powell at Mafeking? Can you imagine any of them being found blind drunk at their post, in the presence of the enemy? Of course not, and I could just as easily imagine Richard Wendover doing it."

The others smoked in silence for a while.

"Very well, then," Ganesh Hazelrigg broke out again. "There must be explanation for what happened —and that black-faced scoundrel of a doctor is the explanation."

"And what about Colonel Maldon and the native officers? What's the explanation of their evidence?"

"The said black-faced scoundrel of a doctor."

"Why?"

"Wendover wasn't drunk. He was drugged."

Major Hazelrigg's listeners literally sat up and took notice.

"My dear chap!" expostulated Colonel Ormesby.

"Mellow Drama. Gee-whiz!" smiled Tommy Dodd.

"Wendover was drugged," repeated Hazelrigg doggedly.

"How can you say that? Why do you . . . ?"

"Because there is no other explanation."

"Melodrama? Black tragedy rather!" exploded Colonel Ormesby. "And poisonous unspeakable villainy. By God, if that were true . . ."

"It is true," asserted Hazelrigg again. "It is true because it must be. Because it is the only possible explanation. Accept the premisses, and it's the only conclusion. Ask yourselves. Accept my word for it that Wendover could not and did not do such a thing, and yet was found apparently dead drunk, what's the obvious and only explanation? That he was drugged. Given that he was shut up, for months on end, with the sort of man who'd jar upon him incessantly, who'd irritate him every time he opened his mouth, who'd offend him at every turn, who'd undoubtedly anger him by laziness and bad work—and what's the unavoidable result? Friction, trouble, bad feeling, mutual antipathy.

"Breckinge would deservedly get the rough side of Wendover's tongue; and when occasion required, that side of Wendover's tongue could be very rough. And what happens when that class of mongrel is told off? He takes it badly. Instead of thinking how he can improve, he thinks how he can 'get even.' And what would be the method and weapons that would appeal to that type of cur when it happens to be a doctor? Breckinge's one idea—and mind you, Breckinge would be in an abnormal state of mind, too, for conditions were almost as nerve-racking and debilitating for him as for Wendover—his one idea would be to get even. Well, Breckinge is a doctor.

"And Breckinge got even," added Major Hazelrigg, and never did that ponderous man speak more weightily.

Again a silence in the moonlit verandah.

"By Jove, Ganesh," said Colonel Ormesby at last, "what an appalling accusation. What a perfectly ghastly thing . . ."

"For Richard Wendover," interrupted Hazelrigg.

Silence again.

"Well, my son," said Tommy Dodd at length, "you've said something."

"And I'm going to prove it," replied Hazelrigg.

PART III

CHAPTER I

Inayatullah Hussein, the Afghan horse-coper, continuing his devious journey, which he had recently broken at Khairabad, rode along on his Kabuli stallion, with his new acquaintance, Gul Mahommed, the friend and retainer of Inayatullah's patron and customer Shere Khan, son of the Khan of Khairastan, chatting merrily of the only three important and interesting subjects of conversation, horses, war and love, the greatest of which in the opinion of Inayatullah Hussein was obviously horses.

Afar off, at a turn of the high mountain road, they beheld a flag-bedecked and deserted *ziarat*.

"We'll halt there and rest awhile," quoth Inayatullah, "for I have placed certain things therein for safety, a sanctuary which the wicked robber would not violate."

"Nay," added he caustically, "nor the holiest saint. Not even the Singing Hadji of Sufed Kot, should he pass this way."

"Which is not likely!" exclaimed Gul Mahommed.

"No, it is not very probable, but one never knows. One never knows. I have heard of even more impossible things happening."

The men rode on in silence.

"Have you heard any talk of this same Singing Hadji of Sufed Kot?" enquired Inayatullah casually.

"There is some talk about him," replied Gul Mahommed.

"Yes, there seems to be talk about him everywhere. What are they saying in this part of the world?"

"Oh, I don't pay much attention," replied Gul Mahommed, "but the Khan and his counsellors were speaking of him the other day."

"He had sent a messenger, I suppose?"

"I believe so."

Gul Mahommed was obviously not interested in the

sayings and doings of the Singing Hadji of Sufed Kot, but apparently Inayatullah was.

"I am a gossip," he said. "Part of my business is to know the news. Helps the patter when I am selling the horses. Everybody is talking about the Singing Hadji. He's going to cause trouble again."

"Yes?" yawned Gul Mahommed.

"Yes. So men say. I thought he had been quiet for an unusually long time. I wonder if he wants your Khan to join in the trouble?"

"I wonder."

"They say there's going to be fighting. They say he's going to proclaim a *jehad*, and start by having a shot at Giltraza Fort."

"Well, it's all good for trade," he added. "Armies mean horses. I wonder if any of the Afghan cavalry regiments will be moving toward the Border?"

"Why should they?"

"True. One should not talk like that. A gossip has to be careful how he mentions the Amir. But I can talk freely to you, oh, Gul Mahommed, friend of my friend and friend of my heart."

Gul Mahommed turned an impassive face toward the garrulous man, and with raised eyebrows considered this effusiveness.

A very sudden friendship. What did the rogue want? What was the Pathan tag? '*Honest as an Afghan horse-coper*'? Yes, and wasn't there one to the effect that a fool trusts a snake, a wolf, a woman and—an Afghan? The Pathan ought to know, for they could do a little in that way themselves.

"Well, I shan't report it to the Amir," he said sarcastically.

"No. Nor to anybody else. I was only wondering, because there is a talk of war, and war means horses, and horses are my living. Will the Khan move when the Singing Hadji gives the signal? Or will he pay off old scores by taking the rascal in the rear when he attacks Giltraza?"

"How should I know?"

"By hearing the Khan's words, as a man does hear

the words of the father of his friend, with whom he lives as a brother."

"Well, I haven't heard any words on the subject."

"Ah, you are not a leaking *mussuck*, Gul Mahommed. Now I did hear some words in Peshawar. Very interesting. The Sirkar wants to be able to march troops quickly to the Singing Hadji's part of the world, should need arise again—as surely it will. And there was a talk about a Road coming up in this direction, and about an offer of a fine subsidy to the Khan of Khairastan if he would be the guardian of that Road, and guarantee it. Keep it open for everybody two days a week like the Levies do the Khyber. They say in the bazaar that Sahibs are coming to Khairabad . . ."

"*What?*" ejaculated Gul Mahommed.

". . . to talk with the Khan of Khairastan, and to say that if he will make his *jowans* into a *pultan*, the Sirkar will give him a fine *pinson*, and give the *jowans* the same *puggarh* that they give the sepoys of the Indian Army, as well as issuing rifles, rations and ammunition to them. That's fine *khubbar*, isn't it?"

"Did you tell the Khan Saheb?"

"No. I had it on the tip of my tongue, and then I remembered the fate of a friend of mine, also a poor dealer in horses, who told some news to the Amir at Kabul."

Inayatullah fingered his beard and laughed fatly.

"Yes. He must have been drinking *sherab*, or something of the sort. If he had been drinking of the Forbidden, what happened served him right, for in his loose-tongued loquaciousness he said to the Amir who was looking over the string of horses my friend had brought:

"'Oh, King of Kings, I am from Penjdeh and there men say that the grey-coats are coming. The great Russian Bear is moving south, going to invade Afghanistan.'

"'Is that so?' said the Amir. And then: 'Climb that tree, oh man, and keep watch against their coming.'

"Well, it does not do to delay when the Amir gives an order. So, to humour the merry Amir, my friend climbed the tree that stood near-by, in the Palace grounds. And then the Amir turned to an officer and said:

"'Station sentries beneath that tree with loaded rifles, relieving them every two hours, by night and day; and when our watchman descendeth, or perchance falleth, from that tree, they will shoot him in the stomach. On thy head be it.'

"So there he stayed until he fell from the tree. And the Amir inherited the horses.

"No," concluded Inayatullah, "it is not always wise to bring news to people in whose power you are. If the news is stale they think you are a fool and bid you depart while the gate is yet open; and if the news is unpleasant, they may forbid you to depart, even though the gate be open. But you, being the friend of his beloved son, could well give him the news about the coming of the Road."

"Is it true?"

"Allah knows! But how often is bazaar gossip wrong? I have never found it to err, save in small detail. Undoubtedly the Sirkar is going to make a Road that would pass through the Khan's country of Khairastan, and as the Khan Saheb is the biggest chief for fifty *kos*, it is certain they will offer to subsidize him as its guardian. Either that or make war upon him the first time his young men come down upon the working-parties and destroy them, or waiting until the Road is made, come down and plunder the *kafilas*, or collect heavy toll from them."

"I will tell him what you say, Inayatullah," said Gul Mahommed.

"It will interest him," observed Inayatullah. "You know the Sirkar is wise as well as strong. And just too. Very just. Understanding that a man must live, and that the Khan and his ancestors have lived for many centuries by guaranteeing the safety of the caravans— at a price—the Sirkar realizes that if it takes away his means of livelihood, it must compensate him. Rather would it pay him the equivalent and keep him as a friend, than beggar him and turn him into an enemy, an outlaw and raider, who will not only exact yet heavier toll than before, but will be as a thorn in the side, attacking their Forts, cutting off their convoys, yea, even raiding into Peshawar itself. . . . Here's the *ziarat*. Let's off-saddle and rest the horses awhile, as we eat and drink."

And dismounting, the two men loosened their saddle-girths, raised and lowered the saddles a few times, removed the bits from the horses' mouths, and dropped the reins over their heads.

Unfolding and spreading upon the ground a saddle-cloth, Inayatullah lowered his heavy frame to it, sighed luxuriously, crossed his legs and fumbled in a big bag slung beneath his *poshteen*.

"Will you break bread with me and share a cold *chupatti* and mutton?" said Inayatullah hospitably, as Gul Mahommed seated himself beside him.

"No, I thank you. I will return to the fort of my friend Shere Khan from here, and a meal will be awaiting me."

"Ah," smiled Inayatullah, smacking his lips. "Lovely Patna rice, each grain bigger and softer than the last. With saffron. And curry of the tail of the fat-tailed sheep. Allah! Or a *pilau* of chicken-livers, rice, raisins, pistachio nuts, shredded onion, cloves, chopped fruit. A mountain of it, rising from a lake of *ghee. Ah-h-h-h* . . ."

"What is there better?" agreed Gul Mahommed somewhat unenthusiastically.

"Why, my son," replied Inayatullah, in English, laying his hand upon Gul Mahommed's knee, "a lobster-claw and a glass of Veuve Cliquot, at Ascot, say—or . . ."

It speaks well for Gul Mahommed's nerves and self-control that he did not start or exclaim.

"What did you say?" he asked apathetically, in Pushtu.

"I said, don't be an ass, Wendover. Come off it. I'm Hazelrigg."

And Wendover came off it.

"Congratulations," said he coldly. "Damned clever."

And extending his hand, added, as though they had just been introduced:

"How do you do, Hazelrigg."

Hazelrigg laughed.

"The same to you, old chap. How do you do and how do you do it? For it's very very good. You ought to join us. If I hadn't known, you'd have taken me in completely, and that's saying something."

"You certainly took me in," snapped Wendover.

"Well, it's my trade, as you know. I am a professional. And if you are an amateur, I can only say you ought to turn pro forthwith. Come on along with me, now."

Wendover shook his head.

"You know me, Hazelrigg, and you know my story, presumably."

"And that, my dear Wendover, is precisely what I do. I know your story. The truth of it, I mean."

"Well then, what's the good of suggesting that I should join you?"

"Because I intend that everybody else shall know the truth of your story."

"That's awfully good of you, Hazelrigg, but I don't know that *I* do. I am not greatly interested, either way. On the whole, I'm a good deal happier here, now, than I used to be," lied Wendover.

"Not you, Wendover. Though it is a splendid idea to think you are—if you do think it. And though I couldn't offer you a permanent post straight away, why not come along with me until I can? Think of the times we'd have together."

"Yes, and think of the times I should have when I ran into people who knew me when I was Wendover of Napier's Horse."

"Yes. But all that would come later. You can stay as much a Pathan as my Mahbub Ali or Shere Khan until the time comes."

"What time?"

"The time when I've done what I am going to do. Got to the truth of the matter and published it."

"Didn't the Court-Martial do that?"

"You know they didn't."

"Well, they thought they did, anyway. So does everybody who ever heard of the case. Wasn't I found blind drunk—with a couple of empty whisky bottles?"

"No, you were found drugged—with a couple of empty whisky bottles planted on you."

"I've often wondered."

"But damn it all, man, you know perfectly well you didn't go to bed with a couple of bottles of whisky and drink them, neat, don't you?"

"To be quite honest, Hazelrigg, I don't. As a matter of actual fact, I don't know at all what I did that night. I can remember feeling frightfully ill, tired and sleepy, and taking a good stiff peg of whisky-and-soda to pull me together; and that's the last thing I do remember. Whether I emptied the bottle and got another one, I don't know. If I did, you can't blame the Court-Martial for their finding and sentence. And yet, in a way, it doesn't seem a very heinous crime, for it was unconscious. I'm not blaming Colonel Maldon for saying I was dead drunk, nor Colonel Matheson and the others for believing it, but you really might just as well blame a somnambulist for what he did when he was sleep-walking."

"Of course you might," agreed Ganesh Hazelrigg. "But that wasn't it at all."

"What I mean to say is," continued Wendover, "I should never, in my right senses, and knowing what I was doing, have dreamed of such a thing as drinking half a bottle of whisky, much less a whole one, least of all a couple. And yet—there it was."

"No, it wasn't," contradicted Hazelrigg. "Of course it wasn't. Did you ever get drunk in your life?"

"No. No. I can't say I ever did. Of course I have known many a very wet night in Mess, special occasions and big guest-nights when the fun went on until daylight, and that sort of thing."

"Yes. Yes. Like everybody else," agreed Hazelrigg.

"But I've always put myself to bed," continued Wendover, "and been bright and early for parade in the morning; and I have always clearly remembered everything that happened the night before. No, I've never been drunk."

"Got a pretty good head?"

"Yes, very good. Not that I've ever tried it to the limit. On a night of uplift, I have had, say, a couple of sherries or cocktails before dinner, a bottle of champagne with dinner, a couple of glasses of port after dinner, and then, later in the evening perhaps, a couple of brandies-and-soda over snooker. And a night-cap to help the last guest off, sort of thing. That has been about my wildest and wickedest effort in the debauchery line."

"And none the worse for it?"

"Bless me, no. Could have sat down and written next day's orders for the Colonel, if he had wanted me to; or filled up a dozen Army forms in triplicate; or danced three rounds with the General's wife."

"Then it was something pretty tough that knocked you out, at Ubele?"

"Yes. I shouldn't have thought even a couple of bottles of whisky would have put me under so completely and for so long. Not if I had drunk them nicely and quietly between drinks . . . I wonder what it was?

"Well, there's one thing," he added, yawning. "We shall never know."

"Shan't we? I'm not so sure," replied Hazelrigg. "Not by any means so sure. I've talked about it, not mentioning your name, of course, but as a hypothetical similar case, to lots of doctors; and I've got some ideas."

Hazelrigg sat silent for awhile.

"Had that doctor chap, who gave evidence against you, got any special grudge against you?" he asked suddenly.

"Grudge? No. Why should he? I had to twist his tail a bit, but . . ."

"But not to that extent, eh?

"Had you had any dealings with him before you were shut up together in Ubele?" he added.

"Dealings? No. I had met him in Madrutta when I was seconded there from Napierpur. Used to see him at

the Club and Gymkana, and came across him officially, now and then, when I was Staff Captain."

"Ever met his father, the Superintendent of Police?"

"No. Heard a good deal about him. Great lad, wasn't
he?"

"Wonderful policeman. Wonderful. Of course he had
a big pull over a man from Home, being bred and born
in the country, and knowing the native from inside, so
to speak. They all loved him, even those whom he
pinched. Quite a hero with the criminal gangs, though
they used to shoot him up, occasionally. The police
sepoys worshipped him. They'd have done anything for
him.

"*Or for his son,*" he added.

"Yes? Fond of him too, were they?"

"I don't know so much about that, but . . . for the
father's sake, I mean. I fancy he could have got away
with anything, so far as the police sepoys were concerned."

"Valuable asset for a young man about town."

"The town of Madrutta, yes. I fancy he made use of
it too."

"Eh?"

"Yes. I've been taking quite an interest in him. Do
you know where he is now?"

"No. Where?"

"Up in Killa Giltraza with the same old lot. Half-
battalion garrison."

"Oh, he's still doing regimental work, is he?"

"Yes. He's not *persona* peculiarly *grata* to the
authorities."

"What's he been up to?"

"That's what they don't know. But there are funny
tales; and he's got some funny friends. Nothing against
him much—officially. And precious little for him."

"I never liked him," observed Wendover.

"No, I don't think anybody does much, but that's
what I'm getting at. Did you show it very plainly?"

"Well, as I say, I had to twist his tail."

"For what?"

"Oh, general slackness and an absolutely wrong

attitude to his job, not only as a doctor but as a gazetted officer. Thick as thieves with his Indian pals, and they weren't too satisfactory. Quite one with them, if you know what I mean. Definitely much more their friend than mine."

"Any special and particular row when you went for him bald-headed and said the sort of thing he'd never forget—although you might forget it next minute?" asked Hazelrigg.

"Well," said Wendover. "If there was, I've forgotten it. Of course, one's nerves were a bit on edge and one's patience wore a trifle thin, what with one thing and another. And I am apt to say quite what I mean."

"Yes. But you don't remember any special row?"

"No. No. It was just one damned thing after another. Oh yes, I do remember telling him just what I thought of him when he connived with the Subedar-Major to conceal from me the fact that, owing to the blighter's laziness and damned disobedience, a good sepoy had been drowned and his rifle and ammunition lost. I'm not altogether in favour of the drowning of sepoys at any time, but a man was a man just then, and a rifle was a rifle."

"Oh! Connived with the Subedar-Major, did he?"

"Yes. And as luck would have it, two of the other native officers were the Subedar-Major's brother and brother-in-law or something of the sort. There were no less than three native officers in that battalion, who were related, by birth or marriage, and of course they all hung together. And our Breckinge made himself a fourth. You'd have thought a fellow who had got such an almighty swipe of the tar-brush would have been all the other way, wouldn't you? Stood on his Englishness and all that. But no, he was as Indian as any of them—especially after I had had to tell him off, once or twice . . . Well, I happened to miss this sepoy, and I had the deuce-and-all of a job to find out what had happened to him. Up against the usual brick wall of blind native *What-do-I-know?* and although Breckinge knew all about the case, those were the very words he used when I questioned him. And then I *did* go for him.

Good and proper."

"I've no doubt it was good," smiled Hazelrigg, "but was it proper? Or was it vulgar abuse? Nasty words like *banchūt*?"

"Oh, no, no. Nothing of the sort. I don't go in for *gulli* when talking to a native, or a Eurasian. I spoke to him as Lieutenant Breckinge, I.M.S., just as I should have spoken to any other Lieutenant who had been guilty of gross breach of duty on top of thoroughly unsatisfactory work and conduct."

"Just cut him to ribbons in correct and well-chosen English, eh?"

"Yes. I told him exactly what I thought of him, and promised him a Court-Martial."

"Ah! You did, eh? And the Subedar-Major whose laziness and disobedience had caused the drowning of the sepoy—did you promise him a Court-Martial too?"

"I did."

"And how long was that before you took to drink?"

"Oh, a day or two before."

"Very interesting . . . And a messenger arrived—got through and said that the relief was close at hand, and would arrive next day—and that the siege was practically raised."

"So they said at the Court-Martial. I knew nothing about it."

"No, you were asleep. Wrapped in sottish swinish slumber. And thus the message went to Breckinge, who acknowledged its receipt in writing, with signature in full; and sent the runner back with it, eh?"

"So I learned at the Court-Martial."

"And that night you went on the booze—and never lived to tell the tale."

Wendover glanced at the speaker.

"To tell the tale of the misconduct of the Medical Officer and the Subedar-Major—to a Court-Martial."

"No, got the Court-Martial myself, instead," said Wendover.

"Yes; very very interesting."

"Well, it's all over and done with, now," yawned Wendover.

"And that's just what it's not, my son. Just what it's not."

"Well, I hope it is. What would be the good of raking it all up again? Supposing what I have always imagined was true, and that Breckinge put half a dozen morphia tablets in my tea-pot—there wasn't any coffee —you don't suppose he did it before witnesses, do you?"

"No; nor that he'd ever confess to having done it. It isn't likely, is it?" admitted Hazelrigg. "Nevertheless, that's what happened, Wendover. Only it wasn't morphia."

"How do you know it wasn't?"

"Because I've talked with better and bigger doctors than Breckinge. It wasn't morphia. And it's a bit of a puzzle to know what drug it was that gave you not only forty-eight hours' heavy sleep, but various other symptoms that you displayed."

"How do you know what symptoms I displayed?"

"Well, I made it my business to study the report of that Court-Martial pretty carefully."

"Well, there were no symptoms described in the report, were there?"

"No; but having studied the report of the Court-Martial, I then also studied the members. Every man of them. And one or two of them were men with gleams of intelligence; especially a chap named Brace. I had a long talk with him. Nice feller. He told me that, had he been sole judge, his verdict would have been '*Obviously guilty but patently impossible,*' with a rider, '*Dead drunk, from cause or causes unknown, especially to the prisoner himself.*'"

"Why? Did he have a notion that I had been drugged?"

"Yes. He told me that that most certainly occurred to him; and that he rejected it as palpably absurd— unless you had a private store of some such narcotic as opium or laudanum or morphia or something like that, and had taken a more or less suicidal dose of it. And that struck him as being every bit as bad as taking a suicidal dose of whisky."

"Yes, I suppose it would. Come to think of it, a gentleman who seeks oblivion from care, with knock-out drops, is every bit as bad as one who seeks it with a bottle of the Old and Bold."

"Absolutely, provided it was a definite and intentional attempt at escape from sin and sorrow, grief and pain."

"That's the actual evidence," he mused. "I suppose if you had drunk two cases of whisky instead of the alleged two bottles, and it had had no more effect than half a pint of cold water, no one would have had a word to say about it. You would have committed no offence, provided you were on the spot for duty every time."

"Quite so, and if I had taken one tablet of morphia, knowing that it would put me out for forty-eight hours, I should have deserved all I got. But I didn't. I neither drank two bottles of whisky, so far as I know, nor did I take morphia or any other drug. For one thing, it is not a habit of mine; and for another, I hadn't got any to take, if I had wanted to do so."

"Therefore . . ." prompted Hazelrigg.

"Therefore, I was drugged by someone else."

"And that someone else?"

"Somebody who stood to gain by my not being in a position to get him Court-Martialled and broke."

"And he was? . . ."

"The doctor—and the Subedar-Major."

"And of those two the likely one was . . ."

"The doctor—because he'd have the drugs and know the proper use of them. Or the improper use."

"Obviously. There's no shadow of doubt in my mind; no possible question about it," asserted Hazelrigg.

"There is in mine, though," smiled Wendover.

"Why? How?"

"It is just possible that I was so very near the end of my tether—and mind you I had had less sleep, more work, and ten times more responsibility than anybody in the place—that I went on drinking unconsciously, took a second drink without noticing what I was doing, and then a third absent-mindedly, and a fourth

179

subconsciously. And then was so affected, in my abnormal physical and mental condition, that I simply didn't know what I was doing, and went on drinking; and, having emptied one bottle, went and fetched another and uncorked that, and drank that, too. It's possible."

"Oh, anything's possible, my good ass; but we have got to take count of probabilities. Is it probable?"

"No. Neither is it probable that an officer of the Indian Medical Service should do a thing like that."

"Does a leopard change his spots if you give him a coat of paint? Does the Eurasian, of very bad maternal stock, change his fundamental nature because you give him a coat of Service cloth? Had he been a white man, the ordinary normal British doctor, the idea would not have entered my head."

"No, and it didn't enter the heads of the members of the Court-Martial either," said Wendover.

"More's the pity. I wish to God I had been on the Court-Martial."

"My dear chap, suppose you had. Would you not have accepted the fact as they did, that Colonel Maldon found me drunk? Found the evidence of the cause of the drunkenness? Empty bottles, and a beautiful stink of whisky; and the testimony of a dozen people, one of whom was a doctor? Of course you would."

"Do you think so?"

"I do."

"Well, I don't. I'd have rejected all the evidence, and the evidence of my own eyes, on the strength of your record, your personality, habits, standards."

"Aren't judges supposed to keep an absolutely open mind, and to be utterly unprejudiced, whether by a previous bad record or a good record? Haven't they got to judge on the facts put before them?"

"Well, weren't you yourself one of the facts? Didn't they know that you . . ."

"They didn't know me, nor anything about me, except that British officers, brothers-in-arms and all that, had seen me snoring, hoggish, drunk, cuddling an empty whisky bottle, with another one on the floor beside me."

"Well? That would merely have presented me with an interesting problem—the question of how that state of affairs came about. I should have started with the premise that most certainly and unquestionably you had not drunk the whisky, and that you were not drunk, and that the whole thing was a plant. Then I should have started looking for the gardener and, to find him, should have enquired for reasons, objects and motives for the planting of the plant. And I'd soon have had the little weed up by the roots and had a look at 'em."

"And I wonder what you'd have found."

"I'll tell you what I should have found. Precisely what I'm going to find, yet."

"And if you did, there isn't much point in locking the stable door after the horse is gone, is there?"

"Hardly the metaphor. There'd be some point in going and finding the horse and fetching him in out of the cold, and then locking the door, wouldn't there?"

"If you could catch him. Some horses prefer—freedom."

"Wild horses, perhaps—or asses."

The two men smoked in silence for awhile.

"Yes," said Hazelrigg suddenly. "I wish I had been on that Court-Martial. It is perfectly maddening to think that Brace actually had the idea and nothing came of it. But there again, your luck was out. You were fated, my son. Kismet. It had to be for some good reason."

"Good reason?"

"Yes. Everything is for a good reason."

"My God! The good part is pretty well hidden sometimes, isn't it?"

"Yes. But among the few things of which I am certain in this uncertain life is the great truth that we don't know our blessings from our curses."

"Get a pretty good idea, sometimes, don't we?"

"We think we do—at the moment. And sooner or later—sometimes a lot later, I admit—we say, or we ought to say, *'Well, well. But for that apparent catas-*

trophe, this excellent state of affairs could never have come about.'"

"I'll remember it next time I stub my toe in the dark," promised Wendover.

"You were saying," he continued, "that my luck was out over Brace. How was that? It wasn't merely luck that he rejected the idea of a drug unless it were a self-administered one."

"That's the whole point. I went to see Brace in Bombay. Asked him to dinner; and, afterwards, we fairly got down to it, and I turned him inside out, on the subject of the Court-Martial. He was only too willing to talk and be helpful, for he's a man with a conscience as well as gleams of intelligence.

"And when we came to the point of symptoms, and he said that it actually had occurred to him to wonder whether it might not have been some other narcotic than alcohol that had put you under so completely and for so long, he remembered an incident that had impressed him rather deeply at the moment, but had receded towards the back of his mind as time went on. Being on active service, he had had something else to think about, and wasn't, moreover, particularly receptive of impressions. And the incident was this.

"He was in charge of part of an advancing firing-line, and during a lull he was walking up and down behind his men, who were lying in open order at the edge of a belt of jungle, waiting for the word to jump up and dash across a belt of open country into the bush on the other side. Before the order came to advance, word was passed along for the doctor, and a messenger came by, looking for him. He said the Colonel Sahib had been wounded, but intended to go on. He wanted the doctor to come and bandage him.

"Brace directed him to where he had last seen a peripatetic Red Cross outfit, a doctor, a mule with panniers, a medical-subordinate and stretcher-bearers. A little while after, the man came back, leading the medical party. Just as they passed where Brace was standing looking through his glasses into the jungle I across the wide glade, heavy firing suddenly broke out again from over the way, at about a hundred yards range, and several people were hit, not to mention the mule, which promptly stampeded.

"Brace shouted his orders for 'rapid-independent,' and the firing, from over the way, died down. When he looked round, he saw that the doctor himself had been hit, and that he was lying on his back and trying to get at something in the breast-pocket of his tunic.

"The rest of his party were either hit or chasing the mule which, after all, was nearly as important as the doctor, as it had got all the bandages and surgical implements in the panniers.

"So, bending over the doctor, Brace asked if he could do anything for him.

"'Yes,' was the reply. 'Small phial here.'

"And, unbuttoning the pocket which had a rather small tight button-hole, Brace found one of those little cylinders of white tablets. The doctor held out his open hand, not to take the bottle, but with fingers and thumb tightly together, obviously wanting him to give him some of the contents.

"'*How many?*' asked Brace.

"'*The whole lot,*' said the doctor.

"'*All of them?*' asked Brace, to be quite sure.

"'*Yes, all of them,*' said the doctor most distinctly.

"So Brace tipped the lot into his hand. About a couple of dozen of them, he said, whereupon the doctor put them in his mouth—the whole lot, every one of them, and swallowed them. And died soon afterwards.

"Brace learned later that the doctor had swallowed a whole bottle of morphia tablets; and that, although he had been hit twice, neither of the wounds was in the least dangerous. He had committed suicide. He was an experienced, fully-qualified doctor.

"Also a full-blooded Indian," added Hazelrigg.

"H'm, I see the point," observed Wendover. "Brace had rather got self-administered drugs on the brain, eh?"

"Yes. We talked for hours, and I don't think there was a thing left unsaid that had any bearing on that Court-Martial and your appearance, conduct and demeanour. I refrained from saying 'Why the Hell didn't you say so, if you had the slightest suspicion that it might have been a case of drugging?' because it was quite evident that, although the idea had crossed Brace's mind, he had dismissed it as ninety-nine people out of a hundred would have done, because the evidence for drunkenness was so very, very strong; because there was medical evidence which was really irrefutable by a layman as to the cause of your unconscious state; and because the drug idea merely passed through his mind without effecting lodgment. And for those two reasons—first, because, if it were drugs, you had obviously drugged yourself as he had seen that doctor do; and, secondly, if it weren't drugs, it was alcohol, as this doctor testified."

"And who shall blame the blameless Captain Brace?" observed Wendover. "Nobody. Especially when one remembers that he was a very junior Captain in the presence of his seniors, including two Majors and a Colonel, and that the evidence was overwhelming—the fact being proved by a Colonel and the cause proved by a doctor."

"No, it's impossible to blame him," agreed Hazelrigg. "Nevertheless the drug idea entered his mind, thank God, and he remembers it."

"And if he had had the courage or impudence to say what he thought," observed Wendover, "what would he have got but a metaphorical kick in the pants for presuming to know better than a doctor and a Colonel, not to mention the other witnesses?"

"Exactly. It wouldn't have made the slightest difference if he had said that, in his wisdom, he doubted the accuracy of the doctor's diagnosis and suspected drugs. But—and thank God once again—he did have the audacity to mention his suspicion to another member of the Court-Martial afterwards. He did say to Captain Marvin, a friend of his, that he had a sort of feeling there was something queer about the business, because the accused most certainly did not strike him as a man who used liquor to that extent, and he did look like a man who had had an overdose of something like opium or hashish, or chloral, or morphia."

"Yes," mused Hazelrigg, "Brace had gleams of intelligence, and an eye in his head. At times, positively observant."

"What did Marvin reply?" asked Wendover.

"Apparently he uttered a coarse and monosyllabic ejaculation, expressive of derisive dissent, and bade Brace get up and make a speech. Said that thereafter Brace had better write a monograph on the extreme difficulties of deciding whether a man was drunk or not; because if there was any doubt, he might not be; and when there wasn't any doubt, he probably wouldn't be, because he'd be drugged.

"And when Brace made a feeble effort to pursue the subject, Marvin told him he had better go and see the Commander-in-Chief about it; that so far as he, Marvin, was concerned, he'd trust old Maldon to know a drunk when he saw one; and he'd also be strongly inclined to accept the evidence of a couple of empty whisky bottles and a doctor's testimony."

"And, once again, who shall blame him?" observed Wendover.

"True. Far from it. Let's praise him. For it may make all the difference, some day, that he raised the point."

"How? Difference in what way? To whom?"

"You wait and see. Well, then I pursued Marvin, who was up at Poona; contrived to run into him in the bar at the Club of Western India, and talked about *shikar*, which is his subject. And so from Indian tigers to African lions, ,and the fate of one Wendover who was eaten by a lion. And thus to the Court-Martial. Oh, yes; he remembered all right. Nasty business. One of the most unpleasant and painful affairs he ever had anything to do with.

"'Had he quite agreed with the verdict and evidence?' I asked.

"'Good Lord, yes. No possible question of the justice of the verdict or, in point of fact, the leniency of the sentence. Oh, yes; plain case of drunk on duty. Blind drunk on active service, too. And there wasn't anything to be said in mitigation. It wasn't as though Wendover had known that relief was near and certain, and that he could therefore let up and hand over. It was quite clearly proved that he was dead to the world when the runner got through with the news that Maldon had won a victory, turned the enemy's flank, got them on the run, and would be at Ubele in a day or two.'

"Then I asked him if he remembered Brace's theory. Fortunately he did. Remembered it with a laugh. Yes, if he hadn't put a spoke in the silly beggar's wheel, he'd have made an everlasting ass of himself. Seemed to think that he might know better than the doctor, not to mention Maldon, who presumably knows a drunken man when he sees him, even if he isn't surrounded by dead bottles and a powerful stink of whisky. And so forth.

"Well, there were two of the five who had, at any rate, had the drug idea before them at the trial.

"And then I set myself to try to instil doubts to that undoubting mind.

"'Did Wendover look like a habitual drunkard?' I asked Marvin.

"No, he wouldn't say that. No, certainly not.

"Had he ever heard of him as a drinker?

"No, he hadn't.

"Did he think it likely that a man of Wendover's sort would go to bed with a couple of bottles of whisky, at a critical point in the siege of a place he had defended most ably for weeks and weeks?

"No, it was incredible.

"Well then, if it were incredible?

"Exactly. Nothing but cold solid proof could make it credible. And there it was. Can't get away from facts. An amazing case. Last man in the world he would have suspected of doing such a thing as that. But you never knew. You never knew. 'Look at that case of So-and-So. Devoted husband, charming wife. Known 'em both for years. You'd say they had never had a wry word. And then, one day, he went home and shot her. And then went to the D.S.P., gave himself up and said he wondered he hadn't done it long ago.'

186

"And now," continued Hazelrigg, after a slight pause, "I intend to set about finding the 'cold solid proof.' To have you reinstated, put once more in command of your men, in charge of your own job, among your own people."

"In command of my men," repeated Wendover slowly. "Yes; almost you persuade me that it would be worth while; that I would do anything . . . *anything* . . . to get back to all that I have lost. My men, my work, my friends—all that made life worth living. But of course, it's no good. It's too late."

"Wait," said Hazelrigg. "You wait a little longer."

"*Wait!*" Wendover laughed, without conspicuous merriment.

PART IV

CHAPTER I

Captain Alexander Breckinge of the Indian Medical Service, was a worried, anxious and, if truth be told, a frightened man.

Fate was indeed playing him a dirty trick. Enough is as good as a feast, and sometimes a great deal better, or worse; and Captain Breckinge had had very much more than enough. To be shut up in a besieged fort once is quite sufficient for a lifetime—Captain Breckinge's lifetime, anyway—and here he was for a second time in that extremely parlous and uncomfortable predicament.

Damn it all, he wasn't a soldier and didn't wish to be one. He was a doctor, and it is no part of a doctor's business to be shot, slashed, starved or tortured to death.

And not only was Fate playing a dirty trick but it was trying to be funny into the bargain. It was being what is termed ironical; for, on the former occasion when he had been besieged and suffering every kind of discomfort, privation and danger, he had been only too anxious to undermine and thwart the authority of the man in command, and actually to terminate that authority as soon as he knew that relief was at hand. And now, when he would have given anything to support the Commanding Officer, to strengthen his position, and to see him in fullest control, not only of the situation, but of his great faculties for command, the wretched man was *hors de combat*.

Not only that, but in spite of all Captain Breckinge could do, he was getting worse, mentally and physically. Instead of being a tower of strength, a host in himself, and the main-stay of the defence, he was lying there on his string-bed in his quarters, alternating between delirium, when he could only babble non-sense, and a state of semi-collapse, in which he could only whisper half-audible replies to half-comprehended questions as to what was to be done.

If he didn't soon recover sufficiently to take command, the Fort would undoubtedly be captured—and Captain Breckinge put to death with the rest of its defenders.

And though Subedar-Major Ganga Charan was the doctor's admiring and obliging friend, the very man to back him up in any little business where native cunning, artfulness and convincing witness were required, he wasn't exactly the man whom Captain Breckinge would have chosen as a sure shield and stout defence in time of trouble of this sort, a desperate situation of the gravest physical danger. The Subedar-Major was getting a bit elderly now, a bit on the fat side, and not precisely an ideal leader of forlorn hopes or desperate defences.

Nor were his relatives and henchmen, Subedar Gopal Mangal and Jemadar Rama Narayen or Jemadar Ganpat Mahadeo, just quite the supports whom Captain Breckinge would have chosen when his life depended upon having about him men of the highest courage, the stoutest heart, and greatest resource and initiative. Fine staunch fellows to back one up in a little *banao*,[31] and see one through an awkward little business of a different kind, but not perhaps quite the perfect opponents for hordes of ferocious Pathans, deadly, determined and relentless.

No, it was a horrible position to be in.

What right had the British Military Authorities to occupy a fort in theoretically tributary country, all these miles from India and from any military base? And if not hundreds of miles, it might as well be that, when you came to consider the passes, one of them snowed up for most of the year; the unbridged rushing torrents; the wretched road which, in places, was under water, in others, under avalanches of shale, and in some parts, was supported on rotting props as it clung, crumbling, to the sheer side of a perpendicular mountain, with a thousand feet of precipice on one side and an overhanging unscaleable cliff on the other.

---

[31] *Plot; swindle; frame-up.*

The Man of a Ghost

What right had they to occupy so isolated and distant a fort with so small and unsupported a garrison?

All very well to say that it was connected by telegraph and telephone with the Khyber. A lot of good that was, when the wild tribesmen were out, and the wires were cut as a matter of course.

And the rations, too. One would have thought that however callous was the fool who decided that the place was to be occupied, he would have realized that it might be besieged, and would at least have taken the trouble to see that it was always kept stocked and provisioned against such a possibility.

But no, he was never likely to be caught here.

And what was the result now? Half-rations, and if the siege went on long enough, it would be quarter-rations, and both food and ammunition dwindling to vanishing point.

And the only means of communication with the Base was by means of messengers who were either promptly captured by the besiegers or, having got through them, succumbed to danger and hardship, and fell by the wayside.

All except one, that was to say. One of them would reach his destination all right.

And besides, if telephone and telegraph had been working, and suppose there had been anyone who could have seen the heliograph when there were signallers to operate it, everybody knew it was only possible for a relief force to cross the snowed-up passes at one season of the year.

It was abominable.

Bad enough, in guaranteed peace-time, to stick people like Captain Breckinge down here to die of boredom, but in the event of war . . . It didn't bear thinking about.

And yet here it was, an actual reality, and here was Major Denbrough—not to mention a score or so of other ranks—down with typhoid, and doing about as badly as could be expected, in view of the fact that there was nothing left in the place but bully-beef and biscuit. And what with the relapse and the fact that the fool was always trying to get out of bed and resume command, it was pretty certain that he'd have a perforation and bleed to death.

And no doubt they'd blame the medical officer for the outbreak of typhoid, as usual. Say he hadn't chlorinated the water properly or something of the kind.

It was a burning shame. Some of those fat Generals at Peshawar or 'Pindi or Simla ought to be in the place, starving to death, and with the yelling tribesmen picking men off all day long and making sudden assaults all night—or, at any rate, very frequently at night, as well as at dawn.

And there was no doubt that since Major Denbrough had collapsed, having carried on as long as he could stand on his feet, sit on a chair, or give an order from his bed when he could no longer sit up, the defenders had begun to go to pieces.

No, Subedar-Major Ganga Charan was not the man he had been.

And the sepoys had definitely got their tails down. Not only was there a terrible lot of genuine sickness, what with typhoid, malaria and the usual illnesses of a starving, confined and despondent force, but there was undeniably a good deal of malingering.

So what was to happen? What was to happen? The enemy were getting ever bolder and more active, and while the numbers of the defenders decreased, those of the besiegers were augmented daily.

There could be but one end to it. And it was not as though these terrible mountaineers were a civilized enemy. There was no question of an honourable captivity, and release at the end of the war. When, at last, they succeeded in burning down the gate and bursting through, or in swarming over the walls, it would be slaughter, butchery, a massacre. The survivors would be put to death in cold blood. Quite possibly tortured, too. He had heard horrible tales.

And Captain Breckinge shuddered.

§2

Major John Denbrough, D.S.O., or the remnant of that once brawny, brilliant and forceful man, lay and gazed at the bare baked-clay walls and ceiling of his room in Giltraza Fort, his body almost too feeble for the moving of a finger or the speaking of a word, his mind clear and his thoughts coherent.

So this was the end.

A good end in a way, for he was dying at his post. Not too bad, but it might have been better. He would have preferred to die in his boots and to be killed by bullet, *tulwar*, or tribesman's knife to dying of sickness, killed by a foul water-borne germ.

Still, although lying undressed on a *charpai*, he was dying in harness, and he had held the Fort as long as he could stand and see; he had led the defence night and day until he lost consciousness; and although he had gone down, had been carried to bed, had been either unconscious or delirious for so much of the time, and in the intervals too weak to move, he had kept the flag flying, and saved the Fort.

For relief would soon come.

The authorities must have suspected that something was wrong as soon as communication ceased; and must, before very long, have discovered that it was not merely a case of a break-down in the line owing to snow in the high pass, or to gales.

And surely at least one of the heroic messengers must have got through.

And if not a single runner had survived, with a few words pencilled on a cigarette-paper, or merely a verbal message, rumour must have reached the Khyber and Peshawar that the Tribes were out in the far North-West, the passes closed, and Fort Giltraza besieged.

The chances were that some Military Intelligence agent, British or native, in some such place as Kunar, Dir, Drosh, Chitral, Hunza, or Gilgit, had heard a bazaar-rumour of a confederation of the notorious Singing Hadji of Sufed Kot and the Tribesmen being on the war-path and having a shot at mopping up Fort

Giltraza, wiping out the garrison, and collaring the rifles.

Yes, of course relief would soon come; and although he would not be there to see it, to hear what the Brigadier had to say, or to read agreeable things in the papers when he got back to civilization, he could die in peace, if not in comfort; he could die content, if not happy, in the knowledge that he had done his duty.

Rough on poor Helen and young Anthony and Dorothy, but . . .

The dying soldier closed his eyes.

The door opened and Breckinge entered the bare, comfortless ill-lit cell that was Major Denbrough's sick-room.

Hullo, had he passed out?

The doctor took the sick man's wrist.

H'm. Collapse temperature. Heart only just beating.

Major Denbrough's eyes opened and his lips moved as he whispered inaudibly.

"What did you say?" asked Breckinge, bending down to catch the words scarcely formed by the white lips. "What's that?"

Silence.

What about an injection of . . .

Ah, that was better. Speaking quite distinctly.

"They are coming. I *know* they're coming. They'll soon be here . . . Hold on . . . Hold on tight, Breckinge . . . Stiffen the men up . . . Stiffen them. Tell them I know that British troops are coming . . . They are near . . . Go and fetch Subedar-Major Ganga Charan."

"Yes, yes, that's all right," replied Breckinge.

Easy to talk. Denbrough had been saying that they were coming, that they were quite near, for days. Every time he had had a lucid interval.

'Stiffen them up!' Fat lot of good talking like that. How could you stiffen up starving men who knew they hadn't a dog's chance; knew they were completely surrounded, cut off, and couldn't possibly last out until relief came. Food and ammunition for a few weeks. No relief for months, perhaps. It was wicked, criminal, abominable. *'Stiffen them up!'* Pah!

"Do you hear me?" whispered the dying man. "Go and fetch Subedar-Major Ganga Charan . . . I'll see the others after . . . One at a time . . . Speak to each of them . . . They'll hold on . . . They must . . . The only thing to do, even for their own sakes . . . It's their only chance . . . Fetch Subedar-Major Ganga Charan."

Breckinge turned and went from the room.

Talk! Easy to talk. Denbrough was out of it, without getting his throat cut.

'*Hold on!*' *The only thing to do!* It was the one sure and certain way of being butchered! There was at least a chance the other way.

When he returned to the sick-room, a couple of hours later, Major Denbrough was lying on the floor, dead.

CHAPTER II

"*Sahib!*" called Subedar-Major Ganga Charan, opening the door of Breckinge's room, his voice quivering with excitement, "there's a Pathan at the gate. The sentry says the man marched straight up the track, with both hands above his head, holding up a white cloth in one of them. He's unarmed; and when the sentry called out that he'd shoot if he came any nearer, the man shouted that he wanted to speak to the senior Officer. Said he had got a message from the Singing Hadji of Sufed Kot, Commander of the *lashkar.*"

"Quite alone? Unarmed? No chance of treachery?" asked Breckinge quickly, hopefully.

"No, Sahib. None at all. Nobody with him. There can't be anybody nearer than their *sangars* and *the* trench on that side."

"Mightn't there be a sudden rush if you opened the gates and let him in?"

"No. They could only make the usual attack. He could be admitted in half a minute. He'd be inside before they were a few yards from their position."

"Come and talk to him from the wall, Sahib," added the Subedar-Major.

"What, and get shot? It's a trick."

"You could shout to him from cover, all right, Sahib. Or someone else could talk to him—saying what you told him to say. But they wouldn't take all this trouble on the chance of getting a shot at one man on the wall.

"It would be quite safe to bring him in," he added, with something of eagerness in his tone.

"All right, then. You should know best. You can take every precaution. If he slips in quickly, there cannot be any harm in admitting him, and hearing what he has to say."

"*Bahut achcha,*[32] Sahib," replied the Subedar-Major, apparently pleased with this decision, and hurried from the room.

It was not the doctor's habit to venture upon the walk behind the embrasures of the high walls of the Fort, or otherwise to risk his life, so valuable to the health and general welfare of the defenders of the place. Nor, since the collapse of Major Denbrough, the last of the combatant officers, had he in any way accepted a position of responsibility for anything but the medical services of the Fort. Nevertheless he had not only given his advice when it had been sought by the Subedar-Major, but had insisted upon that responsible officer consulting him in all matters outside his regular routine military duty.

In the extremely distressing situation resultant upon the death of Major Denbrough, the position which Captain Alexander Breckinge, I.M.S., preferred to establish was one in which he had ultimate unquestioned authority, and Subedar-Major Ganga Charan sole responsibility.

Let Captain Breckinge freely pull the strings and Subedar-Major Ganga Charan fully answer for the results.

The Subedar-Major returned.

"I have admitted him, Sahib," he said, "and there was no ruse about it. No enemy moved, and no shot was fired. The man will not talk. What he has to say, is to be said to you."

"Well, I don't command this Fort. I'm the Medical Officer."

"He says his message is for the Doctor Sahib," replied the Subedar-Major.

"They don't think I'm going out to attend to any of their wounded, do they?" said Breckinge. "What the devil next?"

"It would be just like the Pathan," he mused aloud. "They have a sense of humour all their own. Besiege us here, do their damnedest to kill the lot of us, and then send us a message to say:

---

[32] *Very good.*

"'Oh, by the way, we should be much obliged if the Doctor would call, some time this morning, as the Hadji has got a bullet in his stomach, and it wants attending to.'"

"Perhaps the Sahib could make some sort of terms with them, in return for doctoring their leader," suggested the Subedar-Major.

"How do you mean?"

"Perhaps if you did what they asked, they'd give us a week's truce in return for their leader's life, or something of the sort."

Breckinge thought a while. The Subedar-Major knew nothing of the message that had been sent to the Hadji. Doubtless this envoy brought the Hadji's answer and terms. No need for the Subedar-Major to know anything about the matter.

"There is something in that," he said.

And there might be something better, he reflected. If he could save whomever it was they wanted him to operate on, they might treat him well; might keep him there until their Hadji or Khan or General or Chief, or whoever he might be, was out of danger. They might keep himself a (willing) prisoner until the Fort fell. Thus he would escape the massacre. He might make himself invaluable to them, until he got a chance of escape. They must have a lot of wounded. And when he got back to civilization he could tell his own story as to what had happened.

Anyway, it was a chance, and there was no chance of anything but a beastly death if he stayed here in the Fort—assuming that the Hadji refused to accept the terms he had offered him.

Or another idea—this man had come under a sort of flag of truce. Suppose he sent him back with it and a message to the effect that if they brought the wounded leader under a flag of truce, it would be respected, the leader would be taken into the Fort, and would be given every medical care and attention—provided hostilities were suspended.

They could make a hostage of him.

Directly the besiegers wished to end the truce, he

could tell the Subedar-Major to take him up to the watch-tower above the gate, rig up some sort of a gallows, and threaten to hang him the moment a shot was fired. And do it, too. For if they were going to attack in any case, at least one of them should hang and it should be their leader, too. They'd get that much of their own back on them, anyway.

But it wouldn't come to that. They'd bargain, and exchange the leader's life for the Doctor's.

"Bring the man up here," he said. "Take good care that he is not armed, and see that he is blindfolded."

"I had him blindfolded immediately he was admitted, Sahib," replied the Subedar-Major.

"Why not have him permanently blinded?" he added, as he went out again.

Captain Breckinge took a loaded Service revolver from a holster which hung from a nail on the wall, and placed it on the rough table. This and a roorkie chair and a camp-bed were the main articles of furniture in the room.

A few minutes later, the Subedar-Major returned, accompanied by a file of sepoys, escorting a Pathan in *poshteen* coat, dirty grey cotton shirt and baggy trousers. On his feet were thick-soled heavy heel-less shoes with upturned toes; on his head a huge *puggri* loosely and roughly wound about a conical *kullah* cap.

The Subedar-Major removed the cloth that covered this envoy's eyes.

The man was heavily bearded, of unprepossessing appearance, grievously afflicted with a squint, and burly of person. His empty hands were raised to the level of his shoulders, palms outward.

"*Salaam aleikum,*" said he ingratiatingly, and smiled greasily upon Captain Breckinge who, seated in his chair, his right hand lying on the table close to the butt of his revolver, stared at him without reply.

"This is the man, Sahib," said the Subedar-Major.

"Who are you?" asked Breckinge, in Pushtu.

"Ghulam Hyder," replied the man with a thick-lipped smirk that did nothing to improve the unprepossessing cast of his countenance.

"What do you want?"

"To speak with you, *Huzoor*," replied the Pathan in good Hindustani. "To bring a message and to take back an answer."

"Well, what's your message?"

"*Huzoor*, it is for you alone."

"You say what you've got to say, and be quick about it," replied Breckinge.

The man again smiled uneasily, looked down at his feet, shuffled uncomfortably, and looked up again at Breckinge.

"The *hukm* was that I speak to you with no one present, *Huzoor*. It is to be private between the Hadji and the Sahib.

"The Sahib's messenger reached the Hadji," he added meaningly.

Breckinge glanced up quickly.

"The Hadji's words are for the Sahib's ear alone. No one else is to hear them."

Breckinge thought quickly. Was this genuine? Was it an overture or an attempt at assassination? No. The man was unarmed, and he wouldn't try anything of that sort with his bare hands, against a man with a revolver. He could make him stand in the far corner, and keep the revolver pointed straight at him the whole time.

No, it wouldn't be an attempt at assassination. It wasn't as though he were Major Denbrough. They might have tried something of that sort with him, if they had thought of it, and could find a man willing to sacrifice his life to do it.

And it wouldn't be just a request for medical help if the Hadji or his only son or somebody of that sort was dying for want of it. They wouldn't make any secrecy or mystery-mongering about that; nor if they merely wanted to cadge some bandages and antiseptics in return for a short truce.

If it had been that, the man would have said so, straight out.

No, there was something behind this, and he would be a fool not to look into it. It might be extremely advantageous. In plain words, it might be a chance to save his life. The only chance, too. Besides, there was no need for the Subedar-Major to know what Breckinge's messenger had said to the Hadji. It was annoying that this fellow had referred to the matter before the Subedar-Major and the sepoys. However, he could easily deny it and say the man was a liar. All Pathans were well known to be most shocking liars.

Yes, he had better hear what the scoundrel had got to say, in private.

"All right, Subedar-Major Saheb," he said in Hindustani. "Leave him alone with me, and put a sentry ten paces from the door, with loaded rifle and fixed bayonet and instructions to rush in if I shout or if he hears a shot . . . You are taking special precautions, of course, while this man is here, in case the cunning devils have got some game on, that we haven't thought of."

"*Han*, Sahib," replied the Subedar-Major. "I have ordered *Stand-to* and every man who can hold a rifle is on the walls."

Breckinge nodded and the Subedar-Major retired, taking the sepoys with him.

As he did so, Breckinge took up the revolver and pointed it at the Pathan's chest.

"Stand over there," he said. "Over in that corner. And keep your hands in front of you. If you move one step forward, you'll get six shots into you. Understand?"

"*Bé-shak, Huzoor,*" smiled the Pathan.

What an ugly, truculent and dangerous-looking tough the scoundrel was, thought Breckinge, as the man backed away and took up his stand in the corner of the room.

"Well, what have you got to say?" he snarled.

"Oh, much, *Huzoor*. Much. About your message. Proposals to make."

"From whom?"

"The Hadji and the leaders of the *lashkar*. That is to say, of the two *lashkars*. Three really. And another one is expected to arrive next week."

Breckinge was conscious of that sense of physical discomfort known as a sinking of the stomach. Three *lashkars*, and a fourth one coming. What hope was there? What possible chance?

"Yes. Our leader doesn't like the Commander of the new one, the Mehtar of Lohistan and Halzit. He's a bad man."

"Oh, he's a bad man, is he?"

"A very bad man, *Huzoor*. Untrustworthy. Treacherous. And our Hadji wants this business finished before he comes."

"Oh, he does, does he?"

"Yes. And he's going to take this place at all costs, so that when the Mehtar of Lohistan and Halzit comes with his *lashkar*, he'll find the fruit has been plucked and is safe in our Hadji Saheb's pocket. I mean, he'll find us inside the Fort. He'll be a day after the *mela*. He'll find he's too late. We shall be inside the Fort and the Mehtar will be outside, and he can turn round and go home again."

"Oh, you think you'll be inside the Fort, do you?"

"Without doubt, *Huzoor*. Why not? We know that half the garrison have been killed and half the rest are sick; and that you've got barely enough left to man the walls; and we have known for weeks that the British officers were sick, wounded or dead."

"And how did you know that?"

"By using our eyes. We haven't seen a helmet among the turbans for over a month. Also the last of your messengers—the messengers to the British, I mean—that we caught, had a lot to say. There wasn't much that he hadn't told us by the time we had finished with him."

"Well? What about it?"

"Why this. Why not save trouble, *Huzoor*. And the lives of your men and your own life."

"The Singing Hadji of Sufed Kot, as you call him, is anxious to save life, is he?" sneered Breckinge.

The Pathan leered, grinning.

"Anxious to save the lives of his own men, *Huzoor*," he replied. "He has lost quite enough already. He knows he can take the place now, whenever he likes, but he wants to do it as cheaply as he can. Naturally."

"And what makes him think he can take the Fort whenever he likes?"

"Because he knows exactly how many rounds of ammunition you have for each man. He knows how small your numbers are; and how weak from hunger and sickness are the few men left on the walls. And as he knows this, and that there are no British officers, he also knows that he can take the place by assault whenever he wishes."

"Oh, does he?"

"Yes. And he wouldn't bother about an assault if the Mehtar of Lohistan and Halzit weren't on the way with his *lashkar*. He'd just starve you out."

Breckinge eyed the man in silence.

"Nothing on earth can save the place, *Huzoor*."

No. There was no doubt of it. Nothing on earth could save it, and nothing in Heaven would. A determined assault could not fail, and if the besiegers waited for the reinforcements already on their way, the certainty would be yet the more certain; their easy task the easier by reason of their overwhelming numbers and the yet further weakened state of the yet further depleted garrison.

It would be the sheerest folly to drive this man away with a defiant answer. Obviously they knew to the last detail the condition of the defence; and what he had said about it, and about the capture of the place, was the simple truth. The Fort could now only be held until it was resolutely attacked. And if the story of the approaching *lashkar* were false, and there was not going to be an assault, the end was only postponed, the agony prolonged. The enemy had but to sit there until they could scale the walls or burn down the gate unopposed, and walk straight into a place tenanted only by the dead and the dying, by scare-crow skeletons too weak to raise themselves, much less their weapons.

Breckinge's over-vivid imagination showed him a hideous picture.

He achieved a somewhat unconvincing laugh.

"Well, *budmash*," he said, "suppose every word of what you said were true—which of course it isn't—what about it? What's the proposal?"

"That you save your life and the lives of all your men by opening the gates and marching out."

"What? To be shot down, outside!" sneered Breckinge.

"No. The Hadji Saheb will give you safe-conduct."

"Where to?"

"Wherever you like to go."

Again Breckinge laughed.

"I think I know where we should go, once we were in your leader's hands, eh?"

"No, no, *Huzoor*," expostulated the Pathan. "What does it matter to our Hadji Saheb what happens to a handful of sick sepoys? What he wants is the Fort, and he wants to get into it before the Mehtar comes with his *lashkar*. The Mehtar is jealous of him, and he's not a real friend."

Breckinge laid the revolver down, ready to his hand, and leant back in his chair.

An idea! Suppose the scoundrelly Mehtar of Lohistan and Halzit were going to join in the next assault on Giltraza Fort, might not the besiegers quarrel among themselves before attacking? Might not the Hadji and the Mehtar fight a pitched battle?

Well, and what if they did? The victors would assault the Fort, just the same, afterwards. The garrison was, of course, far too weak to attempt a sally while the Tribesmen were fighting among themselves; and in any case, their doing so would only cause the enemy to sink their differences until the sepoys were disposed of.

No, there was nothing in that.

Still, he might see what this man had to say about it.

"Well," he said, "I think I'll wait until the Mehtar's *lashkar* arrives and attacks your Hadji."

"Attacks the Hadji Saheb?" replied the man, in apparent surprise. "Oh, he'd never do that, *Huzoor*.

They are not enemies. It's only that the Mehtar is jealous of the Hadji, and would want more than his share of the credit and the loot. He'd spread the news all over the Border and Afghanistan and the countries round, that it was *he* who had captured the place. That's what he would do. Turn up at the last minute and take a hand in the final assault, and then pretend that nothing had been done until he came."

Yes, that was probably the truth of the matter. The Singing Hadji of Sufed Kot and the leaders of this confederation of Tribesmen would join forces with the Mehtar and they would not quarrel until it came to a division of the spoils. And this Singing Hadji of Sufed Kot, mullah or agitator or prophet or whatever he was, knowing that the Fort must fall in any case, was determined that it should do so before his rival came.

But could he be trusted?

No, of course not. Nevertheless, there was a chance, and a chance of life is better than a certainty of death.

"And you say that the Hadji offers to let us go free?"

"That's it, *Huzoor.* You open the gates and march out and go where you like. Not a shot will be fired. It is an even better chance for you than what your messenger proposed to the Hadji.

"Or was the messenger only a spy?" he added, leering.

"No, he wasn't a spy. He made a genuine offer . . . But who was ever fool enough to trust the word of a Pathan—without regretting it?" sneered Breckinge.

"Well, it's as you like, *Huzoor.* The Hadji Saheb could take the place to-morrow with the loss of a few men, and then the garrison would of course be put to the sword."

"Every man of them," he added, with a sinister grin at Breckinge.

It was the truth. God knew it was the truth.

"Why, I don't even know that you come from the Hadji with this foolish talk," Breckinge temporized.

The man laughed.

"Why should I risk my life?"

"And if you do come from the Hadji, you come to

spy. As you say my man did."

The Pathan laughed again.

"Why should the Hadji Saheb need to send a spy, *Huzoor*? Do we not know everything? Did I not tell you at once that but a quarter of your men are fit for duty, that you are on half rations, that you have only a few rounds of ammunition per rifle, and that the British officers are sick, wounded or dead? What need have we for a spy within the walls? We are not fools. We can count, and we can see all that we need to see from without. Also we have tortured your other messengers until they spoke. And they all told the same tale."

"Then since you can take the Fort when you wish, why are you so anxious to persuade me to evacuate it?"

"Because I want to please the Hadji Saheb, my master, who has sent me here for that purpose.

"Again I say he is a humane man," added the Pathan with a grin. "He wishes to save life. The Fort is his for the taking, but he wants it without further cost of life—the lives of his men and yours. . . . Well, there it is, *Huzoor*. Take it or leave it."

And Breckinge knew that he would take it.

Life was dear.

He was not a combatant Officer.

The Fort was bound to fall, and it was his duty to save the lives of the garrison. Clearly it was his duty.

Besides, after all, it was Subedar-Major Ganga Charan who was responsible, surely. He was the senior combatant Officer. Naturally he'd do what Breckinge told him to do; but that wouldn't relieve him of responsibility. So if they did get back to India safely, and a Court of Enquiry awarded blame and punishment for the surrender of the Fort, obviously it was Subedar-Major Ganga Charan who would deserve, and get, the blame and the punishment.

And why should there be any blame?

How many times had it not happened before, that a besieged place had fallen because the Commandant preferred surrender to massacre?

How many times had not a besieged force made

honourable capitulation, and marched out with the honours of war, drums beating, flags flying, arms . . . Arms. Yes, what about the rifles? They could not be expected to march from Giltraza to the Khyber without a weapon among them.

Suppose this Hadji fellow kept his word, as he might do, and let them pass through the besiegers and march away, they would fall a prey to the first tribe that chose to attack them, if they were unarmed.

Why, they'd hardly get through the Khyber itself if they had no rifles, much less get from Giltraza to the Khyber.

And of course there was a chance that the Hadji might spare their lives, not only to save unnecessary fighting, but to be able to boast for the rest of his life that a British force had surrendered to him and he had contemptuously let it go.

"And what about the rifles?" he asked suddenly, shooting what he intended to be a penetrating and intimidating glance at the man.

"The rifles, *Huzoor*? Well, I don't know about that. I don't think the Hadji could let the rifles go. No, I'm afraid you'd have to surrender the rifles."

Ah, that was rather reassuring. That certainly looked as though the Pathan leader was making an honest proposition; wanting to get the Fort and the rifles without any further trouble. Now if this *budmash* had jumped at the proposal that the garrison should march out under arms, it would have looked very suspicious. If the whole thing was a trick and a trap, he would have agreed to anything. Yes, that he troubled to bargain was very reassuring. Nevertheless, they might as well stay where they were, as set forth to march down through Tribal Territory unarmed.

If they marched out to-morrow and did an average twelve miles a day, the high pass would be open by the time they reached it.

And much good that would do them, if the pass led them down into country where any band of outlaws could make mincemeat of them at long range.

No, they must keep their rifles.

And another point. They must have enough ammunition, too. He wasn't a soldier, but he did know that rifles weren't much good without ammunition, and that they must have enough to put up a fight if they were attacked.

In point of fact, it was extremely improbable that a considerable party of British troops, marching in military formation, would be attacked at all, unless, to their incredulous joy, the brigands and bands of outlaws, not to mention ordinary Tribesmen, saw that they were all unarmed.

"But talk sense, man. Don't speak as one afflicted of Allah and devoid of the understanding of a child. What would it be but another way of killing us, to make us march out from here unarmed? Suppose I trusted your Hadji, and did so. How far should we march before we were fallen upon and slain? Why, a dozen outlaws living in a cave could come down the mountain-side and shoot us all like dogs."

The Pathan shrugged massive shoulders.

"I could not go back to the Hadji Saheb and confess that I had agreed to your taking the rifles," he said glumly.

The two men eyed each other in silence.

"Not all of them," added the Pathan.

A ray of hope, almost of joy, shot through Breckinge's mind.

Not all of them!

"Well, how many, then?" he asked.

"Dead men need no rifles, *Huzoor*," leered the Pathan.

No, of course they didn't. And surely nobody could blame him—or rather Subedar-Major Ganga Charan—for not attempting to load, with the weight of an extra rifle, men already enfeebled by a siege? Of course not. Surely one would hardly care to ask the strongest troops, in the best of health, to march with two rifles per man?

"And rifles are useless to the sick and the wounded, *Huzoor*," observed the Pathan

Of course they were. Men who couldn't carry themselves couldn't carry a rifle.

And what about these same sick and wounded?

It would be a sufficiently difficult and dangerous march for those who were neither ill nor wounded. It would be impossible for the rest, and quite obviously out of the question, for those who could march, to burden themselves with the transport of those who could not. He couldn't turn the whole force into stretcher-bearers.

No, the best of them would make but poor progress encumbered with nothing more than their arms, kit and provisions.

Rifles only for those who could march.

Of course. The rifles made a fine bargaining point. He could make great use of what was useless—the remainder. Since they couldn't take all the rifles, they'd buy the necessary with the superfluous, so to speak.

"Look here, *Huzoor*," said the Pathan, "I think perhaps the Hadji Saheb would agree to these terms—that he lets you go free with all those who are fit to march, each man with his rifle, and you leave behind the rifles of the dead and wounded. You open the gates and march away—so many men and so many rifles. The rest are the Hadji's."

"Which means that he gets at least three-quarters of them."

"You cannot take them with you."

"No. But we could take the bolts. Or we could smash them or burn them."

"No, *Huzoor*. The Hadji will not agree to that. He may even be angry with me for allowing you one rifle per man; but that I think I can do because he is offering you your lives, and without your rifles you would lose them."

"And what about ammunition?" asked Breckinge.

"You can take the ammunition of the dead and wounded, up to twenty-five rounds per rifle."

"Twenty-five?" exclaimed Breckinge. "Make it fifty."

"But why, *Huzoor*? It only means extra weight for your men to carry. And who is going to attack a company of sepoys, marching with arms, in military formation, with their scouts and flankers and rear-guards, as the Sirkar's troops always do? Twenty-five rounds is enough, *Huzoor*."

"And what about the sick and wounded whom we leave behind?"

Again the Pathan shrugged his shoulders as he threw out expressive hands, palm upwards.

"They'll have to die," he said.

"What, be put to death, do you mean?"

"What use to keep them, *Huzoor*? What can we do? We have no *hakims* and no doctors' stuff. We have no medicines nor the means of dealing with wounded men. What happens to our own wounded? They live or they die, as Allah wills. And as for enemy wounded . . . Besides, how can we feed useless mouths—and why should we, if we could—the mouths of our enemies? No, *Huzoor*, the sick and the wounded will have to die.

"But they will die quickly," he added cheerfully. "They will come to no harm."

"What do you mean—no harm?"

"I mean the Hadji would not treat them unkindly; would not cut off their hands and feet, or put their heads in the fire. He is not a cruel man. No, do not fear that he would torture them or let them die a lingering death of their wounds and their sickness. They will die at once, as soon as you have marched out."

"But even without a doctor or medicine or any attention, some might recover," objected Breckinge.

"None will recover, *Huzoor*," replied the Pathan curtly.

Then, as Breckinge eyed him, an unpleasant smile spread over his unprepossessing countenance as he observed:

"And it is to be remembered that dead men tell no tales!"

Yes, just what he himself was thinking, damn the fellow's impudence. Dead men tell no tales, and even if they could, what reproach would their tales be? The sick and wounded would die just as certainly, if dragged out on to the road for that long weary march, as they would if left to enjoy the mercy of that compassionate man the Hadji. As the Romans themselves always said—*Væ victis*.

Somebody had got to suffer; and they themselves who marched out would have plenty of suffering, even if they ever reached safety.

And if they stayed there, they'd all die, anyway. Of course, it was his duty to save as many as he could; and obviously the only ones he could save were those who could march.

Yes, the sick and the wounded would have to die.

"I offer you those terms, then, *Huzoor*," repeated the Pathan. "You march out with those who can march, each man carrying a rifle and twenty-five rounds of ammunition."

"And food?"

"Yes, and food. Each man to take as much as he can carry in his haversack—their parched grain, sugar, cooked *chupatties* and any of that food that the Sirkar issues in tin boxes. But only what can be carried in haversacks."

"And they'll be too weak to carry much," he grinned.

"And how long do you give me to think it over?" asked Breckinge.

"Until sunrise to-morrow, *Huzoor*. At sunrise, as soon as it is light, I will come to the gate, holding aloft a white cloth, and bringing with me the two sons of our leader; the beloved sons of the Singing Hadji of Sufed Kot himself. They will have the fullest powers to agree to . . ."

"If there's any treachery . . ." interrupted Breckinge.

"Treachery, *Huzoor*? What need for treachery? We are a hundred to one, and can take this Fort in ten minutes and put all within it to the sword. Treachery!"

The man laughed.

"Why, if, in half an hour from now, the Singing Hadji chose to lose a few more men, this place would either be a smoking ruin, occupied only by the dead and the dying, or a fortress fully manned by the *lashkar* of our leader."

No, reflected Breckinge, there was no need for treachery at sunrise, and the only question was whether they would all be butchered later on, as they marched out. But that was unlikely. If they were to retain their arms and twenty-five rounds of ammunition, there would still be a fight, and many would be slain before the last sepoy died. It was plain that the Singing Hadji felt that he had already lost too many of his *jowans*, and that to lose any more would be to pay too high a price for the Fort, the rifles, the money, accoutrements and other loot. Once again, it was the only chance, and it was a good one.

"So be it," he said, again looking up at the Pathan— it not being his habit to look anyone in the face for long. "So be it. At sunrise to-morrow you come with the Hadji's answer, bringing no more than two men with you, and those two, his own sons, empowered to make final agreement with me. And should there be more than three of you, or the least sign of anything suspicious, we shall open rapid fire—and you three will be the first to die."

"If Allah wills," agreed the Pathan piously. "I go now to tell my master that you will surrender the Fort and march out, provided he allows every man, *who can march*, to go free, bearing his rifle and taking twenty-five rounds of ammunition and such food as he can carry. The force to go unmolested where it will."

Breckinge rose to his feet, picking up the revolver as he did so.

"There's one other thing, *Huzoor*," said the Pathan, advancing from the corner of the room. "You do command here, do you not? Your words are heard and your *hukm* obeyed? The Native Officers will agree to whatever you say, and do exactly what you direct?"

"Of course I command here. Absolutely," replied Breckinge. "I am the Doctor Sahib, but I hold the rank of Captain and give orders to the Subedar-Major."

"And all other ranks will obey him, *Huzoor*?"

"Of course. Absolutely."

"It is well. I ask because I do not want to receive blame from the Hadji Saheb. If I tell him that I have made an agreement with you, and then it is discovered that you have no powers . . ."

"No powers! Of course I have powers."

"Look, *Huzoor*, you spoke of treachery. Now, I would not use such a word in speaking with the *Huzoor*, but in all business arrangements there may be mistakes, misunderstandings. If, for four hundred rupees, I buy a horse that belongs to two men, both those men must agree to my price, otherwise when I go to pay, one of them may say, '*What is this? Five hundred rupees is the price*,' whereas his partner had agreed to four. And so I have to pay at least four hundred and fifty and . . ."

"Peace. What's all this talk of horses and partners?" interrupted Breckinge. "I command here, and I have spoken."

"*Huzoor*, I am but an ignorant man and do not know the customs of the Sirkar's army. You are both *hakim* and officer Sahib, and yet not really a *jangi nafar*, a man of war. When the Hadji Saheb questions me, he will be angry if I bring not a word of the chief *jangi nafar*, and it is not well to anger the Singing Hadji of Sufed Kot. Let me, therefore, have the word of the Subedar-Major Saheb that he will do as the *Huzoor* bids, and order his men to march out of the Fort."

"I tell you that he will," snarled Breckinge.

"Then let me hear him say so, *Huzoor*. For my master is a hard man; and I fear lest, making a mistake, I offend him."

Without turning his back to the Pathan, Breckinge went to the door, opened it, and called to the sentry standing a few paces from the door.

"*Subedar-Major Saheb ko salaam do*," he snapped.

Saluting and hurrying off, the sentry returned, a minute later, with the Subedar-Major.

Subedar-Major Ganga Charan understood English perfectly and spoke it intelligibly, two accomplishments which he was wont carefully to conceal, but of which Breckinge was well aware.

"Look here, Ganga," said the latter quietly. "This fellow is quite *pukka*. They sent him to offer terms. I have had to agree to them. We march out with rifles and ammunition, and they march in and take the Fort.

215

They could do that in any case, so it is only a matter of saving more bloodshed. And there's another big force coming to join them in a few days, the Mehtar of Lohistan and Halzit and the Powindah Mullah. We simply cannot hold the place if they assault again, especially with three times the number."

"No, Sahib, we cannot," replied the Subedar-Major.

"There's plenty of ammunition, but it is a case of numbers. And the men are tired. And even if, when they are reinforced, the enemy do not assault, they can starve us out. Yes, of course. We haven't a chance, and they can do what they like with us; starve us out or butcher us. It's a damn shame." Breckinge's voice rose.

"We've got to look after ourselves," he cried, almost hysterically.

"What about the sick and the wounded?" asked the Subedar-Major.

"Well, the longer we are here, the more sick and wounded there'll be. Until we are *all* sick or wounded, starving and dying. And then they'll come and hack us to pieces. It's our duty to save those whom we can save, those who can march," was the reply.

The Subedar-Major eyed Breckinge speculatively. How different was this dark-skinned half-caste from the Major Sahib whose last words to him had been:

"We'll beat them, Subedar-Major. We'll beat them yet. We'll hold this Fort as long as we can hold a rifle."

Yes, a very different man . . . But life was dear and pension near.

"Who'll give the order, Sahib?" he asked. "Who'll be responsible for the surrender?"

The old, old question of the Indian to the European; the old, old necessity—a *hukm*, an order; the old, old fear, bugbear and stumbling-block—*Responsibility.*

Give me an order, begs the faithful Indian subordinate of the European master, and faithfully I will carry it out. Make any demands, give me any commands, give me any punishment, but do not give me responsibility.

"Who will give the order?" he repeated.

"You will give the men their orders, of course,"

replied Breckinge. "You will give the command to open the gates and march out, naturally."

"If we are allowed to go, and we get safely back to India, you will take the blame for . . ." began the Subedar-Major.

"The blame?" snarled Breckinge.

"The responsibility, Sahib. It is you who tell me what is to be done, and I who see that the men do it."

"Yes, yes," replied Breckinge. "I will tell you that it is our duty, to save the lives of the garrison. All will surely die unless . . ."

"Then it is your order to me, Sahib?"

"Yes, yes, all right. That will be all right," Breckinge reassured the Native Officer.

Yes, of course it would. If they lived to face an enquiry—and better live to do that than be butchered here—the senior combatant Officer would of course be responsible. The fact that he was a Native Officer had nothing to do with it. He himself was only the Doctor, and was in no way answerable for what the 'competent local military authority' did. The Subedar-Major was the competent local military authority, of course. It was the Doctor's business to look after the health of the men, to go where they went, and do everything he could for their physical welfare.

He would testify that Subedar-Major Ganga Charan gave orders for evacuating the Fort; that he himself, while refraining from urging his views either way, realized that it was a terrible decision to have to make, but that the decision having been made, all that he himself could do, was to continue in his duty as Medical Officer attached to the unit.

Another thought entered his mind as he studied the face of the Subedar-Major; a memory of a good omen. Dr. Brydon. He accompanied the retreating garrison from Kabul on its march to Peshawar through the Khyber Pass, and was the sole survivor of that massacre. What a wonderful thing if Alexander Breckinge should be the sole survivor of this garrison, and should ride alone into Landi Kotal as Brydon rode alone into Jellalabad, the only man who escaped, the only man who could tell them what had happened.

Anyhow, his evidence as to what had happened would be accepted, of course; and it would be merely of academic interest, so to speak, inasmuch as he was not concerned in any way with the military aspect of the matter.

And somewhat similar thoughts passed through the mind of the Subedar-Major.

After all, it was not as though he could be held responsible. He could say—and the Subedar and two Jemadars would of course support him—that the order to evacuate the Fort was given by the Captain Sahib, who was a doctor, of course, but who was a Sahib, or ranked as one, and who was a *pukka* Captain, and of a rank far, far higher than that of Subedar-Major.

And if a Court-Martial pointed out that, as Captain Breckinge was not a combatant Officer, responsibility fell upon Subedar-Major Ganga Charan, which surely would be most unjust, and was most unlikely, he could still say with perfect truth—as it happened—and with the full support of his subordinate officers, that the Doctor Sahib had said that they must go, or they would all die of sickness and starvation; that he gave an order to that effect; and that as he was a Captain Sahib, the Subedar-Major had no choice but to obey him.

How fortunate it was that the Major Sahib was dead. He would never have agreed to this. Rather would he have shot any man, with his own hand, who so much as talked of surrender.

Yes, he'd have held on until they were all dead of the bad belly-sickness, of starvation, or of wounds— except the few who survived to be hacked to pieces by these devils of Pathans when they burst in.

Only a fool trusted a Pathan, but there was a chance, since they were to be allowed to keep their rifles. And there was a good chance, a very good chance, yea, far more than a chance, a certainty, that the Captain Sahib would be held responsible.

And if the Captain Sahib never survived to reach India, Subedar-Major Ganga Charan could say that it was by Major Denbrough Sahib's orders that he marched the survivors out of the Fort. Yes, just before he died, the Major Sahib agreed to surrender the Fort, to save the lives of the few who had defended it for so long.

"Very good, Sahib," he said. "I'll give the necessary orders. When do we march?"

"To-morrow, if the Hadji agrees to my terms that all who can carry a rifle do so, and that we take twenty-five rounds of ammunition and what rations we can carry. This man's coming back at sunrise with the answer, but he is quite sure his master will agree. Better order the *Stand-to* before dawn."

"Don't trust them, Sahib."

"No. He's bringing only two others with him—the Hadji's two sons—to bring their father's answer."

"Why should the Hadji make any terms with us at all, since nothing can prevent his taking the Fort?"

"So that he can get it without any further fighting. He has lost too many men already."

"Why should he not fall upon us and slay us when we have marched out?"

"Because we shall march out with loaded rifles and fixed bayonets. And still he would lose men if there were a fight."

"Why should he not continue the siege until we die of starvation?"

"Because his rival and enemy, the Mehtar of Lohistan and Halzit and the Powindah Mullah are on their way here, and he means to have the Fort before they come."

"*'The faith of a Pathan, the mercy of a wolf,'*" quoted the Subedar-Major sententiously.

"Yes, I know, I know. But . . ."

"*'Trust a Hur, an Afghan, a woman, a panther, a snake—and a Pathan,'*" again quoted the Subedar-Major.

"Yes, I know. And don't suppose I'm going to trust them because it amuses me. It's our one chance to save our lives."

Silence fell in the little mud-walled room as the

Pathan watched the two men who were talking in English.

"I'll give the necessary orders, Sahib," said the Subedar-Major at length.

"Yes, tell the Jemadars and Havildars to-night, and let them tell the men. I'll have a talk with Subedar Gopal Mangal myself."

"I'll see to all things, Sahib. Ammunition and rations. Twenty-five rounds—and as much more as can be concealed. And cooked rations as well as . . ."

"Yes, let each man carry two haversacks. I don't suppose they'd say anything. Try, anyhow."

"I'll see to everything, Sahib."

"Right. Now, blindfold this man again, and turn him out."

The bandage having been removed from his eyes ere he was thrust out through the briefly-opened gates, the Pathan, his hands raised above his shoulders, as though deprecating treachery and a consequent shot in the back, hurried along the track leading from the Fort, dropped into the trench from which a steady fire had been for so long maintained upon the gate-tower, and crawled to cover behind *sangars* which flanked the trench.

Arrived at dead ground in the shelter of big boulders, he rose to his feet, made his way to the bivouac of the Singing Hadji of Sufed Kot, and begged that His Holiness, if not asleep within his cave, might be informed of his return.

The scowling, truculent and extremely dirty member of the Hadji's special retinue and bodyguard to whom he gave the message, replied that the Hadji Saheb was not only very much awake but awaiting his return.

"Well, give me back my rifle and belt and take me along to him," said the Pathan messenger who had called himself Ghulam Hyder.

No Pathan cares to be separated longer than is absolutely necessary from his rifle, which is to him what his spectacles are to a short-sighted man.

"What have you done with it?"

The man grinned.

"See the Hadji Saheb first," he said, and led the way to the big hill-side cave, at the mouth of which the Singing Hadji of Sufed Kot held *jirgah.*

"*Salaam aleikum*, Hadji Saheb," said the messenger, raising his hands to his forehead in salute, as he approached.

"Well?" growled the Hadji, ignoring the salutation.

"*Tobah!* The accursed unbelievers are still stiff-necked and defiant, Allah smite them. They refused thy terms with laughter, Hadji Saheb."

Frowning, the Hadji, a fighting priest of most secular habit and appearance, stroked his beard.

"Have they ammunition?"

"Unlimited. They have not yet begun to think of touching the reserve supply, of which alone there is enough to withstand a siege."

"Food?"

"Ample. Of that again the reserve is untouched. A go-down full of sacks of grain, sugar, salt, flour; all things. They have even *ghee* and *turmeric.*"

"Then what of the messenger who came hither offering to make terms?"

"A trick, Hadji Saheb. A clever *banao.* If the man is caught by your Holiness, he tells that tale. If not, he goes on and carries a message to the nearest Angrezi fort or telegraph or relief, that all is well, and that if they hurry up there will still be time to catch you."

"Who commands there? A *hakim*, as the messengers said?"

"No. More trickery. A Sahib. A *bahadur* and experienced man of war."

"What is their strength?"

"They have lost but few, and there is no sickness, owing to the skill of the *hakim.*"

"There is a *hakim*, then?"

"Yes, verily, the messengers spoke that much truth. A very *hushyar hakim.* He has kept sickness from them and quickly healed their wounds."

The Hadji eyed the messenger long and thoughtfully, with narrowed eyes and pursed lips.

"Then why so few at the loop-holes and on the walls?"

"More cunning and trickery. Only one-half are ever on duty, the other half resting, sleeping, eating."

"How many?" asked the Hadji.

"I could not count, Hadji Saheb. I did not see much, as I was led from the gate to the Colonel Sahib's room. But, being prepared for a sudden rush, there was a man at every loop-hole, a man at every embrasure round the walls, and a reserve of men waiting ready in the courtyard."

"You seemed to have learned a lot, nevertheless."

"The Sahib hid nothing. He was willing, nay desirous, that the Hadji Saheb should know the strength of the place."

"Why have we seen no *topis* among the *puggris*? Why has the fire from the walls been weak, as though there were but few rifles, and ammunition scarce?"

"Cunning, I say, Hadji Saheb. To lead you to make an assault. The Colonel Sahib wants your *lashkar* to come out in the open, that the garrison may rush to the walls and open rapid fire and mow your men down."

Still eyeing his man, the Singing Hadji of Sufed Kot continued to stroke his beard, in anxious thought and some perplexity.

"So we are tricked, are we? Fooled by these Infidel sons of noseless mothers. Allah blacken their faces on earth and burn their souls in Hell. They let you in, let you sniff around their Fort like a pariah dog round a courtyard, and then kicked you out again like the dog you are—and laughed. They would laugh at me, would they?"

The messenger raised deprecating hands at this shocking thought.

"Laughter is not the attribute of the wise, Hadji Saheb," said he meaningly.

The Hadji looked at the messenger. This man had interested, and slightly intrigued, him from the first; a man of parts, with a brain under his lousy turban.

"Eh?"

"It is the sound emitted by fools, as is braying by asses," continued the man, "but as I passed through the gates of their Fort, I smiled."

The Hadji looked yet more interested as he waited for more.

"For to-morrow I return taking two others with me."

"Why?"

"In fulfilment of the tale I told their Colonel Sahib, that to-morrow I would come back with the two sons of the Hadji Saheb to make a treaty with him, whereby *the Hadji Saheb will raise the siege and depart*, in return for a gift of fifty rifles with a hundred rounds of ammunition for each, and all the rupees that are in the Treasury of the Fort."

"What is this? Say that again," requested the Hadji.

"Having seen all I could, and received a contemptuous reply to the offer of safe-conduct if they would surrender, I thought of a plan. Knowing that the Colonel Sahib would not give up the rifles, nor the money, I made him think that if my mission failed, as I must know it would, I would try to make him think that the Hadji Saheb was tired of breaking his teeth upon a rock, and was about to depart. And being about to depart, was trying to get what he could. Anything he could.

"'*How do I know the Hadji Saheb would keep his word?*' asked the Colonel. '*Who would trust a Pathan? And how do I know that you are empowered to make this offer?*'

"'*Look Sahib,*' said I, '*if I return to-morrow with the Hadji Saheb's own sons—the light of his eyes, the pride of all his days, the joy of his life, who will be the support of his old age—will you make agreement with them? The Hadji Saheb will keep faith. If he will trust his two sons to you, knowing that you will not slay them or even seize them and bind them, will you not, in like manner, trust him?*'

"And after thinking for a moment the Colonel Sahib, smiling, said:

"'*Bring them to-morrow at sunrise.*'"

The messenger smiled ingratiatingly.

"Well?" growled the Hadji, who was not amused.

"Then to-morrow at sunrise I again present myself at the gate, taking two with me—and there will be three of us inside the Fort. And who knows what three bold and resolute men may not be able to do?"

The Hadji started up.

"*Ghazi! Ghazi!*" he cried. "You will? You will slay the Sahib, run amok, kill the *hakim*, kill the Native Officers, give your lives—and gain Paradise? Oh, thrice blessed are they who gain Paradise in the dawning. Seven times blessed are they who do so with the blood of the Infidel upon their hands."

"We are *ghazis*. We would acquire merit and attain Paradise," admitted the messenger. "We would have a treble *ziarat*, for ever to be known as the place of holiest pilgrimage, the Tomb of the Three Pirs who died for the Faith."

"Unless your courage fail you at the last moment and . . ."

"Nay, nay, Hadji Saheb," expostulated the candidate for martyrdom and Paradise.

"Well, in any case—to hold them in converse, yea, and to get them altogether in assembly, all officers, that you may rush upon them and slay and spare not —make play with thy tale of a bargain. Give them to think that I am weary and would raise the siege, but that I hope to go not empty-handed away."

Smiling, the messenger bowed his head.

The Hadji re-seated himself upon his heels as the light of enthusiasm died from his eyes.

This wasn't good enough. Or, rather, it was too good. Too good to be true. If this man was a genuine fanatical *ghazi*, the Hadji was the more mistaken.

On the other hand, what had he to gain by trickery? His shrift would be short inside that Fort if anything went wrong; and the best he could hope for would be to be slung out with a heavy boot behind him, to return to his friends like a beaten cur with its tail between its legs. The worst—to be hanged from the walls.

And what about treachery to himself, the Singing Hadji of Sufed Kot?

No, what could the fellow hope to gain by going over to the British? Apart from the fact that they would not want him, would not have him at any price. They were much too wily; and besides, it wasn't their way.

Still, it looked as though there was nothing to lose, and that there might be everything to gain by agreeing to the scheme.

What about a rush at the gate as it was held open for the three of them to walk in? A picked score or two of his best men silently assembled in the darkness before dawn, each bearing a dead thorn-bush and lying flat, and still as the dead, behind stones and boulders. Let the three men hail the gate just at dawn, and, as it was opened, let this Ghulam Hyder and the other two —if he could find two to go with him—keep the gate open while the rest sprang up and rushed it. Then a prompt fusillade at the walls and a general assault while the chosen men fought their way in.

It might be done at not too great a cost.

Better still, if the three could get in and go *ghazi* inside. The sepoy people would almost certainly surrender if they had neither Sahibs nor Native Officers, no leader at all. And if they did not, their defence would be but poor and half-hearted.

Yes, it really looked like a case of nothing to lose and everything to gain. A bargain after the Hadji's own heart.

"And two other *bahadurs* would go in with you?" he asked Ghulam Hyder.

"They have agreed, willingly. They yearn to gain remission of their sins."

"Doubtless their sins are many," smiled the Hadji, and again pondered the matter as his fingers scrabbled in his bushy beard.

No, he could see nothing wrong, see no opportunity or reason for treachery. The Pathan proverb, '*The friend of a friend is a friend, and the friend of an enemy is an enemy,*' applied here; and this man's gang had joined him well-recommended. Men of his own knew

225

that one of them was the son of a Khan and married to the daughter of a Chief whom they themselves had known.

No, undoubtedly the gang had come and joined the fight for the love of a fight and in hatred of the intruding Unbeliever. And now they desired to gain fame on earth and *houris* in Heaven. Far be it from him to hinder them. Especially as the place might be taken without assault, almost without further cost.

And already the cost had been high. Far too high, in point of fact, and he had reached that anxious and difficult point at which it was debateable as to whether it would be wiser to cut his losses or to endeavour to turn them to profits in a final effort.

Undoubtedly his prestige was suffering, and though his statement—that the bullets of the Infidel turned to water as they approached his sacred person—was not disproven, it was painfully evident that they did not do so when they approached the persons of his followers.

And though he had preached *jehad*, and his *jowans* knew that to fall in a Holy War was to go straight to Paradise, there was a deplorable number of them who appeared to prefer to enjoy the pleasures of this earth for yet a little longer.

If he raised the siege, abandoned the place and departed, his fame would suffer eclipse, his prestige be grievously lessened. Perhaps be destroyed, yea and himself with it.

And another unsuccessful assault could mean nothing less than the defeat of all his plans, the failure of his campaign, the extinguishing of the torch that was to set the whole Border alight.

Should he fail now, what hope that the Amir would send his best General and an army of *khassadars* to join him? What hope that the Mahsuds, Afridis, Mohmands and the Shinwaris would flock to his banner?

No, it would be the end of his great dream of leading, beneath the famous green banner of the Singing Hadji of Sufed Kot, a vast army that would sweep down the Khyber, overwhelming the Forts of the

Infidel, occupy and loot Peshawar, cross the Indus, and come down upon the plains of Hindustan like locusts upon a field of *jowari*.

At first all had promised well. The Amir had sent an evasive and ambiguous reply that, like a nut of unattractive exterior contained a sweet kernel of nourishment.

'Unto him that hath much, I will add more. Unto him that needeth not help, I will give my aid without stint, and will see to it that success shall further succeed. But from him who hath not, I will take away, and for him who faileth, I will increase failure.'

Yea, a blow is as good as a kick to a blind donkey.

And at first, all had indeed promised well. Parties, large and small, of Tribesmen, had joined him from all directions: and gangs such as this would-be *ghazi* and his friends. Messages of goodwill had come from far Herat, Jellalabad, Kandahar and every Province and Governorship of Afghanistan. Messages—and promises. And from beyond Penjdeh had come more. Not only messages of goodwill and promises, but good minted money and European rifles, a convoy led by a curious and interesting man who spoke excellent Pushtu, Hindustani, Russian and English, a most encouraging and useful man, whose advice had been invaluable until he disappeared.

Yes, all had promised exceeding well at first; and the Singing Hadji of Sufed Kot had conceived himself to be the great boulder that starts the avalanche which sweeps all before it and overwhelms the valley.

And here this Fort was delaying his plan, frustrating his ambition and threatening to ruin it.

Either the Fort, or the Hadji's soaring schemes must fall.

"So be it," said he, slowly nodding his head, as he considered the messenger. "At dawn to-morrow. And I will have a party of other devotees ready to rush the gate."

The messenger smiled and sadly shook his head.

"No, Hadji Saheb, the whole plan will fall to the ground if there is the slightest suspicion. They will not

227

open the gates until the sun is up and daylight full. They are wily and watchful men. Instead of opening the gate, they will open fire, if they be in the least suspicious, and our plan will miscarry. Let all be as it was this morning; and make no assault until there be a signal. The firing of a shot, shouts and commotion; or one of us running to the wall, waving a cloth and crying aloud."

"Where were you brought face to face with the Sahib?" asked the Hadji.

"In his room, an inner chamber."

"And who were present?"

"He and the other Sahibs, the Kaptan and Liftenant Sahibs and the Doctor Sahib and the Indian Officers of the *pultan*."

"Then, if suddenly going *ghazi*, you three fall upon them, and there is a slaughter, how shall I know of it?"

"There will be outcry and men will come running. There will be loud *bumbuljo* and *hullagula*."

"And if there were not? If there were silence all about the walls?"

"It will still be plain that we have succeeded, inasmuch as we shall not return. The fact that we come not out again will be proof that we have not acted as peaceful messengers, and have been slain for our treachery. It is well known that the Sahibs would never seize and imprison envoys coming in good faith?"

Again the Hadji slowly nodded his head.

"It is true. And if, suspecting you, they search you for weapons and, having taken them from you, parley with you while rifles are levelled at your breasts, what then?"

"Then, Hadji Saheb, we can do nothing with our hands and our weapons, but can do much with our tongues and our cunning. We will again offer to raise the siege in return for rifles and money, and artfully make it clear to the Sahib that the siege is to be raised and the Hadji Saheb about to depart."

"And then?"

"And then, returning, I will make full report to the Hadji Saheb.

"And the Hadji will raise the siege and depart—*a little way*," he added. "And suddenly, when they have become bold, and thankfully take their ease, he will reappear in the middle of the night, silently as a wolf. And like a wolf will he make his spring."

The reply of the Hadji was an expansive smile, a fat chuckle, and something very closely resembling a heavy wink.

He must keep an eye on this fellow. Undoubtedly he was a *jangi nafar*, certainly he was something of a *ustad*, and clearly he was a wily counsellor. He must have him about his person, promote him, and use him to the uttermost.

But he was forgetting. The man was *ghazi*, was going to sacrifice his body for the good of his soul, was going to step straight to Paradise over the corpse of an Infidel. A pity in a way, but a good bargain.

Yes, the Hadji was more than willing to exchange the life of the excellent Ghulam Hyder for that of the Commandant of Giltraza Fort. Indeed, the three of them, with luck and judgment, cunning and courage, might make a clean sweep of the lot, Sahibs and Indian Officers, too.

Yes, a grand bargain. Three strangers, no kith or kin of his, in exchange for Giltraza Fort and all that it contained; a resounding victory over the Infidel; and a tremendous impetus to the avalanche that should sweep him, like so many of his forerunners, from the hills of the Border, adown the valley of the Indus, and on to the gates of Delhi itself.

Dili dur ast. . . .

But many a conqueror had reached it by the road that the Hadji and his vast conglomerate army should begin to tread, as soon as this Fort had fallen and the flames of its burning lit the Border from end to end, and cast their bright glow upon the palace of the Amir in Kabul itself.

CHAPTER III

After an endless-seeming sleepless night of acutest anxiety, doubt and fear, Captain Alexander Breckinge betook him before dawn to the loop-holed guard-house beside the gate. Through a narrow iron-shuttered loop-hole he peered out into the paling darkness.

Would this Ghulam Hyder return, bringing with him the two sons of the Singing Hadji of Sufed Kot? Would they be fully authorized to make agreement for the surrender of the Fort in return for the lives of the able-bodied, and would they allow them to march out with rifles, ammunition and food?

Should he at the last moment refuse the terms, seize the Pathan leader's sons and hold them as hostages, threatening to hang them the moment a shot was fired against the Fort?

And of what avail would that be, if he did so, and no shot were fired, but the siege were continued until they all died of starvation, or at any rate had no longer the strength to man the walls? The leader's sons would outlast them easily, since the garrison was already in a semi-starving condition, whereas the two sons would enter the place well-fed and in most robust health and strength.

No, it wouldn't do. Besides, what hideous reprisals the Hadji would exact when he took the Fort, as eventually he must.

Calling to a sepoy, he bade him ask the Subedar-Major Saheb to come to the guard-room.

"Salaam Sahib," said that officer, as he entered the room. "The sun will be up in a few minutes."

"Do you think there may be a dawn attack?" asked Breckinge.

"No, I don't. They know we should be ready for them, and they'd lose a lot of men in the first few minutes if we gave them five rounds rapid, as they rushed from their position. No, I think our only danger is treachery when we open the gates and march out."

"But even then," he added, "there would be a lot of killing, as they are leaving us our rifles and bayonets."

"They don't like bayonets," observed Breckinge. "And I think it's a very good sign that they bargained for the spare rifles and did not pretend to agree to everything I said."

"Oh, no, we shall be all right," he continued, more to encourage himself than his hearer. "Do the men know?"

"Yes, Sahib. I talked to the Native Officers and non-commissioned Officers and told them you were certain it was our one possible chance, the only way to save our lives, pointing out that the Fort must fall, in any case, and we be slain, to a man, unless we did this thing."

"And all agreed with you?"

"All save that *takrari* fellow, Havildar Umrao Singh. He tried to show what a *bahadur* he is, and said he'd sooner lose his life."

"What did you say to that?"

"I told him he was quite welcome. If he chose to disobey orders in time of war, and to be hacked to pieces by the Pathans, he could do so. Just as well that as be Court-Martialled and shot for mutiny and inciting to mutiny."

"How—inciting?"

"He said there were men in his Section who'd say the same, and do what he did—refuse to surrender and to march out. Said they'd shut themselves up in the gate-tower and fight to the last cartridge."

"Fight? The fools! The Pathans would burn them alive in the tower."

"That's what I told him, and he said that they . . ."

"Look, look," interrupted Breckinge, who had been peering through the loop-hole as he talked. "Here they come, three of them!"

The sun had risen with the same amazing swiftness as that with which it sets; and, in the light of its bright rays three Pathans were seen to leave the cover of the rocks and boulders that lay beyond the nearest sangars and advance with raised hands, the leading one waving aloft a white cloth.

"You are keeping a sharp look-out for treachery?" said Breckinge.

"*Han*, Sahib, *bé-shak*. One blast of my whistle and they'll get 'rapid independent' from every man who can fire a rifle."

The men advanced and halted at the loud challenge of the sentry above the gate.

As they did so, the three raised their hands yet higher, turned about and presented their broad *posh-teen*-clad backs to the Fort, waited in that position for a minute, turned about again, and continued their slow march towards the gate.

"Be careful, be careful, Subedar-Major," urged Breckinge, toying nervously with the flap of the revolver-holster which he had buckled on, ere leaving his room.

"Have no fear, Sahib," was the reply. "The gate will be opened but a couple of feet and for a couple of seconds. They will be shot instantly, if there is the slightest attempt to open it further or to cause delay."

"Bring them to my room," said Breckinge, "and keep strictest watch and look-out while they are with me. Blindfold them, of course, and search them for weapons, and station four men with loaded rifles outside my door."

§2

As on the previous day, Breckinge seated himself at the table in the ill-lit cell that was his room, placed his loaded revolver in front of him, and waited.

Was it safe to interview them alone? He had six shots in the revolver; but there were three of them, and these Pathans were terrible men. Quite probably a revolver-bullet would not stop one unless it took him through the heart or the brain. If they made a simultaneous rush at him, he wouldn't have a chance, even though they were unarmed.

Perhaps he had better have a sepoy. Yes, two

sepoys, with loaded rifles and fixed bayonets, standing behind his chair. Probably there was no real danger, but it was as well to be on the safe side. One couldn't be too careful in dealing with these treacherous swine.

The door opened and the Subedar-Major entered, followed by Breckinge's visitor of yesterday, Ghulam Hyder, two other Pathans, and four sepoys.

Directing the Subedar-Major to place the three Pathans on the opposite side of the room and to remove the bandages from their eyes, Breckinge bade him station two of the sepoys behind his chair with loaded rifles at the 'ready,' and orders to shoot instantly, if any of the three moved a step in his direction. The other two sentries were to wait without, and were to rush in, the moment they heard a shout or a shot.

Matters having been arranged to his satisfaction, Breckinge, revolver in hand, studied the two new-comers.

Both were big and burly men.

One, of the ordinary fair Pathan type; the other, darker.

All three looked to Breckinge as though they might well have served in a Pathan or Baluchi regiment of the British Army, a remarkably truculent, forbidding and sinister-looking trio.

To think of hundreds and hundreds of such men, swarming over the walls, each with a terrible Khyber knife in his hand, the weapon with which the Pathan loves to fight at close quarters.

Khyber 'knife'! The thing was as big and heavy as a sword; and used like a sword, to cut and hack and slash, as a Gurkha uses his *kukri* or a jungle man his *machête*. Absurd to call them knives. They weren't much used for stabbing, those dreadful blades, a yard long, two inches across, half an inch thick at the back, razor-edged and needle-pointed.

Again Breckinge's over-vivid imagination caused him to shudder, at a picture of hands, feet, arms, heads, being lopped off, each with a single flail-like swishing blow of one of those dreadful weapons.

"Salaam, *Huzoor*," said the Pathan calling himself Ghulam Hyder.

"Are these two the sons of the Hadji?" replied Breckinge.

"*Han*, Sahib, *bé-shak*. Amanullah Khan and Allah-dad Khan."

"They don't look to me like brothers," growled Breckinge.

"Different mothers," observed Ghulam Hyder, grinning.

"And they've come to confirm the Hadji's acceptance of my terms, eh?"

"They have, *Huzoor*. In his great mercy, the Hadji Saheb agrees that you may march away with your men, unmolested, each bearing rifle and bayonet, twenty-five rounds of ammunition, and what rations he can carry. All else, including the rifles of the sick and wounded and dead, and the spare ones in the armoury, to be left behind; all money, clothing, accoutrements, stores. Everything. It is agreed, *Huzoor*?"

"It is agreed."

"And are all the Native Officers willing and obedient? And all the men, too?"

"One non-commissioned Officer refuses, and says that a few of the men of his Section, relations doubtless, will not obey the order."

"Perhaps, being dishonest men, they distrust the word of the Hadji," smiled Ghulam Hyder.

"Perhaps. But I am told that the man says he would rather die than take part in the surrender.

"Let him die," he added.

"With those who support him and the sick and wounded," said Ghulam Hyder. "When will you be ready to open the gates and march out? To-day?"

"To-day."

"It would be better that all who can do so, should march out before the Hadji's men enter," suggested Ghulam Hyder significantly.

"Yes. We shall march out with fixed bayonets and loaded rifles, prepared to fight to the last, if necessary," said Breckinge, looking as fierce and dangerous as he could. "In the event of treachery we shall sell our lives dearly."

"The Hadji Saheb wishes to prevent bloodshed," was the reply.

"It is agreed, then," continued Ghulam Hyder. "But it is the Hadji's wish that all Officers and Native Officers swear in the presence of these, his sons, that they will obey the *Huzoor*, will do as he orders, and will —give no trouble."

"You can take my word for that," replied Breckinge curtly.

"No, that I cannot do, *Huzoor*. I must return with the Hadji's sons, and they must assure their father that all have made surrender, in their presence—or been dealt with."

"And the Havildar and his men who will not do so?" asked Breckinge.

"That little difficulty can be dealt with, *Huzoor* . . . *They* will be dealt with."

With a word of warning to his two supporters to be watchful and ready, Breckinge went to the door and bade one of the sentries, waiting without, to request the Subedar-Major Saheb to come to him.

"It seems that this Hadji fellow wishes his two sons to receive your surrender personally," he said in English, when the Subedar-Major arrived. "Your own and that of your officers."

"Mine, Sahib? I? I am not making the surrender," objected the Subedar-Major.

"Well, we can't split hairs now, man. What does it matter, so long as they let us go? Anyway, they want to be quite sure that you and the other Native Officers are agreed about it. I want you to tell them, and then to send Subedar Gopal Mangal and Jemadar Rama Narayen and after them the Havildars."

"Tell them in Hindustani," he added, turning to the three Pathans, "that you surrender."

And facing the three grim men, standing side by side along the wall, Subedar-Major Ganga Charan said, in Hindustani:

"It is the Captain Sahib's order; and I obey. I and

235

the Native Officers and sepoys under my command surrender as the Captain Sahib says. We will march out with our rifles and twenty-five rounds of ammunition for each man, without fighting—unless we are attacked."

Breckinge said nothing.

"Do you understand that?" asked Ghulam Hyder of the fairer of his companions, in Pushtu.

"I do," replied that man in the same language. "He says that by the Captain Sahib's orders he surrenders and will march out without fighting, unless attacked."

"Tell him you understand," said Ghulam Hyder to the Pathan.

And in good Hindustani the man addressed himself to the Subedar-Major.

"I hear your words," said he. "It is well. You surrender and will not fight. *Achcha.*"

"And you?" asked Ghulam Hyder in Pushtu, turning to the darker of his two companions.

"*Han,*" grunted the man. "I understand," and addressing the Subedar-Major, used much the same form of words as the other Pathan had done.

"It is well, *Huzoor,*" said Ghulam Hyder. "This man may go. Bid him send the other Native Officers."

"All right, Subedar-Major Saheb," said Breckinge. "Send in Subedar Gopal Mangal . . . You will keep a sharp look-out, won't you?"

A minute or two later the Native Officer, brother-in-law and second in rank to the Subedar-Major, entered, and him Ghulam Hyder immediately addressed in Hindustani.

"Are you willing to surrender," he asked, "and to go out from here, promising that the men under your command will not fight my people unless they are attacked?"

"It is an order," replied the man. "I obey it."

"Whose order?" asked Ghulam Hyder.

"The Captain Sahib's."

"If the Captain Sahib and the Subedar-Major Saheb gave you different orders, which of them would you obey?"

"The Captain Sahib," replied the man.

"Let this man go, and send in the next," directed Ghulam Hyder.

"Are you giving orders here?" asked Breckinge. "The Fort isn't surrendered yet, you know."

Ghulam Hyder smiled, and murmured the usual formula.

"It is as your Honour pleases."

"All right, Subedar-Saheb. Send Jemadar Rama Narayen," directed Breckinge.

Jemadar Rama Narayen, the Subedar-Major's relative, also stated his intention of obeying the orders of his superior officer.

"Which officer?" enquired Ghulam Hyder.

"The Captain Sahib," replied the Jemadar with a glance at Breckinge, who made no comment.

As the men turned to depart:

"*Subbr karo*," ordered Ghulam Hyder, and enquired whether there were any other Native Officers.

"Only those three on duty," replied Breckinge. "The rest are sick, wounded, or dead."

"And clearly these three will obey your orders, *Huzoor*," smiled Ghulam Hyder.

"Without doubt," agreed Breckinge.

"And now the lesser people, the Havildars and Naiks and such."

"Why waste time? You don't want to see them all, do you? They'll do as they are ordered, all except the one I told you about."

"We wish to see them all," replied Ghulam Hyder. "It is the Hadji's order to us."

"Is it not so?" he added, turning to his companions.

"It is our father's order," replied the darker one.

"And it must be done," added the other. "All, in any authority, must surrender to us personally."

"Send the Havildars in, one by one, then," Breckinge bade the Jemadar, who, saluting, departed, looking less dejected than when he entered.

Two Havildars, looking emaciated, weary, and as sick as only a sick Indian can look, gave prompt assurance that they would certainly obey orders, and could undertake that the men under their command would do that too.

The third Havildar appeared to be of different mettle.

"Now then, you," Breckinge addressed him in Hindustani. "It has become necessary to surrender this Fort and save such lives as can be saved. The Subedar-Major Saheb tells me that you were disobedient, insolent, and mutinous when he spoke to the Officers and non-commissioned officers yesterday and told them what it was their duty to do. Well, you know the punishment for such conduct. I have sent for you to say that, in the circumstances, I will overlook it, if you return immediately to duty, and set your men an example of prompt and cheerful obedience to the orders of your Commanding Officer—the Subedar-Major Saheb. What have you to say?"

"Sahib, I will not surrender," replied the man instantly.

"Then you will surely die."

"Sahib, my face will thus not be blackened. I am not *bé-ittibar.*"

"And are your Officers? Is not their *izzat* as . . . ?"

"Sahib, I will not surrender," interrupted the man, standing erectly to attention, and looking Breckinge squarely in the face.

"Nor will the men of my Section," he added.

"How many of thy men will refuse to surrender?" asked Ghulam Hyder.

The Havildar ignored him.

"Answer the question," ordered Breckinge.

"I heard no question, Sahib," replied the man.

"Then hear mine, *béwakuf.* How many other fools wish to die with you?"

"There are seven brave men who . . ."

"Let me have no insolence from you," cried Breckinge. "You are a mutineer. I have the right to shoot you where you stand and . . ."

"Shoot, Sahib," replied the man with gross insolence or high courage, according to the point of view.

"Have the men disarmed and brought here,

Huzoor," said Ghulam Hyder in the manner of one who gives an order that he knows will be obeyed.

"How do I know it is not a trick?" replied Breckinge. "No men shall be disarmed and brought from the walls and loop-holes until this matter is settled."

Ghulam Hyder shrugged his shoulders.

"Let this man go and get their names, then," he said; and Breckinge ordered the Havildar to go and do so.

"Without doubt you command here," smiled Ghulam Hyder as the Havildar departed.

"Of course I do."

"Send those two sentries away, then."

"Why?"

"Why not? Allah! You have a revolver and we are unarmed, and you will have four of them outside the door ready to enter if you call.

"*Daro mut,*" he jeered, as Breckinge hesitated. "Don't be frightened. You will still be five armed men to three unarmed."

With a laugh that was intended to be contemptuous, Breckinge bade the sentries wait outside the door, and to enter instantly with the others if he shouted or fired his revolver.

The sentries went out of the room; the door closed; and Captain Alexander Breckinge was left alone with his three visitors.

"Well, Breckinge, my lad," said the man who had called himself Ghulam Hyder, as he removed the turban from his head and the squint from his eyes. "So you'd surrender this Fort, would you? Run away—even though you've still got food, water, ammunition and enough men to defend the walls. *You cowardly little hound!*"

Breckinge stared open-mouthed and wide-eyed, his dusky face paling as the obviously English voice continued in a tone of bitterest contempt and unconcealed disgust.

"You are a credit to your name and to your Service, aren't you? What have you got to say for yourself? Let that pistol alone, you miserable cur, or I'll . . ."

239

Breckinge passed his tongue across his lips.

"Who are you?" he whispered as he stared in bewildered fear at the three men who closed in upon him.

"Major Bartholomew Hazelrigg; Indian Army; Intelligence Department," was the brusque reply.

"This gentleman you have met before," he added, indicating the fairer of the two alleged Pathans, who also removed his *puggri* and stared Breckinge grimly in the eye.

"*Captain Richard Wendover*, formerly of Napier's Horse. Remember him?"

Breckinge sprang to his feet and Hazelrigg picked up the revolver.

As Wendover took a step in his direction, Breckinge literally staggered back, his eyes staring, his face livid with fear.

"*It's a lie!*" he screamed. "*He's dead! He's dead!*"

"Oh no, he's not," replied Wendover quietly. "But I shouldn't be surprised if you soon were, Breckinge."

"Who . . . ? How did . . . ? I . . . You . . ."stammered Breckinge, as his hand went to his throat. "This is . . ."

"Pull yourself together, man," said Hazelrigg. "Here, sit down in that chair and listen to me . . . I've caught you fairly and squarely, and before witnesses. Unfortunately several of them Indians, too. Your own subordinates and friends—not to say accomplices. Trying to surrender this Fort while it is defensible. And just to save your miserable life."

"I'm a doctor. I'm a doctor," gabbled Breckinge. "I have no authority to . . ."

"Come now! None of that!" interrupted Hazelrigg. "That won't do. Haven't you just been negotiating with me for the surrender of the place? Haven't you just been saying and proving that you were in complete authority here, and that the Native Officers would do exactly as you told them?"

"I am only the doctor. I . . ."

"Yes, and a pretty doctor. What were you going to do about the sick and wounded, when the place was evacuated? Stand by them and do your best for them? No, you were going to clear off, save your precious skin, and leave them to be butchered, as you thought."

"You cheated me."

"I did. Most successfully, eh? No doubt about that, Breckinge."

Breckinge glanced about the room like a trapped rat, his gaze resting on the door.

"Call those sentries in, if you like," said Hazelrigg. "I shall be calling them myself in a minute, to put you under arrest."

Breckinge's shifty gaze darted from Hazelrigg's face to that of Wendover.

"It's a trick! It's a lie! How do I know who you are?" he began. "How do I . . . ?"

"You don't. But you can take my word for it. And it doesn't matter whether you do or not. Do you recognize Captain Wendover? And do you remember the Fort at Ubele? And do you remember the charge brought against Captain Wendover? Do you remember what happened to him there—and how it happened? Do you remember the evidence you gave? Eh, Breckinge?"

It was painfully evident that Breckinge did remember Captain Wendover. Also that the sudden shock following upon the strain of the previous days had been too much for him, and that he had completely gone to pieces. He was trembling violently.

"You cannot prove . . ."

"Cannot prove what?" asked Major Hazelrigg; and without waiting for Breckinge to reply, continued:

"But that's where you are wrong, Breckinge. We can prove it. Not only that; but you are going to admit it."

Breckinge, like a trapped beast, dashing about its cage, made another attempt.

"And *you*! What about you?" he shouted. "Haven't you come here and cheated me, lied, made a plot, undermined my authority?"

"Oh, but you haven't got any, Breckinge. You're only a doctor," interrupted Hazelrigg.

"You call yourself a British Officer and you've trapped the garrison of this place into surrendering," chattered Breckinge. "You've come in here and persuaded the Subedar-Major to surrender, and proved to me that it was the best thing; and that I ought to support him; and that I ought to save as many of the garrison as I could."

Hazelrigg laughed aloud.

"Why," continued Breckinge hysterically, "I should never have thought of such a thing. The word 'surrender' would never have entered my head if . . ."

"That's enough, Breckinge," interrupted Hazelrigg again. "You are not doing yourself any good. Confusing heads, aren't you? Yours and mine."

"What d'you mean?"

"I mean the possibility of your surrendering this place would never have entered *my* head, but that your messenger came to the Pathan leader with your proposals for surrender."

"I had a good talk with that messenger," added Hazelrigg.

Breckinge sat down as though his legs would no longer support him.

"Anything more to say? No. There really is nothing to say, is there? You convicted an innocent man once, Breckinge, and now you've convicted a guilty one—yourself—and out of your own mouth. You've done your best to surrender this Fort to me, to abandon it to the enemy, and to desert your sick and wounded.

"I'm not quite certain as to what your responsibility is in the matter of the defence of the Fort, in the circumstances. Doubtless you can plead at the Court-Martial that the fact of the British combatant Officers being dead did not leave you in military command of the place or make you responsible for the conduct of the defence.

"I don't know about that," he continued, "but we shall find out all about it at your trial. What I do know is that every decent white man will think you are the yellowest cur that ever bore a British name and wore the British uniform. For attempting to surrender, I mean."

Breckinge took his hands from before his face, which he had rested in them.

"I am only a doctor," he said again, moistening his

lips.

"*Only!*" said Hazelrigg quietly. "Did you ever hear of Doctor Whitchurch? Like you, he was in a siege. He added British Officer's duty to Doctor's duty. Did them both magnificently, and was awarded the Victoria Cross—as a soldier. As a soldier, Breckinge.

"Now the second point," he continued. "Setting aside the question as to whether the defence naturally devolved upon you as the one surviving white man and British official, what about the question of your being the support and main-stay of the responsible defenders, the power behind the Native Officers?

"Had you any duty to inspire the defence? To be what is called the life and soul of the garrison? To strain every nerve to keep the Subedar-Major and his two worthy relatives up to their job? To keep the men hopeful and stout-hearted? To keep their tails up? Was it in any wise your duty—merely as a doctor—to fight the spirit of defeatism, as you would any other foul microbe? Any part of your duty to show the sort of spirit that that Havildar showed just now?

"What will the Court-Martial have to say on that point, supposing for a moment that you did escape on the technical point that you weren't a combatant Officer?"

"I . . . I . . ." stammered Breckinge. "The men's lives . . . It was my duty to save . . ."

"My God! I could wring your neck," growled Hazelrigg. "Men's lives, you rotten hound. What about those poor devils on their backs with typhoid, dysentery and malaria, and those with wounds. Wounds *in front*, Breckinge. What about *their* lives, you dog?"

Again Breckinge's face went down into his hands and his shoulders began to shake.

"And that's the third point that the Court-Martial will deal with, Breckinge. Suppose, as a Gazetted Officer, bearing a military rank and title, you had no responsibility for the defence; suppose, as the Medical Officer attached to the garrison, you had no responsibility whatsoever for trying to keep up the men's courage and fighting-spirit, and for inspiring a stout

243

defence; what about your responsibility to your own sick and wounded? Can you evade that? Suppose that were the only charge brought against you at the Court-Martial, how would you defend your conduct?"

There was no reply but the now uncontrolled sobbing of the accused man, completely broken and abjectly terrified.

"Yes, it's pretty bad, isn't it?" observed Hazelrigg with a shrug of the shoulders and a glance at Wendover. "Pretty bad—entering into treasonable correspondence with the King's enemies. It won't be a mere case of ruin and disgrace, and your name a by-word in your Service, in the Indian Army, and among all decent people, European and native . . ."

"What will they . . . ? What shall I . . . ?"

"Don't know, I'm sure. I should think they'd shoot you. I certainly would. Anyhow, a long term of imprisonment is the very least you can hope for. Depends on the view they take; but whether, in the circumstances, you were responsible for the defence of the Fort or not, there is no getting away from the fact that you did your utmost to surrender it."

Suddenly Breckinge shot out a hand and pointing finger towards the face of the other Pathan, and in a voice rising almost to a scream:

"*Who are you? Who are you?*" he cried. "*Why does he stare at me like that?*"

And in point of fact, the hungrily ferocious glare with which Shere Khan had been regarding Breckinge's face, from the moment of his entry into the room was, to a person in a condition bordering upon hysteria, sufficiently daunting.

"Never mind who he is, for the moment," replied Hazelrigg. "What he knows is of more importance."

In pitiable anxiety and terror, Breckinge continued to stare at Shere Khan. How could this man know more than Hazelrigg and Wendover, of his attempt to surrender the Fort and abandon the wounded?

"He knows the truth of what happened at Ubele, Breckinge," continued Hazelrigg. "He knows the part you played in what happened there."

"I didn't . . . I didn't . . . I never . . ." began Breckinge.

"Oh, yes, you did," interrupted Hazelrigg. "It'll be a pretty story on top of this one, won't it?"

"There's no evidence. There can't be evidence. Nobody but myself knew . . ."

"What about?" asked Hazelrigg quickly.

"I had been experimenting for years. It was purely scientific research and . . ."

"What a twister you are!" growled Hazelrigg. "What a liar. First about this Fort, and then about that one . . . We know exactly what happened there, just as we do about what happened here. It's no good, Breckinge."

"But you can't know. Nobody but me could possibly know. There's no evidence."

"Of what?" snapped Hazelrigg.

Breckinge's eyes fell.

"No, it's no good, Breckinge. Wriggling won't help you. Far better make a clean breast of it, and help yourself that way," urged Hazelrigg.

Breckinge rose to his feet.

"Major, I swear," he began.

"I've no doubt you do," interrupted Hazelrigg. "But swearing won't help you. You are caught, Breckinge . . . No evidence! You've got a surprise coming."

"And now, there's another little matter," he continued. "Remember Azizun at Madrutta?"

Breckinge literally recoiled.

What was this? Now what other dreadful thing was coming up from the past? Was this man the Devil himself?

"Azizun?" he whispered.

"Yes, charming girl; but it doesn't do to trust them. Notoriously unreliable people. Give their own father away for a handful of rupees. You let her know too much, Breckinge."

Breckinge plucked up spirit and strength for another twist.

"The evidence of a bazaar woman? Haven't you yourself just said that . . ."

"Oh, quite. Quite," replied Hazelrigg. "Wouldn't

hang a dog on the word of a *dasi* like Azizun. But they often have very interesting information. Information that one can investigate. Yes, they can often tell you interesting little stories that you can investigate—and prove. Remember Abdul Ghaffar, the Gulf Arab; the pearl merchant, eh?"

Evidently Breckinge had received yet another shock. He sat speechless and shaking.

"Well?"

"Major Hazelrigg, you don't surely believe . . . ?"

"No. I don't believe. I know. I know what it was that disagreed so violently with Abdul Ghaffar that night in Azizun's house, when he lost the little wash-leather bag of pearls that he always carried about with him. Lost his pearls as well as his life. I know what it was that upset him Breckinge, *and I know where it came from.*"

"Major, before God, I swear . . . I didn't mean . . ."

"No; Devil doubt you. I don't suppose you did. Azizun overdid it, didn't she? Careless. Clumsy. What she asked you for, was a little sleeping-draught for her boy friend, wasn't it? A few knock-out drops. But they knocked poor old Abdul Ghaffar off his perch, once and for all. Seemed to get drunk suddenly; stayed drunk; and died drunk. And Abdul Ghaffar was a strict Mussulman who never touched alcohol in his life."

Again the dark face, now of an almost olive green, sank into the brown pink-palmed hands, as the wretched man groaned aloud.

"Allah! Is it a woman or a pariah dog," wondered Shere Khan aloud, in Pushtu.

Hazelrigg glanced at Wendover, who shook his head deprecatingly.

Yes, it was pretty painful, agreed Hazelrigg silently, as he correctly read Wendover's look.

"Now Breckinge," he said, with a change of voice in which there was a hint of human-kindness. "Just understand, quite plainly, once and for all, that it's no good. You may as well confess. I don't want to give you any false hopes, or to deceive you in the matter. You have no defence whatever. You haven't a leg to stand on, and the one and only thing you can do for yourself, is to make a clean breast of it—that is to say, to admit, fully and freely, what I can prove clearly and completely.

"There's no need for you to do so in the matter of this Fort, for you've shown your hand to me yourself. You had put your cards on the table before you knew who I was. About the other matters, I have, as I've shown you, complete knowledge and more than sufficient evidence. Now then, I'm going to put you under arrest and give you time to think it over."

Breckinge looked up.

"Major Hazelrigg, I am not a soldier," he began.

"You are not," agreed Hazelrigg.

"First of all," he continued, "go to the door and tell those four men to report to the Subedar-Major for duty; and tell one of them to send that Havildar here. The 'mutinous' one, I mean."

Breckinge rose to his feet.

"And by the way," added Hazelrigg, "don't do anything foolish—for your own sake."

Breckinge glanced at the revolver in Hazelrigg's hand, went to the door, and gave the requisite orders to the sentries.

"Close the door and come back and sit down," said Hazelrigg, when this had been done.

"Listen—and be very careful. When that Havildar comes, tell him who I am. D'you hear? Tell him I am Major Hazelrigg of the Indian Army, that I have made my way into this Fort in disguise, and have taken command of it. Understand? Then send him to fetch those men of whom he spoke, the men who were going to back him up in his refusal to join in the surrender of this Fort.

"There will be no risk in withdrawing them," he added. "The place won't be attacked yet awhile.

"Not while 'the Hadji's sons' are here," he smiled grimly.

The door opened and Havildar Umrao Singh entered.

"Now then, Captain Breckinge," said Hazelrigg in

English. "Stand up. Tell this non-commissioned officer who I am."

Havildar Umrao Singh stared in astonishment to see the apparent Pathan standing there bare-headed, and to hear him speaking English.

Breckinge obeyed, explaining the situation clearly in Hindustani.

The Havildar turned and stared incredulously at Hazelrigg.

"It's the truth, Havildar," said Hazelrigg. "I am Hazelrigg Sahib. I am a Major Sahib of the Indian Army; and I have got in here with this other Officer Sahib in disguise. I have sent for you to say 'Shábash.' Well done. I am pleased with you. And the General Sahib will be pleased with you. I shall give you promotion to temporary rank of Jemadar, and without doubt, the General Sahib will confirm you in that rank."

"I don't understand, Sahib," faltered the man.

"No; a bit sudden for you, eh? You will understand better when you see me and this other Officer Sahib in uniform."

He turned to Breckinge.

"Now Captain Breckinge, you yourself tell the Havildar to bring the men of his Section here, those upon whom he said he could rely to refuse to surrender."

Breckinge gave the necessary orders, and apparently doubting the evidence both of his ears and his eyes, the Havildar saluted and left the room.

"Now then, Breckinge," said Hazelrigg. "I want a tunic, shorts, puttees and boots, Sam Brown belt, and so forth. There must be plenty of kit that belonged to Major Denbrough, Captain Scott and Mr. Henderson. One tunic will have a crown on the shoulder-strap and the other a Captain's stars—for Captain Wendover. After I have twisted the Native Officers' tails and spoken to the men, I'm going back to the Pathan camp —for a little while—leaving Captain Wendover in command."

"But he's not . . ."

"Don't let that worry you, Breckinge," interrupted

Hazelrigg. "I am the Senior, and in fact, only, British Officer in this part of the world. I am the 'competent military authority' in Giltraza Fort and for a few hundred miles round it; and I am going to take it upon me to reinstate Captain Wendover—whom I know to be innocent of the charge of which he was found guilty—until such time as my action is confirmed. He will command this Fort.

"There will be no surrender, Breckinge," he added.

Again Breckinge rose to his feet and, apparently plucking up courage and attempting protest, began:

"I shall not accept . . ."

"Nobody asked what you would accept," interrupted Hazelrigg. "You will be under open arrest, and you will hold no communication whatsoever with any of the garrison except the sick and wounded; and you will not leave this room except to carry on your medical duties."

The tramp of feet was heard outside the door, and the Havildar entered, followed by a *naik* and a squad of sepoys.

"Good," said Hazelrigg. "Line up over there and stand easy until I come back."

"Now Breckinge," said he in English, "these are the 'mutineers,' one of whom you talked of shooting. Stay where you are until I come back—and don't talk to them. Understand?"

And he gave further orders in Pushtu to Shere Khan who received them gladly.

"Don't do anything foolish while I am out of the room, Breckinge, for your own sake," he added, nodding towards Shere Khan. "Come on, Wendover, and we'll rig ourselves out for the next act."

The remaining Officers' Quarters yielded all that was required, though the largest tunics were somewhat tight for Hazelrigg.

"You had better have this one when I push off, Wendover," he said, "but the one you've got will do for the present. You look all right in that."

"What about appearing in shirt and shorts with stars on the shirt shoulder-straps?" said Wendover, as he hastily shaved in cold water, with a dead officer's razor.

"No. Better have the tunic, I think, even if it's not too good a fit. It isn't a General's Inspection, after all.

"Gad, what a small head poor Denbrough had," he observed as he put on the late Major Denbrough's helmet.

"Or else what a fat one you've got," replied Wendover.

"Let me try that one . . . Ah, that's better. You can have it afterwards, with the tunic. Now then, what about boots? Amazing how much more of a man one feels, with boots on. It's what I miss most when I go native."

"Same here," agreed Wendover. "Good job young Henderson was a tall man."

"Lord, I can't get into these. Wonder if Henderson had a spare pair?"

"Must have done."

A few minutes later, Major Bartholomew Hazelrigg and the *ci-devant* Captain Wendover returned to Breckinge's room, correctly and fully dressed as British Officers on active service, in lace-up brown boots, putties, shorts, tunics with rank-badges on their shoulder-straps, regulation khaki shirts and regulation khaki ties, Kitchener helmets, Sam Brown belts, sword-frogs and revolver holsters.

The sepoys stiffened to attention and stared in stolid amazement.

Hazelrigg addressed them.

"Listen, men. There has been an arrangement, a plan on the part of the Sirkar, to fool and defeat the enemy. Relief is coming soon; and if it were not, I know that you are the sort of stout *bahadurs* who'd fight to the last. Havildar Umrao Singh will give me your names, and I shall recommend you all for promotion to *naik* as quickly as possible.

"Now then, Captain Wendover Sahib is going to take over command of the Fort. I am going out to play a trick upon the enemy and to hasten the relief. The enemy shall not take Fort Giltraza. The Captain Sahib will defend it from within, and I shall be helping it from without. Remember that, and be of stout heart, if many more days go by and the enemy seem to prevail. But they will not. Dismiss, Havildar, and give my salaams to the Subedar-Major Saheb and tell him I wish to see him here."

The sepoys clattered out, the light of new hope entirely changing the weary expression of their gaunt faces.

The sight of Hazelrigg and Wendover dressed and accoutred as British Officers had had a prompt and powerful effect on Breckinge.

When they had gone from the room dressed as Pathans, he had seemed to be recovering something of his manhood, plucking up a little spirit and gaining some control of his nerves.

Now it was evident that he realized the hopelessness of his position and fully understood that he was lost. Here, before him, was the first of those judges who would try him, convict him, condemn him and sentence him to he knew not what. Here were his accusers, provided with irrefutable evidence. And one of them was his former victim, the man whom he had thought to be dead, the man whom he had brought to ruin and disgrace—now re-habilitated, re-instated.

Again a rigor of trembling seized him.

"Before the Subedar-Major comes, Breckinge," said Hazelrigg as the last sepoy closed the door, "I think I ought to inform you that he was not a loyal and trustworthy accomplice. As I said before, I don't want to deceive you and take advantage of your position, and there is no need for me to do so."

And placing his hands upon the table, leaning his weight upon them and approaching his face towards that of the trembling Breckinge, he added, with mien and voice of the utmost solemnity, gravity and significance:

"I *have had a talk with him*, Breckinge."

"But he never knew. He never knew," began Breckinge. "I swear to you, Major . . ."

"No, he didn't actually know the nature of the drug. I don't pretend that he did; but he knew perfectly well that you administered it, didn't he? You had better confess, Breckinge. It's the one chance you have of, in any way, mitigating the severity of your punishment."

Breckinge stared idiotically, opening and closing his mouth without making a sound.

"Besides," added Hazelrigg, "it's about the one and only thing that you could do to improve my opinion of you.

"Or," he added significantly, "to change my attitude towards you. At the present moment, I fully admit, I am all for the utmost rigour of the law."

A quick look of intelligence came into Breckinge's eyes.

What was this? A hint that this terrible man Hazelrigg might possibly be inclined to bargain with him, might offer something in return for an admission? Possibly let him get away with it? His defences would be down, his cards would be on the table, once he had made the confession, but what of that, if he got something in return? Clearly Hazelrigg knew enough to destroy him completely, apart from his catching him out, in the matter of the surrender of the Fort.

Yes, he was utterly done for, if it came to a Court-Martial, with Hazelrigg giving evidence against him. There could be neither help nor hope. Nothing could save him. Whereas if Hazelrigg offered anything, promised anything, he would keep his word. Better get what he could out of the wreck. Better something than nothing. But he must keep a hold upon himself, must not go to pieces; and above all, he must walk warily, must not be precipitate.

Yes. Better something than nothing. He might save his life if that were in danger; might save himself from gaol; might even escape scot-free, if he bargained well —with proof of Wendover's innocence as purchase-price. He might. But—he'd wait and see what the Subedar-Major said.

The door opened and that officer entered.

The sight that he beheld struck him almost as a

blow.

He could not believe his eyes as he stared at a British Officer, a Major of the Indian Army.

"*Jadu!*" he whispered. "*Jadu!* It is magic."

And then as he glanced at the other figure in khaki, he shrank back, his face taking that tinge which, in a European, would be a loss of colour and a paling to whiteness.

"It's a *bhut!*" he whispered. "It is the ghost of Captain Wendover Sahib."

Hazelrigg addressed him sharply in Hindustani.

"Now then, Subedar-Major Saheb," said he, "what have you got to say for yourself? Is this the way you carry out the Sirkar's orders; obey the last instructions of Major Denbrough Sahib? Is this how you uphold the *izzat* of your Regiment, and of the Indian Army? What have you got to say for yourself? Nothing?"

"It is the Pathan, Ghulam Hyder!" murmured the astounded officer.

Yes, the Major Sahib had made his way into the Fort disguised as a Pathan. For though he wore Major's uniform, and obviously was a Sahib, he still had the beard, and, beneath his helmet, the shaggy hair, of Ghulam Hyder. But the Subedar-Major had often seen British Officers with beards and shaggy hair, on active service.

But the other!

The other was Captain Wendover Sahib himself.

Almost exactly as he used to be.

How had he got into the Fort?

This was witchcraft, devilry, magic. There was no end to the cleverness of the Sahibs.

"Well, what have you got to say for yourself?" snapped Hazelrigg. "There is nothing to say, is there? You are caught in the act of trying to . . ."

"Sahib . . . I . . . It was the Doctor Sahib's order . . ."

"Oh, you are trying to shift the responsibility on to the doctor, are you? Aren't you the Subedar-Major, commanding the men of this garrison since the last British Officer was killed? Aren't you the Senior Officer, and isn't the doctor—the doctor?"

"Sahib, Doctor Breckinge Sahib is a Captain Sahib and ranks above me. It was he . . ."

"And suppose, when the doctor told you to surrender you had replied:

"'*You are the Doctor Sahib. I shall not surrender this Fort at your order.*' Do you suppose that you, the Subedar-Major, the officer in command of the sepoys, would have been punished for disobeying the doctor?"

"Sahib, it was an order."

"Then what about Havildar Umrao Singh? He had an order, and from you, his own officer. But he refused to obey it, and said that several of his men would support him, and would also refuse to obey it . . . Now then; what do I do, do you suppose? Punish him, or see that he is promoted, rewarded, decorated? Well?"

The Subedar-Major's eyes fell.

"Sahib, it was an order," he said again. "The Doctor Sahib said the lives of the men must be saved."

"It's a lie," cried Breckinge springing to his feet. "It's a *banao*. You said the men could not fight any longer, and that you'd have to surrender, and that the best thing was to get terms. It was you who first spoke of surrender, and I said it was your business to defend the Fort and mine to look after the wounded."

The Subedar-Major turned, scowling, to Breckinge.

"Those are not true words," he said. "My brothers are witnesses to . . ."

"Yes, there are too many 'brothers' here, altogether," interrupted Hazelrigg. "Is that all you've got to say before I put you under arrest?"

"It was the Doctor Sahib's order," repeated the Subedar-Major, doggedly and sullenly, once again.

"You are a liar," cried Breckinge again. "You came to me and said . . ."

"Look here, aren't you both forgetting that I was Ghulam Hyder the Pathan, and heard all that was said?" interrupted Hazelrigg.

"I mean, before you came, Sahib. Before you came as Ghulam Hyder," replied the Subedar-Major. "The Doctor Sahib sent for me and said we must surrender, and that we must send a messenger to the Hadji."

"You liar!" screamed Breckinge.

"Oh, he's a liar, is he?" observed Hazelrigg. "And was he lying about what happened at Ubele?"

Breckinge's glance fell as the Subedar-Major, with a quick glance at Hazelrigg, uttered an exclamation.

What had the Doctor Sahib admitted to this devil of a Major Sahib? Had the doctor told a foul lie about that, too, and brought false accusation against his faithful friend and . . . helper?

And as, almost insanely, he bit at his finger-tips, Breckinge similarly wondered. What had this scoundrel already said to Hazelrigg, incriminating Breckinge, in order to exculpate himself? Had he admitted knowledge of the drugging of Wendover? And when had Hazelrigg talked with the Subedar-Major? While he was out of the room, changing from Pathan dress to uniform?

What had been said? . . . What had been said? Where was he? He was in the dark. What should he do? What should he say?

"Sahib, I don't know what the doctor said about what happened at Ubele," replied the Subedar-Major, "but if he said that I knew anything of the putting of *dawa* in Captain Wendover's Sahib's *khana*, it is false."

"Then how do you know that something was put in his food?" snapped Hazelrigg.

The man looked utterly confused.

"Sahib . . . afterwards . . . he told me . . . I didn't know that he was going to do it or I would have warned the Captain Sahib. I didn't know. I . . ."

"Come with me," ordered Hazelrigg curtly. "Stay where you are, Breckinge."

"Major Hazelrigg, I . . ."

"Hold your tongue.

"I'll leave him to you, Wendover," he added grimly, as he led the way from the room and into the neighbouring one, which had been Major Denbrough's.

"Now then, Subedar-Major," said he, closing the door. "You are in a very dangerous position. First of all, you try to surrender this Fort . . ."

"Sahib, I didn't wish . . ."

"Silence. Listen to me. First of all, you were, at any rate, willing to accept Captain Breckinge's order to surrender this Fort, instead of refusing, as a brave man would have done. In the second place, you admitted that you knew that Captain Wendover Sahib was drugged when he was accused of being *béhosh* through drinking too much *sherab*, and you gave false evidence at the Court-Martial."

"Sahib, it was afterwards that I came to know about it."

"Well? And did you immediately go to your Colonel and tell him the truth? You know perfectly well that a man who is an accessory after the fact is as bad as one who is an accessory before it. To know afterwards, and say nothing, is as bad as to know beforehand and to say nothing."

"Sahib, I feared that . . ."

"Yes, you are great at fearing. Now listen to me. Your one chance of saving yourself from prison and disgrace, with the loss of your rank and your pension and of your *izzat* for ever, is to tell me all the truth, to make the fullest confession. As a matter of fact, if you don't do so, and I decide upon it, I can have you shot for cowardice."

Quickly the man knelt and placed his turban at Hazelrigg's feet, making a motion as of pouring dust upon his head.

"Mercy, Sahib," he whispered.

"That's all very well. Listen. If you want any mercy from me, you will tell me the whole truth; and after that, you will show that you are not what I think you are, a coward as well as a rascal. This Fort is not going to surrender. It is going to fight until the relief comes. You are going to be Court-Martialled after the relief, and a full confession *now* will be your chance, your only chance, of getting any mercy from me. Now then, out with it."

And the badly frightened man gabbled his confession.

But in spite of physical weakness and mental strain; in spite of the terrible shock he had suffered at the discovery that Ghulam Hyder was a British field-officer; that Captain Wendover was alive; and the fact that this terrible man had caught him in the act of trying to surrender, his admissions were both garbled and guarded.

Nevertheless, it was abundantly clear that he was perfectly well aware that Wendover had never been in the habit of drinking to excess; had not been drunk when found unconscious at Ubele; and that the state in which Wendover had been found, was entirely due to "treatment" by the doctor.

What, even in his extremity of misery and fear, the Subedar-Major would not admit, was that he was a party to, and an accessory before the fact of, the deliberate drugging of Captain Wendover.

Nevertheless, Hazelrigg obtained his completest admission that he knew that Wendover did not drink; had never been drunk; and that, after the Court-Martial, he had learned that Wendover had been rendered unconscious by the use of a drug. How this interesting information had been received he could not say; and when Hazelrigg corrected that form of words to '*would* not say,' though agitated, confused and desperate, he professed to be wholly unable to remember how he had come by the knowledge.

Hazelrigg summed him up as a man of character and standards far inferior to those of the average Native Officer; far more cunning than clever; and, though probably not a definitely despicable scoundrel like Breckinge, a fairly worthy friend, disciple and confederate of the abler and wickeder man.

Nor did Hazelrigg feel that there was anything to fear from the Subedar-Major's gang-loyalty and staunchness; from his fidelity to his leader in rascality. He was certain that, could he bring about a position where the man must either sacrifice Breckinge or suffer equally with him, there need be no doubt as to his line of action.

"So it comes to this then, Subedar-Major, on your own admission, that you at any rate knew of the *banao*; you knew, either before or afterwards, that

Captain Wendover had been drugged. You knew perfectly well who did it, and why that person did it. For reasons of your own—not unconnected with the fact that you were under threat of Court-Martial—you said nothing. Well, that's pretty bad. Bad enough to ruin you absolutely.

"And on top of that you, as responsible officer temporarily in command of the Fort, wished to surrender it . . . Yes, yes, I know you want to put the blame on somebody else, but you cannot do it. Now then, the line that I shall take when this fighting is over, will be largely—very largely—determined by your effort to get justice for Captain Wendover and by your conduct during the remainder of the siege. As I have told you, Captain Wendover will be in command of the Fort. You will be his Second-in-Command, and he will report to me—and you know perfectly well that he will report with the utmost fairness—on the way in which you support him."

"Sahib, I will do anything . . ."

"Well, see you do it. Now then, I'm going to send for your two relatives. While they are present, don't speak, except to answer any question I may ask you."

The man looked up with pleading eyes.

"Sahib, there is one other thing. Suppose that, most unfortunately, Captain Wendover Sahib should die . . . be killed . . . during the siege."

"Then that will be just too bad—for you—Subedar-Major. That will be bad luck. For nothing on this earth can do you any good now, but your confession and Captain Wendover's personal report to me, that your conduct has been absolutely splendid. Not merely ordinary, good and correct carrying on of duty, mind, but worthy of the highest commendation. If he tells me you've really deserved special mention in despatches, and a decoration, I might consider letting that cancel out the rest—provided you make a full confession to me and speak the truth, at the proper time, about what happened at Ubele. Understand?"

It was clear that the Subedar-Major understood; and Hazelrigg felt that Wendover would be able to count upon the utmost that was in the Subedar-Major —for what it was worth.

After considering the man coldly and quite unfavourably for the space of a minute, he said:

"Come with me," and led the way to the room in which he had left Breckinge, Wendover and Shere Khan.

Opening the door, he discovered Breckinge sitting in a state of apparent collapse, his folded arms upon the table, his head upon his arms, his face concealed.

Watching him, with stony face, stood Wendover, while with a face anything but stony, Shere Khan gloated in triumph.

"Stand over there, Subedar-Major, and don't forget that I wish you to hold no conversation with your brother-in-law and other relative, nor to make any observation whatsoever except in answer to a question from me," ordered Hazelrigg.

And to the sentry who was closing the door, he called:

"*Oh, Sepoy! Subedar Sahib ko salaam do.*"

Raising his head, Breckinge stared in silent and abject misery at Hazelrigg.

Saluting, the sentry hurried off in search of Subedar Gopal Mangal, the Subedar-Major's brother-in-law.

When this man entered, a minute later, the shock that he received, as evinced by his physical start of surprise, would, at a less serious and tensely dramatic moment, have been ludicrous. Literally, he seemed unable to believe his eyes as they beheld two British Officers, one of whom was—no, could not be—yes, undoubtedly was—the long-dead officer who had been the victim of the plot at Ubele, Captain Wendover Sahib. His wide-eyed, gaping, open-mouthed look of amazement changed to a quick glance of anxious suspicion as he caught sight of his brother-in-law. Immediately he adopted an attitude of stolidity and impassiveness, assuming the Indian '*You-are-my-father-and-my-mother-I-am-a-poor-man-and-I-know-nothing*' look that Hazelrigg knew so well.

"Salaam, Subedar Saheb," said the latter coldly,

fixing the Native Officer's eyes with a hard and penetrating stare. "So you are the Second-in-Command of
this Fort—and equally willing to surrender it while still
defensible."

"Sahib, it was an order."

"Yes. Your brother-in-law's order."

"Sahib, it was the Doctor Sahib's order."

"Oh? Well—whosesoever order it was, you were
quite ready to obey it. I've heard no protest from you."

"Sahib it was an order and . . ."

"Yes. It was an order, and like a well-disciplined
soldier you accepted it without a word, and were prepared to obey it. You weren't like that mutinous fellow
Havildar Umrao Singh, were you?"

The man's glance fell.

"Anything to say?"

And again the man repeated the talisman that it
was a *hukm*.

"Well," replied Hazelrigg patiently, "I'm not holding
you responsible. I am merely observing that you made
no protest against the surrender of the Fort of which
you were Second-in-Command. You agreed with your
brother-in-law in this matter, exactly as you agreed
with him *in the other matter—at Ubele Fort*. Now . . ."

Breckinge sprang to his feet, uttered an inarticulate
sound, and sank back into his chair as Shere Khan
growled and motioned to him to be silent.

"Sahib . . . I . . ." began the Subedar.

"It's only fair for me to tell you, Subedar, that your
brother-in-law has made complete confession about
that. He has admitted to knowing that Captain Wendover was poisoned, drugged; that he was the victim of a
villainous and scoundrelly *banao*."

Sliding sideways, Breckinge slumped heavily to the
ground as he fainted.

The look upon the Subedar's face was now genuine
enough. Another quick glance at his relative, a moistening of lips, and a shocked and shame-faced quailing
before the accusing eye of this Officer who stood in
judgment.

"Sahib, I . . . I . . ."

"Well . . . ? Well . . . ? No, there isn't much to say, is there? Since your brother-in-law has confessed. I've got something to say, though; and it is this—that you haven't exactly shone and distinguished yourself by your stout-heartedness during the siege of this Fort. Also that you will hear some very unpleasant things, including a sentence, when a Court-Martial learns that you knew perfectly well, fully and completely, what happened at Ubele, and never said a word."

"Sahib, it was after . . ."

"It's no good, Subedar. You won't improve the position a bit, either by lying or by wriggling and twisting like a trapped snake. Even supposing, for one moment, you were speaking the truth, and you didn't know until afterwards, does that excuse you in the slightest degree for not immediately going to your Colonel and telling him what you had learned?

"Now listen. I am considering exactly what I shall do with you and your brother-in-law. What it will be I don't yet know, but I do know this. It will depend very much on your making a full confession to me, as your brother has done; on your conduct during the rest of this siege; on the support that you give to Captain Wendover; and the example you set to your men. In fact, what happens to you will, to a very great extent, depend on yourself and the report that Captain Wendover gives me."

And having puzzled, terrified and admonished the Subedar, Hazelrigg again opened the door of the room and bade the sentry give his salaams to the Jemadar.

To this man also, it evidently appeared that magic had been done, miracles worked, when before his astounded and incredulous eyes appeared two British Officers, both of whom must have impossibly materialized from within the Fort itself, and one of them returned from the dead.

Towards him, Hazelrigg was less severe but equally contemptuous, and by implication, contrasted his ready acquiescence in surrender with the refusal of the Havildar to obey his superior officer's orders.

Him also Hazelrigg accused of being accessory before or after the event, if not of actual connivance and complicity, in the matter of the plot against Wendover; and when he would have defended himself, told him that defence was vain, inasmuch as his relative, the Subedar-Major, and the Subedar had both confessed. As neither of these men denied it, but merely stood in dumb and shamefaced misery, making no attempt to defend themselves, the Jemadar accepted the rebuke both for his easy acquiescence in surrender and his guilty knowledge of the crime committed at Ubele against Wendover.

Justified of his faith in his ability to obtain partial confession from the Subedar-Major, more comprehensive admission from the Subedar and even less guarded admission from the Jemadar, Hazelrigg, with final exhortation, bade them go, and from that moment change their own attitude, and strain every nerve to change that of their men towards the question of the continuation of the defence of the Fort.

"I shall shortly make the rounds," he concluded, "and shall have a word with every non-commissioned officer. I will then address one half of the men in the courtyard, while the others remain at their posts. When the latter are relieved, I will then speak to them also. And I shall have a word with each of the sick and wounded. I shall tell all the men that Captain Wendover Sahib has come to take command of the Fort, and to guarantee its successful defence until the arrival of the Relief Force, and final victory. You may go."

Breckinge sat up and stared stupidly about him.

"Now then, Breckinge," said Hazelrigg when the Native Officers had departed. "I think I have, to some extent, undone your good work; and I don't think we shall hear any more of defeatism and surrender. Now listen to me.

"If it comes to my knowledge that you say one more word in that direction to anybody, I will have no mercy on you; and I will take prompt and drastic action. You know what I mean, don't you? Now about the other matter.

"The Subedar-Major, your accomplice, or tool, has

given you away about what happened at Ubele. I am going to have that in writing. You heard what his relatives have said. I will have their depositions in writing, too.

"I have held out to them a little hope of there being some chance of their improving their position somewhat, by their conduct during the remainder of the siege. Also by doing their utmost to assist Justice afterwards, when the question of Captain Wendover's reinstatement arises; and when, in view of my report, a Court-Martial enquires into your conduct both here and at Ubele.

"I haven't the slightest doubt in my own mind that the three of them will be only too anxious to assist me in every way, also, when Captain Wendover's case is re-opened on the strength of my statement as to my discoveries, and my action in putting him in charge of the defence of Fort Giltraza.

"Now, I want you to grasp this clearly. I shall be leaving this place in an hour or two, alone, and shall not return until the relieving force arrives, when it will be too late for me to do anything for you—anything whatsoever—even should I be disposed to do so. You will remain in this room until I leave the Fort. Before I do so, I will come and ask you if you've anything to say.

"It will be your last chance of helping yourself," he added.

Leaving Shere Khan in charge of the situation, Hazelrigg then returned with Wendover to the adjoining room. Closing the door, he heaved a sigh of relief.

"Wendover, my son," he said, "we shall do it. We've got him. Now he thinks that the others have given it away, he'll make a clean breast of it and throw himself on my mercy. And I don't think he'll find I have got much of that in stock, until he has made a full confession—in writing."

"He'd never do that," said Wendover.

"Well then, if he doesn't, we've still got him. What with the fact of its being my word against his that he confessed verbally, and the evidence of the Native Officers, I don't think there can be a shadow of a doubt of your completest exoneration and reinstatement, even apart from the fact that you are going to save the situation here. Going to do all sorts of wonderful dags. England will ring with the story. There won't be a newspaper in the civilized world that won't have the account, both of the cruel wrong and of the brilliant exploit. My dear chap, it will be a front-page feature of every newspaper in the British Isles, India and the whole British Empire. And America, too. Talk about clearing your name! It'll be immortalized. You will not only be rehabilitated and reinstated, but reinstated in a blaze of glory."

Wendover smiled.

"My dear chap, I would hate to seem ungrateful, but do you know, I haven't the very slightest desire to be—er—immortalized. As to being reinstated . . . well . . ."

"Now, don't talk like that. Whether you want it or not, it's going to be done. And if you honestly don't care about glory for yourself, what about your friends?"

"Shere Khan and his family? They're my friends. And they don't . . ."

Hazelrigg seized Wendover by the shoulder and shook him.

"Come on," he said; and the drooping spirits of the garrison of Fort Giltraza were galvanized to new life by the incredible apparition of two British Officers making the rounds at *Stand-to*, with a cheery word to each man they passed.

After complete inspection, Hazelrigg, in the presence of Wendover and the Native Officers, addressed the sepoys at two parades, praising them for their defence of the Fort, telling them that the siege was practically over, that relief was at hand, and that all they had to do was to put up a stout defence for the few remaining days. What they must do for the short time of danger, trial and hardship that remained, was to keep sharpest watch and ward; to fight desperately if the Fort were attacked again; and to see to it that all they had undertaken was not brought to nought through the capture of the Fort almost in the very presence of the relieving force. But that of course would not happen.

And it was a force endowed with new life, hope and courage that resumed the defence when dismissed to carry on.

Nor was the effect of the visit of the British Officers to the miserable hospital less marked. To most of the wounded and stricken sufferers, it seemed that the relief had come; and nothing was said to disillusion them. Let those who must die, die the happier; and those who might recover, recover the more quickly.

Anyhow, British Officers had entered the Fort, and if all were not now well, it soon would be.

And having accomplished everything that could be done, Hazelrigg bade Wendover take over full command of Giltraza Fort.

"I'll see Breckinge again, before I change my kit," he said.

An orderly approached and saluted, saying that the Doctor Sahib sent his salaams.

"He sent you?" asked Hazelrigg.

"*Nahin*, Sahib," replied the man. A sepoy standing outside his door had called him and told him that the Doctor Sahib wished to speak to the Major Sahib.

"That's interesting," observed Hazelrigg to Wendover. "Looks hopeful. I wonder if he wanted to come out, and Shere Khan wouldn't let him. Anyhow, he has got something to say. I'll see him alone. Then I'll change back to Ghulam Hyder, and have a word with you at the gate before I go back to the Hadji."

"But I say," expostulated Wendover, "is it safe to . . ."

"Safe?" smiled Hazelrigg.

"But I mean . . . well, what are you going to tell him?"

"Why, that the wicked people in here covered us with rifles, heard what I had got to say, and kept the other two as hostages."

"So the idea will be that Breckinge is still commanding the Fort and has pinched a couple of the deputation, eh? A dirty trick."

"Yes," agreed Hazelrigg, "the Hadji's respect for him will go up enormously."

"Why not stay inside? Stop here till the end. Why not stay here till the relief comes."

"Because I can do more good outside. Besides," he grinned, "the relief may not come at all, my son. I am not going to be bottled up here and done in, along with you."

"In fact, you mean me to have the credit of defending the place, eh? Noble in failure and glorious in death —or a brilliant success, eh? Whitewashed either way," laughed Wendover.

"Gold-washed," corrected Hazelrigg.

"No, that's not it. Not a bit of it," he continued. "Don't flatter yourself that I'm considering you in the least. You keep the works going here until I have brought off the job outside," and turning away, he crossed the courtyard of the Fort to the entrance of the corner tower in which the Officers' Quarters were situated.

§3

Meanwhile, Breckinge, in a state of terror and panic bordering upon insanity, sat shaking and trembling as he avoided the fierce accusing eye of the gaunt giant who stood over him, his face, attitude and every movement a threat.

He remembered the brute now, the Pathan orderly whose outburst at the trial had amused him, had given him the satisfaction of knowing that the one witness for the defence had done the accused man more harm than good. Instead of doing his utmost to convince the Court that his master had never drunk to excess in all the years that he had known him, the best the jungly clown could do was to promise to murder witnesses for the prosecution.

Yes, a terrible and truculent ruffian and, like all Pathans, neither a respecter of persons nor of the sanctity of human life. No, a savage who would kill a man as willingly as he would an insect.

Had they left him here intentionally, to be his executioner as well as his gaoler? And of course he was armed. He could have half a dozen daggers and a Khyber knife under all that loose clothing . . . And after all, would that not be the best way out of it?

Death. What other way was there but death?

For he was caught . . . caught . . . caught.

These dogs of Native Officers had turned against him to save their own black hides.

And to curry favour with this man, Hazelrigg, in the hope of saving themselves, they'd implicate any of the other false-witnesses who were at Ubele and had not been killed here. They'd all hang together against him, and blame him. Say he had made them do it; and they had obeyed because he was the Doctor Sahib and they supposed he knew best. That sort of lying evasion . . .

And that she-devil Azizun. What had she told Hazelrigg? What *hadn't* she told him? What a fool he had been. What a mad fool to trust a dancing-girl, a *dasi*; to lay himself open to blackmail by a bazaar-woman; to let a creature like that know anything against him.

And how had this devil of a Hazelrigg got hold of her? It looked as though he himself wasn't above spending his time in the bazaar, too. But how could a white man become a *habitué* of Azizun's house, become sufficiently intimate with her to find out things like that? But doubtless he was one of those supermen, Secret Service marvels, who could pass as an Indian among natives, although pure European. Well, obviously he could, for he had not only taken-in him, Breckinge, as Ghulam Hyder the Pathan, but obviously he had fooled the Pathans themselves.

Yes, he must have frequented Azizun's house in the guise of a rich Afghan horse-dealer, a Turkoman carpet-merchant, an Arab pearl-broker, or something of that sort; and bought information from her; or perhaps frightened her by disclosing himself as an agent of the Sirkar, a policeman, or C.I.D. chief, or something of the kind.

Anyhow, he knew, obviously he knew, about Abdul Ghaffar, whose death in her house had caused the big scandal.

God alone knew what he hadn't found out.

He must be the Devil himself.

Doubtless he had handled her as he had these damned Native Officers; shown how much he knew or professed to know; and got further confessions from her by a mixture of threats and promises; so that, between fear and hope, she had told him, partly intentionally and partly unintentionally, all he wanted to know.

Still, who was going to believe the word of a bazaar woman, a notorious *dasi*?

No, but she could give him information that he could use, and by means of which he could get all the evidence he wanted, without any reference to its tainted source.

Yes, Azizun had evidently told Hazelrigg that she had drugged Abdul Ghaffar in order to get his famous pearl-bag, and had sworn, what was quite true, that she hadn't had the faintest intention of killing him. As she would point out to Hazelrigg, why should she? She didn't want a terrible scandal, the Police in the place, and the risk of a gaol sentence, not to mention a rope.

And evidently she had told Hazelrigg what they had put in Abdul Ghaffar's cups of coffee, and had also told him the name of the man from whom she had obtained it. She'd point out that the fact that she was innocent of any intention to kill the man was quite obvious from the fact that she had asked Breckinge for some drug that would render Abdul Ghaffar completely insensible without killing him.

Then Hazelrigg had put two and two together, and jumped to the conclusion that the same thing had happened to Wendover. Which it had. Only that in Wendover's case the drug had been carefully administered in the proper doses. Nor would clods like these military people on Courts-Martial ever understand that the whole thing was research, scientific experiment, the testing of most important theories by an authority on toxicology, who was devoting his life to the study of the action of combinations of poisons and narcotics.

Then Hazelrigg had bluffed the Subedar-Major into the belief that he, Breckinge, had made full confession, and that the Subedar-Major's one chance of pardon, or at any rate of amelioration of his position and mitigation of his sentence, would be to speak the truth and add his confession to that of Breckinge his confederate.

That was it.

And even suppose he got off on that charge; suppose, however strong suspicion might be, he was not found guilty—because no one had seen him introduce the drug either into Azizun's house or into Wendover's cooking-pot when he was inspecting the Ubele kitchen —there was quite enough to ruin him utterly in this Fort business, where undeniably Hazelrigg had fairly caught him.

He had obviously talked with Breckinge's messenger, and got evidence of Breckinge making private and personal overtures to the enemy; and he himself had received Breckinge's own agreement to surrender, and his own assertion that he had the power to make the Native Officers follow his example.

No, he hadn't a chance, and this last charge would weigh heavily against him with a Court-Martial that was considering the question of his guilt in the matter of Wendover at Ubele.

And then the death of Abdul Ghaffar at Madrutta. Why, that might be a hanging matter; and certainly the drugging of his superior officer, followed by his charge —and his medical evidence—of drunkenness, would be a gaol matter.

And now this last? Surely that might be a shooting matter. High treason or something of the sort. No, probably not that. But they shot men for cowardice in the face of the enemy in time of war.

But no, no; his fears were getting the better of his common sense. He wasn't a combatant Officer, and they couldn't punish him with anything more than dismissal, for abandoning the sick and wounded, could they?

But oh, the awful publicity, disgrace and shame. It would mean utter ruin.

Only dismissal! Better death than the unthinkable degradation of that. His name a by-word. It would be the worst case ever known in the . . . No, unthinkable. Better death.

Death. Yes. That was the real escape. Sudden, swift and painless.

And it would fool them, too. No proof that Wendover was innocent.

Death. Yes. What about the sort of dose that Abdul Ghaffar had had? And then sleep; prompt, painless oblivion; and no waking. Overdose of a sleeping draught, really.

And suppose he did wake? But he wouldn't. He had experimented fully enough to make sure of that. It was the fool Azizun's own fault that Abdul Ghaffar had died in her house. If she had done what he had told her, "followed the directions on the bottle," in short, Abdul Ghaffar would have awakened after thirty-six or forty-eight hours of apparently drunken coma, none the worse, except for a head and a mouth and a hang-over.

And the dose he had given Wendover had been absolutely accurate. It had acted perfectly. Suppose he gave himself double that dose; there would be no fear of waking, nor would there be any pain.

That was it, escape.

He'd escape them yet, himself unpunished; and themselves no better off. For nothing could really exonerate Wendover, except Breckinge's own confession. Their case would fall to the ground if they attempted to bring it and win it on the strength of the evidence of the Subedar-Major and his relatives.

For after all, they could prove nothing; they knew nothing; no one saw him do it; and all they could say would be lies . . . lies . . . lies . . .

And suddenly, to the surprise of the stolid Shere Khan, the unbalanced tortured man struck his forehead violently with his fist.

Fool that he was! Fool, fool, in his fool's Paradise. Where was he to get the drugs he wanted? Why hadn't he brought a supply of *tafu* and *dhatura* with him?

But whoever would have supposed that he would have wanted it here in Giltraza when, so far as he knew, he hadn't an enemy in the world, and war was the last thing of which anyone thought? How was he to suppose that he should ever be contemplating suicide?

But there were other things. There were other things, painless and swift. Cyanide of potassium; there was a stock of that, thanks to photographic work. There was some morphia.

He rose to his feet.

"I want to go to my other room. Dispensary," he said in Hindustani.

"Doubtless," sneered Shere Khan.

And the smile and the tone of his voice left no doubt as to his meaning.

"I must go to the '*ispital.*'"

"Doubtless," agreed Shere Khan. "Doubtless you will, before long. To the *ispital.* Then to the gaol. Then to the gallows."

Was this why they had left the ruffian here—to watch him, because they feared he might commit suicide? Would they prevent him? Would they deliberately keep him alive?

The devilish cunning; the brutality!

"Go and tell the Major Sahib I wish to speak to him."

"Anything else?" enquired Shere Khan.

"Didn't you hear the Major Sahib say he wished me to speak to him when I was ready."

"*O, Sipahi!*" called Shere Khan, "*ither ao,*" and as the sentry opened the door, bade him give salaams to the Major Sahib and tell him that the Doctor Sahib wished to speak to him.

CHAPTER IV

As Hazelrigg entered Breckinge's room, he found Shere Khan standing with folded arms; smiling still, and still unpleasantly, as he regarded the cowering figure of the man who had so grievously injured his friend and master, and about whose throat his sinewy hands were itching to close.

"Well, Breckinge," said Hazelrigg coldly. "You want to speak to me?"

"Yes, Sir. Send this man away," replied Breckinge.

Hazelrigg bade Shere Khan join Wendover, whom he would find near the gate.

"Are you going to take my advice and do the only possible thing, Breckinge?" Hazelrigg enquired as the door closed.

"What about? What about?" gabbled Breckinge, gnawing at the knuckle of his forefinger like a dog at a bone. "You accuse me of surrendering this Fort when I am only the doctor attached to the garrison. You bring a ridiculous charge against me about being concerned in the death of some wretched Arab in a Madrutta brothel. You say that, years ago, I was responsible for Wendover being found drunk. Man! Didn't Colonel Maldon find him? . . . Didn't he have a fair trial, I say, man? I am ill, I tell you, I'm ill. I want to go and get some medicine."

"I don't wonder you're ill, Breckinge, and I don't doubt you'd like to go and get some medicine. I can quite understand that you'd like to take some of the 'medicine' that you've given to other people, including Abdul Ghaffar and Captain Wendover."

"I tell you I . . ."

"Yes, and I'm telling you something. You are going to take your medicine all right, but I'm going to administer it. If you don't like it, there's one way in which you can avoid it. And that is, write a confession of what you did at Ubele."

272

"Confession of what I did at Ubele? What do you mean?"

"Don't be a fool, Breckinge—and don't waste time. I'm in a hurry. Now pull yourself together and concentrate on this. Get it clearly in your mind. If I leave this Fort without your confession, nothing on earth can save you from a long sentence of penal servitude, or worse—if hanging is worse than penal servitude. It's a matter of taste. Personally I'd I sooner be dead than in prison for life."

"Dead. Dead. Yes, *dead*!" shouted Breckinge hysterically. "And that's what I want to be."

"No doubt. But you are not going to be, until I have your statement, or until you have faced a Court-Martial. And you know what that'll mean."

"Major, I . . ." began Breckinge, and to Hazelrigg's astonishment, burst not only into tears but a torrent of Hindustani, an impassioned appeal for mercy, couched in the language of his childhood, of his mother, of his sweeper grandmother; a reversion to type indeed.

Hazelrigg, his thoughts upon the devilishly cruel deed that had ruined the life of his friend, eyed him unmoved.

"Mercy!" he said, as the prayer ended in a sob. "What mercy had you on a man whose boots you weren't fit to clean? What mercy had you on the wretched Abdul Ghaffar? And on the woman Amelie Pereira, the Eurasian nurse-probationer whom you got into trouble when you were House Surgeon at the Dufferin in Madrutta?"

Quickly Breckinge looked up, as his jaw fell.

What was this? What *didn't* this devil know?

"She died, didn't she? Under your medical care. Died in her sleep. Like Abdul Ghaffar did. Yes—your little friend Nurse-Probationer Pereira was going to have a baby. So she died, eh, Breckinge?"

"Major," whispered Breckinge hoarsely, "let me die, too, I beg you, implore you, *let me die!*"

"I haven't the slightest objection to your dying. In fact, I think you'd be far better dead. But you don't die, unless it's on the gallows, until you've admitted that you drugged Captain Wendover."

"Major, I admit it. I admit it. *I did give him a drug*, a very, very clever . . ."

"Why did you do it?"

"Because I hated him, damn him! Who's *he*, that he should be so superior? Who am *I* that he should despise me? Why was he always finding fault with me?"

"Probably because you gave him cause. But there's more to it than that. Nobody—not even your sort—does a thing like that because fault is found with him."

"He treated me like dirt, I tell you. Always so superior. Half the time, you'd think I wasn't there. You'd think I was mud. Who was he to look down on me? And he stole my girl! She loved me till he came. Then she looked down on me—as he did. Who were they to look down on me? *My grandfather was a British General.*"

"Yes? I should think he's proud of you."

Hazelrigg's hard streak was definitely in evidence.

"Grandson of a British General, eh? Well, pull yourself together and act accordingly. You've lived like a reptile—now see if you can't die like a man, since you are talking about dying. Do the decent thing by Wendover, and then die if you want to. Die like the grandson of a British General, since you are one!"

"Let me die! Let me die!" moaned the broken half-demented wretch again.

"Believe me, Breckinge, I shan't hinder you, once you've made what amends you can. You wouldn't die without doing that, would you—you . . . *you General's grandson?*"

"You'd use the confession. You'd use it against me."

"Of course I should use it. What do you think? But that needn't worry you. You'd know nothing about it."

"My name . . . my reputation . . ."

"Well, what price those, when it comes to being Court-Martialled for desertion of your sick; for cowardice, and for treason; and then tried by a civil court for murder? What about your reputation then, Breckinge?"

"Let me die," moaned Breckinge, and there was that in his voice which showed Hazelrigg that he had won.

"Got any writing materials here?" he asked quickly.

"There are some temperature-charts in that *yak-dan*."

"Pen and ink?"

"Here's an indelible pencil," replied Breckinge sullenly, fumbling in the breast pocket of his tunic.

"Get a chart. One'll be enough."

Breckinge obeyed.

"Now then, write as I dictate. Head it *Giltraza Fort* and the date. Write this—and write small:

"I, Captain Alexander Breckinge I.M.S. do hereby fully and freely confess that I introduced a drug into Captain Wendover's food at Ubele Fort, thereby rendering him unconscious, and apparently drunk, for about twenty-four hours. He was found in this condition by Colonel Maldon, Court-Martialled, found guilty and cashiered. I gave evidence that he was in the habit of drinking to excess, and I suborned the Native Officers of the garrison to give similar evidence, all of which was entirely false. I never knew Captain Wendover to drink alcohol except in extreme moderation, and I never heard of his doing so. I never saw him drink, even at meal times; and it is my sincere belief that he drank only one peg of whisky, as a pick-me-up, each night. He is wholly innocent of the charge that was brought against him, and I alone am responsible for the condition in which he was found.

"That's about what we want," observed Hazelrigg. "Let me read it . . . Yes, that meets the case, I think. Now we'll have your signature witnessed."

And calling to the sentry, Hazelrigg bade him give his salaams to the Subedar-Major Saheb and tell the Pathan that the Major Sahib wanted him.

Should he also send for Wendover and give him his great moment of complete triumph? No. It should not be said that Wendover had any hand in the obtaining of this confession, and Wendover wasn't of the type that takes much stock in great moments of complete triumph.

In fact, he rather gave the impression of a man who had completely finished with triumphs, was indifferent to the opinion in which he was held by his world, and careless as to his fate and future.

Out of that calm indifference, not to say dull apathy, he must be stirred—for it was unnatural, deliberately cultivated.

Nevertheless he would not send for him now; and when the time arrived to bid him triumph, he should find it to be a time when all men, while deeply sympathizing with him and deploring his cruel fate, proclaimed him a hero; admiring his fortitude under adversity and his courage in time of trial. And if he died in the defence of this Fort, as well he might, to prove him innocent and rehabilitate his memory should be one of the main objects of Hazelrigg's life.

The Subedar-Major, followed by Shere Khan, entered.

"I want you to hear me read this confession, for two reasons, Subedar-Major Saheb," he said. "First because I wish you to witness its signature, and second because it will give you a good idea of the sort of form in which your own confession should be written—if I require you to write one. Understand me?"

"*Han*, Sahib," mumbled the Subedar-Major.

"Listen then," and first in English and then in Hindustani, Hazelrigg read the document.

"Sign it please, Breckinge, with your usual signature, and then write, underneath, your full name and rank, Alexander Breckinge, Captain I.M.S., in case your signature is of the illegible variety.

"Now write at the bottom left-hand corner here, '*Signed in the presence of* . . .'

"Now, Subedar-Major, your signature."

And with a few scratches made from right to left, the Subedar-Major signed his name in Hindustani characters.

"Now, Shere Khan, I want you to witness this.

You've heard it in English, and now I'll read it in Pushtu," he continued, and proceeded to do so. Whereafter Shere Khan, writing also from right to left, made the hieroglyphics which represented his name.

"That'll do, thank you, Subedar-Major. I'll talk to you on this matter again later. You have my permission to go.

"Now then, Breckinge," he said, turning to where the Eurasian rested his head upon hands that covered his face, "You said just now that you wished to die. You've my full permission to die, how and when you like, and I shall take no steps to restrain you from doing so.

"In the completest certainty," he added, "that you will do nothing of the sort. Not you.

"Now then. You've made what little reparation can be made in the matter of Captain Wendover. See if you can make some in the matter of your conduct here as a responsible member of this garrison. Do your utmost for the sick and wounded, and don't forget that an important part of your duty is to do what you can to keep up the spirits of those who are still able to fight. A good report on your behaviour is the one thing that may dispose me to do what I can in your favour when the time comes."

"And what can you do?" groaned Breckinge. "If you produce that confession I'm done for, am I not?"

"You are, undoubtedly. But I could choose whether I would bring charges against you which would probably result in your being hanged or sent to penal servitude for life; or whether, on the other hand, I should bring such charges against you as would result merely in your being cashiered—as Wendover was.

"It's up to you, Breckinge. You can either make me the most bitterly relentless enemy, utterly vindictive and implacable; or you can make me a prosecutor disposed to let the accused down as lightly as possible in the circumstances, and to recommend him to mercy.

"And I can assure you that there will be a wonderful difference between the effect of the two attitudes."

Turning on his heel, Hazelrigg went from the room.

As he was about to close the door he looked in again and said:

"Don't forget that you are 'a General's grandson,' Breckinge."

CHAPTER V

A little later, the gate was cautiously opened, while the garrison anxiously watched for any signs of treachery.

Wah, wah! This was a man, this Major Sahib, who was so *hushyar*, so cunning, that he could utterly befool the *hushyar* and cunning Pathans themselves, masters of strategy, trickery and guile.

With a quiet:

"*Shahbash, my brothers,*" to the men about the gate, a "*Remember your destiny is in your own hands,*" to the Subedar-Major and—in English—to Wendover:

"So long, old chap. Happy days," Major Hazelrigg, once more the Compleat Pathan, Ghulam Hyder, marched forth, his hands held high, as one who would earnestly draw attention to the fact that there is not the slightest need to shoot him in the back.

Down the track leading from the Fort, he marched, dropped into a trench, scuttled along it, ran crouching behind *sangars* and vanished into the shelter of great rocks.

As he did so, heavy fire was immediately opened from all directions upon the Fort. But its defenders, having expected just that, presented no target.

Making his way to the cave which was the G.H.Q. of the Singing Hadji of Sufed Kot, Ghulam Hyder requested the watching surly sentry to announce his return. The sudden burst of fire having already done this, the Hadji appeared upon the spacious platform that stretched before the mouth of his cave to the edge of the *khud*.

"Come hither, oh man," he called, and seated himself cross-legged, his un-sacerdotal rifle athwart his lap.

"*Aré*, where are thy brethren, *ghazi*?" he jeered. "In chains or in Paradise? What has happened?"

"*Tobah! Tobah!*" exclaimed Ghulam Hyder. "Alas,

alas! The treacherous Infidel dogs. They have seized them, and they keep them as hostages."

"And what of the rush of the three brave *ghazis* upon the Sahibs? What of the slaughter of all in authority?" sneered the Hadji.

"Hadji Saheb," replied Ghulam Hyder, "who casts his rifle into the river? Who throws his life away for nothing at all? As we entered the gates, with our hands raised, men held their rifles a few feet away from our breasts. To die uselessly and in vain, we had but to move. Then, with men holding fixed bayonets that pricked the skin of my back, and others that held rifles almost touching my sides, I was taken to the room of the Sahib commanding the Fort. What could I do? To move was to die. Men with bayonets behind me, men with loaded rifles beside me, the Sahib with a revolver pointing at my heart. What could I do?"

"What did you do?"

"Fooled him. Gave him untrue answers. Filled his mind with false information."

"Such as?"

"The swift approach of great *lashkars* to join you, Hadji Saheb; of great stores of ammunition and rupees secretly sent to you by the Hadji of Turangzai, by the Kings of Munza, of Panel, of Mandol, of Putistan, of Mazristan, of regiments of the Ben-i-Israel, the fierce Duranis, ordered by the Amir of Afghanistan to march, without his knowledge, to your help."

"It is well," observed the Hadji. "And what of the Fort? Are not the garrison all *pasmandas*[33]—those who are not smitten with disease and wounded with our bullets?"

"Heavy is my heart and reluctant is my tongue, Hadji Saheb. But all is even as I told you but yesterday. Their feet are not tired. Behind their walls they are safe. They eat and grow fat. They laugh and sing and dance. While but few are upon the walls, many are making merry or resting below. Nor will they ever surrender."

"And why should they sing and dance when they

---

[33] *Men with weary feet.*

are ringed about by enemies who will surely slit their throats?"

"Because they have news, Hadji Saheb. News of the approach of British troops."

"And where will they be when the British troops arrive? In Hell."

"Allah grant it, Hadji Saheb; but I fear. And that is not the only news. An army of those thrice-accursed sons of noseless mothers who serve them for gold, those traitors of the Border who undertake to protect the Farungis' roads and keep the Farungis' peace in return for rifles and for money—a *lashkar* of them is coming to attack you."

The fingers that strayed in the Hadji's beard closed upon it in a grip.

"Who are they?" he asked.

"They did not tell me, Hadji Saheb, but undoubtedly they have news of them."

"How?"

"By the marvellous and incredible ways of the hell-doomed Infidel. Messages seem to come to them through the air when they have no *tar* wires."

"They are in league with the Devil," growled the Hadji.

"Doubtless."

"Well, what of the other two would-be were-not *ghazis*?"

"Hostages, Hadji Saheb. Should you assault the place again, they will hang them from the gate-tower."

"And thus will they obtain Paradise—perchance," observed the Hadji. "You have my permission to go. I will send for you later, and we will talk again."

Salaaming, Ghulam Hyder departed in search of others of the band whom he had led to the support of the *jehad* of the Singing Hadji of Sufed Kot.

As they huddled together about a cooking-pot, Ghulam Hyder conversed in whispers with a man, known elsewhere and at other times as Mahbub Ali, prominent and invaluable ornament of the Secret Service and past-master player of the Great Game.

"Well, that would make about twenty rifles in all, wouldn't it?" observed Ghulam Hyder. "Not enough really to make a useful diversion."

"No," agreed Mahbub Ali. "They couldn't do much in the way of an attack on the besieging force, but they might create a very useful distraction in the middle of a fight . . . Suppose I led them, with the other attackers, when an assault was being made on the great gate, and then suddenly we started shooting our poor brethren. It would throw that particular party into some slight confusion!"

"Yes. Done in the right way at the right moment, it might do some good. Might save the gate from being burned down, for example," agreed Ghulam Hyder. "But it would be almost certain death for the lot of you and . . ."

"And it is a game that can be played only once, of course. But our lives would be cheap at the price of the Fort," said Mahbub Ali.

Ghulam Hyder thought a while.

"No," he said at length. "I think we will scatter. All go in different directions, but generally east by south, each with a message and big promises to any Khan who might be useful, and bring a band of men. They know the Relief Force has reached the Tangit Pass. Gather them all together. And if they did nothing else, they'd look like an enemy *lashkar* coming."

"Yes, they would, especially when some of our people came in, one by one, and announced them to the Hadji as such."

"That's it. Then, when you send me word that a fair number have gathered together, I can come and talk to them, making promises of the benevolence of the Sirkar and the impossibility of the success of the Hadji, and get them to elect a leader."

"The Khan of Khairastan," observed Mahbub Ali.

"Yes, he should be here soon," agreed Ghulam Hyder. "Go you yourself and urge him on, Mahbub Ali. If his men and those of his confederation arrive secretly and in time, and make sudden onslaught while the Hadji is attacking the Fort, it would be well."

"Yes, very well," agreed Mahbub Ali. "The Hadji's men are getting discouraged. Much was hoped of you and the other two *ghazis*," he smiled, stroking his red beard, "and you have returned alone, with nothing accomplished. Now there will be no on-fall while the garrison is in utter confusion following upon the slaying of their leaders by the fanatical *ghazis*!"

Both men laughed.

Ghulam Hyder produced a *biddi* from beneath the side of his turban, lit it with an ember of the cooking-fire, placed it between the outer sides of his cupped hands, so that it projected where the bases of the little fingers met, and inhaled the smoke from between his thumbs in approved native fashion.

"Yes," he agreed, emitting a cloud of the stinking acrid smoke which always reminded him of his earliest days of vice when he smoked China tea in a pipe made with an acorn-cup and a straw; cigarettes of brown paper and dried clover; yea, of newspaper and bootlace —possibly a useful early initiation that stood him in good stead now, for but few Europeans can smoke the *biddi* in native style and with every evidence of appreciation of its undeniably peculiar and powerful flavour.

"Yes. I think the good Hadji is feeling depressed with what he knows of his losses, and what I've told him of the state of affairs inside the Fort."

"Natheless, he will make one more assault upon the place, I suppose, before he raises the siege," observed Mahbub Ali.

"I expect so. I'm afraid so," replied Ghulam Hyder. "I'm going to stay here for a while and do my best to discourage him, and to give any warning and information that I can to the Captain Sahib. I wish I could be in two places at once, Mahbub Ali, but I can do the next best thing—be in one place and send thee to the other. Soon I must go down to the Pass."

Mahbub Ali smiled.

"I will bring those who wish to help the Sirkar if the Sirkar is winning; and as quickly as it can be done," he said.

"If it can be done thou wilt do it," agreed Ghulam

Hyder. "Start at once. In the direction of Khairastan."

"And meeting them on the way," said Mahbub Ali, rising to his feet, "I will tell the Khan of Khairastan that his beloved son is now besieged in Giltraza Fort, and should he wish ever to look upon his face again, he must indeed hasten. That will make the lazy old devil hurry his weary feet."

CHAPTER VI

And with a speed incredible to those who have had no experience of the rapidity with which the spirit of the Oriental will rise with the hope and promise of success, and sink with the appearance and threat of failure, the mental attitudes respectively of besiegers and besieged underwent a change.

Within the Fort, the difference in the psychological atmosphere was almost as marked as that in the physical at the rising of the sun. The health of almost all improved. The general cast of countenance changed from morose gloom to smiling cheerfulness. The backs of weary men straightened almost visibly, their shoulders squared, their chests protruded.

As always, with the personnel of an Eastern force, the spirit of the leader was the spirit of the men; and that of the new Commandant of Giltraza Fort was one, not so much of hope, as of certainty, of victory; one of calm and confident self-reliance, and of belief in the worth and worthiness of his sepoys. Tireless, ubiquitous, strong, he never seemed to sleep; and every man felt that the eye of his Commander was upon him; that he was at his side; that he knew not only what the soldier did, but what he thought; that while he commanded them, led them, disciplined them, watched over them, thought for them, fought for them and with them, they could not and would not be defeated.

This was a Sahib. This was a man. And victory would be theirs. Of his tireless energy it was as though he gave every man a share.

And even the soul of Breckinge could scarce forbear to cheer, his mind forbear to admire and to approve. Cursing him, he yet wished that he could have been such a man as this. Was it his fault that he had sweeper blood? *Is it my fault that I am a da Sousa's son*? Damn and curse and smite and blast Wendover, for the English Sahib that he was.

285

Breckinge, after one brief interview, Wendover treated as he would have done any other Medical Officer attached to the garrison.

Immediately after the departure of Hazelrigg, he had entered Breckinge's room.

"Look here, Breckinge," he said. "We are in the same boat—again. Let's pull together so long as it floats. Do your damnedest for the sick and wounded, and I'll do mine for the others. While the siege lasts, at any rate, let bygones be bygones. Until we are scuppered or relieved, let us absolutely forget anything but the defence of this Fort and—er—start from scratch, what?"

"I shall do my best," replied Breckinge sullenly.

"Good. I'm sure you will."

"What's this about my being under arrest?"

"Nothing. I want you to carry on. With an absolutely free hand. Back me up, Breckinge, and—we'll talk again later."

Breckinge gazed sullenly at the ground.

"Come on, man. Here . . ."

And Wendover held out his hand.

Breckinge looked at it.

"Is there any need for heroics?" he growled, thrusting his hands into the side pockets of his tunic.

"None whatever, Breckinge," replied Wendover, eyeing him coldly. "As you please."

"As you please," he said again. "Carry on. You are not under arrest, open or close. Do your best. Outside the hospital as well as in. Do your damnedest and play the game; and I shall be—grateful.

"But," he added, as he turned to go, "if you don't, and you make trouble again, I'll shoot you myself, Breckinge. See?"

§2

For a time the siege continued monotonously, a weary round of routine duty, anxious watchfulness and slow but steady losses on the part of the garrison.

But suddenly this state of affairs was changed.

It was evident that something had galvanized the besiegers into renewed activity; probably, as Wendover hoped and tried to believe, the approach of a British relieving-force, or of a Pathan *lashkar* of doubtful intentions and yet more doubtful cordiality towards the Singing Hadji of Sufed Kot.

In addition to heavy morning and evening shooting, the daily volume of sniping fire increased, and there were evidences of a projected attack which was to be pushed home.

The moonless nights, which had hitherto been reasonably quiet, were now times of great activity, and each day's dawn saw a new *sangar* constructed during the hours of darkness; and each new *sangar* was nearer to the Fort.

One morning, the new *sangar* of the previous night was immediately opposite the main gates of the Fort; and evidently a considerable number of men must have worked with enthusiastic vigour, for this latest field-fortification was more of a redoubt than a mere *sangar* of piled boulders and stones.

From the fact that nothing whatsoever could be seen of the men who manned it, Wendover decided that there had been a busy night of digging as well as of stone-carrying and building.

Why should this new field-work be so big and strong and sited exactly where it was?

Very much more commodious than other *sangars* and trenches, it still could not be big enough to serve as the assembly-point for a large assaulting force; nor, armed as they were with excellent rifles, did the besiegers gain much, from the shooting point of view, by having this post a few yards nearer to the Fort.

What was the game?

It did not take Wendover long to decide; but he kept his counsel. There was no need to publish his conclusion and spread despondency and alarm a minute earlier than was inevitable.

It was thus with no surprise, but considerable misgiving, anxiety and doubt, that he received a report one morning from Havildar Umrao Singh that, during the night, there had been curious and inexplicable sounds; sounds that "came from nowhere"—in other words from a source and direction unidentifiable by the listeners.

That night Wendover heard the unmistakable noises of subterranean digging; and, lying prone with his ear to the ground, knew that his suspicions had been justified. The enemy was mining the main gate of the Fort, tunnelling from the new redoubt, and had almost reached their objective.

At any time now, a mine might be placed and exploded beneath their feet.

§3

Wendover decided that there was but one thing to be done.

They must make a sortie.

It was the only chance of saving the gate, and it was a poor chance.

Oh, for a half-company of fierce Gurkhas who would charge, *kukri* in hand. They'd go through that mob like a knife through butter, and hunt them back to their trenches. Oh, for fifty fighting Sikhs, burly, dour and determined. They'd show the Pathan something with the bayonet. Let him see how the Khyber knife stood up to that.

But these men were different. They had their virtues, undeniably, and they'd improved a lot recently, but there was no doubt about it, the Pathan had put their tails down for them, and man for man, they were inferior in strength and skill, if not in courage. Still, he could probably pick a score or so who would put up a good show; and undoubtedly Havildar Umrao Singh and his Section would acquit themselves like men; be almost as good as Ghurkas, Sikhs, Baluchis or Punjabi Mahommedans, and set an example to the rest.

It would be a bit of a forlorn hope, and they'd probably lose heavily; but the alternative was losing the Fort and everything else.

The Man of a Ghost

What about the Native Officers?

Better leave the Subedar-Major inside, in case anything happened to himself. After all, he was the most experienced soldier there; and he had learned his lesson. There'd be no more talk of surrender. Besides, he wasn't really equal to a physical rough-and-tumble, after a smart sprint. No, he'd have to stay inside. And his brother, Subedar Gopal Mangal? He should come. Give him a chance to distinguish himself and to set an example.

Yes, he'd take Subedar Gopal Mangal and Havildar Umrao Singh—those two good *naiks*—and a party of selected men, beginning with Umrao Singh's lot.

Hurrying, crouching, along the *banquette*, he found the Subedar-Major.

"I'm going to make a sortie, Subedar-Major," he said, "with the best and strongest of the men. If I don't come back, my instructions are, of course, *Carry on.* You will be in sole command—and responsible. Understand? Make no mistake about it, then. The relief force will be here before long. Let them find everything all right—and you will be a famous man. It's a chance that doesn't come to many soldiers, Subedar-Major . . . I am going to take Subedar Gopal Mangal and Havildar Umrao Singh and the best of the men. Most of them will come back, of course. Don't spare ammunition, until we are well into them. There will be a good chance to give it them hot, as we charge, for they'll be attending to us, and not firing at the loop-holes and embrasures. So back us up well."

Sending for Subedar Gopal Mangal and Havildar Umrao Singh who was in charge of the in-lying picket, he bade them quickly pick the best of the men, the strongest and the healthiest, and those with the best stomach for hand-to-hand fighting, to parade at once at the western postern, from which they were to pull away the buttressing baulks of timber and big stones that closed it.

He then went to the hospital and called the doctor to the door.

"Going to make a sortie, Breckinge," he said.

"Bound to be a rush of wounded. Make what preparations you can for them here; and get some stretchers down to the west postern, with half a dozen good men who can make themselves useful with any of the badly wounded we can lug away with us. You will know just what to do, won't you?"

Presumably silence gave consent, since Breckinge made no reply.

Wendover eyed him coldly, and then glanced at his borrowed wrist-watch.

"I shall open the postern in fifteen minutes, and probably the survivors will be back in ten more, walking wounded in less."

"And by the way," he added, ere he closed the hospital door, "Subedar-Major Ganga Charan will be in sole and responsible command, if I don't come back. Hearten him up all you possibly can. And the men as well. The Relief Force must be almost here."

And turning, he clattered down the rough wooden stairway, out across the courtyard and through the main building of the Fort to the little door in the western wall. Here, a working party was pulling away the materials of its temporary walling-up.

The work completed, Wendover bade the men fall in. He then divided them into two parties, the larger one under the Subedar, the other, a quarter the number, under the Havildar, and gave brief clear instructions. They were to file out through the postern, follow him round the wall and, having arrived at the corner from which the attackers of the main gate would be in view, were swiftly to extend and, at his signal, advance at the double.

As soon as they were seen and the redoubt-party turned to meet them, he would shout the order to charge, and they would do so with all their might. No rifle was to be fired. They had not come from behind their defences to shoot in the open. They were to charge the new *sangar* or redoubt, drive the enemy from it, and well beyond it, then retire to the redoubt and defend it until he gave the word to retire.

Once they were into the redoubt, Subedar Gopal

Mangal and his party were to keep up as heavy a fire as they could, to prevent the re-capture of the place.

Meanwhile, Havildar Umrao Singh and his party were to follow Wendover into the tunnel, and deal with the men who were mining. That would be bayonet work. As soon as he had placed the bags of gunpowder, fired the fuse and come out of the mine, the whole sortie-party would run as hard as they could back to the Fort, round the wall, and in at the postern door. Any man who was badly hit and could walk or crawl, was to get back to the Fort at once.

Having described the operation as simply and succinctly as he could, Wendover repeated his orders, and then bade Subedar Gopal Mangal describe exactly what his duties were.

It was plain that he quite understood that his business was to clear the redoubt, drive the enemy out, and keep them out while the others dealt with the mine itself.

Wendover then made sure that Havildar Umrao Singh understood what he had to do. Yes, he was to charge with his men, help bayonet the Pathans out of the redoubt, and when this was done and the rest of the party maintaining rapid fire, he and his men were to help the Captain Sahib to clear the tunnel of its occupants, so that he could place his charge and light the fuse.

That being done and the order being given to retire, he and his men would join the Subedar's party in a swift rush back to the Fort.

That was it. And speed would be everything. It must be a surprise attack. Within a minute of sighting the sortie party, the Pathans in the redoubt must be running for their lives, and the heavy fire of rapid-independent must prevent their return with reinforcements, until the work in the tunnel was completed.

Being satisfied that he had done all he could in the way of preliminary, Wendover bade the Subedar see that magazines were charged and cut-offs closed, and that no man had a cartridge in the chamber of his rifle, and that, with bayonets fixed, everything was ready for the party to leave the Fort.

He then hurried to the ammunition-magazine and taking a long hose-like roll of fuse, hung it round his neck, hoisted a fifty pound bag of powder on to his left shoulder and clasped another beneath his right arm.

But that would put him out of action as far as fighting was concerned. He ought to have his revolver-hand free . . . What about giving one of the bags to Havildar Umrao Singh and telling him to stick close to him? No, he had better leave him to look after the mine party. He'd give one of the bags to a selected sepoy. Better still—to Shere Khan, who would never forgive him if he left him out of such a lovely scrap as this promised to be.

Yes, he had better be in a position to use his revolver. Might make all the difference to the success of the somewhat forlorn hope, as the sortie would prob-ably fail if he were killed. And there would certainly be some hand-to-hand rough-housing before they got the redoubt and tunnel to themselves. Silly—to be unable to defend himself, at any rate until the redoubt was cleared . . .

Returning to the postern, he found that everything was ready, the men with bayonets fixed, and the pos-tern unfastened. To Shere Khan he gave one of the bags of powder and instructions to stick to him closer than a brother sticketh. Also to get a couple of the oil-soaked pine-flares that had been provided for emer-gency illuminations.

"Now then," he said in Hindustani, "who's going to win the Order of Merit? Come on."

And pulling open the gate he led the way.

Glancing back as he reached the south-west corner, he saw that the Subedar and Havildar were behind him, and the men in double file were following them closely.

It looked a pitifully small party to undertake so big a venture.

What a curiously exposed and naked feeling one had, here, outside the walls; and how much stranger it must seem to the rest, to find themselves outside after so many long weeks of confinement; for they had been cooped up in there three times as long as he had.

The very air seemed freer and fresher.

Of course it did. They were away from the appalling stench. That was probably what caused the wonderful difference.

How long the wall seemed.

Apparently they had not been observed from the southern side at all. Doubtless the attention of the whole Pathan force was concentrated on the main gate and the eastern side of the Fort.

He reached the south-eastern corner.

Now for it!

Turning to the little column behind him, he gave a signal to right turn into line. To left wheel. To extend. To double.

To Wendover's delight, the sepoys obeyed coolly and steadily, and the whole party was advancing in good order at a steady run before the enemy appeared to realize what was happening.

Suddenly there were loud shouts from the redoubt, heads appeared, men in incredulous astonishment exposed themselves recklessly.

"*Ch-a-a-a-r-ge*," roared Wendover; and himself dashed forward, his left hand steadying the heavy bag of powder on his shoulder, his right extended, pointing the way with his revolver.

Now your Pathan, be he Afridi, Mahsud, Mohmand or what not, is as brave as any man alive and, in his own place and manner, as well as in most others, is as good a fighting-man as any in the world.

But we all have our little fancies and dislikes, and the Pathan dislikes the bayonet. It isn't that, like some stout fighting-men, he has a distaste for cold steel. *Au contraire* his yard-long Khyber knife is his favourite weapon, and he will as soon face it as use it. But determined and deadly as he is at hand-to-hand fighting, he knows nothing of the art of parrying a thrust. With his sword-like knife he cuts and slashes, but does not thrust; and, being unaccustomed to the receipt of thrusts, has neither needed nor learned to parry one. So that against a well-used rifle-and-bayonet he has no chance. He does not understand it; he does not like it; and wisely he considers that the best thing to do with the opponent who uses such an outlandish weapon is to go away from him.

And as, with the greatest *élan*, the charge was pressed home, the defenders of the redoubt went away.

In the opinion of the charging, cheering sepoys, it was defeat, rout, flight. In that of the swiftly departing Pathans it was strategic withdrawal to a place where they could use the proper weapon, the rifle, in a proper manner: though had these khaki-clad servants of the Sirkar suddenly swept down upon them in this impetuous manner, waving Khyber knives, they would have dashed out and met them with Khyber knives and fought them on equal terms—he who got his slash in first being the better and the luckier man . . .

Over the breast-work of the demi-lune redoubt leapt Wendover, his men close behind him; and immediately all but he, Shere Khan, the Subedar, and the Havildar, flung themselves down behind the dry-stone wall which was very low on the side facing the Pathan position, and opened a heavy fire upon the fleeing and swiftly-disappearing enemy.

After a quick glance round, and seeing that, so far, all was going well, Wendover jumped into the big hole or pit that had been dug in the centre of the redoubt.

Yes, this was the entrance to the mine-shaft.

Taking the powder-bag under his arm, he made his way, crouching low, for some distance along the tunnel, still closely followed by Shere Khan carrying the other bag.

Should he make his way as far along the tunnel as he could go?

No, it would suffice if the explosion took place halfway between the redoubt and the Fort gate. A huge crater would result from the explosion, and the whole long roof of the shallow tunnel would undoubtedly cave in, as the result of the tremendous concussion and vibration. And even if it did not do so right up to the gate, the enemy would have to construct a new redoubt before they could use the small portion that would remain intact.

No, he mustn't go too far. It would be too funny for tears if he himself blew the gate in.

This would do. Dumping the heavy bag and bidding Shere Khan place the other beside it, he began to tamp the hundred-pound charge.

Were there any men working at the end of the tunnel; and, if so, could he deliberately doom them to such a death, to be blown to pieces or buried alive? On the other hand, what were they doing but their very utmost to provide such a fate for the defenders of the gate? As soon as the mine was ready, they would touch it off at some hour of the day or night, when it would result in the greatest loss of human life, with every hope and intention of blowing to pieces and burying alive beneath the ruins of the tower as many as they could of its defenders.

Still, he needn't accept their standards; and there was something particularly horrible about the kind of death that would result if his own explosion brought down a length of tunnel in such a way that the workers at the other end were entombed alive. Or if this didn't occur, how horrible nevertheless to lie at the end of that tunnel, in pitch darkness, wounded and bleeding to death for want of help. And probably the men working down there knew nothing of what was happening in the redoubt.

How many of them would there be? Probably several, working in shifts of two or three, at the 'face.'

As he thought, a man came towards him from the black depths, evidently in a hurry, as he charged along, doubled and crouching like a bear rushing out of its den. Evidently he had gathered that something was wrong, as he held a drawn *tulwar* before him.

At the same moment, behind Wendover, Shere Khan struck three or four matches in a bunch and lit a pine-flare. Wendover fired his revolver and the man fell.

Now they'd come.

There were exclamations; a sound of pick-axe and

spade being thrown aside; and then a rush.

Waiting until he saw a gleam of white and a flash of steel, Wendover fired. Again. And again.

Having emptied his revolver he threw himself down, took his knife from his belt and slashed the protruding corner of a powder-bag.

"Shoot, if they come, Shere Khan," he said, as he thrust the end of the fuse well into the bag. Having done this, he continued tamping. Opening the corner of the other bag, he worked the end of the second length of fuse well into the powder, and then coolly continued his tamping work.

If one fuse failed, the other might succeed.

Suddenly Shere Khan's rifle banged, just above his head, making a tremendous din in the enclosed space.

Glancing over his shoulder, he saw that Havildar Umrao Singh, beside and behind Shere Khan, held his rifle at the 'present.'

As Shere Khan worked the bolt of his gun, the Havildar fired.

That surely must have accounted for the occupants of the tunnel. Anyhow, he could wait no longer.

"Get out," he bawled in Hindustani. "Quick. I'm going to fire the mine."

And as Shere Khan, the Havildar and the men behind them turned about and, hurrying from the shaft, climbed out of the pit, Wendover unrolled the two lengths of fuse to their full extent.

Having done so, he dashed from the tunnel and, at a glance, took in the situation.

The enemy were about to attempt the re-capture of the redoubt.

To the Pathans, a charge of yelling devils, each with a gleaming bayonet levelled before him, was one thing; but a handful of sepoys shooting from behind a low breastwork of rocks was another. They'd soon deal with them. And while a heavy fire was maintained upon the redoubt, a considerable body of Pathans steadily advanced to the assault, making use of cover as only Pathans can. From bush to bush and rock to rock, they crept and wriggled; each man, while making amazingly swift progress, scarcely offering a target to the quickest sharp-shooter.

And as Wendover was well aware, none of these sepoys would ever shine in the art of taking snap-shots at the "running-man" on the rifle range, much less when under heavy fire themselves.

It was time to go.

Pulling out his whistle, he blew a long-continued blast with all his strength, the agreed signal for retirement, that instantly turned the brave defence into a *sauve qui peut*.

Leaping to their feet, the sepoys ran for their lives, Subedar Gopal Mangal and Havildar Umrao Singh urging them on, and, as Wendover had time to note, bravely doing so until the last man was over the redoubt wall and running, as hard as he could go, towards the south-west corner of the Fort.

Derisive howls, yells and cheers rose from the attacking Pathans who, fortunately for Wendover, instead of leaping up and charging in pursuit, as some troops would have done, sought comfortable rest for their rifles, and fired steadily at the swiftly-disappearing foe.

Splendid. Exactly what he had anticipated, and everything going according to plan. It might possibly have spoilt things had the enemy made a rush for the redoubt, though even then it was hardly likely that, in the excitement of driving the intruders out, any of the Pathans would have entered the tunnel . . .

A minute after emerging from the shaft into the shallow pit, Wendover turned about and dashed back again.

Taking a box of matches from his pocket he struck a small bunch of them and carefully lit first one fuse and then the other. For a moment he watched to see that both were burning satisfactorily.

Yes, all was well, and in another minute the Singing Hadji of Sufed Kot would get one of the major surprises of a doubtless surprising life.

Well, it was time for him to go, too, and the sooner the better.

Hurrying from the shaft, he scrambled out of the entrance pit, which was some four feet deep, noted with great satisfaction that not a single sepoy had been too badly wounded to leave the redoubt, sprang over the breast-work, and ran as hard as he could go in the direction of the corner of the Fort, from whose walls loud cheers greeted his appearance . . .

Hullo, that was bad—several men must have been hit while running from the redoubt to the Fort. Bright splashes of blood showed here and there on the grey stones, where wounded men had fallen and lain awhile, ere struggling to their feet and continuing their retreat. Here and there were the bodies of those who had been killed outright, or too badly wounded even to crawl. But this was to be expected, of course. Behind the protecting walls of the redoubt they had been comparatively safe. In the open, running in the direct line of fire between the enemy and the Fort, some were bound to be hit.

Throwing himself down beside the first of these inert bundles of khaki, Wendover saw that the man was dead, a bullet having taken him squarely in the base of the skull.

Scrambling to his feet, Wendover dashed on.

As he ran, bullets struck the ground all round him and he marvelled that he was not hit.

Again throwing himself down, by the next prostrate man, Wendover saw that for him also nothing could be done, a soft leaden bullet, probably from a Martini-Henry rifle, having entered between his shoulder-blades and made a hideous wound as it mushroomed ere passing out through his chest. If not dead, he was unconscious and quite beyond help.

Again springing up, Wendover dashed on and, after running a few yards, received a violent blow that sent him sprawling, the sensation reminding him of that resultant upon stopping a swift cricket ball with his knee.

Pulling himself together and attempting to rise, he found that this was impossible.

Bad luck . . . Since he had to be hit and knocked

out, it was a pity they couldn't either have made a clean job of it, or got him anywhere but in the legs. If they caught him alive, the Singing Hadji of Sufed Kot would teach him a lesson. He'd "learn" him to butt in upon his private affairs in the guise of a Pathan, and then thwart his plans, and perhaps bring them all to nought, in the guise of a Sahib.

Better load the old revolver again, and lessen the number of the Fort's assailants by five when they came to gather him in. And keep the last shot for himself. There'd be no harm in that, surely?

That yelling, howling row he had heard as he crashed must have been a roar of triumph from the Pathan trenches and *sangars* when they saw him go down. How many would claim the honour of having winged him, when the Hadji made kind enquiries on the subject? A few score, doubtless. Probably a few hundred.

But . . . What was he forgetting? What had happened? No, he was a bit confused . . . It was rather a question of what hadn't happened . . . Yes, what hadn't happened?

Good Lord! The mine!

The fuse must have failed.

Both of them.

And wasn't it just his luck? Wasn't it just the devil's own luck that he couldn't go back and re-light them? If only he had been knocked out with a whack in the body in a non-vital part, he could have got his breath again, pulled himself together, and then made a swift dash back and into the place, before the Pathans guessed what he was up to.

Or if only he could have crawled, he might have managed it. Once he reached the redoubt, he would have been safe from interference. There wasn't a man in the Hadji's army who would have risked, not merely death here, but utter damnation in the Hereafter, by being blown to pieces. It was the one death that the *ghazi* himself feared, knowing full well that it was useless to appear at Heaven's gate in a thousand pieces and ask permission to enter as a good

Mussulman.

As these thoughts passed through his mind in a flash, he raised himself on his hands, sat up, turned towards the redoubt, painfully moved his legs, and lay with his face turned to the enemy.

Now then, if he didn't bleed too fast, he could work himself slowly along in the direction of the redoubt, use his hands, forearms, elbows, his knees, his toes, yes, his teeth and his eyebrows, but what he would contrive to edge himself along . . . inch by inch . . . back to the redoubt.

Of course, if the Pathans rushed, there would be an end of the matter, but if they feared a trap, as undoubtedly they did, he might last out, might find sufficient strength to drag himself there somehow, fall over the breast-work, roll into the pit, crawl to the fuses, light them again—and then take his chance. Possibly he could crawl away sufficiently far to avoid being himself blown up.

And if the fuses failed again?

Well, damn it all, he'd set fire to the gunpowder itself, "and go to his God like a soldier."

And then—since dear old Ganesh was so determined to reinstate him—he could do it posthumously. He could rehabilitate his memory.

He really hadn't much cared whether he were cleared and re-established, but it would be rather nice to have his memory sweetened.

Yes, doubtless there were a few people, men like Ganesh, who had believed in him, in spite of the evidence; and it would be rather a score for them. Otherwise it didn't matter really. He didn't care a damn for those who had assumed his guilt and loudly condemned him. Not that one could blame them, in view of the fair, impartial and public Court-Martial.

He hadn't made much of his life, and this would be a little compensation. If he had been living like a dog, he'd be dying like a man.

Finish in style.

How the bullets rained round him.

Damn the beggars, they'd get him before he started,

if they weren't careful!

Painfully he raised himself slightly from the ground, and stretching his hands as far forward as he could, he seized a slightly projecting stone. Flexing and tensing the muscles of his arms, he drew himself a few inches forward, tried to use his toes and knees to increase the distance, and found that he could not do so.

That was bad. Was he paralysed from the waist down? Been hit in the spine as well as the legs?

Well, he must manage with his arms. Or perhaps, if he could slew himself round broadside-on to the redoubt, he could roll. Yes, almost certainly he could roll, and thus keep up a steadier and quicker progress than by dragging himself along by means of his hands and arms.

But it was devilishly painful.

And suddenly his somewhat scattered wits were for the moment totally paralysed by a terrific, shattering, earth-shaking roar as the powder exploded and a tremendous fountain of smoke, stones and earth rose up into the sky.

Thank God! The fuse had been all right.

As he lay still, with closed eyes and swift laboured breathing, a heavy rain of earth and stones crashed down all about him; and, for a full minute, a great silence fell, as besiegers and besieged stared at the smoking ruin of what had been a redoubt, a tunnel and a mine.

And then tremendous outcries broke forth simultaneously as one side cheered with all the strength of its lungs and the other howled savagely in rage and dismay.

A wave of joy surged through Wendover's mind.

Now nothing mattered much.

God willing, the Fort was saved.

Easily disheartened as are all Orientals, whatever be the temper of their courage and *élan*, the Pathan host would continue the siege but half-heartedly, if at all. This mighty explosion would be the death-knell of their hopes of a sudden victory and slaughter ere the arrival of the relief.

Had they succeeded, they would have slaughtered the survivors, occupied the Fort, repaired it quickly, and garrisoned it with picked men. These would have made a most stout resistance if besieged, while the remainder of the *lashkar* would have harried the British force, cut its communications, destroyed the road before and behind it, immobilized it, weakened it by attack after attack until it was overwhelmed.

Now, between the undefeated, evidently resourceful and courageous garrison on the one hand and the approaching Relief Column on the other, they would feel themselves between the hammer and the anvil.

The Singing Hadji of Sufed Kot would quickly find that nothing fails like failure, and one more Commander would discover the inherent weakness of all heterogeneous forces and of plans that depend for their success upon confederations and alliances.

Well, this was the end of Richard Wendover, and incidentally a damned good one! Lucky at last—and at the last.

But from another point of view it might not be so good, if they got him alive.

What rotten shooting. They ought to have got him before now. They must be all dithered by the sortie and general misconduct of what should have been a despairing and defeated garrison.

God! That was a near one. Cut his ear. Bit of a marksman. One or two more from that chap and his troubles would be over. Rather a wonder they didn't make a rush, and either hack him to pieces with their knives or drag him into the nearest trench for future treatment.

Shoot straight, you devils, shoot straight and get it over.

With considerable pain and effort, Wendover raised his body until he was in a sitting position facing the enemy, his hands and straightened arms supporting him.

There you are. You are supposed to be good shots. Can't you hit a sitting man at two hundred? . . . Make a dash for the crater where the redoubt was, and it will be one hundred.

That heavy fire the good fellows were maintaining from the Fort was unfortunate for him, really, keeping most of the Pathans' heads down and spoiling their aim. On the other hand, while the Fort kept up that rate of 'rapid independent,' there would be no rush at him.

Come on, come on. Aim straight, you rotten shots.

Hullo! What the devil! Somebody running. And running towards him, from behind. He must turn round.

That fool Shere Khan coming out to be shot.

And then subconsciously he realized that he had been wondering why Shere Khan had left him to it; and had decided that it must have been because the poor chap was hit. Otherwise Shere Khan most certainly would have come back for his friend when he realized that he hadn't followed the rest into the Fort.

The fool. He'd be hit and then there would be two of them.

And the thin time they'd get when they fell into the hands of the Singing Hadji of Sufed Kot!

Unless he could persuade the Hadji that Shere Khan was a genuine *ghazi* kept as a hostage by the Commandant of the Fort.

But no, the fact of his coming out and trying to rescue his friend would prove that he was a fraud.

As these thoughts passed through his mind, Wendover fell back into a recumbent position, painfully rolled over and raised his head.

Good God in Heaven! What was this?

Breckinge . . .

Had he lost so much blood that he was seeing things? Yes, surely. This must be an hallucination, if ever there was one.

Breckinge? Rushing out from safety to rescue a wounded man under heavy fire? And that man his hated enemy; the man by whose death he stood to save his life—or at any rate, to save himself from the heaviest punishment, from utter irreparable ruin and disgrace.

No, it couldn't be.

The running man checked his pace, slithered, and flung himself down beside Wendover.

Breckinge it undoubtedly was.

"Where are you hit?" he gasped as he fought for breath.

Wendover stared, incredulous.

It *was* Breckinge. There was no possible shadow of doubt.

"Good God, Breckinge! What on earth made you do this? Get back, man, get back at once. Wriggle or crawl or run zigzagging."

"Are you hit in the body?" asked Breckinge.

"No, only the legs. But I can't get up."

Breckinge, recumbent, made swift examination.

"Missed the femoral artery," he said. "Not been bleeding too badly. I'll get you into the Fort before I do anything."

"Get inside yourself, man," replied Wendover. "They'll make a rush in a minute. Especially when they see you trying to get me away. You can't do it."

For reply, Breckinge rose to his feet, seized Wendover about the body beneath the arms, and dragged him several yards in the direction of the Fort, from which came renewed cheers, loud and prolonged, while from the Pathans' position arose howls, shrieks and imprecations and increased volume of fire. All about the two men, sand, earth and stones leapt into life as does the surface of a pond under the assault of a hailstorm.

"Stop it, man," shouted Wendover. "Drop me. Lie down."

And as Breckinge continued to drag him:

"Put me down, I tell you, and run," he urged. "Put me down."

Breckinge obeyed, but only to bend over Wendover, to get his left arm beneath his knees, his right under him, below the shoulders, and with a mighty effort and an output of strength of which Wendover had not supposed him capable, to lift him from the ground and, leaning well back, to totter onward in the direction of the Fort.

"Stop it, Breckinge," begged Wendover again. "Put me down, man. Look, I can do the rest myself . . . I can roll. Run for it. I shall be all right now."

Breckinge, reeling, stumbling, swaying, staggered on.

"Look, Breckinge," said Wendover, "if you must do it, put me down, kneel in front of me, and I'll get on your back, somehow. Give me a pick-a-back. It'll be far easier for you."

"What? And protect my body with yours!" panted Breckinge.

"Rubbish. It would save us both. You could go twice as fast."

A burning pain seared Wendover's dangling arm. They'd get Breckinge in a moment.

It must have been a full minute since he threw himself down beside him.

Well done, the garrison. They were giving the enemy something to think about. But for that really heavy fire, there would have been a charge long ago; or they would have been hit for a certainty.

Well done, Breckinge!

A few yards more, and they'd reach the corner and be in safety, unless the Pathans, enraged beyond discretion, swarmed out of their trenches and *sangars* and made a rush for them. They certainly weren't showing the spirit they had displayed up to date, and in most of the Frontier shows. Either they were fed-up with the whole business, or none too pleased with the result of the Singing Hadji's prophecies and promises. No, they showed more dash and indifference to death than this when their country was invaded and they were fighting in defence of hearth and home. Even so, and allowing for the tremendous firing from the Fort, he and Breckinge had been amazingly lucky so far and . . .

Crash! God, that was painful! It also meant that Breckinge was hit.

Turning himself over, Wendover saw that Breckinge was lying on his face. Yes, the poor chap had stopped one . . . badly. What could he do for him?

Better turn him over, perhaps.

Edging himself along a few inches, with hand and elbow, Wendover contrived to turn Breckinge on to his back. His dusky face was livid; greenish; his eyelids fluttering; a stain of blood was spreading over the front of his khaki shirt.

This was the very devil. He could roll himself to safety, but he couldn't move Breckinge.

What an amazing thing for the man to do.

Talk about finishing in style, and a good end to a bad life!

Breckinge opened his eyes.

"Not too bad, I hope, old chap," said Wendover.

"*Shot in the back*," whispered Breckinge. "Oh, my God, *shot in the back*, after all."

And a bitter sardonic smile showed for a moment upon his face.

"Shot in the back be damned," replied Wendover robustly. "Shot while giving your life for another man."

"*Shot in the back!*"

"Look here, Breckinge, you'll bear the most honourable wound that ever a man . . ."

Breckinge groaned.

"Anyway, you were shot saving my life and . . ."

"Saving *your* damned life, curse you! *Your* life? You blasted swine."

Wendover's mouth closed tightly.

So that was it!

No, no, the poor chap didn't know what he was saying.

Lying down, Wendover rolled a couple of feet away, stretched out his arm and seized Breckinge's collar.

With a mighty effort he dragged him a few inches nearer.

"Stop it, damn you," groaned Breckinge. "Let me alone. Get back . . . since you can move. Go and . . . collect . . . your damned 'confession.'"

So that was what the poor chap was worrying

about.

This was awful. He must do his best for him.

And slowly, for his shattered leg hurt hideously and the bleeding had broken out afresh, Wendover rolled over, again extended his arm, seized Breckinge by the collar once more, braced himself and pulled.

Breckinge cried aloud in pain, but a few inches had been gained.

And every few seconds a bullet struck the ground close by.

Another effort. But damn it all, at this rate it would take the rest of the day to reach the corner of the wall, and they'd certainly be shot within the next few minutes. It couldn't be more than a few minutes since he himself had been knocked over.

Another agonizing roll, another heave at the completely helpless Breckinge, a few more inches gained.

Once more.

But this time as he hauled there came a gush of blood from Breckinge's mouth. Did that mean the end? If so, he'd better leave him, and get back if he could.

Breckinge opened his eyes and said something. Wendover shifted himself closer to him.

"What's that, old chap?" he said.

"I'm dying . . . I'm dying . . ."

"Not you. Stick it out. We'll get back all right. And, Breckinge, listen . . . Can you hear me? Stick it, Breckinge. Listen! *I'll get you the Victoria Cross for this.* That's something to live for, isn't it?"

"You can keep it. I'm . . . I'm . . ." whispered Breckinge.

"You are a brave man. I won't try to thank you. But you are."

"I am a General's grandson," whispered the dying man.

"By God you are—and he is proud of you. And I am proud to be your . . . your . . . friend, Breckinge."

"*Friend!* To Hell with you . . ."

"You came out to save me."

"To save *you!* I came because I—had to," said Breckinge clearly. "Suddenly something made me

307

come."

And turning his head sideways and looking Wendover full in the face:

"I am . . . a . . . General's . . . grandson," he said distinctly, and died.

There was a rush of feet.

A band of sepoys, headed by Havildar Umrao Singh, dashed round the corner of the Fort, swooped down upon Wendover and bore him to the shelter of the south-west wall.

Ere he fainted, Wendover caught sight of a huddled heap. A man in Pathan clothing. Shere Khan. His eyes were open.

"Stop," Wendover whispered, summoning up his strength.

"Stop, I tell you," he cried. "Bring him in."

And a minute afterwards, he and Shere Khan were carried in through the postern gate.

§4

A couple of hours later, his legs roughly but not unskilfully bandaged by a sepoy whose sister had married a stretcher-bearer, and who was, therefore, something of a surgical authority, Wendover lay and listened to Umrao Singh's report.

The Subedar-Major had, most unfortunately, been killed. A bullet had struck him between the eyes as he superintended the firing before the explosion of the mine.

Subedar Gopal Mangal had been hit, just before the sortie party reached shelter, and had been dragged in by his men. He was in a bad way.

As Havildar Umrao Singh explained, he would himself instantly have rushed out with his Section to bring the Sahib in, but that the Doctor Sahib had absolutely and peremptorily forbidden it. The Doctor Sahib had made the sortie party wall-up the postern gate, and had threatened the Havildar with his revolver when he had expostulated and said that the Captain

Sahib should be rescued.

The Doctor Sahib had then directed the defence from the safety of the courtyard, shouting to the men to fire faster and faster, and cursing men who fell wounded.

Then suddenly he had gone mad; had come up on to the parapet; had climbed through an embrasure above the gate; had hung by his hands—and dropped. His feet must have been a man's height from the ground when he let go.

The Havildar had himself snatched up a rifle and fired at every Pathan whom he could see, while shouting to the defenders to continue rapid fire.

The Sahib knew the rest.

He did.

And an amazing thing it was.

Again poor Breckinge had 'reverted to type'; and this time to the higher type. If, for much of his life, he had lived as the son of outcaste degenerate Hindus of the lowest and basest stock, he had died as a European of army-tradition and fighting heredity.

Breckinge, the perjured liar, the cowardly back-stabbing murderer, the treacherous, cowardly villain, had died a brave man, doing a deed worthy of reward with the Victoria Cross.

Poor Breckinge. The irony of Fate! Shot in the back, as Wendover once had mockingly foretold. Shot in the back and in the doing of so brave a deed. And in the saving of the man whom he hated so bitterly; hated to the last.

§5

The firing from the Pathan position dwindled, became desultory and died away.

For the first time in the long story of its siege, Fort Giltraza had a peaceful night.

And in the morning, new life inspired its weary garrison as, clear, unmistakable, heard and recognized by all, came boom after boom of the guns of a mountain battery.

The relief force was at hand, was shelling the enemy—probably a retreating enemy, in full flight, disappointed, discouraged and disheartened.

And, a few hours later, hours of incredible peace, quiet and release from stress and strain, bugle calls were heard.

The Relief Force, unopposed, was marching on; was marching in; was here.

CHAPTER VII

What a day! . . .

How nice the Brigadier had been, and how utterly British in his discomfort; his anxiety to deal adequately with the situation, to say the right thing, and completely to conceal the right emotion.

And how extremely nice his Staff and all the other Officers had been. Charming. In spite of its being so difficult a situation for them—in the circumstances.

An experience as delightful as it was painful.

And Ganesh Hazelrigg, with his marvellous sympathy and loyalty.

§2

And having heard Wendover's account of what had happened since he left the Fort, Major Hazelrigg told his own story; thereafter making clear all things that had been hidden.

He then had his great moment.

"There it is, my son," he concluded, taking an envelope from an inner pocket, extracting a paper and handing it to Wendover, "and the Brigadier shall read it to-night—and then every Officer in this force, before I send it off to Simla."

Richard Wendover took the paper and read Breckinge's confession through from beginning to end, and read it through again.

"I wonder if you'll think I'm mad," he said, and holding it in both hands, rested them on the bed before him, as he gazed smiling at his friend.

"I won't try to thank you," he continued. "That would be just futile, silly."

"Very silly," growled Hazelrigg.

"But it cannot be done, old man."

"Can't be done? What d'you mean—can't be done?

What can't?"

"This can't be used."

"Can't be used? Why, it was written in my presence; signed in the presence of the Subedar-Major and Shere Khan, who both witnessed it. It is perfect evidence; irrefutable; absolute final *proof*. What more do you want?"

"Nothing more, old chap. There couldn't be more. It's marvellous. It is, as you say, perfect. And I couldn't begin to tell you how grateful . . ."

"Don't begin."

"I won't. But . . . but . . . Will you think me ungrateful?"

"Ungrateful? No. Why? What are you driving at?"

"I'm trying to say that—I'm not going to use it, Ganesh."

"*What?* You're not well. You're not . . . sane."

"Never saner. But I can't."

"*I* can."

"Yes, but you won't. We're going to burn this."

Hazelrigg stared wide-eyed and open-mouthed.

"What are you talking about?" he asked.

"We're going to burn this."

Hazelrigg continued to stare in silence.

"I was lying out there, being absolutely peppered; and he dashed out and began to drag me away. And then that wasn't good enough for him. Damned if he didn't get me up in his arms and carry me. Carried me, Ganesh—with his body between me and the enemy. And he was shot in the back. I don't think either of us begins to understand what it meant to poor Breckinge to be shot in the back. I once taunted him with it—said that if ever he were shot—in spite of his wonderful care of himself—he'd be shot in the back. He was a great coward, you know, really. I mean, up till now. And the coward died as brave a death as ever a man did."

Still Hazelrigg said nothing.

"He deliberately gave his life for mine," lied Wendover. "To make amends. Doesn't that wash out—everything?"

Silence fell in the little mud-walled cell, Hazelrigg

saying nothing because he was unable to speak.

This was a greatness beyond the greatest—that this innocent man, who had suffered so immeasurably, this man who had lost everything, lost all that made life worth living—that he should refuse to take it back, refuse reinstatement in his own proper place, resumption of the life which was his by right. Refuse everything. Because his enemy had made reparation—given his life in redemption. Refuse to *come back*—because coming back meant the exposure of the man who had died for him. And refuse to come back because he was merely pardoned—forgiven for the crime he had never committed. Refuse.

It was impossible. Incredible. Absurd.

And in silence Wendover wrestled with temptation.

How could he lose Life a second time? When it was within his grasp. This life that he so loved; this life that he now knew was the only life for him? Fate had really been rather cruel—to give him this brief taste of it again. The work he loved. Duty. Command. Discipline. His army. His friends. His country. His England . . .

But he couldn't use the confession.

No, it couldn't be done.

"I am a General's grandson."

Poor devil! He had given his life—that he might die as a General's grandson; that he might have, for a brief moment, at the last, self-respect, honour. He had died for an ideal; for worthiness; for honour.

Let him have it.

In his way, and in his last moments, he had been great.

Yes, his death had cancelled out that beastly confession.

Poor devil. Weak, vacillating, cowardly; damned and doomed from the moment of his birth. A victim far more than a villain.

No, that confession must not be used.

He, Wendover, had never yet really done anything of which he was utterly ashamed; anything that had made him feel dirty and degraded. If he published and used that confession now he'd feel *filthy* for the rest of his life.

"Ganesh," he said, "I feel ashamed to ask it of you. I feel an incredibly ungrateful hound—but I beg you, let me tear this up."

"I understand," replied Ganesh Hazelrigg, gentleman.

He knew his man. And, with a sigh, he rose, and from his pocket produced a box of matches.

With slightly trembling hand, Wendover held the paper out beyond the bed.

Hazelrigg struck a match and set it to a corner of the document.

It flared up, and Wendover dropped it to the floor, where it burned itself out.

Hazelrigg set his foot upon it, his face grave and sad.

"How's Shere Khan this morning?" asked Wendover.

"Doing splendidly," replied Hazelrigg.

"See you later," he said, and went from the room.

And Richard Wendover lay and thought of Sybil Ffoulkes. She would have approved, he decided—and then doubted that decision.

WORTH WILE

Lady-in-waiting: Madam, methinks he is not worth your while.

Princess: Nay then, Filomena, I think he is worth my every wile.

Masuccio.

To

DR. MAURICE CAMPBELL

PHYSICIAN

To

GUY'S HOSPITAL

LONDON

PART I

For Flying-Officer John Vere-Vaughan, the day began as unpromisingly as most others.

Subconsciously, he noted that it was a good day for flying, that being really the most interesting and important aspect of any day; for to the airman, the weather is as important as to the seaman.

And that this day, from the meteorological point of view, was satisfactory, appeared to be the one satisfactory feature in a generally unsatisfactory existence.

To the earth-bound it must seem extraordinary that those whose haunt is the empyrean, should ever be bored. Nevertheless, to men, young, restless and eager, boredom comes inevitably when the scene of their activities is an ugly khaki-coloured terrain, flat and featureless, surrounded by distant khaki-coloured hills; their home a khaki-coloured Fort, their days and doings monotonous. For there can be a monotony of anything; and deeds, experiences, events, however exciting, become boringly monotonous by endless repetition.

So, to Flying-Officer John Vere-Vaughan, the news that there was trouble beyond the Frontier was welcome.

According to rumour, the trouble—news of which had been brought by a wandering *fakir* known to certain British Officers as Ghulam Hyder—was of the kind that, not so long ago, could only have been cured by such drastic measure as the use of a Brigade of all arms; trouble that, growing with incredible speed from bad to worse, would have involved the Government of India in costly expenditure in money and in the lives of men, before it could have been dealt with, arrested, and cleared up.

What formerly necessitated the employment of Generals, British Regiments, Sepoy Regiments, Squadrons of Bengal Lancers and British cavalry, Batteries of field-guns and mountain artillery, detachments of Sappers and Miners, the Signal Corps and the Royal Army Service Corps, not to mention thousands of camels and mule-carts, and a horde of camp followers, sutlers, syces and servants, could nowadays be dealt with by a dozen young men and a half-dozen aeroplanes.

A case indeed of nipping trouble in the bud; almost one of prevention being better than cure.

To Flying-Officer John Vere-Vaughan it was interesting and curious that there should be people at home—and not only the usual capital-making, vote-catching, or doctrinaire politicians—who, while raising no objection whatever to admittedly necessary punitive or defensive Expeditions of the old-fashioned kind, raised flapping hands and shrieking voices of protest and horror at the doing of the work by a thousandth part of the personnel at a thousandth part of the cost and a thousandth part of the loss of life on both sides —by the use of the aeroplane and the bomb.

To him, the idea was strange that the bullet might kill its thousands, but the bomb must not kill its tens.

"Heard the glad news, Vera?" asked John Vere-Vaughan's friend, Flight-Lieutenant Thomas Blake Lucke, overtaking him as he entered the Mess.

"Yes," replied Vere-Vaughan. "You are gazetted Air Vice Marshal, aren't you, Tommy?"

"By Gum, *vice* is about right!" he added.

"No, I wasn't referring to my doubtless imminent promotion. And unlike yourself, I think of other things sometimes. Higher things," replied Lucke loftily.

"Not higher than that, surely."

"Yes, ten thousand feet. We are going to lay eggs on the Singing Hadji, after all."

"What, is he out again?"

"Yes. He's at it again. And Ghulam Hyder is on to him again. Now, we're going to be. It was about time, when they pushed us up here."

"Us? You, you mean," grunted John Vere-Vaughan with his mouth full.

"Quite," agreed Flight-Lieutenant Lucke. "You are right . . . Wonder when I shall have to take the matter in hand?"

"Oh, go at once," replied Vere-Vaughan, emerging from his coffee-cup. "Nobody would notice."

And while the young men ragged and wrangled, with jeer and jest, the *fakir* Ghulum Hyder, who was also Major Bartholomew Hazelrigg, known to his friends as Ganesh, talked urgently with the Commandant of Hunzana Fort.

§2

In a row stood six two-seater fighting scouts, and busy about them worked the armourers, fitting detonators to the bombs, of which each machine carried eight.

The armourers having completed their work, into the cock-pits climbed the young men who nowadays answered the raiders with raids, the young men who replied, coming down from the air, to those who, coming down from the mountains, harried and slew the King's lieges, breaking the *Pax Britannica* and the brittle peace of the Border.

Having adjusted goggles and harness and settled into their respective seats, the pilots taxied the machines into the position for taking off, and, at a signal from the leader, the engines roared, the machines took off and, flying in great circles, gained height sufficient for crossing the many miles of lofty mountains which lay between Fort Hunzana and Sufed Kot, the stronghold of the notorious Singing Hadji and his ever turbulent and war-like sect.

To Flying-Officer John Vere-Vaughan, the extreme cold of the morning was the chief concern. Everything was familiar and usual; and, at present, his only duty as gunner was to keep a sharp look-out and warn his pilot of any change in the formation of the flight and of any signals made by its leader.

All was as usual until, a hundred miles from home and at twelve thousand feet, a most unusual morning

323

cloud-bank was encountered, a fog, white and dense and of a blanketing thickness worthy of London itself. And looming above it and through the fringe of it were the peaks of the mighty Lushgai chain of mountain ranges. As the machine disappeared into the fog, Vere-Vaughan, already half-frozen, cursed. Why had he joined the Air Force? What was wrong with the Cavalry, the Gunners or the Infantry? Lucky beggars, down there on *terra firma* or on good horses. All nice and warm. Damn this sitting in a mouse's cage wrapped up in white cotton wool, for that was what the fog was like.

Yes, and it wasn't as though one were merely flying blind in a dense fog, which is quite sufficiently beastly, but what about flying in it with other machines barging about a few inches away? And what about flying in a thick fog among damned great mountains a few miles high? They'd be right in among them in a minute. Like being in the middle of a greatly-magnified Switzerland. And what about it in this "tropical" atmosphere which was so disgustingly bumpy?

What a life! Who'd be an airman? Thank God Tommy Lucke was such a great lad at the joy-stick. One of the best pilots ever. Still, if another machine barged into him, or a mountain got up and hit him, what good would his skill be?

God, that was a pocket! Big, deep, and empty as his own. What a funny noise a machine always made going through a thick fog. Swishing. Almost like a speed-boat on the water.

Did Tommy hate it as much as he did, flying like this when one couldn't see the wing-tips? It must be as much as he could do to see his instruments. He himself couldn't see them, even from where he was.

Well, there was one thing. Nobody could accuse him of missing signals, and there was no need for him to stand up in the draught from the propeller and keep on dodging about and looking round for them. Just crouch down in the cock-pit and try to keep warm.

Did Tommy know where he was and what he was

doing, and whether he was upside down or inside out or flying sideways; or backwards, like a sooner-bird which proceeds in that direction during a sand-storm so as to keep the sand out of its eyes? Or was it because the sooner-bird would sooner fly that way so as to see where he has been?

Well, he and Tommy would never see where they had been, and they'd never be where they had seen if this fog lasted much longer. They'd crash into the side of a mountain and that would be that.

Sad . . . Two promising young officers . . . Always promising something or other.

How curiously one's mind worked in such circumstances. Or wasn't it working? A strange thing, the human make-up. Presumably, he ought to be terrified. And really, if you came to think of it, one couldn't be in much greater danger than buzzing along at this speed in a jumble with five other machines and five hundred mountain-peaks. Couldn't possibly.

Oughtn't Tommy to give it up and turn back? No, Tommy wasn't of the turning-back sort. Besides, how could he, even if he wanted to. It would be more dangerous than going on. Bound to fly slap into a mountain-side if he left his course and tried to turn now. They must be at ten or twelve thousand and these mountains must go from fifteen to eighteen thousand . . . Were they climbing? And would they neatly knock the top off Sufed Mountain . . . and the souls out of their bodies?

He ought to feel frightened to death, for it was ghastly, this waiting for sudden and certain destruction.

And yet he wasn't frightened, although he felt that he had every reason to be, and that, in any other danger equally great, he'd have been jibbering with terror.

Perhaps not, though. Tommy had told him how once, when out hunting, he had fallen off his horse— Tommy was quite good at falling off a horse, and could fly any breed of plane better than ride any brand of horse—had fallen off his horse and been dragged.

There was the horse, galloping Hell-for-leather across country, and Tommy bumping along on the ground, being worn to a shadow by friction with the bare earth, the hard going which was not grass but the usual gravel, sand, stone, and baked soil of the Indian maidan, and with the horse's hooves clattering and smashing close beside his poor old bumping head. And on being asked as to his sensations, Tommy had sworn that he had not been frightened in the least. And not merely because he hadn't had time to be, or that he was stunned and stupid, or stupider than usual. He said his mind had been a kind of blank, blanker than usual. And that he had merely wondered what was going to happen.

What had happened was that the stirrup leather had come adrift from the saddle, and the horse had galloped on, leaving Tommy the worse for wear. And it was only then that he had begun to feel frightened, he said; or rather, to realize what a frightfully narrow escape he had had.

But the point was that Tommy had survived all right.

He had come out of that nasty scrape with only a few—scrapes.

And so they would, this time. They'd be all right. Tommy's luck would hold. And they'd neither hit another plane nor a mountain-side. It would be just like good old Tommy's luck to fly blind, straight through a defile with a few thousand feet of mountain-side sticking up a few yards away on either wing; go through it like a train going through a deep cutting. Nobody else but Tommy would ever have found the entrance or kept straight through.

But, God, how he wished something would happen . . . This was really beginning to get on his nerves. He had wondered what it would be like to fly through these mountains if ever they were caught in this country in a fog—and now he knew.

How long had they been in it? What had happened to the rest of the flight? Had they been as lucky as Tommy, or had they all . . . ?

Worth Wile

Why didn't something happen?

What did happen was that the fog thinned, a break occurred, and, far below, the ground was dimly visible. They were through the mountain range and flying over a wide tract of level country.

And also they were alone.

John Vere-Vaughan groaned in spirit. That almost certainly meant that there were five wrecks behind them; that, in five steep-sided *nullahs*, lay five tangled masses of fabric and machinery; five mangled messes of flesh and blood and bone.

And the best one could hope for them was that death had been instantaneous.

The only comfort was that almost certainly it had.

But no, it would hardly be a case of tangled masses. Smithereens, more likely. For each machine carried eight bombs. Yes, death would be instantaneous all right. No burning . . .

Hullo; Tommy was diving sharply.

Did he know exactly where he was; or was he going down to pick up a landmark? Presumably he knew this country pretty well, but . . .

A quarter of an hour or so later, Vere-Vaughan saw a big fort or fortified village on a plateau.

Evidently Tommy recognized the place.

Yes, this was it; or he would not have dropped to a thousand feet and turned.

Now for business.

Four times the machine flew across the plateau, on each occasion dropping a couple of bombs. That the eight explosions would cause much loss of life was extremely improbable, as the Pathan villagers would long ago have made for their caves and natural bomb-proof dug-outs, which required no digging, deep in the solid rock of the sides of the *nullah* that flanked the plateau near the village wall.

That was all to the good. One did not want women and children to suffer for the deeds of their outlaw-raider husbands, fathers, sons and brothers. What was highly desirable was good luck and good judgment in getting some of the bombs on to the big watch-towers, and to do all possible damage to the walls and battlements of the fortified village.

But for the fog there would have been forty-eight bombs instead of eight, for carrying out the work of destruction and teaching the Singing Hadji of Sufed Kot that times were changed and methods improved—from the point of view of his enemies, at any rate.

Still, eight hearty explosions in the right places would give him and his followers something to think about, and damp their aggressive ardour. Raiding; the fomentation of discord, trouble and strife; and the preaching of *jehad*,[34] would appear less attractive pastimes and pursuits now that this new weapon could and would be used against them.

The fourth trip and the eighth explosion.

And what now? Would Tommy try to fly back through that fog, trusting to his wonderful luck and skill once again? Not that skill was going to be much good, when they were into that stifling all-enveloping mist again. Like a blind man trying to run headlong through a trackless forest of trees. They'd certainly share the fate of the other five planes on the return journey. Those five—and the ten men who . . .

It didn't bear thinking of.

Hullo! What was that?

There was a ragged volley of rifle-fire from below, several bullets striking the plane.

Did the beggars know that the machine only carried eight bombs and had dropped them all? At any rate, they had evidently swarmed out from their caves, dugouts and hiding-places under the great boulders, on the explosion of the last bomb.

Good. The lesson could be driven home and the outlaws taught that there was danger to more than their watch-towers and walls, if they came out into the open.

They'd forgotten the machine-gun, or perhaps were ignorant of the fact that the strange bird that laid the explosive eggs carried such a thing.

---

[34] *Holy war.*

A brief duel. Machine-gun *versus* a few score rifles, would be an exhilarating bit of sport. And not exactly sport without danger, either; for these fellows were very fine marksmen.

But surely Tommy was going to turn, dive at them, and give him a chance of getting off a pan of ammunition at them?

Yes, there was quite a crowd of them in their dirty-white and grey clothing, streaming up from the *nullah*, some shooting as they ran, others kneeling and resting their rifles on convenient boulders. Now it was his turn to show the Singing Hadji something.

As these thoughts flashed through his mind, Vere-Vaughan rose in his seat, seized the gun-ring of his Lewis, and glanced at his pilot.

Things happened quickly.

Good God! What was Tommy doing?

Tommy was sinking down, as it were, in his cockpit. Tommy was collapsing; sagging; and swaying in his seat and harness. And Tommy was bleeding copiously.

Tommy had been hit. His head was nodding.

Was he dead?

No. For suddenly he had pulled the joy-stick back, and put the nose of the machine up.

Thank God for that! First of all, flying through lofty mountain and dense fog and then flying with a dead pilot at a few hundred feet!

But he was badly wounded. Could he last out, to get home?

What would be the best thing to do?

Had he better climb across and . . . ?

Suddenly Vere-Vaughan's heart seemed to stand still, his blood to freeze in his veins, as he realized that the machine was out of control; that, for no reason, it was banking with terrific suddenness and steepness, so that the rigging throbbed like harp-strings, vibrated and strained as though everything must come adrift.

And then it fell, spinning; spinning dizzily, like a whirling dervish.

Flung against his gun and pinned there by the force of the speed of the spin, he clung, sick, giddy and suffocated, with closed eyes, gasping for breath, and waiting for the inevitable crash—and, as he did so, had time to think of those others who had crashed with eight bombs beneath them. There was a chance, an infinitesimal chance, for him. For those others, there had been none.

How many minutes had passed since Tommy had been hit? Only a few seconds, probably. One couldn't have been falling at this speed for longer than that.

Suddenly the machine heeled over and dived head-long, nose downward, at a speed too great for the air-indicator to record.

The end . . .

No! Tommy had moved; had come to life; had pulled himself together; and was working with joy-stick and rudder-bar.

Just as the ground seemed to rush up at Vere-Vaughan to strike with hideous impact, the machine answered stick and helm, and though with horrible jarring shudder, righted itself, swooped forward, and began to climb.

And as Vere-Vaughan drew thankful breath of relief, and felt as though his heart had resumed its beating, new danger loomed ahead. Tommy was steering straight for the fog-blanketed mountains. Suppose he lost control again?

He had done so already. Again he lurched sideways, his head falling forward on his chest. Dead.

No! He was all right again.

Now what? What would be the best thing for Vere-Vaughan to do? How bad was Tommy feeling? Was he done in?

Again Vere-Vaughan rose to his feet. No. Tommy had pulled himself together once more. And about time, too, as the machine, swift and straight as an arrow, flew towards the mist through which now loomed the vast wall of a mountain-side.

Straight into the fog. Straight at the mountain, whose face, towering up to its peak, sloped slightly from them.

What was Tommy doing? Quick! Tommy was lurching, sagging, slumping again, his head falling sideways to his shoulder.

Another second and . . .

For the last time, Tommy's brave soul came up from beneath the swirling waters of Lethe, peered through the swiftly-closing mists of death. He raised his head, opened his eyes, grasped the control-column and changed the angle of the plane's direction in time to prevent a head-on crash; changed it so that the angle of the aeroplane's climb almost coincided with that of the mountain-side, so that, as he died, and nerveless eye and hand and foot ceased to function, the crash was more that of a terrific landing that sends the machine bounding and bouncing to its final somersault, than that crash which drives it in one final and tremendous impact to utter splintering smash and complete disintegration and destruction.

Flying-Officer John Vere-Vaughan suddenly realized that it was all over; that he was at rest; at peace; and unhurt.

Also that he was in the uncomfortable and undignified position of hanging upside-down.

Yes, Tommy had been right about that being frightened business. Once he himself had realized that he was for it, he hadn't been frightened. He had felt, so far as he felt anything at all, resigned; remote; rather like a spectator; as though he himself stood by, watching himself about to be killed, and not very greatly interested in the matter.

While there had been a chance, he had been terrified at the thought of Tommy being hit and the machine being out of control; and at the thought of their having to try to fly back through the fog-wrapped mountains with Tommy bleeding to death. But from the moment he had seen that the crash was inevitable, he had not been frightened.

He decided that, on the whole, he had felt rather glad that the business was over, the threat and the danger past—although it wasn't past.

Perhaps the knowledge that nothing could be done and that the inevitable end was now imminent, had had an anodyne effect. Nature's mental-anæsthetic.

But what a long, long second, fear or no fear, it had been between the realization that the crash was now coming, and the actual hitting of the ground; and again, between the first hitting of the ground and the end of the terrific bounce up into the air. They must have leapt thirty feet high; and God alone knew how far, before they bounced again, and then somersaulted and lay still. Quite a voyage, from the first crash of the under-carriage to the somersault and final smash.

But that meant that Tommy must actually have attempted a landing on the steep mountain-side.

Splendid Tommy!

How long had he been dangling here upside-down? Not a dozen seconds, probably. Well, a dozen too long, anyway, especially for poor Lucke.

"*Tommy!*" he shouted. "Hi, *Tommy!* You there?"

What a silly thing to say. Of course he was there.

"*Tommy!* Are you all right?"

What an idiotic thing to ask. How could he be all right when he had been so badly hit that he had collapsed twice?

Feeling for the safety-belt catch, Vere-Vaughan found it, released himself from his safety-harness and fell, head first, from his seat in the cock-pit to the ground beneath, his helmet saving him from anything worse than an uncomfortable neck-jarring bump.

Scrambling out from under the machine, he rose to his feet, stooped beside the pilot's cock-pit and again called,

"*Tommy!* Are you badly hurt? *Tommy* . . ."

There was no reply.

Crouching, he crawled under the over-turned aeroplane, felt about until he found the catch of Lucke's safety-belt, released it, and vainly endeavoured to do something to break his friend's fall, as the sharp click told him that he had unfastened him.

Crawling out again backwards from under the machine, he dragged Lucke after him, turned him over on to his back, unbuttoned his tunic, and, ere long, realized that he was dead.

Yes, Tommy was dead.

A bullet had struck him in the right side, and evidently passing upward, must have pierced his liver and lungs; probably gone very near his heart.

With a lump in his throat, Vere-Vaughan realized that Tommy, mortally wounded, had flown the machine; had, with a supreme effort, in the very article of death, summoned the strength and skill and courage deliberately and accurately to do the one thing that could be done. Coming out of a brief faint or passing coma or unconsciousness, he had seen that they were flying straight into the steep mountain-side; and, even as he died, had put the machine's nose up so that, instead of smashing, like a bullet against a wall, it had landed.

As he died, Tommy had saved his friend's life.

And now what? Here he was, with a smashed machine, over a hundred miles from home and on the wrong side of the mountains, in the heart of the enemy's country—and might as well be a thousand, for all the chance he had of finding his way back, without a guide and food.

What had he better do first? Set fire to the machine, of course, and then give poor Tommy some sort of decent burial.

Producing a box of matches from the side pocket of his tunic and a field pocket-book from another, Vere-Vaughan tore out several pages, made a little heap of them underneath a wing, near where its tip rested on the ground, set fire to the paper, and discovered that, owing to the mist, the fabric was too wet to burn.

A quick look round the machine showed that every part of it was covered in drops of moisture as though after heavy rain, and that in its present condition, it would be impossible to set the wreck alight with matches.

Well, then, something must be done with the petrol. Or, in the present state of affairs, if he sprinkled petrol and lit it, would it just burn itself out, without setting fire to the machine?

Of course not. He must be more shaken and rattled than he had supposed. He had overlooked the fact that the machine was upside-down. Still he had only to turn on the petrol, spill plenty on the ground, and then fire a light from the Very pistol into it. Wasn't the seat specially made of inflammable material? But if the petrol-tank blew up and there was an explosion and then a lot of smoke as the machine burned, it would give his position away.

Well, that couldn't be helped. It was his duty to destroy the machine.

Then there was the ammunition. That would make a good row, popping off, when the fire burned up. A row of that sort would soon bring the Tribesmen down on him. Or up to him. Anyhow, it must not fall into the hands of the enemy.

Then there was the machine-gun too. He had better climb back into the wreckage and put the gun out of action. He could do that pretty effectively with a couple of minutes' work on the lock, and by banging the sights with a stone.

Yes, and when he had made a good job of the plane and the gun, he'd take the Very pistol and lights away with him. Might come in very useful when search planes came over, as they would be sure to do, sooner or later, when the mist cleared out of the mountains.

What could he do about poor Tommy? It would be impossible to get his body away. No plane could ever land anywhere near here, even if the place could be spotted. Perhaps he could find a suitable cave handy. Pile up a little cairn of stones, anyhow.

Well, this wouldn't do. The longer he stood staring, the worse he'd . . .

Bang!

A bullet struck a boulder close beside his head. After him already, were they? The vultures and the feast.

As he flung himself down, another rifle was fired. Another. And another.

Were they going to shoot him up, at long range, and

then come across for the loot? Better that than being taken alive. They were nasty people in this part of the world. The ordinary Border outlaws and *ghazis* who were in the habit of raiding Peshawar; attacking convoys in the passes; shooting British officers in the back, from behind the Khyber rocks and bushes, and those kinds of games, were bad enough, but they were sufficiently sophisticated and civilized to consider a captive British Officer from the ransom point of view. And if they decided to do him in, they would shoot him or just cut his throat—without frills.

But it would be rather a different matter with the wild men in this part of the world, so far from the Border. They might have neither the experience nor the facilities for sound financial use of prisoners.

And, by Jove, if one fell into the hands of the Singing Hadji of Sufed Kot, one would know all about it! Particularly after his unfortunate Giltraza experience of what happens to those who wantonly attack the outposts of the British Raj.

With a swift wriggle, roll and scramble, Vere-Vaughan got behind a boulder. Well, they couldn't hit him there—from that direction, at any rate—but the firing would of course bring others, and they'd soon get all round him. If only he could have got his Lewis-gun into action! But those Pathan marksmen would make a sieve of him long before he could dismount the gun, get it out of the wreckage, and mount it, after a fashion, with sticks and stones and string. Where it was, upside-down in the machine, it was absolutely useless.

Even if he lived long enough to do anything of the sort, and got the gun into action, resting on some stones, it would bound about like a flea in a frying-pan, and there would not be the slightest chance of his doing any execution among scattered sharp-shooters who were also past-masters at the art of taking cover.

On the other hand, they'd never close in on him so long as he had got the dreaded "bah-bah-rifle" waiting for them. For there is no weapon that the Tribesman, however brave, fierce and fanatical, respects and fears more than he does the machine-gun.

No, they'd work round into positions whence they could see him, and take pot-shots at him while they starved him out. And, incidentally, he realized that he was already feeling pretty empty, and was possessed of a thirst which, at the right time and place, would have been beyond all price.

Hullo; that was a close one. Somebody had got round to a flank where he could enfilade him.

What about when it grew dark? They'd rush him, of course. Yes, close in at dusk, like vultures round a dying beast.

What had he better do? If only he could keep them off until relief planes came over and he could make a dash for the plane, get the Very pistol and fire a signal.

Not very much hope then, though, unless it were at night, which it wouldn't be, of course. And anyway, no machine could land and take off again within miles of this awful spot.

No, perhaps the best thing would be to wait until the sun got to the plane and dried it. Then he'd have another try at getting it alight, before they killed him. That would be the best thing.

Yes, with good luck and good judgment he might make it a pretty barren victory for them. Two dead Sahibs, a burnt-out plane and a smashed Lewis-gun.

Suddenly his helmet was jerked sideways.

By Jove, that was a near one. He had better edge round the boulder a bit. Or would that expose him from the front?

If only the machine were dry, he'd make a dash for it now. Get round behind it, and have it all burning merrily before they pipped him.

The sounds of sniping suddenly increased, and so grew in volume that it was as though an attempt was being made to prevent his doing precisely what he had intended.

Forestalling his rush, were they? Going to make him keep his head down?

Precisely that.

The firing ceased suddenly and completely.

There was a pattering of horny feet, and, with a

rush, a mob of tribesmen swarmed up from below, over the curve of the mountain-flank; while simultaneously, two other crowds swiftly converged, on either side, upon the boulder behind which he crouched.

That was that, then.

Vere-Vaughan rose to his feet as the three hordes of huge and hardy mountaineers, active as cats and strong as buffaloes, with wild yells and brandished rifles, bore down upon him and engulfed him.

It was like being overwhelmed by a wave, each drop of which was a devil; like being borne down beneath a surging avalanche of great savage apes that clutched and tore and snatched and rent, as though their one desire was to tear him asunder.

But even as he fought desperately, driving his fists into open-mouthed wild-eyed hairy faces, he realized that the great Khyber knives, the small needle-pointed Pathan daggers, the heavy rifle-butts, were not being used, and that he was to be taken alive.

Before a blow on the head knocked him senseless, he saw that what had seemed about to happen to him was actually happening to the plane. It was being literally torn to pieces, rent asunder, destroyed, by the wild triumphant masses that swarmed upon it and covered it, like a million ants upon the body of a fallen bird.

And the devilish brutes were hacking Tommy's body to pieces.

When he recovered consciousness, he found that he was lying on the ground, his clothes in rags, his nose bleeding, an eye closed, his head one agonizing ache, but otherwise undamaged, unwounded, his arms and legs unhurt.

That was something to be thankful for. While one can walk, one can escape—perhaps.

But what was the idea? Ransom or torture? If they took him to the Singing Hadji of Sufed Kot, as presumably they would, his fate would depend entirely on whether the Hadji would prefer to get a considerable sum in sacks of silver Indian rupees, or whether he'd prefer to get a little of his own back on the British Government in the person of one of its officers, in revenge for his heavy defeat after the siege of Giltraza Fort.

It had been a humiliating end to his wonderful *jehad* which, starting at Sufed Kot, was to have taken Giltraza and then swept like an avalanche through the passes, over the Border, down into the Indus valley, to lay waste the country of the Infidels from Peshawar to Calcutta, harrying and slaying the Hindu *mlecchas*[35] and overthrowing the Government of their white Infidel rulers.

As he scuttled home with his tail between his legs, with a punitive column after him, the Hadji must have made himself some promises—to be kept when the time was again ripe and his Russian friends ready to help him once more.

Yes, there would be considerable rejoicings in the valleys of the Sufed Kot when a European officer was brought in alive, as a gift to the Singing Hadji.

A nasty situation. Probably the British had no more venomously vindictive enemy than this *Mullah*. And, apart from him and his personal hatred, the attitude of all Pathans towards flying-officers was peculiar. Apparently, they regarded them as persons of tremendous importance and value to the British Government, and considered them as a breed of supermen whose marvellous gifts, powers, and knowledge, enabled them to fly about the sky, and, from the safety of their altitude, to rain death upon their enemies beneath.

Well, that might be all to the good, and weigh sufficiently with these people to decide them upon a course of action of their own, independent of their spiritual suzerain, the Singing Hadji of Sufed Kot. They might, after all, know enough to do a deal with the British Government on their own account; and that might be the reason why they had only knocked him about, and not slashed him to pieces with those awful Khyber knives, which were really swords.

On the other hand, they had been doing some

---

[35] *Out-casts, unbelievers.*

pretty useful shooting, and had undoubtedly put one bullet through the top of his helmet; but there again, the close shooting might have been just clever Pathan marksmanship, to pin him down where he was, while the others surrounded his position and rushed him. Also to keep him from setting the plane alight and putting the machine-gun out of action.

And that was a bad business, the machine-gun. They'd get that all right. And the ammunition. They'd have plenty of .303 S.A. stuff of their own too, to use in it.

The plane didn't matter. They had made about as big a mess of that as he could have done by burning it. By the sounds of rending, cracking and crashing, they were going to reduce it to matchwood and scraps, each man securing a souvenir. What about the engine? A pity there wasn't a bomb or a hand-grenade there that they could smash too.

What were this lot all wrangling about, and squabbling over? How different their fiercely gabbled Pushtu was from the Peshawar *munshi's* measured cadences and slow considered speech. He had thought he was making good progress with his Pushtu, but he could hardly understand one of the sentences that these people were screaming at each other.

Probably quarrelling as to whether they should cut his throat or not.

What had he better do? Lie doggo, or sit up and put in a word for himself; suggest ransom, and appeal to their greed.

Owing to the extreme poverty of their soil and the hardship of their lives, the Pathans were about the most avaricious and grasping fellows on the face of the earth. If they would only keep him themselves, and not pass him on to the Hadji, surely he could persuade them that he was more valuable alive than dead; or rather, that he was valuable to them alive, and that his death, if they murdered him, would lead to heavy punishment; that sooner or later, the long arm of the law of the British Raj would reach out as far as here.

Could he put that into Pushtu? Probably they wouldn't listen. They considered that this air-fighting was an abominable business. Most unfair. It was openly said in Peshawar that, once upon a time, the British had been fine and honourable foes who fought man to man, rifle to rifle, and bayonet to knife. Foes who scrapped up and down the Border, through the passes and over the hills, and, by no means always winning, gave good sport. They had liked the Sahibs very much in those days, and had enjoyed the various shows, Black Mountain, Tirah, Malakand, Tochi, Afghan wars; all of them. And what with their perfect knowledge of the terrain, their mountaineering skill and hardihood, and the fact that their rifles were every bit as good as the British rifles—and in point of fact, very often were British rifles—things had been fairly equal; and when not equal, had, at any rate, been very good fun.

And now the British, who considered themselves sportsmen, and war the best of all sports, had gone and spoilt war. Spoil-sports, that's what they were.

Thus the talk of the bazaars of Peshawar, and what is said in the balconied houses of the bazaars of Peshawar is what is thought throughout not only the Border but throughout Afghanistan, Baluchistan, the Sarhad, Chitral, Khurassan, Turkestan, the Pamirs, and all that Asian world.

Hullo, that was plain enough. Someone had shouted.

"Bring him to the *Malik*, I say."

And someone else:

"No, to the *Mullah*. The *Mullah*—who is as ten *Maliks*."

The *Mullah* presumably would be the Singing Hadji of Sufed Kot himself, and the *Malik* the local Chief or Khan. Or possibly the *Mullah* wasn't the Hadji, but the local Holy Man; and so far, perhaps, it was a case of State versus Church; the secular party, the *Malik's* henchmen, wanting to take him to that individual's fortified village, presumably nearby, for ransom; and the ecclesiastical party wanting to run him off to the *Mullah*, who would most certainly have him handed over to the Singing Hadji, probably for execution. And by all accounts, the Singing Hadji's executions were apt to be drastic and slow.

What a hellish din. They'd be fighting among themselves in a moment. How long had he been lying there? Probably a whole minute or less. Might be as well to get up and try to weigh in on the side of the *Malik's* lot. For somehow, he felt that, if there were a chance at all, it would be rather with State than Church, be rather with the *Malik's* greed of gain than the *Mullah's* greed of vengeance. Much more likely that the *Malik* would be a bit of a sportsman than that the *Mullah* would— with his odium theologicum added to his natural enmity toward the invader.

By all accounts, nine-tenths of the Border trouble was fomented by the *Mullahs*, who had the most fierce-ly fanatical religious hatred of the Infidel, whose liberal and tolerant ideas of education were undermining the blind belief of the Sons of the Prophet in their spiritual leaders.

To this *Mullah*, whether he were the Singing Hadji himself or not, the British Officer stood for what was even more detestable than invasion—innovation; what was even more horrible than political intrusion— religious deterioration.

It was the might of the *Mullah* that was threatened, his hitherto unquestioned arbitrary and complete pow-er in a country where, except for the hereditary Khans, other potentates and powers were not tolerated. In the Free Country of the Border no man was king, but every *Mullah* was a monarch in the district that he ruled through the religious faith and obedience of his fanatical flock.

Hullo, it was warming up . . . A man, unusually big, brawny and active, even among those huge moun-taineers, had suddenly whipped out his Khyber knife, seized the beard of a man who was thrusting his furious face into his own, as he screamed,

"The *Mullah*! The *Mullah*! The *Mullah*!" and slashed him across the neck, the broad blade sinking down to the bone. There'd be a free fight in a minute, and the captive would get the benefit. Somebody would give him a swipe with one of those ghastly butchers' knives —one of the *Mullah* lot probably, to spite the *Malik* men. He had better do something about it.

God, how his head hurt! Would he go giddy and fall down again, if he scrambled to his feet?

A diversion came from the direction of the wreck of the aeroplane. Someone had found the Very pistol and fired it off. As the scrimmage was suspended while all heads turned that way, Vere-Vaughan rose to his feet, his aching head seeming to spin upon his shoulders.

"*Hi!*" he shouted in the momentary lull, as he swayed. And as all heads turned toward him, he bawled in Pushtu:

"Listen! The Sirkar gives big rewards for the Sahibs who fly. Ransom. Take me to the *Malik.* Rupees. *Backsheesh* for everybody."

And led by the man who had slain the *Mullah's* representative, the *Malik's* party, grouping themselves about him, began to hustle him down the mountain-side. Evidently these had chosen the better part—or hoped they had. Let those who wished to waste their time in tearing the magic flying devil-carriage to pieces, do so; let those silly fools who wanted to hand good money over to the *Mullah,* say so; but let wise men see that their *Malik* and their village got the rupees. They'd take the cash and let the credit, of slaying an Infidel, go. So—on to the village.

Staggering, stumbling and falling, Vere-Vaughan was shepherded down the mountain-side; and, by the time he was shaking with fatigue, reached the plain and a distant view of a village which, from the aeroplane, he had not seen, whether by reason of intervening mountain or impenetrable mist, he did not know.

Thank God, they had flown a long way from the fortified place that they had recently bombed! There might be a certain amount of personal feeling in the minds of the inhabitants of that particular spot. Not that any of them had been killed, but as householders they must have suffered a good deal of damage and loss. And moreover, they might claim that he was their lawful prey—although this gang had actually caught him—inasmuch as it was a shot from one of their rifles that had hit the pilot and so brought down the machine. Yes, it was truly lucky that that Fort and village were quite a good many miles away, as they must be, for poor Tommy had flown the machine, or it had flown itself, for quite a while after they had turned and left the place.

The people there would be bound to hear all about it though. The news of the bringing down of a flying devil-carriage would be known throughout the whole Border country, in a day or two.

However, by the time they came to claim him, the *Malik* of this village would have made up his mind, and made his little arrangements too; and if he had decided to hold the prisoner for ransom, he would jolly well hold him; At least it was to be hoped he would; though it seemed a bit improbable that he would be able to defy the Singing Hadji of Sufed Kot when he came to hear of it, and demanded the prisoner's surrender, as surely he would.

Hullo; he was going to faint. He could go no further. He was done. That must have been a proper blow he got on the head. Probably a swipe from a gun-butt. And, but for his helmet, he'd have been out for the long count, with concussion of the brain, if nothing worse. He must sit down.

He fell rather than sat, and at once discovered that, in thinking he could go no further, he was mistaken. For promptly his captors started to beat him unmercifully; and by the time he had been violently struck across the face and head by horny hands; kicked in the ribs; and had received a few heavy blows across his. arms and shoulders from sticks, shoe-heels and the cleaning-rods of Martini rifles, he realized that he could go quite a long way yet. It was humiliating beyond speech, painful beyond words, but probably, these callous and ruffianly brutes were saving his life.

For, down the mountain-side after them came a

smaller but violently vociferating crowd of *Mullah's* men, evidently nobler souls than these his captors, inasmuch as they put blood before *backsheesh*, punishment of the Infidel invader before ransom and reward.

Thrusting the others aside, the big leader who had already killed one man that morning, seized Vere-Vaughan by the arm, jerked him to his feet, and shouted in Pushtu:

"Come on, you fool. They'll slash your guts out if they get you."

And with an effort of will which was a triumph of mind over matter, Vere-Vaughan pulled himself together, rose to his feet, and again staggered on.

§3

The village was a Fort and the Fort was a village; and in the curious and mediæval way of life of its inhabitants, John Vere-Vaughan would have been more interested, had his own fate and future been more certain and settled.

Definitely he was not popular, for as the party approached the fortified gate, and certain ardent spirits running on ahead spread the glad news that one of the *feringhis* who had come down in the wounded flying-bird had been captured alive, a mob of women and children, hobbledehoys and girls, streamed out, shrieking insulting epithets and horrid threats.

Mingling with his captors, they endeavoured to get sufficiently near to the helpless prisoner to strike him, spit upon him, and to claw at his face.

One woman, knocking off his helmet and seizing his hair, dragged his head back and scratched him fiercely, causing him excruciating pain; and by the time that a laughing stalwart had pushed her away, Vere-Vaughan's sentiments were not chivalrous.

Evidently the women-folk would be on the side of the *Mullah* party. And what were those lines that had come into his mind as the horde of shrieking hags had borne down upon them from the village gate?

> *"When you're wounded and left on Afghanistan's
>   plains,*
> *And the women come out to cut up what
>   remains,*
> *Jest roll to your rifle and blow out your brains*
> *An' go to your Gawd like a soldier."*

Yes; if, in the end, the *Mullah* triumphed over the *Malik*, and handed the abhorred Infidel prisoner over to the women, he'd have cause to envy poor Tommy, and to wish that he himself had been shot while trying to destroy the machine.

The Pathan might be a magnificent enemy, a foeman worthy of one's steel, but he did not shine as a generous captor. There was nothing of "a lion in the fight, my boy, but a lamb when the fight was done" about the Brothers Mahsud, Afridi, and Mohmand.

And as the mob struggled through the gate, a beastly thing occurred, an event which Vere-Vaughan found it difficult to forget by day, and that haunted his dreams by night.

From the low doorway of the guard-house, there rose up an aged man. His beard was long and white; his wrinkled face cadaverous and filthy; his trembling hands, long skinny claws; and he was blind. Toothless and blind and old beyond the ordinary span of life of the Pathan—who is very apt to be cut off in his fighting youth or prime—this man, whether by age or renown, evidently enjoyed the respect of the populace; for, as he tottered forward with hands outstretched, they made way for him, even the leader standing aside and halting.

"What do I hear?" quavered the ancient. "What is this? Great *khubbar*[36]! A *feringhi* prisoner! One of those who slew my sons, yea, and my grandsons?"

Evidently the old man's descendants had died in battle, or perhaps been hanged for raiding, robbery, and murder.

With joyous whoops his captors assured the old

---

[36] *News.*

man that this was indeed a *feringhi*, a white man, a Sahib, and no ordinary one either; one of those who, defying Allah, flew about the sky.

Fumbling, grasping and clutching, the old man seized Vere-Vaughan by the ears, violently shook his head, cuffed his face with all his strength, which was quite adequate to the effort, and then deliberately attempted to gouge out his eyes with his thumbs.

Again humiliating and painful beyond belief.

Violently struggling, Vere-Vaughan freed his hands and thrust the horrible old man from him, refraining, even in his pain and rage and fear, from striking him with his fist.

"Nay, nay, do not blind him, *buddoo*," laughed the leader, thrusting himself between Vere-Vaughan and the old man. "Don't blind him. Not yet. We are going to see what the *Malik* has to say about it. They've done us a lot of damage, curse them. Now perhaps we can make them pay. Yea, tenfold."

"Put out his eyes, I say. Put out his eyes," quavered the ancient. "Tear out his tongue; and, to-morrow, cut his throat."

And at least half the crowd and all the women seemed to be of the same opinion.

"Come on," shouted the leader. "Get him to the *durbar-khana*."

And, headed by the speaker, the men of his more immediate following hustled his prisoner along the street to the gate of a compound on the far side of which stood one of the biggest buildings of the village. This Town Hall or Municipal Offices was very stoutly constructed of sun-baked clay bricks, and like all the rest of the wall-enclosed village, looked fit to stand a siege. Evidently the news had reached the Mayor and Corporation—or the *Malik* and his gang—as rugs and *dhurries* were being spread on the dusty earth before the door of this Durbar-house, and a few tightly-stuffed bolsters, covered in dirty white, laid on either side of an aged cane-bottomed blackwood chair which looked as though it had once adorned a *babu's* office in Peshawar.

And as the scuffling crowd poured in at the compound gate, the *Malik* and his satellites emerged from the *durbar-khana* or Council Chamber and took their places.

Here was evidently a free Parliament, whereof every male inhabitant of the village, young or old, was a self-elected Member.

Glancing round, Vere-Vaughan noted with approval that female suffrage had evidently not yet reached this part of the Afghan Border; for the ladies who had spat upon him, flung mud and stones at him, and endeavoured to get at him with knife or talon, remained at the compound gate, whence they watched the proceedings with savage eyes.

As the *Malik* seated himself upon the chair, and the village elders and office-holders sat down upon the rugs and *dhurries*, the whole assembly squatted, and, gratefully, Vere-Vaughan sank down upon the ground.

Thank Heaven that, whatever was going to happen, he could rest in peace while they wrangled; for rest and peace were what he craved, more even than drink and food.

He had never known what weariness meant until now!

Dully he was aware that his leading captor was haranguing the *Malik* and the assembly, claiming that, inasmuch as he himself had personally directed the capture, and had with his own hand seized the captive, he had the right to make the following proposals, and to expect that they would at least receive careful attention.

Vere-Vaughan realized that, like so many of his kind, the man was something of an orator; and, moreover, that he himself could follow quite easily what was said when the man was making his speech. It was infinitely easier to understand what was solemnly uttered in this durbar than it was to get the meaning of the shrieked gabblings and the frenzied wranglings of the mob that had fought over him.

"Consider, oh *Malik*," cried the man whose name Vere-Vaughan now discovered to be Wali Dad, "that what we want, and always shall want, is rifles. More rifles, and then more rifles still. Never can we have enough. Nor enough of ammunition. What need is there for me to speak of the ever-increasing difficulties of getting good rifles and the ammunition that fits them? Why, when I was a boy and had my first rifle, it cost but thirty rupees, and it was a good one. And what is the price of such a rifle now, a magazine rifle? Its weight in silver will not buy it. And if that is its price to-day, what will be its price to-morrow? Allah knows! Therefore, I say, let us get silver, and with that silver let us buy rifles and ammunition.

"Let us sell this man back to the Sirkar, bargaining fiercely and letting him not go until we have reached the utmost limit of the price that they will pay. And with that money, let us buy rifles. Not the faulty short-lived weapons of the Kabul *lohar*[37] or some *then-ka-bar-then banane-wallah* who calls himself a *banduk-banane-wallah*,[38] but rifles made in Russia if we cannot get those made in England. We all know the Tashkent man from whom the rifles of Russia . . ."

"Silence, Wali Dad," interrupted the *Malik* at this point. And added the equivalent of "That'll be quite enough out of you, on that subject."

"Well, Russian or English, what does it matter, so long as they are real *Belati*[39] rifles, and not bazaar trash?" continued Wali Dad. "Anyhow, I captured this man, and I say let us sell him. Cutting his throat or putting his feet in the fire or handing him over to the women, may be all very well, and I've nothing to say against it with regard to an ordinary prisoner. But in this case it would be simply silly. Who'd shoot his best camel because it had trodden on his foot? Who'd butcher his best buffalo because he wanted a bit of liver with his *kaibobs*? Who'd kill a prisoner worth thousands and thousands of rupees just because he didn't like the man's people? The *feringhi* is an enemy all right, but how could we have war if we had no

---

[37] *Blacksmith.*
[38] *Gun-maker.*
[39] *European.*

enemies? You can't have war without enemies, and who wants to live without war? Very well. Sell him to the Sirkar I say, and buy rifles and ammunition."

And as the man sat down, there was a murmur of applause from the throng about him.

But the old man who had attacked the prisoner rose to his feet, and in a quavering scream, cried:

"*Din! Din!* The Faith! Kill the Infidel. Slay all Infidels, I say. Kill him, as they killed my sons and grandsons."

"All very well for you, grandfather," boomed a deep voice from the other side of the compound. "You don't want a rifle," and at this sally there was a laugh.

"And suppose they did kill your sons and grandsons! What did you expect them to do with them? Fill them up with curry?" asked another. "Wali Dad is right. Let the Sirkar ransom the flying-man, I say, and let us buy rifles and ammunition.

"And then let us go up against the Khan of Khairabad, for harbouring the enemies of the Singing Hadji," he added; a sentiment which met with considerable approval from the audience.

"What will the Sirkar pay for him?" enquired another man, rising to his feet as the last speaker sat down. "That's the question. Let it depend on that. If it is a matter of a few hundred rupees to be divided among the lot of us, I say let us serve him as they served my brother. They hanged him: hanged him in Peshawar gaol. Well, let us hang this man, over the gate. They set us the example. Do what you like to him first, and then hang him."

"What? And give them excuse to bring their flying devil-carriages over, and get the place blown to pieces, eh?" sneered Wali Dad. "Would it be better to have bombs on our houses than rupees in our pockets, you fool?"

"Anybody else got anything to say?" enquired the *Malik*, rising to his feet. "No. Well, listen to me. You heard Wali Dad. He talks sense. Of what comfort will it be to us that we have slain this man, next time our village is ringed about by outlaws, raiders, enemies, and for every hundred shots they fire, we can only reply with scarce a dozen? What will it avail us that we slew this man, when our ammunition is gone, and the enemy bursts in and sets fire to the thatch and slaughters us and our women and children; drives off our horses, our sheep and our goats; and scatters us homeless upon the mountains?

"We will send messengers to Giltraza saying that we have one of the officers of high rank who fly in the air—and what are they prepared to pay for his life? Knowing that it would be useless for them to send the flying devil-carriages or a *rissala* of cavalry to rescue him, inasmuch as neither we nor the prisoner would be here when they arrived, they will bargain with us. For long we will dicker and argue and wrangle, holding out for our price until we settle upon a sum. And it will be a good one."

"And will they pay it?" sneered the old man who had expressed other views for the disposal of the prisoner.

"Having given their word they will keep it. Having promised a sum, they will pay that sum," replied the *Malik.*

"Always provided," he added, "that we hand over the prisoner sound and whole."

"And not with his eyes gouged out, *buddoo,*" shouted someone at the back, raising a laugh.

And at this point it was borne in upon Vere-Vaughan that an evil practice, known in America as high-jacking, was understood by the simple villagers of this remote part of the world. For, rising to his feet, one of Wali Dad's party, a man who had been active in support of the latter's defence of the prisoner from irreparable damage, observed:

"Yea, hear the words of the *Malik* and heed them, for he speaks wisely and for the benefit of all. But let us remember this. News of our wonderful capture of the flying devil-carriage, our slaying of one of the men who fly, and our capture of this one, will swiftly travel abroad and be known far and wide throughout the land. Let us watch, therefore, that this prisoner be not snatched from us by evil-disposed men, who would then go swiftly by secret ways and themselves take him to Giltraza and keep him hidden in a cave nearby while they offer him for sale."

"Yea verily! There you are," screamed a man whom Vere-Vaughan had previously noticed as being a prominent and violent leader of the *Mullah* party. "Exactly! Before we know it, we shall be besieged here, and the place perhaps taken by assault. What, my brothers? Are we to fight and lose our lives in *defence* of this man? Lunacy! He who proposes such a course is afflicted of Allah."

"Oh, he is, is he?" observed the *Malik*, rising to his feet and laying his hand upon the handle of his *tulwar*, the sword of office which he had girded on before taking the chair at these proceedings.

"He is! By Allah, he is!" boomed a great voice from behind; and, as all heads turned in the direction of the gate, Vere-Vaughan beheld a big and ugly man, the appearance of whose fierce cruel and scowling countenance was not improved by the ravages of smallpox which had not only deeply pitted his face, but had destroyed the sight of one eye and eaten away one of his nostrils.

Obviously the *Mullah*, Vere-Vaughan thought, and thanked God that, by all accounts of the appearance of that gentleman, it was not the Singing Hadji of Sufed Kot. He was said to be a hard-faced man of clear-cut features and predatory hawk-like countenance, and certainly not disfigured like this by smallpox.

Could he be the far-famed Hadji of Turangzai? No, it would scarcely be that firebrand, as he'd hardly be in this part of the world; and moreover, he must be an older man than this. A very much older man. Why, his son-in-law Abdul Ghaffar Khan, leader of the pernicious Red-shirts of the Border, must be a man of middle-age. No, this would be the local *Mullah*.

And a damned unprepossessing brute he was, concluded Vere-Vaughan.

Nevertheless, from what he had gathered, the fellow might just as well be the Singing Hadji himself, inasmuch as he would either have the prisoner put to death here and in short order, or hand him over to the Singing Hadji, that that ecclesiastic might have the pleasure of dealing with him personally.

God send that the State stood up to the Church, and that the *Malik's* love of rupees was greater than his fear of excommunication.

Loud cheers from the *Mullah's* party and a noisy ululation from the women applauded the appearance and bold firm statement of the *Mullah*.

"Afflicted of Allah, he is," boomed the *Mullah* again. "For if it were necessary, we *would* fight, and some of us lose our lives, in defence of our right to punish this servant of the Sirkar, that great enemy of God which tramples on the Faith, martyrs its ministers, and invades the sacred soil of Islam with fire and sword, loot, rapine and slaughter."

Vere-Vaughan almost smiled to himself as he thought of the cast-iron British Rules and Regulations which so stringently forbade anything in the nature of the unnecessary use of fire or sword; of the slaying of a single individual, save in the heat of battle; in necessary reprisal and punishment for raiding and slaughter, or after fullest and fairest trial in Court of Law; and of the looting of so much as a rupee's worth of property, however great the provocation caused by the Pathan's cruelty to the wounded, and callous brutality when raiding and rieving on the Indian side of the Border.

"But that will not be necessary," continued the *Mullah*. "The man will be dead, long before there is any question of defending him from capture by irreligious backsliders who would take him from us that they might make profit of him. Moreover, he will be dead long before he could be recaptured by those who sent him hither to slaughter us, destroy our homes and lay waste our fields. Let him die. Let our women torture him through the night; and at dawn we will hang him from a high gallows, with the entrails of a pig looped about his neck. I have spoken."

"You have," thought Vere-Vaughan. "You have

surely been delivered of a mouthful. Now, Mr. *Malik*, it's up to you."

When the applause that had followed the *Mullah's* speech had died down, the *Malik* rose to his feet, smiled sarcastically, and observed that possibly there was a little misunderstanding somewhere.

Was the *Mullah* under the impression that it was *he* who had destroyed the flying devil-carriage, slaying one of its occupants and capturing the other? And if he were not under that impression, but quite realized that it was the *Malik's* excellent son-in-law Wali Dad who had done so, doubtless the *Mullah* was fully prepared to recompense that good man, his friends, relations, supporters and followers, and indeed all the fighting men of the village, by himself paying from the rich revenues of his *ziarat*[40] a sum equivalent to the amount which the Sirkar would undoubtedly pay for the return, alive, hale and hearty, sound in wind and limb, of their invaluable Flying-Sahib.

He had not gone into the matter thoroughly, or even been officially informed, as to the exact sum which the Sirkar was prepared to pay in such a case; but, speaking off-hand, he would be inclined to put the amount at at least ten thousand rupees.

At the mention of this colossal sum, a gasp, a murmur, and audible ejaculations of "*Wah! Wah!*" proceeded from the assembly.

Ten thousand rupees!

Religion was religion, and they were all devout Mussulmans; the *Mullah* was the *Mullah*, and a *zubberdusti*[41] man was he; the *houris* of Paradise were the *houris* of Paradise, albeit somewhat far away; Allah was Allah and Mahommet was his Prophet in Heaven, and no sane man disputed the fact; but . . . ten thousand rupees, here on earth!

Many promptly deserted the *Mullah* faction and joined that of the *Malik* openly. More did so in their inmost hearts.

Yea. Piety was piety—and rupees were rupees. Only

---

[40] *Shrine, holy tomb.*
[41] *Forceful: violent.*

to think of it! Ten thousand!

A very wicked-looking fighting-man, one Nazir Ali Khan—who was here to-day, an agriculturist, and gone to-morrow, an outlaw raider and Border thief—upon whose head was a price, whose ways were very evil, and whose piety very pronounced, rose to his feet.

"Oh, *Malik*," quoth he. "Do you charm our ears with honied words and beguile our senses with foolish talk, or do you speak of that which you know? Does the Sirkar pay ten thousand rupees for one of its fighting Sahibs who fly?"

"It does. Or more," averred the *Malik* roundly.

"Then there is one for sale," observed the robber, and sat down again amid loud laughter.

Upon him the *Mullah* turned his baleful eye.

"Thou dog and son of a dog," he growled. "Behold!" And stretching forth his closed right hand, the *Mullah* extended the index finger and then the little finger, as he held the arm rigid, and pointed at the man who, laying his hand upon the hilt of his dagger, moistened his lips.

"Thinkest thou to tread the knife-edged bridge that stretches across the chasm 'twixt Earth and Paradise, thou fool? Thy feet shall slip; and into Gehennum thou shalt fall and burn . . . and burn . . . and *burn* . . ."

The man's fierce gaze sank before the terrifying glare of the *Mullah's* eye, and he pulled the end of his *puggri* across his face as though sheltering it from the heat of a flame that scorched and seared.

The fearless and ruffianly desperado was cowed, and Vere-Vaughan noted the fact with misgiving.

Turning from the man, the *Mullah* harangued the free parliament of Kurnai village and valley.

"Hear and heed, oh Sons of the Prophet," he cried. "Listen; hear my words, and take note. Of what avail to you in the Day of Judgment are rupees? Will you go before the throne of Allah and into the presence of Mahommet his Prophet, holding a bag of money? Naked, we came upon this earth and naked shall we cross the bridge of Eblis. Nothing that the eye can see or that the hand can touch shall we take into the dread

Presence. But more solid than rock, more real than Earth and Sun and Moon itself, more eloquent than the voice of the Angel Gabriel or Haroun the Brother of Moussa the Prophet, will be the deeds that you have done here in this life.

"And which of you will wish, in that last hour, to have upon his soul the sin of this deed that you would do, the selling of this slayer of the Faithful, this Infidel delivered into your hands for punishment? The man who would do that would steal from a *ziarat*, would use the stones of a prophet's tomb to make himself a cooking-place, the sacred bones of a Saint for fuel to cook his mutton stew. Such a one would pluck the Beard of a Holy Pir[42]—yea, of the Prophet Himself—to stuff a saddle."

He paused, and the deep silence was as that of a great empty place at midnight.

"And," he resumed, "let no man draw nigh unto Mosque or Shrine with this sin upon his soul, after he has heard my warning. Let no such man come into my presence. Let him not dare to prostrate himself in prayer, for his prayers will not be heard. Nay, more, his son will die; his wife will be unfaithful; his horse will break a leg; and the crops of his field will wither away."

Turning about, the *Mullah* of Kurnai made dramatic exit; and for several seconds no man drew audible breath or so much as heaved a sigh.

Then tumult broke loose and chaos seized the orderly durbar. And louder than the voices of the *Malik* and his officials who cried again for order, louder than the voices of the *Malik*'s party and the followers of Wali Dad, louder even than the shrill cries of the women, were the shouts of applause and roars of approval from the followers of the *Mullah*.

Yes, decided Vere-Vaughan, oratory, for the time being at least, had won the day. Oratory, with its appeal to superstition; combined doubtless with the feeling that, even assuming the occurrence of the extremely improbable event of the *Malik*'s obtaining ten thousand rupees for the prisoner, the fact remained

---

[42] *Saint.*

that there is many a slip 'twixt the cup and the lip, 'twixt the money-bag and the empty pocket; and that, after all, the man in the village street might see precious little of the ransom money, if any were paid.

That there still was a stout party of hardy spirits who did see a personal profit—if only in the shape of a brand-new rifle and a thousand rounds of ammunition —was nevertheless obvious. For shout and bawl as the *Mullah's* men might; answering shouts, flashing eyes, bared gleaming teeth, foam-flecked lips and shaken fists were by no means wanting.

And as Vere-Vaughan was well aware, albeit the Pathan is a fanatically religious son of Islam, ready on the least provocation to go *ghazi* and die for the Faith, his nature is also provided with a remarkably practical streak. He is both a religious visionary and a secular realist; and, at the same time, a calmly cunning casuist. Sufficiently an idealist to visualize the green pastures, still waters, and lovely *houris* of Paradise— particularly the *houris*—he is also sufficiently a materialist to know precisely how many *pies* go to a *pice*, how many *pice* to an *anna*,[43] and how many *annas* to a rupee; and it is an unusually dull specimen of the genus who cannot, upon occasion, so arrange matters that his conscience is clear and his debt cleared; his pious heart full and his pocket fuller.

And herein lay Vere-Vaughan's small hope—that, in some way, the followers of the *Malik* and Wali Dad might show those of the *Mullah* a way, albeit muddy, slippery and twisting, whereby they could reach the goal of personal enrichment while not entirely deviating from the general direction of salvation. It should not be difficult, if he read the Pathan aright, for the *Malik* and Wali Dad to persuade, at any rate the unconvinced, that, though their feet might be soiled along such a path, their faces need not be blackened.

Suddenly a rifle banged and a swift silence fell upon the noisy assembly.

Turning sharply, Vere-Vaughan saw that a man standing behind the *Malik* had fired the shot,

---

[43] "Anna" = *one penny. Sixteen to a rupee.*

doubtless by his order, and probably a variation of the idea of ringing a bell for silence, or tapping with a chairman's gavel.

The *Malik* was on his feet.

"Hearken, oh men of Kurnai. The Pir Sahib has said his say; and to the words of so holy a *Mullah* all must give ear, though as Nazir Ali Khan the Outlaw has said, the *Mullah* will not recompense us for the great loss of those sacks of rupees, those mule-loads of minted silver Government-of-India rupees that we should lose by foolishly cutting the throat of this man.

"But the *Mullah* has said that the prisoner must die; he must be *hallaled*; his throat must be cut, as that of a sheep or goat, making him an acceptable sacrifice at the Mullah's shrine and in the sight of Allah.

"If we obey the *Mullah*, we have his blessing and the favour of the light of his holy and lovely countenance. If we disobey him, we have ten thousand rupees.

"Which is it to be? Are we to lose this great sum at the Pir Sahib's whim? Or are we to show him that though he be a Judge he is not a Ruler? For who made him a Ruler and a Judge over us? Are we to lose our money—or our favour in the sight of the one eye of our *Mullah?*"

Applause and laughter from lewd fellows of the baser sort.

"Suppose we do neither?" he asked.

"*And both*," he added, leering round. "Suppose I, in council with the other leaders who forever watch over your interests and consider what is best for you—suppose we use our brains while you use your strong right arms and the keen sight that Allah gave you for the true aiming of your rifles. And suppose we think of a plan whereby we lose not this great sum of money, and yet retain the favour and the blessing of our holy Pir."

The silent crowd was all attention. Hands stroked long beards, scrabbled in short ones, or sought to relieve slight itchings beneath big turbans, as the keen eyes in avaricious or fanatical faces closely watched their headman.

In the *Malik's* oratorical pause, light apparently dawned upon the evil mind of Nazir Ali Khan, the man who had already earned the rebuke of the *Mullah*.

"By Allah!" he guffawed. "That's good, Malik Saheb. Send him out to-night with me and half a dozen more —to have his throat cut. Then, being a mighty *bahadur*, like all these Officer Sahibs, he'll escape from us— and of course we'll follow him. We'll chase him—all the way to *Giltraza*. And a mile or so from that Fort we'll catch him!"

All eyes turned in the direction of the speaker, and on the faces of the quicker-witted, smiles were dawning.

"And we'll come back," continued Nazir Ali Khan, "and show you and the *Mullah* his blood-stained coat— and a few other things. An eyeball or so . . ."

"Out of a sheep," he grinned parenthetically, as he leered round at his audience.

"Yes, we'll bring back plenty of evidence of his death—*and* we'll bring back ten thousand rupees also."

There was a general laugh; and hope dawned faintly in Vere-Vaughan's anxious half-stunned mind.

Yes, that would be like the Pathan. Tell the *Mullah* that the captive had been butchered as requested; whereas he would be safe and sound in Giltraza Fort, handed over in exchange for a certain amount of cash and a credit note for the rest. Of course, the O.C. there would neither have ten thousand rupees nor the authority to disburse it, but he would pretty promptly get on the heliograph to someone who'd authorize him to promise a certain amount, and to hand over part of it forthwith.

"What do you think of my idea, oh *Malik*," insolently shouted Nazir Ali Khan, evidently the *enfant terrible* of Kurnai.

"I don't think of it at all," rebuked the *Malik*, and again added the Pushtu equivalent of "And that'll be quite enough out of *you*."

Nevertheless, Vere-Vaughan thought of it, and decided that some extremely good seed had been sown in remarkably receptive and fertile soil.

Evidently the idea made tremendous appeal to the simple villagers. A lovely idea—to diddle the *Mullah*, keep the ecclesiastical peace, and also collect the cash.

But the glow of hope faded as he realized that the man was a fool to blurt out the suggestion in full durbar like that. Of course there would be plenty of pious and faithful members of the *Mullah's* congregation who would go straight off and tell him exactly what Nazir Ali Khan had said. Whereupon the *Mullah* would take good care that the prisoner was not spirited away in the night, under the pretence of having his throat cut, outside the walls.

The *Malik* again called the assembly to order.

"Now then," quoth he, "you've heard what I have had to say. You have listened to the words of our holy *Mullah*. You have listened to the speech of sensible members of this assembly as well as"—with a glance in the direction of Nazir Ali Khan—"the braying of asses and the bleating of goats. We have come to no decision; and, here and now, at this meeting, we will not come to a decision, the matter being too important for haste.

"Upon every problem the wise man sleepeth. To-night, the prisoner will be closely guarded, and to-morrow we will decide his fate. Discuss among yourselves, and, when we re-assemble, it will be made known by acclamation whether those who are in favour of the village being provided, strengthened, protected, emboldened and enriched, number a majority—as I have no doubt they will—or whether those who would truckle to the *Mullah* and keep us weak and fearful in the face of our enemies, are to triumph over us. I have spoken. The Durbar is closed."

"Come on, quickly," said Wali Dad, seizing Vere-Vaughan's arm and pulling him to his feet. "Follow me . . . Close round him, my brothers."

And while babble of argument and noise of wrangling arose about them, Wali Dad and his followers, with Vere-Vaughan in their midst, thrust their way through the crowd of men and the mob of screaming and reviling women, out of the compound, down the street, across the centre of the village, and to a house somewhat bigger and more strongly fortified than the rest.

"This is the *Malik*'s house," said Wali Dad. "You will be safe here, Sahib.

"Until the *Mullah*'s men storm it and get you out," he added with a malicious grin.

A real Pathan humourist.

§4

The night that followed was not a happy one for Flying-Officer John Vere-Vaughan. The roof, floor and walls of the room in which he was confined, were of unadorned clay, burnt as hard as brick; the thick and heavy door of tough *kan* wood; the light-and-ventilation window, a small barred unglazed aperture, placed high up in the outer wall. Of furniture there was none, save a native *charpai*, a string and frame bed unprovided with so much as a blanket or *rezai*.[44] A prison cell indeed.

But horrible a prison cell as it was, doubtless it was nothing more nor less than an ordinary bedroom, sitting-room or boudoir, of the *Malik*'s house; and regarded by that civic dignitary and the members of his household as an entirely eligible bed-sitting-room for a single gentleman; and, albeit unprovided with gas-fire or running h. and c., undoubtedly attendance was included.

Seating himself on the uncomfortable bed-frame, Vere-Vaughan rested his elbows upon his knees, his aching head upon his hands, and forbore to give way to despair. He had a chance. Definitely there was room for hope that he would be offered for ransom—an offer which, whether eventually modified or not, would undoubtedly be accepted.

His plane was wrecked, his friend was killed, and he himself was in the hands of fanatical and vindictive enemies, whose lives and property he had been in the

---

[44] *Quilted bed-covering of cotton.*

act of threatening and attempting to destroy; but a hope remained.

And incidently, what had they done with the instruments and fittings of the plane that he had last seen them in the act of wrecking and tearing to pieces? Had they been able to dismount the Lewis-gun and bring it along?

Unfortunately there could be little doubt as to that.

And what about the engine and the instruments in the "office"? There was nothing there that would be of any use to them, or that they could use against the British, except the Lewis-gun and the ammunition. He blamed himself severely for not putting the gun out of action. But he had wasted time, or rather lost invaluable time and opportunity, in trying to set the machine on fire, knowing that when it blazed up and became a furnace, the machine-gun would be destroyed along with everything else—or that at any rate, it would be rendered quite useless by subjection to that tremendous heat. When he had found the plane would not burn, he ought to have put the gun out of action at once, by smashing the sights and the lock. But things had happened so suddenly, and he had been all-ends-up, what with the crash, the death of poor Tommy, and the sudden surprise when they had started firing at him.

And before he could decide as to whether he should make a dash from behind his boulder and start wrecking-operations, or wait till the machine dried so that he could set fire to it, they had put down a barrage of bullets, and then rushed him.

A bad business. Perhaps he wasn't to blame, but his father always said that one ought to blame oneself when one can.

To think that only a few hours ago he had been as a bird, and flying like a bird, and now here he was in a prison. The bird was caged all right. What were the chances of getting out of the cage?

Going to the barred aperture, the ledge or sill of which was some seven feet from the ground, he rested his hands upon it and drew himself up, so that he could look out.

A second later a handful of mud and filth struck the bars and spattered his face.

H'm! There was good watch kept on that side, anyhow. Probably the window looked on to the compound at the back of the *Malik's* house, and there would be a sentry under it. A stalwart tribesman with long knife, dagger and rifle. And doubtless the watcher himself was watched by an admiring throng of spectators, women and children, some of whom had flung the mud.

Not much hope in that direction, even if he could dislodge the stout bars and crawl out, the latter feat a itself a pretty difficult task.

And of course, there would be another sentry at the door. How was that fastened?

On the inner side it was not fastened at all, there being no sort of bolt or lock. Doubtless it was one of those doors secured on the outer side by the usual stout heavy iron staple, hasp and padlock. And of course there would always be people in the next room, into which this one opened.

Well, what about investigating, anyway. A foolish waste of time, no doubt, but there was no harm in trying; and one heard all sorts of wonderful tales about unexpectedly easy escapes.

Thrusting his fingers into the considerable crack between the edge of the door and the jamb, Vere-Vaughan pulled, shook the door, and then pushed against it. There was a sound without. A few seconds later, the door was opened inwards, a tall Pathan appeared in the aperture, and smiled upon him. It was a large and cheerful smile, showing a perfect set of shining teeth, but the effect of the smiling lips was somewhat marred by the gesture of the hand, as, swiftly, the sentry drew his finger across his throat from ear to ear.

Enough said; although no word was spoken.

The man slammed the door, and Vere-Vaughan heard sounds as of an iron bar being dropped across it and a heavy padlock being inserted into a hasp.

So that, again, was that. At door and window a watchful active and powerful man armed to the teeth, and numbers of others within call. And, had he been entirely alone in the house, how long would it have taken him to open that inch-thick hard-wood door, with its heavy battens and cross-pieces, secured by a strong bar, iron fastening and padlock, without tools of any kind; or to remove an iron bar from a small aperture seven feet from the ground, and squeeze himself through an opening of circumference smaller than that of his body?

What about the walls? They were only of burnt clay and sun-baked brick, but one cannot dig through even that with one's finger-nails.

And in any case, the idea of escape was mere idle speculation, of course, for he would, naturally, be most closely guarded, day and night, both by those who saw in him an incredibly valuable property, and those who wanted his blood even more than they wanted the blood-money.

Well, well. . . . ! What about a little sleep? If this appalling headache and the extreme discomfort of the unfurnished *charpai* would permit of it.

The wretched thing, a four-legged oblong frame across which fibre rope was tautly strung—taking the place of laths and making a sort of net of four-inch mesh—was more an instrument of torture than of rest, a rack rather than a bed; for, unless his head rested upon the hard knotted rope at one end, his feet extended beyond the frame at the other. And if, to ease his aching feet, he rested his head upon the frame, its hardness and the lumps of the fibre rope soon made the position unbearable.

Having removed his thin khaki coat and folded it up to make a pad beneath his head, he found himself shivering and aching with cold.

Resuming his coat, he lay flat upon the rough floor of beaten earth, and decided that, on the whole, it was more comfortable than the bed.

Nor was it particularly helpful to realize that, probably, the majority of the inhabitants of the village were doing the same thing, lying on the ground with nothing more than a thin cotton *dhurrie*[45] for bed and a dirty cotton sheet for covering.

Doubtless there was no intention, in this particular matter, of inflicting hardship. On the other hand, it must have occurred, even to these savages that, like themselves, Europeans eat and drink. Probably they were gorging themselves with mutton and rice, in celebration of the auspicious occasion; and enjoying it the more for the thought that the sky-riding *feringhi*, haughty and superior, was, in their own expressive idiom, dining on wind.

But they might have given him a drink of water, damn them.

Unlikely as it seemed, he must have slept, for, in the small hours of the morning, he was wakened by the sound of rifle-fire, and he wondered what was happening.

A few minutes later the door of his cell opened, and two men entered, one of whom carried a small butti, a crude oil-lamp which gave forth more smoke and smell than light.

By the flickering yellow flame of this miserable vessel, of which the original pattern might well have been left in that part of the world by the army of Alexander the Great, Vere-Vaughan, sitting suddenly erect, with a jerk that caused his head to throb violently, saw that one of his visitors was Wali Dad, son-in-law of the *Malik* and prominent member of the anti-*Mullah* party. The other was a man he had not seen before, or at any rate had not noticed—a rather good-type Pathan, with something clean-cut and smart about him.

What was this? Midnight murder? Hardly. The fellows were apparently unarmed; and if the villagers had decided to kill him, it was improbable that it would be done in this hole-and-corner fashion, wasting the material and opportunity for a fine tamasha.[46]

---

[45] *Rug or carpet.*
[46] *Show: rejoicing: ceremony.*

No. It was more likely some question of ransom. Probably the avaricious beggars couldn't sleep for thinking of the amount that was to be made out of a perfectly good airman, returned to store undamaged; and they wanted to discuss the question of the price with which they might open the bargaining.

What would be the best policy? To strengthen further their cupidity and determination to secure the ransom, by suggesting some fantastic sum? Or would they be so annoyed when they made application in the proper quarter, and found that the *prix fixe* for an airman was only a miserable thousand or two, that they would cut his throat? No. The Pathan who was not too fanatical to consider ransom, would not cut off his nose to spite his face, or cut his victim's throat to spite that rascal's Government.

Better perhaps accept the *Malik's* estimate and talk of ten thousand, if conversation on that subject were the object of the visit.

But why the second man? Hardly for Wali Dad's safety, in the circumstances, as doubtless there were plenty of others at hand, and probably double sentries at the door and window.

Placing the *butti* on the corner of the bed-frame, where its smoking flame dimly illuminated the mud-coloured room, Wali Dad squatted down, crossed his feet and leant back against the wall. To Vere-Vaughan's surprise, the other man, raising his right hand to his *puggri* in swift and easy salute, greeted him with a friendly, if perfunctory, "Salaam Sahib," ere he followed Wali Dad's example and seated himself beside that stalwart.

That was curious.

Eyeing the man more closely, Vere-Vaughan's first impression was confirmed. He was, in some indefinable way, slightly different from the rest. Perhaps his clothes were cleaner, his *puggri* more closely wound; his moustache and beard more neatly trimmed; the set of his shoulders and his whole bearing more military. That was it. Of course, the man was an ex-sepoy, either a time-expired soldier or a deserter from some

Pathan Corps. Some such Regiment as the 40th Pathans, or the 127th or 129th Baluchis.

Splendid. That boded well; for a man who had served in an Indian Army Regiment would be, at any rate, more civilized, broader-minded, more amenable to the ideas and dictates of decency, and the fair and honourable treatment of prisoners of war, than these jungly savages at the back of beyond, many of whom had never set eyes on India, scarcely even seen the Khyber Pass, or visited Peshawar. Unless, of course, the man were simply a *budmash* who had been the black sheep of his Battalion, and, after well-deserved punishment, had deserted with his rifle. He didn't look a bad sort, though; and had not the general air and bearing of a truculent, treacherous, and seditious envoy who, a tool and emissary of some implacable enemy of the British Raj such as the Singing Hadji of Sufed Kot or the other Hadji of Turangzai, had crossed the Border and enlisted, simply to learn British military methods with a view to using them against those who taught them.

Producing a *biddi* from his cummerbund, Wali Dad lit it, puffed forth a cloud of stinking smoke, eyed Vere-Vaughan lazily through half-closed eyes, and remarked in Pushtu:

"This man talks Hindustani. You'll be able to understand everything now. He learned to speak it in India."

"I suppose he did," replied Vere-Vaughan in Hindustani, a language which he understood and spoke far better than the more difficult Pushtu, as he had studied it on his arrival in India, and constantly spoke it to his bearer, syce and dog-boy. "Learnt it, no doubt, when his Battalion was stationed in Karachi, Bombay and Poona, eh?"

The man grinned disarmingly.

"What is your name and regiment?" asked Vere-Vaughan.

"Khoda Khan Abazai," was the reply. "I was Havildar in the Pathan Company of Sandeman's Rifles."

If this were true, the man would hardly be a

deserter, then, and was probably a good fellow. He must have been of good character and conduct, as well as some ability, to rise to the rank of Havildar. Here was a hope. On the other hand, he wasn't old enough to have served for a pension.

"Oh? How is it you are here, then, at your age?"

"I deserted, Sahib," smiled the man.

"Oh! One of that sort, are you?"

"*Nahin, nahin*, Sahib! It wasn't my fault. I didn't want to go. I loved the Regiment, and would have served the Sirkar until the time came to go on *pinson*."

"Well, why did you desert, then?"

"Khawas Khan of Khairastan shot my brother, and there was no one to carry on the feud," replied the man, as though that naturally accounted for every-thing—as indeed it did, from the Pathan point of view.

Vere-Vaughan had been long enough on the Border to know that it was as imperative and sacred a trust for the Pathan to avenge the death of a relative who died doing his duty in the matter of carrying on the family vendetta, as it was the imperative and sacred duty of an Englishman to feed, clothe and educate his own children.

The slayer might not have the vaguest idea as to when, how, and why the blood-feud started; but what he did know was that there was a vendetta; that his great-great-grandfather had been shot by the other side; that his great-grandfather had avenged the slaying; that his great-grandfather had been killed for taking that vengeance; that his grandfather had avenged the death of the great-grandfather and had been himself killed for doing so; and that the oldest son of the grandfather must slay his father's slayer—and so on, for ever.

Obviously this man, Khoda Khan Abazai, had been a younger son; had served in the Indian Army until news came that his elder brother had been slain by the son of the man whom his father had killed; and had then promptly applied for leave to go to his village and avenge his brother's death.

Sacred as was his duty to the King Emperor, the

Colonel and the Regiment, there was one duty yet more sacred, utterly supreme, the duty of slaying Khawas Khan who had, at long last, contrived to do *his* duty and kill Khoda Khan Abazai's brother. And so, until Khawas Khan was dead, the face of Khoda Khan Abazai was blackened. His name was mud; his family was disgraced; his wife and children were shamed; his very existence a hissing and a reproach; and if leave was not due to him and could not be granted—well, he must take it.

He must take French leave and a British rifle—and go home to kill Khawas Khan.

And having absented himself for so long—and it would take a very considerable time for him to reach his village, creep secretly into his watch-tower, and wait until the wily Khawas Khan exposed himself to the fatal shot that, night and day, he was expecting—he would, by the time everything was satisfactorily completed, have been absent from his Regiment for months, perhaps for years; and to return would be to receive months and perhaps years, of penal imprisonment. So—sad, unfortunate, and deplorable as it was—there was nothing for it but to desert.

And there sat Khoda Khan Abazai, defaulter, deserter, rifle-thief, and man of strictest honour, who had done his bounden duty as he saw it, at the risk of his life and the loss of career, comrades, promotion, success and pension.

Presumably his present task was to talk clear and simple Hindustani to the Sahib, make all things plain unto him, and see to it that there was no misunderstanding between him and his captors on the subject of his position, prospects and chances of ransom.

And as Vere-Vaughan studied the man, he was amazed to see that his right eye slowly closed and opened again, in a most indubitable wink.

But no, he must have been mistaken. The man had either a piece of dust or an eye-lash troubling him, or possibly a nervous affection which caused a spasmodic contraction of the eye. Not that the average Pathan is much subject to nerves, but the man might have received some injury to his head that affected the facial muscles. He had known of such cases.

But there was a chance. There was just the ghost of a chance that it was a wink, a gesture behind which lay intention. He must be careful to betray no surprise if the man . . .

Yes, it was a wink, for, even as he looked searchingly at the fellow's face, the latter yawned, put his hand up to his mouth, murmured some apt quotation or incantation suitable to the occasion of yawning, and, as he did so, placed his right forefinger against the side of his nose and winked again—a gesture unmistakable in any unspoken language and in any part of the world.

The gleam of hope broadened and shone more brightly. This Pathan, brought in by Wali Dad himself, was secretly signalling to him, making covert overtures and signs which were tokens.

"Now," said Wali Dad, having got his stinking *biddi* satisfactorily burning, "I'm going to tell you what I have come about; and then this man, Khoda Khan Abazai, is going to tell you the same thing in Hindustani, so that there can be no mistake.

"It's like this. We have got the *tup-tup* rifle out of the broken flying devil-carriage, and we want to know how to use it. That clever fellow, Nazir Ali Khan, put it up to his shoulder and held it as though it were an ordinary rifle, and pressed the button or pulled the trigger. It fired about ten rounds all in a second and knocked him head over heels. It also broke his jaw. Laugh! How we did laugh.

"Then his brother, Hidayetullah, rested it on a wall and fired it. He got on a bit better, but the *tup-tup* rifle didn't like that, either. It went mad and jumped about like a young goat tethered on a short cord. It didn't half-kill him, like it did Nazir Ali Khan, but he couldn't do any good with it.

"Without the chair it sits on, you couldn't hit a man on a horse at a hundred yards, because you can't hold it still. Now, what we want, is to know how to fix it up, so that we can shoot with it; and then we want to know the proper way to load it and clean it; and we don't want to fix it up over the gate-tower, either, like old Khan Allahdad's cannon. We want to take it along with us when we go raiding.

"This man, Khoda Khan Abazai, says that in the British Army, two men have charge of one of these guns, one carrying the gun and the other the stand and spare parts and ammunition and so on. Well, we want to do that. We want to take it about with us wherever we go; and it's no good while it knocks people over or jumps about so that you can't aim it, is it? Do you understand what I have said?"

"No," replied Vere-Vaughan.

"Oh, haven't you? Well then, that's where this man, Khoda Khan Abazai, will come in useful. He'll talk to you in Hindustani. He'll make you understand all right."

Whereupon the ex-sepoy repeated what Wali Dad had said, making clear that which was already abundantly clear, explaining fully, carefully and patiently, that Vere-Vaughan was expected to get the gun satisfactorily mounted and fully to demonstrate its working and use, care and keeping, to his captors who, every one of them, loved weapons, adored rifles and were prepared almost to worship a real *tup-tup* or *bah-bah* rifle that was a genuine and going concern.

"Well, do you understand now?" asked Wali Dad, when the other had finished.

"No," said Vere-Vaughan.

"You don't?" exclaimed Wali Dad. "I see. But I think you'd better understand before sunrise, because, if you are not going to show us how to mount and use the *tup-tup* rifle, we are going to hand you over to the *Mullah*, and before long you will wish you had done as we asked.

"But it will be too late then," he added, grimly.

"Well, that would be a silly thing to do, wouldn't it?" replied Vere-Vaughan. "It would cost you ten thousand rupees. You could buy a lot of *tup-tup* guns for that, you know."

"Yes, if we could get them," grinned Wali Dad.

"Now look here, Sahib," he continued. "It will be all that the *Malik* and I and our faction can do, to save you from the *Mullah* and his followers, even if you help us about the gun. If you refuse, there won't be a chance. You see, it's like this. Here is the *Malik*"—and he raised his right thumb—"and the *Malik's* men"—and he raised the fingers of his right hand. "And here, look, is the *Mullah*"—and he raised his left thumb—"and here are the *Mullah's* men"—raising the fingers of his left hand. "See? Now then. There are my ten toes. They are on neither hand, are they? Though if they went to the right, there would be fifteen against five, and if they went to the left, there would be fifteen against the other five—and it is those ten toes that'll make the difference between life and death to you. Death with torture. Because they are the people who will come to the *Malik's* side if you are going to show us how to mount the gun and use it; and who will go to the *Mullah's* side if you refuse. Do you understand?"

"No," replied Vere-Vaughan.

"All right. Then Khoda Khan Abazai shall tell you in Hindustani. There is no hurry."

And producing another *biddi*, Wali Dad lit it with a red-topped tandsticker match, which he lit with a flick of his thumb-nail.

And in Hindustani, Khoda Khan Abazai explained that if the Sahib were helpful and obliging, it was extremely probable that the populace would wish to keep him alive and healthy, appoint him Master of Ordnance, and retain him in that rank and office until such time as they could conclude satisfactory negotiations for his ransom. Whereas, if on the other hand, he were contumacious and refused to oblige, the people would dislike him even more vehemently than they did at present, and would hand him over to the *Mullah* who'd teach him not to come bombing peaceful villages in the Sufed Kot country; or hand him over to the Singing Hadji who would be delighted to relieve the *Mullah* of the trouble of punishing him satisfactorily.

"Understand that?" asked Wali Dad.

"No," replied Vere-Vaughan.

Wali Dad yawned and stretched himself.

"Listen, Sahib," he said. "If you think that you are safe because the majority would rather have you held to ransom than put to death, I'll tell you something. I don't know how much the Sirkar would pay the *Malik* to hand you over, but I do know what the Singing Hadji of Sufed Kot would pay."

Vere-Vaughan's heart sank again. For some reason, he hadn't thought of that. Of course, if the *Malik* sent messengers to the Singing Hadji, to ask the Singing Hadji whether he were in the market for a British Officer—the identical one who had just been chucking bombs about, in the Sufed Kot country, the reply would be prompt and affirmative.

Yes, of course these wily rogues would sell him rather than give him—sell him to the Singing Hadji rather than hand him over to the *Mullah* who would make a present of him to his ecclesiastical and temporal over-lord. They would think that they might perhaps get more from the British Government, but that there would be some considerable difficulty about completing the deal; whereas if they sold him to the Hadji, they'd be enjoying the double satisfaction of getting cash and vengeance too.

Yes, it was quite likely that they might turn an honest penny in that direction, but he had been long enough in Peshawar and on the Border, and had heard enough about the Mohmand, the Mahsud, the Afridi, and the other Pathans, to be perfectly certain that anything he did or did not do in the matter of showing them the working of a machine-gun, would have no effect whatsoever upon his fate. While individual Pathans had quite frequently proved themselves models of loyalty and patterns of fidelity to admired and trusted masters, treachery was nevertheless one of the leading traits of the Pathan character. They would no more think of keeping a promise, simply because it was a promise, than they would dream of keeping a dead horse simply because it was a horse.

Other aspects of the question aside, he would gain nothing whatsoever by helping them in the matter of the Lewis-gun. Moreover, he couldn't put those "other aspects" aside.

"Your words are as those of one without sense and understanding, Wali Dad," he said. "Do you compare the incalculable wealth and immeasurable power of the Government of India with those of the Singing Hadji of Sufed Kot? For every *pice* he has, the Sirkar has a *lakh* of rupees, nay a *crore* of gold mohurs. And as for power and strength, when he preached *jehad* and besieged Giltraza Fort, did he not soon flee, yelping like a village cur, before one tiny flick of the little finger of the Sirkar? Why, should it choose to do so, the Government of India could brush the Singing Hadji of Sufed Kot away as you would a fly, or crush him as easily as you could a mosquito."

"First catch your mosquito," yawned Wali Dad, "and a *crore* of rupees in Peshawar is worth less than an anna in Kurnai."

And turning to Khoda Khan Abazai, Wali Dad bade him make it clear to the Sahib that unless the *Malik's* party could get a majority on their side, it was quite certain that he would very soon be sold to the Singing Hadji by the *Malik*, or else would fall into the *Mullah's* hands, and be lucky if the *Mullah* put him to death.

This the ex-sepoy proceeded to do in colloquial Hindustani, and, suddenly pausing, he sneezed, said "Praise be to Allah," sneezed again and said, "Thanks be to Allah," sneezed a third time and said swiftly and almost inaudibly, in English, "*Ask for water*," and continued the torrent of Hindustani.

To say that Vere-Vaughan received a shock is to express but mildly the effect upon his weary and despondent mind of those three words, swiftly and unmistakably spoken in his own tongue.

It was not that there was any inherent improbability in an ex-sepoy knowing a little English. It was in his introducing the words thus quietly and surreptitiously. It meant, almost certainly, that the man wished to help him and befriend him.

But then, he reflected as the pendulum swung, what more likely than that a man who had been in an

Indian Regiment and had known and liked British Officers, should wish to be pleasant and agreeable, provided it cost him nothing.

But no, there was more to it than that, or why should he have suggested asking for water. He could just as easily have said, "I'll help you" or "I am a friend," or something of the sort.

Vere-Vaughan glanced at Wali Dad who was watching him somewhat listlessly and, from time to time, yawning and scratching himself.

Apparently he had noticed nothing. Probably he knew enough Hindustani to follow the gist of what was being said and to understand a word or a sentence here and there. If he had noticed the muttered English, he may have thought it was an aside in Hindustani, uttered with reference to the sneeze. To the Pathan, as to many other Orientals, sneezes are portents, their number and occasion being indicative and noteworthy.

"So you see, Sahib," concluded Khoda Khan Abazai, "it would be better for you to do as Wali Dad says, otherwise he cannot save you, and will not try."

Vere-Vaughan turned to that warrior.

"Look here, Wali Dad," he said. "I thought you Pathans were noble enemies. I thought you were fine fellows, and not just jungly savages. I have been here for hours, and have had neither food nor drink. I am hungry and thirsty. Give me water."

"What did you give us?" sneered Wali Dad, "when you were flying in the sky?"

"Nothing whatever," replied Vere-Vaughan. "I came nowhere near this place at all."

"Well, what have you given other villages? Bombs and bullets from the *tup-tup* rifle."

"Well, it's war, isn't it? You are a fighting-man, aren't you? What do you expect an enemy to give you?"

"I expect them to fight on the ground, with rifle and steel," was the reply.

"Well, how did you fight before you had rifles? You used *jezails*, didn't you? Matchlocks made in Tank and Kabul, with smooth bores. Well, and when the first rifles came, did you refuse to use them? Did you say it wasn't fair to use breach-loaders against your enemies' muzzle-loaders? Of course you didn't. And just as you've gone from the *jezail* and the matchlock to the magazine rifle, so the British are going from the foot-soldier to the flying-soldier. We are using a new thing that flies, just as you used a new thing that repeats, has a magazine and a rifled barrel. You will have flying-carriages yourself some day, no doubt."

"Meantime we have got a *tup-tup* gun," said Wali Dali, "and you've got to show us how to use it."

"Have I? Well, I'm not going to talk to you about that any more. Not a word. I will *not* do it. Now suppose I have something to eat and drink. Get me some water, anyhow, if you don't want me to think you are an ignorant and uncivilized jungle-wallah."

Rising to his feet, Wali Dad went to the door, threw it open and shouted.

Khoda Khan Abazai glanced swiftly towards the open door and then turned to Vere-Vaughan.

"*Khubbardar!*[47] Sahib," he whispered. And then in English, "Be careful. Very bad peoples. Don't make angry. If *Mullah* getting you, burn you alive, perhaps. Sahib make gun go. They soon break it. No good for you to . . ."

Wali Dad re-entered the room carrying a *chatti*[48] containing water and a brass *lotah*,[49] and the conversation continued without the introduction of any new subject to render it in the least degree interesting.

§5

Next morning Khoda Khan Abazai, bringing unleavened bread and a platter of cold rice, entered Vere-Vaughan's cell, accompanied by another Pathan, a grim and silent man.

"Sahib," whispered Khoda Khan Abazai, speaking in a fluent stream of Hindustani, with an occasional spate of English where he was sure of the meaning of the

---

[47] *Look out!*; *beware*; *take care.*
[48] *Water-vessel.*
[49] *Cup, bowl.*

sentences and thought it likely that he might make his meaning the clearer to the British Officer, "let us talk fully and freely, without deceit or double meaning. I will tell you the truth; and do you, being a Sahib, tell me the truth. I will make no promise that I cannot perform; and do you make me no promise that you cannot perform; nor promise me anything on behalf of others that those others will not perform."

"Be it so, Khoda Khan Abazai," replied Vere-Vaughan. "I will make no false promises, nor undertake to do anything that cannot or will not be done. If I promise on behalf of the Sirkar or others, it will be as though I promise for myself. Speak on."

"Sahib, I can save your life and get you to safety and freedom if you . . . if you . . . if you can . . ."

"If I can make it worth your while?"

"Sahib, I can save you, if you can save me."

"What do you mean—'save' you?"

"Why, if I get you away from here, I must go with you. My life would be short if I stayed here after helping you to escape, or if I stayed anywhere in the Free Country of the Border. I must return to India."

"Well?"

"Sahib, I do not wish to go to gaol."

"For what?"

"Sahib, I left the *pultan*[50] without leave, taking my rifle with me. What would it have availed me to go to my home to meet my enemy, unarmed? And it was months and months ere I could slay him. And thereafter, for months and months I had to hide in my watch-tower, lest I be slain by his brother. And then it was too late to return."

"Or to send back the rifle," observed Vere-Vaughan.

Khoda Khan Abazai spread deprecating hands as he shrugged his shoulders.

"Sahib, what could I do? But there it is. If I return to India, I am liable to arrest and punishment as a deserter and rifle-thief, and you know what the punishment would be."

Yes. Very heavy indeed. Deserters and rifle-thieves

---

[50] *Regiment.*

go to penal servitude. This Khoda Khan Abazai would be 'for it,' if he went back to British territory. And it was quite possible that he hadn't told the whole story. He might have killed a sentry in getting away, or pushed his bayonet into his sleeping enemy before he cleared out. But there could be little doubt that if he really did risk his life now, to save a British officer, succeeded in doing so and, returning with him, gave himself up, a Court Martial, sentencing him for desertion, would make the strongest recommendation to mercy, a recommendation which surely would be implemented when the rescued officer gave evidence of the man's redeeming conduct.

"Well," he said, "if there is nothing else against you, except desertion with your rifle—because you could not get leave to go and do what you considered your duty in the matter of the family feud that had devolved upon you through the death of your brother—I am sure I can promise that the offence would be condoned if you put yourself into the power of the British and into danger of punishment, through trying to save a British officer."

The Pathan eyed the Englishman anxiously.

"Yes, I will take it upon myself to promise that you will not be punished for desertion with your rifle," said Vere-Vaughan.

"You really think you can promise it, Sahib."

"Yes, I do; or I would not say so. What I can promise, without the very slightest doubt, is that I will do my utmost to prevent your being punished."

"Absent without leave, eh, Sahib?" grinned the Pathan.

"Yes," agreed Vere-Vaughan. "Pretty long absence and quite without leave; but I feel absolutely certain that we should get away with it, in the circumstances. I expect you'd get a nominal punishment for being 'absent without leave,' and you'd have to complete your period of service, of course."

"Should I be reduced to the ranks?"

"In the circumstances, I should think not."

"Lose my pension?"

377

"I should think not."

"But I might, mightn't I? The Court-Martial might say '*Havildar Khoda Khan Abazai deserted with his rifle. Instead of going to prison he shall be set free because he saved the Sahib at the risk of his life, but his name shall be struck off and he will lose his pension.*' It might go like that, might it not, Sahib?"

"It might. But I honestly don't think you'd be punished at all."

"Suppose I were? Would the Sahib make it up to me?"

"I will certainly undertake to pay you your pension for the rest of your life, if, through you, I escape," replied Vere-Vaughan.

He could most willingly promise that, at any rate. The few rupees a month that a pensioned non-commissioned officer gets would be a very small price for Vere-Vaughan to pay for the saving of his life. What would it be? One or two pounds a month? He could do better for the good fellow than that.

"Yes, I will pay your pension, if you are dismissed from the Army, Khoda Khan," he said, "and whatever happens, whether you are reinstated and earn your pension, or whether you are not allowed to qualify for it, I will give you a thousand rupees as well."

Yes, he could certainly lower his bank-balance to the extent of sixty-six pounds thirteen shillings and fourpence, as a reward for the saving of his life.

And undoubtedly Khoda Khan Abazai's life would be in as great danger as his own was, if he were caught in the act of attempting to free the priceless prisoner of the *Malik* of Kurnai.

"And what about the ransom, Sahib?"

"Ransom? If you enable me to escape, I shall escape instead of being ransomed, shan't I? Can't have it both ways. Either I get away without cost to the Sirkar, or else the Sirkar buys me."

But this did not seem to appeal to the ex-sepoy, and, as Vere-Vaughan was well aware, there is no better bargainer, no more grasping and avaricious dealer, than the Pathan. His religion may forbid usury, but apparently and by his reading of it, nothing is said on the subject of sharp practice, low avarice, and excessive greed of gain.

"*Nahin*, Sahib!" expostulated Khoda Khan Abazai. "Consider. If the Sirkar were prepared to give ten thousand rupees to its enemy the Singing Hadji of Sufed Kot, who otherwise would torture you to death, surely it would give as much, or more, to me, its friend and servant who wish to help it, and who would never do you any harm."

And that was undoubtedly a point of view. Nor would it be very wise to point out to Khoda Khan Abazai that to get the ten thousand rupees, he must be, not a loyal friend, but a bloodthirsty foe of the British and a potential murderer of his captive!

Still, he must play fair by the man and tell him nothing but the truth.

"It's not quite like that," he said. "You can't have it both ways, you know. You've either got to befriend me, help me to escape, and expect as your reward, a pardon for past offences and a money-present from me— or else you've got to stand in with the *Malik* of Kurnai as an enemy of the British and a murderer who says he won't commit the murder, provided he is paid sufficiently.

"And mind you," he added, "if you do that, I doubt whether you will get much of a share of the loot. Probably not an *anna* of it."

And at this, Khoda Khan Abazai, stroking his beard, nodded his head in agreement.

Vere-Vaughan pursued the advantage.

"Suppose, just suppose, that the Singing Hadji sent messengers to the nearest Fort, and negotiated through the Commanding-Officer for the payment of ransom. And suppose I were handed over at that Fort and, in return, a mule, laden with rupees, was brought back to the Hadji. Do you suppose even the *Mullah* of Kurnai would get one of those rupees? I doubt it. Much less would the *Malik* of Kurnai, or Wali Dad, or even any of the *Mullah's* party who tried to keep me themselves and to negotiate on their own account. You yourself wouldn't get an *anna*."

"Perhaps not, Sahib. But you admit that the Singing Hadji might get the reward if he handed you over. Very well then, why shouldn't I get it if I handed you over, or if through me, you got safely to Giltraza Fort? Why shouldn't I, your friend, and the friend of the Sirkar, get the reward, if the Singing Hadji, your enemy and the enemy of the Sirkar, gets one?"

"He doesn't, you fool; he doesn't," replied Vere-Vaughan wearily. "Can't you see a difference between a reward and a ransom? If the only way of saving me is by paying the Singing Hadji, then he will be paid, and that will be a *ransom*. If you like to do your best to save me without any bargaining, and succeed, you'll get a *reward*, which is a very different thing."

"How much would it be?"

"Well, we have a proverb which says that virtue is its own reward. Your reward for saving me would be a pardon for desertion and rifle-stealing; and, whatever else happens, the payment of your pension. I guarantee that. Because, if the Sirkar does not pay it, I will, *and* a thousand rupees in cash, the day I get down to Peshawar. That's your reward."

The Pathan smiled wryly.

"You say there is a difference between a ransom and a reward, Sahib. By Allah, there is! Nearly nine thousand rupees difference!"

Vere-Vaughan was conscious of a feeling akin to disillusionment, disappointment and disgust. Why must this good fellow haggle and bargain like this? Why spoil a fine deed, turning an act of courage and loyalty into a business deal; making a hero into a hireling?

But then, he told himself, what was the use of expecting a Western line of thought and conduct from an Oriental?

He must try to look at things from the Pathan point of view. It was only the man of the West who would prefer the Victoria Cross to be made of copper, value twopence. The Oriental would prefer it to be made of fine gold—and studded with diamonds, too.

Where the Westerner would think it shame to make a cash profit on a courageous act of mercy, the Pathan would consider it a piece of idiotic folly to lose anything that could be gained, whether moral or material. Definitely and literally he would 'take the cash and let the credit go.'

He must put himself in Khoda Khan's place and see the matter from his point of view. Apparently he was willing to save him, and to run the risk of being killed by his compatriots on this side of the Border, as well as of being arrested by the British as a deserter and rifle-thief on the other side of the Border. And in return for this, he wanted something more than indemnity from punishment, if he succeeded in reaching British territory. He wanted all he could get. And who should blame him? But he certainly could not expect to get ransom money, and he must not be encouraged to think it.

"Well, Khoda Khan," he said, "to a noble-minded *bahadur* there are better things than money."

"Are there, Sahib?" enquired the Pathan naively.

"Yes. Honour, fame and the praise of good men."

"Well, the Singing Hadji has those," countered Khoda Khan Abazai. "He is honoured throughout the Border. His fame is known from Kabul to Calcutta, and from Bokhara to Peshawar. And on this side of the Border all men praise him."

"I said good men."

"All Pathans are good men," was the somewhat crushing reply.

Weary to the point of exhaustion and despair, Vere-Vaughan forbore to deal with this proposition or to argue further.

"Well," he said, "since we are to talk as though you were a horse-coper and I an animal for sale, state your terms, Khoda Khan Abazai; if what I have promised is not enough."

"Oh, it is not for myself, Sahib," was the prompt and somewhat reproachful reply.

"Not for yourself?"

"Not for myself only, I mean. I'm quite willing to risk

my life for the Sahib . . ."

". . . And for a thousand rupees and a pension," murmured Vere-Vaughan.

". . . but there are the others. What am I to promise them? You see, if you could have guaranteed that the Sirkar would pay us a ransom of ten thousand rupees, there would have been a thousand for each of us."

"Ten of you?" asked Vere-Vaughan.

"Yes. We shall have to be a party of at least ten, if we are to hope to make our way safely and successfully —or, rather, with the slightest chance of success—from here to Giltraza Fort. We shall have to be a band of good fighting-men, well-armed and ready to fight like devils. You see, not only shall we be pursued by the *Malik's* and the *Mullah's* men, and have to keep them off, if we cannot elude them; but we shall have to fight the Singing Hadji's men and any outlaw bands who see us. Outlaws and robbers will attack us all right, especially when they realize that we've got a Sahib with us. I don't see how we could possibly do with less than ten, if we are to leave a rear-guard to fight, while you and I continue our flight. Ten? Twenty would be more like it. You will need a guide, of course. Or if the Singing Hadji's men take the wrong trail and don't overtake us, we shall want quite a good handful to stave off attack by the outlaws, robber-bands, and raiders."

"Yes, I suppose so," reflected Vere-Vaughan.

"Of course we should, Sahib. Directly a shot is fired at us, you and I and perhaps one or two others would hurry off, while the rest took cover and opened fire on those who attacked us."

Vere-Vaughan studied the face of Khoda Khan Abazai. Like those of all Pathans, it was hard, strong, and ruthless, the face of a man of great determination, courage and cunning.

And suddenly he felt ashamed of his recent attitude. Of course the man would want a considerable sum of money. If he had to bribe and reward a score of others, and it were a case of share and share alike, Khoda Khan wouldn't get much of the thousand rupees. One twentieth, fifty rupees—three pounds six shillings and eightpence—wasn't very much for which to risk your life, even with a small pension thrown in.

But perhaps he really wanted to return to his regiment and rid himself of the reproach of being a deserter, as well as of the gaol-sentence that hung over him.

If all went well, he'd be able to swagger about the bazaars of Peshawar again, fearing no man, and perhaps wearing the mufti or undress uniform of a *Havildar*[51] of Sandeman's Rifles.

That might be the real reason. The *pultan* that had been his home for so many years, might still be his spiritual home; and the flesh-pots, the regularity of the life, the security, the authority, the sound of the bugles and of the feet of the men who drill and march, all those things might be tugging at his heart-strings. And with regard to the rest of the band, fifty rupees each didn't seem much for a desperate venture.

But where was the Pathan who wouldn't do any mortal thing for fifty rupees?

And then another idea occurred to him.

"What about these others who'd join you and go with us? Wouldn't their lives be in danger too, on this side of the Border?" he asked.

"Oh, that won't worry them, Sahib," replied Khoda Khan. "They don't look very far ahead. One or two of them are going across the Border with me; and the rest of them are going to set up as raiders and outlaws."

"Going into the robber business, eh?"

"*Han, Sahib. Bé-shak. Bahut achcha kam bhi*,"[52] grinned Khoda Khan.

"Set up in business with the money they make out of this affair. What are you going to pay them?"

Khoda Khan Abazai smiled artfully. The average Oriental is economical of the truth; the Pathan miserly —in that respect, as in others. A truth-lover, it hurts him to part with it.

"W-e-l-l-l," he said, "it isn't so much what I am *going* to pay them as what I have promised to pay

---

[51] *Sergeant.*
[52] *Yes, Sahib. Without doubt. And a very good business too.*

them. They think we shall get the ransom, share it equally, and clear off out of the Singing Hadji's country, *ek dum.*"[53]

"And how much do they think the ransom to be? Is ten thousand rupees still the figure?"

"That's it, Sahib. They think they are going to get five hundred rupees each, the silly fools."

"And you are going to give them fifty?"

"Not if I can help it, Sahib."

"How much, then?"

"Not an anna."

"But they'll round on you. They'll . . ."

"Don't you worry about them. Sahib; nor about me. Let's get you safely into Giltraza Fort, and I'll undertake to get safely across the Border. We'll meet in Peshawar, and you will give me one thousand rupees and a *hundi*[54] on your bank for my pension, paid monthly, eh?"

"You can count on that. I can give you my word for that part of it."

"And you'll get the Court Martial to pardon me and to send me back to my Regiment?"

"I can't promise that, Khoda Khan. You know I can't. But I faithfully promise I'll do my best; and I honestly believe that you won't be punished if, through you, I escape."

Slowly Khoda Khan Abazai nodded his head, as he studied Vere-Vaughan's face.

"But I tell you frankly," continued Vere-Vaughan, "I wish you'd play fair with the others. I'd much rather you did."

The Pathan laughed aloud.

"Don't you worry about that, Sahib. You leave it all to me. Do exactly what I tell you—and I'll get you safe into Giltraza Fort."

"You will, eh?"

"On my life be it. On the head and the life of my son be it. On the Holy Koran, by the Ninety and Nine Sacred Names of Allah and by the Beard of his

---

[53] *At once.*
[54] *Draft; bill; order.*

Prophet, on whom be peace, I swear it. I swear that I will get you safe into Giltraza Fort *if you do exactly as I tell you*. Will you do that, Sahib?"

"Yes, certainly. Of course I will. And not only will I do exactly as you say, but I'll do exactly as I say, in the matter of reward."

Khoda Khan Abazai rose to his feet.

"Good," he said. "That's settled, then."

Drawing himself up to attention, he saluted formally, in military style.

And then, relaxing, he grinned ingratiatingly.

"And you'll try to get the Sirkar to pay me the ransom too, won't you, Sahib?"

"Oh, get out! You Pathans always want it both ways, don't you?" jeered Vere-Vaughan.

"Of course we do," agreed Khoda Khan in mild surprise, as with his silent companion, he departed from the room.

§6

That night, and thenceforth, the quality and quantity of the prisoner's food improved. Evidently he was now receiving the ordinary rations of the well-fed and prosperous villager or member of a raider-band in good standing and flourishing way of business.

On top of the pile of excellent hot rice was admirably curried mutton; and, above this, three or four well-cooked chupatties.

What was the meaning of this? But for the visit and proposals of Khoda Khan it would have had the painful suggestion of a fattening for the slaughter. But of course it was nothing of the sort, if only for the reason that the captives of the Singing Hadji of Sufed Kot were not likely ever to be fattened for any purpose whatever, since the good Hadji was no cannibal. It was much more likely they'd be starved into a state of misery and emaciation.

In point of fact, it was a good sign, he felt sure. It meant that Khoda Khan was, at his own expense or in some other way, providing him with food that should give him strength for the long and difficult journey.

From what he had seen of the country when flying over it, he realized that it would be a case rather of mountaineering than of marching; and that, however well tracks, trails and passes were known to his guides, they must inevitably climb great mountain ranges, and have but little experience of horizontal terrain.

It was not as though they would be able to use such roads as there were. All roads, and all parts of every road, would be under the surveillance of outlaws, raiders, robbers, and bandits, who lived entirely on the roads by the plunder or the "taxation" of those who used them. None but well-armed *kafilas*[55] could hope to cross the Border country without being blackmailed, or else being completely looted on refusal to pay toll.

And as for a small party accompanied by a European, unless they took precautions, they'd get about as far through the Country of the Gun as would a cow with tallow legs through Hell.

But of course there'd be no need for him to travel in British uniform with helmet, shirt, tie, tunic, Sam Brown belt, and puttees and boots. They could get him up as a Pathan, with *kullah*,[56] *puggri*, cotton coat, long shirt outside baggy trousers drawn in at the ankle, *cummerbund* and *chaplis*[57]; with a rifle slung across his back, bandoliers, and a *lathi*[58] in his hand. No, he'd have to keep his boots and socks. He wouldn't get far in *chaplis*.

Of course, they could disguise him as one of themselves.

On the other hand, it would soon be known far and wide that the Flying Sahib, prisoner of the *Malik* of Kurnai, had escaped, and was, naturally, making his way in the direction of the nearest British Fort. Then every outlaw gang in a thousand square miles would be out on the high-jacking business of looting the

---

[55] *Caravans.*
[56] *Conical cap.*
[57] *Sandals.*
[58] *Staff.*

Malik's loot, capturing his captive, and getting the fabulous ransom which it was well known that the Sirkar always paid for captured flying-officers.

Well, that would be a change for the better, anyhow. An outlaw leader would be particularly concerned to keep him alive and well, instead of torturing him to death as the Singing Hadji was likely to do.

Nevertheless, he had had quite enough of captivity, which was boring beyond belief, humiliating beyond words, and about as miserable and uncomfortable a state of existence as one could conceive.

Anyhow, thank Heaven for a jolly good bucket of curry and rice.

There was a sound of the movement of locks, bolts and bars. The door opened and Wali Dad entered.

"Salaam, Sahib," he said, saluting casually, his manner neither insolent nor respectful. "*Kuch khaire khubbar ahé?*"[59]

"*Khubbar!* How should I get *khubbar?*" growled Vere-Vaughan.

"Well, I've got some, anyhow."

"Oh?"

"Yes. I hear you are going to escape."

"Do you? That's good news, isn't it?"

"Don't know. May be. Depends."

"On what?"

"How it is done and who does it."

So Khoda Khan had been talking, had he? Of course he had. He had to get together a band of sufficient size to give the venture a chance of success. He couldn't do that without talking.

He waited for Wali Dad to speak. A good plan, he considered, as it not only impresses the Pathan who, like most mountaineers, admires taciturnity, but compels him, sooner or later, to come out into the open.

"How do you think you would get from here to Giltraza Fort, supposing I opened that door and said '*You may go. You are free*'?" asked Wali Dad after a long silence.

---

[59] *What's the news?*

"Walk," replied Vere-Vaughan succinctly.

"And how far do you suppose you would walk, without food and a rifle? And what would you do when you got a bullet in your back?"

"Fall down, I expect."

"You would. And a few minutes later your throat would be cut. No one can get through the Sufed Kot country, not to speak of the country beyond, without first getting the Singing Hadji's permission here, and then the permission of about a dozen Khans, not to mention outlaw chiefs."

"No?"

"No. Khoda Khan's been fooling you."

"Yes?"

"Yes. And if he told you that he could help you to escape, guide you safely to Giltraza Fort, he has been telling you lies."

"Has he?"

"Yes. It could only be done by a well-armed party, a proper raiding-party, the sort of band that would be dodged by the outlaws rather than having to dodge them all the time. That's the only way you could get from here to Giltraza, even supposing you escaped," affirmed Wali Dad.

"Yes?"

"It could be done, mind you, if you could find some-body who could get such a band together."

"Yes?"

"Oh, yes. I could do it myself!"

"Yes?"

"It would cost a lot, though."

"Would it?"

"Well, you see, there'd have to be, oh, anything from a dozen to a score—say five and twenty perhaps—to be on the safe side; and even if they were only going to get a miserable hundred rupees each, that would be two thousand five hundred rupees altogether."

"Just that," agreed Vere-Vaughan, once again taking stock of the somewhat unprepossessing countenance of Wali Dad, of whom he had never been really fond. What was the idea? A bargain? The raising of the price of escape; or the worst kind of blackmail—'*Pay me so much, or I'll tell,*' sort of idea? Had Khoda Khan approached this fellow indiscreetly, and let him know too much too soon? Had he tried his luck with him and failed, or what was it?

"Can you find it, Sahib?" asked Wali Dad.

"Find what?"

"Two thousand five hundred rupees."

"Look here, Wali Dad. If Khoda Khan has been talking to you—as he talked to me—he must go on talking to you. Understand? And you must talk to him. I'm not going to talk to you or anybody else, about—escaping."

Wali Dad nodded.

"I quite understand," he said slowly. "You are to make your arrangements with Khoda Khan, and he is to make his arrangements with us, eh?"

"I'm not going to talk to you about it at all. If you want to talk about such matters, go and talk to Khoda Khan, as I said."

"All right, Sahib! It's all right," laughed Wali Dad. "You needn't be afraid. It's not a *banao*.[60] You can talk to me about it just as freely as you did to Khoda Khan . . . What do I get if I join in?"

"Join in what?"

Wali Dad was neither irritated nor surprised. This was how people should talk, not blurt things out as children, idiots, and women do.

"In this plot for your escape," he said. "Khoda Khan wants me and Chimnai the Outlaw, Mahazil, Hakim Khan, Moussa Beg, Yacoub Ali, Ibrahim the Strong and one-eyed Kassim Shah and a few more, to take to the hills—and take you with us. Turn outlaw—with you for our first prize."

Vere-Vaughan looked up sharply.

That had an ugly sound. That opened up a very sinister vista and started a very unpleasant thought. Was Khoda Khan a two-faced double-dealing oily-tongued scoundrel, after all? Were he and Wali Dad and the rest of the gang themselves to be the high-

---

[60] *Frame-up; swindle.*

jackers, steal him from the *Malik* on pretence of helping him to escape, and then hold him to ransom, themselves?

Well, on second thoughts, why not? As he had already realized, he'd be better off in the hands of mere professional bandits, whose main interest would be to keep him whole and hearty, for ransom.

Yes, if that was it, let them go to it, by all means. It would not be immediate escape to freedom, but it would be a good step along the road to escape.

Well, he'd hope for the best while expecting the worst. He'd assume that Khoda Khan was straight; but he would not be in the least surprised if, when they were well away from the Sufed Kot country, he and Wali Dad and the rest, laughing boisterously, smote him on the back and said:

'Well now, we'll settle down in this nice comfortable cave and camp here while Khoda Khan goes on to Giltraza Fort to negotiate for the ransom. And you'd better give him a pretty good chit to the effect that you will never be allowed to leave the cave till we get ten thousand rupees: and that if they play any monkey tricks with aeroplanes, Corps of Guides Cavalry or anything of that sort, we'll cut your throat.'

Yes, on the whole, he'd prefer that definitely; because if the very worst came to the very worst, they'd cut his throat quietly and decently, or shoot him, and there would be no unpleasantness.

These fellows were not malicious and vindictive brutes, like the Singing Hadji, fanatical in religion and politics, who'd prefer his blood to hard cash, the delight of torturing him to the joy of receiving money. They were just honest robbers and ruffians, and he'd be better off with them.

Or was he going too far and too fast? Was Khoda Khan a well-meaning and over-ambitious fool who had given the show away to Wali Dad; and was the latter now going to put the screw on them both?

"Look here, Wali Dad," he said. "If you want to talk business—I don't say what business—you bring Khoda Khan with you, and we'll all three talk."

"Who's Khoda Khan?" sneered Wali Dad.

"I don't know. A friend of yours, isn't he? Didn't you introduce him to me?"

"Why should Khoda Khan manage this business?"

"What business?"

"The business we're talking about."

"I'm sure I don't know."

Wali Dad smiled, with a glance of what was obviously approval, as he rose to his feet.

"That's all settled then, Sahib," he remarked.

"Is it?" enquired Vere-Vaughan in surprise.

And with a nod and a curt chuckle, Wali Dad departed.

What amazing, devious, and amusing fellows these Pathans were.

§7

Next day Wali Dad returned, accompanied by Khoda Khan Abazai and his grim silent friend of yesterday. Apparently the three had come to an understanding, were in complete agreement, and their visit was in the nature of a reassurance and confirmation of Khoda Khan's arrangement with Vere-Vaughan.

Once again they went over the whole business from beginning to end, talked it back and forth, made frequent reference to the ransom, and finally left Vere-Vaughan strongly under the impression that Khoda Khan was honest so far as he, Vere-Vaughan, was concerned; that he fully agreed to his terms; and, though still toying with the idea of the ransom as well as the reward, accepted Vere-Vaughan's refusal to promise anything whatsoever in that direction, or to hold out any hope that it would materialize.

But there he was inclined to think that Khoda Khan's honesty ended, and to doubt that his companions would get anything at all.

However, that was their business; and, so long as he himself absolutely refused to promise them anything, but invariably referred them to Khoda Khan, he need have no qualms of conscience, or consider himself in any way responsible for their disappointment.

Similarly with Khoda Khan himself. If, after having got him to Giltraza Fort, Khoda Khan had to pay the penalty, whatever it might be, of any disingenuousness he had used with regard to his friends, that was entirely Khoda Khan's business.

And once again, that there might be no mistake whatsoever, he made it clear to Wali Dad that he did not believe that any cash payment would be forthcoming from any source whatsoever except his, Vere-Vaughan's, own pocket; that he had agreed with Khoda Khan what that payment was to be; and that he would pay no one else one farthing.

The arrangement was Khoda Khan's, and with Khoda Khan they must arrange.

This, in the end, Wali Dad accepted, and solemnly and voluntarily took the same binding and unbreakable oath that Khoda Khan had taken, swearing upon his life and upon his head, upon the life and the head of his first-born son, by the Ninety and Nine Sacred Names of Allah and the Beard of the Prophet, upon whom be peace, that he would honestly do his utmost to get the Sahib, alive and well, safe and sound, into Giltraza Fort.

And somehow, Vere-Vaughan felt convinced. Only the most evil and degraded Mussulman would break that oath. None would make it voluntarily with the intention of breaking it.

An idea. Insist on their *all* making it, in his presence, Koran in hand. Yes, every one of them. Not even in the innermost arcana of the realm of the Singing Hadji of Sufed Kot could there be a score of men who would voluntarily swear such an oath as that, on the Koran itself, with the intention of breaking it.

"We understand each other, then, Sahib," concluded Wali Dad.

"Yes. But look. Come to-morrow, bringing with you a copy of the Koran, and take that oath again, with the Koran in your hand."

"Do you not trust us, Sahib?"

"Of course I don't."

Wali Dad laughed, in no wise offended.

"Suppose I refuse?" he asked.

"Then that will prove that I am right in mistrusting you, won't it? I shall know that you are a liar and a rogue, a two-faced double-dealing dog."

"Oh, you mustn't think I'm a liar, Sahib. I never tell lies."

"Bring the Koran then."

"I will."

"Shall I bring a copy of your Holy Book also, that you may swear to us upon it?" he grinned as he rose to his feet.

"By all means," replied Vere-Vaughan, "if you can find a copy. And I will swear that, as soon as I get to Peshawar, I will pay Khoda Khan—what I have promised him."

"Khoda Khan and no one else," he added distinctly and deliberately.

"No need to swear an oath, Sahib, no need," laughed Wali Dad, and departed, followed by Khoda Khan who, at the door, turned, smiled and nodded encouragement.

§8

Not in his most optimistic moments could John Vere-Vaughan regard the escape-party as a prepossessing collection of comrades whose faces were their fortunes, and in whom he could confidently put his trust.

Granted that Khoda Khan Abazai was a good specimen of Pathan and a fine fellow, by any standards; Wali Dad a fair one; and one or two others passable types, the fact remained that the majority of these candidates for outlawry and professional banditry were, save for physique, absolutely appalling specimens of humanity.

Of the score or so, he could have taken a dozen and said, 'These are undoubtedly the twelve most ruffianly, villainous, and evil-looking blackguards whom I have ever seen gathered together.'

Chimnai the Outlaw, who seemed to be a man of light and leading among them—or rather of leading, as light was an incongruous and inapplicable term—was, in appearance at any rate, a typical stage robber of melodrama, the perfect bandit of fiction.

A man evidently of enormous forcefulness, his face expressed nothing higher nor better than determination, ferocity and ruthless cruelty. Such notorious scoundrels as he should have broken yellow fangs, exposed by blubber-lips; shapeless noses; should be afflicted with a grievous squint, or be one-eyed; whereas, in point of fact, Chimnai's mouth was firm and thin-lipped, his teeth white and perfect, his nose aquiline, his eyes keen and clear, the whole nevertheless composing a most villainous criminal countenance which Vere-Vaughan distrusted on sight, and whose owner he instinctively disliked, if not feared.

Studying him, Vere-Vaughan decided that here was a strong man and a very evil one; cruel for the sake of cruelty; and wondered that, in spite of his regular and good features, he should nevertheless look so exactly what he was, a savage and bloody-minded bandit.

Even one-eyed Kassim Shah—in spite of his abominable countenance and his ill-wound *puggri*, unkempt hair and beard, dirty shirt over-provided with bandoliers and belts which encompassed him about like a garment—looked less of a stage villain and robber of fiction. Natheless, with his greasy smile and shifty eye, he was plainly a very nasty piece of work.

Hakim Khan, broad as he was long, was the bluff bold hearty; merry and bright; who, roaring with laughter, would dig you in the ribs with blunt thumb or sharp knife, impartially and without malice; a man who would cut your bonds or your throat as circumstances and rupees bade; and would be a fine dependable fellow as long as his interests were yours.

The man introduced as Moussa Beg carried also his condemnation in his countenance, a long gaunt fellow who could not smile; whose lips were frozen into an unchanging sneer that exposed his dog teeth; whose eyes could but glare; his brows but frown; and who must always be the less dangerous, in that his face was a patent danger signal.

Ibrahim the Strong, a silent man, was about the biggest, thickest, and brawniest man whom Vere-Vaughan had ever beheld. Proudly, Wali Dad said of him that he could tear a live goat to pieces with his hands; and confirming this statement, Hakim Khan, with a bellow of laughter, assured Vere-Vaughan that once, Ibrahim the Strong—particularly annoyed with a man whom he thought to have cast sheep's eyes upon his wife, in his absence—had leapt upon the offender's back, pulled him to the ground, placed his feet against the man's shoulders, one on either side of his neck, seized his head in both hands, and twisted it from his body.

"Splendid," murmured Vere-Vaughan, glancing from the laughing scoundrel to the strong one.

"*Han*,[61] Sahib! Like a chicken's head!" guffawed Hakim Shah. "Wonderful!"

"Just like a chicken's," murmured Vere-Vaughan, fascinated, hypnotized, as he met the gaze of the silent Ibrahim the Strong.

Nor towards Mahazil, ceremoniously introduced as one who had wiped out a whole family, from great-grandfather to week-old baby, by way of contribution to the ancestral blood-feud, could Vere-Vaughan feel any warmth of admiration. A cold killer, utterly devoid of any trace of social feeling.

Nor did Mahazil appear to view Vere-Vaughan with any warm regard, and gave him the impression that, on the whole, he'd much rather cut his throat and 'learn' him to be a *feringhi*, than help him to escape, even for the reward of fifty rupees. Mahazil quite successfully gave him the impression that he was accustomed to bigger and definitely better enterprises than this one, into which he had been foolishly and weakly beguiled by the officious Khoda Khan.

Gul Mahommed was a less dislikeable person and

---

[61] *Yes.*

gave Vere-Vaughan the impression of a man who was a proscribed outlaw and robber *malgré lui*; one who had taken to the heather by force of untoward circumstance and bitter constraint, rather than by reason of criminal instincts. He was inclined to class Gul Mahommed with Khoda Khan Abazai as a higher type than the rest; and he had a strong feeling that Gul Mahommed wanted to say something to him privately, but never got the chance.

And, taking them all round and as a party, Vere-Vaughan could not but feel that, since he proposed to entrust himself to their care—he could not say to their tender mercy, for of tenderness and mercy they could have none—it was indeed fortunate for him that their cupidity was engaged to support their honesty—in spite of the solemn oath taken upon the Koran.

For, on the following day, Wali Dad kept his promise, and, on visiting his charge, brought with him a small, ancient, and evidently much-revered copy of the Koran bound in green leather, enriched by a green ribbon marker, and kept in a close-fitting green velvet case shaped like an envelope, the flap being tied down with a green cord.

On this, Wali Dad once more swore the great oath by his life and his head; by his son's life and his son's head; by the Ninety and Nine Sacred Names of Allah, and by the Beard of the Prophet, that he would faithfully do his utmost to deliver Vere-Vaughan, safe, sound and uninjured, into the hands of the Commandant of Giltraza Fort, as quickly as it was possible for him to do so.

The same oath Khoda Khan Abazai took; and, although Vere-Vaughan assured him that it was quite unnecessary, he placed the sacred book upon his head and repeated the oath a second time.

And, that same night, in ones and twos and threes, Wali Dad introduced the rest. First, the terrible Chimnai the Outlaw; then the bluff and burly Hakim Khan and another; after them, the sinister and repellent Moussa Beg with one-eyed Kassim Shah, a most uninspiring pair; then the amazing Ibrahim the Strong and, later, Mahazil, Yacoub Ali with Gul Mahommed, and then others; and every man of them took the oath on the Koran.

Little as he liked them and less as he trusted them, Vere-Vaughan was nevertheless reassured by the fact that each one of these men did severally and with the utmost willingness, swear the oath in a manner that carried conviction. Even the evil Mahazil left him impressed with his sincerity—though it might be the first and last time in his life that he was sincere.

No, he was foolish to doubt. These men, for some reason—and doubtless Khoda Khan Abazai provided good reason—did really and truly intend to take him thence, and as straight and swiftly as might be, to Giltraza Fort.

§9

And on the last night of his captivity in the stronghold of Kurnai, whence escape had seemed impossible, Vere-Vaughan received confirmation of his belief and hope.

For, to his prison-cell, Khoda Khan and Wali Dad brought yet another recruit to the escaping party, a man who gave Vere-Vaughan the surprise of a lifetime, and interested and intrigued him more than all the rest put together.

Of middle height, fair-skinned and grey-eyed, cleaner and neater than the rest of the Pathans, and with a noticeably and definitely different cast of countenance, the man was introduced as Hussein Ali Shah Powindah.

Studying his face, Vere-Vaughan decided that this bird, whatever its note, was not really a mountain eagle. It had neither the same predatory eye nor beak. Somehow it looked more of a domestic fowl. Yes, definitely Hussein Ali Shah Powindah was less of a born savage than the rest of these brutes.

Powindah? Weren't the Powindahs a class of Afghans, and rather more traders than warriors, inclined more to rob from behind counters than behind gun-sights, and to use the trade-routes rather than the robber-tracks?

"*Salaam aleikum*," said the man, touching his forehead with his hand and bowing. "May you never be tired."

Tired! Good Lord! thought the unfortunate Vere-Vaughan.

"*Salaam*," he replied. "May you always be rich."

"And has this man also made arrangement with you?" Vere-Vaughan asked Khoda Khan.

"He has. He quite understands," was the reply.

"And have you made it clear to him," enquired Vere-Vaughan, as he had done in each case, "that I promise nothing to anybody but you? That there is no question of ransom; and that the reward I pay will be paid to you and to no one else?"

"He understands everything, Sahib," Khoda Khan assured him.

"*Bé-shak.*[62] That is so. Very *hushyar*,"[63] agreed Wali Dad, nodding his head. "If it be the will of Allah that I or Khoda Khan shall be slain in our brave attempt to save your Honour's valuable life," he added, "Hussein Ali Shah Powindah will take charge of you and guide you. He knows the tracks; and not only is he a great *bahadur*[64] to fight, but he has a tongue of silver. So, should he and you fall into the hands of evil men, without doubt he will persuade them to let you go, or induce them to come with you to Giltraza Fort and share the reward."

"By the way, that's a point," observed Vere-Vaughan. "Suppose Khoda Khan were killed, which Allah forbid, who is to receive the reward I promised him? What do you say, Khoda Khan?"

"Oh, give it to him who guides you and gets you there, Sahib."

"Well, there will be a whole party of us, won't there?"

---

[62] *Without doubt.*
[63] *Clever.*
[64] *Hero.*

"Yes, yes. I meant if you escaped with only one man while we fought a rear-guard action. If that should come to pass, you will go on with this man, Hussein Ali Shah Powindah; and the money can be handed to him or anyone whom he appoints in Peshawar."

"And if a whole party of us arrived there without you, Khoda Khan?"

"Then pay it to Wali Dad, who will . . ."

"Right. But again supposing that—Allah forbid—neither you nor these two reach Giltraza alive, what then?"

The three Pathans eyed each other, and Vere-Vaughan half suspected that a scarcely hidden smile lurked behind their beards. If so, what were they grinning at? Perhaps the idea of the rare old shemozzle there'd be when it came to divvying up.

"Better give it to the biggest," decided Khoda Khan. "Save a lot of trouble."

"Ibrahim the Strong, eh?"

"Yes. If he's there, I shouldn't care to be anybody else to whom you paid it, Sahib."

Anyway the money wouldn't be there in Giltraza Fort, so the question didn't really arise; and privately he decided that, if he reached the Fort safely, and neither Khoda Khan nor Wah Dad were present, he would guarantee safe conduct to this man Hussein Ali Shah Powindah down into Peshawar, and there pay him a thousand rupees before witnesses, and see him safely back across the Border. Yes, he'd take either him or that other man, whose name he had forgotten—Gul Mahommed, was it?—who had struck him as a quieter, milder, and more amenable specimen of blackguard altogether.

Presently Wali Dad, yawning, clearing his throat and spitting with abandon, arose and departed; and Khoda Khan, after some more desultory conversation, asked whether either of the others could provide him with what he termed *dir-salai*,[65] and finding that they could not, departed in search of matches or other light

---

[65] *Matches.*

for his *biddi*.

It was after he had closed the door that Hussein Ali Shah Powindah provided Vere-Vaughan with his memorable shock.

"Well?" he said softly in English. "Do you recognize me?"

For a few seconds Vere-Vaughan was too astonished to reply, his mouth opening as widely as his eyes.

"Good Lord!" he breathed. "Are you an Englishman?"

"Don't you know me?"

"No. Who are you?"

"Ever heard of Major Bartholomew Hazelrigg, disrespectfully known as 'Ganesh' in certain Messes?"

"Why . . . Yes . . . Of course. Are you he, Sir?"

"Don't you remember me?"

"No, Sir. I have never had the pleasure of seeing you before. Pleasure! Good Lord above us! I wonder whether one man ever gave another greater pleasure."

Hussein Ali Shah Powindah smiled, showing excellent teeth.

"Good. I somehow didn't think we'd met before, though I know your C.O. and one or two of the poor fellows who were killed in that ghastly raid over the Sufed Kot country. You are the sole survivor, you know."

"I was afraid I was. My pilot, poor Lucke, was shot. I suppose the others all crashed going out?"

"The whole lot."

"It's an absolute marvel that we got through the mountains in that fog."

"Yes, a wonderful bit of luck—or judgment. Devilish hard on poor Lucke—being shot, after that."

"Yes. Heart-breaking, but . . ."

"Well, you are all right, anyway, and ought to be safe back, pretty soon. By Jove, you've been lucky, all right, young fellow."

"Yes, Sir. But . . . But this is marvellous. Incredible . . . I can hardly believe it. You are on Secret Service again, sir? I've heard that the Pathans could never tell you from one of themselves. Not even those who'd known you in uniform."

"Well, they haven't spotted me yet, as you see."

"But aren't you in terrible danger here, Sir?"

"Oh, I don't know. Got to be careful, of course."

"But you were in the Singing Hadji's camp actually during the siege of Giltraza, weren't you?"

"Yes, in another manifestation. I was a *ghazi* then, with a squint and a big beard and a different accent."

"Well," he continued, "why I called upon you tonight was to cheer you up. And to tell you to trust absolutely to Khoda Khan—and Wali Dad and the rest of them, as far as that goes. They'll get you there all right, D.V., and robber-bands permitting. But be careful to do *exactly* what Khoda Khan tells you. Of course, they are running tremendous risks themselves, and you've got to put yourself entirely in their hands and be guided by Khoda Khan. He's quite all right. Ex-sepoy, as I've no doubt you know. He's a very good fellow. He hopped over the Border, as so very many of them do, to perform his duty, and rather overstayed his leave."

"Does he know who you are, Sir?"

"Oh, good Lord, no! No. No. No. Get that clear in your mind. The fewer people who know anything about me on this side of the Border, the better. And I shouldn't be here now, except that I want you to get safe to Giltraza."

"It's most awfully good of you, Sir, and I can't thank—begin to thank you."

"No, no. It isn't only for your *beaux yeux*. Naturally I'd do anything to help you—but I'd *give* anything for you to get to Giltraza all right. I want you to take a message to the Commandant, and also a confirmatory note in writing. Do you know Colonel Garstan personally? No? Well, I want to get a message to him. Most tremendously important. That's why I came, as I said, and I wanted to impress on you that the more carefully you do as Khoda Khan tells you, the likelier my message is to arrive. Do you read Russian?"

"No, Sir, I don't. I'm awfully sorry, but I don't."

"Speak it or understand it?"

"No, Sir. Not a word. I haven't been out here very long, and my language-study has been confined to Hindustani and Pushtu. Later on, I hope."

"Yes, yes. All right. It doesn't matter. But I must give you a little sign-and-token scribble that Garstan will understand and that'll *prove* that you and your tale of having come from me are genuine. Then he'll be able to believe the message—which he'll find a bit of an eye-opener. If you are wondering why I'm going to write it in Russian, it's because I am not absolutely certain as to how much English our friend Khoda Khan knows."

"You don't trust him, Sir?"

"I don't trust anybody, my son. First rule of the game. So if by any sad chance, the message fell into the wrong hands, there is much less possibility of it being read and understood, if it's in Russian. Ever heard of the Hadji of Turangzai?"

"Yes, Sir, I've heard of him."

"Well, he, for example, reads English as well as we do; and there are quite a few queer coves, Asiatic and other, knocking about this part of the world, who've been in India and learned English for trade purposes. Not to mention Secret Service Agents."

"I suppose there are Bolshevist agents among the Tribes?"

"Good Lord, yes! The U.S.S.R. people have got some very fine men in Afghanistan, and here as well as on the Border."

"And in India too, as far as that goes," he added, as he sat fumbling inside his *poshteen*.[66]

Hussein Ali Shah Powindah produced a little penny notebook with shiny black cover, such as is sold in Border village bazaars, and a stump of indelible pencil.

"I'll give you a verbal message, of course, but I particularly want this little document to get to Colonel Garstan. The signature and password will prove and confirm what he may doubt, that the message that I shall give you actually does come from me, Major Bartholomew Hazelrigg, Military Intelligence Branch of

---

[66] *Sheep-skin coat.*

the Secret Service. This is the message:—*All these men are known to G5.H8. personally. He guarantees them all—except the one mentioned in the note brought by Flying-Officer John Vere-Vaughan.* Give it him immediately you enter. Otherwise he'll be very hot and bothered, because he knows for a fact that I am sojourning with my friends, the Faquir of Ipi and the Hadji of Turangzai, which, as you perceive, I am not doing."

And as, cool and nonchalant, he talked as quickly and easily as though he were sitting in his chair in his Club or bungalow, the man calling himself Hussein Ali Shah Powindah wrote.

"There you are," he said, a few minutes later, tearing out some pages and folding them together. "Put that inside the lining of your *topi* or under your *puggri*, if you wear one, and give it to Colonel Garstan, or he will doubt that you met me week-ending with the *Malik* of Kurnai in the country of the Singing Hadji of Sufed Kot."

PART II

I

A generation earlier, Richard Wendover on the last night of the long holiday between leaving The Old Ride, his Prep School, and going up to Wellington, was methodically tidying away his treasures.

Having somewhat unnecessarily oiled his air-rifle, he laid his army of leaden soldiers to rest in their great Fort, each wrapped in his martial cloak of newspaper; put away where dusting housemaids and other nuisances and dangers could not corrupt; neither break through nor steal such other treasures as his ignorant seniors called toys, and which he knew to be parts and properties of his own higher and better life, wider, brighter and more glorious than anything known to those adults, so wise, so grave, so earth-bound and so dreary.

Finally he took from its safe resting-place in a big blotter which he kept in his one locked drawer, a double sheet of newspaper, the contents of which he knew almost by heart.

Since he must leave it behind him, he would read it once again.

This, perhaps the most treasured of all his possessions, a sheet of yellowing paper, was fragile and ragged-edged, but among other precious things, contained most priceless of all, the Name—a name, the reading of which he always kept to the last, and then, having feasted his eyes upon it, closed them and indulged in reverie, gave rein to his imagination and allowed his mind to be up-lifted on soaring wings of hope, high resolve, and young brave ambition.

The paper was *Number 9554 of "The Times," London, Thursday, June 22, 1815. Price 6d.*

The first page consisted of amazing and amusing advertisements; the second, Wellington's dispatch from the field of Waterloo; the third, the official Bulletin, headed *Downing Street, June 22, 1815.* And this dispatch, once again and for the hundredth time he read.

Official Bulletin.

Downing Street, June 22, 1815.

The Duke of Wellington's Dispatch, dated Waterloo, the 19 June, states that on the preceding day Buonaparte attacked, with his whole force, the British line supported by a corps of Prussians; which attack, after a long and sanguinary conflict, terminated in the complete Overthrow of the Enemy's Army with the loss of ONE HUNDRED & FIFTY pieces of CANNON and TWO EAGLES.

During the night, the Prussians under Marshal Blucher, who joined in the pursuit of the enemy, captured SIXTY GUNS, and a large part of Buonaparte's BAGGAGE. The allied armies continued to pursue the enemy. Two French Generals were taken.

Such is the great and glorious result of those masterly movements by which the Hero of Britain met and frustrated the audacious attempt of the Rebel Chief. Glory to Wellington, to our gallant Soldiers, and to our brave Allies! Buonaparte's reputation has been wrecked and his last grand stake has been lost in this tremendous conflict. TWO HUNDRED AND TEN PIECES OF CANNON captured in a single battle, put to the blush the boasting column of the *Place de Vendome.* Long and sanguinary, indeed, we fear, the conflict must have been; but the boldness of the Rebel Frenchmen was the boldness of despair, and conscience sate heavy on those arms which were raised against their Sovereign, against their oaths and against the peace and happiness of their country. We confidently anticipate a great and immediate defection in the Rebel cause. We are aware that a great part of the French nation looked to the opening of this campagne with a superstitious expectation of success to a man, whom, though many of them hated, and many of them feared, all had been taught to look on as the first captain of the age. He himself went forth boasting in his strength, and still more in his talents. He had for many years ridiculed Carnot's plan of a Northern campaign, and had openly avowed at Paris his intention to break through the Allied Armies, instead of moving round both their flanks. With as little reserve had he declared that he would open the campaign on the Meuse and Sambre. In short, by a refinement in finesse, he had exposed his true plan, imagining that nobody would believe that such was his real intention. We do not deny that his plan might have been one of considerable ability; but he did not take into the account that he was to be opposed by abilities superior to his own. That unpalatable truth his vanity would not allow him to believe, nor would it easily find credit with his admirers; but the 18th of June we trust, will satisfy the most incredulous. TWO HUNDRED AND TEN PIECES OF CANNON! When, where, or how is this loss to be repaired? Besides, what has become of his invincible Guard, of his admired and dreaded Cuirassiers? Again we do not deny that these were good troops; but they were encountered by better. We shall be curious to learn with what degree of coolness, of personal courage and self-possession, Buonaparte played his stake, on which he must have been well aware that his pretentions to Empire hung. It is clear that he retreated; nor are we prepared to hear that he fled with cowardice; but we greatly suspect that he did not court an honourable death. We think his valour is of the calculating kind, and we do not attribute his surviving the abdication at Fontainebleau entirely to magnanimity.

To the official bulletin we have as yet little to add. The dispatches, we understand, were brought by Major Percy, Aide de Camp to the Duke of Wellington; and we have heard but we hope the statement is premature, that among the British slain was that gallant and estimable officer Sir Thomas Picton. But whoever fell on this glorious day cannot have fallen in vain. The fabric of rebellion is shaken to its base. Already we hear numerous desertions have taken place from the Rebel standard; and soon, it is to be hoped the perjured wretches, Ney and Desnouettes, and Excelmans, and Lallemand and Labedoyere and their accomplices in baseness and treason, will be left alone as marks for the indignation of Europe and just sacrifices to insulted French honour.

And having read it, he turned as usual to that thrilling and even yet, to him, harrowing list headed *"British Killed and Wounded."*

And once again, and for the hundredth time and, as always, preventing his eye from falling upon the last name of this preliminary list, read:

"Duke of Brunswick.
Lieutenant-General Sir Thomas Picton.
Lieutenant-General Sir H. Ponsonby.
Colonel du Plat, K.G.L.
Colonel Ompheta, K.G.L.
Colonel Morrice, 69th Regiment."

And down through Lieutenant-Colonels, Majors and Captains to the end of the list, and then slowly, yet with quickening breath, read:

"Captain Grove, 1st Guards.
Lieutenant C. Manners, Royal Artillery.
Lieutenant Lister, 95th Regiment.
Ensign Lord Hay, Aide de Camp to General Maitland.
Ensign Brown, 1st Guards.
Ensign Richard Wendover, 1st Guards."

ENSIGN RICHARD WENDOVER, 1ST GUARDS.

And he himself was a Richard Wendover. And would some day be, not Ensign, but Second Lieutenant Richard Wendover, and would go to the Indian Army to follow in the footsteps of that Waterloo hero's son and grandson who had fought in every British campaign in India.

Yes, Richard Wendover, son of Ensign Richard Wendover, 1st Guards, who had never seen that son, had served in India for over forty years, distinguishing himself on almost every battlefield from 1835 to 1875, and as Colonel of Indian Irregular Cavalry, numbering his own son among his subalterns; that son who, arriving in India and joining his father's Regiment in 1856, had served throughout the Mutiny and been friend and brother-in-arms of the great Lord Roberts himself.

And the boy, looking up from his treasured scrap of paper and staring, unseeing, through the window of his attic play-room, would think of Lieutenant Richard Wendover of Napier's Horse, winning decoration and swift promotion at the siege of Delhi; of that earlier Lieutenant Richard Wendover winning fame and decoration at Sobraon and Chillianwallah under Sir Hugh Gough, and again at Lucknow; and of Ensign Richard Wendover dying with half his men in the unbreakable square at Waterloo. And he would swear that he would be worthy of these ancestors.

And then his eyes would return to the paper and, once again, with bated breath, he would read the list headed *"Wounded,"* beginning with *"General H.R.H. the Prince of Orange, K.C.B. severely,"* and going on through no less than eight Lieutenant-Generals wounded in the same battle.

He could almost repeat their names by heart.

"General H.R.H. the Prince of Orange, K.C.B., severely.
Lieutenant-General, the Earl of Uxbridge, G.U.B., right leg amputated.
Lieutenant-General Sir Charles Alten, K.C.B., severely.

Lieutenant-General Cock, right arm amputated.
Lieutenant-General Sir C. Barnes, K.C.B., Adjutant-General, severely.
Lieutenant-General Sir J. Kempt, K.C.B., slightly.
Lieutenant-General Sir Colin Halkitt, K.C.B., severely.
Lieutenant-General Adams, severely.
Lieutenant-General Sir W. Dornby, K.C.B., severely."

And, as usual, he would make up his mind that some day there would be a casualty list in all the big papers, and among the names of wounded Generals would be *Lieutenant-General Sir Richard Wendover, K.C.B.*

On gloomy days the name would appear in the list of killed.

Lieutenant-General Sir Richard Wendover, K.C.B.

Yes, he was going to be a Lieutenant-General and a K.C.B., like his friend Lieutenant-General Sir Arthur Ffoulkes, K.C.B., by the time he reached the end of his army career. He liked the sound of Lieutenant-General better than that of mere General, and found it somewhat disappointing that the rank of Lieutenant-General was senior to that of Major-General. Major-General sounded so much more "superior" than Lieutenant-General and full General, but there it was, and one had to put up with it.

Of course, if he did exceptionally well in the Indian Army, he might very well rise to be Commander-in-Chief, with a seat on the Viceroy's Council, the second most important man in the Indian Empire. But that was rather going it a bit, and he'd be quite content to be Lieutenant-General Sir Richard Wendover, K.C.B., and either be killed in battle or, at least, severely wounded.

There was a knock at the door of his attic sanctum. That would be his friend's daughter, young Sybil Ffoulkes. A good kid. A pity she wasn't a boy as she ought to have been, for she could catch a ball almost as well as he could; throw a stone pretty straight— which precious few girls could do; use a catapult and an air-rifle in a most useful manner; and run like blazes. The boy had an uncomfortable feeling that there were one or two things that she could do even better than he, but that was not a thought to dwell upon. And certainly it would not be a good thing for the fact to be demonstrated. Make her cocky, and that would be a pity.

For, at present, though gifted in these directions, she was modest and unassuming, content, nay grateful, to do as he told her. Yes, although on principle he disliked girls, whether sisters, cousins or unrelated, he could not but approve Sybil Ffoulkes (who was hardly like a girl at all) apart from the fact that she was actually a Lieutenant-General's daughter, which made her much more interesting than otherwise she would have been. And of course it was his friend Lieutenant-General Ffoulkes who had taught her to swim like a fish, ride like a jockey, sail a boat like a fisherman, throw a fly, play cricket, fence, and use a gun; brought her up like a boy, in fact.

Yes, come to think of it, he'd miss the kid. Still, she'd be there when he came back for the hols, and would be that much older and more sensible.

"Come in," he said.

"Hullo, Dickie. You said I could come over and say good-bye to-night."

"Well, I'm not stopping you, am I?"

"No, but may I come to the Station in the morning? I'm going cubbing, and I thought . . ."

"Think something else. I don't want a pack of kids hanging about. It'll be bad enough with Mother, and the rest of them."

"Well, you might look out of the window after the train goes under the bridge. I can ride Blaze up to the fence near the Golf Club House and see you go by."

"All right. If I think of it."

"Can I help you with anything?"

"No. I've done it all."

"Can I write to you?"

"Good Lord! What about? Don't be sloppy."

"It isn't sloppy to write letters."

"Depends on what you write. I don't want another proposal of marriage. Suppose some of the fellows got hold of it."

Sybil kicked the chair on which she sat astride.

"Don't be silly. Is it likely I should write that?"

"Well, you said it, anyhow."

And Sybil squirmed as the boy laughed loudly, and she remembered the occasion upon which she, uplifted by the music, dancing, laughter and excitement of her tenth birthday party, which had fallen on Christmas Eve, had decoyed him out into the empty stone-flagged hall and, beneath the huge bunch of misletoe which hung from one of the beams, had flung her arms about his neck and kissed him, a noisy, clumsy and hearty kiss.

"Cool!" the surprised and slightly shocked Richard had observed as he rubbed his lips.

"I'm going to marry you, Dickie," Sybil had whispered, raising herself on her toes, placing her hands upon his shoulders and repeating the offence.

Sybil now stared at her hero consideringly as he folded up his precious newspaper. This farewell visit to Dickie's den was not turning out as she had intended. It was to have been beautiful but poignant. Dickie was to have been sad and depressed at the thought of their separation for so terribly long a period as three months, and she was to have cheered and comforted him by talking of all they would do together in the hols. And here he was, not in the least sad or depressed.

Dickie was a beast, and she hated him.

"Yes, I know I did," she admitted. "I said I was going to marry you and I *am* going to marry you. So there."

"Suppose I don't propose?"

"Well then, I shall."

"And suppose I say no?"

"That won't make the slightest difference. I shall be marrying you, not you marrying me."

"Fair warning, anyhow," jeered the boy. "Shall we have tea first?"

§2

Years later . . .

413

There was a sound of revelry by night, and England's capital had gathered bright, her Beauty and her Chivalry, at the Russian Embassy, where that very popular figure of London Society, the Russian Ambassador, was giving a dance in honour of the birthday and promotion of his nephew and Military Attaché, Prince Nikolas Bailitzin, brilliant young ornament of Diplomatic Society, owner of vast estates and *protégé* and favourite of the Tsar.

Scarcely a Society matron, blessed with a marriageable daughter, viewed the handsome, gifted and accomplished Prince Nikolas Bailitzin with anything but marked approval. Those who had no daughters were apt to be less enthusiastic; and, granting all that was said concerning his eligibility, were prone to observe that he appeared to be an extremely dissipated young man, and that had they daughters, he would be the last person in whose company they would wish them to be seen. And in many cases, their sons and husbands agreed, for, undeniably, young Bailitzin went the pace, seemed to forget that London was not St. Petersburg, and appeared quite anxious to do his best to shock even the most tolerant circles of London Society.

Time after time, the Ambassador admonished him, frequently warned him, and occasionally threatened. One more scandal and back to Russia he should go.

And the sooner the better, replied the ungrateful and undutiful nephew. The sooner the better, save for one small matter.

And how would he like a year or two of garrison life at the back of beyond, eh? How would he like to be stuck down with a *sotnia* of Cossacks somewhere on the wrong side of the Volga, eh? Kick his heels through a winter at Orenburg, or perhaps exchange his present post of Military Attaché to the Ambassador to the Court of St. James's for that of the Russian Envoy to the Court of the Amir at Kabul?

But Prince Nikolas Bailitzin had not taken his uncle's threats too seriously, for he had not the slightest doubt that they were empty, inasmuch as an appeal to the Tsar would result in a permanent and most satisfactory post about the Court of St. Petersburg, and no regimental duty, either. No, not while his father, General Prince Alexieff Bailitzin, late Colonel of the Imperial Body-Guard, was chief of the Emperor's Military Household.

Yes, on the whole, he had had enough of London; enough of England, a stuffy country where the real queen was Mrs. Grundy, and where, even if there were no Secret Police, the others didn't seem to know the difference between an aristocrat and a serf, and it was actually a boast that all men were equal in the sight of the Law.

Still, he didn't want to go back to Russia just yet, because if he did, he'd have to go alone, and that he had no intention of doing.

When he did go, Sybil Ffoulkes should go with him. It was not his habit to take no for an answer, nor his custom to accept defeat and humiliation. For what was refusal, repeated flat refusal of all that he, Prince Nikolas Bailitzin, had to offer, but galling humiliation? He had done this girl the honour of asking her to marry him, and marry him she should, little as she deserved such an honour if she were fool enough to prefer a wretched undistinguished unimportant subaltern who was not only a man of no title or family, but not even an officer of the Guards or some crack British Cavalry Regiment. An utterly obscure penniless Lieutenant of their native Indian Army. She must be mad. If only he could get her over to St. Petersburg and give her some idea of what she was missing by declining to become the Princess Bailitzin! And, according to her own father, whom he had approached, this fellow with whom she was infatuated didn't appear to care tuppence about her.

A pretty state of affairs, that an obscure nonentity like that should be preferred to a man of rank, wealth and distinction, *bien vu* at two Courts, a prominent ornament of the best Society of two Capitals; and, what was more, that he should be indifferent to that which his superior would give anything to possess.

But perhaps she was just being coy, just enjoying her sense of power, keeping so brilliant a suitor on a string for the pleasure of showing everybody that she could; taking delight in imagining the envy of all her friends who would have jumped at the chance with which she was dallying, pretending to despise.

"Let's sit this one out, Sybil. I want to talk to you for your good," smiled Prince Nikolas Bailitzin, as the music began again.

"*My* good—or yours?" enquired Sybil Ffoulkes lazily fanning herself.

"Both. Oh, definitely both. I feel kindly disposed towards each other. No, each of us, isn't it? I want to make you a Princess and a shining light of the Imperial Court, the most brilliant in Europe, and I want to make you the mistress of a huge old house, a *château*, a castle, yes, and of enormous estates."

"And you?" smiled Sybil Ffoulkes, with a faint edge of sarcasm to her deep voice.

"I? Oh yes, I want to make myself the happiest man in the world."

"For how long, Nikolas?"

"All my life."

"Nikolas, it dawns upon me that you are proposing once again."

"I have the honour to ask you to be my wife."

"And I have the deep regret to decline."

"But why? For God's sake tell me why, Sybil. You won't do better."

Sybil Ffoulkes turned her head sharply and stared coldly, as though incredulous, at the Russian.

"I shan't do better?"

"No."

"That's bad news," she observed.

Bailitzin seized the girl's hand.

"Look," he said. "Do you understand all I am offering you? Do you really know what you are doing? Or are you being—what is the word?"

"I don't know what the word is, Prince, but anyhow I'm not being it. Once and for all, and I hope it is for the last time, thank you very much indeed for the great compliment you pay me, but I cannot marry you."

"Cannot?"

"Cannot. Would not. And will not."

"But will you tell me why?"

"Lots of reasons. First of all, I don't love you."

"My dear, I haven't asked whether you loved me. I asked whether you will marry me."

"You don't think that there is much connection between the two?"

"Oh, yes. Yes, surely. What a strange thing to say. How cold you English girls are. I think there is every connection between love and marriage. And I tell you I love you."

"Well, I don't love you."

"And you only marry where you love?"

"Every time. Always," replied Sybil Ffoulkes languidly, as she rose to her feet.

"Good," laughed Bailitzin triumphantly as he sprang up. "I'll make you love me."

And with a swift and practised grace, he flung his right arm about her, seized her right wrist, crushed her left arm to him, so that she was helpless, and with his left hand beneath her chin, raised her face and kissed her savagely upon the mouth. And again—and again—and again.

Sybil Ffoulkes kept perfectly still.

"Done?" she enquired as the Russian released her with a harsh laugh, and raising her right hand, struck him with all her strength across the face. And the hands of Sybil Ffoulkes, golfer, hockey player, fisherwoman, swimmer and horsewoman, could be extremely hard and heavy as well as soft and light.

So unexpected and sudden was the blow that the man staggered back, stepped upon a small rug that slid on the highly polished floor, and measured his length upon his back.

"Our dance, I think, Sybil," said a voice, as the head of the unfortunate Russian smote the parquet with a resounding thump.

Richard Wendover held the curtain of the alcove on

one side as the girl walked out into the corridor; and, with a cool eyebrow-raising glance at the Russian, he dropped the curtain.

"Really! I shouldn't care to be your husband, Sybil!" he said.

"Tastes differ apparently, Dickie," replied the girl.

Richard Wendover smiled.

> 'It's all very well to dissemble your love,
> But why do you kick me downstairs?'

he grinned. "What has the wild Cossack been doing now? Proposing?"

"Just that."

"And do you knock him out every time he does it?"

"Practically."

"Looked a bit—er—practical. As I say, I shouldn't care to be your husband."

"You'll love it."

"I'm no hero, Sybil."

"You are mine, Dickie."

"All mine," echoed her heart.

After the dance, as they sat behind a bank of flowers on the vast marble-paved landing:

"About this Bailitzin feller?" said Richard Wendover. "Does he need—er—slapping or anything?"

"He did, Dickie, and he got it."

"Well, do I have to go and push his hat down over his ears and run away; or snatch his button-hole or something?"

"No. Not even to flap your handkerchief at him. After all, he did ask me to marry him, Dickie."

"Mad. All those Russians are mad," yawned Richard Wendover.

§3

Lady Ffoulkes looked up from her book, and eyed her daughter consideringly, and with anxiety.

What a stubborn headstrong girl she was, and always had been. Never told one anything. If she were suffering, as undoubtedly she was at the present moment, she always kept her suffering to herself. Never sought sympathy. Never had a nice talk, and talked it all out. And not only strong-headed but wrong-headed.

Dickie Wendover was the trouble of course.

And if Dickie Wendover wasn't in love with her, wasn't going to propose to her?

She didn't seem to realize that it was an absolutely boy-and-girl affair that was over and done with. Young people who were children together, grew up together, never married. They knew too much about each other. No glamour and romance left. Just think of the glamour and romance there would be in marrying a handsome young officer of the Russian Imperial Guard, Military Attaché to the Russian Ambassador, a personal friend of the Tsar and *protégé* of the Empress; a courtier. Just imagine a girl having an opportunity of being a real Princess, of living at the Russian Court, seeing that wonderful life of Russian Royalty and Aristocracy from the inside. Probably having a post at Court, Lady-in-Waiting, or something of that sort. Now, that was what one might call really romantic and glamourous.

But no. She must throw herself at the head of a young man who simply did not want her, and who, after all, was a penniless subaltern in an Indian Regiment.

And she made no secret about it, either.

When the Prince had come down for the week-end, and had spoken to herself and the General, and she and the General had spoken to Sybil, the silly girl had, in her most unmaidenly, not to say brazen, manner, stated that nothing on earth would induce her to marry Prince Nikolas Bailitzin, because she did not love him—rather despised him, in point of fact—and had no desire whatever to go to Russia; and, if they wanted to know, it was her intention to marry Dick Wendover. And if she didn't marry Dick Wendover, she'd never marry anybody else; never marry at all.

And had the silly girl a private understanding with Dick Wendover?

None whatever.

And yet she proposed to marry him.

She did.

And supposing Dick Wendover did not propose to her, as he hadn't done so far, and certainly showed no likelihood of doing, what then?

Why then she'd propose to Dick.

And if he declined the honour, refused to marry her?

Then she'd propose again.

She would pester him until he gave in?

Exactly. Wear him down and wear him out, and not give up hope until he had married somebody else. Yes, and then she'd wait till that somebody else died and Dickie was a widower.

"And wanted somebody to look after his children?" Lady Ffoulkes had enquired bitterly.

Yes, that would be her chance, Sybil had declared with an apparently gay defiant hopefulness. Splendid idea.

Lady Ffoulkes studied her daughter's face. Had she got a little thinner since this wretched Dickie Wendover had gone back to India? It might be the shadow from the reading-lamp that made her cheekbones seem a little higher, her prominent chin a little more bony.

What a strong face it was. Almost masculine in its cool firm purposefulness. Amazingly like her father's face had been at that age.

But the smile was very sweet, and the finely lashed eyes beneath their well-marked eyebrows were kindly and friendly, for all their direct straightness of glance, and they lit up most merrily when she laughed.

No, there was nothing hard about the face, nothing peevish or petulant, but it was just a little older than it ought to be, and too apt to fall into the lines and expression of—what should one say? Resignation? That was hardly the word, but you felt that for so young a girl, she was too serious, thought too much about something, as though she had come up against life too young and had been through trouble. Or rather, as though she had had trouble earlier than was right. Too serious, but, thank God, no *poseuse*, the last person in the world to dramatize herself or to let—

> *"Concealment, like a worm i' the bud*
> *Feed on her damask cheek."*

"Don't stare, Mother Ffoulkes. Very rude, dear," said Sybil, looking up suddenly.

"I was thinking about you, Sybil. Do you know I'm afraid you are getting thin."

"Thin? No, not thin yet, if a little thinner. Strangely enough 'thin' is thinner than 'thinner,' if you know what I mean."

"Well, I don't, dear. But anyway, you are thinner."

"You should feed me better. It's a shame."

"Or you shouldn't ride so much."

"So much as what?"

"So much as you do."

"One to you, Mother."

"And another thing, Sybil, you—what shall I say? I don't know how to put it. May I say, you brood too much."

"Broody old hen."

"Well, my dear, I don't want you to be a broody old hen. I want you to be as cheerful and merry and bright and happy as you were when . . ."

"When Dickie was at home?"

"Yes."

"Counsels of perfection, darling. When Dickie was at home the sun shone all day."

"My dear, we had a lot of rain."

"A terrible lot, but the sun shone all day—and all night, too. I grudged the time I wasted asleep because I wasn't consciously happy, sleeping. I was alive in those days. Life was utterly lovely," mused the girl. "Unbearably happy. I was alive."

"My dear, you are alive now."

"Oh, Mother, how can you talk such rubbish. I'm completely dead, dear. In two places."

"Sybil, what nonsense you talk. How could one be dead in two places?"

"Easily. Dead from the neck up, and also from the neck down. Every time Dickie went away to school, I felt perfectly dreadful. Sick. Couldn't eat. Each time he went back to Sandhurst it was the same. When he went to India, I got insomnia, and if I hadn't shaken myself severely, boxed my ears and taken a tight hold, I should have gone into a decline. You know, declined chocolates and the next dance and food and—all that. And now that he's gone back again, oh! I am so happy, Mother. Giggle all day. So happy I literally don't know what to do. But what I think I *shall* do, is to go out to India."

"Sybil! Have you no pride, no self-respect, no shame?"

"Not a bit. Not the least little bit of any of 'em, thank God."

"D'you mean to tell me that you'd actually go out to India with the view to going and staying with somebody who's somewhere near where Dickie Wendover is stationed, so that you can throw yourself in his way?"

"I don't know about throwing myself in his way, Duckie. Unless you mean in front of his horse's hooves when he is out for a morning canter."

"What then?"

"Well, you know the sort of thing. You are a woman of the world, darling. Go to the weekly dance at the Club or Gymkhana or whatever they call it, ask him for a few dances, lead him out to a quiet spot under the moon, and the palms and the dew, and propose to him again."

"Again?"

"Again and again. Wear him down. And if he kept on refusing me, I could, at any rate, see that nobody else got the chance to be refused."

Lady Ffoulkes knitted in silence for a while.

"My dear, what do you see in the man?" she asked at length.

"What do I see in him? Well, I see in him the man whom I love with all my heart and soul and strength, all my mind and body, if that is anything. I see in him the only man whom I could possibly marry, and the man whom I am going to marry."

"Sounds a little selfish to me, not to mention brazen and shameless and unwomanly."

"Oh, I'm all that, if loving a man and admitting it, is brazen and shameless and unwomanly; but I don't think I am completely and purely selfish. You see, there's nobody alive who knows him and understands him better than I do. And mind you, Richard Wendover is a queer cuss. He can be as stubborn as a mule, and wrong-headed as two mules. A horrible ruffian, really. But I understand him, and could lead him on a string. There's nobody alive who'd devote herself so utterly and completely to his well-being and happiness as I should. It would be my happiness to make him happy, to look after him, to take care of bim. You know, to see he washed behind the ears, had a clean handkerchief and wore lots of wool next to his skin. Just think of a wretched bachelor in the hands of thieving servants, and with a cook who'd give him the same dinner every night for ten years."

"In point of fact, I believe subalterns in India do themselves remarkably well," replied Lady Ffoulkes coldly.

"Yes, and are 'done' remarkably well. And they get constant malaria because their mosquito-nets are not kept mended; and enteric because the cook uses water from the nearest drain; and tetanus because they don't take the trouble to disinfect cuts and grazes they get at polo and pig-sticking; and dysentery because . . ."

"I can't say that Richard Wendover looked as though he led a life of constant malaria, enteric, dysentery, and tetanus," interrupted Lady Ffoulkes.

"No, dear. He looked perfectly lovely, and a model of health and strength and fitness, but he's running those risks all the time."

"Well, to come to practical details, whom do you intend to visit in India? All our friends have been home for years. Do you know anyone well enough for you to be able to propose yourself for a cold weather?"

"No, darling. But I know an Organization to which I can propose myself for all the cold weathers that stretch between now and the time when Dickie is able to afford to marry me. That's his present defence."

"Organization? Defence?"

"Yes. Q.A.M.N.S. And whenever I ask Dickie to marry me, his defence is poverty; he says he can't afford to."

"Sybil! You'd join the Queen Alexandra Military Nursing Sisterhood? On the chance of being sent to India and stationed at a Military Hospital somewhere near where Dickie Wendover's regiment is?"

"That's the idea, Mrs. F. I shall qualify, get a nomination or whatever it is, join the Q.A.M.N.S., wangle it that I'm sent to India at the earliest possible moment, and then wangle my way to the Military Hospital at Napierpur."

"But Sybil, it's disgraceful, unthinkable. A girl simply pursuing a man like that. Think of the talk there'd be."

"And of the talks there'd be between me and Dickie," smiled Sybil Ffoulkes. "'Dickie,' I'd say, 'I've come half across the world because I lof you. Lay your head on my shoulder, Sonny, and turn your face to the East and the West; and give up this idea of not marrying me, for, believe me, your Sybil knows best.'"

"I find this sort of talk very distasteful, Sybil," interrupted Lady Ffoulkes.

But notwithstanding this fact, she continued the conversation.

"And supposing you did do anything so shameless as to go to the depôt of Napier's Horse and absolutely pursued and pestered Dickie Wendover, until he very rightly and properly declined to have anything more to do with you, what then?"

"Why, don't you see, darling, I should wait until Napier's Horse went out on a show on the Border, a sort of Tirah or Malakand do, and then, one fine morning—

> *"'Into a ward with whitewashed halls,*
> *Where the dead and the dying lay,*
> *Wounded by bayonet, shells and balls,*

Worth Wile

Somebody's Darling was borne one day.'

"And I am the Somebody, you see, Mother, and Dickie is the Darling, and he's knocked all end-wise. Full of bayonets, shells and bullets. But not so that he won't come right-end-up again. Nothing to spoil his beauty. And they've already given him morphia at the C.C.S. That is the Casualty Clearing Station. And when he comes round, whom does he see bending over him? Me. And ere he fades out again, he whispers one word. I won't tell you what the word is, Mother. It might be rude. But he's got to be in bed in that ward for quite a while. Or perhaps not so long. At any rate, long or short, it's going to be the exact time that it takes him to realize that he loves me; that all else is dross and dripping. And as soon as he can totter, he totters forth with me, and the band of Napier's Horse plays *The Wedding March.*"

And Sybil whistled shrilly:

"You see, I've thought it all out, Mother dear."

"If you could talk sense for one moment, Sybil, would you tell me whether you really intend to apply for admission to the Q.A.M.N.S."

"Most certainly I do. I'm going to become a Nurse, simply and solely so that I can get out to India, and simply and solely so that I can see Dickie. I don't want to talk any modern tripe and flapdoodle about Living my own Life, but I am going to be a Nurse, and that particular kind of a nurse, and in that particular country, and in Dickie's particular part of that country."

"Well, of course, they are all gentlewomen and it is a noble profession, but the scarlet cape, my dear!" objected Lady Ffoulkes. "So unbecoming, with your colouring."

"Well, I must get 'em to change the colour of the cape. Or else change my own colour."

"Still," conceded Lady Ffoulkes, "the cape is only worn out-of-doors. The rest of the uniform is dove-grey, I believe. Most becoming. But of course it is all absurd nonsense."

"What, the Queen Alexandra Military Nursing Sisterhood?"

§4

Lieutenant-General Sir Arthur Ffoulkes, K.C.B., seated in his library, smoking the best pipe of the day, and reading *The Times*, as was his wont for half an hour after breakfast, suddenly came upon an item which caused him to frown, to go back to the head of the column and begin again, and finally to whisper in horrified dismay,

"*Good God!*"

Again he read the appalling announcement, and remained, even then, half incredulous.

It was absurd.

There must be a mistake somewhere. Miscarriage of justice. Or they'd got the name wrong. Or there were two Richard Wendovers in the Indian Army.

Perhaps so, but there weren't two in Napier's Horse.

What a truly dreadful thing!

And for the first time since he lost his old friend, he could be thankful that he was dead. It would have broken his heart. General Sir Richard Wendover, K.C.M.G., K.C.B., D.S.O., was as fine a soldier as ever stepped, and, had he lived another year, would have been Commander-in-Chief of the Indian Army. Yes, it was a mercy he was dead. And his wife, too.

And by Jove, poor Sybil! The boy had been her greatest pal, her life-long friend. People had thought, at one time, that it would come to something. Well, thank God, again, that it hadn't.

He had better tell her himself, before somebody else did, or she heard people talking as they'd be bound to do. Everybody knew him. All the hunting people.

Or had he better tell her mother and get her to break it to her? No, perhaps he had better do it himself. For he had an idea that Sybil's mother might have some difficulty in keeping a very faint flavour of *I-told-you-so* and *I-always-knew-it* out of her voice and manner when she told Sybil. Undoubtedly, like himself, she had been really vexed, only very much more so, when young Prince Nikolas Bailitzin had come to see them and definitely proposed himself as Sybil's suitor, and she had turned him down flat.

And she had made no secret whatsoever of the fact that she preferred Dickie Wendover. When her mother had got at her, to know whether she and Dickie were engaged or had an understanding, she had again made not the slightest secret of the fact that there was nothing of the sort. Had just said quite plainly that if she married anybody at all, it would be Dickie Wendover, and if it weren't Dickie Wendover, it would be nobody at all.

Well, this put an end to that nonsense, anyway.

Yes, he had better tell her himself and tell her at once.

He rang the bell, and when the butler answered it, bade him find Miss Sybil and ask her if she would come along to the library for a moment, before she went out.

A few minutes later, Sybil, in rat-catcher riding-kit, bowler, gauntlets and spurred boots, strode into the library.

"What is it, Daddy?"

"Sit down, my dear. I just wanted to speak to you for a minute. You don't read *The Times*, do you?"

"No, Daddy. Only Marriages and Racing."

"Well, there's an item in it to-day which comes under neither heading. A bit of bad news. Very bad indeed. Young Wendover."

Sybil went white.

"Not . . . not *dead?*" she asked breathlessly.

"No . . . No. Better in some ways if he were."

"Don't talk such rubbish, Daddy. What is it? Tell me quickly."

"Court-Martial."

"Well, that might happen to any soldier. Lot of silly

427

red tape. Jam-returns wrong?"

"Court-martialled for being drunk at his post, at Ubele—besieged; practically under fire. Blind drunk. Dead drunk. Speechless. Utterly unable to speak to the officer commanding the relieving force."

"I don't believe a word of it," interrupted Sybil.

"No? Unfortunately the Court-Martial did, on the evidence. And sentenced him to be cashiered: dismissed the army with ignominy."

The girl sat down on the nearest chair.

"As you know," continued the General, "he was seconded from his Regiment on special duty to Madrutta and thence to the African show, on active service. He was in command of an important post and admittedly put up a very good fight. Then apparently the strain was too much for him and he turned to the bottle, as other fools have done before him, drank to excess and, being the only surviving combatant officer, left everything to the doctor. Went from bad to worse until he drank himself absolutely insensible. And that is how the relieving force found him. Blind to the world on the camp-bed in his hut with two empty whisky bottles."

"And you ask me to believe it?" whispered Sybil, staring wide-eyed and white-lipped at her father.

"I'm asking you nothing, Sybil. I'm telling you the verdict of the Court-Martial. Evidently a properly-convened Field General Court-Martial with everything regular and correct and the prisoner properly represented. Anyway, here it is."

"I don't believe it."

"Do you mean you don't believe *The Times* account of it?"

"I don't believe that Dickie ever got really drunk in his life. And I know as well as I know that I am standing here, that he never got drunk when on duty; when he had responsibility; with other men's lives and the safety of a fort depending on him."

"The Court-Martial believed it, my dear. Look here, I'll write to Witherington at the War Office and ask him to get all the facts."

"Where is he now?"

"Witherington?"

"Dickie."

"How should I know, my dear? He can go where he likes and do what he likes, except ever again serve his country in any capacity whatsoever."

"Do you think he'll come home?"

"Last place in the world he'd come to, I should think."

§5

Yes, the last place in the world that he'd come to.

Where would he go?

She must try to put herself in his place, as far as such a thing was possible, and try to think of the sort of things he might do, the sort of place to which he'd go.

What could have happened, and how could such ghastly mistake have been made?

Because, of course, there was a mistake somewhere.

Perhaps he had been so weak and ill with dysentery and malaria that a little alcohol had acted like a powerful drug, a narcotic?

What would he do?

If she knew anything of Dickie—and surely if anybody alive knew him, she did—he wouldn't blow up and go off the deep end, whether he felt the sentence of the Court-Martial to be just or not. He wouldn't, for example, commit suicide. Of that she was quite certain. There was nothing neurotic or unbalanced about him; nothing unstable or melodramatic.

Of course he would feel it a most appalling disgrace, and it would be a shattering blow, but he'd stand up to it. He wasn't the sort of vessel that was easily sunk, and he'd weather the storm somehow. His life was wrecked and smashed, but he'd pick up the pieces and re-build it.

What would he do, and above all, where would he go?

429

There would be no point now in her keeping on with the Queen Alexandra Military Nursing Sisterhood idea, of course. It would be particularly foolish to get herself stationed in India, and tied down to duty in some particular spot, bound hand and foot by red tape, when she might want to go off in a hurry. For Dickie would not go back to India any more than he would go Home. Of that she felt quite sure. Naturally his first instinct would be to go where nobody knew him; cut himself off as completely as possible from his past, his friends and acquaintances, and start afresh somewhere under a new name.

Would he write to her? After all, she was his oldest friend. His best friend.

His dearest friend?

Dickie was so inarticulate, so undemonstrative, so ferociously anti-sentimental, that he never had used, and probably never would use, such a phrase as "dearest friend." But she felt pretty certain that, little as he had shown her in the way of kindness and affection, not to mention love, he had shown still less to anybody else in all the world; unless he had fallen in love in India, got engaged and said nothing about it. But as he never wrote letters except for an annual brief note at Christmas time, there was no evidence on the subject. Nor, to her, was any really necessary. He would not fall in love. He'd be too busy, too keen on his job, and too indifferent to women.

On the other hand, if she could only write to him, be sure of getting a message to him, she'd feel better.

Possibly Dickie would, too. Even to a person so self-contained and self-sufficient as Dickie, surely it must give some pleasure to know that there was at least one person in the world whose faith and devotion were not in the slightest degree affected. Dickie was everything that was self-reliant and self-confident, an essentially lonely, single-minded, single-handed person, but even to him, in such a time of need, an absolutely staunch faithful friend must be a friend indeed?

Well, she could write to him care of the War Office without much hope; care of his Club and his Bank without much more, and care of his Regiment.

And that reminded one of the horrible fact that he'd no longer have a Club or a Regiment. But still, they'd send on letters if they had any address to which to forward them—and that was just what they wouldn't have.

Innocent or guilty, he would clear out absolutely, and sever all connection with his past life. Knowing Dickie as she did, she could foretell his re-action to calamity exactly. Of that she was perfectly certain.

If he were innocent, he'd be extremely angry, resentful and hurt; and when he had recovered consciousness, so to speak, he'd shrug his shoulders and make the best of things. He was too much of a philosopher and of too tough a fibre, too stout-hearted altogether, to let it break him. He'd emerge harder than ever, and naturally cynical and bitter. Never very expansive and on-coming, he'd be dour, not to say morose.

And if he were guilty, which of course he wasn't, there would be, added to that, more than a touch of desperation and defiance. He'd be a rather dangerous and—but what was the good of speculating about anything so utterly idiotic. Dickie, once again, was no plaster saint, but he was a British Officer of the best type, utterly incapable of doing anything base and mean, and even more incapable of committing a military crime of this sort. Might as well talk about his committing a civil crime, pocket-picking, burglary, or robbery with violence on the King's highway. It was simply idiotic. And if he were guilty—a thing which she would only believe when he himself told her so—it wouldn't make the very slightest difference.

If only she could see him and tell him that. He had always been more or less fond of her, of course, in his way, but if she could really help him now, stand by him in his trouble, might he not become fonder still?

Meanwhile, what could she do? How could she get into touch with him, since she hadn't the slightest faith or hope that letters would reach him?

§6

And then came the second blow—far worse—though that had not seemed possible.

General Ffoulkes had written a number of letters to various people who might be in a position to give him further information on the subject of the tragedy of Richard Wendover. From their replies, he had learned little more than he had from the newspapers, save for one written by a Colonel Matheson who had been President of the Court-Martial—to the effect that Wendover had completely vanished. He had not sailed from Kilindini by the ship in which he had taken passage, and had absolutely disappeared.

And now Colonel Matheson had written what was evidently the last chapter of the sad story of Richard Wendover.

He had gone big-game shooting, or at any rate on *safari* through the lion country, apparently alone or almost alone, and had been killed by a lion. Proof of the identity of the remains of the partly-eaten corpse, discovered by some natives, was provided by the tab sewn on the heavy khaki hunting-shirt, upon which was woven the name R. WENDOVER.

And that was that.

It had seemed best to General Ffoulkes to send for Sybil, give her the letter, without comment, and leave her alone in the library to read it.

"Poor girl," growled the General to himself. She had evidently been very fond of the fellow. Not unnaturally, as they had grown up together. But on the whole, since so terrible a thing had happened to the man, this was perhaps the best way out of it.

In point of fact, it might have been a clever form of suicide, the sort of thing that Richard Wendover was capable of doing, if he decided to commit suicide and was determined that no one should be aware of the fact.

Quite possible, for he was undeniably a tough lad.

Poor little Sybil. Still, she'd get over it, and this would put an end to all that nonsense about believing him innocent and wanting to find him.

§7

A case of "poor little Sybil" indeed, with her double burden to bear, the loss of the friend whom she had loved all her life, and the carrying on of the normal daily round—hiding from relations and friends, from acquaintances and enemies, the fact that she had received an all-but-mortal blow.

Her father, who probably both loved and understood her better than did her mother, realized something of what she was suffering, and admired the stoicism and fortitude with which she was behaving.

As he watched her carrying on with the common task, the trivial round; taking her share in the social life of the house and of their circle, helping her mother to entertain guests, apparently cheerful, light-hearted and care-free, he paid a tribute to courage.

A somewhat unusually imaginative and understanding type of man for a soldier, he was able, to some extent, to do more than sympathize and offer empty consolation. Wisely he forbore to ridicule her refusal, even now, to believe in the disgrace and death of the man whom she loved; and he encouraged the habit she was forming, of coming and sitting on a fireside stool in the library, a room sacred to her father, on her way up to bed, instead of merely looking in to say good night as had been her custom.

Leaning against his chair, she would talk of the subject ever uppermost in her mind, and he would encourage her to do so.

What if it were merely foolish optimism on the girl's part? Surely hope is preferable to despair, and the longer she went on hoping, the better. Time was passing and time is the great healer.

Of course, as she said, the finding of a body, the clothing of which bore a name, was no actual proof that the name was that of the person wearing the clothing; and the more she talked about it, the more he saw her point, and was inclined to accept it.

A shirt on which a tab bearing Wendover's name was sewn, obviously belonged to Wendover. But no Court of Law would accept that as proof that the man wearing it was Wendover himself. It was the strongest circumstantial evidence, and in his own mind there was no doubt that the man was Wendover. But the fact remained, it wasn't proof. He doubted whether, for the purposes of probate for example, an heir would be allowed to presume death on the strength of the finding of a name-tabbed shirt. Not straight away, at any rate.

There was a chance.

And on the whole he thought it was the wiser and kinder plan to encourage Sybil to think so.

For himself, after careful thought and analysis of the matter, he decided that there were three aspects, three possible solutions.

First and likeliest, that Wendover, dressed in African hunting kit, had gone lion-hunting and been killed by a lion.

It was very probable that he would not have a proper *safari*, with an experienced Swahili *neapara*[67] and gun-boys, staunch and reliable, and an outfit of specially-chosen porters. If he had, they would have stood by him; and if he had been killed, would have carried his body to Nairobi or to the camp of the nearest District Officer. Failing that, they would have buried him, and reported to the Police or the nearest Authority. Certainly they would not have allowed their Bwana[68] to be eaten by lions, even if they had not been able to prevent his being killed by one.

No, Wendover wouldn't have stopped to gather a proper *safari*. He'd have just pushed off into the blue with a cook and one or two porters. His one idea would have been to get away from civilization as quickly and as far as possible. He had probably gone lion-hunting on foot, and in the most dangerous manner had followed up a wounded lion into thick bush or high grass and been torn, mangled and killed.

---

[67] *Headman.*
[68] *Master.*

Secondly, he might have thought, "Well, life isn't good enough after this, on any conditions, and I'll get out of it." But Wendover was undoubtedly the sort of man who'd hate to have it known that he had committed suicide and was apparently something of a coward, as well as a blackguard. Suicide would be a very ugly sequel to ignominious expulsion from the Army.

To blow his brains out or cut his throat would be such a very frank admission of defeat as well as of guilt. If he had boarded the ship on which he had taken a berth for England and disappeared overboard one night, it would still have been an obvious case of suicide; but, as had occurred to the General's mind before, it would, to a man like Wendover, be an excellent idea, since he intended to commit suicide, to do it, not with his revolver or a razor, but with a lion! It would please him to do a thing that would take as much nerve as that, a thing which very few suicides would have the guts to do, even if they thought of it.

Yes, he could imagine Wendover in search of secret suicide, deliberately firing to miss a charging lion.

And thirdly, there was the possible solution that he was still alive, and had "planted" the shirt, with the intention of creating the belief that he was dead.

Or the shirt might have been stolen from him by a native servant, sold in the bazaar and bought second-hand by some Portuguese or half-caste trader on whose dead body it had been found.

"Daddy," said Sybil one evening, "I don't believe two things."

"I don't believe millions, my dear. Have a cigarette."

The girl took one from the proffered case. The General lit it, saying as he did so;

"I know what you mean. You don't believe the finding of the Court-Martial was just; and you don't believe he's dead."

"I'm perfectly certain, Daddy."

"Got any reason, or is it the old story of the wish being father to the thought?"

"Well, it's a mixture of reason and intuition. Reason says that Dickie was entirely incapable of doing what he was accused of doing. Even if I didn't love him, but merely knew him as well as I do, reason would tell me that the thing was impossible. Then as to the other, his being dead; well, there I'm afraid it is intuition. Though I don't know why I should say 'afraid.' I believe that intuition is often right where apparently accurate reasoning turns out to be wrong. I just *feel* that he is alive."

"Well, my dear, as I've said before, the evidence points to his death but by no means proves it."

"No, of course it doesn't. I was thinking only last night, that supposing we gave an old shirt of yours to a tramp, and months and months later, he fell into the river while wearing it, and his body was found, the Police wouldn't immediately decide that it was you, would they? There wouldn't be a notice in the newspapers that you had been found drowned."

"No, of course not. And if there were, I'd stoutly deny it.

"And," he continued, "we needn't give undue weight to the fact that Wendover hasn't denied that the shirt was his. Because it is entirely possible, in fact very probable, that he'd be only too glad for people to suppose that that was the end of him."

"Yes. Yes, that's exactly what I am building on. Dickie wouldn't stoutly deny it. Naturally he wouldn't, if he had, as you say, 'planted' the shirt with the intention of creating the belief that he was dead. And if there was nothing of that sort, he wouldn't contradict the rumour of his death, because he'd be only too glad for everyone who knew him to imagine that he was dead . . . Then he could really start afresh somewhere else, and build up his life again.

"That's what I think he'd try to do," she continued. "But what sort of new career would he try to start and where would he go? If one could only guess that, one would have some idea as to what to do."

"And suppose we did know, what could one do about it?" asked General Ffoulkes.

"I don't know that 'one' could do much about it, Daddy, but I know quite well what I should do about it."

"Write to him?"

"Yes, and a little more than that. If I knew where he was, I should write to him and tell him that I was coming to—help him. And without waiting for an answer, I should go straight to wherever he was."

"Well, it seems to me that, in the circumstances, you might not be very welcome. What about that?"

"I'd make myself welcome. He'd probably be most unpleasant and disagreeable, but I am perfectly certain he'd be glad to see me. Wouldn't anybody in such a position be glad to see a—friend? Somebody who absolutely believed in him, and was more than willing to do anything to prove it?"

"Well, yes. That's true enough, but surely it applies rather to a man friend, doesn't it? I mean, supposing Wendover is alive and is 'wilful missing,' has deliberately disappeared and created the belief that he is dead, it is quite likely that he has gone to some place where a 'girl friend' couldn't be much use to him? Except perhaps by staying at home and by writing the sort of letters that a man in such circumstances would like to get. I could imagine their being extremely cheering and helpful—life-saving, in fact. But it is only a man who could go and live with . . . go and be with . . . well, you know what I mean; go and look after him, if he were, well, down-and-out in some god-forsaken hole. Supposing he were beach-combing on Zanzibar Island or Madagascar or in the South Seas; suppose he had gone down to the Transvaal, and were a 'poor white' among white trash, living in a corner of a corrugated iron hut in Tin Shanty Street and working with the niggers at some mine or other."

"Well, if he had gone beach-combing to the South Sea Islands, I should comb the beaches till I found him; or if he were living in Tin Shanty Street in some *dorp* near a mine, I should go district-visiting in the slums of that *dorp*."

General Ffoulkes, a usually undemonstrative man,

stroked his daughter's smooth head and then rested his hand upon her shoulder and let it remain there.

"We'll hope for the best, my dear. We'll keep on hoping and we'll keep on trying, too."

"That's it, Daddy. The first thing is to find out whether he is undeniably dead, beyond any shadow of a doubt. I'll write to someone pretty-well every day.

"Won't it be awful," she added, "when we've come to the end of the list, and can't think of another person to write to? Still, we won't think of that. Have you had any more ideas?"

"Well, yes. There was a chap I used to know very well, named Hazelrigg who . . ."

"By Jove, yes!" interrupted Sybil. "I remember Dickie speaking about him. He did some rather marvellous stunts as an Intelligence Officer. Yes, I remember Dickie saying that he came into the Mess one night, just before dinner, dressed up as a *fakir* or something. Kicked up an awful row and was thrown out, and not a soul recognized him. Then, when he was turned out of the Lines, he went down into the bazaar, made a nuisance of himself there, and when the Police were beginning to get unpleasant, he went on and attended a convocation of filthy itinerant holy men who had assembled in a big camp outside the city walls. Having harangued them and stayed to supper, he felt that his disguise and acting abilities were in good order, and started off for the Border. I gathered that Dickie rather hero-worshipped him. You will write to him at once, won't you, dear?"

"I'll write to-night, but the snag is that Heaven alone knows when he'll get it. He may be anywhere in India, from Bombay or Delhi to Simla or Peshawar, and it is more than likely that he isn't in India at all. Probably somewhere in Afghanistan or Turkestan or the parts adjacent. He's the Russo-Afghan-North-West Frontier specialist, and gets his information first-hand. I'll ring up Colonel Harrington-Spens, first thing in the morning, and see if he has heard from him lately."

"Ring him up to-night."

"All right. You get off to bed now, and I will. Good

night, my dear. Keep smiling. If Wendover is alive, we'll find him."

§8

The days and weeks and the months rolled by, and the light of Sybil Ffoulkes's faith began to burn a little dim, her hope to grow fainter. As she had to admit, it really did seem as though Wendover were dead, had been killed by a lion on the Kathedong plains in East Africa. Letters of various kinds from widely varying people had reached her or her father, and the import of all, without exception, was the same.

The answers to her father's letters, written to each member of the Court-Martial, had made it perfectly clear that no shadow of doubt remained in the minds of the writers about the guilt of Richard Wendover; and as to his ultimate fate, none could give any other information than that he never occupied the berth that he had taken on the ship that should have borne him from Kilindini, the port of Mombasa, and that he had simply vanished.

Colonel Maldon at Nairobi was good enough to write a further letter saying that he had got into communication with the Major Robinson who was in charge of the building of the Tabundi railway, inasmuch as, according to the *Nairobi Chronicle*, it was to him that poor Wendover's torn and blood-stained shirt had been brought.

He enclosed Major Robinson's reply, which was to the effect that, although no European had seen the body that had been found and buried by the men who brought the shirt to him, he had no doubt whatever that the dead man had been Wendover. He had carefully questioned the men who had brought the remainder of the shirt bearing Wendover's name-tab, and they had stated simply and plainly that they had found the body of a Sahib three days previously in the bush out on the Kathedong plains; that the body was that of a European; that it had been partly devoured by a lion; and that they had buried, or rather piled a cairn of stones on it, and put a boma of thorn branches round the cairn. According to these men, the body had only had a shirt, shorts, puttees, and boots. One of the men was actually wearing the boots; and as they had noticed 'writing' inside the collar of the shirt, they had brought the ghastly remnant along with them, to show it to the Police or the authorities at railhead, for which place they were making in search of work.

No, Major Robinson regretted to say that there could be no doubt whatever that the portion of the torn shirt had belonged to Wendover, and that it was Wendover's body that these men had buried. What finally clinched the matter in his mind was the fact that no European in that part of the world had been reported missing. Had any local planter, military officer, civil official, hunter, or other such white man, disappeared, the fact would very soon have been not only noted but notified.

So there was a double reason for concluding that the body had been that of the missing Wendover.

And then one gleam of hope seemed faintly to illuminate the darkness of the settling cloud of Sybil's despair when another man, to whom Colonel Maldon had been so kind as to write, raised the point of the identity of the men who had brought the blood-stained shirt to Major Robinson. This was the Superintendent of Railway Police to whom he had reported the matter, notifying that he held a clue which indicated that the buried corpse was that of the late Captain Richard Wendover.

The Superintendent of Police—after suggesting that it was quite possible that the men who had "found" the shirt had murdered its owner for the sake of his rifle and other kit—had then toyed for a moment with the alternative theory that the two discoverers, apparently Pathans, were actually Wendover himself and a genuine Pathan. But this idea had been laughed to scorn by Major Robinson, who had himself once met Wendover in the Bombay Yacht Club. No, the two men who had got hold of the remains of Wendover's shirt and his boots were Pathans all right. Robinson had given them a job as labourers with his Pathan coolie-gangs working on the railway, and had seen them and spoken with them almost daily while their names remained on his pay-roll.

It was obviously really nothing, this idea of the Police Officer's, but nevertheless Sybil Ffoulkes wrote to him and to Major Robinson to pursue this shadow of a hope.

'What shadows we are and what shadows we pursue.' But better pursue a shadow than do nothing; and, after weeks of weary waiting, had come the reply of the Superintendent of Police to the effect that he did remember saying something of the sort when he visited Major Robinson to investigate the alleged finding of the body of Captain Wendover, but in point of fact he had really rather been manufacturing theories that might possibly fit the facts. He hadn't seen the men themselves, as they had left rail-head before he arrived, and he hadn't the slightest reason for suspecting the men of murdering Captain Wendover; nor for imagining that one of them was Captain Wendover himself, in disguise.

As a matter of fact, it was, of course, extremely improbable that, if they really had murdered and buried a European, the Pathans would have said a word about it to anybody; and it was therefore, in his opinion, pretty certain that they had found the corpse as they said, and that the corpse was that of the man whose name was on the shirt-tab. As to his somewhat idle suggestion that one of them might have been Wendover himself, that was quashed by Major Robinson's statement that he knew Wendover by sight.

Major Robinson's letter which arrived by the next mail, answered all her questions very fully, and told her that the people who brought the evidence of Wendover's death were itinerant Pathans, good type men whose statements he did not doubt. He had liked them both, and far from suspecting them of being murderers, was bound to admit that they had undoubtedly saved his life at some risk to themselves. There had been a plot on the part of the discontented and disgruntled Pathan construction-gang to murder him, and not only had they warned him beforehand, but had stood by him when the trouble materialized.

So great had been the risk in doing this, that they had evidently considered their lives to be in danger, and had disappeared forthwith. Where they went, he had not the faintest idea; and although he had made all possible enquiries among his Pathan and other workmen, he had been unable to obtain any information whatsoever.

Well, that was that, and another will-o'-the-wisp light had gone out. And no further light of any kind was shed by the quite considerable number of letters that her father and she received, from officials and others in Africa and India, who had had anything to do with the case, or had known Richard Wendover, or were in a position to hear anything about him if he were still alive.

Gradually General Ffoulkes adopted the line that everything possible had been done, no stone left unturned, and, inasmuch as no news was forthcoming that gave the slightest reason for hope, the only thing to do now was to accept what was evidently the fact, that Richard Wendover was dead.

"We mustn't let it become an obsession, my dear," he said one night, as Sybil sat beside him.

"An obsession!" exclaimed Sybil in her low, slightly husky voice. "Dickie isn't an obsession with me! He *is* me, if you can understand. He isn't something stuck in my mind. He is my mind. I don't think of him. He is my thoughts. He is myself, my life, my world. Just exactly fills my universe."

"Yes, I can understand," said the General. "But the fact remains, an obsession is an obsession—and that way madness lies."

"I shan't go mad. Or at any rate, madder. No madder than I've always been about Dickie."

"And if it is proven that he is dead, you're not going to let it spoil your life? You aren't going to retire on to the shelf and settle down to be an old maid? You are not going to regard life as over and done with, in the early twenties, are you? You've always been fond of Wendover, but there are other men equally . . ."

"Now don't talk rubbish, Daddy."

"Well, that's the last thing I want to do. I want to talk sense, and I want you to take the sensible view, the long view. I'm not good at this sort of thing, my dear, but you know what I mean. One has to face up to these blows, and realize that Time heals all wounds. Completely heals absolutely everything, you know. Devilish hard for you now. Don't think I don't understand and sympathize, but don't take it too hard. Resignation and . . ."

"Yes, I know.

> "'Should He call me to resign
> What most I prize, it ne'er was mine,'

and all that.

"Well, perhaps he wasn't mine, but I'm damned if I'll resign him, Daddy, or resign hope. Don't squash the poor little hope I've got, because it is what keeps me going, and I'll not believe that he is dead until I know it. And I'll tell you what's a funny thing. I feel glad that I can never really *know* it, supposing he were killed and buried in East Africa. Do you understand what I mean?"

More moved than he cared to show, the General gently patted his daughter's shoulder.

"I know, my dear. Nobody, who ever knew him, has seen him dead, and therefore there will never be any proof that he is dead, eh? And so you can go on hoping that he isn't. But I don't want you to go on hoping too long; hoping all your life, so that it slips by, and, one fine morning, you discover that you are an old maid who has deliberately wasted her life, thrown it away, waiting for a dead man to speak."

"My dear, if Dickie is alive, I shall get in touch with him somehow. If Dickie is dead, then I shall do just what you said. Wait. Wait—for the rest of my life."

"That's foolish talk."

"Yes, I am a fool. I'm one of those fools who only

love once. You wouldn't like me to marry another man, while I loved Dickie, would you? Loved him with all my heart and soul and strength?"

"No," said the General. "I wouldn't. What I should like, if it were possible, is for Wendover's memory to fade gradually. Until you could think of him as a friend; the boy with whom you more or less grew up; and of whom you were very fond. And perhaps, in time, be able to laugh a little at yourself for this tremendous infatuation. It's a good thing for us to be able to laugh at ourselves, you know."

"Yes, I expect I shall laugh like Hell. Would you mind not using the word 'infatuation'? Infatuations don't last twenty years, as this one already has, do they? Don't last a whole lifetime, as this one will."

"Well, my darling child, if it will, it will; but I pray God it won't . . . Isn't that the telephone bell?"

"Yes. I'll tell you something you are losing sight of, Daddy, and that is the intuition, instinct, whatever you call it, that I have, about it. It is a certainty in my mind, at any rate, that Dickie is not dead."

The General sighed heavily.

Youth! Youth! With its incurable optimism and hope; its inevitable refusal to realize that the wish is father to the thought. On the other hand, not incurable, alas! Hope, faith, and optimism get cured soon enough—or rather, die—with the other illusions and with Youth itself.

The library door opened.

"You are wanted on the telephone, Sir," said the footman.

"Excuse me a moment, Sybil."

"I'll come too—in case."

For, nowadays, she haunted the neighbourhood of the telephone cabinet whenever there was a call—only to depart on hearing the first few words—fool that she was, she acknowledged. What did she expect to hear? Someone answering in Dickie's voice, which was saying that he had come home alive and well?

"Hullo!

"Oh, hullo! That you, Harrington-Spens?

"Thanks awfully.

"Very good of you to trouble.

"I'll take it down.

"Yes.

"'*Wendover alive and well. Seen Persian coast month ago. Write Thorburn, Napier's Horse. Signed Ganesh.*'

"Yes, I've got it. I'll read it through to you.

"Well, most awfully good of you. I don't know how to thank you.

"Yes, neighbour of ours. Known him ever since he was a squeaker.

"Yes, most extraordinary affair.

"Will you express my gratitude to Hazelrigg next time you write?

"I'll write to this chap Thorburn. Napierpur, I suppose?

"And to Hazelrigg too, of course.

"Yes, she's very well indeed, thanks.

"And Mrs. Harrington-Spens?

"Good.

"Good-bye. And thanks again. Good-bye."

General Ffoulkes flung open the door of the telephone cabinet, his eyes wide and bright, his face flushed.

"Sybil!" he called.

Oh, there she was in the hall. Sitting bolt upright, still as a statue, staring straight in front of her, clasping the carved arms of the chair.

Poor child! In her white dress she looked like a marble figure, a corpse.

"Sybil, he's alive!"

There was no reply.

The General strode forward and touched her.

"Sybil darling, he's alive."

"I heard, Daddy. I heard," she whispered.

And for the first time in the General's memory, she suddenly burst into a flood of tears, shaken from head to foot by violent sobs.

"There, there, my dear. He's alive. He's been seen. He's all right. Don't cry."

The girl sprang to her feet and fled up the broad staircase.

"Well, well," sighed the General as he returned to the library. "Kittle cattle, women."

And now what?

§9

By next morning, Sybil Ffoulkes was a different girl. A crushing weight of grief had fallen from her shoulders, as though she had dropped a load of lead. Grief, misery, aching despair, had turned to joy, delirious happiness.

He was alive.

What else mattered? What if he had been court-martialled and cashiered, dismissed from the Army with ignominy, publicly proclaimed as unfit ever again to serve the State in any capacity whatsoever.

He was alive.

The next thing was to learn where he was and what he was doing.

Again and again she repeated to herself the words of the telegram which she knew by heart.

Should she cable to this Captain Thorburn of Napier's Horse?

Yes, she'd just use her surname, and Captain Thorburn would think it was from General Ffoulkes. He could think anything he liked. She'd go down to the village Post Office and do it this morning. What should she say?

"*Kindly write giving full information about Wendover, to Ffoulkes, Wealdsfold, Sussex.*"

Yes, that would do. He'd quite understand that somebody was very anxious to know about his meeting with Captain Richard Wendover, and anything that he could tell them as to the latter's movements and whereabouts. He'd know that anybody who took the trouble to cable was deeply interested and that the matter was urgent.

And suddenly her soaring spirits fell. Would Captain Thorburn feel that he had any right to give information about a brother officer who was under a cloud, and who might have deliberately endeavoured to spread the belief that he was dead?

But on the other hand, evidently he had told Major Hazelrigg, because it was he who had cabled his brother-in-law, Colonel Harrington-Spens, who had rung up and told the General last night. Evidently Captain Thorburn had told people in India, so surely he wouldn't mind telling people in England, especially anyone so interested and anxious as to cable.

Well, she could only wait and see.

What she could do, was to write him a letter so that if she got no reply to the cable, she might hope to have one, however guarded, in answer to her letter. Surely he'd reply to it? Of course he would. And if he told her no more, he'd admit that he had seen Dickie, since obviously she already knew it; And if she learned nothing fresh, nothing material, she would at any rate, get a letter with Dickie's name in it, a letter written by a man who had actually seen him.

Yes, and if he were one of those extremely cautious and careful people who would not give information about anybody without their permission, she'd write again and tell him that she was Dickie's *fiancée*. So she was, in a way. She had promised to marry him, hadn't she? She needn't tell this good Captain Thorburn that Dickie had never accepted her kind offer; but she wasn't going to stick at a lie if, by telling one, she could induce him to be more forthcoming and tell her everything he knew. It was quite probable that, Captain Thorburn also being an officer of Napier's Horse, Dickie would have had a long talk with him and told him everything; the truth about the charge on which he had been court-martialled, what he was going to do, where he was going, and all that sort of thing. He might very well have given some sort of address to Captain Thorburn so that he could keep in touch with him. Anyway, she'd write.

And of course she'd write a nice long letter to that marvellous Major Hazelrigg.

How could she ever begin to thank him? He had

saved her life, or at any rate, turned it from dust and
ashes back into joy and loveliness, hope and faith, and
—oh, everything that was glorious.

Dickie was alive.

And with that heartening illuminating joy radiating
her whole being, she contrived to wait until Captain
Thorburn's answer came.

No, he wasn't a bit sticky, bless him, and evidently
saw no reason why he should conceal the fact that his
former brother-in-arms was undoubtedly alive, though
beyond that he could tell her little.

He himself had been on an ibex-shooting expedition, along the Mekran coast. (She had looked that up
in the General's atlas, and discovered it to be the
Eastern end of the coast of the Persian Gulf.) And
having passed a camp of what were, no doubt, Pathan
and Afghan gun-runners, he had suddenly come face
to face, in a narrow mountain defile, with two apparent
Pathans, one of whom was Captain Richard Wendover.

He knew him the moment he saw him. He immediately addressed him in English, and the man replied
not only in English, but in Wendover's voice. He had
said:

"Never mind what my name was. It is Gul
Mahommed now." And when Thorburn had asked him
if there was anything he could do for him, Wendover
had replied:

"Yes; you can bung off."

Then nodding his comprehension of the situation
that Wendover wished to create, he had smiled and
said:

"I see you want me to *wend over* the mountains,
eh?" And Wendover had laughed, nodded and said:

"That's the idea. So-long."

And that was all he could tell. He could give
General Ffoulkes, if it were he who had cabled, his
absolute assurance, on oath if necessary, that Captain
Richard Wendover, late of Napier's Horse, was alive,
and that the writer had talked with him in Mekran.

Beyond that, he could only surmise. His own belief
was that Wendover had made his way up from East

Africa to the Persian Gulf, assumed Pathan disguise and, as he spoke Pushtu perfectly, had joined one of the big Pathan caravans that ply regularly between Kabul and the Persian Gulf. In point of fact, it really looked as though, having come the appalling cropper that he had, poor Wendover had "gone native," turned Pathan, and was turning a more or less honest penny at gun-running. The writer requested General Ffoulkes, or whoever it was that had cabled, to be so good as to keep the matter strictly private. Wendover had said nothing about that, but, in point of fact, nobody outside the officers' Mess of Napier's Horse knew anything of this except Major 'Ganesh' Hazelrigg who was an old friend of Wendover's, and who happened to be staying with Napier's Horse when Thorburn returned there from his hunting-trip and encounter with Wendover.

Well, that was something! Something? It was everything, absolutely everything, to know that he was alive and well; and it was more than "something," to know in what part of the world he was.

Kabul. That was the capital of Afghanistan, wasn't it? Could a woman go there? She must ask her father. But she was very much afraid that she had heard or read that it was practically impossible for any European, who wasn't actually invited by the Amir, to get there. Yes, and of course she had heard Dickie himself speak of the gate across the road where the Khyber Pass ended, the gate on which was painted, "Afghanistan. No admittance," or something humourous like that. And he had told her that that was the furthest point to which any European could go on foot, horseback, camel or motor-car, up the Khyber Pass.

No, there wasn't much hope of her getting to Kabul. Besides, even if it was as easy to get there as to Calcutta, it would be an absolute wild-goose chase. There was no earthly reason for supposing he'd be at Kabul, beyond the fact that he had been seen with Afghans and Pathans. He might, or he might not, go there, and if he did, there was no earthly reason for supposing that he'd stay in the place.

449

And as she sadly admitted to herself, even if he did, wasn't it more than likely that he might regard her presence there as an infernal nuisance? Quite probably he'd have all he could do to look after himself, without having to look after a woman too, in a place that was notoriously dangerous for Europeans, especially British people. In point of fact, she might be a great deal worse than a nuisance. She might be a danger to him.

No, that wouldn't do.

What about writing to him there? To whom could she address it, though, except to the Embassy, Consulate, or Residency or whatever it was, which would be about the last place he'd go to? He wouldn't expect letters at Kabul, and if he did, he wouldn't go to the British Consulate, disguised as a Pathan, and ask if there were any letters for Captain Richard Wendover of Napier's Horse.

No, she'd have to rely on Major Hazelrigg. He was a friend of Dickie's and—why, of course—he must often be at Kabul. Yes, she'd write to him, tell him everything, and beg him not only to tell her anything he could, but to see if he could find Dickie, make Dickie write to her, and tell her where she could get a letter to him.

Yes, and she'd enclose a letter addressed to Dickie, for Major Hazelrigg to give him, if he did find him in Kabul or elsewhere. And moreover, she'd consult Major Hazelrigg about her going out to India, and whether there would be any possible chance of her seeing Dickie, if she were to stay in Peshawar or some place near the Afghan Border.

Hope springs eternal. And it seemed an eternity before any more news came, an eternity through which she lived upon that same hope, refusing to allow hope deferred to make her heart sick.

§10

And then, one day, that dawned just like any ordinary day, there came a letter enclosing one addressed to Colonel Harrington-Spens and sent on for General

Ffoulkes to read, a letter bearing an Indian stamp with the Peshawar postmark, and in it was confirmation of Captain Thorburn's statement, and fresh information.

Actually Major Hazelrigg had seen Richard Wendover in a Pathan village beyond the North West Frontier, and although he had been unable to communicate with him, had had no shadow of doubt that it was really he, alive and well.

Major Hazelrigg, himself in disguise, had had to go on his way to India; but, his immediate job being completed, he had spent his ensuing leave in trying to get to the bottom of the truth of the matter of Wendover's disgrace and degradation—now that he knew for certain that Wendover was alive.

Working on a theory of his own, he had come to a conclusion, and felt sure that he would soon be able to produce evidence that would lead to a re-trial and the establishing of his friend's innocence. But, having followed clues—and people—to Bombay and Poona, he had felt that he must now return to Khairastan, see Wendover again, and get some further information from him on the subject. And he must see him in such circumstances that, this time, he could talk to him without fear of discovery, of exposing either of them as being what they were, Englishmen in disguise.

This he had done, had found Wendover living as a Pathan in the retinue of the Khan of Khairastan, whose son, Shere Khan, had been a trooper in Napier's Horse, and had always followed the fortunes of Captain Richard Wendover, to whom he was devoted.

In the rôle of Inayatullah Hussein, Afghan horse-coper, he had visited the house of Shere Khan which was near the Khan's fort of Khairabad, and had, on his departure, induced Richard Wendover, alias Gul Mahommed, the Pathan soldier of fortune, to ride out with him a short distance and put him on his way.

When they were alone, he had suddenly addressed Wendover by name, told him who he himself was, and forced him to drop his pretence of being a genuine Pathan who understood no English.

Gradually Wendover had thawed to his friend, had

expressed his gratitude to him for devoting a whole leave to going into his case with a view to proving his innocence, but had added that, in point of fact, he really wasn't interested nowadays.

He hadn't the slightest desire to go back to India, or to have anything more to do with the people who had so easily believed in his guilt. The Army had kicked him out, and out he would stay. Besides, he loved his present way of life, and far preferred it to that of "civilization," that of a European in India.

Major Hazelrigg had wrestled with him for hours, told him what a fool he was, and that he ought to be ashamed of himself for being so acquiescent in his own ruin and disgrace, so supine, so indifferent to his fate.

Besides, if he really did not care, as far as he himself was concerned, hadn't he a duty to his friends and those who loved him?

At this Wendover had laughed rather bitterly.

The letter went on to state that Hazelrigg, in spite of what he had said to Wendover, could quite understand his attitude, his injured pride, and his feeling that if *that* was what his brother-officers and everybody else thought of him, they were welcome to do so, and he didn't value their opinion sufficiently to lift a finger to change it.

Not that any lifting of poor Wendover's own finger could have done anything to help him to change it.

And in the end, Hazelrigg had told Wendover that he was going to find absolute and irrefutable proof of his innocence, publish it abroad, and demand enquiry, prosecution of the real culprit, publication of all the facts, and Wendover's exoneration and re-instatement.

As he said good-bye to Wendover, he had begged him not to disappear from Khairabad, but to wait; just to wait a little longer, to which Wendover had, with a sarcastic laugh, replied only '*Wait!*'

And again the brilliant hues of happiness and hope-restored beautified the thoughts and soul and life of Sybil Ffoulkes.

He was alive, he was well, he was known to be

living in Khairastan, and she had a link with him in Major Hazelrigg. Oh, if only this marvellous and magnificent Hazelrigg lived the ordinary life of a regimental or staff officer in garrison, instead of spending most of his time on Intelligence work beyond the North-West Frontier, inaccessible to messengers, un-get-at-able with letter or cablegram; with his habit of disappearing suddenly and emerging suddenly, months, possibly years, later.

Still, she must be thankful for small mercies. No, colossal mercies, really, for wasn't it everything in the world to her to know where Dickie was, and to have a letter from a person who had actually talked to him?

And now what was the best thing to do? Obviously she must go to India and to the town or other inhabitable place that was nearest to Khairastan.

"Where is Khairastan, Daddy?" she asked that night, when she went for her usual session in the library before going to bed.

"North-West Frontier. I'm not absolutely certain as to whether it is on the Tochi River in Waziristan, or the Kurram River farther north. I rather fancy it is that way, between Safed Koh and Jalalabad. I'll look it up."

"Which would be the nearest town in India? Quetta?"

"Oh, dear no. Dera Ismail Khan, or perhaps Bannu, if it's Waziristan way. If it is farther north, Kohat or Peshawar . . . Yes, I remember now. I think one goes up through the Khyber and then turns left, towards Parachinar, to get to Khairastan. Yes, from Peshawar. Why?"

"Because I'm going out India way."

General Ffoulkes laughed uneasily.

"And with whom are you going? I'm afraid your mother and I can't manage the trip."

"Oh, I don't want to go with anybody. I shall go alone."

"Well, you'll have to go to some place where we know somebody, won't you? You can't live alone in an Indian hotel."

"Have a look at your maps and make sure now, there's a dear."

"Well, in point of fact I'm quite sure that Peshawar is the nearest point in British India. As a matter of fact, I remember quite clearly now. I went up the Pass with General Bindon when the Commander-in-Chief was first considering the idea of a strategic road up through Khairastan. I'll show you a map in the morning. But you can take it for certain that Peshawar it is."

"Right, Daddy. Then it is Peshawar for me. Whom do we know there?"

"Oh, lots of people."

"The Commissioner or the G.O.C.?"

"I'm not certain who is Commissioner of Peshawar, or who is Governor of the North-West Frontier Province at the moment; but Archie Vere-Vaughan commands the Peshawar Brigade. He's an old friend of mine. Coming home next year, as a matter of fact. I made a note to ask him to come and shoot."

"Vere-Vaughan. Is there a Mrs. or Lady?"

"No. He's a widower. Got a son and daughter out there. Son in the Flying Corps. I think the boy went out with the first flight or squadron that went East."

"Do you know the General well enough to tell him I am coming out to India and want to see Peshawar and the Khyber Pass and all that, and could he—you know —smooth my way, give me a helping hand and a leg up? I suppose he has got the keys of the Khyber in his pocket."

"Write like that with a view to his replying that he hopes you'll come and stay with him and his daughter, eh?"

"That's the idea."

"Yes, Archie Vere-Vaughan would be delighted, I'm sure. And I've not the slightest doubt that his daughter would be very glad of a girl visitor. I remember her as a toddler, when I was up at Murree one time, after you and your mother had gone home. I went to see her at school too, in England, when she was a long-legged flapper, at Vere-Vaughan's request. Looked after her a bit. Oh yes, they'd be delighted to see you. And what d'you think you're going to do when you get there?"

"Don't know, Daddy. But I've got all sorts of plans and wild ideas, and I shan't come back from India until I've seen Dickie."

"H'm. How are you going to set about that?"

"See Major Hazelrigg, and get him either to bring Dickie by the scruff of his neck from Khairastan to Peshawar, or else to take me from Peshawar to Khairastan."

The General laughed shortly.

"You simply don't know what you are talking about, my dear. Take you to Khairastan!"

"Well, I expect stranger things than that have been done. You've heard of Gertrude Bell, I expect."

"Not a parallel case at all. These Pathans are very exclusive gentry, their motto being 'Here's a stranger. Shoot him dead.' As for a woman—a white woman . . .'"

"Daddy, don't discourage me. I'm going out to Peshawar and I'm going to see Major Hazelrigg, and I'm going to see Dickie somehow. Perhaps I could help Major Hazelrigg."

"What as a female Intelligence agent?"

"No. Help him in finding out the truth about Dickie's alleged crime. You know what he says in his letter . . . I could buck him up if that were necessary, and possibly there might be a financial aspect of it, mightn't there? Expenses in tracing witnesses and all that. And if Dickie is taking the line that he simply isn't interested, Major Hazelrigg won't get any help or encouragement from that direction, will he? Besides, I may be able to persuade the silly boy that it's his absolute bounden duty not only to himself but to everybody else, to get himself re-instated. And whether he agrees or whether he doesn't, I'm going to do my utmost to kick up the devil of a dust. Tell everybody that there are proofs that Dickie is innocent. Get hold of journalists, special correspondents, newspaper editors, reporters, that sort of people, and interest them. Work up a regular campaign so that there's such a lot about it in the Press that the authorities simply have to do something about it."

"Walk into the offices of the *Civil and Military Gazette* and *The Pioneer* and frighten the Editors to death, eh?"

"Well, interest them, anyway. You remember that disgraceful case out of which the Lords of the Admiralty came so badly, when an Osborne cadet was accused of stealing a postal order from another cadet and cashing it himself."

"Yes, a shameful business. Somebody at the Admiralty should have been thrown out into the gutter."

"Well, isn't that a case in point? The poor boy was disgraced and degraded, kicked out of the Navy; and the Lords of the Admiralty, in spite of all his father could do, merely raised a flat fat Stiggins-and-Chadband hand and replied:

"*'Hold your peace, fellow. What we have said we have said, and what your boy has done he has done, because we have said he has.' And it was only when that famous K.C. . . .*"

"Marshall Hall, wasn't it?"

". . . interested himself in the case and kicked up such a dust that it was re-opened. And with what result? That the boy was exonerated, proved innocent, and his name publicly cleared. If I remember rightly, he refused to be re-instated when they offered to take him back. And quite right too."

"Yes, and that's just Wendover's attitude," said the General.

"Well, I'm going to make him change it."

"His position is different. He's not a youngster at the beginning of his career, who can easily adopt another one."

"I'm going, anyway."

"Well," sighed the General, "good luck to you, my dear. But first catch your hare, you know, before you start him off on a different course."

"That's it, darling. First catch him. And I'm going out to Peshawar to catch Dickie, and once I've caught him . . . Well, you'll see."

§11

And then, once again, the long weeks of waiting and hoping; this time for an answering letter from Major Hazelrigg.

The one from Sir Archibald Vere-Vaughan came quite quickly, in little more than six weeks, and contained a warm and kindly invitation for Sybil to visit them at Peshawar as soon as the General returned to his Headquarters there. At the moment, he was just off on an expedition which would last some time. His daughter Charmian was going to Simla, and he would write again when they both returned to Peshawar. Then Sybil must come and stay for the whole of the cold weather—and the hot too, if she liked.

Enclosed was an equally cordial invitation from his daughter Charmian; hoping that Sybil would come as soon as they were in Peshawar again; that she would stay for as long as she could; and promising her plenty of dancing, riding, hunting with the Peshawar Vale, and a good time generally. Charmian Vere-Vaughan assured Sybil that she would find Archie quite a decent sort, and not in the least heavy in hand.

So Sybil possessed her soul in patience, and again settled down to a period of waiting and hoping; hopefully waiting for a letter from India, a letter from Major Hazelrigg that would give her some more news, a letter from General Vere-Vaughan saying he had come back from the little campaign, expedition, manœuvres or whatever it was, and possibly one from Dickie in answer to the one she had sent to Major Hazelrigg for delivery, should he see him again.

And then the Blaze of Glory. The news that thrilled the Empire. The wonderful defence of Giltraza Fort, its relief at the eleventh hour, and the amazing story, of which the papers had got hold, to the effect that the successful defence of the Fort was due to an *ex* British Officer who had been admitted to the Fort in the rôle of a Pathan emissary from the leader of the besieging force!

The two or three British officers of the besieged force had been killed or had died of wounds or disease, and the weary and disheartened garrison of sepoys, half-starved, short of ammunition, and gradually reduced in numbers, were despairing of being able to continue the defence.

The apparent Pathan messenger, admitted to parley with the senior Native Officer, had declared himself a British Officer sent by the Sirkar to their help; had announced the approach of a large relieving force, put on the uniform of one of the dead officers; and galvanized the garrison into new life and activity.

And this officer was said to be a Captain of Napier's Horse.

And after the relief and his recovery from a wound, he had disappeared as suddenly and silently as he had arrived.

The affair caused a tremendous stir, and the story was a nine-days' wonder.

It was recalled that an officer of that Regiment had been cashiered for drunkenness when in a most responsible post, on active duty; had vanished; and had been killed, as was supposed, by a lion.

And now someone, credibly reported, on excellent authority, to be he, had turned up in the wild buffer-state of Giltraza, had saved the British Fort there, kept the Flag flying until relief came, and had then disappeared into the blue as he had come out of it.

And the name was Wendover.

Leaders on the subject were written in the London, Provincial, and Indian Press.

Signed letters appeared, saying that surely his offence should be condoned, the Court-Martial sentence quashed, and he be re-instated. And not only re-instated but rewarded, decorated, promoted.

The affair made an enormous appeal to the public imagination, popular feeling was deeply stirred, tremendous enthusiasm aroused, and there was a nation-wide wave of sentiment which swept across the country and round the Empire. Not since Ladysmith and Mafeking and Chitral had such popular interest been manifested.

It was like a story, and the kind of story that appeals to the British public.

But gradually the tumult and the shouting died, as the Captains and the General departed from Giltraza; and after the nine-days' wonder, there dawned the tenth, whereon some new attraction and distraction occupied the febrile fickle public mind.

And, long after the matter had been generally forgotten, Sybil got a letter from Major Hazelrigg telling her all about it, and that Richard Wendover, flatly refusing to use the occasion as the basis of an appeal for pardon and re-instatement, had declined to return to India with the Relief Force, and had actually disappeared again, presumably into the wilds of Khairastan.

And this, added Major Hazelrigg, in spite of the fact that he had been able to establish with complete certainty and irrefutable proof, that Richard Wendover had been entirely innocent of the charge on which he had been condemned. He had not been drunk; he had been drugged, and Hazelrigg had obtained the confession of the actual criminal.

What could one do with a man like that?

§12

'*What could one do?*' laughed Sybil.

Why, one could go and find him and talk to him for his good, of course.

II

The ancient city of Kharkand is a picturesque and interesting place, but rarely beheld by European eyes, or at least by those of Britons.

The Old Town is a dilapidated dust-heap; the New, a mediæval high-walled city, the two forming the largest town in the southern portion of the Province of Ching-Kiang.

Its inhabitants, mainly Turcomans, are an apathetic people, much afflicted by excessive heat and cold, malaria, dust, goitre, Chinese rulers, Khotanese invaders, and a well-grounded persistent sense of insecurity of life and property. They are great potterers, great believers in the doctrine of *laisser-faire*; a people of little faith, less hope, and no charity.

Occasionally, they turn from their occupation of listening to professional story-tellers, to doing a little leather-work, the making of the soft high Kharkand boots and the skull-caps about which the turbans of Central Asia are wound.

The two Pathans, large and stolid men, who sat cross-legged on a bench in front of a *chai-khana*,[69] watched with apparently incurious eyes and expressionless faces, the crowd that eddied about the stalls and shops of the covered bazaar.

Occasionally they exchanged remarks in murmured Pushtu, as they speculated upon the nationality, status and business of the varied throng of passers-by, Chinese, Turkis, Tungans, Khirgiz, Kazaks, Bhokarans, Afghans, Russians, Indians and assorted Asiatics.

A tall lean man, with drooping moustaches nearly a foot in length, clad in a long and filthy coat, plus-fours of ragged cotton, and a particularly bright and beautiful skull-cap of cherry-coloured silk, stopped to beg,

---

[69] *Tea-house.*

but in doing so, halted too suddenly and too exactly, in the way of a swaggering crop-headed Turcoman, half-bandit, half-soldier, in a bandolier-begirt khaki uniform and red slippers, who promptly knocked him down, kicked him in the stomach, and went on his way rejoicing.

A Chinese of rank, followed by a small boy who apparently drove him along with blows of a yak's tail, stepped over the prostrate beggar without a glance at him, whereas the small boy ceased from his fly-flapping labours with the yak's tail, to spit accurately in the direction of the beggar's woebegone face.

As the beggar was in the act of rising to his feet, a stout and jovial Afghan took advantage of his undeniably attractive and tempting position to bestow so hearty a kick upon his bottom that he shot forward on his face.

As he lay, a peculiarly slovenly-looking Tungan officer of the garrison, mounted on a deplorable horse, endeavoured to trample him into the dust.

The more humane horse having narrowly avoided trampling or kicking the head of the beggar, the latter, sat up, sighed, scratched himself, and again approached the aloof uninterested Pathans, squatted before them, and began to sing in a high nasal voice, a curious song, the occasionally-repeated refrain of which was:

"The British aksakal knows him."

The beggar was not, whether by the standards of the East or West, an accomplished singer, nor his song a stirring aria, neither a gem of music nor of poesy, but it appeared to interest one of the Pathans. Apparently for the first time, he saw the beggar and his glance was keen. Nevertheless his response was not encouraging.

"Go away, dog," he growled.

As the beggar slunk away, the Pathan rose to his feet, yawned and stretched himself.

"Don't lose sight of him in the crowd, Shere Khan," he said, and led the way in pursuit of the unprepossessing mendicant.

Through bazaars of which the roadway was age-old

dust, fine as grey flour, and the shops holes-in-the-wall in which sat apathetic men among their fly-covered stock-in-trade; through streets that were featureless cañons between lofty windowless and doorless houses; across market-places crowded with noisy buyers and sellers of unappetizing food-stuffs, men whose clothing and head-dress showed them to be of a hundred different castes, creeds and nationalities, the two Pathans swaggered along, their eyes fixed upon a cherry-coloured skull-cap that shone like an oriflamme through the dust-haze and disappeared behind camel, stall, booth or pile of merchandise, quickly to reappear.

From time to time its owner stopped to beg, to scrabble in the dust for edible garbage, to sing in a high nasal howl a stave of song, in the obviously ill-founded hope that it might appeal to the charitable susceptibility or musical ear of some stall-holder, purchaser or passer-by.

Finally, seeing that the two Pathans were near and following, he darted through a narrow alley, waited at the further end of it until they appeared in sight, turned to the right and, after shuffling along, with his eyes industriously searching the gutter for such treasure-trove as a Japanese cigarette-end, finally came to anchor by the steps of a clean-looking respectable house.

Ignoring the man, the Pathans entered the verandah, were accosted by a servant, and after brief colloquy, conducted further into the building, which was the house and office of the functionary known as the British *aksakal*.[70] This individual proved to be a Powindah merchant who, having for forty years trodden the roads of Central Asia, from Kabul to Nanking, from Irkutsk to Kashgar, from Srinagar to Calcutta, had at last unwillingly settled down in Kharkand, a Tungan robber's bullet having shattered his knee and crippled him severely.

Having introduced himself and given proofs of his *bona fides*, the Pathan calling himself Gul Mahommed proceeded to question the Powindah *aksakal* on such

---

[70] *A sort of acting-sub-deputy-assistant-adjutant-vice-consul.*

subjects as the state of the road to Kashgar; the best form of transport—camel, horse, or donkey; the news as to changes in the political situation; the latest bazaar gossip, and other matters of interest.

Having then charmed the ears of the exile by praise of the glories of his native Kabul, and delighted him with talk of mutual acquaintances; mutually admired and well-remembered people and places; the scandals of the Amir's Court, and such matters; beautiful shalimars; vineyards where one could pluck the big ripe yellow grapes that dangled from their horizontal lattice-work above one's head; orchards thick with trees that were heavy with luscious peaches, he brought the conversation back to local affairs, and broached the subject about which he had come to talk.

The *aksakal* clapped his hands and, as the servant entered, bade him bring tea. The tea was brought, already milked and sweetened, in a kettle, and poured into large cheap mugs of Japanese make.

For several minutes the three men sat in silence.

Gul Mahommed raised to his bearded lips the mug that stood beside him on the floor, and took a long drink.

"By Allah, that is good tea!" he said, and smacked his lips loudly. "Caravan brick tea, I should say."

"Yes," admitted the *aksakal*, "that is one thing good that one gets in this hole—over-land tea."

"Yes?" murmured Gul Mahommed, and added:

"And Russian cigarettes a few, Russian caviar a little. And Russian pamphlets a lot."

The Powindah shot a quick glance at the speaker.

"*Where has he gone?*" asked Gul Mahommed.

"Who knows the way of a bird through the air, a fish through the water, or of a Russian agent through Ching-Kiang?" shrugged the Powindah.

"Which way did he go?"

"By the Kashgar road."

"For Osh and Andijan?"

Again the *aksakal* shrugged.

"Who knows?"

"I wonder whether you do, my friend," reflected

Richard Wendover.

"Whence came he?" he said aloud.

"From Urumchi, he said."

"My information was that he came through Khotan."

"Yes?"

Silence fell in the small whitewashed room, with its walls and floor of dried mud, its barred unglazed windows, its crude furniture of official desk and bench, its tightly stuffed cushions and bolsters in dirty white cotton covers.

The *aksakal* observed that the weather was very hot, and that there was a lot of sickness in the town.

"Look," said Gul Mahommed suddenly. "The English are better friends than the Russians. Better paymasters."

"Yes?"

"And the *aksakal* at Yardash has just been given the rank of Khan Bahadur, on retirement."

"Yes?"

"I have the ear of a Sahib who speaks with authority, and whose words are heard when he makes recommendations. Would it not be a fitting and a pleasing thing for you if you were transferred to, say, Yarkand, Kashgar, or Srinagar; yea, even to Kabul itself?"

"It would, indeed. It would be a change from the desert to the oasis, from the barren to the sown. To Kabul? It would be a change from Iblis to Paradise. A change from death to life."

"Then which way did he go?" said Gul Mahommed with apparent irrelevance.

"He went to Kashgar," was the prompt reply.

"Ah, that's better. With how many?"

"Absolutely alone, except for a servant, a Kirghiz. He bought four donkeys."

"Where shall I look for him in Kashgar?"

"It would be like looking for a louse in the wool of the sheepskin coat of a Pathan," shrugged the *aksakal*.

"Yes, but if one knew in which seam of the coat?"

"Try the Yangi Hissar," said the *aksakal*.

"Ah! There, eh?"

Again silence fell, pregnant and tense.

Suddenly Gul Mahommed said in English:

"Do you speak English, Abdurraman Powindah?"

The face of the *aksakal* showed the surprise, indeed the shock, that the question gave him, not so much by reason of its being spoken in English, as by its tone; curt, crisp, and commanding; the voice in which the British Officer speaks to the Indian subordinate.

"Have I not dwelt for years in Calcutta, Delhi, Lahore, 'Pindi and Peshawar . . . Sahib?" replied the *aksakal*, in excellent English.

"Very well, then, you'll be able to believe me when I tell you that I am a British Officer. If not, ask any questions you like."

"Sahib, I would not doubt. Yet a minute ago, I did not doubt that you were a Pathan. By Allah, it is clever."

"Do you know Simla?" asked Gul Mahommed.

"I have been to Simla and thence to Darjeeling and thence into Tibet," smiled the *aksakal*.

And for a while the two men talked of India, the remarks of the one showing his knowledge of those things that would be known by a British Officer, the questions of the other directed to the eliciting of facts which would place the status of his visitor beyond reasonable doubt.

"And your friend here, Sahib?" asked the aksakal.

"He is a Pathan, a man of rank and importance."

"Now let us speak with single tongue," he continued. "Tell me things of interest."

"What sort of things, Sahib?"

"Come, come. You know. Tell me about the new road that comes out of Russia in the direction of Kashgar; the truth about the Tortinjis and whether the Russians are really organizing those Kirghiz into innumerable cavalry regiments. Who really rules here, the Provincial Government or Moscow?"

And on these lines the conversation proceeded a little more easily until suddenly Gul Mahommed observed:

"Yes, that tallies with my information. Now then,

about him. Where has he gone?"

"By the ninety-and-nine names of Allah and by the Beard of the Prophet on whom be Peace, I swear to you, Sahib, I know no more than that he set out on the Kashgar road, mounted on a pure-bred Badakshani mare, a bay with three white socks, his servant riding a half-bred Kabuli mare, a flea-bitten grey, long-eared, ewe-necked and somewhat goose-rumped. He had four well-laden donkeys."

"And who looked after the donkeys?"

"An Afghan and three Tungans."

"And who looked after the Afghan and the three Tungans?"

"There was a pair of Turki-Chinese half-castes."

"Oh, our numbers are growing. You are sure there wasn't a *sotnia* of Cossacks?"

The *aksakal* smiled and waggled deprecating hands.

"I'm telling you the truth, Sahib," he said with a note of gentle remonstrance.

"And what were you telling me before?" enquired Gul Mahommed. "Now go on remembering, and tell me everything you can remember; where he stayed, whom he visited, with whom he talked, anything which may be interesting and helpful to me—and to you. Likely to help you along the road to Kabul, eh?"

And the good *aksakal*, smiling inwardly at the thought of the Russian roubles already in his *cache*, frowned in deep thought, as he strove to remember, or to invent, interesting details of the sort desired by his visitor. For rupees are even better than roubles, and both are acceptable in the banks and bazaars of Kabul.

§2

Apparently the only living things in the illimitable space of that howling Central Asian desert, Gul Mahommed and Shere Khan camped that night beside the ancient if almost invisible track that leads from Kharkand to Kashgar.

Gul Mahommed sat huddled in his *poshteen* beside the embers of the fire over which Shere Khan had cooked their evening rice and mutton, their flat *nands* of unleavened bread, and boiled their Russian tea.

Shere Khan, wrapped from head to foot in a dirty sheet that by day was sash, shawl or *cummerbund*, lay stark and stiff as a corpse. The shroud-like suggestion of the sheet was increased by the fact that it covered even his face and hands.

A queer idea, mused Gul Mahommed. It must be some subconscious symbolism, There was certainly no warmth or protection against the bitter wind in that thin cotton covering. And yet, lying on the hot sand of the deepest valley of Taklamakan, or at fifteen thousand feet on the Pamirs, lying on ground so frozen that it was practically ice, Shere Khan's idea of going to bed was to roll himself in that cotton sheet like a caterpillar in a cocoon.

Well, so long as he rested and slept soundly—the faithful fellow. Did ever man in need of a friend have finer truer friend than Richard Wendover had in this ex-sepoy, of birth, breeding, race, caste and creed, so diametrically different from his own; this Pathan, once his servant, now his blood brother? He was more than a brother, he was his friend. What nobler word was there than this; what higher, finer relationship?

He felt ashamed that it should be so one-sided; that the Pathan should be so much the giver; he, so much the recipient. Not only friend, faithful unto death, but body-servant, retainer, watch-dog and his stout fighting-man; cheerful companion, unfailing support. Literally, there was nothing that Shere Khan would not do for him, even to the giving of his life; nay, rather, beginning with that, for he would think nothing of it. It would give him pleasure and pride to die for his Sahib, and greater love hath no man than this.

Why was it? Surely not merely because, when he, Gul Mahommed, had been Captain Richard Wendover of Napier's Horse, and Shere Khan a trooper, the latter's life had been saved by his Squadron-leader. He liked to think that Shere Khan had been really attached to him before that. For it had been nothing. Merely a matter of pulling-up when he saw Shere Khan crash and roll like a shot rabbit, lifting the unconscious man, carrying him to his own horse, and keeping off the nearest Mahsuds with his revolver, scrambling up behind the wounded man and, by the greatest good luck, getting away under heavy fire.

But for himself, had it been good luck? Wouldn't it have been a thousand times better if he had got a tribesman's bullet through his head that day? Better even, if they had taken him alive and finished him off slowly. He would, at any rate, have been finished, and have left a good name and a clean record; something the Regiment could have been proud of.

Yes, he liked to think that Shere Khan's unfaltering, ungrudging, unlimited devotion was not due to that episode only. Naturally, a native *sowar* liked to feel that his British Officer thought him worthy of so much trouble as actually to pick him up, carry him and sling him across his charger, and ride away with him. That's how he'd look at it, the kindness of his Officer in taking so much trouble, not his courage in taking so much risk.

Anyway, there it was. Shere Khan had prayed to be taken with him, as his batman, when his Captain was seconded from the Regiment, the Regiment that he had never seen again.

And when the crash came, when the well-built edifice of his career fell about him in ruins, and he decided that death was far better than the life that had turned so suddenly to dust and ashes, it had been Shere Khan, and Shere Khan alone, who had saved him; the only man or woman, apparently, in the whole world who believed in him, the only person who had stood by him and stuck to him. And he had stuck to him as does a dog to the adored master, as little affected by his fall, ruin and disgrace as the dog would have been.

And when he had decided that there was no road that he could take, nothing that he could do, it had been Shere Khan who had shown him one, and put his feet upon it; Shere Khan who had said:

"Let my people be thy people, my country thy

country, my home thy home. Come and be a Pathan,"
unconsciously implying "and how could man live
better?"

And it had been a good road, a good life upon that
road—apart from the Thing ever present in his mind,
even when he slept. He had not been unhappy and, at
times, had, for a space, enjoyed life to the full, leading
a hard life among hard men as a mountaineer, a
tribesman, a respected member of the hardiest, free-
est, most independent and most war-like people in the
world.

And he had enjoyed the long long journeys, full of
incident and change, danger and difficulty, and had
had the satisfaction of knowing that he had anony-
mously done some useful work thereon.

Yes, if variety and danger are the salt and spice of
life, there was little wonder that he had found the meal
well flavoured. Great times. Great days and nights.
Really exciting periods when he carried his life in his
hand, a thing scarce worth a moment's purchase, and
his only regret the fact that Shere Khan's danger was
almost as great as his own.

And then the awful and unforgettable Thing that
had happened to him.

The Thing . . .

Memories.

The time when he had met the man whom it was
now his life's purpose to meet again; the man whom he
would some day meet, unless one of them died first,
which Heaven forbid.

He had thought that he had borne a pretty heavy
grudge against that fellow Breckinge who had caused
all the trouble; but really he had never hated him as he
did this Russian. And, in the end, he had forgiven
Breckinge. For one reason, he had never really been
sure that Breckinge was at the bottom of it, until
Ganesh Hazelrigg got to work and proved it, and by
that time the wound had healed over and he was a
different person altogether. By the time Breckinge
confessed, it really was as though he had done that

incredible injury to somebody else, some other man whom he, Wendover, had known many years ago. So that, at the end, there had been nothing much more in his mind than the dislike and condemnation, on general principles, of a very dirty dog. Had Breckinge lived, he would not have troubled to hunt him down and see him punished; and as he died in the way he had done, there had been no point in disgracing him posthumously.

But this "Comrade" Bailitzin, as he called himself at Tashkent, was a different proposition altogether. If Breckinge had been a disease-bearing louse, Bailitzin was a scorpion; or, as they were both reptiles and not insects, if Breckinge had been the unobtrusive deadly krait, Bailitzin was the hamadryad, the aggressive man-hunting king-cobra.

And yet, what Breckinge had done to him had been gratuitous, undeserved, the abominable outcome of private and personal malice; whereas Bailitzin could, of course, and probably did, consider that any injury he had done had been in the way of duty.

And to be quite honest, so it had, if a little unnecessary, and in excess of duty.

Nevertheless, he hated him beyond telling, hated him far more than he had done Breckinge; and whereas he had forborne to take action against Breckinge, when it had been the obvious thing to do, nothing on earth would induce him to spare Bailitzin.

However, first catch your bear and then skin it—or then consider sparing him. But he'd catch him all right, for he would devote his life to that purpose until it was accomplished.

And what would he do with him when he got him; when he and Shere Khan and the chosen handful of the pick of the fighting men of Khairastan who followed Shere Khan, had got him all to themselves, nice and comfortable and cosy in Khairabad Fort?

Probably run him down to Peshawar and hand him over to the British authorities, when it actually came to a decision—which would mean a firing party for the dog. Or should he give him a taste of what he himself had suffered at Tashkent, pay him back in his own coin?

A bit banal, and unimaginative, just to do unto Bailitzin as Bailitzin had done unto him.

If he left it to the Pathan *jowans*,[71] they'd probably think-up something far better. But that was the one point on which he had not 'gone native' completely. He still objected to deliberate cruelty to animals, even to such animals as Bailitzin, and he couldn't get the correct Pathan angle on the subject of torture.

And yet it was foolish, sloppy, childish; a weakness which he ought to eradicate. Why couldn't he treat Bailitzin at least as brutally and savagely as Bailitzin had treated him at Tashkent? The thought of it still made him shudder, and that was probably why he hated Bailitzin so. Yes, very likely that was the psychology of it. Bailitzin had broken him, for the time being, and taught him what fear was, screaming fear of pain; degradation; that combination of mental and physical agony that is so much greater than either alone.

Yes, undoubtedly that was it. Against Breckinge he'd have felt no more than a colossal grouse, partly because he had never been sure until the end that Breckinge had done what he suspected him to have done; and partly because Breckinge had never frightened him, never made him grovel. And somehow, although Breckinge had ruined him, he had not humiliated him, certainly had not terrified him; so that when he had known, beyond any shadow of doubt, that Breckinge was the culprit, he had found himself unable to hate him or to want to be revenged on him.

Was his deadly unswerving and insatiable hatred of Bailitzin really a somewhat disreputable passion based on wounded pride and injured vanity? Was it because Bailitzin had frightened him, terrified him, broken him, that he hated him beyond forgiveness.

Whether base and ignoble or not, there it was, and the fact remained a fact. No man had ever hated another more than Wendover did Bailitzin. Inciden-

---

[71] *Young warriors.*

tally, the man who could put an end to Bailitzin's activities in India and Central Asia would have deserved well of his country. That is to say, the Briton who could do so, not to mention the Chinese or Japanese who could contrive it, though to their countries he was perhaps less of a danger.

A great man, Bailitzin, in his sphere, and as valuable to Russia in Central Asia, Afghanistan and India, as Wassmuss had been to Germany in Persia, or Lawrence to Britain in Arabia.

But how different a man from Lawrence!

Or from Wassmuss, who had been not only a patriot of high ideals, but a decent and honourable individual, a gentleman, in fact.

No, Bailitzin was not of the Lawrence or Wassmuss type, not a Colonel Leachman nor a General Gordon. Clever as any of them, perhaps far cleverer than any of them, he was a ruthless savage brute, a Tartar beneath a Russian skin of the thinnest. Had Lawrence or Wassmuss or any of the others caught a dangerous enemy agent as Bailitzin had caught Richard Wendover, they might conceivably have shot him out of hand, had it been in time of war, but they would not have done what Bailitzin did.

And in time of peace it would never have entered the head of any one of them to have done more than arrest Wendover, have him court-martialled and get him a term of imprisonment.

What had made Bailitzin so vindictive? Surely not the little episode at the Russian Embassy in London? Was it just the nature of the brute, racial antipathy, or had the circumstances in which he had caught Wendover at Tashkent had something to do with it, given him a jolt, made him uncomfortable, and decided him to give Wendover a lesson, *pour encourager les autres*?

It couldn't have been only that, however, because, had Bailitzin's intention not been thwarted, *les autres* would never have known what happened to him.

Memories . . .

It must have been a nasty jar for the authorities to

learn that one of the professors at the Russian Officers' School of Oriental Languages at Tashkent was a British Officer and obviously, therefore, a British Secret Service Agent.

That really had been rather a neat piece of work— quite impossible, apparently, and quite simple as a matter of fact.

Of course, it had been Wendover's good luck that there was a vacancy for a *munshi*[72] to teach Hindustani and Pushtu to those Russian officers specially selected for Intelligence work in India and on the Border. Had there been no such vacancy, and had it not happened that he and Shere Khan had made the acquaintance, at the *chai-khana* at which they lodged, of an old gentleman who taught Persian at the school, he would never have known of it.

But when the aged scholar had learned from the courteous Gul Mahommed, over endless cups of tea, that the latter was an educated Pathan of Peshawar who had been at the Alighur College and learned English and Hindustani, and was, moreover, a Russia-loving England-hating firebrand and agitator, he had at once seen in him the ideal candidate for the teaching vacancy that he had been bidden to do his best to fill.

People who spoke Pushtu were not common in Tashkent. Those who also knew both English and Hindustani were most uncommon, and one who knew these three languages and had the correct political orientation was unique. In point of fact, Gul Mahommed was as suitable and desirable for the post as the post was suitable and desirable for Gul Mahommed.

He had been taken by the *moulvie*[73] to be interviewed by the Adjutant of the Officers' School; and— after a certain show of indifference on the part of Gul Mahommed, the obvious over-estimation of his importance and value, and a display of rapacity in the matter of salary, he had been appointed as teacher of Pushtu and Hindustani, with private English classes, on the side, for such Officers as wished to continue their

---

[72] *Teacher, secretary.*
[73] *Teacher, priest.*

studies in that language.

For the Adjutant of the School had found that this fellow—upon whose Pushtu and Hindustani he was not competent to pass judgment—undoubtedly spoke quite fluent, if somewhat stilted and bookish English. But that, as he knew, was the way of all Orientals who graduated in English schools. They learned from books and talked like books. Macaulay, chiefly. And the Adjutant, formerly a prominent Nihilist, who had been, like Lenin, an exile in London in Tsarist days, and whose language was far more colloquial and idiomatic and slangy than that used by Gul Mahommed, decided that the latter's slight accent and Victorian type of English did not debar him in the least from teaching the English language to the officer-students in his charge.

Interesting students, too, Wendover had discovered. Somewhat different from those to be found at Sandhurst and Woolwich, most of them being men of considerable service and experience. Remarkably different, too, from the type of student to be found at the Staff College; for though a few were former Imperial Tsarist Officers—urbane highly-educated and polished men of the world, who knew the Capitals of Europe, and who, in their youth, had seen the palmy days of St. Petersburgh—the majority were tough, if not rough, customers, who knew more of Siberia, Mongolia, China and the life of the fringes of the former Russian Empire than of Courts and Capitals. A motley collection, of widely differing social, as well as geographical, origins, varying from Lapland to Armenia, from the Ukraine to Mongolia, most of them Red regular officers, some of them Secret Service agents from different walks of civilian life.

Yes, it had been one of his least unhappy periods since the smash, that thrillingly interesting dangerous time when he, a British Officer and unaccredited but professional Secret Service Agent, had worked in the very heart of the enemy's camp, cultivated the men who were the most dangerous foes of his country, listened to their conversation, examined with meticulous care the contents of waste-paper baskets gathered by Shere Khan—who had obtained a job as *chowkidar*, a night-watchman, a stupid and ignorant fellow upon whom the students of Pushtu could, nevertheless, practise.

But the stupid and ignorant fellow had the intelligence and ability to note the trend of the subjects of conversation and the line of thought pursued by his interlocutors, who were obviously deeply interested in the matter of Pathan tribal ethnology, customs and politics; of roads and passes throughout the Border country; of bazaar gossip concerning Afghanistan and India; of the present relation between Afghanistan and the Border tribesmen; of feuds and alliances as between Afridis, Mahsuds, Mohmands, Shinwaris, and other tribes; who could raise great *lashkars* of fighting men; of the influence and importance of the Mullahs.

When people are going to converse for the purpose of improving their knowledge of the language in which they do so, they must have some subjects of conversation, and such were the subjects on which they tried to talk with Shere Khan. But to no one was it known that between the burly stupid night-watchman and the brilliant *munshi* who taught three languages, there was any connection whatsoever, or that the one even so much as spoke to the other.

It had greatly interested Wendover to discover that more than one of the students of Pushtu, Hindustani and English were anxious to learn all they could about the Singing Hadji of Sufed Kot, and to note that, whereas to the British he was a truculent fire-brand whose chief interest in life was the breaking of the *pax Britannia* and the fomentation of trouble on the Border, it appeared that he was by these earnest enquirers regarded as a great patriot, one whose yearnings for self-determination ought to be gratified, whose struggles for the spread of his religious and political principles should be assisted by all true lovers of freedom.

Moving cautiously, and with the skill of experience, the Professor of Pushtu, Hindustani and English had contrived to give the impression that he too was not uninterested in politics; that he had ambitions; that greatly as he appreciated and enjoyed the honour of being a Professor of Languages, he would even more greatly enjoy that of being an emissary and an agent who, on the Indian Border could serve Holy Russia, or if they preferred it, Unholy Russia.

Who would be better than he, in that part of the world, once they had trained him for the job, and taught him exactly what he had to do?

Not only could he work among his brethren and fellow tribesmen on the Border, but also in Kabul, which he knew like the palm of his hand. In Afghanistan he could be an Afghan, and could guarantee that a letter written here, in Russian, and sewn between the leather layers of the sole of his sandal would be safely delivered in Kabul, and an answer brought back.

Better still, he could take messages by word of mouth, the only really safe way of sending them, and after having shown his ability and worth, could be admitted as a fully-qualified and fully trusted Secret Service Agent.

And then in India. Look what he could do there. In any town from Peshawar to Calcutta. And he could play many parts. He could be the swaggering truculent and haughty Pathan that he was; and as such, could live and work in the bazaars of Peshawar, Rawalpindi, Umbala, Lahore, or anywhere else; and if in any such place it were necessary for him suddenly to disappear, he could quickly transform himself into a *fakir*, a Mussulman holy man of the most venerable type, a syce, a camel-man, a beggar, a gharry-wallah, a respectable and well-behaved sepoy, on leave from an up-country regiment—anything.

Or again, properly fitted out and provided with the necessary funds to play the part, he could be a small "hill Nawab," visiting, and roystering in, any of the towns that his employers desired him to visit.

Wendover smiled to himself as, in retrospect, he saw the worthy *munshi* Gul Mahommed making steady headway in that extraordinary School for Scandal of a political kind; increasing in importance and the consideration of his superiors and his students; identifying himself with the atmosphere of the place; seizing every opportunity of broadening the scope of his work as teacher of languages until he was as much a teacher of the politics of those who spoke those languages; an authority upon the currents and cross-currents of Border thought, prejudice and intrigue; of Indian Mussulman and Hindu antagonisms and alliances; and above all, of British, civil and military methods and preparedness.

It could not be said that, when the good Professor, forgetting language instruction for the moment, branched into impassioned harangues on politics, he was notable for accuracy of statement. Could his words have been heard in the Secretariat at Simla or Delhi, they could not have failed to cause surprise.

It would have been news to the Viceroy's Council that the perpetual bazaar-clashes between Mussulman and Hindu were faked to lull the Rulers, who dwelt in a fool's paradise, into a fool's sense of security—the truth being that, beneath the surface, there was a swiftly growing and almost accomplished *rapprochement* between these two apparently irreconcilable sects who, when the hour was ripe and aid was certain from outside, would cast aside their trifling superficial and merely apparent differences, and unite into a homogeneous nation, one and indivisible!

It would have surprised the Government of India to learn that the Indian Army was honeycombed with sedition, and ripe for mutiny; that Sikh and Pathan, Mahratta and Punjabi Mahommedan were utterly unreliable; and that powerful and influential members of the British Parliament visiting India, openly said that before long, the great Labour Party, riddled with Communism as it was, had determined to bring about the complete separation of India from England. Also that India, moreover, was a country that longed to be ruled by a Soviet or a congeries of Soviets, inasmuch as Indians, whether Hindus or Mussulmans, hated personal rule, detested autocratic government, whether by

Princes or by Sahibs, and would much prefer government by Babus.

What his hearers wished to think, he had given them grounds for thinking; what they wanted to know and to believe, he had taught them; their wishes were father to his thoughts when preparing his impromptu outbursts.

And, in a surprisingly short time, he had found himself not only the leading authority on the politics of the Border and Northern India, but had somehow come to be accepted as a political refugee; a potential, if not actual, Red Shirt; a friend and follower of the powerful Singing Hadji of Sufed Kot; and an enemy of the British, sufficiently active and powerful to have been in danger of the reach of their long arm until he had crossed the Border, reached Tashkent and entered the Haven—that haven of safety that is happy Russia.

Yes. Without too much inclination to pat himself upon the back, he could not deny that it had been a skilful piece of work, albeit one that could only have been done in those fortuitously fortunate circumstances.

Memories . . .

It had all been amazingly *à propos*, and the little snowball that was the work of his own hands had grown as it rolled, until its size, velocity, and potential power amazed him. Actually, he had imposed himself upon them so gradually, naturally and gently that, imperceptibly, he had changed in their sight from a mere *munshi* into a possible, and thence to a probable, envoi-plenipotentiary to the Tribesmen; to the most important of the Border leaders; the Hadji of Turangzai; Abdul Ghaffer; the Singing Hadji of Sufed Kot; and the nest of militant seditionists known as the Hindustani Fanatics.

But for the coming of Comrade Bailitzin, there was no telling to what heights he might not have attained, to what positions he might not have aspired, what secrets might not have been given him—secrets he would have used to forestall and thwart the schemes of those who would have employed him to work against the British Government, to foment trouble on the Border and to induce the Amir of Afghanistan to sever diplomatic relations with Britain, as a prelude to war. Let India be but engaged in another Afghan war, another Tirah-Malakand-Mohmand insurrection—with military mutiny and civil rebellion co-incident in India with these wars—and Russia's hour would have struck.

But it was Bailitzin who had struck. And very cleverly.

For some time past the Adjutant of the school had been taking notice of the Professor of Pushtu, Hindustani, and English; had made a point of accidentally encountering him; of sounding him as to his opinions; and had one day sent for him to his office and questioned him as to his personal history, compiling a *dossier* for the College records.

He had had to think quickly, and answer each item of the *questionnaire* promptly; and finally the Adjutant had asked him when he intended to return to the Indian North-West Frontier country, and what he proposed to do when he got there.

Was he going to lead the life of a Border tribesman after enjoying the flesh-pots of Tashkent? Or was he going down into India?

And Munshi Gul Mahommed had replied that he was so happy where he was, that he had formed no plans for the future; but how infinitely happy would he be if the Russian Officers under whose kind control he now worked, would send him to the Frontier, or to Afghanistan, or even to India.

Send him on what business, the Adjutant had enquired.

Oh, any business, Gul Mahommed had replied, fingering his beard with sly, deprecating, smile. Any business whatsoever.

And thereafter, on several subsequent occasions, they had gradually got down to it, and talked real Secret-Service stuff.

And then had come the great day when the Commandant of the School himself had sent for Munshi

Gul Mahommed, and given him a prolonged and thorough gruelling.

The leaven was working, and working fast.

What a *coup* it would be, if the man who longed, beyond anything, to be the most invaluable agent of the Military Intelligence Service of the Indian Government, could get himself actually appointed to a post in which capacity he could work and rise to prominence in that branch of the Russian Secret Service that dealt with India, Afghanistan and the buffer States between them!

Had he overdone it, thereby raising the Commandant's suspicion? Surely *that* had never needed any raising, in that home and factory of suspicion, where the teaching and training, and the very breath of life, were double-dealing, deception and suspicion.

Anyway, he had made a bold bid, an audacious throw, staking everything, in obedience to his motto of *l'audace, l'audace, et toujours l'audace*; and, without expatiating to the Commandant, as he had done to the Adjutant, upon his most exceptional fitness for service in India, Afghanistan and on the North-West Frontier, had gone one step farther than ever before.

Again Wendover smiled grimly as in retrospect he saw himself wearing the Oriental dress of a language-teaching *munshi*, raising his eyes (respectfully lowered in the Presence) looking the Commandant full in the face, stepping up to his desk and bending toward him to whisper, in English, which the Commandant spoke colloquially,

"And another thing, Excellency. Do you realize that I could *pass myself off as a British Officer*?"

And the big, bearded, heavily-built Commandant throwing himself back in his chair, had laughed aloud.

"*You?*"

"Yes, I. In their khaki—the tunic, shorts, putties, Kitchener-helmet and Sam Brown belt of a British Officer—I could call on almost any Regimental Mess and be accepted for what I pretended to be, a British Officer spending a week-end or so at the Station; I could live with any Regiment or Battery or other unit for several days, accepted as one of their Service. I could visit any fort or outpost, be given at least one night's hospitality, and spy out the place thoroughly."

"Bosh!" had replied the Commandant. "You'd be spotted for what you are, in five minutes, and shot out of hand, or rather shot into gaol out of sight, in the tender English fashion, instead of being liquidated straight away. Your English is very good; very good indeed. I have never met a native who spoke it better; but you've got an accent, you know."

"Yes, Your Excellency," he had agreed, "but so have a good many British Officers, you may remember. Some are Irish, some Scottish, some Welsh, some are Australian, some Canadian."

The Commandant had eyed him thoughtfully in silence for a minute.

"You seem to know a lot, or to think you do. Personally I've never known that a British Officer was Scottish, Irish or Welsh, by any difference in his speech; and I've met a good many of them."

Yes, this man had once been a Tsarist Officer, and doubtless had visited both England and India.

"I could pass a test, Excellency. I could pass myself off on any officer of this School, or of the Tashkent garrison, as a British Officer."

"That's a very different thing from passing yourself off as a British Officer in a British Mess! Still, we'll see. Meantime, I know that the Adjutant thinks highly of your gifts and capacity for, well—some different kind of work from that which you are doing here. He tells me that you are an ardent Pathan patriot, that you have fought against the British, and that you are anxious to do so again; to engage in a more dangerous form of warfare than that of the battlefield. You know the approaches to the Khyber Pass, of course?"

"As I know the face of my son."

"Hunza and Gilgit?"

"As well as I know Kabul and Peshawar, Excellency."

"And the Road?"

"I have trodden every yard of it, many times. From

here to Kashgar, from Kashgar to Tashkurghan, over the Pamirs to Hunza, to Nagar, to Gilgit, and by Nanga Parbat, over the Burzil Pass down by the Wular Lake to Srinagar, on down to Jammu, and by the Trunk Road to Amritzar and Lahore, and through the Sikh country by Patiala to Delhi."

"And you could make that journey in almost any capacity, eh?"

"Without doubt, Excellency. On foot or on horse-back. As a trader, a coolie, a Powindah gun-runner, an Afghan horse-dealer, a non-commissioned officer of the Corps of Guides pretending to be something else, or . . ."

And again he had looked the Commandant full in the face.

". . . as a Russian officer or a British officer—likewise pretending to be something else."

Again for a minute the Colonel eyed him thought-fully, his bearded face inscrutable.

"Look," he said suddenly. "I will give the Adjutant instructions to assist you to get what kit you will want; and, this time next week, come into this room, dis-guised as a British Officer. Not only dress, but hair, moustache, everything, and I will try you out. And to give you a fair test, without bias, I will have two or three people here, to whom I shall say nothing about you, beforehand. We'll see whether you convince them, in their ignorance, and also persuade the Adjutant and myself that the rôle is perfect. And short of perfection, of course, you must not fall, if you want us to try you in the higher rôle."

Memories . . .

A week later he had endeavoured to give them a surprise. And they had given him one instead. Not only the surprise of a life-time but the shock of a dozen life-times. Wily devils, the Russians. Undeniably the most Westerly of Orientals rather than the most Easterly of Occidentals.

If he had fooled them to the top of their bent, by getting right into the centre of their spy-factory and deluding them, gathering priceless information and forwarding it to Colonel Ormesby, they had certainly fooled him in the end; and in a game of that sort, he who fools last, fools best.

Yes, and he who fools best, fools last too. They certainly had had the last word; and, but for the courage and Pathan cunning of Shere Khan, they'd have had the last word—the last that Richard Wendover ever spoke.

Perhaps, again, that was part of his hatred of Bailitzin.

That first humiliation had been, in some ways, the greatest of all the humiliations he had made him suffer, because Bailitzin had caused the wound to his vanity to be self-inflicted. They, Bailitzin teaching them, had led him on to make such a fool of himself as he, even yet, blushed to think of. For their diversion he, their wretched dupe, had plumed himself on the cleverness with which he was duping *them*. He had positively strutted; and, with grave faces, they had watched and encouraged him, suppressing the derisive laughter that bubbled within them.

It made him almost sick with anger and self-contempt to look back at himself, dressed almost correctly as a Captain of the Indian Army, conducted into the Commandant's room by the apparently admiring Adjutant and being introduced to the assembled officers; the Commandant in his usual chair behind his desk, on either side of him a couple of officers whom he did not remember having seen before, a cavalryman commanding Kirghiz Levies, a Cossack, an artillery officer and an obvious soldier in mufti, who might have been a Secret Service agent or perhaps a Cheka, or other, Government official.

And before them, he had carefully played his well-rehearsed part, that of a British Officer calling on a Mess, to all of whose members he was a stranger, looking the part, he flattered himself, from head to foot; closely cut hair, clean-shaven, save for a toothbrush moustache; a riding-switch dangling negligently in his left hand.

He had acted the part well, oh, hellishly well, the blithering fool, while those half-dozen Russians also played theirs, giving him every help and encouragement. And he had been so colloquial and clever with his English, not too slangy, not over-doing the military idiom, and not over-acting.

And while doing it, he had remembered that, hitherto, he had always spoken English with the accent of the educated Pathan or Afghan, and wondered, even while he played his part, how the Commandant would account to himself for the change in his voice, if he noticed it.

But of course he'd notice it, and, equally of course, fie would realize that the fellow was acting; that he was giving a brilliant impersonation of a British Officer, and, while acting that part, was not only adopting the mannerisms and the appropriate turns of speech, but was actually imitating the accent and tone of voice.

And even as he carried on the light and easy conversation, tapped his breast-pocket for his cigarette-case, accepted one with easy grace and casual thanks from the Adjutant's *tabakier*, lit it and held and smoked it and disposed of the match, precisely as he would have done had he been a caller at a British Mess—being careful to show that there was quite a distinction and a difference of technique between British and Russians even in the nice conduct of the cigarette—he had stood aside and watched himself with a certain admiration, had exulted, and felt that he was giving these crafty fellows a really memorable leg-pull.

And at last, when he had finished his cigarette, had finished laughing in the British manner, which is different from the Russian, had finished his slightly drawled sentences of slightly clipped words, he had risen to his feet, bowed to the Commandant and glanced at the faces of his judges.

Yes, judges indeed.

There had been a grim silence; for him, at first, no more than an awkward pause in the proceedings in which he had taken a leading part. Then the officer in mufti—a man whom he felt sure he had seen before, probably about the School or in Tashkent town—had spoken, softly and quietly, with a pleasant smile playing about his thin-lipped mouth, while the wrinkles about his watchful eyes were not those of laughter.

"Very interesting, *Captain Richard Wendover.* Very well done. But then, of course, you have rather special qualifications, haven't you? Who should play the part of a British Officer better than Captain Richard Wendover—of Napier's Horse, until dismissed from the Army with ignominy?"

Yes, it had been a bit of a shock, though, for the moment it had been that of having his play-acting spoilt, of being made to muff his lines, stutter and stumble, fumble and look silly; that of the actor who had forgotten his cue, or walked on in the wrong act, or walked on in his shirt and slippers.

And then had come the realization that it was something more than that. That it was death.

He was caught, found out, and he'd soon learn how the New Russia treated the spy, caught red-handed within her gates.

The old Russia had had pretty drastic ideas on that subject, but in the treatment of spies, as in so many other things, Soviet Russia had advanced a very great distance along the road of Progress.

And here was not a mere suspect picked up in the street, to be flung into prison until somebody had time to fetch him out, ask him three questions and then shoot him. Here was a viper in the bosom, a serpent on the very hearth, of the spy-school, not only filling a post of trust therein, but actually trying to win a post of the highest confidence and faith, in order that that confidence and trust might be betrayed.

And the Russian officers had laughed, not merrily and heartily, but with amused contempt, fathomless contempt of the poor clown who had tried to fool them. The clumsy stupid Englishman, the oaf, lout, ass, bungler, mountebank, who had actually offered them this sample of his wonderful wares.

Instinctively he had turned to the door, only to find

it opened for him by the Adjutant and to see, in the corridor, a Corporal's guard of stalwart Cossacks with drawn swords.

As he was seized and hustled from the room, he had heard the Commandant say:

"I'll leave him to you, then, Comrade," a remark which had drawn quiet laughter from the others.

And the days that followed had been definitely one of the bad patches in the life of Richard Wendover.

Memories.

One evening Bailitzin had entered the cell into which he, the *soi-disant* munshi and revealed spy, had been thrown, one of the underground cells of this well-equipped School, a small part of whose activities was the "questioning" of spies; of people who might be spies; of people who couldn't possibly be spies but might know something about the spying of others; of people who were not even suspected of knowing anything about the spy-work of others, but who might be possessed of information useful or interesting to the spies of the authorities.

It was an unpleasant cell; dark; damp; verminous; ventilated only by a drain-pipe that sloped upwards, at an angle of forty-five degrees, out to the pavement of the inner courtyard of the School; and recently inhabited by a person of uncommendable habits.

The door had been flung open by the soldier turn-key, and Bailitzin had entered, accompanied by an orderly who carried a chair, a man almost seven feet in height, vast and powerful, and who looked as though he might at some time have been a Sergeant-Major or other ornament of the Preobrazhenski or Ismailski Regiment of the Imperial Guard.

Wendover noticed with a feeling approaching incredulous horror, that the giant carried, coiled in his right hand, a *nagaika*, a steel-tipped black-snake whip, such as is used by the Kirghiz Irregulars and the Cossacks; a terrible weapon or instrument of torture and death.

"Well, Wendover," said Bailitzin, in perfect English,

"'so we meet again,' as the villains of the Adelphi Drama used to say."

"Again?" asked Wendover, involuntarily.

"Yes, my friend, again. Have you forgotten the occasion of our meeting in London? I haven't forgotten *you*—nor the occasion when you grinned at me because I had slipped and fallen—while talking to our conceited little friend. My turn to laugh now, eh?"

"Your luck really was out the other day—that I should have been there."

Bailitzin laughed, with genuine amusement.

"Really very funny," he continued. "There were we, suspecting you for all we were worth, perfectly certain that you were a British Agent—and a damned good one, if you were a Pathan—and then, of your goodness, you make all things abundantly clear unto us. To me, at any rate. I knew you at once, in that British uniform, and with your beard off. I shouldn't have known you as a Pathan. Oh, really damned funny."

And Bailitzin smote his thigh and laughed again.

Suddenly his laughter was cut off as though with a knife.

"Take off that belt and tunic," he said.

Wendover hesitated. Who *was* this fellow?

Bailitzin glanced over his shoulder to where the orderly stood at attention in the corner, and then leered at Wendover.

"Quick," he growled, "Or . . ."

Wendover unbuckled his belt and removed his tunic.

"Now take off your shirt."

Wendover obeyed.

"Sit down," said Bailitzin. "There, on the floor in front of me."

Wendover glanced at the horribly befouled earthen floor and again he hesitated.

To sit there, at this Russian's feet!

Bailitzin again glanced over his shoulder towards the Orderly standing in the corner.

"Paulov!" he snarled, and the giant strode forward, uncoiling the heavy short-handled whip, with its long black lash, pliant as rubber, tough as rhinoceros-hide, pointed with steel.

Wendover sat down.

"You are wise," smiled Bailitzin. "Shortly you will be sad. Yes, go to your grave a sadder and a wiser man.

"And without going out of this cell," he added pleasantly. "*Pheugh!* Your carcase won't make this cell smell any more attractive."

And taking out his case he lit a Turkish cigarette.

"Unless, of course," he continued, when he had puffed an aromatic cloud and sniffed it appreciatively, "you can remove a certain doubt from my mind. *Which* I doubt. I'm going to ask you a few questions. First of all, in the ordinary sense of the term; and then, if I am not satisfied, in the technical sense of the term, I'm going to have you '*questioned.*' Understand?"

Wendover nodded.

"Do you understand, I said."

"Yes."

"Paulov!"

Again the giant strode forward, dropping the coiled lash of the thick but tapering whip to a straight line.

"Yes . . . Sir," said Wendover.

And at a motion of Bailitzin's head, the soldier drew back to his corner, coiling the lash again as he did so.

"That's better. Say 'Sir' every time you speak, or I'll make you do it kneeling, with your forehead on the floor. Now then. I've got your *dossier* pretty correctly and pretty fully, to an extent that would surprise you. So if you want to go out of this cell alive, speak the truth; for I haven't much hope of making any use of you, and I have every intention of making sure that you are of no use to anybody else . . . Paulov!"

And once again the orderly strode forward, un-coiling his *nagaika.*

"*One*, if I raise my hand," he said in Russian, and the giant took up a position beside Wendover, his hand raised to strike.

And Wendover knew that a cut from that steel-tipped whip would be only one degree less effective than a cut from a sword.

He had seen the *nagaika* in use.

"Now then, my friend, if I have the slightest reason to think that you are telling me a lie, you will regret it as long as you live—and that may not be saying much. Are you a Secret Service Agent, employed and paid by the British Government to spy here?"

"I am not," replied Wendover instantly and truthfully.

Watching in horror, and with a morbid fascination, the hand that projected beyond the wooden arm of the chair, Wendover saw it quiver, as though about to rise in signal to the executioner.

"Are you a renegade so embittered against the Government and Army which have kicked you out with ignominy, that you have renounced your country and 'gone native' completely, once and for all?"

"Yes," replied Wendover.

"Ah! That is interesting. It also tallies with information that I have been collecting concerning you since you came here. Now then, Mr. Renegade, have you not only done that, but have you also become an enemy of your own country?"

"No."

"And you are not prepared to assist the enemies of your country?"

"No."

"You are quite certain?"

"Yes."

"Ah!"

And this time the hand that lay along the arm of the chair was raised. There was a sudden swift movement, and Wendover (who had once experienced that sensation) felt as though he had been shot. But the pain was worse, excruciating, unbearable. Almost he screamed; and, only with the greatest effort, half-stifled the cry that was forced from him by the sudden agony.

He tried to spring to his feet and in the act of rising, received a stunning blow from the giant's huge fist, and a kick that, for a minute, prostrated him.

"Sit up," said Bailitzin.

Gasping for breath, Wendover had pulled himself

together, and with a great effort, had continued to sit up.

"Now; I am going to ask you those questions again. . . . Are you a Secret Service Agent employed and paid by the British Government to spy here?"

"I am not," replied Wendover, through clenched teeth.

Again Bailitzin raised his hand, and again the gigantic soldier struck with all his strength.

This time Wendover managed to receive the blow without a cry, and wondered if the pain and shock were less, by reason of the numbing effect of the first blow.

Nevertheless he writhed in agony, and only with the exercise of the utmost power of his will, refrained from again attempting to spring to his feet and smash his fist into the face that smiled down upon him.

But why provoke a stunning blow from the orderly's iron fist, a kick from that great steel-shod boot?

"Are you a renegade, so embittered against the Government and Army who have kicked you out with ignominy, that you have renounced your country and gone native completely, once and for all?"

". . . Yes," replied Wendover.

And with eyes fixed upon the projecting hand, like those of a dog upon the whip of its master, he watched and held his breath.

"Ah!" breathed Bailitzin, and the hand did not rise.

"Now then, Mr. Renegade, have you not only done that but have you also become the enemy of your own country?"

"No," replied Wendover, and as the arm began its languid motion from the horizontal to the perpendicular, shouted:

"*No! No! Don't . . . Don't*"—vainly, as the third blow fell.

This time Wendover could not suppress a cry of agony, nor the feeling of mad rage that impelled him to spring to his feet. But the executioner was a skilled workman. While yet his victim's hands were on the ground, he kicked with all his strength, and, as

Wendover fell sideways, he stooped and struck him a swinging upper-cut on the jaw.

As he recovered consciousness Bailitzin was counting aloud:

"Eight . . . nine . . . ten . . . come on, man, sit up. No? *Out,* then—as we say in England, eh?"

He produced and lit another cigarette, and as he threw away the match, ordered sharply:

"Sit up! *Quick.* Now then. Consider your answer carefully, my good Wendover. Are you prepared to assist an enemy of your country?"

Wendover, dazed, giddy, what is known as 'punch-drunk,' as well as half-insane with pain and wrath, stared like a trapped animal at his captor.

Where was he? Was this a nightmare? What was his tormentor saying? Help an enemy? What enemy? Enemy of his country? What a question!

He shook his head.

"Answer."

If he had shaken his head he must mean no.

"No," he said.

And the fourth blow fell.

He had never imagined pain so terrible, humiliation so utterly degrading. To be beaten like a dog at the order of this dog.

What could he do? If only one of these men had a pistol in his hand, and would shoot him when he tried to attack, he'd soon put an end to it that way. But to be struck down and kicked senseless before he could rise!

"Now, I'll ask you that last question a third time . . . Are you prepared to assist an enemy of your country?"

What should he say? Where was the sense, or what was the use, of heroics in this underground cell in the presence of these two Russians? Where was the wisdom in suffering more torture if it could be avoided—and avoided by tricking this brute?

Bailitzin's hand moved slightly.

"*Yes!*" cried Wendover quickly.

"I thought you would," smiled Bailitzin. "I thought I should be able to make you see wisdom—as well as feel it and taste it, eh, Wendover? You never thought you'd feel the knout on your back, did you, when you were the superior Captain Wendover of Napier's Horse. Of course, you'd work for an enemy country to save your hide and to line your pocket. What else are you disgraced and ruined renegades fit for? What else were you doing but helping enemies of your country when you were gun-running? Yes, gun-running. I told you we knew all about you. What else were you doing in Muscat? Remember the good Monsieur Mamoulian, the Armenian Agent of *Goguyer et Fils*. You interested him very much while you thought you were completely taking him in. He knew you were a British Officer all right, though he couldn't quite spot your game. And do you suppose you fooled Yacoub Ali, the Mekrani? Yes, he's a simple fellow! Lucky for you that Ilderim Durani had been told to see you safe across and up to Kabul. Thought you fooled him, too, didn't you? All this surprises you, does it? Ah! And do you remember Ghulam Shah Powindah? It never occurred to Captain Wendover, the clever Englishman, that Ghulam Shah Powindah was a Russian Agent, and twice as clever."

Yes, pretty clever, if it were true, Wendover had thought wearily. But then, of course, the Russians would have their best agents on the gun-runners' track, right the way through from Muscat and Dozdab to Kabul and beyond, they being equally keenly interested in trying to see that the Tribes on the British border got all the rifles they wanted, and that the Tribes on their own border got none. The more good rifles in the hands of the Pathans the better; and the fewer among the Kirghiz, Usbegs, Tajiks and Kalpaks, the better.

Yes, he remembered Ghulam Shah Powindah, and that Shere Khan had been suspicious of him. He remembered Shere Khan's remarking that Ghulam Shah Powindah seemed a lot too inquisitive.

What was Bailitzin saying?

". . . and the man who will make money out of smuggling guns to be used against his own people, will make money out of supplying information about his own people. Now then, supposing I gave you your choice between being flogged to death with that whip—not half a dozen comfortable little cuts like this, but strung up and cut to ribbons by two experts, until you die—or, on the other hand, an even more lucrative job than gun-running."

Wendover had stared stupidly at the face that he would have given his soul for the power to smash.

"Well, speak up. I'm offering you a chance to work under me as a Secret Service Agent. Will you do it?"

"Yes."

"You will get me information as to military movements; strength of garrison, nature and number of guns and machine-guns in the Khyber Forts; photographs—especially certain photographs—maps, drawings, plans. Or work in Quetta and Peshawar?"

"Yes."

"And, as a Pathan, you'll work among the Tribes, stir up the *Mullahs*, work among the Red-Shirts, take our messages and help to the Hadji of Turangzai, eh?"

"Yes."

"And first of all, will you go to the Singing Hadji of Sufed Kot and help him capture Giltraza Fort?"

"Yes."

"You will, eh? Ah! You've travelled a long way since you were Adjutant of Napier's Horse, haven't you? Travelled a long way since I last saw you—where?"

Yes, where? Where on earth had they met last, if this Russian hound were speaking the truth?

"You still don't remember, eh?"

"No."

"No, to be quite frank I shouldn't have remembered you, recognized you, but for your cleverness in dressing up as a British Officer. It's wonderful how beards and moustaches disguise us. We knew we had got somebody in our clever Munshi Gul Mahommed, but I never dreamed it was our Captain Wendover himself, until you so obligingly shaved and dressed up."

And again Bailitzin laughed with genuine, if contemptuous, amusement.

Wendover stared in stunned bewilderment.

"Do you still pretend you don't remember me?"

"Yes. I mean no, I don't. I can't . . ."

"Cast your mind back to a reception at the Russian Embassy in London, once, when you were home on leave. Do you remember a do at the India Office when the Russian Ambassador and his staff were invited; and a levee at the French Embassy when the Russian Military Attaché . . ."

Ah! That was it. Of course. Of course. What was it this fellow had called himself then? He had had a title in those days. Prince or Count Somebody or other. He had forgotten his name. Why, and of course he had met him at Sybil's. Good Lord, yes! He had been a bit of a joke among Sybil's set. Yes, Mary Harrington-Spens had told him, Wendover, that he'd have to look out, or Sybil would be going all Russian; and he had rather ungraciously replied that Sybil could go anything she liked, so far as he was concerned. And Mary had told him not to be silly. And she had said she could shake him for being so stupid.

But how the fellow had changed. He had had a moustache and a monocle in those days. Wasn't sure he hadn't had a beard. Yes, he rather thought he had.

But why did the man hate him so? Why had he treated him like this? Must be something personal. Sybil? Surely not.

"Remember?"

"Yes."

"Yes, and I doubt if you will ever forget me again, by the time I've done with you. Great man in those days, weren't you? Didn't think you would ever kneel to me. To me, who knelt, yes, *knelt*, to Sybil Ffoulkes—and was refused. Refused for you. *You!* Look at you."

So that was it, was it? But what did he mean—refused for him? Sybil Ffoulkes had never really been in love with him, Richard Wendover; nor he with her. They had never been engaged. What did the fool mean —refused for him?

"Pity she can't see you now, eh? See you—and me."

"Give him another one, Paulov," he had added, in Russian.

And again, as Wendover cringed and shrank and vainly tried to protect himself with his arms, the whip had whistled and fallen like a sword-blade. And Richard Wendover had bitten his hand till it bled, to keep himself from screaming, from crying aloud, from praying for mercy, to this man who could, and quite probably would, have him flogged to death.

"Your turn, then, eh, Captain Richard Wendover? Whose is it now? You won then. Who wins now? She and her friends and you laughed at the love-struck Russian then, didn't you? Who laughs now?"

It was on the tip of Wendover's tongue to swear that Bailitzin was wrong, that Sybil Ffoulkes had never been anything to him, that they had never been engaged, that she had never refused Bailitzin on his account.

But even supposing he could bring himself to say it, what would be the use?

"Where is she now?" snapped the Russian suddenly.

"I don't know."

"Well, there are a lot of things that you don't know that that whip will help you to know, when you are strung up by the wrists to a ring on the whipping-post. And even so, perhaps I know them already. If you don't know where she is, I'll tell you. She's in India. Did you know that?"

"No."

In point of fact he was pretty sure she wasn't.

"Well, she is. She's in Delhi, and I shouldn't be surprised if she came to Srinagar. And I'll tell you something else. It wouldn't surprise me in the least if she came here to Tashkent. And yes, she is by way of being the Intrepid Traveller nowadays. It wouldn't surprise me in the very slightest, if a delightful, charming and obliging gentleman, also a great traveller, a what shall we say—an American journalist—were to help her to carry out a little escapade: a man who knew the ropes and spoke Russian, eh?

"Or possibly a Russian Officer whom she had known in London, formerly Military Attaché, *bona fides* above reproach. Who better qualified to help her? Meet her at this end of the Khyber Pass, and take her to Kabul. Or meet her in Srinagar and arrange disguises, passports and so on, and then give her a bit of the travel she's anxious for. Up through Gilgit, Nagar, and Hunza, by way of Tashkurghan and Kashgar to Andizhan and by way of Ferghana, to wonderful Samarcand, Bokhara and Tashkent—until I have got her where I want her, eh? She might then see you, mightn't she, scratching yourself in this cell, if I choose to keep you alive here with that object. Yes, practically alive, to all intents and purposes. A bit blind and bleary, as well as smelly and lousy, of course. That is, unless I decide to give you a trial as a spy, and to introduce you to my wife in that rôle.

"'Sybil, my love, I think you've met this—er—gentleman, formerly Captain Richard Wendover of Napier's Horse, dismissed with ignominy from the British Army, and now a renegade traitor and spy.' That would be quite amusing, wouldn't it?"

And he had reflected, it would, perhaps, be amusing—for Colonel or Comrade Nikolas Bailitzin—if he could bring it off. But somehow, knowing Sybil Ffoulkes, it didn't seem very likely. It was quite possible that Bailitzin might impress her to the extent of getting her as a fellow-traveller into Central Asia and Asiatic Russia, but it was very doubtful whether he, with all his cleverness, ruthlessness and complete absence of scruple, could ever get her into any sort of a Soviet prison, or any other position from which she would see no way of escape save through marrying him. Of course, he might get her into Asiatic Russia, or some part of Central Asia that was a sphere of Russian influence, and there have her arrested, and then play the *deus ex machina* at a price—but anyone who "caught" Sybil Ffoulkes would be apt to find he had caught a Tartar.

And what was all this? A peculiarly silly dream, or what? Prince Nikolas Bailitzin, former acquaintance and Military Attaché at the Russian Embassy, a red renegade, a Comrade, a Cheka man, a Kommissar, and now his gaoler and torturer—and talking about Sybil Ffoulkes?

"Well, I'll look in and see you again to-morrow and bring Paulov, in case you are still in any doubt as to what you had better do—and in case I am in any doubt as to whether I will have you really flogged or not."

Memories . . .

And on the next day, Bailitzin had again come to the cell, and demanded an immediate answer, as to whcthcr hc was prepared, freely and frankly and wholeheartedly to take service under the Russian Military Intelligence Department concerned with Central Asia, Afghanistan and India, or would prefer to be flogged to death.

And having spent the night in pain and mental agony of fear, anxiety and indecision, he could not believe that Bailitzin would be silly enough actually and genuinely to believe that he, Wendover, would be likely to be of any assistance, or any value whatsoever, to the Russians. Any fool, much more the astute Bailitzin, would know perfectly well that Richard Wendover, as soon as he was free and provided with transport, money and instructions to go to the North-West Frontier of India, would escape to a place of safety. Or, going to the North-West Frontier, would there use his Russian credentials to learn all he could, and promptly send the information to his own people. Become a double spy, in fact.

But one must be a Bailitzin to know exactly how a Bailitzin's mind worked and how he judged other people. He'd judge them by himself, of course. And might it not be that he'd see how a British Officer, kicked out of the British Army, a ruined man and an outcast, might very well turn traitor to his country, not only from savage resentment and hatred, but as a means of livelihood? What was Bailitzin himself but a traitor and a turn-coat? He had been not only an Imperial Officer, but a chosen one, and something of a *protégé* of the Tsar—and here he was, in this galley, not only holding the rank of Colonel in the Red Army, but working as a Secret Service agent hand-in-glove with the Cheka, if not actually an official of that murderous blood-drinking scourge.

Yes, it might be Bailitzin's belief that Wendover, once properly broken by good Russian methods, could be made invaluable.

He was quite capable of endeavouring to extract information under torture, acting upon it, letting it be known from whom it had been received, and then taking the attitude of—

'Now you *have* committed yourself. Now you really *are* a Russian Agent, and your people, who kicked you out, know it. So you'll be well advised not to fall into their hands, for they'd certainly shoot you. And so would we, if we had the slightest reason to suspect you, or if your work wasn't satisfactory.'

And of course, Bailitzin was quite conversant with the double-spy type of Secret Agent, his uses, his limitations, and the difficulties and dangers of employing him.

Naturally, if Bailitzin really believed that Wendover was a staunch incorruptible British Secret Service agent, in good standing, he'd either shoot him out of hand, or flog him to death. But Bailitzin must be of the type that believes that every man has his price, obviously having one of his own; and might argue that Richard Wendover would certainly prefer life, emolument, and the Russian Service, to ugly and obscure death in that cell. Particularly would he be prone to this kind of conclusion in view of the fact that he knew Richard Wendover to be what he was, a disgraced and broken officer who had "gone native."

But that had all been lies that the cur was yelping about Sybil being in India. Of that he had been quite certain.

Memories . . .

There was a clatter and clanging without, the door was thrown open, and Bailitzin, followed by the giant Paulov, entered. Had the fellow been up all night or left his bed at this ungodly hour? Anyway, the idea was doubtless to be-devil his victim when vitality was lowest and resistance weakest.

Wendover had struggled to his feet.

"Get down," Bailitzin had growled, adding in a pleasant voice, as Wendover obeyed:

"We will excuse you from rising while commending your good manners . . . *Paulov!*"

And once again, the huge Cossack had stood over the Englishman with raised arm and whip ready to strike.

"Tell the truth immediately, without a second's delay for concocting an answer—or up goes my hand. Are you an accredited Secret Service Agent of the British Intelligence Service?"

"No."

"What were you doing here, disguised as a Pathan?"

"Earning my living as a *munshi.*"

"Why here, in the Officers' School of Foreign Languages?"

"Where else? I heard from Munshi Amanullah Ibrahim that there was a vacancy for a teacher of Pushtu, Hindustani and English, the three languages that I know."

"What brought you to Tashkent?"

"Wanderlust. I was tired of living in a Pathan village."

"Not gun-running this time?"

"No."

"No, but I'll tell you what you were doing. You were spying all through our Border country. Taking the political temperature among the Turkomans, the Kirghiz, the Tajiks, the Kazaks, and throughout the Khanates, with special attention to the Bokhara country, eh? Very interested to know whether there's going to be a Soviet Republic there, and in a few other Places along the frontiers of Sin Kiang, from the Karakoram to the Altai; from Tashkurgan, Yarkand and Kashgar to Chuguchak; and whether we are raising a real army of those Kirghiz horsemen who are the best light cavalry in the world. That's what you were doing, friend Wendover, and when you had got a nice packet of invaluable information, back you were going with it to Delhi, to lay it at the feet of the Commander-in-Chief of the Indian Army, or rather at those of the Chief of the Political Service, weren't you? In the hope that you might buy your way back to favour and get a job in the British Military Intelligence Service. Show them what a clever fellow you were, and how you could really get away with it; live among the wicked Border tribes as one of themselves; in Kabul as an Afghan; in Tashkent as a Professor of Languages; hoodwink the silly Russians, and get secret information straight from the stable, eh? That was the game, wasn't it, Mr. Renegade?"

"No."

"What, then?"

"I have told you. I had 'gone native,' and I was sick of the life I had chosen."

"And you actually ask me to believe that you were not spying, either by order, or in the hope of selling anything you could pick up?"

"Yes."

"Paulov! *One*, I think. One good one."

And immediately the whip had whistled and fallen, with fearful force and effect.

"We had better have your tunic and shirt off, I think, my dear Wendover, if you are not going to speak the truth. Mind you, you'll come to it, you know, sooner or later. They all do. We get the truth from everybody in the end, except possibly now and then—in the case of those who die first."

"I am telling you the truth," replied Wendover, as soon as he could conquer pain and control himself. "I have held no office or job of any sort under the British Government since I was cashiered from the Army."

"Oh? Well; I'm afraid we have no means of checking-up on that, as they would disown you in any case. Well now, since you've become sufficiently Pathan to play the part you have played here, and in which I fully admit you were not suspected until I came, let's talk again about what we were referring to yesterday. Now then, since you are not a British spy, and you are a disgraced and broken British Officer who has gone native, are you prepared to work for us at a good salary and commission, that is to say, payment by results?"

"Yes."

"You are willing to become an absolutely honest and faithful spy in the Russian Intelligence Service, and willing to do all you can to help the Russians in every way against the British?"

Wendover moistened dry lips.

"*Paulov!*"

"Yes!" cried Wendover. "I am."

"Ah! And if I draw up a document in which you renounce your British nationality and allegiance, and declare yourself to be a paid agent of Russia, a spy in the Russian Secret Service, you'll sign it, eh?"

Wendover thought quickly.

Why shouldn't he, if that were going to save him from being flogged to death? And what harm could it do, even supposing it were dispatched to the Commander-in-Chief in India, or to the Viceroy or any other Indian official.

What did it matter? He had finished with that life altogether. And besides, most people must suppose him to be dead, after "Gul Mahommed" and Shere Khan had provided pretty convincing evidence of the death of Richard Wendover. And there was another thing. He could sign this agreement with the words 'Richard Wendover' but in a handwriting and a form which were most obviously not his own signature.

"*Paulov!*"

"Yes," cried Wendover. "Yes, I'll sign it."

"Ah! I've no doubt you would. And what would your signature be worth? Do you think I'd trust you, you treacherous double-traitor? False to your own country? Then you'd be false to us. And you'd tell everything you knew to the first people who caught you and shook a whip at you, wouldn't you? No, my friend. I've got you where I want you, and a very good place for you, too. Before you die, you are going to do a little more teaching, give a little more information; but this cell will be your classroom, and I will be the class. And you'll tell me absolutely everything you know, about both the British and the Pathan sides of the Border.

"By the time I have done with you, I shall be the best informed Russian in Asia, on that subject, at any rate. And you'll tell the truth too; for at the first lie, or the first suspicion of a lie, I'll make you into what we call a truth-machine. We've lots of them, you know. The moment one of us comes into their cell, their one desire is to babble the truth, the whole truth and nothing but the truth, and to pray to God—and to us—that the truth may be acceptable and accepted. And you'll tell the truth all right.

"Why, my good Wendover, at the first lie that you dare to tell me, I'll give you such a flogging as will hurt your great-grandchildren. Your ultimate descendant will jump like a flea at the sound of a whip . . . Employ *you*, you disowned, disinherited, dismissed refuse. I'd as soon employ a cobra to scratch my back . . . Pheugh! What a filthy stink."

Comrade Colonel Bailitzin produced his cigarette case, lit a cigarette and smoked in silence for a minute or two.

"Now then," he said, "this is the position. You were caught here spying. That's obvious. You came here, and you'll stay here; and whether you get any more food, and particularly any more water, depends on the information you give us. And how much of the *nagaika* you get every day, and how soon I have you flogged to death, will depend on your usefulness. When I have learned all you know, I may still find a use for you. In this cell, *bien entendu*. I may bring a man to you and ask whether he's absolutely correct in whatever disguise he is wearing; whether he's word-perfect, and so on. I don't profess to know everything there is to be known about India yet, and there you may be worth your—bread-and-water.

"Yes, I'll send you one or two of the genuine articles, and one or two of the fake ones, and see if you can spot which is which; and if you fail, I'll reward the man who gets past you, and flog you for letting him do it. If, on the other hand, you denounce the genuine article as a fake, you'll get another flogging.

"Oh, you are going to have a great time here, friend Wendover, and going to be very useful—while you last. In point of fact, you may last quite a long time, if I feel you are really doing your utmost to give me every satisfaction. For a start, I'm going to give you pencil and paper, and you are going to do the best you can—the best you can, mind, my dear Wendover—to sketch the interior of the forts at Landhi Kotal and Ali Masjid, just to show us what you can do in that line; and as you have been stationed in both of them, you ought to be quite useful. Anyway, you'll get a useful flogging if you are not."

And the first use that he had made of the paper and pencil brought to his cell by his gaoler, had been to write Shere Khan's name in Pushtu on a narrow strip of it, and then to wrap it about a tunic button and, after many failures, to throw it up the sloping pipe which conveyed a little air and a lot of water, when it rained, from ground level down into his dungeon.

The wily Shere Khan would, of course, be spending most of the hours of the day and the night in finding out where his friend was; and it was more than probable, first, that he would patrol this particular courtyard at night; secondly, would walk close to the walls; and, thirdly, would see—by the light of the hurricane lamp which, as watchman, he would carry—the paper wrapped about the button. He could read his own name and would guess the rest.

There was nothing showy and brilliant about Shere Khan; of books he was ignorant; he could barely read or write; but his superior in wiliness and cunning did not exist. No better man on this earth at plots and plans and the strategies of peace or warfare.

It would be as surprising as disappointing if, one day, a pebble did not roll down that wretched drain or ventilation-pipe or whatever it was that was the only communication between the dungeon and the outside air.

But what then? Suppose Shere Khan did discover where he was, what could he do? He couldn't dig him out through six feet of stone foundation.

But he could talk to him. Yes, and Shere Khan could send a weapon, sliding down that sloping pipe, or drain or whatever it was, that ran through the thickness of the wall up to the blessed light of day. A Khyber knife.

And then what? Suppose he could spring on Bailitzin and split his skull, or drive it through him before Paulov could prevent him. It was hardly likely that he could do as much with the gigantic Paulov. And suppose he killed them both. Was it to be supposed that he could then walk out of the cell, out of the underground-prison part of the building, out of the school itself, into the streets of Tashkent?

Memories . . .

Day after day, Bailitzin had visited him, always accompanied by Paulov and sometimes by another officer who was, he gathered, Bailitzin's right-hand man, and a specialist for work in India—a man who was known in the school as *"Feodor the Monk."* From time to time, an apparent native would accompany Feodor the Monk and, in the rôle of a Hindustani *bunnia* or *sanyasi*, a Mussulman *fakir* or merchant, a camel-man, a Pir, a horse-dealer, a pedlar, a carpet dealer, an itinerant musician, a snake-charmer, a juggler, would set him the problem of finding out whether the man was the genuine article.

Sometimes he undoubtedly was genuine so far as Wendover could discover; sometimes he was a palpable fraud who would only deceive an ignorant and unobservant European.

And on some days Wendover received a stroke or two of the whip; on some days, several; on others none at all; but always there hung over his head the threat of a real flogging, being tied up by the wrists to the ring of the whipping-post, and suffering the worst that could be done by two executioners cutting criss-cross, and so putting an end to this unspeakably humiliating, degrading, and agonizing business.

And then Bailitzin had over-reached himself, and by his own cleverness, cunning and malice, had enabled Wendover to escape, or rather, Shere Khan to effect his rescue.

For one day—it being usual for Bailitzin to torment and torture his victim at two in the morning as often as at two in the afternoon—the door of the cell was thrust open and a Pathan was thrown into the room. From the peak of his *kullah* to the soles of his *chaplis*, he looked an authentic Afridi.

After examining the cell as a rat might its trap, cursing under his breath and invoking Allah, he squatted on his heels and glowered in silence, hawked and spat, lighted a *bidi*, blew clouds of acrid stinking smoke, and then addressed Wendover in a harsh and croaking voice, speaking guttural Pushtu.

Very clever indeed, admitted Wendover to himself. Most creditable and convincing.

But just the striking of the match had spoilt the show for this particular audience, inasmuch as it had shown, on the man's right eyeball, a tiny thickening of the cornea, a sort of colourless spot that was almost like a tiny bubble, and that Wendover knew only too well.

The man was Bailitzin and, but for that almost unnoticeable eye blemish, he would have deceived him completely. The acting, like the dress, was perfect, as was the use of the vernacular. The nasal and guttural accent, idioms, oaths, were all admirable. Freely, and with a respect tinged with a sense of apprehension, he admitted that it was wonderful. What would this man not be able to achieve when spying in disguise!

But Wendover had looked into those hateful eyes too often and too long to be deceived. How many times had not Bailitzin thrust his fiercely menacing face into Wendover's as he growled a threat, and how often had not Wendover noticed that spot beside the iris of the right eye, that little oval lump that was transparent, like a very tiny pimple of glass on the white of the eye?

And now what? Should he let him know that he had

recognized him, or pretend to be deceived? Be deceived, of course. Lead him on. He might get a chance to do himself a bit of good, or to mislead Bailitzin.

"*Salaam aleikum*," said the Pathan at length, as though noticing the other man for the first time.

"*Salaam.*"

"Why are you dressed like one of the *gora-log*?"

"To keep myself warm. Are you a prisoner too?"

"Looks like it, doesn't it? Allah burn the bastards."

"What's the charge?"

"None that I know of. I suppose they think I'm a spy. They've got spy madness here."

"Yes, they seem to think I am one, too."

"Whom do they accuse you of spying for?" asked the pseudo-Pathan.

"The British. And you?"

"Why, I came up here to find this place and bring a message to the Masters. From the Singing Hadji of Sufed Kot. Ever heard of him?"

"Oh, yes. I've heard of him."

"And now they want to make out that I don't come from him at all; that I am a spy."

"Spying for whom?"

"Allah knows."

"You did come from the Singing Hadji, I suppose?"

"Of course I did. Where else should I come from? I can prove it, too; easily. I've got some writing. Down in the bottom of the sheath of my Khyber knife. They'll let me go to-morrow. Yes, when the fools have read my writing, they'll cast dust on their beards, and will send me back with a good *kafila*. Yes, a fine well-laden *kafila*. Do you know Giltraza Fort?"

"I have seen it. Yes, going up from Khairastan to Hunza, I saw it from the Road."

"Never been inside it, I suppose," asked Bailitzin.

"Well . . . That's as may be."

And Bailitzin, after long and close questioning of Wendover, was taken away; in other words, a couple of turnkeys obviously instructed to that effect, came, and roughly hustled him out of the cell, as though for further interrogation.

A very good performance. No fault could be found with it at all.

And evidently Bailitzin either enjoyed playing that part for Art's sake, or else hoped to learn something from Wendover or to trap him into some admission. Or again, perhaps he did it simply for the practising of his Pushtu and impersonation of a Pathan under the eye of a competent judge, for he came again the next night and the next, and whatever he learned from Wendover —which was precisely nothing—Wendover himself had gained the very strong impression that the Singing Hadji of Sufed Kot was the present friend, *protégé* and ally of the Russian Army in Asia.

That India was the bright particular star of its most sanguine hopes and the goal of its ambition, Wendover had learned before his discovery and downfall; that the lives of a corps of very able Russian officers were devoted to the study of the subject of the invasion of India, and another corps to the fomentation of internal trouble in India, he had known vaguely for years; that the work of the latter *cadre* was very highly organized and successful he had discovered without surprise, in the spy-school. What had surprised him, had been the scope and thoroughness of the staff-work of the officers responsible for preparing and maturing plans for external invasion.

What he had learnt in this dungeon was that one of the levers to be used in the moving of the rock of British defence was the Singing Hadji of Sufed Kot. And a sinister aspect of the freedom of Bailitzin's talk in the rôle of Pathan, was shown by his conscious, or unconscious, assumption that it did not greatly matter what his prisoner thought or learned, inasmuch as he would never again be in a position to make use of anything he might learn.

The *soi-disant* Pathan had never actually said in so many words:

'*I don't mind telling you this, as you'll never leave your cell alive,*' but he had contrived to imply that they could converse quite freely together because, whereas the Pathan was a bright and chatty fellow who'd shortly be setting out on the delightful journey over the Pamirs, the prisoner was, to all intents and purposes, a dead man.

And the end had come rather suddenly. After a longer talk than usual, the Pathan had risen to his feet, removed his *puggri*, smiled pleasantly at Wendover and drawled in his excellent English:

"Well, Mr. British Agent, who scored this time? Recognize me now? Not quite so clever as you think, are you? Not the only man in the Trade who can do a bit of hoodwinking, eh? And don't you pretend that you knew me all along, or I shall be disposed to send for my good Paulov."

Bailitzin's tone had changed.

"Wendover," he yawned, "I think I've about finished with you now. I think I can have you liquidated without loss—to ourselves or to anybody else. So think this over until to-morrow. I have made you offer to betray your country; to beg on your knees to be allowed to take Russian roubles in return for doing it; I have had you whipped like the cur you are; I have picked what you call your brain; and I have taken you in completely, a dozen times. For you had no more idea that your Pathan visitor was Colonel Bailitzin than that he was the King of England. And further, I am going down to Peshawar, and I'm going to meet all your Army friends—in the rôle of a Foreign Correspondent—and I'll tell them how you were executed by the Russians for trying to double-cross them while spying on the British; shot like a renegade dog, even by the enemies of the British, who had disowned you and kicked you out."

And again the voice had changed and became hearty and reassuring.

"But of course we are not really going to shoot you, my dear Wendover. No, no. We wouldn't dream of such a thing. We don't believe you when you say you were spying on us in the hope of selling information about us at Delhi, in return for some sort of re-instatement; we don't believe you when you say you will turn your coat and spy for us; nor do we believe that—if we spared your life in return for your most solemn oath that you would serve us honestly—you *would* serve us honestly.

"No, we sum you up as the sort of creature that would serve neither side honestly, but would try to make a profit from both, and swindle both. We doubt very much whether your own people would employ you after having dismissed you with ignominy and a sentence expressly stating that you should *'be permanently disqualified from ever serving the State in any capacity whatsoever'* . . . Once a renegade, always a renegade . . . And since you have come here, and doubtless learned a good deal about us in the past year, we feel that we cannot let you depart now, in possession of that information. No, really. But—shoot you, my dear Wendover? Of course not. As I have said, we wouldn't dream of such a thing. No, no."

And here, once again, the voice had changed and abandoned silk for steel.

"No, we'll flog you to death. And I shall have the greatest pleasure in superintending that little matter myself, to-morrow. Somewhere about sunrise, eh? Or perhaps a week hence—or a month."

And laughing pleasantly, Bailitzin had left the cell.

Memories . . .

And an hour or so later he had returned, or at least, some sort of a Pathan had pulled back the bolts, turned the key and walked in.

Wendover had eyed him wearily.

More play-acting by that unspeakable Russian dog? Hadn't he triumphed enough? Or was it 'Feodor the Monk' again? Or, good God! Was this the end? Had the executioners come to fetch him to the whipping-post? No, the man was alone, and . . . and unless he were dreaming or had gone mad, it was Shere Khan.

And Shere Khan it had proved to be. Shere Khan, looking slightly bulkier than usual, by reason of the fact that he was wearing what might be termed "two of everything."

With little waste of words and none of time, he had

unwound a spare *puggri* from about his waist, produced a flattened conical *kullah* cap and slippers from
beneath it, thrown off the two coats and a long Pathan
shirt, stripped off the outer pair of baggy trousers, and
provided Wendover with all the articles of clothing
necessary for his resumption of the rôle of Gul Mahommed.

Within five minutes of his entering the cell, the
change was effected, and Wendover, whose hair, beard
and moustache had grown again during the period of
his incarceration, looked as tough and genuine a
Pathan as did Shere Khan himself.

"Listen, Huzoor," Shere Khan had whispered, his
one-track mind seeming to have suffered upheaval by
the sight of his friend in the khaki, albeit dirty and
dishevelled, of a British Officer. "There were only two
sentries to-night. One never gave me a second glance,
thinking me to be the Russian Officer playing Pathan
as usual, and the other is suffering from a broken
neck. I didn't want to get any blood on my clothes. Now
walk boldly forth. All doors are open, save that of the
entrance-hall, and the key of that is on the inside. The
outer gates are shut but unlocked. Walk out as though
you are the Russian Officer. It is known that he comes
here almost nightly, dressed as a Pathan. There is but
one man for you to pass, and he is sitting, between
sleeping and waking, on a bench at the inner door of
the hall. If he is awake and sees you, he'll say nothing.
If he does . . ."

Shere Khan offered Wendover his Pathan dagger.
Not the great Khyber knife, but the dagger which is
perhaps the best-shaped and most efficient in the
world, with its combination of razor-edge, thick strong
back, and almost triangular point of needle sharpness.

"And what about you?" asked Wendover.

"I shall follow in a few minutes. Here's the key of
the compound gate. The watchman mustn't see two
Pathans at once, or he'd actually wake up and do a bit
of what he is paid for. But if we go separately, he'll
think you are the Russian Officer disguised as a
Pathan again. If he is still awake and sees me a few

minutes later, he'll think you went back when he was asleep, and have just come out again. And if, for a change, he's wide awake, and starts thinking when he sees me, I'll put an end to his thinking for good."

And Shere Khan tapped his left side where, beneath coat and *cummerbund*, was his Khyber knife.

And as simply and easily as though walking out of his own bungalow, Wendover had left the cell, ascended a flight of stairs, gone down a corridor, crossed an empty class-room, passed along another corridor, and entered the hall where, by the light of a hurricane lamp, he had seen a man squatting on a bench and leaning against the wall.

Whether awake or asleep, this Turkoman *chowkidar*, fellow night-watchman of Shere Khan, had said nothing. If awake, doubtless he supposed the Pathan to be either his colleague or Colonel Bailitzin, whose strange humour it had been lately to array himself in those clothes when visiting the prisoner below.

Opening the big hall door he had stepped out into the blessed open air, breathed deeply of its sweet freshness, looked up at the starry sky, and marched confidently across the court-yard to the entrance gate and unlocked it. Outside this, he had strolled up and down in the shadow of the wall, until the gate had again opened and closed behind Shere Khan.

"Any trouble?" he had asked.

Not the least. The other night-watchman had yawned loudly, cleared his throat, spat and grunted:

"Who was that who went out?"

And Shere Khan, as his hand went to the hilt of his Khyber knife, had replied:

"Whom do you suppose? Didn't you challenge him?"

"No, I thought it was you."

And with a malicious snigger:

"You'll be for it to-morrow," Shere Khan had replied. "It was the Colonel, of course."

And scarcely believing the evidence of his senses, doubting whether he were awake or dreaming, Richard Wendover had attempted to thank and praise Shere Khan, as the two of them had slunk through the alleys and by-ways of the sleeping city, to a dark corner of the *kafila serai* by the Yarkand gate where, among the sleeping beasts they held converse with a friend, a dirty camel-man who, strangely enough, spoke English, Hindustani, Bengali and Russian, and who answered better to a certain number than to any name.

Memories . . .

And as honest, hard-working, if filthy, camel-men, they had taken service under a merchant travelling west to Khiva, through the Qizil Qum and the Kara Kalpak to Khiva, and thence North, skirting the Sea of Aral to Orenburg on the Ural River, down which river they had come to Uralsk, and thence across the Steppes to Saratov, and from there, peacefully down the Volga River to Astrakhan, by a little rusty steamer to Baku, and thence, by road again, to Tabriz, Teheran, Meshed, Herat and so back to Kabul, and there, after hearing and seeing many things, Gul Mahommed had written a long letter to Colonel Ormesby of the Intelligence Department. A letter which was wrapped about the wooden strut of a camel-saddle frame, from which the leather had been unpicked, removed, and then sewn on again; and so it had travelled safely to Peshawar and to the house of one Moussafa Shah who had once been Rissaldar of the Cavalry Regiment of the Corps of Guides; and by Moussafa Shah it had been taken safely to a secluded and inconspicuous little bungalow at the back of the military cantonment of Peshawar, and placed by him in the hands of 'Tarmi Dard' Sahib, known to Colonel Ormesby, Major Ganesh Hazelrigg and a few others as Tommy Dodd.

And from Kabul, Gul Mahommed and Shere Khan, being for the moment weary of travel, had proceeded to Khairabad in Khairastan, of which small part of the Border country, Shere Khan's father was the Khan.

Memories . . .

Of Ganesh Hazelrigg coming to Khairabad in the guise of a Holy Pir, and there being some talk of keeping him permanently, that he might occupy a shrine which should become sacred as a place of pilgrimage and a source of revenue to Khairabad.

Of how, as he had learned from Ganesh Hazelrigg, the latter had recognized him, largely through his humming a stave from *The Mikado*; though he had not recognized Ganesh.

Of how, on general principles, he had opposed the suggestion that the Holy Man should be butchered to make a Khairabad Holy Day and be the *pièce de résistance* of a shrine, and had bidden Shere Khan to warn the Holy Man in the morning that it would bc a splendid idea for him to go while the going was good.

Of how Ganesh Hazelrigg, coming again in the rôle of an Afghan horse-coper, visiting Shere Khan's fortified house and without disclosing his identity, asked him, Wendover, to set him on his way for a few miles as he wasn't sure of it.

And then, when they were alone together, and miles from the nearest human being, how this Inayatullah Hussein, Afghan horse-coper, had suggested that they halt, rest and eat, had talked of local politics and rumours concerning the Singing Hadji of Sufed Kot, and then had almost frightened him to death by suddenly speaking English and addressing him, the dyed-in-the-wool Pathan, Gul Mahommed, as Wendover.

Yes, he would never forget Ganesh's quiet:

"Don't be an ass, Wendover. Come off it. I'm Hazelrigg."

And it had only been then, when he spoke like that, in his own natural English voice, that he had realized that this really was his old friend whom he hadn't seen since he left Napierpur, a couple of years before his crash, Court-Martial and ruin. The first Englishman to whom he had spoken since he had disappeared and turned Pathan gun-runner, except for those few words with Thorburn at Godoz.

And so it had been Ganesh Hazelrigg, whom he had saved, in the guise of a Holy Man when they had wanted to martyr and canonise him at Khairabad!

And that was an amusing thing, that he, Richard Wendover, as Gul Mahommed the Pathan, should have saved the life of Bartholomew Hazelrigg as the Pir Saleh ud Din Ali Moussa, without knowing who he was.

For the old Khan and his counsellors had for once quite agreed with the hot-headed young *jowans* of the Tribe that it would be just as well to put the visiting Holy Man to death, because if he were a bandit spy, dead spies tell no tales, and if he were the genuine Holy Man, well, martyrdom and canonization were all in his day's work and what a Holy Man was supposed to hope for, weren't they?

And then, there was Ganesh, trying to save him in return; not to save his life, but his *way* of life.

It had been rather splendid, old Ganesh's faith in him; probably the only man who hadn't accepted the Court-Martial's finding as correct and its sentence as just; the only human being except Shere Khan, excluding possibly one woman. Sybil Ffoulkes might have had doubts. Yes—he had been sure she would.

Well, it cut no ice now, of course, but it was heart-warming to know that Ganesh had believed in him all through—as it was interesting to wonder whether Sybil Ffoulkes had done so.

And Ganesh had talked about digging the whole thing up again, and he had told him he didn't want any exhumation whatever; to let what was buried stay buried, for it stank, and it was only recently that he had been able to breathe pure air, uncontaminated by that stench of devilish villainy and cruel, if inevitable, injustice.

No, he had told Ganesh: he had put all that behind him. He had turned Pathan and he'd stay Pathan, and a damned good job too.

In point of fact, he simply did not regret it, for he far preferred this life of glorious freedom. He didn't want to be whitewashed and reinstated. Didn't care a damn whether his name were cleared or not. And a lot more such lies.

For even to Ganesh he could not bring himself to tell how he had been frightened and flogged, degraded and humiliated by Bailitzin, compared with whom he now regarded Breckinge as a poor rat, a rat that had bitten his hand pretty badly, no doubt, but compared with whom Bailitzin was a vast saurian reptile that had dragged him, wallowing, through the foulest mud and filth, with intent thereafter to destroy him utterly, kill him most cruelly.

Then Ganesh had asked him a number of questions about his being found dead drunk, and exactly what had been the relations between him and the Eurasian Medical Officer who had been in the Fort with him at the time. And although he had been pretty restive under Ganesh's cross-questioning, that astute and wily man had confirmed in his mind, as a certainty, what had hitherto been a conjecture, that Breckinge, the Eurasian doctor, had given him a powerful narcotic that had not only put him to sleep for forty-eight hours, but poisoned him sufficiently to affect his mind and memory for quite a while.

And ponderously shaking his wise old head, Ganesh had gone off about his Intelligence business, very angry with him, and bidding him *wait*; just wait and see.

And then, weeks or months later, had come Ganesh's subordinate Mahbub Ali, bidding him join Ganesh as quickly as he could, and with as many staunch men as he could bring, to swell the army of the Singing Hadji of Sufed Kot, who was about to besiege Giltraza Fort.

Memories . . .

Giltraza Fort. By the time he had reached Ganesh, half its defenders were dead, including Major Denborough, Captain Scott and Lieutenant Henderson, leaving no one in charge of the native officers except Captain Alexander Breckinge, I.M.S., the Eurasian doctor.

And then Breckinge's amazing deed. No one would ever know whether he went mad, *berserk*; whether he hoped to rehabilitate himself; or whether, in those tremendous moments, the spirit of his grandfather, General Sir Percy Vereker Breckinge, had risen up within him and seized the captaincy of his soul. Probably all three motives had contributed, with the last-named most powerful, as his dying words had been '*I am a General's grandson.*'

Yes, and when the relieving force had marched in, and Ganesh had come to his bedside, overflowing with joy, congratulations and triumph, how the good chap's face had fallen when he had told him that he wasn't going to use Breckinge's confession. Nor get himself reinstated in a blaze of glory, as the innocent hero of a shameful miscarriage of justice, and the noble hero of the defence and salvation of the Fort that Breckinge had wished to surrender to the Singing Hadji.[74]

Nor had he been quite honest with Ganesh. Although he had told him the truth and nothing but the truth, he had not told him the whole truth. He had pretended that his main reason had been that he really couldn't use the confession, and blacken and damn for ever, the memory of the man who had died in the act of saving his life.

In point of fact, he felt pretty sure that, other considerations apart, he couldn't have done it, in spite of the fact that Breckinge had died cursing him. He would have felt bad about it for the rest of his days, because, whatever Breckinge had done to injure him, he had died trying to save Wendover's life.

No—whether that fact would have weighed with him sufficiently as a motive for refusing to use the confession and accept re-instatement at the cost of Breckinge's memory, he couldn't really be certain. For there had been other reasons.

In the first place, he shrank from the idea of more publicity, another Court-Martial, and going through the sort of thing that poor Dreyfus must have suffered when he returned to France from Devil's Island. He had always loathed being conspicuous, and, for a man of reticence, a certain shyness and a hatred of publicity and prominence, he had had a pretty good belly-full already, when his Court-Martial and disgrace had been a nine-days' wonder, published and discussed in al-

---

[74] "*The Man of a Ghost.*"

most every newspaper in the world.

No, he hadn't wanted to face any more lime-light, whether as villain or hero, and there was always the chance that the authorities might either refuse to open the matter, or, as Breckinge's only witnesses were dead, to accept this document, a scribble on the back of an army hospital case-sheet.

And again, especially after the horrible confinement of the siege, he longed for the mountains. Infinitely preferable to him were Khairastan, Khairabad Fort, Shere Khan's own Fort, and that glorious open-air life and that wonderful mountain air. Yes, infinitely preferable to the plains of India, garrison towns, and the narrow life of a regimental officer, cribbed, crabbed and confined by routine discipline and duty, like a blind-folded ox revolving about a well-head or a threshing-floor.

No, whatever it may have been at first, life as a Pathan was now better than existence as an Englishman.

He was a hill-man now, and—

> "*So and no otherwise—so and no otherwise, hillmen desire their Hills.*"

And then there was Shere Khan. Could he turn to him, after all they had seen and done together, dared and suffered together; after each saving the life of the other at the risk of his own; could he turn to Shere Khan and say:

"Well, I'm off. I'm going back to India and the Regiment," knowing that there was no return to the Regiment for Shere Khan? He had deserted when Wendover was cashiered and kicked out; had stood by him and shown him how to make a new adjustment to life. Shere Khan had brought Richard Wendover to a new home and people and country, when he needed them. He had been accepted there, had become a Pathan— and a Pathan he would remain. Besides, Shere Khan had married: and probably, before very long would be the Khan of Khairabad. He could not return to India—

to be Richard Wendover's domestic servant until he was arrested and gaoled as a deserter.

And should Richard Wendover have left the ruins of his life lying blackened in the mud for this semi-savage Pathan, this "native"?

Yes, he most certainly should and would, rather than break his heart with gross ingratitude. Pathan? Native?

> '*There's neither East nor West, Border nor breed nor birth,*
> *When two strong men stand face to face, though they come from the ends of the earth.*'

And Shere Khan was a strong man if ever there was one, and Richard Wendover could be strong enough to put this temptation behind him and continue to stand face to face and side by side with the man who had saved him from suicide after his downfall; had shown him the way of escape, kept him alive, and given him a life to live; saved him again at Tashkent and had been servant and friend and brother, giving him that love than which there is no greater, the love that offers the laying down of life for that of the friend.

And lastly, what was possibly the strongest motive, probably the *real* motive—for which of us can honestly and unerringly pick out his real motive for any abnormal act—had been his consuming hatred of Bailitzin, his insatiable yearning to deal faithfully with Bailitzin; to catch him alone; to wipe out in some measure a stain; to cut out the canker that corroded his soul far more than had the injury which Breckinge had done him.

Breckinge was—*Nothing.*

And how impossible he had found it to tell even Ganesh the truth. Not even to him could he admit that he had been whipped like a dog, had been made to lie and to grovel—for that was how he regarded it—at the feet of this Russian.

Probably it would have been the wise thing to have got it all up and out, to have made full confession to

Ganesh, and to have uncovered the ever-festering sore and let in upon it the mellow light of reason, the light of Ganesh's sanity and wisdom.

At the time, he had felt that nothing could help him, cure him, except action, his own action against Bailitzin.

And so he had said nothing whatsoever to Ganesh about the matter, and had given him the impression that his sole reason for refusing to "stage a comeback" had been his objection to whitening himself at the cost of blackening the memory of Breckinge who, in his last minutes had surely made atonement for his wretched life, the life for which the sins of his grandfather were to blame more than Breckinge's own.

It had been a rather mean trick, and the only salve he had had for his conscience was the thought that, had there been no Bailitzin and no other consideration, he might perhaps have acted as he did, for no other reason than the one he gave to Ganesh.

And Ganesh was no fool. He saw further through a brick wall than most men, and no doubt thought his own thoughts and had his own ideas about what Shere Khan was to Richard Wendover; and also as to what Richard Wendover, detected spy, must have suffered at the hands of the Russians whom he had so long and successfully fooled.

Anyway, he had stuck to his point. He had gone his own way and, in spite of what the Brigadier and Ganesh had said to him after the relief of Giltraza, he had slipped quietly away from the Fort, with Shere Khan, as soon as they were both fit for travel, and had returned to Khairastan. And after terrific rejoicings feastings and gorgings at Khairabad Fort, he had retired to Shere Khan's Fort and settled down to the peaceful life of a Border clansmen whose rifle is never far from his hand.

But he had said unto his soul "Peace!" when there was no peace; when, in his thoughts by day and his dreams by night, appeared the face of Bailitzin, the man who had turned the ex-British officer—the hardy venturer who had made good among gun-runners, bandits, outlaws, brigands, fierce fighting-men—into a little whipped dog, cringing in fear at his feet.

'*Breckinge!*' he brooded—what that miserable Eurasian had done to him had been as nothing compared with what the Russian had done. Ten Breckinges could not have warped and seared his soul as Bailitzin had done. The harm that Breckinge had worked had merely been to his reputation and career. That which Bailitzin had done had been to his very being, his essential self, his immortal soul. "*Who steals my purse steals trash,*" and Breckinge now, in retrospect, appeared to him but as some poor pick-pocket. "*But he that filches from me my good name robs me of that which not enriches him, and makes me poor indeed.*" And Bailitzin had stolen something not only irreplaceable but immeasurably valuable, something that left him poor indeed, something absolutely essential to his peace of mind.

How, for example, could he possibly turn his thoughts to Sybil Ffoulkes while his mind was warped and twisted, blackened and blasted by memories of what Bailitzin had done to him, and had made of him, *Richard Wendover*, who had once been a proud man.

Memories . . .

Brooding over his shame, nursing his sense of injury until it became an *idée fixe*, possessing his longing for vengeance so that it became an obsession, darkening his thoughts and destroying his peace until he had become more saturnine, grim and gloomy than the grimmest Tribesman of them all.

And again Shere Khan had helped him, had saved him, restored his sense of proportion and mental balance.

That winter morning, when as they sat sunning themselves upon the Fort wall, suddenly, as though reading his very thoughts, Shere Khan had said:

"*Huzoor*, the hour has struck. He himself has come south, and is even now in Kabul."

"*Bailitzin?*"

"None other. Last night, ere we returned from hawking, one came with a message, left it and passed on in haste. By the *durwan's* description of the man and what he said, 'twas that Mahbub Ali, Hazelrigg Sahib's man, who was with us at Giltraza before we got into the Fort."

"Mahbub Ali? And what was the message?"

"The Bear has come out of his forest; seek for him in his den, in the bazaar of the gun-smiths wherein is the house of Ilderim the Gun-runner."

And he had known at once that Bailitzin was in Kabul and, probably in the guise of a prosperous Afghan merchant, was staying in the house of the Russophile agent, the good Ilderim the Afghan, with whom he himself had once crossed from Muscat to Persia.

And quickly as he had risen to his feet, Shere Khan had been as quick, and without waiting to be asked to do so, had immediately given orders for the saddling of horses, the preparation and packing in haversacks of cooked rations, and had said good-bye to his beloved Bibi Jan, his wife—and what was more, the admired and cherished mother of his son.

But if *Dili dur ast*,[75] so is Kabul, and by the time they had reached the bazaar of the gun-smiths and the house of Ilderim the Gun-runner, the Bear had left its den and had taken the road again. As he had given out that he was going north-westward to Kushk and the ancient city of Merv, capital of the Turcoman country, the wily Shere Khan had accordingly watched for him on the road that went south-east, had seen him and his well-armed *kafila* pass, and, having set a man to follow, had discovered that he was making for the turbulent land ruled by the Singing Hadji of Sufed Kot.

And thence Richard Wendover and Shere Khan had made their perilous way, only to learn that, having sojourned with the Singing Hadji, Bailitzin had departed again, leaving behind him certain small but heavy sacks which, unladen from camel, mule and donkey, had clinked melodiously as they fell to earth.

And so north-west once more; by Jalalabad to Kunar, to Dir, and by Chilas on the Indus River to

---

[75] *"Delhi is far away."*

Gilgit, where they lost the trail entirely, and returning to Chilas, learned that their quarry had turned east, for Drosh, where they had followed him, picked up the trail again through Chitral, and so through Kafiristan to Banu and north through Kataghan to Tashkurgan, where they were hot upon his trail.

Memories . . .

And so at last, in Kharkand, they had found themselves but two days behind him as he rode to Samarcand, mounted on a pure-bred Badakshani mare, a bay with three white socks; his servant riding a half-bred Kabuli mare, a flea-bitten grey, long-eared, ewe-necked and somewhat goose-rumped; followed by four well-laden donkeys looked after by an Afghan and three Tungans, themselves looked after by two Turki-Chinese half-castes.

And in the Turki-Chinese half-castes there was hope, for it was entirely possible that, like the long lean beggar, clad in filthy coat, plus-fours of ragged cotton, and a particularly bright and beautiful skull cap of cherry-coloured silk, who had watched for Wendover in the Kharkand Bazaar, these "Turki-Chinese half-castes" might be men belonging to Ganesh Hazelrigg's marvellous organization, that thin and widely-cast network of spies and sub-agents that sparsely covered the Border, Afghanistan and south-eastern Central Asia.

§3

So thus, and now, Gul Mahommed, the Pathan who had been Richard Wendover the British Officer, came to be sitting raking over his bitter memories, huddled in his *poshteen* beside the embers of the fire over which Shere Khan had cooked their evening rice and mutton, their flat *nands* of unleavened bread, and boiled their Russian tea.

Suddenly he heard a sound, snatched up his rifle, and sprang to his feet. Almost as quickly, Shere Khan, wrapped from head to foot in a dirty sheet, sprang from the stark stiffness of his corpse-like rigidity and knelt beside him, rifle at the ready.

"Who's there?" cried Wendover.

And a cracked and quavering voice replied from the darkness.

"Only me and another ass," as into the light cast by the fire upon which Shere Khan threw a handful of dry grass and twigs, rode the cherry-coloured-silk capped beggar of the Kashgar bazaar, upon a potter's donkey so small that the toes of the tall lean man seemed painfully to be turned upward, lest they drag upon the ground.

Shivering, with each hand thrust up into the opposite sleeve, the ragged beggar with the foot-long moustache, as strange and bizarre a figure as could be found in even a Central Asian bazaar, nevertheless spoke excellent English.

"M.I.15 blew in just after you left," he said. "He's on his way to see the British Resident at Kashgar—on a rather more important matter. Russo-Chinese Ching-Kiang stuff. Told me that your man is for Jalalabad and the Border by way of Yarkand and Badakshan. He's meeting a *kafila* from Tashkent there, and there are going to be great doings in the Singing Hadji's country again. Apparently they are not going to Kabul for fear the bullion, that is going south with them, stays there for good. I should think your best plan would be to get straight down into the Singing Hadji's country. Get there before he does, and lay for him there. You can get word to G.5.H.8. from there, and he'll get a move on. I should think a few of these bombing-planes they've sent to India would make the Singing Hadji sing a different tune if they could hover over his home-town occasionally. If they could make it, from Hunzana, that is. Anyway, you'd have earned your corn for the rest of your life if you could put Bailitzin out of business."

"Yes. Nothing like combining business with pleasure," growled Wendover. "What about a pot of good hot tea."

"For the love of God!" shivered the cherry-capped beggar man, who spoke such admirable English and knew so much of the affairs of Comrade-Colonel Nikolas Bailitzin, Richard Wendover, Ganesh Hazelrigg of the Intelligence Department and of the local Anglo-Russian-Chinese situation.

III

Major Bartholomew Hazelrigg, who could afford to make such confessions, freely admitted that the Hadji of Turangzai was one of the people whom he did not understand.

When that notorious and potent ecclesiastic had been a *Mullah* in the Charsadda district of Peshawar, he had been noteworthy and respected for his justice, impartiality, and incorruptibility as a *kazi*, a judge administering Mohammedan law and custom.

On several occasions, when keeping close watch upon certain political suspects, fire-brands, agitators, terrorists, and those who aided and abetted terrorists; and when unravelling obscure and interesting problems connected with his work, Major Hazelrigg had attended sessions of this *Mullah's* court. Nor, of course, had he paid these visits in his own proper person and the uniform of a British officer. The worthy *kazi* had been entirely unaware of the honour paid to the Court; and if he had noticed the quiet and unobtrusive man with the henna-dyed beard, *kohl*-encircled eyes and solidly respectable appearance, he had supposed him to be an idle member of the public, enjoying a free show; or some ordinary man-in-the-street sort of person interested in a case; one of its principals; or perchance one of its many witnesses.

And squatting quietly, with closed eyes, rocking gently to and fro, fingering a rosary, and occasionally murmuring, *sotto voce*, to himself, Major Hazelrigg had noticed, among many other things, that the *Mullah* of Charsadda was not only a very sound judge who had Mussulman law and custom at his finger-tips, but was patently honest and impartial. It was also evident, from the conversation of litigants, witnesses, and people in and about the Court, that he was widely known and esteemed for these qualities, and generally regarded as a poor-man's Judge, being no respecter of persons and, unlike the majority of his kind, utterly unbribable. Not only had the rich man no pull in the *Mullah's* Court, but the Hindu, or other person of different religious or political opinion, suffered no handicap.

And further, sitting silent and somnolent, Hazelrigg learned that, although the Charsadda district was a hot-bed of intrigue and sedition, of feud and faction, the *Mullah* of Charsadda cared for none of these things, rendered unto Cæsar the things that were Cæsar's, upheld the Law as established, and was apparently entirely free from racial and political bias.

When upon occasion, some hot-headed loose-tongued litigant gave angry utterance to sedition, to his own political views, or to condemnation of those of his opponent, the *Mullah*, eyeing him coldly, would observe;

"I know nothing of that. Keep to the matter in hand, please."

And, talking one day with the Commissioner of the Division, Hazelrigg learned that that officer, a man un-usually well-informed, considered the *Mullah* of Char-sadda to be an admirable and valuable friend of the Government, if only because he was a stout upholder of Authority and the scourge of all who defied it and broke its laws.

What, then, was Major Hazelrigg's surprise to learn, on his return to Peshawar after an absence in Afghan-istan and Turkestan, that the *Mullah* of Charsadda had fallen from grace, had changed completely; and, from being a pillar of society, a prop of authority, an impar-tial judge and loyal subject of the King Emperor, had become a violent agitator against the Government, an embittered seditionist, and an active and dangerous enemy of the British.

Anything that surprised Major Hazelrigg interested him; and of all things that interested his tenacious mind, he made a close and careful study.

What had so changed the admirable *Mullah* of Charsadda, that from a firm friend, he had become a bitter foe?

The Commissioner could not tell him: no one could

tell him: and Hazelrigg determined to find out for himself; not only because the failure to solve the problem bothered him, but because he felt that when he knew what had caused this *volte face* on the part of the *Mullah* of Charsadda, he would know something very useful.

And to gather knowledge useful to him as a player of the Great Game was the main occupation and chief interest of his life. For the Secret Service was not only his profession but his hobby, his only joy, the ruling passion of his existence.

Sojourning in the houses of the *houris* of the Peshawar bazaar; loafing and sleeping in the *serais* where *kafilas* end the journeys begun in Khiva and Bokhara, Tashkent and Samarcand; smoking his hookah about the camel-dung fires; dipping into the sooty flesh-pots wherein bubbled the luscious stew of the tails of fat-tailed sheep; while he exchanged the news of the day with Afghan horse-coper, Bokhara rug-pedlar, Samarcand silk-merchant, and silver-tongued Persian vendor of jewellery and of lies, he talked of this and of that, of Kings and Khans, of Amirs and Emperors—and of the *Mullah* of Charsadda who, formerly an upright Judge, was now a fugitive in the Mohmand country; a fire-brand, agitator and fomenter of rebellion, who had given his daughter to the notorious Abdul Ghaffar Khan, outlaw and terrorist, son of Bairam Khan, known for intrigue and subversive activities.

And winnowing the grain from the chaff, Hazelrigg came upon what he considered the truth.

Listening on balcony and in upper chamber; by camp-fire, among the munching camels; in bullock-cart and railway-carriage; in caravanserai and market-place; under the roadside *peepul* tree; on railway-platform and village watch-tower; in mosque courtyard and compound of toddy-seller's shop; vacant-faced and empty-eyed, apparently heedlessly hearing answer to idle question, he followed threads of discourse, and by patient and skilful weaving, he plaited a cord that connected the downfall and disappearance of the *Mullah* of Charsadda with the activities of that, to him, peculiarly poisonous person, the Singing Hadji of Sufed Kot.

By the time he had himself to leave Peshawar, he had learned from Bazaar rumour what was as convincing as anything proven through impeccable witnesses in a High Court of Justice.

Whatever anybody else thought or knew or thought he knew, Hazelrigg knew that the mystery of the *Mullah* of Charsadda, now notorious as "the Hadji of Turangzai," could be solved by the Singing Hadji; that the man who could answer the question was the man who, at the instigation of the Singing Hadji of Sufed Kot, had brought charges, absolutely false, against the *Mullah* of Charsadda, and had apparently proven him to be a two-faced plotter and seditionist.

It had been cleverly done.

Foolishly the *Mullah* of Charsadda had struck back violently at those who smote him under the cover of darkness; and had gone about, loudly denying that he had done things of which he was accused by no one save the base and cowardly wretch who had written anonymous letters concerning him. Hurt and indignant, he had gone to British officials, angrily accusing them of believing evil against him; and when he had been, perhaps somewhat coldly, informed that no evil had yet been heard, he had become yet angrier, had shouted, contradicted, accused, expostulated violently, and given offence.

All were in league against him and were listening to the abominable lies which were the absolute inventions of his enemies. He was innocent—and it was a damnable shame to doubt him.

With the cleverness and skill that had made him one of the best of his Service, Hazelrigg had ferreted out the fact that, in the Court of the *Mullah* of Charsadda, the Singing Hadji of Sufed Kot, or his representative, had lost a case, had been verbally scourged and excoriated for offering the *Mullah* a bribe, and publicly threatened with prosecution and punishment.

Here was motive for enmity. Here was the beginning of the trail that led from the excellent *Mullah's* Court to the abominable Hadji's stronghold; and that trail

Hazelrigg patiently and accurately followed, discovering upon it the gang who, in Peshawar, were the agents, representatives, spies and creatures of the Singing Hadji.

On the whole, the vengeance was a very pretty piece of work, and worthy of the brain that had conceived it; for the neat little plot, nicely carried out, had not only ruined the life and work of its victim, but had turned him into an active enemy of the Hadji's own great enemy, the British Raj!

How the Singing Hadji must have chuckled and crowed at the success of his cleverness, when he learned that the *Mullah* had been fool enough innocently to inculpate himself, and the British fools enough to let him do so—the *Mullah*, fool enough to shout from the house-tops,

"Since you think me a seditionist, I'll be one," and the British, fools enough to say:

"If you do, you must take the consequences."

The pity of it!

And now to make useful practice of his theory; to consider a way of turning his discovery to account.

Suppose the Hadji of Turangzai—albeit far too heavily involved and indeed embittered and perverted ever to return to his allegiance—could be persuaded of the fact that the secret enemy who had borne false witness against him, blackened his character, and driven him desperate, was none other than his present would-be ally the Singing Hadji of Sufed Kot, might not far-reaching consequences ensue from such a revelation?

Since the Hadji of Turangzai was now doing his best to raise the Mohmands against the Government, the fewer allies that he could find to help him in starting another Border war, the better for the Sirkar; and the likeliest and most powerful ally with whom he could combine, would be the Singing Hadji of Sufed Kot.

Suppose the Hadji of Turangzai could be convinced that the anonymous enemy who had wrecked his career was the Singing Hadji of Sufed Kot, there would be no such alliance.

'*Divide et impera*' is good political policy and, better still, is 'Prevent an alliance of enemies whose union would be dangerous strength.'

Particularly, when the Government is pursuing a policy of extremest conciliation—which to the Pathan is nothing but weakness, feebleness and fear—and is playing with fire kindled by a Red-shirt leader, the longer anything approaching actual war could be postponed, the better.

Oh for the days of the strong men who said '*Let us rule, or go*'; and—when Ajab Khan behaved in precisely the same manner and incited the Bunerwals to invade British territory—took him, tried him, and promptly hanged him for what he was, a pestilent breaker of the peace and a maker of war.

Such strong men the Pathan could understand, respect and heed. For weak men and their 'conciliations,' he had nothing but amused contempt.

One of these days some flabby theorist would simply abandon Peshawar City to the mob and proclaim, to the Border and Beyond, that the British are degenerate, are neither willing nor able to defend those whom they resume to govern.

Yes, a visit to the Hadji of Turangzai was indicated. After a tour of the Sufed Kot country.

Incidentally, Hazelrigg would have an opportunity of discovering whether the villainous Chimnai the Outlaw and his notorious band of robbers and raiders were being harboured by the Singing Hadji; for the sooner the fire-brand Chimnai the Outlaw was captured and brought to justice, the better.

§2

And in due course Major Bartholomew Hazelrigg, in his famous impersonation of a red-bearded Afghan horse-coper of the name of Inayatullah Hussein, paid his proposed visit to the Hadji of Turangzai, informed him that he had just been sojourning in the Sufed Kot country, and had there learned that the wicked and violent man known as the Singing Hadji, was gathering a *lashkar* that he might make war upon the Turangzai Pir of whom he was notoriously jealous, and against whom he had so maliciously wrought when the latter was the Judge of Charsadda, known to and admired by all, for his even-handed dispensation of pure justice.

And should emissaries from the Singing Hadji come bearing beautiful letters written on silk, or at least wrapped in silk, from the Singing Hadji, proposing that he and the Hadji of Turangzai should join forces and once more proclaim *jehad* against the Infidel, it would be wise and well to treat the messengers with contumely and their master with contempt. Yes, send them back like beaten dogs with words of wrath and messages of insult. For Inayatullah Hussein had certain knowledge that the Singing Hadji was the secret foe of the Turangzai Hadji and had been the cause of his downfall.

And the Turangzai Hadji listened to the wise words of the widely-travelled Afghan.

And where was that excellent and interesting patriot and raider known as Chimnai the Outlaw? Gossip said that he had been sojourning with his good friend of Turangzai.

Chimnai the Outlaw? Well, in point of fact, he had been staying here with the Hadji of Turangzai, but had departed quite recently, on receipt of some *khabbar* or other, brought by a man of Kurnai.

Oh, Kurnai, in the Sufed Kot country. Inayatullah Hussein must have just missed him then. What a pity. He had the very horse for such a man as Chimnai the Outlaw. Such a horse as bore Mazeppa.

And now, having enjoyed the good Hadji's hospitality, Inayatullah Hussein must take to the road again; gird up his loins and betake him to Kabul, and thence probably to the Kirghiz Steppes in search of more wonderful horses.

Ah, what a public benefactor he was, bringing these magnificent beasts from their home, hundreds and hundreds of miles away, down to the markets of the Border, that his fine friends and patrons might be worthily mounted.

But Inayatullah Hussein apparently changed his mind as soon as he was out of the sphere of influence of the Hadji of Turangzai; for to the Sufed Kot country he returned, and there, visiting Kurnai by night, learned that once again he had missed the elusive Chimnai the Outlaw, who, with a band some twenty strong, had quietly disappeared one night—taking with them a prisoner, a Sahib, one of the wonderful Men who Fly. Yes, he had been brought down by the clever men of Kurnai and his flying devil-carriage had been destroyed.

IV

The gentleman whose neat visiting cards bore the legend

> SYLVANUS H. STUYVESANT,
> 4406 Lakeside Drive,
> Chicago.
>
> *United American Press.*

and whose idiom and intonation accorded therewith, strolled unconcernedly past the Kabuli gate and along the Suddar Bazaar of Peshawar. As he observed to the educated and English-speaking Mussulman gentleman who had been deputed by the authorities to accompany him, his luck was in. For there was every indication that trouble was brewing, if not indeed already brewed.

The Bazaar had declared a *hartal*,[76] in token of its disapproval of the conduct of the British. Precisely what that conduct was, the inhabitants of Peshawar were unaware, still more unaware were the visitors from the hills, who were in the city in large numbers.

But that the British had misconducted themselves, as indeed they had done, any time and every time for the last hundred years, the Pathans of Peshawar were well aware. For one, Badishur Gul, had said so.

Loudly he had proclaimed the fact, far and wide, throughout the whole Mohmand country; and now in Peshawar itself.

Did the Peshawaris desire still to call themselves men; to walk with a swagger; to keep their shirt-tails out; to earn and deserve the continued approval of

---

[76] *Strike.*

their wives, and, more important, of the Ladies of the Bazaar who were not their wives? Then they must shut up their shops, sulk, curse, shake their fists at Europeans and in the general direction of the European Cantonment, go about in crowds singing seditious songs; and, if things looked fairly propitious, they must start rioting,

Naturally, if it were one of the days when the funny British did not want any nonsense, and were going to turn out a Battalion, a *Rissala*,[77] and a few armoured cars, the rioting had better be postponed to the following week, when doubtless the funny British would clear out of the city; scuttle into Cantonments; shut themselves up behind the charged perimeter wire, to touch which was death; and leave the rioters to it.

For, of course, you never knew nowadays, and had to take your chance. The British might shoot you for rioting, arson, murder, and seditious proclamation, or they might just cringe, tell you how frightfully sorry they were about everything, and give you some money.

Queer, aggravating people, the British; you simply never knew where you were with them.

From time to time, Mr. Sylvanus H. Stuyvesant's companion asked a question of a passer-by; of a burly bearded shop-keeper squatting cross-legged before the door of his lock-up shop; or, for a few minutes, joined a corner knot or strolling group of truculent tribesmen, passed the time of day, swapped lies and exchanged news.

"What's the latest about the Afridis?" Stuyvesant asked the Mussulman gentleman as the latter rejoined him after a brief conversation with a pair of swaggering Pathans, obvious wild men down from the hills.

"Two *lashkars* of them, Sahib," was the reply. "Approaching Peshawar, one on each side of the Khyber. One of them is going to attack the Forts and close the road, while the other comes down on Peshawar."

"And the city boys will join them, I suppose?"

"Surely; unless the British patrol the streets with armoured cars."

---

[77] *Native Cavalry Regiment.*

"They do that sometimes, do they?"

"Yes. Only last month there was rioting, and the mob was looting the *bunnias'* shops. News was sent quickly to Cantonments and an armoured car came. Unfortunately someone shot the driver and the engine."

"Shot the engine?"

"Well, something happened, and the car stopped and could not go on."

"So what?"

"The mob built a fire under it."

"Well, well! Rough stuff. Will the boys go out and meet the Afridis, or wait for them down here?"

"It's not known, Sahib. Sometimes they do one thing, sometimes another. There are many rumours."

"Do all the Pathans, Mohmands, Mahsuds, Afridis—can't remember all their names—do they all hate the British equally? Or do some tribes hate them more than others do?"

"They don't hate the British, Sahib."

"*What?* Don't hate them?"

"No. They fight them, of course. But they don't hate them. It's like when one regiment plays football against another regiment, or one native *pultan* plays a hockey match against another. They strive with mights and mains to win, each to conquer the other, but they don't hate."

"Yes. But that's different. That's a game."

"Well, fighting is the Pathans' game; and there is no bad feeling, really. Why, there was a General here who was always fighting the Tribesmen. Killed hundreds of them and burned their crops and their villages and blew up their watch-towers. He died here, during the campaign; and the people he had just been fighting—I think they were the Mohmands—sent envoys with a flag of truce, to ask whether ten of their chief *Maliks* could come and pay their respects at his funeral. They were willing to give up their rifles and trust to the British not to take them prisoners."

"And what did the British say to that?"

"They said, yes certainly, they'd be very pleased;

and the deputation came down to Peshawar, attended the funeral, and then went home again."

"Gee!" observed Mr. Sylvanus H. Stuyvesant.

For a time the American gentleman asked the usual general and obvious questions concerning the infinitely interesting city of Peshawar, and of the prophylactic measures adopted by the British to counteract the feverish symptoms so frequently and painfully displayed by the tribesmen.

The English-speaking Mussulman gentleman, kindly and helpfully detailed by the Authorities to bear-lead the Special Correspondent, show him all he wanted to see, and provide him with every facility for discovering everything that he wanted to know, gradually discovered that this tripper, tourist, or three-week collector of the information requisite for the compilation of an exhaustive and authoritative examination of all the problems of India, was not as other men; not as other visiting Sahibs who presented credentials, and were handed over to him for treatment.

These, be they men or women, be they English, French, American or what not, came with open minds, open eyes and indeed frequently with open mouths, listened to what he had to say, took a carefully-conducted trip up the Khyber, looked somewhat vacantly at what he bade them observe, thanked him politely, went their way and wrote their book.

But this gentleman had evidently studied his subject before coming to see Peshawar and the Khyber Pass; knew exactly what he wanted to see; where he wanted to go; and those things concerning which he wanted to know more. On some points he was, indeed, better informed than the Mussulman minor-official himself.

And to that quite astute servant of the British Raj it was clear that the American Special Correspondent was extremely well-qualified to do the work with which his Newspaper Syndicate had entrusted him.

He was a nice man too, a very agreeable Sahib, and able to show his appreciation of services-rendered without causing any uncomfortable feeling on the part of the recipient. Not like some of the blatant trippers who openly and crudely proffered a tip, as though an educated Indian gentleman, B.A. of Allahabad University, were a luggage-carrying coolie, a gharry-wallah or a hotel waiter.

And in addition to his delicacy and good manners, he was generous. Most generous.

§2

"Well," said Mr. Sylvanus H. Stuyvesant, one evening, as the car, in which he and his *cicerone* were seated, drew up at the hotel, "I guess we're through for to-day."

"Yes, Sir. Thank you. And what about to-morrow? Will my services be required?"

"Well now, they will and they won't. I'm going to stroll around on my own to-morrow; perhaps take a run out to Shabkadr. I'm told there's a simply wonderful view from the Fort there, and I've got a letter of introduction to the Commandant. But what I would like you to do, is to see if you can find out the address of a man whom I was advised to meet up here, if I could. A distinguished Native Officer of the Corps of Guides. He was a good friend to a friend of mine who was in India some time ago, and I promised to look him up. He can tell me something I want to know too, about this very wunnerful Regiment, this Corps of Guides. I understand they're unique; and that the Cavalry Regiment serves as an Infantry Battalion while the Infantry Battalion takes its turn as Cavalry. I'd certainly like to write an article on the Corps of Guides, and I want to go and see their location at—what's the place, Marden? I want to call on their Mess and I want to see that famous cemetery."

"And what is the name of the Native Officer, Sir?" enquired Mr. Stuyvesant's guide.

"Well now, what is it? Wait a minute."

And Mr. Stuyvesant dived into his capacious pocket for his notebook.

"I've got it here, somewhere. Wait a minute. Now where did I put that letter? Ah, here we are. Rissaldar-Major Moussafa Shah. What rank would that be now? Rissaldar-Major. What's Rissaldar?"

"It means he is, or was, chief superior Native Officer to Cavalry Regiment, like Subedar-Major of Infantry Regiment.

"Or," added the learned clerk, making a bold shot, "like Sergeant-Major in British Regiment."

"Well now, you find out where he lives. And then I'll get you to take me and show me his house, and one day I'll just drop in and have a talk with him. I guess we'll make out, with my bit of Hindustani and his bit of English . . . Got the name right? Rissaldar-Major Moussafa Shah."

"Yes, Sir. I will endeavour to discover his house."

"And I shall feel much obliged."

And this was a euphemism which the Mussulman gentleman fully understood.

"Well, goo' night. Be around on Saturday morning about ten, and we'll go some place."

"And by the way," added Mr. Stuyvesant, as he turned away to go into the hotel, "not a word to anybody about this Rissaldar-Major Moussafa Shah. It just occurs to me that perhaps some of the British officers or officials might feel I was kinda going behind their backs, if you know what I mean, in getting the story of the Guides from one of the Native Officers instead of from a British Officer. But you see, I want the real low-down on the subject. I shall have plenty of talks, of course, with the Colonel and Officers, but I want what we newspaper men call a story; the real dope straight from the horse's mouth, if you know what I mean, about this unique Corps. I want to get a new angle on it, and just write down an actual conversation between me and a real live guy who has been through it from recruit to Senior Native Officer. That'd be mighty interesting."

"Yes, Sir. I quite understand, and I'll endeavour to find the house of Mister Moussafa Shah."

But somehow or other, the gentleman from Allahabad University entirely failed to find the house of Rissaldar-Major Moussafa Shah, and Mr. Stuyvesant also failed to make his acquaintance.

This, until more urgent affairs distracted his attention, was a matter of considerable chagrin to the gentleman calling himself Sylvanus H. Stuyvesant.

§3

"Well, young woman, what's the latest news on the Frontier?" enquired General Sir Archibald Vere-Vaughan, commanding the Peshawar Brigade, as he looked up from his plate of porridge, and sternly eyed his daughter Charmian.

"Social? Political? Or Military?" replied Charmian Vere-Vaughan.

"Any. All. Keep me informed and up-to-date."

"Well," considered the girl. "I think the most important is that I've got a boy-friend."

"Poor fellow. Is he the eighth or the eighteenth?"

"Twenty-eighth, and brightest and best. A lovely boy. Such a beautiful name. Sylvanus H. Stuyvesant."

"Splendid. What does the 'H' stand for?"

"Heliogabalus, I should think."

"Really? What's he like?"

"Oh, forty-ish, fairish, fondish."

"What d'ye mean?"

"Sweet."

"Where does he come from?"

"Chicago."

"That's in America, isn't it?"

"How bright you are, Daddy. He's writing a book or a newspaper or something. I'm going to bring him to lunch. You'll love him."

"I love him already," replied General Sir Archibald Vere-Vaughan, rising, and going to the side-board whereon silver dishes sizzled above little spirit-lamps.

"What, for my sake? And on my description?"

"No. For his own sake and on Rawalpindi's description. He's . . ."

"Oh, you know him? Well, why couldn't you say so."

"I am saying so. Yes, I know him all right. He actually presented himself and his credentials to me, before making *your* acquaintance. Even went to the Governor, the Commissioner, and the Political Agent first, also. He is as you say, writing a newspaper, or for a newspaper, giving America what I believe is known as the low-down on the Anglo-Russian-Afghan-Border situation."

"Writing up the shemozzle, in fact," observed the girl, helping herself to marmalade.

"You've said it, sister," said the General to his daughter. "And he is your latest boy-friend, is he? Were you 'At Home' when he called at Flagstaff House and wrote his name in the book? Or how did you get to know him?"

"Tommy Dodd. Last night. While you were out on night manœuvres—by your own account. He dances beautifully, and is a most interesting chap to talk to. Been everywhere, done everything—if not everybody. I like him terribly."

"Does Tommy Dodd also like him terribly?" enquired the General.

"Loves him, I should think. Bad taste if he doesn't."

"Ask you to vet him?"

"No. Not in so many words, but I prophesy that before long Thomas'll want to know what I think about him."

"Do you think?"

"Yes, Daddy. Of course I do. I think you are a funny man."

"And you think Mr. Sylvanus H. Stuyvesant *is* all he pretends to be, eh?"

"That much, at least, because, so far, he only pretends to be an American journalist 'covering India' and a regular fellow."

"And he's that, eh?"

"You've said it, brother," replied the young lady.

V

Charmian Vere-Vaughan was accompanying her admired friend Major Bartholomew Hazelrigg, at his earnest invitation, "just for a ride," in Colonel Ormesby's fast car, up the Khyber Pass. The car was driven by one Tommy Dodd, beside whom sat a British soldier, a loaded rifle between his knees.

"And the leader of the escort is a bit of a lad, eh? Something out of the top drawer?" asked Charmian Vere-Vaughan.

"Well, I'm not given to the making of rash statements, Charming, but I don't mind saying that he is the most extraordinarily attractive and intriguing man of all the men you have ever met or ever will meet," replied Major Bartholomew Hazelrigg.

"Present company excepted, of course, Lord Ganesh."

"God Ganesh, please. Elephant God."

"'Attractive and intriguing'! What are his attractions and—intrigues? With the Sons of War, or the Daughters of Men?"

"Now, now, don't go putting wicked ideas into my blameless mind. Dirty words into my clean mouth and evil thoughts into my innocent soul. Daughters of Men! He's a misogynist."

"What's that? Sounds foul."

"A woman-hater. Or rather, he doesn't trouble to hate 'em."

"Shows he's got sense. Got some wisdom, anyway. Tell me about him, Ganesh."

"And yet at least one woman loves him utterly and completely—desperately in fact. I gather she'd do anything in the world for him," continued Hazelrigg.

"Who is she?" asked the girl.

"A Sybil Ffoulkes. Daughter of General Sir Arthur Ffoulkes. She and Wendover grew up together. Boy and girl affair."

"There's always one who loves and one who is loved in every love-affair," observed Charmian didactically. "And she did the loving, eh?"

"Apparently."

"Tell me all about him."

Major Hazelrigg, usually terse and taciturn, waxed eloquent upon the subject that, next to his job and Miss Charmian Vere-Vaughan, interested him more than anything in the world.

"Tell you about him! Take me a long time. He's—er —one of the best."

"Oh, well, every man's friend is that. Sum him up. Without feeble *clichés*."

"*Clichés!* Well, in cold blood and plain English he's —if you'll excuse the word—the noblest man I've ever met."

"Tut!"

"The bravest and the finest."

"You've known some stout chaps in your time too, haven't you, Ganesh?" said the girl, eyeing her companion.

"Yes. And he's easily first by a long way."

"Rest also ran, eh? Tell me about him."

"I'm trying to. He did the biggest thing I've ever known a man do. Not only that, but the biggest thing I've heard of, or read of."

"What was that, Elephant?"

"I'll tell you. Tell you from the beginning. We've half an hour yet."

"You could talk about him for half an hour?"

"Yes, or half a day. To you."

"To me?"

"Sort of person who could understand and appreciate a man like him."

Yes, he thought to himself, studying the girl's face. Yes, understand and appreciate Richard Wendover. And fall in love with him too.

But what of that other girl at Home—who was so deeply interested and desperately concerned about him —judging from her letters. There had never been any

542

signs that Wendover was either desperately concerned or deeply interested in her. He had never mentioned any girl at Home.

"And if he ever falls in love, it will be with someone like you, my dear. And that's the only chance, the only lure. The only way to get him back. The one and only," he said.

"Thank you, Ganesh. You say the nicest things—and yet never pay compliments. That's why I love you so, darling old Elephant."

And tucking her arm through that of her admired friend, the girl snuggled up to him affectionately.

"Go to it, pup," she said.

"Well, he and I were at the same Prep School, though I was considerably his senior. In fact, I think I was Captain of the school when he came. Stout kid. And I noticed him at his first Rugger efforts when we tried him in the First XV. Pluck! Game as a fighting-cock. I can see him now. Knocked silly and trampled flat. So hurt that he was white and crippled and gasping, but wouldn't own it."

"Had guts," murmured Miss Charmian Vere-Vaughan.

"As you observe, in the modern fashion," agreed Hazelrigg. "Yes, richly endowed with—guts. Same when he took up boxing. You could defeat him on points, or you could knock him out, but you couldn't beat him, so to speak . . . Then he came on to my Public School. Same there. Not brilliant. Not clever, even. But Lord, how solid, sterling, and—what shall I say—resolute, determined. And fine. Mind you, he was no marble-browed Eric, or Little by Little. He got into as much trouble as anybody, and was no favourite with the masters. But the Head, investigating a nasty business once, said to him:

"*Give me your version of this, Wendover, and I will accept it.*'

"He did; and when the Head questioned him, he knew perfectly well that every answer he got was the absolute truth, without a shade of prevarication; and when, once or twice, Wendover refused to answer, the

Head didn't get angry or press the point. For he was a sportsman, too, and he knew that Wendover would have been sacked, expelled with ignominy, rather than tell a damned lie on the one hand, or inculpate anybody on the other. Fact! He was no good at lying—try as he might."

"Well, thank Heaven Galahad could get away with a Bit of Sin, anyway," yawned Charmian Vere-Vaughan.

"Get away with a Bit of Sin? I tell you, except for truthfulness and an extraordinarily high code of personal honour and self-respect, he was a bad hat," defended Hazelrigg. "One or two form-masters loathed him, and his House-Master referred to him, in front of me, as a Perfect Curse. He was very fond of him, nevertheless.

"Same at Sandhurst. Far from brilliant, and of by no means blameless record—pretty low on the lists; and extremely popular as a fine sportsman and a fearless outspoken blunt fellow who was as straight as a die, a wonderful friend and, oh, well—one of the best. And he got very keen on his profession. Although he was very good at games, especially Rugger and boxing, a distinguished Army representative at both, and played a lot, he did not lose much time on the social side. Didn't dance; didn't binge at all; took no interest whatsoever in girls—of either kind; didn't go to race-meetings and that sort of thing; and rather concentrated on his work.

"Then he came out to India and made an uncommon good impression and a good start in a good Regiment."

"Which?"

"Napier's Horse. They were a good crowd with a good Colonel; and it was considered no disgrace to a youngster to be keen on his job and really to work at it. And although I wasn't able to see as much of him as I should have liked, he was evidently the same old Richard Wendover, self-contained and self-sufficient; tough and resolute; just a little dour; no social light, not heading for hill-captaincy at Simla; and quite inexpert at poodle-faking, carpet-knighting, and even at dancing and amateur theatricals. Kind of chap at whom lesser men sneered."

"'Adjutant to Adjutant-General in three moves,' sort of thing, eh?"

"But it was behind his back that any sneering was done. He wasn't the sort of chap to whom anyone was openly rude; for he had a short way with him, and I don't deny it. But although he was never what I call a generally popular man, he was something very much better. He was popular with the right people. By which I don't mean the 'best people.' I mean the *right* people, who rule India and the Army professionally rather than socially. Not that the matter interested Wendover either way."

"He was popular with women," observed Charmian Vere-Vaughan sapiently.

"If so, he didn't know it. They simply didn't interest him. He was a man's man. And I think he preferred horses and dogs to men, even so. Well, Napier's Horse were in a Frontier show."

"The Dochi or the Malai one?" asked the girl.

"Well, both, as a matter of fact; and Wendover distinguished himself."

"Not buckling swashes, I suppose?" enquired the girl.

"No. Solid good work, and a remarkably fine piece of rear-guard doings."

"Nothing more difficult," murmured Charmian.

"Quite so," smiled Ganesh Hazelrigg. "Anyhow, General Bligh noticed him, and it didn't do him any harm. Or did it? Did it lead to his utter ruin?"

"How?"

"I'm telling you."

"Well, get on with it, then, Ganesh, and don't interrupt."

And there was no interruption while Hazelrigg told Charmian Vere-Vaughan the true story of Richard Wendover. . . .

§2

". . . And so he stayed native. Absolutely refused to say one word against the doctor; and most peremptorily forbade me to do so; tied my hands completely. And without inculpating the doctor he can't clear himself, of course," concluded Hazelrigg.

"I don't think I would have given way to him if I had been you, Ganesh."

"Yes, you would. You don't know Wendover."

"No, but I'm going to! By Jove . . . I . . ."

Words seemed to fail her.

"What does he call himself?"

"Gul Mahommed."

"And is he really going to remain Pathan for the rest of his life?"

"He says so."

"Going to marry into his friend's family and settle down in Khairastan for good? It's absurd."

"Well . . . I don't know. If he prefers that sort of existence to the joys of 'civilization,' as we are pleased to call our present remarkable way of life . . . He didn't get much out of that, did he?"

"But it's ridiculous. It's wicked. It's such a criminal waste, apart from anything else," protested Charmian Vere-Vaughan.

"Oh, I don't know about waste. He does wonderful work, of course, for Military Intelligence. Worth a dozen ordinary agents, or a battalion of troops."

"Oh, I've no patience with such nonsense!" interrupted the girl. "Why can't he come into the Service properly? Either go back to his regiment or into the Political Service? It's just stupid. Why can't he behave as any ordinary sensible person would in such circumstances?"

"Because Wendover is not ordinary. Especially since his life was smashed. You yourself said you wondered he didn't go mad."

"I said 'ordinary sensible person.' It seems to me he's neither ordinary nor sensible."

"Well, there it is. Either he honestly does prefer the

life he leads, or else he sticks to his bargain with himself about the dead doctor. As I say, he knows that the matter couldn't be completely cleared up and cleaned up, and himself publicly re-instated, without the utter blackening and blasting of the doctor's reputation and memory."

"Well, and why should the character of an innocent living man be blasted and blackened, as you call it, rather than that of a dead scoundrel? It's insane."

"I quite agree."

"You did your best, of course, to persuade him to let you use your proofs and clear his name."

"I did my utmost, of course."

"It's quixotry gone mad. Knowing you as he does," said the girl, "I should have thought he could have accepted your point of view, been advised by you."

"Yes."

"I can't understand it, can you, Ganesh?"

"I can't—but then, my dear, it was not for me that the doctor gave his life."

Silence fell between the man and the girl. It was broken at length by Charmian Vere-Vaughan.

"Why did you want me to come with you and meet Captain Wendover?" asked Charmian Vere-Vaughan suddenly.

"Well, for the pleasure, no, the joy and delight, of having you all to myself for a few hours, my dear, and . . ."

"Yes? And . . . the real reason?" smiled Charmian.

"And I wanted Wendover to see you, and have a talk with you. Or rather, I wanted you to have a talk with him, if you know what I mean."

"Vamp him?"

"Mildly. Mildly. I wanted you to give him a glimpse of one of the wonderful things of life—from which he is so wilfully cutting himself off. I shan't rest happy until I see Richard Wendover back on the right side of the Border, back in British uniform, back to his Regiment, and in his right and proper place in the world."

"Decoy duck, am I?"

"Perfect duck. And if you could get him back, what a work you'd have done."

"I'd do anything for you, dear old Ganesh."

"I'm sure you would, my dear, except marry me, and a few little things like that. Anyway, you'd be doing a wonderful thing for me, and for a man worth ten of me, if you could weigh-in sufficiently to make this wrong-headed lunatic return to his proper muttons. Why, suppose he fell in love with you at first sight—as I did. He'd just follow us home."

"Sure he would! You've said it, brother, as Mr. Stuyvesant would observe. And you could call me Little Bo-Peep for the rest of my days."

"Well, perhaps it is too much to hope that he will fall in love with you so violently and suddenly that he'll come right home right now (as Mr. Stuyvesant would say), but although I don't want to pay you compliments and turn your young head, and make you vainer than you are already, I firmly believe that the sight of you will give him something to think about, in addition to what I have got to say to him. Not so much *you* as all you stand for, my dear."

"Yes, all right, Ganesh. No need to elaborate it. I'm the World, the Flesh and the Devil."

"You certainly can be a little devil, and you represent the world to which I mean to make him return.

"If only he would fall in love with you," he mused. "But it's too much to hope."

"Left-handed compliment! Thank you. And there's another small matter, my good Ganesh. What about the girl he left behind him?"

"Well, he did leave her behind him, didn't he, and apparently has never written her a single word since. One can hardly hope to play her as a trump card."

"And have you the idea concealed at the back of your tortuous and scheming mind that I may perhaps remind him of the girl he left behind him? Remind him of her so much that it will stir up all his lovey-dovey feelings—so that he will listen to you this time?"

"Yes, my cute child. It certainly was and is at the back of my mind, and at the front too."

"You're a cunning old beast, Ganesh."

§3

In a cloud of dust, the car came to a standstill within a hundred yards of where, seated motionless on horseback, was a large group of gaily-dressed Pathans, their shirts and baggy trousers dazzlingly white in the sunshine, their velvet waistcoats of red and blue and mauve heavily embroidered with gold lace, their conical gilded *kullahs* gleaming, where they protruded through the top of the big loosely-wound *puggris*, their weapons glinting, the embroideries of their saddle-cloths, the metal ornaments of their saddles, reins and bridles, glittering.

In front of them, on a fine Kabuli stallion, sat, straight and upright, like the Lancer he had been, their leader.

"Well—here's Gul Mahommed, formerly Richard Wendover of Napier's Horse," said Hazelrigg quietly, as the fine-looking horseman trotted toward the car.

"I say, Ganesh," whispered the girl. "Let's go all English. Introduce him as Captain Wendover, and refuse to have any Gul Mahommed nonsense."

"Righto. It'll be all serene with Shere Khan, of course, but I'll talk Pushtu to him in front of the men. No doubt they are a hand-picked lot and have a pretty good idea that Shere Khan's *purdeshi*[78] friend isn't all he pretends."

"Morning, Wendover," he said, as the latter rode up to the car. "How's tricks?"

With a cold stare at the speaker and ignoring his companion the apparent Pathan replied in Pushtu with the usual greeting,

"*Salaam aleikum.* May you never be tired."

"Come off it, son," grinned Hazelrigg. "I want to introduce you to Miss Vere-Vaughan. You've met her father, of course."

Wendover frowned at the girl.

"How d'you do, Captain Wendover," said Charmian,

---

[78] *Foreign.*

extending her hand. "Please don't go all Pathany and too-Push-tu with me. I've been hearing all about you from Ganesh. And I do so want to know *you*; not Gul Mahommed."

For a moment the frown on the dour hard face, cold and forbidding, deepened.

"*Do*," said the girl with a smile which proved irresistible.

With a laugh, Wendover raised his hand in a salute, took that of the girl, looked her in the eyes, and then glanced at Hazelrigg.

"A low and dirty dog," he said, eyeing Hazelrigg. "Corrupt, cunning and devious by trade."

"No, it's my fault entirely," laughed the girl. "Ganesh is as wax in my hands. Always has been. I made him talk, and I made him tell."

"Well, come along," replied Wendover.

"Everything all right?" asked Hazelrigg.

"So long as we are back here in time for you to get home in daylight. By the way, I've just heard that the neighbourhood of the pontoon bridge across the Battu branch of the Kabul River delta isn't going to be a healthy spot to-night. Safe as Piccadilly this end."

"Tell Granny!" smiled Hazelrigg. "Yes, that's all right, old chap. We are not going round Matta way; and, anyhow, this is a best-behaviour day for my Afridi pals."

"I expect you'd like to see Piccadilly again, one of these days, wouldn't you, Captain Wendover?" said the girl, getting out of the car.

"I? No," was the short reply. "Prefer peace and pure air."

"Snubbed," laughed Charmian Vere-Vaughan.

"Couldn't raise a side-saddle, of course," said Wendover as Shere Khan rode forward leading two horses.

"Never use one," said the girl, throwing off a dust coat and displaying the fact that she was dressed in boots and riding-breeches.

"Good."

"Don't suppose I could ride on one," she added,

measuring the stirrup length by putting the tips of her fingers against the saddle-girth and the stirrup under her arm. "I could do with that a hole longer."

Having adjusted the stirrups Wendover held the slightly restive horse's head while the girl mounted.

"I think you'll find him all right," he said, "as you've no whip or spurs. Doesn't need anything of that sort."

"A soft mouth, eh?" said the girl, noting the snaffle bit.

"Yes. Broke him myself," replied Wendover. "Never had a curb in his life."

"And what about this brute?" asked Hazelrigg, climbing somewhat heavily into the saddle of a raw-boned raking country-bred, rather above the average in height, as its curiously long and puckish ears swivelled round almost completely, as though loosely screwed to its head.

"Kathiawari. Bucks, bolts and bites; rears, plunges and rolls," replied Wendover.

"But doesn't talk," he added with a malicious grin, glancing from Hazelrigg to Charmian.

"Good," smiled Hazelrigg. "Sort of horse I love. Come on, Chatterbox."

And, followed at a couple of horses' length by Shere Khan, and at some ten horses' length by the escort who, as the girl noted, rode in military formation, the party trotted away in the direction of Wendover's temporary camp.

At the early off-saddling and picnic in the shadow of a great rock by a deep *nullah*, the wily Ganesh turned the conversation into the channels in which he wanted it to go; and, after a really admirable meal which offered a choice of *kaibobs*, *pilau*, curried mutton, chicken and variously cooked eggs, followed by peaches, nectarines, a melon, walnuts and *hulwa* sweetmeat, he, under pretence of examining the country with his field-glasses from an eminence at the mouth of the *nullah*, left Wendover and the girl together.

Not a question did she ask, not a pointed comment did she offer; but with the skill and wisdom of an older and more experienced woman, tried to induce Wend-over to talk of his amazing life and extraordinary adventures; while she, in her turn, spoke of all those things that she imagined he must still hold dear; and indirectly and by implication, talked of a fine world ill-lost for love of solitude, a world foolishly forgone for false ideal and quixotic sentiment.

By the time Ganesh returned, though neither knew how it had come about, Charmian Vere-Vaughan was entreating Richard Wendover to resume his proper place, to be what he ought to be, and to do his duty to himself.

"Hullo, here comes dear old Ganesh," she said, breaking off suddenly from deep seriousness, "just when I was thinking of my very first copy-book."

"Oh? What reminded you of that?" asked Wendover.

"Why, licking my pen, protruding my tongue, and inking my fingers, I had to write, Heaven knows how many times:

> "*'To thine own self be true,*
> *And it must follow as the night the day,*
> *Thou can'st not then be false to any man.'*"

"Yes," nodded Wendover. "Noble sentiment. I quite agree. Can'st not be false to any man—alive or dead. Especially dead.

"He having lost his life in the act of saving you," he added.

§4

The cavalcade having returned to where the car, with its armed chauffeur and escort awaited it, Char-mian Vere-Vaughan, taking farewell of Richard Wend-over, endeavoured to extract from him a promise that he would come down to Peshawar and pay a visit to her father, the General, who, she assured him, was not only most anxious to make his acquaintance but was very desirous of a long talk with him concerning Fron-tier affairs.

To this Wendover, smiling, made evasive reply.

Ganesh Hazelrigg, having seen the girl comfortably and warmly wrapped up, against the rapidly falling temperature, turned back to Wendover and, as soon as the latter had finished answering a number of questions put to him by Tommy Dodd, spoke with him aside.

"What I really came up for, Dick. Listen. It's now finally decided that the road shall run through Khairastan. We want you to get the Khan and the *Mullahs* and the leaders of the congregation accustomed to the idea; also the tribesmen generally, throughout the Khanate. You can hint at great favours and blessings to follow; so that when it is publicly announced that the road is coming, it will be to the sound of a great Amen—because lots of rifles and rupees will come with it."

"Bribery and corruption, eh?"

"Yes, and better still, the 'King's Own Khairastan Levies,' or what not. And you can do an invaluable work by making a pick of all the lads-of-the-village who'd like a brand-new rifle, a brand-new uniform, and regular pay. So that when Colonel Ormesby comes along finally with drums and trumpets and a big escort, to talk turkey with the Khan, it will be more or less plain sailing, and we can raise the Regiment straight away. We'll take it that any man on your list is good enough; and we'll make Native Officers of the men you recommend; chaps who've got local influence and personal power, and who'd be the right men in the right place as Subedars and Jemadars. You know the sort of thing I mean? Well, O.K. by you?"

"I'll get down to it," replied Wendover.

"And then, of course, you'll come down to Peshawar and attend a pow-pow with the Political people and all that. Stay with me and put in a bit of civilization, eh?"

"Funny old boy," smiled Wendover.

Nevertheless, ere he said good-bye, Ganesh Hazelrigg gave Richard Wendover the very clearest directions for the finding of a sure haven of refuge, where the two of them could meet in native dress and talk in peace

and privacy—the house of one Rissaldar-Major Moussafa Shah in a by-lane of Peshawar city.

VI

"Yes, Thomas. Astounding, amazing and incredible are the words," agreed Colonel Ormesby, head of the Intelligence Department, as he lit his cheroot. "I frankly admit to being surprised; even I, and I thought that nothing on God's earth, particularly His Indian earth, would ever surprise me again."

He and Thomas Dodd, obscurely prominent member of the Military Intelligence Branch of the Secret Service, sat side by side after dinner in the lamp-lit verandah of the latter's humble little bungalow, unobtrusive, screened and unnoticed in a quiet corner of the Peshawar cantonments.

"Garstan always was an extraordinary bird," he continued. "A damn good fighting soldier. But of all the bull-headed blundering asses! Yes, apart from routine or running a show on active service, if a thing could be done the wrong way, you can rely on Garstan to do it."

"Prehistoric animal," murmured the other man, who spent most of his life in native dress, and who was known as the Great Tommy Dodd to the few people who knew him for the amazing Englishman he was. "You'd have thought even he would have known more about Court-Martial routine than that."

"You would," agreed Colonel Ormesby. "Though, mind you, when the average soldier-man gets on to that line of country he generally lands in a bog. The best of them need a signpost in the shape of a Judge-Advocate. Somebody from the Judge-Advocate General's department to shepherd them along."

"Only natural," observed Tommy Dodd. "After all, they aren't lawyers. Still, the best of them realize the fact and walk warily, knowing that the legal part consists entirely of pit-falls for the layman."

"True, but you'd have thought that even Garstan would have known that a Judge-Advocate must be appointed at a General Court-Martial. Though you can

do without one at a District Court-Martial," agreed
Colonel Ormesby.

"Yes, he really is a Bee of the Effest description.
Fancy not knowing that a District Court-Martial can't
try an officer."

"Yes. Even he should have known that."

"What'll happen?" asked Dodd.

"Of course the whole thing will be quashed, and
Garstan will get a real rough raspberry. But I suppose
they'll have to hold an enquiry since the funny feller
convened a General Court-Martial, which he had power
to do as he was a field-officer and not of the same
Corps as the members of the Court, and could get four
members of the rank of Captain or higher and not of
the same Corps," said Colonel Ormesby.

"Yes, all right so far," he added. "He only fell down
on the trifling fact that he had no jurisdiction whatsoever."

"Never mind. He thoroughly enjoyed himself,"
smiled Tommy Dodd.

"Yes, but what about the poor devil he tried? He
must have enjoyed himself!"

"Damn' disgraceful. But of course he'll get a proper
Court-Martial?"

"Yes, he'll get one all right. His father'll see to that."

"Bit rough on the General."

"Most abominable scandal."

"You don't believe the charge, do you, Sir?"

"Good Lord, no. Of course not . . . Nevertheless,
impossible but true' seems to be the verdict. Of course I
don't believe it—but at first sight it seems to have happened. I suppose that, in the circumstances, there will
have to be a proper General Court-Martial, if only in
young Vere-Vaughan's own interests. There couldn't be
a verdict of *Guilty*? Not from a properly conducted
show? But you can hardly blame Garstan's lot for
bringing it in so. What a Fred Karno's Army of land-
lawyers!" he snorted indignantly.

"Yes, it's a beastly business. Awful for the General.
It's so extraordinarily hard to overtake a lie and stop a
scandal. Unless the thing is properly handled now, it

will stick to Vere-Vaughan as long as he lives. He'll be 'that chap who was found guilty of cowardice and treachery by Court-Martial, and wasn't punished because the thing was quashed on a mere technicality.'"

"Yes. 'Hushed-up' is the word that will be used though."

"Exactly. And they will say it was because his father is a General that it was hushed up. I hope Garstan gets it good and proper, precisely where the chicken got the axe."

"I suppose if Garstan's burlesque had been *pukka*, the sentence would have been carried out?" mused Dodd.

"Some kind of sentence. Not the death sentence, I should think. But quite possibly penal servitude. Certainly dismissal from the Army, at the very least."

"Wonder what the fellow whom they put up to defend him pleaded?" mused Dodd.

"Goodness knows. Extenuating circumstances I should think."

"Trying to save his life, you mean?"

"Yes. Probably pleaded that he hadn't the nerve to shout a warning and take what was coming to him, and that no fair-minded person could blame him. Something of that sort," replied Colonel Ormesby.

"Yes. Yes. I suppose so. And if it had happened like that, it is a line, anyhow."

"I think so. If he pleaded that he knew that the first squeak out of him would be the last, and therefore he didn't squeak, the Court might take the view that he certainly hadn't shown the highest form of self-sacrificing heroism, but on the other hand it wasn't precisely cowardice and it certainly was not treachery.

"No. Can't you imagine Garstan sitting in judgment in a case like this. I don't know who the others were, but if they were men like Garstan they'd be about as fitted to try a case that turned on a point of psychology and temporary nerve-failure and that sort of thing, as a herd of bulls. No, Garstan wouldn't bother about the finer shades of guilt or innocence, error of judgment or failure of nerve. He'd just say, here was a man who got five and twenty of the worst and most competent Border ruffians into this Fort, as his friends, by guaranteeing them; personally vouching for each one; and that he did this knowing that it meant the almost certain capture of the Fort. And all to save his own hide."

"Yes," agreed Colonel Ormesby. "Sounds nasty, put like that, doesn't it? And by Jove, they were the Devil's Own, the absolute pick of the Singing Hadji's worst men, including Chimnai the Outlaw himself, probably the most 'wanted' individual between here and Kabul, next to the Singing Hadji."

"Not only Chimnai the Outlaw, either," observed Tommy Dodd. "There was the Singing Hadji's own son, as well as the notorious Mahazil and Hakim Khan."

"Yes. And Kassim Shah too. Not to mention Ibrahim the Strong, the poisonous Moussa Beg, and Yacoub Ali."

"By Jove, there's one thing about it. However narrow an escape Garstan and his merry men had, it turned out pretty useful in the end."

"It did indeed," agreed Colonel Ormesby. "Quite a case of 'all's well that ends well.' About the biggest haul we've ever made. If only the Singing Hadji of Sufed Kot and the Hadji of Turangzai had been there too, the Border would have been quiet for a generation."

"By Jove," said Tommy Dodd. "It is a pity young Vere-Vaughan couldn't plead that that was the whole idea! Strike an *Alone I did it!* attitude and modestly deny that he deserved the D.S.O., not to mention the Victoria Cross. A great pity."

"As it is, thanks to the bull-headed Garstan, he's in the middle of a most unpleasant stink," observed Colonel Ormesby.

"Yes, and he'll smell for the rest of his days if we're not careful."

"Well then, let's *be* careful," said a voice from behind them.

And as the two men sprang erect in their long legrest chairs and turned to the doorway that led out from the sitting-room to the verandah, they saw a bulky and beaming Pathan whose bearded face smiled kindly upon them.

"Hullo, Ganesh," greeted Tommy Dodd casually.

"I *wish* you wouldn't do that!" expostulated Colonel Ormesby. "Very clever and pat and *à propos*, Hazelrigg, but really . . . You are much too solid to materialize like that just behind one's chair," he grumbled.

"Sorry, Sir," laughed Hazelrigg. "I didn't know with whom Tommy Dodd was plotting. Don't trust him, you know."

"No," agreed Dodd. "Only person you trust is yourself. And then you're generally mistaken."

"And if you want to sit down," he added, "you can damn well squat on the floor. See Mahbub Ali in the back verandah?"

"Yes. Completely took him in, too. Called me a horrid name. New one on me. I must remember it."

"What's the news?" asked Colonel Ormesby.

"Vere-Vaughan's the news, Sir," replied Hazelrigg. "I was coming to see you about him. That blasted fool Garstan . . ."

"Yes, we were just talking about it. Tell us exactly what happened."

"Well, I wasn't there till afterwards, but I can give you a pretty accurate account. Get me a cheroot and a drink, Tommy Dodd," demanded Hazelrigg, "and you lug another chair out, while you're about it. I've had all the floor-squatting I want, lately."

And Ganesh having lit his cheroot and almost emptied his pint tumbler, settled himself in comfort while the others awaited his account of the happenings at Giltraza, an account which they knew would be what he had described as pretty accurate.

"Half a minute, before you begin," said Colonel Ormesby. "I suppose it is true that that ass Garstan convened a District Court-Martial, appointed himself President and tried Vere-Vaughan?"

"Yes. Did the whole thing in style. Got down to it and spread himself, and then sent off duplicate, triplicate and quadruplicate copies of the Proceedings all over the shop. Or at any rate, to Peshawar and 'Pindi, to the Judge-Advocate-General at Delhi, and probably to the Commander-in-Chief, the Viceroy, and all his Council."

"He actually sent a copy here to the General—to the boy's father?"

"Yes. A wonderful bird, our Garstan. You'd have thought he would have been out of harm's way up there. The right man in the right place, wouldn't you?"

"He is too. He *is* the right man in a Border fort really."

"I think on the whole I'd rather be young Vere-Vaughan than he, when Delhi says its say," observed Tommy Dodd.

"Not you, my son. He has landed poor young Vere-Vaughan properly. No doubt he'll be able to clear himself officially, but . . ."

"Quite so. Tell us what happened. Reconstruct the crime."

§2

"Yes. I'll reconstruct the whole business for you," promised Ganesh Hazelrigg.

"In the very small hours of the morning, the sentry over the main gate of Giltraza Fort was suddenly surprised . . ." he began.

"Or awakened," murmured Tommy Dodd.

". . . to hear a hail from the darkness below. He says that he immediately shouted back 'Harlt! *Who com dar?*' which he probably did."

"As he rubbed the sleep from his eyes," whispered Tommy Dodd.

"And the voice from the darkness replied in Hindustani: '*O Siphai! Darwarza kholo!*[79] *British Officer Sahib hai.*'

"This apparently flummoxed and flabbergasted the sentry; for, as he says, he knew that the voice was that of a Sahib and not of a Pathan. So instead of taking a

---

[79] *Open the gate.*

pot shot at the Voice, he shouted, and roused from his slumbers the Havildar of the Guard.

"Extremely annoyed at being awakened from his deep dream of peace, the Havildar came cursing, and when the sentry told him that there was a Voice down there, the Havildar, it seems, replied that he had better damn well shoot it in the neck next time he saw it, and not be such an illegitimate son of a noseless mother and a burnt father; and concluded with a statement that he was perfectly certain that there was no voice there except the Havildar's, and that the sentry would hear it in the Orderly Room and to his disadvantage, in the morning.

"Whereupon the Voice immediately arose from the black darkness below bawling to them to hasten.

"'*Jaldi! Jaldi!*' it cried. '*Darwaza kholo! Main British Officer Sahib hoon. Hum ander ana mangta. Kholo! Jaldi!*[80] Damn and blast your eyes . . .'

"'That's a Sahib all-right,' observed the Havildar. 'By what he says and the way he says it. Who but a Sahib would want the Fort gates opened in the middle of the night? And in a hurry too. And it's a Sahib's voice. What shall we do?'

"Whereupon the sentry, according to his own account, very sensibly suggested that the Havildar of the Guard should consult his Officer on the subject of correct procedure when a British Officer knocks up a Fort in the middle of the night.

"This did not immediately commend itself to the Havildar who began to parley with the Voice, asking who it was, whence it came and what it wanted, only to receive very urgent and stringent instructions to shift like Hell and get someone to open the gate.

"Anyhow, by this time the Sergeant decided that he had better 'pass the buck,' and it seems to have gone from Havildar to Jemadar and from Jemadar to Subedar and from Subedar to Subedar-Major until a British Officer came to see what the row was all about, and soon settled the matter.

"It was MacIntyre, who's not a very bright lad.

---

[80] "*Quick! . . . I want to come in. Open!*"

Sound, sober, and serious, but much too cautious. Sort of chap who'll hardly make a move for fear of making a mistake.

"'Hullo,' he called down. 'Who's there?'

"'Vere-Vaughan.'

"'Voice from the grave. Vere-Vaughan's dead. Try again,' jeered MacIntyre, too wise and knowing a bird to be had like that.

"'I am Vere-Vaughan, I tell you. I've been a prisoner. I wasn't killed when we crashed. I was taken prisoner.'

"'Who by?'

"'The Singing Hadji of Sufed Kot.'

"'And he let you go?'

"'I've escaped. There's a party of us, and we've got to get in at once. We've been chased the whole time, and they can't be far behind.'

"'How many of you?'

"'Twenty-three. I say, for God's sake buck up and let us in, or we shall be scuppered yet. They may be close enough to hear.'

"But MacIntyre, as I've said, is of the real old dour and carefu' breed, ye ken. Goes slow, mak's sikkar, ca's canny, looks before he loups—and then doesn't.

"'If you're Flying Officer Vere-Vaughan, who was your pilot?' quoth he.

"'Lucke.'

"'How many machines in the flight?'

"'Six.'

"'What were the names of the other pilots?'

"'Gordon-Johnson, Hewitt, Wilbur-Miller, Featherstone, Cresset.'

"'What's your father's christian name, profession and rank, if any?'

"'Oh Lord, how much more? General Sir Archibald Vere-Vaughan.'

"'Got any brothers or sisters?'

"'Sister. Charmian.'

"'Who commands this Fort?'

"'Colonel Garstan.'

"'What do they ca' him?'

"'Gog.'

"'God? Wrong.'

"'Gog, I said. And so they do.'

"'Eh! Mind he doesna hear ye. What do they call his dog?'

"'Magog. For the Lord's sake open the gate and let us in.'

"'Aye, aye. All in good time. How many do ye say ye've got wi' ye?'

"'Twenty-three. And they've saved my life at the risk of their own.'

"'Aye? Twenty-three. All Pathans?'

"'Yes.'

"'H'm. Are you in uniform?'

"'No, I'm not.'

"'In Pathan kit, eh? Why?'

"'Oh, for God's sake! You don't suppose I was going to run about these hills in uniform, do you? Simply asking to be captured again, or shot up? Look here, can't you show a light or something and have a look at me?'

"'And give you a chance to have a shot at me, eh?'

"'We could have fired a volley up at where you are standing long ago, if we had wanted to do that.'

"'Think of that now! Bide ye there a minute, and don't so much as scratch your head for I've trained a machine-gun on ye.'

"Thus the good MacIntyre—or words to that effect.

"Anyway, taking it by and large, and adding up the probabilities and giving due weight to the fact that the Voice had answered all questions correctly, MacIntyre thought it was good enough to risk knocking-up Garstan, who simply hates being knocked-up at three o'clock in the morning.

"One can imagine him going to Garstan's quarters, tapping at the door, being asked who the Hell he was, and what the Hell he was making that row for, and what the Hell he wanted; informing Garstan that there was a British Officer outside, and being told that the British Officer could sanguinarily well stay outside— while Garstan snuggled down to sleep again.

"But the tenacious MacIntyre must have stuck to

his point, and at the risk of his life, fetched Garstan up from the depths again, to tell him that apparently, so far as he could make out, it really was the supposedly dead airman, Flying-Officer Vere-Vaughan, the son of General Sir Archibald Vere-Vaughan; that he had been captured by the Singing Hadji of Sufed Kot, and had escaped with a faithful band of rescuers; had been pursued for days, and was in imminent danger of being recaptured under the very walls of Giltraza Fort.

"Doubtless the magic names of General Sir Archibald Vere-Vaughan and the Singing Hadji of Sufed Kot brought him from his bed like the sound of the horn of—the Archangel Gabriel.

"Anyhow, Garstan, probably calling MacIntyre and Vere-Vaughan and the Singing Hadji peculiar names, pulled a British Warm over his pyjamas and went down to open the front door.

"Of course he parleyed with Vere-Vaughan, asked him a few questions that pretty well established his identity; and, being satisfied that he wasn't dreaming dreams and that there were no visions about, admitted Vere-Vaughan and his rescuers—for whom, individually, Vere-Vaughan vouched, giving Garstan his word that he knew each one of them personally, and guaranteeing him as a friend of the English, only too anxious to get out of the reach of the Singing Hadji and only too thankful to be in the safety of Giltraza Fort.

"As Vere-Vaughan pointed out to Garstan, it would be a pretty ghastly thing to leave the good fellows outside to be scuppered at dawn by the *lashkar* of the Singing Hadji's men who had been pursuing them, and from whom they had only escaped by clever rear-guard tactics by day, and dangerous and difficult cross-country travelling by night.

"According to Vere-Vaughan, they were all dead-beat, hungry, thirsty, foot-sore, weary and worn-out.

"Well, anyway, Garstan was persuaded to let the whole party in, gave orders for them to be fed and dossed down, and took Vere-Vaughan along to his quarters for a drink and a feed while a bed was knocked up for him.

"What had given Garstan pause, of course, was the fact that they were a scarecrow-looking band of scallywags, and Vere-Vaughan as bad as the rest of them, in dirty Pathan kit, unshaven and unshorn.

"Of course, in spite of this, he was obviously an Englishman, and quite able to convince Garstan that he was whom he professed to be.

"And then, unfortunately for poor Vere-Vaughan, two things happened almost simultaneously and rather dramatically—two things that, taken together, suddenly turned Garstan from the bluff and hospitable host and sympathizer into an outraged and ferociously indignant accuser and captor.

"For just as Vere-Vaughan had produced from the lining of his Pathan *kullah* cap, about which his *puggri* was bound, a little piece of paper, and handed it to Garstan, there came a knock at the door, and in came MacIntyre who, with a curious and incredulous stare at Vere-Vaughan, more or less whispered in Garstan's ear something that caused that bull-dog jaw to drop yet lower and those prominent eyes to bulge yet more. For they were already doing it—and for damn' good reason, as I'll tell you.

"'*What?*' said he. '*What? Chimnai the Outlaw? And the Singing Hadji's son?* My God! Then this letter is genuine—and this fellow is a fraud—or a traitor! *Chimnai* himself?'

"'Yes,' said MacIntyre, 'and One-eyed Kassim Shah, Hakim Khan, Moussa Beg, Ibrahim the Strong, Mahazil, Yacoub Ali, Wali Dad *and* Khoda Khan Abazai, according to Usman Shah.'

"And here was an example of a bit of the Standing Luck of the British Army," observed Hazelrigg, "for Usman Shah, who was Garstan's orderly and white-headed boy and, in point of fact, an extremely smart chap, had been bred and born in the Sufed Kot country. Also, before, for excellent reasons, he had skipped over the Border and enlisted in Garstan's regiment, he had been an outlaw and raider himself, and had known all about everything and everybody in that part of the world. And by the mercy and grace of

God he had been on duty that night and had seen Vere-Vaughan's 'rescue-party' file in and get the once-over from Garstan, MacIntyre and the rest.

"And who should the good Usman Shah immediately recognize but his old pal and former comrade, one Khoda Khan Abazai, deserter from Sandeman's Rifles with whom Usman Shah's battalion had been brigaded at Quetta or 'Pindi or somewhere.

"Anyway, Usman Shah recognized Khoda Khan Abazai; and, of course, being a brother Pathan and fellow riever and raider under his skin, or his uniform, he didn't give him away. Not immediately. Thought he'd say 'How's tricks?' later on, and have a *bukh* with him about the old folk at home in Sufed Kot.

"And then glancing around, the on-the-spot Usman Shah, bright and observant, noted a one-eyed gent, and without change of countenance or turning a hair, recognized his old pal, the far-famed fire-brand, One-Eyed Kassim Shah.

"Yes, surely that blackguardly hang-dog countenance could belong to nobody else? And, by the Beard of the Prophet, who was that beside him but Ibrahim the Strong? There could be no other, surely—of that bulk. And, merciful Allah, who was that coyly lurking behind the big man, if it wasn't the great Chimnai the Outlaw himself!

"And then Usman Shah really stood up and took notice; and as each face came into the light of the guard-lantern, he fairly studied it.

"By the time he had seen the whole twenty-three he was sure, beyond peradventure of a doubt, that here was a most lovely *banao*, with the great Chimnai the Outlaw in the middle of it, and, doubtless, running it.

"For there, before his very eyes were not only Chimnai the Outlaw and One-eyed Kassim Shah, but Mirza Khan Iskander Khan Juma, beloved son and heir of the Singing Hadji himself; not to mention Ibrahim the Strong; Hakim Khan; Moussa Beg; Mahazil; Yacoub Ali; Wali Dad; Khoda Khan Abazai, the man whom many a time and oft he had seen in British khaki in the bazaars of Quetta, Peshawar and 'Pindi; and nearly a score more of the most notorious brigands of the Border country.

"How Usman Shah must have chuckled to himself; first, in admiration of the marvellously clever trick whereby Chimnai had got this big band of braves inside Giltraza Fort; secondly, at the really amusing kismet whereby Usman Shah should have been, not only in the Fort, but on duty that night; thirdly, that Khoda Khan Abazai should have been with the band, and fourthly, that Usman Shah should not only have been in Giltraza Fort and on duty that night, but should have seen and recognized Khoda Khan Abazai in time.

"For if he hadn't recognized Khoda Khan, he would probably not have recognized anybody else, being bored, sleepy, and not particularly interested.

"Yes, very amusing; for, by daylight it would have been too late. Those twenty-three *budmashes*—each notably resolute and resourceful even among notoriously resolute and resourceful fighting-men—would have made their hay before the sun shone. Twenty-three of them loose inside the Fort—and all but the guard sleeping!

"Clever. Really clever. And almost a pity to spoil it.

"And now he must do some quick thinking, and then act promptly.

"Go straight to the Colonel Sahib? No. Better not. The Subedar-Major? No. The wily old devil would take the credit himself . . . The best plan would be to tell MacIntyre Sahib. Yes, that would be it. Tell MacIntyre Sahib and ask him to take him with him to the Colonel Sahib, and he'd tell the Colonel Sahib the names of almost every one of them.

"Well! If Chimnai the Outlaw survived this (which wasn't likely) his fame would be illuminated with a blaze of glory that would dazzle all men. The sound of his name would be heard from the Border far across Hindustan, Afghanistan and the lands beyond.

"Wonderful Chimnai the Outlaw to get himself and a picked band into Giltraza Fort! Unlucky Chimnai the Outlaw to have run into *the one man there* who could give the show away! Unfortunate Singing Hadji of Sufed Kot, who had so nearly captured Giltraza Fort before, when it was in the act of being surrendered; and who had so nearly got it again now, when it was in the act of being seized!

"Well, well! A sad pity. But a man must look after himself; and Usman Shah would certainly do much better out of this by saving the situation and being the hero of the occasion. For the British could, and would, reward him much better than the Singing Hadji of Sufed Kot ever would. Moreover, the British kept their promises. They were bound to win in the long run, and the Singing Hadji had had a pretty long run already.

"Besides, Usman Shah liked the Colonel Sahib who although *takrari*[81] and *zubberdusti*,[82] was a good fighting man and could laugh and joke with a fellow.

"So off went Usman Shah to MacIntyre and told him the tale.

"Try to imagine the mysterious mien and portentous pompousness of the good Usman Shah as he unfolded the plot to the dour, sceptical, and over-cautious MacIntyre.

"Here was the great Chimnai the Outlaw, legendary figure of fame on the Border, locally a compound of Robert Bruce, William Wallace and Hereward the Wake; the greatest thorn in the British flesh; who was constantly bringing-off coups of which the success was due solely to his amazing courage, resource, daring, and determination.

"Here he was, inside Giltraza Fort with seven devils each worse than the other. Seven and thrice seven.

"And the incredible thing was that they had been brought into the place by a British Officer, or by a European masquerading as a British Officer. Moreover this man, whoever he was, had personally vouched for the raiders; had sworn that he knew every one of them himself; and that they were good men, friends of the British and, in the present venture, were risking their lives to save a British Officer from captivity and death.

---

[81] *Difficult, quarrelsome.*
[82] *Violent.*

Further, that they were in the gravest danger, having been pursued night and day by a horde of the Singing Hadji's men; *and the Singing Hadji's own son and heir was one of the gang for whom this alleged British Officer had vouched; the Singing Hadji's son Mirza Khan Iskander Khan Juma, bitterest of England's bitter enemies!*

"Imagine the state of mind of the excellent MacIntyre.

"He knew that Usman Shah himself, albeit now a British sepoy, was no virtuous innocent of blameless life, and no ordinary village yokel either; but a man with a well-known and not unadmired record as a riever, raider, and outlaw himself, before he skipped across to the British side of the Border. Yes, his was quite a case of—

> "'*Last night ye had struck at a Border thief—tonight 'tis a man of the Guides!*'

"Now, was Usman Shah making, as a native loves to do, a mountain out of a mole-hill—in the hope of getting credit out of it, somehow? pondered MacIntyre.

"Was it an absolute *banao*[83] and leg-pull, a thing of which Usman Shah would be quite capable? Was it a shot-in-the-dark fired by reason of vague suspicions that he had seen one of these fellows before; just a hundred-to-one bet on a rank outsider, on the chance of its coming in? No harm done if the horse was a non-starter; and a magnificent scoop if it won.

"Or was the whole thing absolute fact, and Usman Shah speaking the plain ghastly truth—that a large band of the biggest desperados on the Border was at this moment in Giltraza Fort? Aye—and might be acting while he was scratching his head!

"Well, it was up to the Colonel.

"And wouldn't Lieutenant MacIntyre hear something to his disadvantage if he lugged the Colonel out of bed again, and on a wild-goose chase! He wasn't apt to mince matters if he thought he had been fooled.

---

[83] *Frame-up, plot.*

But, damn it all, what was that, compared with the risk of the fort being captured? Besides, he might not have gone back to bed yet. He had not, in point of fact.

"Of course, the band had been made to give up their rifles, in spite of Vere-Vaughan vouching for them; but that wouldn't worry them. It wouldn't take a gang, led by Chimnai, long to get them again. Trust the wily Pathan to bring off a trick like that. They'd all lie down, go peacefully to sleep, snore loudly, and in about a couple of hours' time, open one eye. Then, silent as ghosts, they'd arise and get the unsuspecting sentries, one by one; and they'd never know what got them.

"Yes, if he took no notice of Usman Shah's tale, and lay down for forty winks, he'd probably never wake again, or wake to find a Pathan hand over his mouth and a Khyber knife half-way through his neck.

"No. There was no doubt about it that, if this were a ruse and he did nothing, the Fort would be captured, the gates would be opened, and the alleged 'pursuers' would also be inside, long before dawn.

"Probably they were all round the Fort, waiting for a rifle-shot to tell them that the gates had been opened, and that all they had to do was to rush in.

"Why, even if things went wrong with Chimnai's plan and he didn't scupper the sentries, get the rifles, butcher the Officers in their beds, and slaughter the unarmed sepoys, it would be an absolute hell of a business for the garrison to have a fight going on inside the Fort while it was being assaulted from the outside. Of course, the first thing that Chimnai would do would be to open the gates the moment the sentries and guard had been done-in.

"And so the cautious man decided that it was his duty to run the risk of making a damn fool of himself, and getting the rough side of Garstan's tongue.

"So having given orders for the extremest care to be taken of the honoured guests—by a guard with loaded rifles, charged magazines and fixed bayonets—off went MacIntyre to that stout warrior and whispered the tale in his ear."

"And what was Garstan doing at the moment that MacIntyre came and reported what Usman Shah told him?

"He was in the very act of reading the little piece of paper that Vere-Vaughan had just produced from the lining of his Pathan *kullah* cap, the little piece of paper with a message on it, written in Russian. And that message as I have said, was already making Garstan's bull-dog jaw drop and his prominent blue eyes bulge. Not a doubt of it.

"Garstan listened to MacIntyre and then pulled himself together, and became his cool phlegmatic self once more, as the dropped jaw closed again and his mouth set hard as usual.

"'You don't read Russian, do you?' he asked MacIntyre.

"'No, Sir.'

"'Nor presumably do you, Mr. Whoever-you-are,' he said, turning his menacing glare on Vere-Vaughan.

"'No, Sir,' replied Vere-Vaughan. 'I don't.'

"'Huh! I imagine not!' was the reply. 'Well, I do. And I'll tell you what it says here.

"'*To O.C. Giltraza Fort.*

"'*Arrest bearer, Flying-Officer John Vere-Vaughan immediately. Under pressure he has given great help and invaluable information to Singing Hadji of Sufed Kot. I have rescued him and am sending him to you with my men—reliable and trustworthy. Please reward them and keep them in Fort till I come.*
                    "*B. Hazelrigg. (G.5. H.8.)*'

"It was Vere-Vaughan's turn to stare open-mouthed.

"'But . . .but . . . There must be some mistake, Sir. Major Hazelrigg wouldn't write that. He helped me to escape.'

"'I'm sure he did. Succeeded, too. Got you into the best place for you, moreover. Very clever. Cleverest man in the Intelligence. Heard of some of his coups before . . . Well, we've got you all right . . . Now then, what became of the other men—those that Major Hazelrigg must have sent you off with—his own men, our agents?'

"Why, I . . . I . . . I brought them in here, Sir. They are here in the Fort.'

"'Oh, are they? Well, my information is that they are not. The information I have just received from Mr. Mac-Intyre is that you've brought into this Fort *on your personal word and absolute guarantee*, a collection of the biggest scoundrels, outlaws, agitators, terrorists, and most dangerous enemies we've got.'

"'You are looking after them, I suppose?' he inter-rupted himself, turning to MacIntyre.

"Yes, Sir. I thought I had better speak to you before putting them under arrest; but I turned out the guard and told the Havildar to see they keep as they are, lying down, where they are, until I came back.'

"Colonel Garstan stared at the paper in front of him, and then at Vere-Vaughan.

"'Anything to say before I put you under arrest?' he asked.

"But I . . . I . . . I don't understand, Sir. Major Hazelrigg, disguised as a Pathan, came into the cell where I was imprisoned and said that these people were all right, and that they'd get me to Giltraza Fort, and that he'd give me a note to you, which he would write in Russian, in case anything happened and it went astray.'

"'Quite so,' smiled Colonel Garstan unpleasantly.

"He said he had got a most important message for you about the Hadji of Turangzai and the Singing Hadji of Sufed Kot, and that he'd let you know that my escort were good fellows who—though doubtless with some hope of reward—would see me safe here. I promised one of them a thousand rupees and . . .'

"'And all the rest of it,' interrupted Colonel Garstan. 'And you actually mean to tell me that Major Hazelrigg who has spent most of his service on the Border here, disguised as a Pathan, didn't recognize the infamous Chimnai, the man he has been after for months? Why,

I know for a fact that he saw him in Peshawar and very nearly got him. One of Chimnai's narrowest escapes. Do you mean to say he doesn't know One-eyed Kassim Shah, Hakim Khan, Moussa Beg, Ibrahim the Strong, Mahazil, and all the rest of them?'

"Vere-Vaughan stared in amazement.

"'Do you mean to tell me that he doesn't know the Singing Hadji's own son—Mirza Khan Iskander Khan Juma? Why, bless my soul, Major Hazelrigg lived in the Singing Hadji's camp.

"'Like Alfred the Great among the Danes,' he illustrated brilliantly. 'Lived in his camp and was actually sent by the Singing Hadji into this very Fort as an envoy, and got Captain Wendover in here with him.'

"John Vere-Vaughan, almost worn out; weary in mind, body and soul; stared stupidly, amazed and incredulous, frowning in hopeless perplexity.

"'Of course he knew them all,' continued Garstan, 'And I haven't the slightest doubt that he was in Sufed Kot simply because Chimnai and his gang had taken refuge there. Followed them there from the Hadji of Turangzai's place. Well, once again, have you anything to say before I put you under arrest?'

"'I can only say, Sir, that I cannot understand what has happened. I can't tell . . .'

"'I can, though. I can tell you exactly what happened. You got away from Sufed Kot with Major Hazelrigg's help *and* with some of our people, his agents. You got away all right—but you were followed, and the whole of your lot were scuppered, all except you, by Chimnai and the rest. And they gave you the choice of having your throat cut or coming along here with them. Isn't that it? Something of that sort?'

"'No, Sir. Absolutely nothing of the sort, I swear.'

"'Well, you can do that before a Court-Martial. Here's Major Hazelrigg's message—which you brought me yourself and which you admit that he gave to you—written in Russian so that you couldn't read it, requesting that you be arrested at once. And so you will be. You'll have every opportunity of explaining how it is that you left Sufed Kot in charge of Major Hazelrigg's

men and turned up here with a big band of the most
desperate and dangerous ruffians on the whole Border,
under the leadership of the most notorious fire-brand
in the country.'

"Colonel Garstan rose to his feet.

"Well, you are under arrest. I'll see to you when I
come back. I'm now going to hand-cuff your friends—
whom you guaranteed and brought in here with their
rifles loaded. Before I do so, are you disposed to—er—
give me any help?'

"'I'll give you every possible help I can, Sir. Why
shouldn't I? I can't understand . . . I . . . What can I
do?'

"What can you do? Identify each one of these men
you brought in. Confirm what my orderly, Usman Shah
—who knows every one of them personally—has told
Mr. MacIntyre. Point out Chimnai and the Singing
Hadji's son, and Hakim Khan, Moussa Beg and
Mahazil and Wali Dad and Khoda Khan Abazai. Ibrahim the Strong and One-Eyed Kassim Shah won't need
any identification.

"But I don't know them, Sir. I only know—er—Wali
Dad, who was the leader of the people who originally
captured me; and Khoda Khan Abazai who admits to
being a deserter from Sandeman's Rifles. I never knew
the records of the others at all. Wali Dad and Khoda
Khan said they'd try to rescue me, in return for a
reward; and I think they hoped to get some ransom
money, though I assured them they would not. And the
whole lot swore on the Koran that they were speaking
the truth, and were going to rescue me; and then Major
Hazelrigg came to me and assured me I could trust
them all, and that, provided we weren't captured on
the way, they'd get me safely here.'

"'Indeed?' sneered Colonel Garstan. 'And can you
tell me why Major Hazelrigg wrote this message directing your immediate arrest?'

"'No, Sir. I can't understand it. I only know that he
wrote it and that he told me I should be safe with the
rescue party.'

"'I've no doubt he did. Not the slightest. And still

less do I doubt that your party was overtaken and captured, and the whole lot of them killed. And I haven't the slightest doubt that you were given the choice of being taken back to Sufed Kot for the Singing Hadji to deal with, or being brought to Giltraza Fort for them to deal with—under the walls—unless you guaranteed them at the gate. You knew perfectly well that your life hung by a thread outside there, and that if you said the wrong thing they'd shoot. Shoot you first, and MacIntyre and me next. Didn t you?'

"'Absolutely nothing of the sort, Sir. The party that came in here with me is the party that left Sufed Kot with me.'

"'Indeed! Is that so, now? Then why are they the very pick of the Border firebrands and the enemies of the Sirkar? And once again, can you explain why Major Hazelrigg writes here that you are immediately to be arrested, as soon as his people have got you here?'

"'No, Sir. I can't.'

"'No. I'm sure you can't,' was the reply.

"And the stout Garstan with his one-way mind, his forthright simple and honest stupidity, stood for a moment staring at Vere-Vaughan in deep thought, an unwonted exercise for the good fellow.

"'What puzzles me,' said he—and the whole thing puzzled him pretty nearly to death—'is why you didn't give the show away (their show, of course I mean) directly you were in this room, in safety.'

"Poor young Vere-Vaughan's face lit up.

"'But of course, Sir! If I had thought my only way of getting safe in here was to come in with these men, and I had done such a cowardly, foul, fool thing, shouldn't I round on them the moment I was safe from them?'

"'Aye,' murmured MacIntyre, nodding his wise head.

"'Well you didn't, anyway,' snapped Garstan.

"'Oh God,' protested Vere-Vaughan. 'Of course I didn't! Because I never was in any danger from them. I tell you, Sir, they are my friends. They have helped me to escape. We have had a running fight more or less the whole way, three parts of them doing rear-guard action while I pushed on with the others.'

"'Look here, Vere-Vaughan,' replied Garstan. 'Here's the test. Do you give me your word of honour, as an officer and a gentleman, that you know each one of these men to be what he says he is, and to be what he pretends to be—an enemy of the Singing Hadji of Sufed Kot and a friend of the Sirkar? Do you guarantee that they are all escaping from Sufed Kot and genuinely taking refuge in this Fort? And with no other object or hope but to get safe across the Border before the Singing Hadji catches them?'

"'*Yes, Sir, I do*,' replied Vere-Vaughan immediately. 'I guarantee that Wali Dad, the leader, comes from Kurnai; that he was the leader of the men who caught me when the plane crashed; saved me then, as long ago as that, from being killed by the followers of the *Mullah* of Kurnai; and took me to the *Malik*. In the end, the *Mullah* of Kurnai would have got me, and handed me over to the Singing Hadji; but Wali Dad was in charge of me, and more or less prevented me from being put to death, protected me, both on the way and at Kurnai.

"Then, while I was in Kurnai, expecting to be handed over, for the Hadji to cut my throat at any moment, Wali Dad brought another man with him, Khoda Khan Abazai, when he brought my food one night. This man admitted that he was an unwilling deserter from the Indian Army, and wanted to go back and asked if I would do my best for him if he helped me to escape. Of course I said I would, and bargained with him. Then, as he very reasonably pointed out, it would be quite hopeless for one or two of us to try to get out of Kurnai and the Sufed Kot country and safely here. There would have to be a big enough party to fight, not only if pursued by the Hadji, but attacked by outlaws, bandits, raiders and robber bands; and he and Wali Dad got to work and no doubt promised all sorts of things to friends of theirs whom they knew could be induced to come in with them. They all wanted me to promise something, but I took the line that this man, Khoda Khan, was my agent, so to speak, in the matter, and they must deal with him. I've no doubt he bribed them with all sorts of promises, and encouraged the belief that there would be a big ransom to divide.'

"'And you mean to tell me that you believed all this?' asked Colonel Garstan.

"'I'm telling you everything exactly as it happened, Sir,' replied Vere-Vaughan. 'I hadn't implicit faith in any of them—unless it were Khoda Khan who had been a sepoy and seemed a good chap, and in Wali Dad—until I found that every one of them was willing to take the most solemn oath, with the Koran in his hand, that they would get me safely here. Each one of them was brought to my prison at night, by Khoda Khan, and willingly took the oath on the Koran. Then I did believe that, whatever sort of people they were, they'd keep that oath, and that for their own reasons, they intended to get away from Kurnai to Giltraza and to get me away with them—doubtless in the hope of substantial reward.'

"'You believed that, eh, and expect me to believe you?'

"'I did believe it was all right, Sir; and just before I got away I was quite sure it was.'

"'Why?'

"'Because Major Hazelrigg himself guaranteed the men; and told me that, with any luck, I should reach Giltraza Fort safely; and that I was to tell you that he was in the Sufed Kot country, and give you a message.'

"'And what does the message prove to be? That you are to be arrested on sight for a traitor who has been giving help and information to the King's enemies,' interrupted Garstan.

"'I can't understand it, Sir.'

"'No, I'm sure you can't, and we won't go round that circle again. Now then—last chance to do yourself any good, Vere-Vaughan. With Mr. MacIntyre as witness, I ask you again if you will admit that you know who these men are and will help to identify them. At present I've nothing but the word of my orderly.'

577

"'Exactly, Sir,' cried Vere-Vaughan. 'If it is my Word against your orderly's and . . .'

"'*And* Major Hazelrigg's,' interrupted Garstan, pointing to the paper that lay before him, 'Major Hazelrigg's secret message, written in Russian with the perfectly obvious intention of denouncing you. No, it won't do, Vere-Vaughan. All right then—I arrest you in accordance with Major Hazelrigg's written request and the evidence of a witness who knows the men you've brought into the Fort. The prisoner is in your charge, Mr. MacIntyre, until I return.'

"And then Garstan, who is a man of action—and no better man alive when that sort of action is needed—promptly got down to it with the outlaws. And one has to admit that Usman Shah was able to clear away any lingering doubt that might have remained in what we must call Garstan's mind.

"The Colonel made his little arrangements and told Usman Shah what to do.

"From the door of a disused store-room that happened to be empty and that had been allotted to Vere-Vaughan's friends, Usman Shah suddenly whispered '*Chimnai!*' And Chimnai, doubtless thinking it was one of the band, promptly answered, 'What's up? Who is it?'

"It's I, Usman Shah. Don't you remember me, Chimnai? I recognized you, at once. What do I get if I don't betray you, Chimnai? What do I get if I help you?'

"One imagines the feelings of the unfortunate Chimnai, trapped in the middle of Giltraza Fort—or, rather, in grievous danger of being trapped unless he could deal promptly and effectively with this Usman Shah. If only he could get his hands on the fellow's throat, or better still, the hands of Ibrahim the Strong!

"'Come in here,' whispered Chimnai.

"'No fear,' replied Usman Shah. 'Not I. You come out here, Chimnai, if you want to talk business.'

"And out crept Chimnai, to find a powerful electric torch turned on him, and to see Colonel Garstan, revolver in hand, and a business-like firing-squad standing at the ready.

"'Hands up, Chimnai! *Quick!*' ordered Garstan, raising his revolver. Chimnai who had escaped out of that sort of fix before, put them up, and was promptly seized by half a dozen hearties who had been waiting on either side of the doorway.

"Of course that again was good enough for Garstan. Obviously this was the great Chimnai the Outlaw himself, self-declared; nor was there any doubt in the Colonel's mind as to all the others being who and what Usman Shah said they were.

"Although he had taken full precautions to deal with a sudden rush, he hoped there would not be one, for he naturally wanted to get this lot alive, every one of them. For it would be the coup of a life-time, the biggest haul ever made on the Border. Not just a notorious leader and his band, but a collection of such leaders.

"After waiting a few minutes, a score of loaded rifles pointing at the doorway, Garstan told Chimnai to call to Mahazil and tell him to come out. And on Chimnai's taking no notice of the order, he promised him faithfully, on his word of honour as an officer and a gentleman, that he'd hang him at dawn—and more than hinted at the sort of hanging that is particularly unattractive to a good Mussulman.

"Chimnai, knowing his Garstan of old, called Mahazil, and, answering to the name of Mahazil, a man came out, and was promptly seized.

"Yes, Usman Shah had not been mistaken.

"'Now tell Mirza Khan Iskander Khan Juma, son of the Singing Hadji of Sufed Kot, to come out,' said Garstan, 'and just mention that if there's a rush, there will be a volley—from twenty rifles. And that the survivors, if any, will be hanged in about an hour's time. And you with 'em.'

"Chimnai, as would any Pathan have done in like circumstances, did his best to save his own hide. And in about five minutes from leaving his quarters, Garstan had got the lot of them trussed up.

"He then made Chimnai, who seemed to have quite a good grasp of the principles of turning King's Evidence, name each one of them; and, sure enough, the name he gave to each, corresponded with that already given by Usman Shah.

"Well, there it was, and Garstan being Garstan, what followed was inevitable.

"I suppose, knowing the man, one can hardly blame him. For what with the fact that he had caught a large party of the biggest firebrands of the Frontier, inside his Fort, and Hazelrigg's urgent request that he should arrest Vere-Vaughan, there was nothing else for it. Of course he must arrest Vere-Vaughan. It was as imperative that he should do it as that he should arrest the Border outlaws whom Vere-Vaughan had brought into the place.

"And, mind you, a more intelligent man than Garstan would have been puzzled; and Garstan's is the type of mind very much open to occupation by the *idée fixe*.

"Vere-Vaughan had brought the order for his own arrest, argued Garstan, an order written in Russian so that Vere-Vaughan couldn't read it—a very neat catch-out—and he had brought these scoundrels too. Of course Vere-Vaughan knew them, and knew what he was doing. Obviously he did. It would have been a funny enough business without Hazelrigg's message, and nothing could have saved the Fort and the lives of everybody in it, if it hadn't happened that Usman Shah was on duty, and had recognized the deserter from Sandeman's Rifles.

"And as it went round and round in Garstan's mind like a squirrel in a cage, the conclusions to which he had jumped while talking to Vere-Vaughan became more and more certain, the explanation more and more inevitable, until the big idea became the *idée fixe* and it was unshakably established in his mind that Vere-Vaughan, caught out by Major Hazelrigg, had nearly spoilt the show by arriving with a different party. Doubtless Hazelrigg had heard that Vere-Vaughan was in the Singing Hadji's hands; had gone there in disguise to see what could be done about it; and had found that Vere-Vaughan, to save his wretched life, had turned traitor. And Hazelrigg, with the help of his spies and agents, had got Vere-Vaughan out of Kurnai, and sent him off with the message. And the party had, as Vere-Vaughan himself admitted, been pursued. Also it had been overtaken and caught.

"And though Vere-Vaughan would not admit the fact, it had been destroyed; wiped out, to a man. And to save his own life, Vere-Vaughan had done as his captors told him. They had brought him to the gates of Giltraza Fort and there, with the point of a knife against his liver, he had guaranteed them as friends.

"But why? Why, in Heaven's name, when he was safe, hadn't he immediately told the whole truth?

"Presumably because he was ashamed of the part that he had played. Of course that was it. He hadn't the guts to own that he hadn't had the guts to yell to MacIntyre;

"'*It's Vere-Vaughan, and I'm with a gang of the Singing Hadji's biggest blackguards. Open fire at once. Don't mind me.*' Something of that sort. If he had shouted in English, they wouldn't have known what he was saying.

"Yes, they would though. Apparently that deserter fellow understood English. Still, the right sort of man would have done it, nevertheless.

"But wait a minute. Wouldn't it have been better to have got them all safe inside the gates, and then said:

"'*There you are, Sir. The pick of the prize fire-brands of the North-West Frontier. Arrest them—quick?*'

"No, of course it wouldn't. Over a score of them. With loaded rifles. With the gates open. No, that wouldn't have done. That would simply have been admitting armed enemies.

"No, the other would have been the right thing. But then they'd all have escaped in the dark, if he had simply shouted the truth.

"Oh, Hell, what a brain-addling puzzle.

"Anyway, Garstan hadn't got to solve it, thank goodness. A Court-Martial would do that. That would be the thing of course. Thrash it out before a Court-Martial, and let Vere-Vaughan show good reason—if he could—why, once he was safe and sound and out of reach of the gang, he didn't immediately say what had happened."

§3

"Look here, my dear Ganesh. I wouldn't interrupt you for worlds," interrupted Colonel Ormesby, "but, really, I can't sit on it any longer. *Did* you hear that Vere-Vaughan was in the Singing Hadji's hands? *Did* you go and rescue him? And *did* you give him that message, in Russian, for Colonel Garstan?"

"I did none of these things," was the reply.

"Then who the devil was it?"

"That's what I want to know; and intend to find out."

"And how is it you've come to learn all this?"

"Because by the best of good luck and the worst of bad luck, I barged into Giltraza Fort just too late, the day after Garstan had sent off the *budmash* gang under heavy escort; and young Vere-Vaughan as well. It was the greatest good luck that I went there then, and learned everything there was to learn from Garstan, MacIntyre, Usman Shah, the Havildar, the guard, the sentries, the arrest-party and everybody else who had the slightest knowledge of the least thing that occurred that night. And, of course, I talked it all out with the members of the alleged Court-Martial, though they couldn't shed any fresh light. They could only tell me what the witnesses had told them; and I had myself just heard it all.

"What I got from the members of the Court-Martial was a side-light on Vere-Vaughan—Vere-Vaughan's attitude and account of it all. And that gave me some ideas."

"Did you tell Garstan what you thought of him?" asked Dodd.

"No. In Giltraza Fort he's on his native heath, and is my superior officer. I didn't tell him what I thought of him; but I told him what I thought of the case, and what I thought of his Court-Martial. And I think I

582

succeeded in making him damned uncomfortable. However, he blustered bluffly. Said he had done his duty according to his lights. Which he had; though he thinks they are million candle-power arc-lights instead of farthing dips—and said that the matter was now out of his hands; which unfortunately it is.

"And, naturally, he is almighty cock-a-hoop at having collared Chimnai the Outlaw, the Singing Hadji's son, One-Eyed Kassim Shah, Hakim Khan, Moussa Beg, Ibrahim the Strong, Mahazil, Yacoub Ali, Wali Dad, Khoda Khan Abazai, and all the rest of them. And of course that is a feather in his cap."

"A whole peacock's tail in his blooming hat," growled Tommy Dodd.

"I'll tell you a thing that strikes me as queer, and as being just one weak spot in Vere-Vaughan's story," Tommy Dodd continued. "And that's this. It doesn't ring true to me that the whole of that lot took the Pathan oath, Koran in hand. You might conceivably find one irreligious and completely abandoned, blackguard, such as yourself, Ganesh, but I don't think you could find a score of them in the whole Border, nor yet in all Islam who would take an oath like that, intending to break it."

"No! But don't you see, my good fat ass," replied Ganesh, "that those bright boys pledged their souls, their salvation, and their hopes of the *houris* of Paradise *that they would get Vere-Vaughan safe and sound into Giltraza Fort.* . . . And didn't they do it?"

"One to you, Ganesh," admitted Tommy Dodd. "By Gad, isn't that the Pathan all over? Can't you see them all grinning in their sleeves as they swore the never-broken and unbreakable oath that they'd rescue him?"

"And that would have been the only weak spot in the story too," observed Colonel Ormesby. "To me it is perfectly clear that they took him in, from first to last, and that he hadn't a suspicion of them. I don't know the boy, but I'm quite certain that Archie Vere-Vaughan's son would never have bought his life at the price of the slaughter of a garrison and the loss of a Fort. Of course he wouldn't."

"By Jove, what a damned clever trick," he added, "and how nearly it came off. It would have succeeded—must have—but for that Usman Shah chap. I should think it's the Indian Order of Merit for him!"

"Yes. And it might have been the D.S.O. for Garstan, if he hadn't been so very Bee an Eff in the matter of the Court-Martial, and refused to believe Vere-Vaughan."

"I don't know," mused Tommy Dodd. "I don't know. It's very easy to be wise after the event. But, speaking for myself, if I had been in command of that Fort, and the youngster had rolled up, accompanied by a score of the biggest blackguards and most dangerous fire-brands on the whole Frontier, and with written directions for his arrest, from the most famous Intelligence Officer in India, I'm not at all sure I shouldn't have done exactly as Garstan did."

"Not you, Tommy," objected Ganesh. "You'd have arrested the outlaws, and you'd have kept the officer—possibly under open arrest—until the situation clarified itself."

"Mind you," said Colonel Ormesby, "Garstan, fool or not, acted very smartly, one might say cleverly, over the business of the outlaws. Some people would have pooh-poohed Usman Shah's tale. In fact, most people would, in view of the fact that the men were guaranteed by a British Officer. It's all very well to sneer and jeer at Garstan, but by being the Bee Eff you call him, he struck about the best blow at the source of Border trouble that has been struck for a generation."

"No, with all sympathy for young Vere-Vaughan, and every regret that this should have happened to him, I don't think that a really impartial person can blame Garstan," he continued. "Not if you keep in mind the written instructions for Vere-Vaughan's arrest. No, damn it all, taking that in conjunction with the outlaw band, you can't blame him. Personally, I think the only mistake he made was to exceed his Court-Martial powers. Of course he is ignorant of Military Law. Most of us are. He knew he had power as a Convening Officer, and could call a District Court-Martial. And there he had jurisdiction over Khoda Khan the sepoy. If he had liked to amuse himself thus, presumably he could have held a Summary Field District Court-Martial that could have given the man two years' rigorous imprisonment: and he could have convened a British, an Indian, or a Mixed Court."

"But he didn't Court-Martial the sepoy, did he?"

"No. Just sent him down with the gang and a note to the effect that he was not only one of the Singing Hadji's men, who had fired on a British aeroplane, killed a British Officer and taken part in the capture and imprisonment of another one, but that he was also a deserter and rifle-thief. No, what he did do, was to try poor young Vere-Vaughan by what he called a District Court-Martial."

"Well, there's one thing," remarked Colonel Ormesby. "If he had convened a General Court-Martial under the Indian Army Act with himself as President, and with four British officers and the other requirements fulfilled, the findings of the Court would have been quashed on technical grounds, if only because there was no properly appointed Judge-Advocate. Not only that, of course, but as soon as Ganesh Hazelrigg notifies the Judge-Advocate-General that he has never seen the prisoner and never written the alleged request for his arrest, the evidence will be invalidated."

"Well, I should think that Garstan will get a colossal crack over the knuckles."

"I doubt it. His tuppenny Court-Martial proceedings will be quashed just as a matter of official routine, and he will get the honour and glory of the round-up which undeniably he has brought off—with Vere-Vaughan's unintentional help!"

"And what about Vere-Vaughan?"

"Well, he'll now get a proper Court-Martial of course. Anyway, the General will damn-well see that he gets one."

"Yes, and for evermore he will be the Flying-Officer who was Court-Martialled for some funny-business— treachery and cowardice—and had the good luck to get away with it."

"'Fraid so. Like the innocent party in a divorce case. He or she is thenceforward the man or woman who either brought the divorce or was divorced, or, anyhow, was mixed up in a divorce case."

"By the way, I suppose there's no fear of the real General Court-Martial going wrong, is there?" asked Tommy Dodd.

"Oh, surely not," replied Colonel Ormesby. "By the time a really experienced officer, thoroughly acquainted with the rules of evidence and Court-Martial procedure, has made the Summary of Evidence and laid it before the Convening Officer and handed it to the Prosecutor to form his plan of action on, and to the accused to form his plan of defence on, the thing ought to be as clear as daylight and all plain-sailing."

"I suppose so," agreed Tommy Dodd. "Hope so, anyway."

"But, mind you, you never know," he said. "If you get an extremely able chap, of the K.C. type, a Barrister-at-Law whose speciality is prosecution, he might make things look ugly. In the circumstances, very ugly indeed. You see, for very much of it there is absolutely nothing but Vere-Vaughan's unsupported word, against the fact that he did bring those beauties into the Fort, and that only by the merest and most amazing chance they were recognized in time."

"Oh, don't croak," began Hazelrigg.

"Croak! I'm talking sense. If you could clear your mind of all preconceived ideas and actual knowledge, I rather fancy the whole thing would strike you as very much fishier than it does at present."

"Doesn't strike me as fishy at all," protested Hazelrigg.

"No, but it would if you were a completely detached stranger, sitting on a Court-Martial listening to a very clever prosecuting-counsel who invited you to ask yourself, as a man of plain common sense, whether it was for one moment likely that the accused did not know what sort of company he was in—after having dwelt in their midst at Kurnai in Sufed Kot, travelled with them for days, and had every opportunity of seeing and realizing the kind of people they were."

"Yes," replied Hazelrigg impatiently. "And what about when I bob up and testify that the message which he, in obvious innocence and ignorance, handed to Garstan, is an utterly bogus one? Also that I never saw him at Kurnai in Sufed Kot."

"Yes, and by Jove, we're rather forgetting the significance and implications of that little touch," observed Colonel Ormesby. "Since you say you didn't write it, Ganesh—and we'll give you the benefit of the doubt—I ask, once again, who the devil did?"

"Well, on the whole, I think it's one of the biggest mysteries I've run into," was the reply. "And that's saying something. In the first place, who on earth would there be in that barbaric nest of savagery who could write Russian correctly—grammatical convincing Russian that took Garstan in? And in point of fact, Garstan's a very good Russian scholar, to call him a scholar. Had a Russian mother or governess, or grew up in Russia, or something. Yes, that was it. I think his father was Military Attaché to the Tsar. Or am I thinking of somebody else? Anyway, the father was either that or head of a British concern in Russia; and Garstan grew up speaking Russian as his mother-tongue, or at least was bi-lingual . . . And this Russian letter was good enough for him."

"And there's more to it than that," remarked Tommy Dodd. "Not only does somebody in Kurnai in Sufed Kot—where there's obviously nothing but wild Pathans who can neither read nor write their own language, much less a foreign one—write correct Russian, *but* knows the name and initials of Major Bartholomew Hazelrigg of the Intelligence Branch, and knows that it's quite a feasible and reasonable thing for him to be sending chits from the Sufed Kot country to the Commandant of Giltraza Fort."

"It is utterly amazing," commented Colonel Ormesby.

"Yes, and so much so," pointed out Tommy Dodd "that the prosecution may make some rather uncomfortable use of it."

"As how?" asked Hazelrigg sceptically.

"Why, as being a most obvious lie on the part of Vere-Vaughan. How could there be in the Sufed Kot country anybody whom he could possibly imagine to be Major Bartholomew Hazelrigg of the Military Intelligence Branch of the Secret Service; and who could tell him a wonderful tale—in English, mark you—that caused him to put all his faith and trust in some of the biggest blackguards in Asia; and could also write him a chit in Russian? . . . You could hardly blame the Court if they decided then and there that the youngster was a plausible but obvious liar."

"Bosh!" replied Hazelrigg. "Is it likely that Vere-Vaughan would produce anything so damning as an order for his arrest, if it hadn't been given to him under the most convincing circumstances? Surely it's plain to the meanest intelligence, even to yours, Tommy, that Vere-Vaughan couldn't have known what was in the chit, and that therefore it must have been given to him by somebody who took him in completely."

"And then we come back to the 'who' problem," observed Colonel Ormesby. "*Who* could there be in Sufed Kot who would do a thing like that?"

"And that leads us on to the 'why' of it," he added. "*Why* should the feller want him arrested? Assuming—what I haven't the slightest doubt is perfectly true—that Vere-Vaughan was taken in as he says, acted in all good faith and brought this chit from somebody who completely duped him, why should that somebody have written a note in the name of Major Hazelrigg, in Russian, and with that curious request? One can quite understand his writing that the outlaw band were all the best of good fellows and stout friends of the English, but why the other part?"

"Well, that seems pretty clear to me, Sir," replied Hazelrigg. "Whoever did it, not only wanted to see the garrison scuppered and Giltraza Fort captured by the Singing Hadji, but—supposing that failed—wanted to provide the British Army with a first-class scandal. A regular Dreyfus case. Shake the faith of the Higher Command, the rank and file of the Army, and of the

British Public, in the dependability of the British Officer. I suppose that the character—for honour, loyalty and incorruptibility—of the British Officer class stands as high as that of any in the world. Well, what a very useful piece of work for an enemy of Britain to undermine that! To do for the British Officer class what the foul swine who falsely accused Dreyfus undoubtedly did for the French Army Officer class. That's how I look at it. And that's the line the defence must take."

"You'll suggest it to them, of course, Ganesh."

"Rather. I'm going to have my say when the Summary of Evidence is being drawn up."

"What is the exact procedure with regard to that?" asked Tommy Dodd.

"Why, the Convening Officer consults an independent person who's the best informed and most conversant with the whole case; and then the whole story of it, in chronological sequence, is written out, with a list of names of the witnesses whose evidence will prove each point. Then, when this has been done, the officer concerned will carefully record the statement of each individual whose actual personal knowledge is entirely relevant, and obtain his signature. And as Colonel Ormesby said before, the whole trial is built up on this Summary of Evidence, and nothing is more important than that it should be thoroughly, properly, and legally taken by a lawyer or by somebody from the Judge-Advocate-General's office, who knows the rules of evidence."

"By the way, with regard to Garstan's funny Court-Martial, does he reckon that it was a case of On Active Service, and that it was therefore his right and duty to convene a Summary Field General Court-Martial?" asked Colonel Ormesby.

"Lord knows, Sir. I suppose he could reasonably take the view that his was a force acting against armed assailants and, inasmuch as there was scrapping going on all round—the Hadji of Turangzai having a whang at the Singing Hadji of Sufed Kot and the winner being quite likely to have a shot at Giltraza—he could call it Active Service. As far as that goes, it is always Active

Service on that part of the Border, isn't it? . . .

"Well, anyway, I don't see that Vere-Vaughan has the worst to fear from the Court-Martial," he added.

"No, nor do I," agreed Colonel Ormesby. "What he has got to fear is the gossip of the ignorant and ill-informed; not to mention the innuendoes of the malicious."

"And what I will move Heaven and earth, to do," said Hazelrigg, "is to see that nothing goes wrong at the Court-Martial, and that he gets a thumping verdict in his favour. Leaves the Court without a stain on his character.

"And then," he added, in a quiet voice that his hearers knew and respected, "I'm going to take a trip into the Sufed Kot country and get my hands on the gentleman who writes notes in Russian. I'm going to explain to him clearly that I prefer to write my own letters."

Colonel Ormesby smiled.

"I've no doubt he will see your point, Ganesh."

"And probably feel it," added Tommy Dodd.

VII

The house in the Peshawar Bazaar was tall, narrow, and silent; its parapeted roof flat, its few windows permanently shuttered, its door but rarely opened.

Nor was its proprietor, Moussafa Shah, formerly Rissaldar-Major of the Cavalry Regiment of the Corps of Guides, a man of whom local acquaintances asked idle questions. Such acquaintances were few and intentionally discouraged by the dour and dangerous-looking occupant of the silent and secret house.

To Major Bartholomew Hazelrigg, living the life of a Pathan in the name and rôle of Ghulam Hyder, came Rissaldar-Major Moussafa Shah, as his admired superior took his ease upon one of the cushioned mattresses on the roof. Here, where none could overlook or overhear, Ganesh Hazelrigg was wont to interview divers curious persons, usually by night, privacy being completely ensured by the sinister and forbidding watch-dog Rissaldar-Major Moussafa Shah.

On rare occasions, one knocked upon the heavy door, that opened on to the narrow fetid lane, with the wrong kind of knock, proffered the wrong pass-word, and received summary discouragement from Rissaldar-Major Moussafa Shah, a man given to the use of extreme measures, contemptuous of the Civil Law, and, moreover, well aware that such people would be the very last to appeal to it.

But when the nocturnal visitor knocked correctly, did the right things with his hands when the door was opened, made the correct, if remarkable, answers to the curious questions asked by Rissaldar-Major Moussafa Shah, and completely satisfied this Guardian of the Threshold that the Seeker for Admittance was of the Elect, he would introduce him to a bare and empty room on the ground floor, lock him in, and inform his Sahib that "One came."

Among the retired Rissaldar-Major Moussafa Shah's

virtues of loyalty, fidelity, staunchness, obedience, and cleverness, was that of incuriosity. A fine soldier, worthy Native Officer of his magnificent Corps, duty and discipline were his gods, orders his guiding stars. All he wanted from his officer was to be told exactly what to do. The rest would follow as the night the day. His not to reason why; his not the very faintest desire to reason at all, or to know anything whatsoever about his master's business.

"One comes, Sahib," he said, emerging from the doorway that led from the stairs on to the roof, standing to attention and saluting.

"Who is he?"

"One Gul Mahommed."

"Bring him."

And silently Rissaldar-Major Moussafa Shah disappeared.

By Jove, here was a piece of luck for Bartholomew Hazelrigg. The very man of all men whom he wanted to see; the man who could tell him most about what he wanted to know, and help him best in what he wished to do.

Gul Mahommed!

But what on earth had brought him down to Peshawar?

And suddenly a great and brilliant idea illuminated Hazelrigg's mind and made instant appeal to his subtle scheming brain.

By Gad, that was an idea! That really was a thought. Now to work with care, cunning, and all the cleverness he had. Really to work, for a great end—for two ends, entwined, united, woven into one.

Yes, the idea of a lifetime. And to carry it out should be the work of a lifetime, if necessary.

And now to begin, for footsteps sounded on the wooden stair. Now to begin the work.

But though he knew it not, the work was already begun; was more than half done.

Hazelrigg rose to his feet as a big Pathan stepped

from the shadows into the bright moonlight, and Rissaldar-Major Moussafa Shah closed the staircase door behind him.

"*Wendover!*" he said, extending both hands, taking that of the Pathan in his right, and laying the other upon the man's shoulder.

Wendover's grip was sufficiently eloquent and painful reply to Hazelrigg's unwonted display of emotion.

"I can hardly believe it . . ." he said. "This is an answer to prayer—not yet prayed. Still, wishes are prayers. Thank God, anyway. Sit down and don't talk so much."

Smiling grimly, Wendover seated himself.

How extraordinarily handsome he had grown, in his cold, severe, and classic style; a little repellent and forbidding, perhaps; but how that smile lit the hard face up—like a burst of sunlight on a grey rock. And how strong the face had grown. 'Sweet are the uses of adversity.' Poor Wendover didn't look as though he had found them very sweet—but here was iron that had been in the furnace of adversity, and turned to steel.

Yes, a rock of a face. Chin and jaw of granite. A man neither to hold nor to bind; neither to lead nor to drive. Certainly not to drive.

What a triumph for the man—or woman—who could lead him home; lead him back to his proper place again; to a way of life, right and natural, and accordant with his birth and breeding, education and training.

A criminal waste—this man living as a semi-civilized Pathan tribesman.

Now to be wary and wise, if ever Bartholomew Hazelrigg had been wary and wise.

"Well, you remembered what I told you about the house and how to find it; and all about Rissaldar-Major Moussafa Shah and how to handle him," he said cheerily.

"Yes, I made careful note of that and of the pass-words, Ganesh, and I'm glad I did. Mahommed has come to the mountain this time."

"And the mountain's damn glad to see Gul Mahommed. But however much it laboured and rumbled, it could only bring forth a mouse's squeak of welcome."

"So you are glad to see me, old chap, eh?"

"You've said it, Son."

And saying much, while telling nothing; asking nothing while hoping to learn much, Ganesh Hazelrigg waited. It was no small matter that had brought Wendover down from his mountains, and he would speak of it in his own way and time.

Meantime, he, Hazelrigg, would talk of the matter nearest to his own heart.

"Have a cheroot," said Hazelrigg. "I've got some Lotuses here, in pretty good condition."

"A-a-a-a-h! One of the things I miss . . . Thanks . . . Gad, that's good!" sighed Wendover, leaning back on the cushioned mattress, and relaxing, as he exhaled luxuriously.

"City seems pretty quiet," he said.

"Yes, pretty peaceful—under the surface. Border quiet too," replied Hazelrigg. "While the two Hadjis are licking their wounds. And all the bad men are away from home just now. On their travels. A Week in Lovely Lucerne—or Twenty Years in the lovelier Andaman Islands. Yes, all dull and quiet on the Frontier now."

"Won't be for long, though," said Wendover.

"No? Just One Damn Thing After Another on the Border, isn't it? Where's trouble coming next?"

"Khairastan. And the Faquir of Ipi."

"What—the Road? I thought the old Khan had seen the light—that shines on the Sirkar's silver rupees."

"Yes. He had," replied Wendover. "Sees a brighter light now. Paradise."

"Oh-h-h. Gathered to his fathers, is he?"

"Yes, that's what I came to talk to you about, because the new man regards the Road as the Scots preacher regarded Sin. He's against it. And he has got all the young men of the Tribe with him, and most of the elders too. And the Ipi Faquir. They definitely don't want any Road through Khairastan."

"Don't blame them, either," admitted Ganesh.

"And what's more," continued Wendover, "we are being corrupted."

"We are, eh?"

"Yes. Khairastan is all of a bubble. What is known as 'seething with discontent'."

"Who's behind it?"

"That's the other thing I came to tell you. There's a very clever man indeed behind it, and a mighty powerful force behind him. Quite a weighty person."

"Weight of terrorist and seditionist rupees—from the Indian side of the Border?"

"No, weight of roubles from the other side."

"Ah! And you've spotted him? By Gad! Good man!"

"Spotted him? He's an old friend of mine—though he doesn't know it. An old pupil, in fact. And now the rôle is reversed. I used to teach him Pushtu and Hindustani; and now he's teaching me Bolshevism, Communism, Terrorism, Agitation and the science and art of the Fomentation of Trouble and Warfare. He has corrupted me utterly. Turned me from a peaceful inhabitant of Khairastan and member of the party of Law and Order into a bitterly anti-British agitator and firebrand. Corrupted Shere Khan too, and all his clan."

"And you think it has gone on long enough, eh?"

"Just exactly long enough."

Ganesh Hazelrigg possessed his soul in patience. No good hurrying Wendover, but if he didn't get on with it, a little quicker, something quite other than patience would possess his soul, for a change.

An old friend? An old pupil?

Of course—Tashkent. Wasn't it there that Wendover had actually had a job as *munshi*, as teacher of Pushtu and Hindustani in the Russian Officers' School of Oriental Languages which was also a school for Intelligence Agents and spies? Of course.

This Russian Secret Service agent who had come to Khairastan to take advantage of the trouble caused by the Ipi Faquir and the expected coming of the Road, must have been at the School, learning the languages necessary for him to carry on his Intelligence work in Afghanistan, in India, and among the Border tribes.

"And you are going to put an end to it? And to him?" asked Hazelrigg.

"Yes. I'm going to put an end to this particular agitation and agitator. That's one of the things I wanted to see you about—which would be the better plan from the British point of view? That misfortune overtake him among the wild mountains and wicked men, or shall it be a 'Catch-'em-alive-O!'? I can arrange either."

Ganesh Hazelrigg smoked silently in deep thought.

"I didn't know whether you might say, '*Oh, what a pity you wasted him,*' if he came to a sad end in Khairastan. '*What a pity you killed the goose that might have laid us a lot of golden eggs—of information—in return for reprieve and commutation of sentence.*' And then I pondered whether you'd say, '*Why on earth couldn't this poor fellow have fallen off his horse or out of bed or something, and broken his neck, instead of being sent down to Peshawar for trial as an enemy spy and agent—wasting time and causing an unpleasant smell; unpleasant but dear to the nostrils of our pacifists, disarmists, communists and those who raise the roof of Parliament when we do anything in defence of India, not to mention of our humble selves.*'"

"Y-e-s-s-s," murmured Hazelrigg, puffing luxuriously at his cheroot and saying one thing while he thought of another. "Yes. The leopard is a wicked beast."

"Eh?"

"Used to be three leopards on the English flag."

"What about it?"

"'*C'est un animal très méchant. Quand on l'attaque il se défend*'."

"Yes," smiled Wendover. "Used to, anyhow."

"And so this clever man, this weighty person who's an old friend of yours, though he doesn't know it, an old pupil in fact, is attacking. And you are going to be *un animal très méchant.* And he's in your part of the Border, and his name is Bailitzin."

Hazelrigg sprang to his feet.

"Comrade Colonel Bailitzin," he whispered. "I understand everything now! *He's* the gentleman who writes notes in Russian—and in my name . . . And you actually know where he is."

"Well, he's on the Khairastan Border, stumping the country, with headquarters at Kurnai, and he's not likely to leave before I return. And what's more, he won't leave—alive—before I return."

"Suppose he tries."

"Shere Khan'll look after him. Shere Khan is in Kurnai now, with the best of his men. Shere Khan's a big man these days, and there's either a modest majority or a very big minority who'd far rather see him Khan than his elder brother. No. Shere Khan'll see to it that Colonel Comrade Bailitzin doesn't leave Kurnai until I come back. Shere Khan and the men of his own village have appointed themselves the Comrade Colonel's personal body-guard. They'll guard his body all right, alive or dead.

"Which is it to be?" he added.

"I'll tell you later on, Dick. It depends on you, to some extent," replied Hazelrigg.

"Well, if you don't want him, say so. Because I know exactly what to do with him. I've got a very big account to settle with the gentleman, and he might, or might not, survive the settlement. If he didn't, there's an end of the matter. If he did—and I didn't—then I'd like you to take him over, because there are three courses open.

"One—Shere Khan's men execute him, which they'd be delighted to do; two—they give him safe conduct out of the Border country and warmly advise him not to return; or, three—they bring him down to Peshawar gaol, where he gets fair trial for what he is, with all the publicity attendant upon such a trial, and the gratis information to his employers as to where he is and what has become of him. Then the smiling and ever-truthful representative of the U.S.S.R. in London will call upon our Foreign Secretary and, in the course of conversation, mention that the Minister for Foreign Affairs at Moscow makes a special point of requesting that the Russian subject named Bailitzin, who has been arrested and wrongfully imprisoned in India, be immediately released . . . Otherwise, etc. . . . . And Our

Foreign Minister will gallop round to the India Office and tell the Secretary of State for India all about it. Questions in Parliament; especially from the member who plays outside-left on the Left Wing: long and urgent cables to the Viceroy; release of Bailitzin."

"With a substantial donation from the Poor Box," murmured Hazelrigg. "So that if it depends on you, he won't be handed over to us at all. Personally, you don't actually yearn to see him awaiting trial in Peshawar Gaol."

"No, I want to see him awaiting trial in Heaven," replied Wendover.

"Very well, then, my son. It's up to you. Now listen. You know all about what happened in Giltraza Fort."

"No, I don't know all about what happened, and that's another of the things I want to talk about. One more account to settle with Comrade Bailitzin. Let me tell you my end of the story—up to the time when Vere-Vaughan and the outlaw band got into the Fort. Then you can carry on."

"Right," said Hazelrigg. "We can get the whole thing straight between us, and lighten each other's darkness."

"Well, it was like this," began Wendover, "I was on the track of a very bad lad of whom a lot more will be heard later, known to you as the Faquir of Ipi. He's going to give as much trouble as the two Hadjis put together, some day. I had heard that he was week-ending with the Hadji of Turangzai, so Shere Khan and I went along and joined the party. That was soon after you had visited the Hadji of Turangzai, as I learned from the Hadji's description of the excellent horse-dealer, Inayatullah Hussein the Afghan, who had just sold him a fine Kabuli stallion.

"We were sure of three days' hospitality, anyway, even if we couldn't ingratiate ourselves and stop on and interest the Hadji of Turangzai in some little schemes, one of which was the forestalling of an alleged treacherous attack upon him, which was being arranged by the Singing Hadji of Sufed Kot.

"Well, having made the acquaintance of the Faquir

of Ipi and learned his interesting views upon the very best ways of making real trouble for the wicked infidel British; and having succeeded in thoroughly interesting the Hadji of Turangzai in what, according to our tale, the Singing Hadji of Sufed Kot was proposing to do to him, news suddenly came of the disaster to the Flight stationed at the new Hunzana Fort Aerodrome.

"According to the account, arriving quicker than if Turangzai possessed the telegraph, five planes had crashed in a fog among the mountains, and one had been shot at by the Singing Hadji's people and had actually come down at Kurnai, the pilot having been mortally wounded and—the great point of the story and the cream of the jest—the observer had been captured alive and unhurt, and was now in the hands of the Malik of Kurnai who rather proposed to keep him there.

"With profuse apologies to our host, we cut short our visit at Turangzai, told him how much we had enjoyed ourselves, but must return to Town first thing in the morning.

"To tell you the truth, I was in a mortal funk at going into the Sufed Kot country, for fear I should run into the Singing Hadji himself, and be recognized as the unspeakable villain who had diddled him at the siege of Giltraza."

"Yes, by Jove," smiled Ganesh. "The Singing Hadji would pay quite handsomely to have you or me just where he wants us, wouldn't he?"

"Yes. So I went very unostentatiously to Kurnai, by roundabout tracks over the mountains, giving Sufed Kot Fort as wide a berth as possible. And, by Gad, I was glad I had gone. There was as nice a situation, and as neat a little job being hatched, as you could ever imagine.

"First of all, I discovered that young Vere-Vaughan was alive and well but was a bone of contention—a bone that was likely to be picked pretty clean. There were two parties in the lively city of Kurnai, one of which was for doing its plain religious duty and handing the Infidel over to its spiritual overlord, the

Singing Hadji, for treatment; and the other was for keeping him for ransom.

"This party wanted to run him along to the nearest Fort, Giltraza of course, and hand him over C.O.D. or part cash and three months Bill of Exchange, or in return for an I.O.U. for ten thousand rupees. And into the middle of this squabble who should stroll but . . ."

"Comrade Bailitzin," murmured Ganesh Hazelrigg.

"Exactly. Whereupon I had to ride my evil passions on the curb, and fight my almost uncontrollable desire to let urgent private affairs take precedence of high matters of state."

"Go for him, in short, and remove his stuffing," murmured Hazelrigg, taking the cheroot from his lips and blowing a thoughtful cloud.

"Very much so. However, I was in a pretty dangerous situation myself, and as I say, behaving most unobtrusive and inconspicuous-like. Also, the first thing—the thing that I was there for—was to rescue young Vere-Vaughan. So, far from introducing myself to the Comrade and inviting him to 'come outside,' I avoided him like the Devil. It would have been a different matter on my native heath of Khairastan, but here, Bailitzin was sitting as pretty as though he were still in Russia. If he should chance to recognize me, one word from him, and I should be for it."

"And he would have said the word all right," observed Hazelrigg. "How was it that you recognized him and he didn't spot you?"

"Oh, that was an easy one. He was being the big Hussein Ali Shah Powindah, self-proclaimed. All open and above board. The accredited emissary of the U.S.S.R., the incalculably mighty country that could, at any moment, and would, at some moment unspecified, eat up Afghanistan and India too, and would let the Border tribes in on the ground floor. Let them lead the van on the great march down to the Loot of India . . . No, he made no secret of who he was, at any rate to the Singing Hadji of Sufed Kot, who introduced him in solemn durbar to a great *jirgah* of Mullahs, Maliks and Khans.

"So at Kurnai, he moved in the fierce light that beats upon the bringer of rifles and rupees, whereas I was an insignificant hanger-on, a wandering *budmash* who was probably a fugitive from justice and therefore a nice man to know, and deserving of asylum."

"*Asylum's* right for you, Dick," observed Hazelrigg. "But we'll get you back to sanity. Before long, too."

"So you see, Comrade Bailitzin filled the picture—or rather, was the picture. And I was only one of the little spots that go to make it up.

"And talking of spots," continued Wendover, "Bailitzin has got a tiny one beside the iris of his right eye. A very minute blister, like a transparent pimple."

"Thanks. I'll put that in his *dossier* in case we lose him this time."

"We won't lose him," Wendover assured Hazelrigg. "Why, he's my hobby, Ganesh; my chief interest in life. I shall be almost sorry when he's dead."

Hazelrigg laughed.

"I should be extremely grieved if anyone else caused his death, and I think Bailitzin would be sorry if anybody but himself killed me. Anyhow, he didn't kill me this time, didn't even see me, for I was one of a hundred, all pretty much alike."

"No, of course he wouldn't be expecting to meet you in the Singing Hadji's country, and would be too busy to see what he wasn't looking for."

"Yes, and he had a great game on. A really neat scheme. And he was playing for high stakes. For as Shere Khan and I learned from one Wali Dad, leader of the Keep-the-prisoner-for-ransom party, Bailitzin intended, or rather was proposing, to use Vere-Vaughan for his own purposes, which were neither execution by the Hadji, nor ransom by the British, but as a sprat to catch a mackerel."

Hazelrigg nodded.

"And the mackerel was to be Fort Giltraza," he said.

"Yes, and they'd still have the sprat inside the mackerel. Very neat."

"Well," continued Wendover, "Shere Khan and I cultivated the expansive Wali Dad, learned all about everything that was going on, and put ideas into his head. So that when the plot for capturing Giltraza Fort was all nicely cut and dried, I, the outlaw Gul Mahommed, and Shere Khan his brother, offered to join the party that was going to march into the British lion's den. In other words, introduce itself into Giltraza Fort.

"Wali Dad mentioned this to the Committee, and guaranteed us as stout citizens, old friends of his.

"What was our game, instantly enquired the great Chimnai the Outlaw. And if Bailitzin was the brains of the scheme, Chimnai the Outlaw was the brawn and the guts."

"Yes," agreed Hazelrigg. "Chimnai's a man as well as a devil."

"And all the congregation—and as you know, they were the real cream of the villainy of all the Border . . ."

"The concentrated essence," agreed Hazelrigg.

". . . said, yes, what was our big idea. Whereupon Wali Dad told them not to ask silly questions. What did they think our game was, except to be in on the ransom money, get a new rifle, and, at least, have a nice day in the country, anyway.

"And Chimnai the Outlaw and the other blackguards, the plausible Khoda Khan Abazai, the appalling Moussa Beg, Ibrahim the Strong, Kassim Shah, and the rest of them, grinningly agreed that the outlaws, Gul Mahommed and Shere Khan, should certainly come along and fight, do any dirty work that was going, and get not one rupee of ransom money or anything else.

"And so we joined the band. And my next effort was to get into personal touch with young Vere-Vaughan who was evidently keeping his end up splendidly. But do you think I ever got a chance to say a word to him alone?"

"No," laughed Hazelrigg. "It's only in the storybooks that the Secret Service Agent is selected to stand sentry over the door of the man with whom he wants to get in touch."

"Quite so. I never got a chance of so much as winking at him. Now and again I got into his prison by just lounging in behind Wali Dad and Khoda Khan Abazai, but the whole scheme would have been ruined if I had uttered a sound or made a move that showed I was in collusion with Vere-Vaughan, or interested in him in any other way than that in which the rest of his captors were.

"And in point of fact, it really did not matter, although I should have liked to give Vere-Vaughan a cheering word and let him know that he had got a friend at hand.

"In the same way, Shere Khan went into his cell once or twice with Wali Dad, who was his especial gaoler, but he could never get in alone.

"It would have blown the gaff too, for either of us to have suggested a private colloquy with the prisoner. As you know, there's no more suspicious bird on this earth than the Pathan; and although Wali Dad had fallen for us to the extent of guaranteeing us as good honest murderers, robbers and outlaws, we were the merest wandering strangers.

"Nevertheless we were allowed to join Wali Dad's gang and attend the meetings of the plotters, and I thought I knew all there was to know—except anything that Bailitzin might have said to Vere-Vaughan. That he visited Vere-Vaughan quite alone, and for quite a long while, I knew; and I was pretty sure that it wasn't for the sake of Vere-Vaughan's *beaux yeux.*

"Naturally, Bailitzin had some deep game of his own. I'd have given almost anything to have had five minutes alone with Vere-Vaughan, for I was worried. I was playing my own game against Bailitzin, and to some extent, playing it blindfold. His game was to get Giltraza Fort by introducing inside its walls a force big enough to capture it if they could suddenly take the garrison by surprise in the middle of the night. A damn' clever scheme too, and putting Vere-Vaughan to magnificent use.

"My game was to allow Bailitzin's to go just as far as I wanted it to, and no further. I, of course, wanted to get the said party—all men with prices on their heads, and absolutely our most dangerous enemies—

inside the Fort, there to be caught like rats in a trap. It would make a clean sweep of all our firebrands, and be a crippling blow for their employers. It would mean peace on the Border for years, not only by reason of the actual loss of the firebrands but from inevitable damage to morale . . . It was worth the slight risk of losing Giltraza Fort."

"Almost," demurred Hazelrigg.

"But I knew that the risk was negligible. Bailitzin must have talked to Vere-Vaughan in such a way that his suspicions were not aroused, and that he had not the vaguest idea that he would be introducing human dynamite into the Fort, and with the fuse lighted too.

"You should have heard Chimnai and Co. chuckling, rolling with silent laughter at Vere-Vaughan's simplicity, at the way they were taking him in. And none chuckled louder than Shere Khan and I.

"Nor was my laughter wholly false when I looked round that circle of faces—to call them faces—and thought how I was going to double-cross them, high-jack them and make the *coup* of a century, and land the whole lot behind bars in one fell swipe.

"But while they chuckled at the thought of the innocent pink-cheeked Vere-Vaughan making them all swear on the Koran that they would deliver him safely at Giltraza Fort, and I chuckled at the thought that I'd damn well see *them* safe inside the Fort, I still had an occasional qualm and uncomfortable feeling when I thought of Bailitzin.

"Of course I entertained the hope that he'd come along too, and I should be able to add him to the bag—a real prize—but meanwhile what was he saying to Vere-Vaughan?

"I wondered whether his confabulation with Vere-Vaughan had some reference to what the latter should do in the Fort during the night, or immediately upon entry; and whether he were convincing Vere-Vaughan that he was a British Secret Service Agent. Something of that sort."

"And not a bad shot, either, my son," observed Hazelrigg. "I'll tell you in a minute. Go on."

"Well, when everything was settled, the gang waited for the first dark night; and when it came, Wali Dad went in and fetched Vere-Vaughan. Everyone else in the place, except the conspirators, was asleep. Wali Dad took some Pathan kit into Vere-Vaughan's cell, and a few minutes later brought him out. That was simple enough, of course, because Wali Dad was his gaoler and responsible for him, and could come and go as he liked. There were always three or four *budmashes* loafing about in the room and passage outside Vere-Vaughan's door, and Wali Dad saw to it that on this night they were men of the 'rescue' gang.

"Well, they led Vere-Vaughan out of the village to where the rest of us were waiting, and we got away without a sound.

"Of course it was necessary to do the job in this way, as there was quite a strong party in Kurnai who wanted him taken to the Singing Hadji at the Sufed Kot Fort, as a burntoffering and bloody sacrifice, and . . ."

"About what he would have been," observed Hazelrigg.

"Well, we weren't molested that night, made what pace we could in the dark, and by daylight were well away from Kurnai, on the other side of the hills. It was a bitter disappointment to me, when I made my way up to the front of the *kafila* and then let them all pass me again, to find that Bailitzin was not with us. There was one good thing about it, though; by remaining at Kurnai, he could probably prevent any serious pursuit. What he said went, both with the Malik and with the Mullah of Kurnai, as the Singing Hadji had told them quite plainly in durbar that the friend of Hussein Ali Shah Powindah, as Bailitzin called himself, was the friend of the Singing Hadji.

"Nevertheless I would have given a lot, a real lot, to have had him with us. It would have given me a greater sense of justification in the risk I was taking."

"Can't have everything, Dick."

"No, that's what I tried to tell myself. But supposing that, unknown to me and Shere Khan, the gang had decided to start business five minutes after Vere-

Vaughan had got them inside, and before I could get at the Commandant and put him wise, it might be touch-and-go as to what happened. At best it would have been awkward, with two and twenty of those fighting fiends well inside the place, and nobody knowing what was happening.

"Yes, I thought more than once of the proverb about the cup and the lip, because even if something of the sort took place without the conspirators being success-ful, there would probably be a good many casualties on the British side and a good many escapes on the other side. I did not want the thing to fizzle out in a rough-and-tumble from which the best part—or the worst part—of the gang escaped, and the whole show a muck-up. I wanted it neat and clean, and the lot of them nicely trapped, without a blow struck or a shot fired.

"And of course the probabilities were that I could bring it off. A certainty almost. The gang would arrive under the walls in the middle of the night. Vere-Vaughan would say his piece as he had been told, and in all good faith would take his rescue party, his friends and saviours, inside, and Shere Khan and I would go with them. I, knowing every inch of Giltraza Fort, would go straight to the C.O.'s room, while Shere Khan would stand ready to cover Chimnai if he started anything immediately. Not that I had much fear of this, as it was definitely understood that the whole place was to be allowed to settle down to sleep again before Chimnai gave the word to start the slaughter.

"Well, man proposes! And God disposed—a stone, on the edge of a narrow path as we crossed the Kara Koh Mountains.

"It was loose, fell as I stepped on it, and I went with it, a most awful purler. Sudden as a thunderclap . . .

"And the next thing I knew was that I was lying on my back in a cave, with Shere Khan smacking my face with the wet end of his *puggri* and calling impartially upon me, the Devil and Allah, to do something. And when I opened my eyes, he cursed me foully and fero-ciously for being such a clumsy fool as to fall down a precipice—like a mother smacking her kid for not getting run over. The good chap was really frightened. Thought I had broken my neck, and it was a marvel I hadn't. I found later that the earth was eroded from under the stone on which I had trodden, so that it was overhanging; that I had fallen about thirty feet; had bounced off the sloping side of the mountain and landed all of a heap on a wide ledge of stone, one of those millions of flat-topped rocks, really, with which all those mountain-sides are strewn.

"Can you imagine my state of mind when I recovered complete consciousness and grasped the situation? I had taken a ghastly thump on the head and I wasn't sure my skull wasn't fractured. My left shoulder was dislocated. I wasn't at all certain that I hadn't broken most of the ribs of my left side; and, what was really worst of all, from my point of view, my left ankle was so badly sprained that I thought it was broken.

"God knows what I didn't think, those few first minutes. There was I, an absolute wreck, and there was the band well on its way to Giltraza Fort. To the capture of Giltraza Fort, in point of fact.

"I tried to shout to Shere Khan to run like hell, catch up with the band, get into the Fort with them and warn the C.O. that what Vere-Vaughan Sahib thought to be his rescue-party was a band of the worst *budmashes* and outlaws on the whole Frontier, and that they intended to seize the Fort in the night. Then, whether it was the pain, or the smash on the head, or concussion and shock, or the horror of the thought that I had lent a hand in the capture of Giltraza, I don't know, but I passed out again and was unconscious, off and on, for the rest of that day.

"When I came round again and got things straight in my mind, I said to Shere Khan, who was sitting beside me:

"'*Have you been? . . . Did you get in? . . . Is the Fort safe?*'

"And Shere Khan's only reply was to bid me keep quiet, keep still, and not to try to talk.

"No need to tell me to keep still. I tried to raise my

head, tried to get up, but it was useless. For one thing, as I soon discovered, I was pretty well tied up, as Shere Khan had set my shoulder, bound my arm to my side, splinted my left leg and put a cold compress round my head. Amazingly good work too, as he had nothing to work with but a few yards of cotton *puggri* and our long Khyber knives and their scabbards for splints.

"Then I noticed that it was getting dark. Soon I began to collect my faculties. When what brain I have was functioning normally and coolly, I realized that it must be several hours since I fell, and that the raiding-party must be twenty miles away. Also that they would soon be bivouacing for the evening meal, and that Shere Khan, by a great effort, could overtake them to-morrow.

"Yes, if he ran all night while they slept, he could come up with them, make a casual remark, to anybody who asked him, to the effect that he had abandoned me, as I couldn't walk. And he could go on with them, and play my part as soon as they were all inside the Fort. Having warned the Commandant and waited till the gang were all safely in irons, he could then tell the C.O. that he had left a friend on the track, and must get back and look after him. They could hardly refuse to let him go, after the service he had rendered; although of course they'd send someone with him to see that he came back as a witness at the trial of the raiders. If there should be any among them who couldn't be convicted in a British Court of Law on his past sins, he could get a death sentence—or a life one in the Andaman Islands—for being in this little show.

"So, when I had got everything straight in my mind, I turned on Shere Khan and rent him; talked to him exactly as I used to do when I was his Squadron-Leader and he was a trooper in the ranks. Fairly blistered him.

"And the angrier I got and the more ferociously I insulted him and cursed him, the more gently he soothed and humoured me, and bade me 'drink a drop of this.' He had been in Dr. Bennell's Hospital in Pannu, in his time, and knew the bed-of-sickness drill and book of the words. You'd have thought he had got a draught of bromo-chloral in one hand and a hypodermic syringe full of morphia in the other, instead of a drop of dirty water in an old tin mug.

"It was no good raving and cursing at him, so I again began to do my damnedest to get up, observing that if he were afraid to rejoin the *budmashes* and get into the Fort with them, I should have to go myself if I had to hop the whole way on one foot.

"I did manage to get upright this time, and found it was indeed a case of 'on one foot,' for I could no more put any weight on the other leg than I could have done if the foot had just been hacked off with an axe. Nor do broken ribs and a broken skull lend themselves much to the exercise of hopping. Problems of breathing and giddiness arise; and it wasn't many seconds before I was full length on the ground again. Then I really gave my whole mind to moving Shere Khan, who is more obstinate than a dozen army-mules when he has made up what he calls his mind. When I found I could do nothing at all by flat *hukm*,[84] by appeal, threat and insult, I tried to make him see what it would mean to me if the Fort fell. I must have risen to heights of eloquence, though that is not exactly a habit of mine."

Hazelrigg grunted.

"Damn it, I waxed sentimental, though I'm not what you'd call a really sentimental man."

Hazelrigg laughed.

"'Did we not fight together in that Fort, Shere Khan?' I wept. 'Did we not bleed there together? Were we not both shot down? Did we not save the Fort? And now, are you the man who is going to lose it, see it fall—and fall into the hands of the Singing Hadji of Sufed Kot himself? And you—you who have followed me, lived with me, loved me, been my blood brother all these years—you would now blacken my face forever? You . . . you . . . you foul dog: you Pathan. If you do this thing, we part, I will never set foot again in Khairastan. Now go.'

"And Shere Khan?

---

[84] *Order, command.*

"'There, there!' he said, 'drink a drop more of this.'"

"I might as well have been talking to the rock on which I had fallen. If I had pulled out my automatic and taken my solemn oath that I would shoot him dead unless he went, I should have been quite welcome to do so. He would not leave me in what he considered danger, and no doubt I looked pretty bad, apart from the fact that I couldn't move. I suppose he realized that if he went and anything happened to him and he couldn't come back, I should either starve to death or come to some other sticky end.

"Well, can you imagine how I felt, Ganesh, as the hours went by, and that maddening lump of stupidity wouldn't leave me?"

"Yes. Nasty position," grunted Hazelrigg. "One of the high spots of a spotty career."

Wendover laughed shortly.

"Well, I suppose I must have passed out again—or else there is a gap in my memory owing to concussion—but the next thing I knew, I was out of the cave, out in the open, and for the moment I thought I was riding a camel. For I found I was being joggled and jolted along in a way that made my whole body one ghastly agony, head opening and shutting with a bang, every breath a stab, and an almost unbearable pain in the left ankle and leg.

"Once again I pulled my wits together—and realized that Shere Khan was carrying me. Not slowly striding along, doubled up, with me on his back, but carrying me in his arms, precisely as a woman carries a child. And he was running. What d'you suppose I weigh? Twelve stone?"

"Thereabouts, I should say. You are tall and broad, but you are lean and hard. Say twelve stone seven."

"Well, believe it or not, Shere Khan was running—like a horse with a twelve stone handicap—and, by gad, it was a contest between his power to carry me and my power to be carried. Time after time I was on the point of begging him to stop and lay me down, but I was ashamed to—though I freely confess that I wished to God that his strength would fail and he'd have to put me down.

"Uphill he strode. On the level he ran. And downhill he bounded.

"It was utterly amazing, and of course, utterly hopeless. However seldom he rested for a *chupatti*[85] from his haversack and a drink from his water-bottle, he couldn't possibly overtake the band now, nor reach Giltraza Fort before them. Hopeless. But there was some sort of comfort in feeling that I was moving, moving towards Giltraza, and moving more quickly than the band themselves.

"And on went Shere Khan. I don't want to pretend that he did anything that is sheerly impossible, nor that he did what no other man on this earth would have the strength, endurance, and spirit to do; but I truly believe, Ganesh, that there are few men alive who could equal, and none who could excel, his performance. That I'll swear. From time to time he put me down, lay with his head on his arms and breathed as though his lungs would burst; and when he had recovered breath, he fed me with *chupattis*, took a bite himself, had a drink, puffed a *bidi*, picked me up, and was off again.

"I had talked to him to some purpose!

"We slept a little while that night, but for how long I don't know, for we lay down in darkness and it was still dark when he picked me up again. As he laboured on, that day, my agony of mind grew steadily worse.

"I couldn't let my *friend* run till he died, as he might have done, like a horse.

"I couldn't bring myself to stop him while there was a ghost of a hope of a chance of catching up with the outlaws.

"There always was a possibility that they would change their plan to the extent of halting and bivouacing, while one of them went on and reconnoitred; or possibly of their camping in some convenient cave while two of them took news of Vere-Vaughan up to the Fort in broad daylight and dickered for the ransom.

---

[85] *A kind of pancake.*

They could, of course, take a note from Vere-Vaughan, saying he was alive and well, and guaranteeing that it was a genuine offer. If the outlaws had decided on anything of that sort, we might yet save the situation. In that case, we were, of course, both prepared to take our chance of going up to the gate and being shot down by the gang while we bawled '*Arm, arm, Auvergne, the foe!*' or words to that effect. There'd be plenty of time to put a spoke in their wheel before we were done in.

"And while I clenched my teeth to bear the pain, and prayed to whatever gods there be, to bear the problem—instead of leaving it to me—Shere Khan ran on.

"Talk of the men who, unencumbered, ran the thirty miles from Salamis to Athens!

"Well, in a way, my prayers were answered, for, that afternoon Shere Khan put me down and rested with increasing frequency. His great strength was giving out, and he was coming to the end of even his incredible powers of endurance.

"Then, suddenly, while he was running blindly into the sunset, he began to stagger, tottered, swayed from side to side, partly stooped to put me down and partly fell—and that was the end of it.

"D'you know, Ganesh, for a moment Giltraza Fort and everybody in it could have been blown to Hell for all I cared, if this meant that Shere Khan was dying . . . Have you ever ridden your horse to death? To save your own life? Well, you'll remember how you felt, and you can multiply it by ten thousand and not realize how I felt.

"And what do you think I did, Ganesh?"

"Get on," growled Ganesh, who for the first time in his life was hearing his friend really talk.

"I fell asleep. Can you believe it?"

"Of course. What one does do when one is worn out, mind, body, and soul."

"When I woke I turned my head, and literally thanked God to see that Shere Khan was alive, lying there beside me breathing, asleep. And since you know so much, Ganesh, what did I do then?"

"Woke him up."

"Yes, I did. I woke him up.

"'*Blood brother*,' said I, '*run on—alone.*'

"And Shere Khan, moving stiffly, like an old man, prostrated himself, after smearing his face and hands with water, with his back to the rising sun and his face toward Mecca, and prayed. Then he took the remaining *chupattis* from our haversacks, divided them equally, and began to eat.

"'*Eat mine too*,' said I, '*that you may have the more strength to run.*' But he wouldn't do anything of the sort, and while I was explaining to him that, if he'd just shove me under a bush and run on, he'd be able to reach the Fort (if he didn't overtake the band) and warn the garrison, if it were not too late. But if it were
. . .

"And while I was still talking he bent over me and once again, but with obviously painful effort, gathered me up into his arms."

"What followed was epic, Homeric. For Shere Khan, with frequent rests, continued all that day. He was barely conscious of what he was doing and was in a state very similar to that of *ghazi*; his body was up-borne by his spirit, like that of the *ghazi* is; and just as the *ghazi* can fight and carry bullets, long after he ought to be down and out and dead, so Shere Khan, in this ecstatic and self-hypnotized state, ran on, long after his lungs and muscles should have failed him. He was glorified, uplifted and, I believe, heard nothing that I said to him.

"And so he ran on until suddenly we crashed, and personally I felt as though I had fallen down the cliff again.

"When he had recovered breath, Shere Khan sat up and looked round. Nearby was one of the thousands of caves with which those mountain-sides are honey-combed. Into this he dragged me, and as soon as his laboured breathing would allow, finished what he considered his share of the water and *chupattis*—about a quarter of the total.

"Having eaten and drunk, he rose to his feet.

"'*Do not attempt to move, Gul Mahommed,*' he said. '*I will return if I live. Should I not return—you have your pistol.*'

"And without another word he staggered out of the cave.

"As he said, I had my pistol and I need not put up with the troubles and trials of this weary life for more than a week. The food and water would last me for two or three days with careful rationing, and I could wait two or three more, in case Shere Khan were 'unavoidably detained.'

"Well, that was another bad time, Ganesh, lying in that cave, with the world's best headache, ribs that felt as though they were penetrating my lungs, and a leg that looked as though I had got elephantiasis, and felt as though I had got a bullet in the ankle—lying there and wondering exactly what had happened in Fort Giltraza.

"I could see that vile crew of human tigers, most of them with a murder-score that topped the hundred, beginning their job inside that Fort an hour or two before dawn, getting the sentries silently, rushing the guard-room before a rifle could be fired, making a shambles of the sleeping sepoys' quarters.

"They could do it all right and they would do it, once they were admitted, unsuspected, under the deluded Vere-Vaughan's guarantee. And I was responsible, the fault entirely mine, with my big ideas about nabbing the lot of them at one go. And lying there in the dark, almost unable to move, I saw myself for what I was, a swashbuckler who had once 'saved' Giltraza Fort, the clever would-be Secret Service man who had been caught and flogged and humiliated almost to death by a cleverer man."

"*What?* Flogged? What do you mean?"

"(I'll tell you in a minute.) I was the artful plotter who was going to double-cross the double-crosser, trap the trapper, and clear up the Border in a single move. Yes, I got a quite unpleasant glimpse of myself that night, Ganesh, and I realized that why I had taken this risk of letting the Fort be captured wasn't really because I was so damned keen on my self-appointed job, so filled with a burning sense of duty and patriotism, but just because I hated Bailitzin so. That was the hitherto unconscious motive of why I took that line, and now I was conscious of it, and a mean poor thing I felt. It wasn't so much that I was for England as that I was against Bailitzin. I had really gone on with it until it was too late to change my plan, because I hoped and believed that Bailitzin would go with the outlaws (as Hussein Ali Shah Powindah, of course) and get into the Fort himself. And *then* I should have had him. Had him just where I wanted him. That was the height and the depth and the real measure of my taking the chance of using the safety of Giltraza Fort as a pawn in my game."

"Bosh!" growled Hazelrigg. "You did exactly what I or any other agent in similar circumstances would have done. Made a bid to catch the whole gang of them."

"Well, anyway, there I was, properly on the rack, physically and mentally. And sometime or other, long after I had begun to dream dreams and see visions and point my pistol at things that weren't there, Shere Khan, or the skeleton of Shere Khan, came back, and I think that the sight of him and what he said, saved my life.

"'*It's all right*,' he said, as he sank down beside me. '*Nothing has happened, not a shot fired. Not a sound. The flag's flying, the sentries are at their posts and the gates open and shut to let men come and go. A scouting-party under a British Officer marched out this morning and disappeared into the hills. And later, a Company came forth, picketed the hills, and then did attack drill, followed by retreating under fire, and rearguard drill back to the Fort.

"'*Then I waited about, trying to get* khabbar *and at length had speech with a camel-sowar who rode from the Fort. Him I approached with empty hands raised above my head, and gave him money for news. Huzoor, they were captured! They are in chains! The Colonel Sahib was much too* hushyar[86] *to be fooled by that banao. Or else Vere-Vaughan Sahib, knowing all the time and holding his peace until they were inside the Fort, privately told the Colonel all things and delivered those evil men into his hands.'*

"Ganesh, I could have got up and danced for joy, only I couldn't move. Then came re-action and I passed out again. I suppose I really had sustained concussion of the brain, falling down that precipice."

"H'm," mused Ganesh Hazelrigg. "One would have thought you'd have been safe enough, in falling on your head, Dick."

"Well, you're wrong—for the first time in your life, doubtless. I had not only fallen on my head but on my ribs and my left ankle. Well, the Lord alone knows how long I lay in that cave, with Shere Khan feeding me as the ravens fed Elijah."

Richard Wendover yawned like a man weary almost to death.

"And now I have come down to have a talk with you about the projected Khairastan Road, about Bailitzin, and to hear what really happened at Giltraza Fort."

"You didn't come because you yearned to see me then, Dick?"

"No," grinned Wendover. "Knowing what a nuisance you can be with your 'Won't you come home, Bill Bailey.'"

"Ah! You've come to have a talk about the Road, about our Comrade, and about Giltraza. Yes, and you've come for a bigger purpose than that, my son, although you don't know it. *You've come to save a man from what happened to you.* You are going to prevent a youngster from crashing utterly, and bringing one or two others down with him, including his father, who happens to be a distinguished General."

"What, Vere-Vaughan?"

"Yes, Vere-Vaughan. You are coming Home, Bill Bailey, and you're going to bring Vere-Vaughan home—or keep him there. However, one thing at a time and

---

[86] *Clever.*

first things first, especially as they lead naturally up to the last, the important matter. Well, about the Road. That's decided on; the money appropriated and Superintending Engineers and such, appointed. And it is going to run through Khairastan, below Khairabad, and by Hunzana to Hunzana Fort, and thence to Giltraza, even if the Khan and every man in Khairastan and the Faquir of Ipi object. Yes, Giltraza. And now— do you believe in God, Dick?"

"Mind your own business, Ganesh. Why?"

"Oh, nothing, except that young Vere-Vaughan safe-conducted his 'rescue' party into Giltraza Fort where everybody but a sentry or two was asleep, and, but for the mercy and grace of God, there would by now have been no Giltraza for the Road to go to. But He had seen to it that one Usman Shah, Colonel Garstan's orderly, ex-Border-thief, raider and outlaw, should be in Giltraza Fort."

"Naturally he should, since his Sahib was there," interrupted Wendover.

". . . *and* that Usman Shah should be up and about and awake, very much awake, *and* by the light of the guard lantern, should have seen, not only a British Officer in Pathan kit talking English and introducing his friends, *but* should have recognized, in the British Officer's friends, dear old friends of his own; old pals along with whom he had made many a raid, cut many a throat, set fire to many a thatch, trotted home in the small hours with many a sack of loot. Yes, none other than his old cullies, Chimnai the Outlaw, Ibrahim the Strong, one-eyed Kassim Shah and a score more.

"*Well, well! Here's doings!*" thought Usman Shah. "And, there being no such good husband as a reformed rake, and no such honest game-keeper as a reformed poacher, off he marched in a prompt and soldierly manner and blew the gaff—to Colonel Garstan.

"Meanwhile, what do you think Vere-Vaughan had done in the cosy comfort of Colonel Garstan's boudoir? Produced a note, a passport, a *laisser passer*, letter of introduction in fact, from—whom do you think? None other than Major Bartholomew Hazelrigg, G.5 H.8 of

617

the Indian Army, Military Intelligence Department, not wholly unknown to fame."

"A letter from you in your handwriting and with your signature?" asked Wendover in amazement.

"No. That's the cunning part of it. A letter from me in Russian, which eliminates the hand-writing difficulty; and with my personal initials and Secret Service number."

"Huh! Bailitzin, of course!"

"Pretty cute, eh! Written in Russian, not only so that there should be no give-away if Garstan happened to know my ordinary handwriting, as he very well might, but written in Russian, so that poor young Vere-Vaughan would have no idea of the contents."

"And what did the letter say?"

"Why, '*Arrest bearer immediately, as a renegade and traitor*' and more to that effect. And the third devilish clever point about the whole scheme was that it caused Garstan naturally to jump to the conclusion that the escort who had set out from Kurnai with Vere-Vaughan, were Major Bartholomew Hazelrigg's men, detailed to get the traitor safely into British hands, that he might suffer British justice."

"By Jove!" murmured Wendover. "That's what he was doing when he visited Vere-Vaughan in prison. Impersonating you, and giving him a chit which Vere-Vaughan thought was to make everything all right. My God! I'll deal with Comrade Bailitzin when . . ."

"When you've dealt with poor young Vere-Vaughan's business, Dick. That comes first, you know. You, and you alone, can make it absolutely crystal clear to a Court Martial and to the dirtiest back-biter in India or anywhere else, that the boy was absolutely innocent of any intention of saving himself at that price, as well as absolutely ignorant of what was going on."

"And of course Garstan was completely taken in too," said Wendover.

"Absolutely. It is very easy to be wise after the event, and say that he shouldn't have been taken in, but wouldn't you or I have been deceived, in like circumstances? We might have acted in a different manner from that in which Colonel Garstan did, subsequently, but I think we should have accepted a letter brought to us by Vere-Vaughan *and guaranteed as genuine* by Vere-Vaughan. You see, the poor chap assured Garstan, with all his powers of persuasion and with all the truth that was in him, that Major Hazelrigg himself had written that note, in his presence, handed it to him, and said that he must get it safely to Colonel Garstan at Giltraza Fort. And who else—as Garstan would argue—speaking perfect English and introducing himself as Major Hazelrigg, could have got into touch with Vere-Vaughan in Kurnai, right in the heart of the Singing Hadji's country?

"No," continued Hazelrigg. "Since Vere-Vaughan himself insisted that the letter was genuine, well, it must be genuine, and Garstan had no option but to act upon it, and put Vere-Vaughan under arrest."

"And but for this Usman Shah, the thing was done, eh?" observed Wendover. "Thanks to my damned stupidity."

"Yes. Well, the best-laid schemes of mice and Bailitzins gang oft agley. And it was Usman Shah who was the 'agleying' instrument—instead of you, this time."

Hazelrigg glanced at his friend's sombre face.

"Cheer up, Dick," he said. "You can't expect to have a monopoly of the fort-saving industry, you know. But if Usman Shah was chosen as the instrument for that job, you were chosen for another one; and that was why you were moved to get up from Turangzai and go to Kurnai. It was that you might be able to testify for young Vere-Vaughan and, as I say, to save him from suffering what you've suffered. There's no one else can do it, and surely there's no one else who could be more anxious to do it? There's no one better qualified than you to know what such a thing as a false accusation and wrongful sentence means to a man. And another thing, Dick, he's younger than you were, and he's not of as tough a fibre. You'll stay and tell the Court of Enquiry all you've told me, won't you? Every one of those outlaw blackguards will swear that Vere-

Vaughan was in the know. They'll have been primed by Bailitzin to say that, and they'll do it—if only for the fun of the thing. You'll not only have saved the youngster and his family, you'll have saved the Army in India from a scandal and disgrace as bad as the Dreyfus case."

Wendover eyed his friend thoughtfully for a moment. "Yes," he said. "Of course I'll stay."

"Of course you must, since nobody else can give your evidence. Court won't let me tell them that you told me this; won't listen to hearsay evidence. It'll have to come direct from you, on oath . . . I must let Vere-Vaughan and the General and Charmian know at once. You don't look a Lump of Joy, Dick, but by Jove, you are a joy-bringer on this occasion! Thank God you came down out of the Sufed Kot country or wherever you were, in time.

"That's settled, then, Dick. You'll testify," he added, holding out his hand.

"I will," replied Wendover quietly, giving his friend's hand a brief shake.

Hazelrigg sank back against his cushion with a deep sigh of relief. *Now he had got him.*

He took another cheroot and struck a match.

"When will you come and see the General?" asked Hazelrigg, as he threw away the match and blew a long cloud of smoke.

"General? I don't want to see any Generals."

"No, and I don't suppose any Generals want to see you. Don't suppose anybody wants to see you. *But* you don't think I'm going to produce, as the prize witness for the defence, a dirty-nosed Pathan, lousy and smelly, who looks as truculent a *budmash* as Chimnai the Outlaw himself, or any one of his gang, do you? Good Lord, man, I can hire them at fourpence a day to say any mortal thing I tell them to say! Do you know who's going into the witness-box to end the whole case with a few words? Why, *Captain Richard Wendover of Napier's Horse*, the man who, once upon a time, got into Giltraza Fort, galvanized the defence, and saved it; the man whose name is familiar throughout the British Empire, Europe and America. You are coming with me to see the General. I'm going to introduce you and guarantee you to be whom you are—and he's going to re-instate you, as he has power to do, pending confirmation by the Commander-in-Chief. You'll be gazetted back to your old rank with a brevet and a decoration, and as Brevet-Colonel Richard Wendover, D.S.O., you'll give evidence that, of your own personal knowledge, Flying-Officer John Vere-Vaughan was approached, deluded, and deceived, by a European impersonating a Secret Service officer, Major Bartholomew Hazelrigg. You'll testify that, to your own personal knowledge, the outlaw band who accompanied him to Giltraza Fort did, at the instigation of this same European, pretend to be villagers of Kurnai who were anxious to share the ransom money, if any, paid by the Sirkar for the rescue and return of their prisoner. You will then tell the Court precisely what you intended to do, and exactly what happened, the result of which was the successful entry of the outlaws into Giltraza Fort."

"But look here, Ganesh . . ."

"Now, that's quite enough, my son," interrupted Hazelrigg, sitting bolt upright. "You leave this to me.

"You'll then inform the court," he continued, "that the European who, disguised as a Pathan, impersonated Major Bartholomew Hazelrigg, was a Russian—hence the note written in Russian and signed with my initials. You can then testify that he is an old friend of yours; that you knew him when he was Military Attaché in London; that you met him again at Tashkent when you were actually working there as a *munshi*; and that now he is a Russian agent working in Sufed Kot.

"I shall go and see the General this very night, and take a load off him that will make him ten years younger," he added.

"Yes, but look here. You listen to me," expostulated Wendover. "I said I'd give evidence that would clear Vere-Vaughan absolutely. I said nothing about making a public show of myself, and getting re-instated and all that. And what's more, there is to be no mention whatsoever of Breckinge. I'll not agree to your using what you know about him. I've said I'll stay and clear Vere-Vaughan, and I will, but . . ."

"And I said that you are no earthly good to me or to Vere-Vaughan in your present rôle and guise. Look at yourself. Who's going to listen to you? The Court would look at me, not at you—and grin:

"'Hullo! What's this? One of old Ganesh's budmashes saying his piece. Disgraceful attempt to interfere with the course of Justice. What's the old devil's game in trying to get Vere-Vaughan off? Why, of course, he's after Charmian Vere-Vaughan himself.'

"No," he continued, "you are going to do this, as in common decency you must, and you are going to do it properly, as in ordinary common tactics you must. You are going to give your evidence as a British Officer."

Hazelrigg lay back again.

Yes, thought he to himself, and I'm going to do a bit of testifying, too. This 'Spare poor Breckinge's memory' nonsense has gone on long enough. I'm going to tell all I know . . . Let the dead bury the dead . . . No, I don't mean that. Still less do I mean de mortuis nil nisi bonum . . . No. I mean mort main. The dead hand of Alexander Breckinge on Dick Wendover's throat. Well, there's no hand on mine; and the whole story is coming out now. God moves in a mysterious way. If Dick hadn't pushed off into the blue after the relief of Giltraza; if he hadn't been caught and flogged as he was, by this man Bailitzin; if he hadn't been on his track as a wandering Pathan budmash, he wouldn't now have been able to save Vere-Vaughan and his family from disgrace. And, on the whole, I think this brings him back in an even bigger blaze of glory than that in which he would have returned with the Giltraza Relief Force. . . . Now then, the quicker things move the better. The General will be back in Peshawar to-night.

He rose to his feet.

"Look, Dick. You'll give me your word not to leave this house till I come back, won't you?"

"Suppose you never do come back?"

Hazelrigg laughed.

"You get more and more Pathan every day, you know. You won't leave to-night, anyhow, will you?"

"No, I won't."

"Shout for Rissaldar-Major Moussafa Shah if you want anything whatever. He'll get a room ready for you and lay out some khaki. You'll find a tunic and slacks that'll more or less fit you. And the trimmings."

"Hurrying things a bit, aren't you, Ganesh?"

"No, no . . . By the way, what was that you said just now about being flogged?"

And Richard Wendover told that story fully.

"And I tell you, Ganesh," he concluded, "I shan't feel clean, whole; I shan't feel my back's healed; I shan't feel I'm a *man* until I have put that little matter straight between me and Comrade Bailitzin."

"No . . . No . . . I can understand that, Dick. Well, you leave it to me, and I'll bet you a small sum that you will see him in Peshawar before long; see him in the prisoner's dock; and what's more, on the scaffold in Peshawar Gaol. . . . You shall see him hanged."

"I should hate to."

"Didn't know you were squeamish, Dick."

"No, I don't think I am exactly what you'd call—squeamish. Nevertheless I should hate to see Comrade Bailitzin hanged.

"I don't say I wouldn't like to hang him myself," he added. "In fact, there are very few things that would give me greater pleasure."

"Well, funnier things than that have happened. You've got whisky and soda and cheroots by you."

VIII

Charmian Vere-Vaughan sat on the arm of her father's chair and stared, unseeing, as he did, into the glowing log fire. Thus had they sat since their silent dinner.

What more was there to say?

Nothing. However, there is always vain repetition of what is hope-inspiring, comfort-giving.

"They won't believe it, Daddy," said Charmian at length. "They can't. Is it likely that Jack would do a thing like that? *Your* son?"

"Courts of Law, Military or Civil, don't go by what is likely, my dear," was the curt reply. "They go by facts."

"But surely they go by probabilities."

"They go by evidence, and evidence is against him. Major Hazelrigg didn't give him that note, and when he is asked who in God's name *did* give it to him, he can only say, in effect, '*Some man gave it me.*' How does that sound?"

"Well, when Jack says some man gave it him, we know that some man did give it to him."

"Yes, but *they* don't. If I were on a Court-Martial, and the prisoner had some amazing document or what-not, for which he had to account, and all he could say was '*Some man gave it to me,*' I know what I should think. Why, it's what the pickpocket says, to account for the possession of the gold watch. '*Someone gave it to me.*' And of course he cannot say who gave him the gold watch. Nor can Jack say who gave him the Russian note, except that it was 'some man.' Without doubting Jack's word for one second, one has to put oneself in the place of the Court-Martial, and admit that it sounds thin."

"But Daddy, look here. When that note ordering his arrest is produced, and Major Hazelrigg testifies that it is a forgery, and that he never wrote it, isn't that all in Jack's favour? Obviously it is bogus, and was written

624

by an enemy, and is all part of the plot to get those outlaws into Giltraza."

"Might have been written by a friend—of the British, I mean—who was on Intelligence work there, and thought Jack was playing for safety too cleverly. I haven't seen the document, of course. Such a person might have been a subordinate agent whose name carried no weight. Might have been a *babu* like Hurri Chandra Gosh. He might have written it, and realized it would carry weight and achieve its purpose if it had Major Hazelrigg's initials and official number. Besides, my dear, Jack was inside the Fort with the outlaw band, before he produced it."

"Well then, they can't say he used it to get them in, can they?"

"No, and that does him no good. He got them in by personally guaranteeing them."

Silence again.

Charmian sighed deeply.

"That girl arrives to-morrow, Daddy," she said suddenly.

"Oh Lord!" groaned the General. "Wasn't time to put her off, I suppose?"

"No. Couldn't very well do that after she had started. And one couldn't possibly stop her at Bombay, not knowing whether she had anywhere else to go."

"No, of course not," agreed General Vere-Vaughan. "Damn nuisance though."

"Oh, I don't know. She may be all to the good. Start an affair with you, Archibald, and keep you young and fresh."

Glancing up at her father's face, she realized that there was need of some such rejuvenating process. He'd be an old man in a few months, unless something happened, instead of the young-for-fifty pal that he had been until this blow had fallen.

§2

Sybil Ffoulkes rose to her feet as the train slowed

down, and tried to shake some of the dust of North-West India from her white dress.

In a few minutes the train would be in the station and she would have reached the end of her long journey, of which the rail-road from Bombay to Peshawar seemed longer in retrospect than the sea journey from Marseilles.

In a few minutes she would see the place that Dickie knew well, tread the streets that he—perhaps recently—had trodden.

Why, he might be in Peshawar itself at that very moment.

And what was she going to do now that she had reached Peshawar? Strain every nerve, use every wile, to get in touch with him, to see him and to get him to come back, back to India, back to the Army, back to her. For she was quite certain that to whatever else he came back, he must come back to her whom, in his queer way, his strange inarticulate grudging way, he had always loved. Of that she was absolutely certain.

Of course he did not love her in the way that she loved him, with all her heart and soul and mind and strength; but he loved her after his own fashion, and that would have to be good enough. It would be good enough.

The train drew to a standstill and a spick-and-span young officer, followed by an orderly, approached the first-class carriages and seeing a girl standing by an open door, saluted.

"Miss Ffoulkes?"

"Yes."

"Oh, good morning. The General, Sir Archibald Vere-Vaughan, sent me to meet you. Place you under military escort, you know. And Miss Vere-Vaughan is awaiting you at Flagstaff House, and asked me to say how sorry she is that it was quite impossible for her to come to the station."

And he murmured something about an invasion of Great Ones for luncheon.

And ere Sybil could reply, he bade the orderly see; that the Miss Sahib's *saman*[87] was loaded on to the mule-cart *ek dum*[88] or quicker.

Taking her dressing-case, he led the way through the noisy throng to where, outside the station, a big car, driven by a soldier-chauffeur, awaited them.

Sybil glanced about her. Richard Wendover had come to this railway station many times. He must know it nearly as well as he did the little station at Home.

Dare she ask this young aide-de-camp whether he knew him? No. And she must cease behaving and thinking like a fool.

On second thoughts, was there any real objection to her thinking like a fool, seeing that it was the only comfort and pleasure that she had in life.

Nothing could have been warmer than her welcome. Both the General and Charmian were kindness itself, expressed the greatest pleasure at having her, and the hope that it would be for just as long as she cared to stay.

As Sybil thanked them, she wondered what they would say if she had spoken up truthfully and said:

"That'll be just as long as it takes me to find Dickie, and to decoy him here."

But in spite of their warm and kindly welcome and obvious wish to make her feel at home, she was conscious of an 'atmosphere.' And to atmosphere she was extremely sensitive.

What was it? The fear that hangs over Peshawar as part of its very life, the sense of living on the edge of a volcano?

Probably not, in the General's own house. On the other hand, who better than he would know the danger and feel the strain?

Or was it something domestic, this sense of constraint, tension, this feeling as of iron self-repression, of vital words unuttered?

---

[87] *Luggage.*
[88] *At once.*

Sybil decided that it was the absent-mindedness of minds that were pre-occupied by trouble.

§3

Yes, the General and his daughter had got something on their minds. Well, so had she, and they could all be absent-minded together.

Thus Sybil Ffoulkes, as she sat in the drawing-room after dinner that night, and studied her host and hostess as they moved about among their guests. As these were all senior officers and two or three wives, she felt that there might be among them somebody who had known Richard Wendover. For she saw Life in terms of Richard Wendover; Time itself, as the time since she had seen him, and the time that was to pass before she should see him again; Space as the distance that separated her from him; and she divided People into those who had, or might have, seen and known him, and people who could not have done so.

And as she sat fighting against the long sickness of hope deferred, but never pitying herself, a man who had been at the far end of the dinner-table approached her, took her empty coffee-cup, and said,

"We haven't met before, I think, but we have corresponded, Miss Ffoulkes. Major Hazelrigg."

"*Oh!*" gasped Sybil. "Oh, I'm *so* glad. Thank you very very much indeed for your kindness in writing. I was so hoping to have this opportunity of trying to tell you how grateful I am. But I didn't think it would come on my first evening in Peshawar. Do you know where he is now?"

Ganesh Hazelrigg patted the clenched hand that lay on the sofa beside him and forbore to ask who '*he*' might be.

"I do," he said.

"Oh, where? Very very far away? Is it a place that I could get to? . . . Oh, where is he?"

"He's in Peshawar, my dear," said Hazelrigg, nodding his head in ponderous re-assurance.

It being part of his arduous, dangerous, and thrillingly interesting profession to study faces and read the minds to which they were indexes, Hazelrigg decided that this particular face, dead white, its large and brilliant eyes now burning with a fierce flame, was the index of a one-way mind of tremendous determination and inflexible will-power, of a mind simple, sincere and direct; honest, unswerving and faithful unto death. Here was a person worth meeting, a person to interest such a man as himself, and a woman to move the immovable Richard Wendover.

Hazelrigg's eyes lit up as he watched the girl.

Why, this was a gift from Heaven, a god-send. Surely Wendover must be ripe and ready for such a venture and for such a woman, after these years of lonely self-repression, these years which he must have spent in eating out his heart, almost utterly alone, more alone really than any *sadhu* sitting in his Himalayan eyrie. For there is no loneliness like that of being alone in a crowd of strangers, especially alien strangers, men of antithetic outlook upon life, religion, home, marriage, women, law and everything else. No, Ganesh Hazelrigg knew something of that loneliness, and wondered how a man could stand it without respite, without relief; and with the intention of suffering it as long as he should live.

Yes, this was a God-sent chance and hope, for though honours, praise, reward, re-instatement, re-compense would not bring him back to his own again, this woman might—in the likely event of his relapsing after he had saved young Vere-Vaughan.

She should have the chance, anyway.

And straightway the subtle and intriguing mind of Bartholomew Hazelrigg began to work with thoughts of the best uses for this tool delivered to his hand. So far as he could remember, Wendover had never mentioned Sybil Ffoulkes to him, but then, Richard Wendover was very good at not-mentioning.

In the happy days before red ruin overtook him, he had been, to say the least of it, uncommunicative, reticent, and somewhat taciturn. And since then, this trait had increased tenfold. When he was with him on the road, in the Singing Hadji's camp outside Giltraza, and elsewhere, speech had seemed to be not only difficult but distasteful; and, until his outburst of the previous night, it had really seemed that he was losing the faculty of talking in his own tongue.

Now then, if his sense of duty forced him out into the open, forced him to accept acknowledgment of identity; forced him to the acceptance of publicity and praise, might not this girl be able to make that condition permanent?

The Return of Richard Wendover.

Ganesh Hazelrigg, in spite of his training, his way of life, and all that he had seen and done, remained at heart a Romantic. How delightful when Romance went hand-in-hand with business, his business of plotting, spying, intriguing, and serving his country in secret and devious ways. Yes, most certainly this Sybil Ffoulkes should meet Richard Wendover, and have the best possible opportunity of bringing that stubborn, quixotic, and pride-ridden fool to his senses.

"*Here!* In Peshawar?" whispered the girl. "*Oh!* . . . Could I see him . . . I must see him . . . Could you take me to him?"

"I can. I will. Just exactly how and when, I must think. But you shall see him."

The girl's hand tightened on his wrist with a grip iron. Gad, how strong she was! Muscles and will both of steel. The right sort of mate for Richard Wendover.

Yes, it looked as though one of Ganesh Hazelrigg's jobs was going to succeed. Gloriously and soon. This was answer to prayer; the wish that is a prayer.

Yes, he had got him where he wanted him now, and the girl would keep him there.

"Oh, Major Hazelrigg—soon? I can't believe it. I . . ." whispered the girl, and seemed unable to say more.

This would want a little arranging—going down into the Bazaar in uniform or in mufti with a European woman. The house was too carefully watched. And even the sinister and forbidding Rissaldar-Major Moussafa Shah would be questioned by his neighbours if a Miss Sahib were seen going into his silent and secret house.

No, he had better go in Pathan kit, and she had better wear a *bourka*[89] over her European dress. That would merely cause the keen-eyed watchers to grin and speak evil of the chaste Rissaldar.

And on the way up to the roof she could take off the *bourka* and come upon Wendover as what she was, a beautiful English girl. That would knock him off his perch; whereas the appearance of a *bourka*-covered native woman would not interest him in the least. What he would register, to that vision, would be annoyance.

From what he had seen while, in the rôle of Inayatullah Hussein the Afghan horse-dealer, he had been a guest in the house of Shere Khan in Khairabad, Richard Wendover had had no use for, and no dealings with, native women. It had interested him to note that Wendover had not married a Pathan girl, and that he led a completely celibate life. Shere Khan had rallied him on the subject in the presence of the said Inayatullah Hussein.

Yes, it would be bad staff-work, bad stage-management, to take this girl to Rissaldar-Major Moussafa Shah's house in native dress, and lose the element of surprise; of shock, in fact. By the time it had been explained that the bundle was Sybil Ffoulkes, an Englishwoman and not a native, the whole thing would be spoilt. It was the sudden jolt that was wanted.

"I'll take you to see him to-morrow," he said.

And strong as was her grip upon his wrist, it tightened perceptibly.

"To-morrow," she breathed.

"Yes. You—er—dress as you like, and I'll bring a *bourka*, and if you don't mind being escorted by a native, I shall be in the dress of a Pathan. Nice respectable Pathan, you know. A sort of Nawab. I had better mention it to the General—I shall be having a talk with

---

[89] *Garment covering a woman completely from head to foot.*

him to-night—and perhaps you had better tell Char-mian all about it. I think you'll find her more than sympathetic. She has met Dick Wendover, you know, and admires him tremendously. Yes, we'll go to-morrow."

"How can I thank you? I can only . . ."

"No, no. Quite the other way about. I shall have cause—I hope—to thank you. I want to see my friend Richard Wendover back in his proper place. We all do. Dreadful waste of a life. A magnificent man like that. Not but what he's most devilish useful where he is, but still . . ."

"I'd do anything. Anything," whispered the girl.

"Would you? Would you walk from here to Khaira-bad on foot, sleeping on the ground and eating what you carried?"

"Of course I would. I'd walk from here to Khairabad to see Dick for five minutes."

"In danger of capture by bandits?"

"In danger of anything."

Hazelrigg laughed and patted the hand which had relinquished its hold upon his wrist.

"That's the spirit. We'll get him back."

§4

That night, after the departure of the other guests, the General took Hazelrigg to his sanctum that he might hear fuller particulars of the good news, a brief outline of which Hazelrigg had whispered to him on arrival.

"Well, there it is, Sir," he concluded. "For the second time in his amazing life, Wendover plays *deus ex machina*. He is here in Peshawar, and he is, of course, ready to do his duty in the matter of removing any suggestion of suspicion as to your son's motives and conduct. Working at his self-appointed task as Secret Service agent and Intelligence spy, he went to the place where your son was held captive, with the view to negotiating ransom; and there he saw the chance of not only getting him safe into Giltraza, but getting nearly all the leaders and fomenters of Border trouble as well.

"And in his own proper person as Captain Richard Wendover, of not only unblemished but brilliant record, he will testify that your son was the victim of an extremely accomplished and astute Russian agent who impersonated me, and hatched the plot of giving your son, for his supposed escort, the men who were to seize the Fort.

"Wendover was present at the interviews between some of these men and your son; was filled with admiration at the way the boy dealt with them, getting them to swear on the Koran that they would loyally carry out their undertaking to him; and at the way in which he had flatly refused to show them how to work the machine-gun they had taken from his aeroplane.

"In fact, he can do more than exculpate and exonerate him, he can show him worthy of the highest praise. Thanks to Richard Wendover, your son will get a decoration rather than a Court-Martial sentence, or any sort of stigma."

"Thank you, Hazelrigg," said the General. "I can't say more than that, but I mean it."

And Hazelrigg knew that from General Sir Archibald Vere-Vaughan, this was as good as a speech of perfervid gratitude.

"I remember the matter of Wendover's court-martial, of course," the General added, after a pause.

"And you get the point, Sir?" smiled Hazelrigg, "that, for his evidence to carry full weight, it *must come from Captain Richard Wendover of Napier's Horse*. Better still, from Major and Brevet-Colonel Richard Wendover, D.S.O. That'll be a very different thing from evidence given by a renegade white man who has 'gone native.' He must get *now* what he would have got—if he hadn't been such a fool as to run away—after the Giltraza show."

"Of course. Exactly. Naturally," mused the General. "He must be re-instated; and, as you say, promoted and decorated; and he must appear at the court-martial in the uniform of his Regiment . . . Why did he disappear after the Giltraza show?"

"Oh, I think one can understand it, Sir. He had taken a terrible knock and he was pretty bitter—as you or I would have been—since he was absolutely innocent. Think what a man, wrongfully hanged for murder, must feel as he stands on the scaffold with a rope round his neck. It must have been like that for him when he was cashiered. And another thing, he's a naturally shy man. I mean, he's the last person in the world to enjoy *réclame* and publicity and the lime-light. And I really believe he does enjoy the Pathan life; the absolute freedom and the untrammelled unconventionalism. I do myself, when I am on a job in disguise, up there."

"Yes, but you don't 'go Pathan,' so to speak. You act Pathan, and you come back to Civilization. You can throw it all off, and there you are, in the Clubs and Messes, and the bungalows of Society."

"And get that variety which is the spice of life? Quite so, Sir. And I am perfectly certain that at times, just occasionally, Wendover must still get an unbearable nostalgia, must feel suicidal, especially when he thinks not only of what he left, but of the reputation he left behind him. Broke, cashiered, disgraced . . . Yes, and that brings me to something I particularly wanted to say to you, Sir, in the very strictest confidence."

"Yes?"

"In the very strictest confidence, might I repeat that, Sir? Rub it in, so to speak."

"My dear Hazelrigg, you don't suppose that if once I gave you my word, I should . . ."

"No, Sir. Of course not. Please don't misunderstand me. I only said what I did, in order to make it very plain and clear that what I am going to say is in the very strictest confidence. I mean, absolutely between you and me, and not to go outside this room unless and until Wendover makes it public—which he never will do."

"I understand," said the General.

"Well, like everybody else, I supposed Wendover to be dead, killed by a lion in Africa. When I had proved

634

that he was alive, by seeing him myself, I made up my mind that on the very first opportunity, I'd go into his case and arrive at the facts, for I knew, as well as I knew my own name, that the Court-Martial had not arrived at the truth. And to cut a long story short, I found that I was right; and I obtained irrefutable proof that Wendover, who was cashiered for being drunk, had been drugged. Moreover, I got the written confession of the actual criminal, the doctor who had compounded the drug."

"But why didn't you publish it?" asked the General.

"Because Wendover wouldn't allow me to do so. He burnt it."

"Good God!" exclaimed the General. "What an unspeakable fool. But why? *Why?*"

"Because the guilty man gave his life saving Wendover's. Died for him, in point of fact."

"I see. I see. What a situation! . . . Your friend Wendover is a man."

"My friend Wendover is a man."

"And we must save him, Hazelrigg. Get him back."

"Yes, and I think it can be done. Our hands have been unexpectedly strengthened. At least, I think they have. A woman."

"Oh! That's interesting. Who is she? Not . . . ?"

"Yes, Sir. Miss Ffoulkes. They grew up together. Boy and girl sweethearts, I believe. I imagine they were engaged when the crash came, and that he ran away from her as well as from everything else. If I'm right in thinking he did so, then obviously he did it rather than 'drag her down' as he would imagine. If she had been coming out to marry him, he wasn't going to let her come and marry a—well, a criminal. A disgraced and degraded outcast. Still less, a renegade, as he considered that he had made himself when he turned Pathan."

"He couldn't have loved her very desperately," observed the General, "or he'd have considered her when he had the chance to return in a blaze of glory, triumphant over his enemy and his detractors—and all that."

"No, I shouldn't think he ever loved her—er—very desperately. Not that kind of chap. I imagine that most of the loving is on her side."

"And she stuck to him, eh?"

"Absolutely. She and her father got at me through Colonel Harrington-Spens, to see if I could give them any information. Of course I let them know, directly I discovered that he was alive and—well, here she is."

"And do you think she'll have some influence, although he neglected her for so long?"

"Yes, Sir, I do. Surely she must epitomise all that he has lost. When he sees her and hears her, when she talks of the past, I mean, she must be the very spirit of England, Home, and Beauty, to a man who has lived as he has, since he was cashiered. And inasmuch as he's 'coming back' to do his duty in the matter of your son, I think he'll stay put, as a matter of common decency, if not duty, to this girl. But—and this is the point, Sir—there must be no mention of Breckinge."

"Breckinge?"

"Yes, the doctor who ruined his life and whom he forgave when he afterwards saved it. Knowing my Wendover as I do, I'm perfectly certain that, having made up his mind not to use Breckinge's confession then, he won't do it *now*. I mean he won't damn the fellow's memory and blacken his name, to clear his own. No. We shall have to get him to do what he will very much dislike doing, and what he flatly refused to do before—be given a full and free *pardon* and re-instatement. Pardon for what he never did. Re-instatement, honour and reward, for what he did at Giltraza."

"And there, the girl can, and will, help, eh?"

"She'd literally give her right hand to do so. I'm taking her down to the Native City to-morrow to see him."

When Major Bartholomew Hazelrigg said good-bye to General Vere-Vaughan, the hour was small and the hopes of both these gentlemen were great.

§5

In the ground-floor grim reception-room of the silent secret house of Rissaldar-Major Moussafa Shah, Sybil Ffoulkes removed the all-enveloping *bourka* which, like an extinguisher, covered and hid her from the crown of her head to the soles of her feet; tidied her hair; strove to keep her throbbing heart from deafening and choking her; and then followed Ganesh Hazelrigg up a narrow wooden stair which, after numerous twists and turns, ended at a closed door.

Opening this, Hazelrigg stepped out on to the roof, stood aside, announced in butler-like voice and manner:

"A lady to see you, Sir," closed the door and clattered down the stairs, leaving Sybil Ffoulkes face to face with Richard Wendover who had sprung to his feet from the native *charpai* on which he had been sitting.

"*Dickie!*"

He stared incredulous.

With shining eyes and transfigured face she came to him.

"Dickie!" she said again, and put her arms about his neck.

"Good God! Sybil!" said Wendover, and in kindly brotherly fashion, kissed her.

For a while she clung to him, her cheek against his breast.

"Oh, Dickie, how could you?"

"How could I what?"

"Not write to me."

"How could I not write to you? Why, by not writing to you."

"Oh, Dickie! . . . But I have got you now."

"Yes. Break away. And don't kiss coming out of the clinch."

"Aren't you glad to see me, Dickie?"

"Oh, yes. Rather. Frightfully."

Richard Wendover, taking the girl by the shoulders, and holding her off from him, looked into her shining eyes.

"But what the devil are you doing here, young Sybil? Who asked you to . . . ?"

"What am I doing? I'm 'doing' India, Dickie. Visiting the country."

"So am I," replied Wendover. "I'm down here for a few days. How long are you staying?"

"Depends on you, my dear. Oh, Dickie, how *could* you?"

"Now don't start that all over again. And don't snivel. Come on. Sit down."

Comfortably seated side by side on the cushioned *charpai*, the two talked of old times, talked as they had done a thousand times in childhood, when the girl had been the boy's inseparable companion, fag, henchman and willing slave.

Slowly he thawed and warmed towards the woman of whom he had always been quietly fond, whom he had always admired without praise, and had approved without acknowledgment.

And when he realized that she had come to India with no other object or reason than to try to find him, to help him in any way that might be possible, and to advise him wisely and induce him to return, he was more moved and touched than he would admit, even to himself.

A fine lass, a stayer, he was feign to confess. The child who had been a good scout, a sound pal, had grown up into a remarkable woman. For it was remarkable, surely, that a girl should have wished to come half-way round the world to look for a man who was under a cloud, to tell him that she loved him—had always loved him—especially when he was disgraced, ruined, *déclassé*, as even the general public knew; and now she had come with the object not only of helping him, but of joining him, throwing in her lot with his.

For this was abundantly clear from what Sybil had been saying.

Well, doubtless she and Ganesh Hazelrigg were right, and it was his duty to himself, as well as to quite a lot of other people, to have his name publicly cleared and himself publicly re-instated. Incidentally, it was—

as General Sir Archibald Vere-Vaughan had said to
Ganesh—his duty to the British Army. But of course
the General had an axe to grind, since the worthier the
witness, the more valuable his testimony before the
Court-Martial. No, that was an unworthy thought. The
General quite honestly wanted the stigma removed
from the officer's name and thereby from the fair fame
of the Army.

Nevertheless, it was the Army that had kicked him
out.

But, oh Lord, he mustn't start all that again for the
millionth time. When would this bitterness be purged?

Yes. He would of course do the proper thing by
young Vere-Vaughan and do it handsomely; appear in
Court with a brand new halo, shining bright.

And then?

Wasn't he, on the whole, happier on those wild
hills, with those wild men? Weren't they fitter companions for Richard Wendover as he now was, than the
over-civilized inhabitants of British cantonments?
Would he not rather live and die a free tribesman, die
eventually with a bullet through his brain, make a
good end in hot blood, than eke out his dwindling
strength, with whitening hair and stiffening joints in
some dull village in England?

England—that green and pleasant land.

The Border—that wild fierce stark mountain-group.

England, Home and Beauty. The beauty of this
wonderful woman by his side.

England on a fair May morning. Leafy England in
summer. Cubbing at dawn on a fine October day.
Hunting thrice a week through the winter. Hunting,
shooting, fishing, golf.

The Border, stark and grim, harsh and cruel; the
treachery and savagery, the squalor, the dirt and the
unimaginable poverty, narrowness and restrictions of
native village life.

And loneliness, the utter awful loneliness which, at
times, drove him almost mad; that unbearable monotony of life which was undoubtedly affecting his mind
and character.

Yes, but his friend Shere Khan. The man to whom he owed his salvation from madness, from despair, death and damnation, when he had not a soul to whom he could turn for a word of friendship and faith. How could he leave him? How should Richard Wendover leave Shere Khan and retain his self-respect, knowing that nothing on earth would ever induce Shere Khan voluntarily to leave Richard Wendover, in any conceivable circumstances whatsoever?

If he rejoined his Regiment at Napierpur, he could not take Shere Khan with him. Shere Khan, the deserter, who had deserted that he might help and save his Sahib. And he *had* saved him. Saved him from Hell and suicide, as a man saves another who is drowning.

And suppose he insisted on the inclusion of Shere Khan in his own amnesty and forgiveness? . . . God damn them! How dare they 'forgive' him for what he had never done? But no, that was his own fault and misfortune and pride. He would not make Breckinge's memory a bridge to his own immaculate return, proclaimed blameless and therefore in no need of forgiveness.

No, he couldn't do that, since by his own decision he was receiving a pardon for his alleged crime. His pardon would be an act of grace on the part of the Authorities in return for his saving Giltraza, and he would not be in a position to bargain about Shere Khan.

Besides, it would be merely postponing the parting. If he returned to India and took Shere Khan with him as friend, orderly or anything else, the day would come when Richard Wendover would have to retire, to whatever rank he might rise. And then he must leave India —because if he decided to go back to the Regiment, he would marry Sybil—and he couldn't ask Sybil to 'retire' in India. They'd have to go Home when he retired, of course. He must give Sybil a fair deal. And quite unconsciously, he put his arm about her shoulders and drew her to him.

"Oh Dickie. You do forgive me?"

"Yes," replied Richard Wendover. "Yes, I'll forgive

you, young Sybil—this once . . . Here, don't strangle me!"

§6

That evening as Sybil dressed for dinner, she found herself singing aloud, and wondered how long it was since last she had done such a thing.

He was alive; he was well; and he was amenable. Amenable to Major Hazelrigg's insistence that he should accept pardon and re-instatement; and, so far as she could tell, to her insistence that he should return permanently to his proper way of life as what he was, a British Officer of not only unblemished, but most distinguished, record.

And when everything was straight, and the affairs of Captain Richard Wendover and Flying-Officer Vere-Vaughan were finally settled, she would ask Dickie whether he realized *now* that he needed someone to look after him; and she would remind him of the promise of marriage made long ago—her promise. And if he said he didn't want to marry, she'd tell him that, not having tried it, he knew nothing about the matter, and couldn't possibly know whether he liked it or not. And she'd make him a fair offer that, if at the end of— what should she say, one, two, three, five years—he found he didn't like it, she'd set him free. (And she'd make him love it, beyond anything he had known.) But she'd promise to set him free if he wanted "freedom." Having married him, she would divorce him.

Yes, that's how she would talk to him.

Hurrying downstairs lest she should be late for dinner—and for a big dinner-party—late in the General's house of all places, she found that she was first in the drawing-room.

A car drove up to the steps on the far-distant side of the vast verandah. Two orderlies sprang to their feet, and a man in evening-dress stepped out of the car, gave his hat, scarf and light overcoat to the Goanese butler, who, handing them to an underling, advanced to the drawing-room, announced into the emptiness of the great drawing-room:

"Mr. Stuyvesant Sahib," bowed and retired.

Looking round the room for his host and hostess, and seeing no one, the man, with assured manner, strode across the shining parquet in the direction of the log fire, and suddenly saw Sybil Ffoulkes seated in a high-backed chair.

"Good evening," he began. "I . . ."

And suddenly stopped open-mouthed.

"*Prince Bailitzin!*" said the girl. "*Why!* I had no idea that you . . ."

And also stopped.

For, to her amazement, the man turned on his heel, hurried from the room and called for his car.

"But what an extraordinary thing!" thought Sybil; and, a minute or two later, dismissed Prince Bailitzin from her mind, as her thoughts returned to their ever-constant subject, Richard Wendover.

At dinner, a large periodical affair at which there were usually from twenty to thirty guests—many of whom were birds of passage who had called and entered their names in the Visitors' Book at Flagstaff House—there was a vacant place. But all traces of it being swiftly obliterated by the competent butler, no-body noticed the absence of that active, inquisitive, and very interesting American journalist, Mr. Sylvanus H. Stuyvesant of the United American Press.

IX

And, as the world soon knew, Captain Richard Wendover was pardoned, re-instated, promoted and decorated, in recognition of the great courage and ability, initiative and fine example, that he had shown in the successful defence of Giltraza Fort.[90]

All that the Brigadier-General commanding the relieving force had recommended at the time was now: carried out in full, the unfortunate officer having been happily re-discovered living in Peshawar.

People thought none the worse of him for having modestly disappeared from Giltraza, as soon as he was able to travel in a camel *cacolet*, and decided that few men had earned a better D.S.O.

The nine days' wonder of his re-appearance and re-instatement became at least eighteen when, his blushing honours thick upon him, he testified publicly and effectively, that Flying-Officer John Vere-Vaughan had behaved with the utmost courage, coolness and competence while a prisoner in the hands of the fanatical followers of the Singing Hadji of Sufed Kot; and that he had been completely deceived as to the true character of the men whom he had introduced into Giltraza Fort in the belief that they were honest Tribesmen, solely desirous of rescuing him, albeit in return for ransom money.

This young officer was complimented, decorated and promoted—a sufficient answer to the malicious scandalmongers who had been more than hinting that he had tried to buy his own safety at the expense of that of a British outpost.

---

[90] *See "The Man of a Ghost."*

X

The hospitable dining-room of Flagstaff House could rarely have contained a happier family than that which gathered about its great table on the eve of the departure of some of the members of its house-party to their respective destinations.

Almost *en famille*, there sat down General Sir Archibald Vere-Vaughan, his daughter Charmian and her friend Sybil Ffoulkes; his son John; Major Bartholomew Hazelrigg; Major and Brevet-Colonel Richard Wendover; Colonel Ormesby and Mr. Thomas Dodd.

It needed not the General's best champagne to make conversation flow, wit sparkle, and laughter bubble. The General beamed, thanking Heaven for his son's happy issue from his afflictions, and eyeing leniently his daughter's outrageous flirtation with Ganesh Hazelrigg—God bless him. Him and that splendid feller, Richard Wendover. Amazing chap. It was to be hoped he'd settle down now to regimental duty. Though probably he'd hanker for the old life sometimes. Well, if he did, he could go off on a shooting-trip in Kashmir or somewhere, and work it out of his system that way. Could that girl hold him—if the *affaire* came to anything? According to Charmian, she was absolutely mad about him. But if Wendover suffered from any of the same sort of madness, he certainly concealed it well. He might settle down. There was one thing. Napier's Horse would give him and her a warm welcome.

By Jove, an idea! Suppose Wendover really loathed the thought of returning to regimental life as much as he thought he did, what about the new job for which he, General Vere-Vaughan, had been asked to recommend somebody. Colonel of the new Khairastan Levies, when they were raised, to guard and guarantee the peace of the Khairastan-Giltraza Road. Now that would be a job for such a man as Wendover. He knew the country like the palm of his hand; spoke the language as well as he spoke his own; knew all the leading people in that part of the world; could get inside the skin of the Pathan and think his thoughts. And of course he'd have the most perfect Intelligence Service. There could not possibly be a better man for the post, or a better post for the man. He'd talk to him about it after dinner.

If he didn't want to go back to a British India cantonment, he'd jump at it, surely.

And what about Sybil Ffoulkes? No doubt she'd jump at it too, because it was just the sort of job that would keep him happy and keep him in the place and the way of life that he loved. If he married her, came back to India, and hated it, she'd always have the feeling that it was, to some extent, her fault that he was discontented and miserable; and that she had been the cause of his giving up the only life that suited him. On the other hand, what about the girl herself in such circumstances? How would she get on, in Khairastan? Probably get on well enough anywhere, so long as she was with Wendover who, according to Charmian, had been the one love of her life and her life-long love. She certainly must be devilish fond of the feller to come out here and go for him as she had done. Some people would call it chucking herself at his head, and say that she ought to be ashamed of herself.

Well, the girl was far above that sort of shame; and she was about the best thing that could be chucked at Wendover's head.

Glancing at them, he noticed that, as usual, Sybil was talking and Wendover listening—or not listening. She must find him damned irritating. Or was it a case of whatever he did was right?

Well, probably she knew him better than anybody else did, and it was a credit to his personality and character that he had inspired a love like that.

And the General heaved a deep sigh as he looked back over the barren years behind him.

"I say, Dickie, I've just thought of such a queer

thing that happened here, a little while ago," Sybil was saying to Wendover, as the General was watching them.

"Oh? It didn't strike you dumb!"

"It did though—for a moment. Who do you think walked into the drawing-room while I was sitting there alone? Do you remember that Prince Bailitzin?"

Wendover's eyes turned sharply toward hers.

"Yes, I do remember a gentleman named Bailitzin," he said.

"Well, I was sitting in the drawing-room alone just before dinner and he walked in."

"Did he now?" said Wendover quietly.

"Yes, and the curious thing was that the butler called out '*Mr. Stuyvesant, Sahib,*' most distinctly."

"Oh, yes? And what happened?"

"The man came across the room, saw me and gave a start. It must have been Prince Bailitzin because he obviously recognized me immediately and just stared— gaped. I said '*Why, Prince Bailitzin!*' and then he turned about, and marched out of the room. And he must have gone straight away because he wasn't at the dinner."

"Did you say anything to the General?"

"No, there was quite a big party that night, and I didn't get an opportunity of speaking to the General or Charmian in private, until we were going to bed. When the women were in the drawing-room she was doing her job as hostess; and when the men came in, the General joined in a bridge four on the verandah. Not that I thought it was of any particular importance either, but when Charmian came to my room, as she always does to say good night and see if I have everything I want, I just mentioned it. She was partly puzzled and partly inclined to pooh-pooh it altogether, and said:

"'*Well, was he Stuyvesant the Special Correspondent playing Russian Bears, in London; or is he the Russian Prince What-d'you-call-him playing American Stuyvesants, in Peshawar?*'

"I said, '*Anyhow, he is the man who was a Russian*

attaché in London before the War and he was quite well known to my people and everybody in Town, as Prince Bailitzin. He came to our house.'

"'Then I'll tell you what it is, my child,' said Charmian. 'It's one of those extraordinary doubles you hear of. Two men exactly alike. Mr. Stuyvesant was actually recommended to Daddy's loving care by Head Quarters, Rawalpindi.'

"'Then,' said I, bringing down my trump card heavily, 'why did he turn round and walk out of the house when he saw me? And if he was invited to dinner, why didn't he stay?'

"'Oh, well, as for that, he's a journalist and a Special Correspondent, and liable to rush from the dinner table, let alone the drawing-room, if he suddenly thinks of something, or hears some news. One leap to the Telegraph Office to cable to his paper.'

"'And why should the sight of me give him the idea of cabling to his newspaper?' I asked.

"'Who shall say?' laughed Charmian. 'You may have reminded him of some other catastrophe, and he rushed off to cable it. Don't go and queer my Mr. Stuyvesant's pitch. He's rather a bright spot in my dull young life, and quite a change from these military-minded men. He's a good guy.'

"'Well, anyhow, mind you tell the General what I've told you,' said I, and left it at that."

"And did she tell him?" asked Wendover.

"I don't know, Dickie, and I haven't thought about him from then till now."

"I think about him quite a lot," observed Richard Wendover.

"Why?" asked Sybil Ffoulkes.

"Tell you, some day. Perhaps."

"Are you still jealous of him, Dickie?" asked the girl, though she feared that it was highly improbable that the sentiment of jealousy was one that Richard Wendover was likely to entertain.

So the good Bailitzin had been down in Peshawar had he, reflected Wendover, and in the rôle of an

American Special Correspondent! And he had, more-over, satisfied G.H.Q. at Rawalpindi as to his *bona fides.* Assured of his genuineness, G.H.Q. at Rawal-pindi had passed him on to G.H.Q. Peshawar (with what he would, in that rôle, have called their O.K.) and with full permission to "cover" the North-West Frontier for the American newspaper syndicate that he repre-sented.

Yes, one had to hand it to Bailitzin as a very astute, clever, accomplished man, as well as a very brave one.

For Comrade Bailitzin of the Russian Military Intel-ligence to call at G.H.Q. Rawalpindi, and actually to visit and dine with the General at Peshawar, put him one up on Richard Wendover, who had only been a teacher in the Russian School that taught the art of spying upon India. Or were they quits? Anyway, they were not quits yet in the matter of the *nagaika.* It was Comrade Bailitzin who held the whip-handle still.

He must have come down through Peshawar to Rawalpindi after seeing young Vere-Vaughan off to Giltraza Fort.

What a shock he must have got when he walked into the General's drawing-room and found Sybil Ffoulkes there!

And he must have done a little hurrying that same night—back to his hotel, change into Pathan kit, away down to the Bazaar, and off to the hills with his hench-men. They'd probably be assorted Usbeg, Kazak, Tur-coman and Afghan swash-bucklers, with a picked handful of the Singing Hadji's best *budmashes.*

And that's where he'd probably go and lie-up, for a while. He'd be safe in Sufed Kot with the Singing Hadji as long as the supply of roubles and rifles lasted, and that would be indefinitely, while he continued his anti-Road agitation in Sufed Kot and Khairastan.

Bailitzin! What a cruel pity. It made one *sick* to think that he had been so near, so recently. He must have given Shere Khan the slip after all. Perhaps Shere Khan had found out and followed him, and might be in Peshawar even now.

And now if he, Gul Mahommed of Khairabad, were

permanently changed back into Major Wendover of Napier's Horse, he'd never see Bailitzin again; never get him where he wanted him—that he might talk to him for a while, on the subject of *nagaikas*—with a *nagai-ka.*

XI

To Major Richard Wendover and Tommy Dodd, seated at the latter's dinner-table over a glass of excellent port, entered Major Bartholomew Hazelrigg.

"Hullo, Ganesh! Come and sit down and have a liqueur brandy or a glass of port. Be your last chance for a little while, what? When are you off?"

"One thing at a time, Tommy Dodd," replied Ganesh Hazelrigg ponderously. "Don't hurry me. Will I sit down? Yes. Will I have a glass of port? Yes. Will it be my last for some time? Yes. When am I off? To-morrow. Now be quiet a minute. Good evening, Dick Wendover."

"Good evening, Ganesh."

"It was you I came to see," continued Hazelrigg. "Not this noisy feller Dodd. I want to know, once and for all and finally, whether you've made up your mind about the Levy job. I don't want to say my piece about it, get it offered to you, and then you refuse it, you know. I've had a talk with a certain lady friend of mine, and she's quite ready to take it and . . ."

"What the devil do you . . . ?" began Wendover.

"I was going to say when you interrupted, she's quite ready to take it and anything else with which you are thrown in, pound-of-tea *ke mawfik*."[91]

"Yes, quite definitely," said Wendover quickly. "I'm more than willing to raise and command a regiment to be called the Khairastan Levies which, in return for pay, rifles and uniform, will guarantee to protect the Khairastan-Giltraza Road . . . I'd want an absolutely free hand, of course; the irreducible minimum of red tape, and to pick my own officers."

"Oh, they'll be only too glad to give you a free hand," replied Hazelrigg. "Save somebody the deuce of a lot of trouble. And while your blaze of glory lasts, you can ask for anything you want—and you'll get it. Only

---

[91] *In the manner of.*

got to mention it to General Vere-Vaughan and he'll give it to you on a golden platter. In anticipation of sanction. Meantime, you'll rejoin Napier's Horse while the mills of God and Delhi grind as slowly as usual, I s'pose?"

"Yes, to-morrow."

"Thorburn's Major now," mused Hazelrigg, twisting the slender stem of his wine-glass between the finger and thumb of his large and powerful hand. "It only seems the other day I heard him telling them that he had seen your ghost at Godoz."

"Warre's gone, I suppose," said Wendover.

"Yes. Sampson's commanding now. Nasty man. I expect they'll offer you the command when he goes."

"Shouldn't care to take it until Thorburn has had his turn," replied Wendover.

"Shouldn't care to take it at all, in point of fact," he continued. "Much rather command a 'Catch-'em-alive-O!' Battalion, over the Border."

"I suppose you would. When there was nothing doing on the Road you could make a little private war of your own, of course."

"Invade Afghanistan," observed Wendover. "Russia later."

"Gather in China too," observed Tommy Dodd, as he rose and went out into the verandah on business of long chairs, whisky decanter, siphon and cheroots.

"Talking of China," said Hazelrigg, "when you are gazetted to come up here again, to start raising and organizing the Khairabad Levies, you had better bring some china."

"China?"

"Pots and pans. Two of everything, you know."

"'Fraid I don't follow," said Wendover coldly.

"Well, she's going to follow you, old son, anyway, so do the thing properly."

Wendover laughed shortly.

"Let's have an engagement before we have a marriage, shall we?" he said.

"Yes, let's," agreed Hazelrigg. "I'll start putting it all over the place to-morrow."

"Rather awkward for whatever lady you have in mind."

"For the lady? Not at all. It's going to be awkward for you, Dick, by the time you've told your cowardly version of the disgraceful story."

"Yes? Well, anyhow, you won't mind butting in on my private affairs, will you?"

"Oh, not a bit. Not a bit. Besides, they'll be public affairs by to-morrow."

"Dick," continued Hazelrigg, laying his hand on Wendover's shoulder as he rose to his feet, and speaking with the ponderous solemnity which had earned him his nick-name of Ganesh the Elephant God, "Dick, don't be a Bee-er Eff than God made you. That was a bad enough job, as He would be the first to admit. Haven't you the sense of an afflicted louse? Can't you see an inch in front of your besotted nose? Don't you know a diamond when you see one? My dear chap, if you've ever had any ill-luck in the past, believe me, you've got some good luck now that more than wipes it all out. Come off it, you damned fool. Why, if I thought it would be any good, I'd go on my knees and beg her to marry me to-morrow."

"Who?" enquired Wendover.

It is better perhaps that Major Hazelrigg's reply be not recorded.

§2

That night as Major Richard Wendover of Napier's Horse sat on the side of his bed in Mr. Dodd's spare bedroom, and yawning, wound up his watch, there came a light tapping at the open window. It might be a branch tapping the frame or glass—and then again it might not, in view of the fact that the tapping was regular and rhythmic. The owner of a hand accustomed to beating a tom-tom with finger-tips and wrist was intent upon attracting the attention of the occupant of the room.

The eyes of Major Richard Wendover raised toward the window became those of Gul Mahommed as, dropping to the floor, he moved, crouching low, towards the lamp that stood upon the bare dressing-table.

Having turned this out, he took his revolver from where it hung beside his bed, and still keeping below the level of the window-sill, which was some seven feet above the outside ground, enquired in Pushtu and a harsh whisper:

"Who's there?"

"It is I, Dost Mahommed, brother of Shere Khan," was the reply.

"Perhaps, and perhaps not. But if thou art the young brother of Shere Khan, tell me the name of his wife."

"Bibi Jan."

"And of her father?"

"Ali Abdullah."

"Raise both thy empty hands above the window-ledge that I may blow them to pieces if thou art a liar."

The man outside obeyed.

"Now, seizing the window-ledge, draw thyself up that I may see thy face."

And a moment later a turbanned head appeared, silhouetted against the moon-lit night.

Wendover struck a match and as quickly blew it out.

"Salaam, Dost Mahommed," he said, "What's the matter?"

"Sahib, my brother Shere Khan . . ."

"Yes? Quickly. What of him?"

"Sahib, the Police have got him."

"The Police? What for?"

"A killing, Sahib. He has slain a man."

"Where is he?"

"At the Police *thana* in the Sudder Bazaar. The Police cannot get him to Peshawar Gaol because of the mob, but soldiers will soon come and take him. He'll be hanged for murder, Sahib."

"Whom did he kill?"

"A Powindah. He was bargaining with the man for a

lungi,[92] and they got angry. Suddenly the *borah* or *bunnia* or whatever he was, snatched the *lungi* from Shere Khan's hands, called him an evil name, thrust him over the step of the shop and spat upon him. So Shere Khan killed him, of course."

"Of course," agreed Wendover, and climbed out of the window.

---

[92] *Silk shawl.*

XII

At the request of Colonel Ormesby, Major Hazelrigg postponed for a few days his departure from Peshawar.

"Well, there it is, Colonel!" said he, as he strolled up and down the verandah with that retiring and little-known, but enormously important, official.

"He's gone. And thank God he got away. I don't quite know what would have happened if the Police had managed to run him in to Peshawar Gaol. The mounted Military Police may get him yet," said Colonel Ormesby.

"Not a hope, or rather, not a fear. Once he got into the hills with his men, no Police, mounted or un-mounted, would ever catch him."

"I suppose he'll make for Khairastan," mused Colonel Ormesby. "Thank the Lord that 'on no condition is extradition allowed in' Khairastan. Nothing short of a war could get him out of that country—and by the time troops got there he'd be gone."

"What a hopeless, incredible *fool!*" he growled.

"Yes. Greatest fool that ever lived—and one of the greatest gentlemen. Shere Khan would have hanged if Wendover hadn't dashed down there, organized the mob, rushed the Police *thana*, and got away with him."

"Couldn't he have waited and done things decently, by process of law and . . ." began Colonel Ormesby.

"And seen his friend hanged 'by process of law,'" sneered Hazelrigg. "What earthly chance would his Shere Khan have had, once he was in the clutches of the Law? Nothing on earth could have saved him. From our point of view, what he did was plain bloody mur-der, and by our law he would have hanged. Wendover saved him from death by hanging, just as certainly as though Shere Khan had been sinking in a whirlpool, and he had saved him from death by drowning."

"Well, he has saved him at a terrible cost."

655

"Yes, at the cost of everything. That's why I mentioned the word 'gentleman.' To us, this Shere Khan may be a lousy Pathan; a half-civilized semi-savage tribesman; a wild mountaineer, half-brigand, half-cultivator; a liar, a brute, a rogue and a robber. But to Wendover he is a friend, and the word 'friend' means something to him, and you may take it for granted that Wendover's just as prepared to lay down his life for him as he is to lose everything else."

"What'll they do with him if they catch him? Wendover, I mean."

"Lord knows! They wouldn't hang him, I should think. There were one or two lives lost in the shemozzle. If anyone was killed by a revolver bullet, he was killed by Wendover. It was a case of *lathis* and knives against the Police truncheons. Luckily it wasn't the armed Military Police who pinched Shere Khan; but so far as I can gather from a dozen different stories, the Police-Havildar at the *thana* telephoned, and a squad of Military Police came down and chipped in, and some of them may have used their carbines."

"Anyway, he'd be Court-martialled and broke, once again," observed Colonel Ormesby, "and then turned over to the Civil arm to be tried for rioting and leading an attack on a Police *thana*; obstructing and wilfully hindering the Police in the execution of their duty; if not for wounding or killing any of them. And he'd get a life-sentence—if not a death one."

"Yes, or the other way about," agreed Hazelrigg. "Either that or they'd chuck him into Peshawar Gaol, and keep him to be tried before the Judicial Commissioner, and, after receiving sentence of imprisonment or what-not, he would be cashiered from the Army automatically."

"Well, he's done it now!" he added with a sigh.

"Yes, he's done it now," agreed Ormesby.

"You know, Sir, I think it's a damn' shame," said Hazelrigg, "that we should apply our Western standards and ideas to these Oriental people. It's as sacred and solemn a duty of one of these Pathans to kill a man who flirts with his wife as it is to say his prayers.

It's as much his duty to kill the man who has done that, or who has killed his father or brother in the blood feud, or who has blackened his face in some other way, as it is our duty to feed and clothe and educate our children. How should we like it, if an alien race, who were in a position to do so, hanged us every time we committed the offence of feeding and clothing and educating our children? And the Pathan cannot understand it, you know. They admire us for many things, but they have nothing but the uttermost contempt for a man who goes to law against somebody who has done him certain injuries, instead of punishing the fellow himself."

"Yes, I know, I know," agreed Colonel Ormesby. "It's one of the problems of the Frontier. But there it is. If the Pathan comes on to our ground, he comes under our Law . . . Anyway, what you say doesn't apply to Wendover, even if it does to Shere Khan—and from what one can gather, it doesn't. He seems to have committed an absolutely wanton and unprovoked murder. They say he was bargaining with a *dukandar*,[93] snatched away the thing they were wrangling over, and when the *dukandar* snatched it back, Shere Khan just pulled out a knife and stuck it in his neck."

"Yes, but there would be more than that to it," said Hazelrigg. "The man must have used some unforgivable insult. Not merely the *gulli* abuse of the bazaar, but something that—leaves a mark—that can only be washed out in blood."

"Well, that may be all very well in Kabul, but we can't have it in Peshawar," said Colonel Ormesby. "And we've got to realize that the man is now a wanted murderer, and will be arrested as such, if he crosses the Border. Also that Wendover—who fought like a wild beast against the forces of Law and Order to rescue him—did rescue him, and fled with him. That's the position, isn't it?"

"That's it, Sir. I'm afraid that's it. Can we hush it up, I wonder? The fact that Wendover got him away and went with him, I mean."

---

[93] *Shop-keeper.*

"No, we can't. He was recognized. The fool was in uniform. Apparently someone dashed off to Tommy Dodd's bungalow and told Wendover, just as he was thinking of going to bed; and he must have got out of the window and rushed off straight away. Tommy says he heard nothing; and the verandah doors were still bolted on the inside, back and front, when he got up this morning."

"And that's an end of the Khairastan Levies for some time, I suppose," said Hazelrigg. "I had been building a lot on having a solid *entente* with Khairastan. It would have made all the difference in the world if we could have counted on complete peace and safety for the Road and for the building of the Road, right through Khairastan; not to mention the fact that we should have all the labour we wanted, and all willing and contented."

"Yes," he continued, "with the Khan of Khairastan, our well-beloved (and well-paid) friend, and Colonel Richard Wendover commanding a fine battalion of picked riflemen, the equal of any *Alpini* or *Bersaglieri* regiment in the world, we should have been sitting pretty—in that part of the Border at any rate. And now with Shere Khan on the run and, perforce, an enemy . . ."

"He's nobody, is he?"

"He's the present Khan's brother, anyhow! And at any moment may be Khan himself. The current incumbent is not popular, and Shere Khan is something of a national hero."

"Well, well! Kismet!" he concluded. "What is written will come to pass. Poor old Wendover."

"Well, the man's a most . . ."

Colonel Ormesby halted for the *mot juste*.

"Yes, Sir," interrupted Major Hazelrigg. "A most gallant gentleman—and a most bloody fool—whichever you were going to say."

§2

General Sir Archibald Vere-Vaughan was genuinely

concerned.

Indeed, although he would have denied it stoutly, he was extremely shocked. He was sorry for this amazing Richard Wendover, to whom he was under such deep obligation, sorrier still for what he had done, and sorriest of all for the way in which he had done it.

It wasn't the clean potato.

It wasn't the act of an officer and a gentleman, to go scrapping up and down the Bazaar with a gang of Pathans, knocking the Police about and rescuing their prisoner. One could only attempt to excuse such conduct by remembering that the man had lived as a Pathan, with Pathans, for so long that he had become one himself, at heart.

He had utterly ruined his career, the new career that lay shining bright before him; he had done a ruffianly and blackguardly thing; and he had done it in a most disgraceful and caddish manner, in view of the fact that he was practically engaged to a girl who was the General's guest; that he had actually just been staying in the General's house; and had been visiting it daily, up to the time of the occurrence.

Really, if he had no thought whatsoever for his host and General, he might have had some for the charming delightful girl who had stuck to him, stood by him, and wanted to come out from Home to do anything she could in order to help him, at a time when he was an outcast.

It wouldn't be a pleasant job, breaking it to her that her *fiancé* had—relapsed. Relapsed into criminality, he was going to say, but one could hardly speak of the man as a criminal and a recidivist, when admittedly his first Court-Martial had made a most grievous error, and his life had been not only blameless but brilliant—up to last night.

Yes, up to last night. And then, with everything before him, and the world at his feet, he had ruined it all; he had gone down into the Bazaar and got mixed up in some 'disgraceful *fracas*,' resisted the Police, rescued a prisoner they had arrested, and bolted. One injured policeman was said to be on the danger-list.

Suppose he died as the result of a blow from Wend-over's fist!

Talk about 'conduct unbecoming an officer and a gentleman'—or even conduct likely to cause a breach of the peace! This *was* a breach of the peace, and a damned serious one.

And he had actually used a revolver, threatened the Police with it, if he hadn't shot 'em up, as well as knocking down those who tried to prevent him from rescuing their prisoner—who had just committed a callous murder.

The chap must be queer in the head: that was the kindest construction to put on his conduct. The defence might plead that in a Civil court, or before a Court-Martial, in mitigation of sentence; but any Court that accepted the plea might well do so only on condition of his being consigned to a military criminal-lunatic asylum. Much would depend, of course, on whether he had actually killed anybody in the fight. But whether he had or not, the penalty for causing and abetting a violent attack upon a Police Station, and the rescuing of a murderer, must be pretty drastic.

Poor devil.

And poor little Sybil Ffoulkes. Best plan would be to tell Charmian, and get Charmian to break it to her.

Yes, and she had better advise her to go Home at once. Go home—and the sooner the better, for there would be the most awful scandal.

Poor little girl. The chap must really be a bit of a blackguard.

§3

"Thank you so much, my dear," said Sybil, dry-eyed, white-faced and tight-lipped, "but if you would keep me a little longer, I should be so grateful."

"Why, of course, my poor darling. You must stay just as long as ever you like. Daddy only thought—we thought—that you'd like to get away, get out of it all."

Sybil smiled.

"Get out of it all? I've been doing my utmost to get

into it all—from the moment I heard about the Court-Martial in Africa. I'm going to stay in this part of the world so long as he is in it, and I'd love to stay in Peshawar, here in Flagstaff House, as long as you will have me."

"And that's as long as you like, Sybil. Do believe that. Daddy looks on you as a daughter. And, personally, I shall be truly sorry when you go."

And Charmian kissed her guest warmly.

"*And we don't forget what he did for Jack,*" Charmian continued. "In point of fact, if he hadn't come here on Jack's account, this would never have happened, would it?"

"No, and I shouldn't have found him again. And, to me, nothing else really matters. So we're quits."

"Why did he do it?" wondered Charmian.

"For some good reason of his own, I suppose," was the reply, "though I admit it might not seem a good reason to anybody else."

"The leopard and his spots, eh?" said Charmian.

"Quite so. And he always was a bit of a leopard."

"I wonder where he'll go?"

"Back to Khairastan, I suppose."

"We'll get hold of Ganesh, and have a talk with him," said Charmian. "He and Colonel Ormesby will be coming to lunch, to talk to Daddy, and we'll get him to ourselves for a little while afterwards."

"I wonder if a woman could get to Khairastan," mused Sybil.

"Yes, in a tank or an armoured car, with a cavalry escort, I suppose. Though I doubt it."

XIII

And by devious ways known only to the Border riever, the outlaw, the brigand and the raider, Wendover and Shere Khan, with the band of Khairastan men who were Shere Khan's retainers and bodyguard, came roundabout to Khairabad, eventually approaching the Fort from the North.

And there they went to ground and licked their wounds, which were many, though not fatal.

And one day, as Gul Mahommed and Shere Khan sat in an embrasure of the wall and talked,

"Tell me again what happened" said Gul Mahommed, "that thou, a civilized man, a trained trooper, father of a son, became as a mad jackal in the Peshawar Bazaar."

"What happened? Nothing to make a fuss about. I did but go up to his stall that I might buy a lungi to bring back to Bibi Jan, to show that she had been in my mind, even when I was in far distant places, and upon matters of high importance beyond the understanding of women. And picking up the *lungi*, I offered the dog five rupees, whereupon, snatching at it, he replied, '*No, nor ten times five rupees.*' Whereat I laughed and told him he was the father of all robbers, and offered him fifteen. Thereat he pulled the harder, and said one hundred; and thereupon I offered him twenty, and said that I was a fool to do so and that he was the last descendant of a very long line of hanged thieves. And then, instead of bargaining like a gentleman, the *soor* snatched the *lungi* and insulted Bibi Jan and my son."

"Insulted them? But had he ever seen or heard of them?"

"No. But he said, '*Oh, husband of a whore and father of a leper* . . .' so I just stabbed him. Wouldn't you, Gul Mahommed?"

"Well," temporized Wendover, "I don't know that I

662

should have been at pains to stick him through the jugular vein. Couldn't you have given him a quiet poke in the shoulder or somewhere?"

"Ah!" smiled Shere Khan. "Now you're asking another question. First you wanted to know why I stabbed him, and I told you. Now you're wanting to know why I killed him, and I'll tell you. As I was in the very act of raising my knife, just to give him one in the chest, from which he could recover or not, as he thought fit, he spat on my beard. So then, of course, I gave him one for keeps."

"So you slay everybody who spits on your beard, eh?"

"Well," replied Shere Khan in a somewhat surprised, not to say scandalized, voice, "don't you, Gul Mahommed?

"It was written on his forehead," he shrugged, "that I should be thinking of Bibi Jan, should see the *lungis* in his *dukan*,[94] should stop and bargain, that he should insult my house, and that in the very moment of raising my knife, he should spit upon my beard."

"And because he spat upon you, you gave it him where it would do most good, eh?"

Shere Khan smiled.

Wendover fell silent and reflected. Shere Khan had meant well, and had done well, by the code of Pathan honour.

Yes, but Shere Khan hadn't done so well for Richard Wendover.

And he laughed aloud, a brief harsh bark of mirthless merriment, as he thought of how, at one minute, he had been the white-haired boy, the bright particular star of the garrison and, indeed, the Army—and the next minute, had fallen so far from grace as to be back at the very bottom of the pit from which he had just been digged. One minute, Major and Brevet-Colonel and future Commandant of the King's Own Khairastan Levies—and the next minute a criminal fleeing before the Police, wanted for being an accessary after a murder; for resisting and wounding the Police; and for

---

[94] *Shop.*

effecting the escape of the arrested murderer.

And another amusing thought was that Shere Khan took it as a matter of course, all in the day's work or the night's diversions. Quite obviously he could see nothing in it but a lark following upon a righteous act.

And now what? *"Back to the lashkar[95] again Sergeant. Back to the lashkar again,"* eh?

Well, there was one thing. They were both safe enough, here in Khairastan; safe anywhere on this side of the Border, but it would be more than Shere Khan's life was worth to go down into India again. And more than his own freedom was worth. What would they do to Richard Wendover if they caught him? Presumably the very least that he could expect would be a good substantial jugging, ten years or so.

Yes, he was a criminal now, all right. Neither the Indian Penal Code nor the Law of England took a light and lenient view of the snatching of murderers from the scaffold, nor even of rescuing arrested prisoners from the hands of the Police.

What was the price mentioned in the tariff—for storming Police Stations? What a lovely array of charges could be made out, by a really up-and-coming Public Prosecutor or Attorney-General or whatever it was.

And again Wendover laughed.

Let's see, he thought—there'd be accessary after the fact of murder; incitement to riot; siege, assault and capture of a Government Police *thana*[96]; assault, battery and malicious wounding of uniformed Police; wanton and wilful damage, to wit, the smashing of doors and windows and other articles of Government property; the using of a lethal weapon, to wit a revolver, for the threatening and intimidation of the Police; the hindering of the Police in the execution of their duty while attempting to arrest rioters when attacking the said Police with stones and *lathis*; and for rescuing, succouring, and removing their lawfully arrested prisoner; and—God knew what-all.

[95] *Irregular undisciplined forces.*
[96] *Station.*

Shere Khan interrupted this sombre train of thought by bursting into a loud guffaw.

Yes, that was it. A great lark. Very funny indeed! Positively gloating over the lovely *tamasha*, the neat punishing of a face-blackening scoundrel, a nice dust-up with the Police, a run for dear life, and a few days taking to the heather.

But what else could he have done? Left Shere Khan to go quietly and respectably to the gallows, while he himself went quietly and respectably to his honours and his Regiment? Left Shere Khan to the Law, that couldn't understand and wouldn't understand, that when a man's wife and oldest son have been insulted, his beard spat upon, his face, and the face of his family, blackened, nothing could wash away the horrible stain but the blood of him who had been guilty of the unpardonable crime?

Nor would he have counted it any sort of a price to pay for the life of his friend, had it not been for Sybil. He had halted for a moment, with his hand on the window-sill of his bedroom window; had stood in thought, ere climbing out to join Dost Mahommed, as he realized that he would be making Sybil pay as well.

And then, did she but know it, he had paid her a compliment, for he had told himself that she would understand, nay, agree—indeed, approve. For had not Shere Khan saved him from he knew not what, in the worst hours of his life? Had he not more than once saved his life at the risk of his own? Was Shere Khan not his *friend*? Would she now have him abandon Shere Khan to a shameful death?

And ere his feet had reached the ground outside Tommy Dodd's bungalow he had put her from his mind.

But now that they were safe and had nothing more to do than think the matter over in all its bearings, he was unable to put her from his mind.

Poor Sybil!

Yes—poor Sybil. And could it be that he was

665

beginning to miss her—wanting to see her again?

§2

And at this time, it came to pass that Khan Mian Gul Jan, the new Khan, who was the son of Khan Khudadad Khan Hassan Ali Khan and elder brother of Shere Khan, rose early from his *charpai* in the great fort of Khairabad, and rode forth with hawk on wrist, followed by a cavalcade of his favourites, with falconers, huntsmen, retainers and men-at-arms. He had informed his hawking *shikari*, the previous night, that he would ride to a certain tarn in a broad valley, upon which wild duck of all kinds, geese and other aquatic birds, were wont to take a night's rest as they broke their long journey from the north to warmer southern climes.

And the Khan's intention having been noised abroad, certain of the young men of Khairastan—who, by reason of their birth, warlike qualities and their renown for horsemanship and swordmanship, had service at Khairabad, about the person and beneath the eye of the Khan—held council together.

As is by no means unusual in those parts and circumstances, the council ended in a plot. Or, to put it more exactly, in that council, a plot that had been in existence since the accession of the young Khan, came to a head, and it was decided that if, on the morrow, the Khan went hawking, as he proposed, by the Talar Jhil, he should not return.

It was an unhealthy place for Khans of Khairastan. One had entrusted himself to its placid bosom in a frail craft, which was meant to be a duck-punt, and had been drowned. Another had fallen, in battle, by the shores of the Talar Jhil while opposing the invasion of Khairastan by the men of Sufed Kot; and yet another, while shooting duck, was himself "accidentally" shot.

So, of course, really, the whole thing was a question of *kismet*. Nothing to do with the plotters, of course. If it was the *kismet* of Khan Mian Gul Jan to go hawking there to-morrow—well, that was just too bad.

How many men were in the plot is not known; and how many men that night were aware of the interesting fact that the shores of the Talar Jhil would be profoundly unwholesome for the Khan, will never be known. But what is absolutely certain, is that Shere Khan who, by the death of his older brother Khan Mian Gul Jan, would himself become Khan, neither knew, nor ever had known, anything whatsoever about the intentions of the plotters.

In the first place, it was a generally accepted and well-recognized fact that if Shere Khan himself had been consulted on the subject of his brother's death, he would not only have refused to have anything to do with it, but would have promptly and peremptorily prohibited the carrying out of the great idea.

Admittedly he was a queer man, and had picked up strange notions in his extensive foreign travels in India and Africa; and, through his long association with Europeans and particularly with his bosom-friend, known as Gul Mahommed, he had grown strangely intolerant of some of the good old customs of his people.

Nevertheless, he was the man they wanted for Khan. He was a man. If, on his travels, he had perhaps lost a little of the tart cathartic virtue of the true Pathan and some of their finest traits and characteristics, he had nevertheless learned a very great deal about the art and craft of war.

If Khairastan were to flourish and survive the encroachment of the Singing Hadji of Sufed Kot on the one hand, and of the British on the other, as well as the constant raids and attacks from North, South, East and West on the part of envious inimical Tribesmen or merely playful raiders and rievers, they must have such a man as Shere Khan at their head, to give advice in council, leadership in war, and the final word when, in open *jirgah*, there were two or more opinions, and parties supporting those opinions.

In short, the new Khan, Mian Gul Jan, had proved himself no good, and Shere Khan, his natural successor, was known to be very good.

Secondly, Shere Khan was absent from Khairastan,

so that if any liar hereafter denied that Shere Khan was ignorant of the plot, he could scarcely, however malicious and evil-minded, pretend that Shere Khan had had any personal hand in the death of the brother whom he would succeed.

And thus it came to pass that, the *kismet* of Khan Mian Gul Jan of Khairastan decreeing that he should ride to the Talar Jhil for his hawking, the aged but very serviceable gun of his chief fowler accidentally went off as its owner was marching just behind the Khan's horse. And as the muzzle of the duck-gun happened at the moment to be pointing straight at the middle of the Khan's back, the sinister shores of the Talar Jhil once again proved fatal as the Braes of Yarrow.

Khan Mian Gul Jan Khan Khudadad Khan Hassan Ali Khan was dead, and his brother Shere Khan reigned in his stead—the jovial and noisy rites and ceremonies of his induction being necessarily postponed for a while as he was absent upon affairs of state in the country of the Singing Hadji of Sufed Kot.

§3

However, news being taken to him of the sad event, Shere Khan returned quickly to Khairabad, and having briefly and somewhat skimpily mourned his brother, he was, with a great and memorable *tamasha*, seated upon the *gadi*[97] of his fathers, and reigned in his brother's stead.

§4

"Huzoor! Gul Mahommed! Awake and arise," shouted Shere Khan's great voice a few days later, at the door of the room that Wendover now occupied in the big Fort of Khairabad. "Great news."

"Come in," cried Wendover as he yawned, stretched himself, and sat up on his *charpai*.

Now what was the wild fellow bawling about,

---

[97] *Seat of judgment.*

waking him from a deep dream of peace, in the small hours of the morning.

"Great news?" growled Wendover. "What? Have you murdered somebody else?"

"Not yet, Gul Mahommed. Not yet. But only wait. Listen. *They've got him*, and they are bringing him along. Seized him yesterday evening, between Kurnai and our Border. Young Dost Mahommed rode swiftly ahead to tell the good news."

Wendover sprang out of bed.

"Bailitzin!" he whispered.

"Bailitzin," grinned Shere Khan. "What shall we do with him? Whip him to death with a *nagaika*, or feed him, feet first, slowly into the fire? Or what about a cauldron of boiling fat?"

"You leave him to me," growled Wendover.

"*Bé-shak*, Huzoor. He is your man, for you to kill as you please. I did but offer suggestions. Doubtless you will think of better ones though—for it was you whom he evilly entreated and brought to shame. It was your face he blackened."

"And what would you do with him, Shere Khan, had it been you whose face he had blackened?"

"Who shall say, Huzoor? I should think of many punishments, and one day, in my wrath and in my haste, I should do unto him one of those things. But I would keep him alive for a long time. Yes, he should die many deaths."

"It will be enough for me if he dies one," said Richard Wendover. "Send me young Dost Mahommed."

XIV

Removing bolts and bars from the outside of the room in which Bailitzin was imprisoned, Richard Wendover flung open the door and strode in, followed by Shere Khan, who bore in his right hand a heavy whip.

"Well, Bailitzin," said Wendover, "*so we meet again, as the villains of the Adelphi Drama used to say.*"

Bailitzin rose from the *charpai* on which he had been sitting.

"Yes. Your turn now, Mister Renegade. Your turn, for the moment. What is it going to cost me to get away?"

"I don't know, Comrade Bailitzin. That remains to be seen, but I think, I somehow think, it will cost you your life."

"What, murder?"

"W-e-l-l-l, did we call it that when I was in the cell beneath the spy-school at Tashkent? If you remember rightly, the promise was that I should be flogged to death with a *nagaika*, after prolonged and considerable treatment—somewhat humiliating treatment."

"Look here, my good ex-British-Officer, let's talk sense and talk business, shall we? Your treacherous blackguards turned on me last night, and here I am. Well, I made a mistake, at Kurnai, and I'm ready to pay for it. That double-faced *soor*[98] Shere Khan—who tells me that he was a door-keeper and *pattiwallah*[99] at Tashkent when you were a *munshi* there—took me in, when he was there at Kurnai. Well, serve me right for trusting anybody. I'm not complaining, and as I say, I'll pay the price."

"You will, Bailitzin," replied Wendover, eyeing the

---

[98] *Pig.*
[99] *Messenger.*

Russian grimly.

He was a brave man, but he was very uncomfortable. That was shown by his talkativeness. Positively garrulous. Well, he should be made a little more uncomfortable.

Turning to Shere Khan, Wendover took the terrible whip from his hand.

"Not a *nagaika*, Bailitzin, but perhaps, in its different way, as good as a Russian knout. Better possibly— in Shere Khan's hands. He's one of the strongest men in Asia, you know. Ran with me in his arms for miles."

"Listen, Wendover," interrupted Bailitzin. "Don't be a fool. Do you realize that I can make you a rich man? That I can supply your whole tribe with new rifles? . . . Do you hear that, you Shere Khan?" he cried, turning to that stolid man. "Tell the others outside there. Tell everybody in Khairabad and Khairastan that I can give them all new rifles. Yes, and money."

Shere Khan, with a wolfish smile, showed brilliant teeth gleaming whitely between moustache and short bushy beard.

Wendover laughed contemptuously.

"And at what price do you assess your valuable life, Bailitzin?" he asked, running the lash of the whip through his fingers.

"I'll give you, personally, ten thousand roubles, and five hundred rifles."

"Quite a valuable life," observed Wendover. "Worth that much to you, is it? Well, it is worth a great deal more than that to me, Bailitzin."

"How much?"

"Suppose I said a million roubles and ten thousand rifles?"

Bailitzin, biting his lip, clenching and unclenching his fists, stared white-faced at his captor.

"Talk sense, Wendover," he said. "A hundred thousand pounds ransom, and ten thousand rifles. You value me highly. Make a reasonable proposition."

"I only wanted to discover how highly you valued yourself. Tell me the absolutely ultimate utmost that you could and would pay me, to set you free."

Bailitzin thought for a moment.

"Look, Wendover. Twenty-five thousand roubles and one thousand rifles."

"You could and would pay that, eh?"

"Yes."

"But they wouldn't be your roubles and your rifles, Comrade Bailitzin. Surely the good Commissar, or whatever you are, wouldn't rob the State of all that money and munitions. You are a patriot, Bailitzin, and not only a patriot, but a genuine, convinced, believing and honourable Red; a stern sea-green Incorruptible; a true-blue gutter-snipe proletarian Bolshevist official."

"Never mind about that," snarled Bailitzin. "Do you accept my offer?"

"No, Comrade, I don't. Nor any offer you could possibly make. There's not enough money in the world to buy you."

"So it is murder, eh?"

"That's not what you called it at Tashkent. I went to school there, Bailitzin. A hard school under a hard master, and I learned a very hard lesson. I was starved and beaten, beaten like a dog, Bailitzin, in a dark stinking lousy cell—for weeks. And I should have been buried under the floor of that cell, if I had not escaped; having been flogged to death when you had done with me.

"Well?" he added.

Bailitzin sat down heavily upon the *charpai* and licked dry lips.

"Anything to say?"

"You'll regret it, Wendover. You'll regret it as long as you live. And that mayn't be very long, either. I tell you that what happened to me is known in Sufed Kot. The Singing Hadji himself knows by now that I was seized by the bodyguard with whom I was riding, and was taken to Khairastan. You'll have the Singing Hadji and the whole of his *lashkar* here in no time, if I don't return to Sufed Kot. He'll eat you up, wipe you out, the lot of you, and annex Khairastan."

"Won't that be just too bad," observed Wendover.

"And now, strip to the waist," he added in a voice

that cut like a whip.

"Wendover, I can make you a rich man. I can . . ."

"Quick!" interrupted Wendover. "I can scarcely keep my hands from . . ."

"Wendover, you have your price. Name it, and . . ."

"Shere Khan!" said Wendover over his shoulder.

And Bailitzin threw off his Pathan coat, gold-embroidered velvet waistcoat, and drew off his shirt.

"Kneel down," growled Wendover, "before I knock you down and put my foot on your neck."

Bailitzin obeyed and Shere Khan stepped forward with great clutching hands.

"A-h-h-h!" breathed Wendover. "That's better, Bailitzin. That's what I wanted. Wanted, night and day, since I crouched in the filth of your cell at Tashkent and was whipped like a dog. Now then. You're a Russian, aren't you?"

"You know I am."

"Yes, and I'm an Englishman. You know I am. And if you don't, you can know it by *this*," and he threw the whip away from him.

"One of the differences between Bolsheviks and Britons. We don't flog and murder captives. Get up. Put your clothes on."

"Murder without the flogging, eh?" said Bailitzin, as he faced Wendover.

"No, we don't murder prisoners either."

"No. Kill them—and call it 'execution' instead, eh? Truly British!"

"Yes, execute them after fair trial. If they are found guilty of murder—or are caught behind the lines in disguises, spying, in time of war."

"Well, foregone conclusion, anyway. Shoot me and be done with it."

"You'd prefer that to being sent down to Peshawar, to be tried and hanged? For there are one or two hanging matters, Bailitzin, aren't there? Remember Captain Crombie? We happen to know who shot him. Remember Burton?"

"He was a spy. He was . . ."

"And Mrs. Burton? And the two children? They

spies too! Well? Here and now, or Peshawar?"

Bailitzin glanced round the windowless room, at the doorway blocked by fierce-faced burly Pathans; looked at Shere Khan; and, lastly, at Wendover. Better here and now, than after lingering in a British gaol. Better here and now, than prison life-sentence in India, or perhaps the Andaman Islands. This sloppy fool, this British "sportsman," would see he was not tortured.

"Here and now," he said.

"To-morrow morning, then," replied Wendover and, turning on his heel, left the cell.

"Shere Khan," he said, as that worthy replaced bolt and bar. "Khan or no Khan! On your head be it if he escapes."

"As we escaped from Tashkent," he smiled grimly.

"I'll spend the night with him, Gul Mahommed," grinned Shere Khan. "He won't escape."

"Please yourself about that," replied Wendover, "but no—er—unkindness. Understand?"

"I wouldn't injure a hair of his head," replied Shere Khan fervently. "And I'll see he's fed on the best, and that he has a good night's rest, in comfort, with a nice *rezai*[100] to keep him warm."

§2

Next morning, soon after dawn, Wendover, followed as usual by Shere Khan, again entered the room in which Bailitzin was confined.

"They gave you all the food you wanted, last night?"

"Yes."

"Have you had food this morning?"

"No."

"Shere Khan, see that the prisoner has tea, bread and fruit and a *lotah* of milk."

"I don't want you to have a heavy breakfast, Bailitzin," he added, turning to the Russian.

"No?"

"No. Not just before violent exercise. You are going to fight."

---

[100] *Quilted bed-cover.*

The somewhat weary and apathetic look faded from Bailitzin's face, and his eyes brightened as he looked up at Wendover.

"Fight? How? Whom?"

"Me."

"You? What with? Pistols?"

"No. I want something nice and intimate. Something personal, Bailitzin, if you understand me. Hand-to-hand and man-to-man stuff. Good rough stuff. I've dreamed of it, Bailitzin. Woken many a night from a dream of it."

"And if I win, I suppose your bully there takes it up?"

"No. If you win, Bailitzin, you'll have a chance, a very fair chance—of getting away."

"And if I lose?"

"Well, you will have lost, Bailitzin. And Russia will have lost Bailitzin, too."

"And if I am too badly wounded to . . ."

"Then I'll take every care of you, Bailitzin. Everything possible will be done for you. It will be my one desire to nurse you back to health.

"And then we'll fight again," he added.

Bailitzin stared at Wendover, evidently thinking hard.

So that was it, was it? The rat was not in a trap to be put in a pail of water. There was a chance.

But no. The mob would tear him to pieces as soon as he had killed their leader.

"More of your English hypocrisy and trickery, eh?" he said. "You'll play cat-and-mouse with me if I'm laid out—and if you are, your mob will hack me to bits."

"The Russian speaking," sneered Wendover. "You and I are going to fight privately—intimately, if you know what I mean, Bailitzin. No seconds, no spectators, no 'gate,' no ring-side seats, no nothing—but just you and me. And if you win, it's up to you. As I said before, you'll have a chance."

Bailitzin stared with parted lips.

"A chance? A fine chance!" he jeered.

"Well, beggars can't be choosers; but, anyway, you'll

have one."

"A chance to get from here into the Sufed Kot country on foot!"

"You won't be on foot; you'll be on the best horse I can give you."

What was this? Where was the trick? Of course he wouldn't have a chance. On the other hand, one knew what fools these English were.

"And another thing," he said quickly. "I've never used one of those Khyber knives, and I suppose you are an expert with them."

Yes, that was it. It would be a vulgar bloody rough-and-tumble with butchers' knives, and doubtless Wendover had had plenty of practice, and fancied himself at the sport of lopping.

"Wrong again, Bailitzin. There will be no Khyber knives nor Pathan daggers. No pistols, carbines, or rifles."

"What, then?"

"A pair of cavalry swords, Bailitzin. Any objection?"

By God, the fool! If he were speaking the truth, which doubtless he was. A fast horse and a cavalry sword. His favourite weapon. Did the "sporting" half-wit know that Prince Bailitzin had been a noted swordsman among the Officers of the Imperial Guard? Could it possibly be that he was going to be given the chance to cut down this insolent English fool, and then ride for his life, with a fair start?

What was he saying?

"That's the idea, Bailitzin. We are going to have two of the best stallions in Khairastan; and we are going to have two perfectly good regulation cavalry-sabres. British Army swords, taken from their dead owners after some Border scrap."

"And what'll be wrong with the one that I am to use?"

"That I can't tell you—for you shall have the choice of the two sabres."

And so it came to pass.

§3

"Listen, Khan Shere Khan Khudadad Khan Hassan Ali Khan of Khairastan," said Wendover to Shere Khan, as they left Bailitzin's well-guarded prison. "For I am about to say words of great import. Listen and heed, and fail me not. Do all things as I say, for you will take an oath upon the Koran so to do them. In a few minutes' time, I ride out alone with the Russian. Follow me not, and see that no man follows me—neither you nor any man going beyond the pass out of the valley, but halting by the *ziarat*. If I return, Bailitzin will be dead, and we will give him burial where he dies. If I return not, within an hour, then I shall be dead or badly wounded. Should that be so, bring me back here and do what you can for me, at the same time sending mounted men in pursuit of Bailitzin. Let them catch him, if that be possible. Doubtless he will ride for Sufed Kot Fort or Kurnai and, as you know, the same track serves for both, for many miles.

"And this is the important part. If you take him alive, do him no further harm, but deliver him safely at Giltraza Fort with the letter that I shall leave."

"Yes," mused Wendover aloud. "That would be very appropriate, very fitting. Let the writer of notes delivering prisoners to the good Garstan, be himself delivered with a note to Garstan. He will welcome him with open arms, when he knows it is the man who was the cause of his making such a blazing fool of himself with his childish court-martial, and condemnation and sentencing of an innocent man."

"Understand?" he continued, noting the doubtful and disapproving look on Shere Khan's dour face. "He is to be taken to Giltraza Fort alive, and, as far as possible, unhurt. Fetch the Koran and swear."

"There's no need of oaths between thee and me, Huzoor," grumbled Shere Khan.

"So be it, then; but put your hands between my hands, and swear upon the head and life of your son that you will do as I bid."

And Shere Khan reluctantly gave the promise,

677

which Wendover knew would be binding, that no vengeance should be taken upon a victorious Bailitzin, if re-captured; and that he would take him with a strong escort, and deliver him at Giltraza Fort.

"Good! Are the horses ready? . . . Bring me the swords . . . Have you had them sharpened, edge and point?"

The cavalry swords proved to be in excellent condition, having been cared for, as weapons are cared for, by the men of the Border; hilt and blade as speckless and shining as when found in the hands of the fallen Hussars before whose earth-shaking, irresistible charge the Tribesmen had broken and fled, only to re-assemble to cut off the rear-guard squadron of the column that, towards nightfall, had broken off the engagement and returned to its camp.

Taking one of them, Wendover hefted it, weighed and balanced it, made long lunge and swift recover, swung it, whistling, in glittering arcs; and rejoiced that, when a Squadron-leader of Napier's Horse, he had practised and trained so long and keenly to win the cup for the "Officers' Mounted Sabres" event in the tournament of the Divisional Competition.

Yes, he'd be able to give Bailitzin a run for his money when it came to "mounted sabres," with sharp edge and point; no rules or regulations, no umpires, and no rests between hits. If this were the last thing he ever did, one thing was certain, he'd very thoroughly enjoy the doing of the last thing he ever did.

"Take a revolver," advised Shere Khan.

"What for?" enquired Wendover coldly.

"In case he flees for his life, once he and you are alone and his horse proves the faster."

"He'll be welcome to try," smiled Wendover, "but to do him justice, I don't think he'll try to run away. And if he does, he won't get far . . . Come on. We'll let him choose one."

§4

"There you are, Bailitzin. Choose one of those swords, re-sheathe it, and don't touch it again until I say 'Draw swords,'" said Wendover, a few minutes later.

Bailitzin took, and drew, a sword.

Ha! This would do. Long and strong and straight and heavy. Suit him beautifully. Perhaps he'd have preferred one of the slightly curved pattern to which he was accustomed; but this would do. He had been afraid they'd produce a pair of the short unhandy *tulwars* worn by the Indian Lancers. More like an old-fashioned naval cutlass. But these were gentlemen's weapons.

Drawing one, he too hefted it like a swordsman, felt grip and balance and weight, put the point upon the ground and tried the spring of the blade, the while Shere Khan, a distrustful man, covered him with the heavy old-fashioned revolver of which he was so proud and fond.

Bailitzin then tried the other sword, bending the blade into a semi-circle. Nothing to choose between them.

"Have you any choice?" he said, eyeing Wendover and intending to be sure to ask for the one that Wendover professed not to prefer. Of course, the stupid Englishman would say 'I'll have this one,' thinking that the Russian would immediately say 'No, I'll have it.'

Yes, if there were anything wrong, Wendover would secure the good one by pretending to want the other.

But apparently there was nothing in it, for, to Bailitzin's faint surprise and chagrin, Wendover replied:

"Not the slightest."

"All right, I'll keep this one, then," and Bailitzin returned it to its steel sheath.

"Don't make a mistake and draw it again until I tell you," warned Wendover, "and when you do, you can throw the sheath away. Follow me."

And with Shere Khan and four other Pathans close about him, Bailitzin proceeded by narrow corridor and stair, rampart-walk and court-yard, to a gate about which stood a crowd of the *jowans* of Khairabad, two of whom held the saddled and bridled horses.

One of these Wendover mounted.

"See your stirrups and girths are right," he said to Bailitzin.

"I was about to, especially the girths," was the reply. "Queer things are apt to happen to saddle-girths in these circumstances."

And raising the saddle-flap he assured himself that the girths were stout and strong and properly buckled. Then putting the finger-tips of his right hand against the saddle and straightening the right arm, he raised the stirrup and placed it beneath his arm-pit.

"Good guess. Exactly right."

And placing the reins in the left hand that grasped the sword, he mounted with easy grace.

"Nothing under the saddle," he observed, finding that the horse neither reared nor bucked as his weight came down upon it.

"Only the horse," replied Wendover. "What did you expect to be under it?"

"Oh, a spur or a bent nail or a sharp stone or two. What do you generally put?"

"I expect you know more about those things than I do, Bailitzin," replied Wendover. "Ride on in front of me."

The gate was open, and the two horsemen rode forth on to the track, followed by Shere Khan and a great crowd of Khairastanis.

"These all your seconds?" enquired Bailitzin, turning his head.

"Neither mine nor yours," was the reply. "Don't be afraid. Ride on."

Bailitzin laughed aloud, and Wendover paid him the compliment of admitting that the laugh sounded spontaneous and genuine.

Along the upward-sloping track, the cavalcade wound its way, mounted or afoot, with much commotion of chatter, laughter, and shout.

Arrived at the *ziarat*, the Pathans fell silent as

Wendover reined in his horse, raised his hand and addressed the men of Khairabad, as all, save Bailitzin's more especial escort, gathered about him.

"Hear, oh men of Khairastan," he said in Pushtu. "I have asked a favour of your Khan and he has granted it, swearing by the head and the life of his son, that he will keep his word to me, the which I know he will do. He has sworn also that you will hearken unto his words and obey. No man is to follow me, for I would fight my enemy alone. If I see you not again, farewell. And may each one of you, when his time comes, have as happy a death as mine will be."

And turning to Shere Khan, he grasped his hand.

"Whatever may befall, let no man pass this *ziarat*," he said. "Farewell, Shere Khan, my friend and brother."

"Dismount, that I may embrace thee, Huzoor," replied Shere Khan. Wendover did so, and each took farewell of his friend in his own fashion.

"Shouldst thou fall and he ride, then we also may ride?" asked Shere Khan. "If thou returnest not within the hour, then we may come?" he asked.

"At the end of an hour," replied Wendover.

"Ride on, Bailitzin," he said. "There's a valley a couple of miles on, at the turn of the track, level and grassy."

And Bailitzin rode on at a sharp trot, Wendover following close behind him.

"This horse is a little faster than yours," he added meaningly.

Suppose Bailitzin broke into a gallop and tried to draw away? Well, he'd shout to him to draw swords, and he'd go for him. They were about of equal weight, and Bailitzin would have little chance of riding away from him.

What a hell-for-leather gallop it would be if he tried, and kept his start. Better close up on him, perhaps.

He must ride carefully, though. It would be unbearable, unthinkable, that his horse should put his foot in a hole, or tread, as once he himself had done, on a stone that moved, bringing him down with a crash while Bailitzin rode to safety.

What was Bailitzin thinking? Doubtless thinking what fools these English were, and particularly the man Wendover, that he should have left the heavily-armed escort of Pathan horsemen behind, and had not ringed the valley about with his sharp-shooting riflemen.

So he was a fool, doubtless. But man does not live by bread alone. No, that wasn't what he meant. What did he mean? "Thrice armed is he who hath his quarrel just." Was that it? More like it, anyway. Besides, fool or no fool, he wanted Bailitzin to himself. He wanted to cleanse himself from the foulness that Bailitzin had put upon him, purge his blood of the poison in it, throw off the incubus that he had borne since Bailitzin had flogged and humiliated him in that foul prison. That was why he was here alone with the Russian, behaving with what Ganesh Hazelrigg would call madness, sheer lunacy, childish quixotic folly.

But as he had told him, it wasn't merely Bailitzin's death that he desired. It was the killing of Bailitzin by Richard Wendover that was necessary.

No, it wasn't revenge. It had nothing whatever to do with revenge. A mere desire for revenge could be gratified by seeing Bailitzin hanged, shot or imprisoned by process of law. Revenge was really an evil thing, the thing that decimated the Tribesmen, with their blood-feud vendettas.

No, honestly, genuinely and unequivocally, it was not vengeance that he desired, but purification, moral and spiritual rehabilitation, recovery of his self-respect. That Bailitzin's death was essential to this was not the fault of Richard Wendover. It was Bailitzin's own fault. By his own act, Bailitzin had rendered this rite inevitable, ineluctable.

While that man in front of him was alive, he would feel almost physically sick every time he remembered the whippings and his own involuntary cries of pain, his cringing, his grovelling for mercy almost, at the feet of the man who held the steel-tipped whip . . .

The path began to descend towards the little valley

with its central plain, not more than twice the size of a polo-ground.

Yes, this would do. Nay, more; it was obviously the appointed spot, the place where the agony of his spirit would end in death or healing cure.

He inhaled deeply and sighed with content. Here was the scene and setting of his release, the place either of his victoriously throwing off, or thankfully laying down, the burden that . . .

There was a sudden rasp of steel and a whirl of dust as, in one movement, Bailitzin swung his horse about upon its haunches, drew his sword, and rode at Wendover, a Cossack cry upon his lips, the glare of his fierce eyes no less bright than the flashing sword above his head.

A treacherous dog.

Had he been wearing spurs, wherewith to cause the fiery stallion to leap more swiftly upon Wendover, the fight would have been finished without beginning. As it was, he had but time to parry the sweeping downward cut with his sheathed sword, and with a turn of the wrist to deflect it and drive his own scabbarded point at Bailitzin's throat. A lucky fluke that, for the thrust, catching him beneath the chin, had almost knocked Bailitzin from his horse.

Swinging his own horse to the near side, Wendover whipped his sword from its scabbard, rode at Bailitzin, feinted at his head and, as Bailitzin's sword came up in parry, dropped his point and thrust again, tearing, as he did so, the side of Bailitzin's *poshteen* coat.

Good! For all his treacherous attack, he was rattled, and hadn't been as clever as he thought. As with knee and rein, Wendover again swung his horse, Bailitzin, with a back-handed stroke, missed his neck by a hair's-breadth, recovered, caught Wendover's answering slash upon the forte of his sabre, lowered his point and, in his turn, thrust, the sword grazing Wendover's shoulder.

Dashing past him, Bailitzin galloped a short distance, pulled his horse up suddenly, swung it about and charged.

Yes. It was fortunate indeed that neither was wearing spurs, for obviously Bailitzin missed them badly, and would have been much more dangerous had he been so equipped.

Evidently this was a swordsman who, fighting mounted, was one with his mount, a Cossack centaur whose horse's limbs were as his own, for swift change of stance, elusion, charge and withdrawal.

And the bits the horses were wearing were too powerful, and the Russian's horse, with wrenched cut mouth, was fighting his rider.

Willingly Wendover admitted that had Bailitzin been mounted on his own charger and equipped with the accoutrements he knew, he would have been the better man. As it was—it remained to be seen.

As Bailitzin charged, his sabre across his left shoulder, he aimed a mighty horizontal blow which, unparried, would have half-severed his opponent's head from his body.

Wendover was quick and cool. Now, to duck under that, drop his point and thrust—and he'd have the Russian spitted on his sword. But in the act of striking, Bailitzin's blow became a feint, his sword changed direction and, like lightning, descended full upon Wendover's head, the Russian rising in his stirrups as he brought down the heavy sword like hammer upon anvil.

Yes, thought Wendover as he parried, and that's where he has forgotten what the Pathan *puggri* is like. No good cutting down on that, friend Bailitzin. A nasty-unpleasant thump, but no sword can cut through that solid mass of tough yielding cotton stuff. Next time, you'd better try a drawing cut.

But the force and weight of the tremendous blow spoilt his next thrust, diverted it, so that it passed harmlessly behind Bailitzin's back.

Also it had annoyed Wendover, woken him up, turned him from a sternly active and aggressive foe into a fighting fury whose sword, like a fiery flame, seemed to flicker like forked lightning about his enemy's head.

The clattering clashing rattle of the swift rally had more of violence, ferocity, and force than of elegant and academic sword-play, as when two mighty boxers, abandoning finesse and skill of defence, stand face to face, toe to toe, breast to breast, exchanging smashing blows without thought of guard and self-defence.

And suddenly, Wendover's sword, swung in fierce horizontal cut from across his shoulder but slightly deflected upward by Bailitzin's parry, struck the Russian's *puggri* from his head, sending it flying to earth some yards away.

Reining back and holding his sword on guard, Wendover bade Bailitzin dismount, recover his *puggri* and bind it again securely about his head.

"What?" panted the Russian. "While you ride me down?"

"Don't be a fool," shouted Wendover. "Get your *puggri*—or don't blame me if I split your skull next time."

No, he thought. Bailitzin wouldn't do much blaming of him or anybody else, if once he could give him "cut one" straight down on his unprotected head.

"Ride away, then," answered Bailitzin. "If you mean it, ride to the other end of the ground and give me time to fix the thing."

With a contemptuous exclamation, Wendover turned about, rode on in a direction which would place him between Bailitzin and his line of retreat in the direction of the Sufed Kot border, changed his sword to his left hand, to flex, rest, and relax, the muscles of his right, and was instantly aware of the thudding of hooves behind him.

He might have known it.

If he swung about, Bailitzin's horse would catch his, broadside on, and send him sprawling.

Swerving right, without checking pace or attempting to go about, he turned in his saddle, tried to give Bailitzin his point as he came up, and received that of Bailitzin's sword through his left shoulder.

So that was what it felt like to be run through with

a sword. Rather like being burnt. Not nearly as painful as one would expect. That would come later. How soon would he weaken, cough blood and turn giddy? Perhaps it was nothing. He hadn't seen the point sticking out through his chest.

Well, first blood to Bailitzin. And now anything he could do, were best done quickly.

As the thought passed through his mind, he swung his sabre far behind him, felt it strike and thud, wheeled his horse full right, and realized that he had slashed Bailitzin's side.

Good! That would even matters up; might more than even them, as the play of the Russian's sword-arm would be affected.

Again the two men were face to face, almost right knee to knee, with raised swords feinting and flickering.

A swift and powerful downward stroke of Bailitzin's sabre fell harmless on Wendover's hilt and was swiftly changed to a thrust that pierced his chest. Very quick and neat; and dangerous—for Bailitzin. For ere the thrust could be recovered, Wendover's sword-point had dropped, and he had thrust with all his strength and weight, driving the sword home to the hilt.

And now to finish.

Wheeling his horse and drawing back his sword, he raised it above his head, stood up in his stirrups, struck back-handed, and sideways at Bailitzin's neck, with all his strength, even as the Russian's point again went home—too late.

With labouring lungs, breathless, and feeling as though his heart would burst, Wendover dropped his sword-hand, leaned forward on his horse's neck, and watched with staring eyes his enemy collapse, drop his sword, reel in the saddle, and fall to the ground, there to lie motionless beside his horse, as his life blood gushed from his neck like water from a tap.

Dead . . .

He'd never move again after such a stroke as that; a stroke delivered with all a strong man's strength, almost a madman's might, with sharp-edged heavy sword, in so vulnerable a spot.

A stroke that had cut him free; free from shame and horror.

Free—and dying . . . blind . . . falling . . .

With a heavy thud, Wendover fell from his horse and lay motionless in the blood of the man whom he had killed.

§5

Khan Shere Khan Khudadad Khan Hassan Ali Khan, Chief of Khairastan, glanced at the sun and the shadow thrown by a rock.

"Mount and ride," he said.

And leading the cavalcade of horsemen and the almost equally swift foot-men, dashed headlong down the track by which his friend and his enemy had disappeared but a short hour before, an hour that had seemed like a lifetime.

Rounding the hillside at breakneck pace, and thundering down into the valley beyond, he saw what he had feared to see, a sight that by strange premonition, he had expected; two horses standing still, with hanging heads, two men lying yet more quiet.

"By Allah! Both are dead," cried his cousin Hussein Shah, riding beside him.

"Both? Liar and fool, I will slay thee, if it be so," shouted Shere Khan, driving his horse ahead of the rest.

First to reach the fatal spot and first to touch the ground, his horse still galloping, Shere Khan knelt beside his friend, raised his head, placed his ear upon his heart, and praised the One True God.

"He is alive," he said. "Make a litter, thrusting rifles through the sleeves of two of your *poshteens* . . . No. He is too big a man."

"Lift him on to his horse and two of us will support him," said Dost Mahommed.

"And start the bleeding again? Stand clear. I will carry him.

"Look you, Dost Mahommed," he added, "take my horse and ride. Halt at Khairabad Fort long enough to bid Bibi Jan make ready for my wounded brother. Hot water, cloths, a bed. And bid the *hakim* Rahimtullah make ready too. Then, without losing a minute, ride. If your horse falls dead, run you, until you also fall dead. But don't fall until you have had speech of the Sahib who dwells in the house whence you called Gul Mahommed on the night that the Police seized me. Tell him all things, and he will tell Gul Mahommed's friend —known to-day as Ghulam Hyder and to-morrow as Inayatullah Hussein, and who is the Sahib that is the friend of Gul Mahommed. Hazelrigg Sahib. Bid him come, bringing an English *hakim*, a Doctor Sahib. And say that I will have men and picked horses waiting at this end of the Khyber Pass. Ride, for the life of Gul Mahommed who is sorely wounded. Look, there is blood upon his lips. Go."

And Dost Mahommed, a boy of sixteen, who had killed his man, married his girl, begotten his son, broken-in his horse, and won his spurs on raid and foray, sprang into the saddle of the best horse in Khairastan (noted for the speed and endurance of its breed of horses) and started on a ride that became legendary, as famous in its way and place as the rides of Paul Revere and of those who brought the news from Aix to Ghent.

XV

Major Bartholomew Hazelrigg, calling at an unusually early hour at Flagstaff House, gave his card to the
accomplished Goanese butler, bidding him take it to
Ffoulkes Miss Sahib.

A minute later, Sybil, dressed in riding kit, entered
the drawing-room white faced, firm lipped.

"Not been sleeping too well by the look of her,"
thought Hazelrigg, "since he went."

"Good morning, my dear. Just had a messenger,"
said he.

"From Dickie?" asked the girl.

"Well, in a manner of speaking. From his boy
friend. I thought I'd just let you know that he is safe
back in Khairabad."

"Oh! He is, is he!" said Sybil. "And there he sits for
the rest of his life, I suppose?"

"Well," replied Hazelrigg weightily, "Peshawar and
the parts adjacent won't be too healthy for him, for
some time to come. I'm going up that way."

"When?"

"To-day. Now as a matter of fact. Any message for
him?"

"No. Unless you tell him I hate him."

"Don't wonder at it. Unreliable changeable flighty
sort of fellow."

"And that's exactly what he isn't. As you must
perfectly well know, since you've known him for so
long."

"Sit down, my dear. You look like a ghost."

"Why *did* he do it? How *could* he? It's incredible."

Hazelrigg changed his tone and manner.

"I'll tell you why he did it. His friend, the man who
saved his life more than once—and saved a great deal
more than his life—committed a murder here in Peshawar. The Police had got him—and he was for it. He'd
have been hanged by the neck until he was dead. And

the man's brother came and told Wendover that the Police had got his friend. So what must the fool do but rush straight down to the Bazaar, gather the Khairabad gang and, with the street mob, attack the Police thana, rescue his friend from the clutches of the Law, and then do the only thing possible."

"His *friend*? What, Shere Khan, of whom he was never tired of talking to me?"

"That's it. Without a second's hesitation, he threw up everything, career, happiness, home, friends, you . . . everything. Isn't he a fool? No wonder you hate him."

"Fool?" said the girl. "Hate him? Yes, it's no wonder I hate him—like you do."

"A bad business," said Hazelrigg ponderously, shaking his head. "And he has made it worse."

"*What?* How?"

"Got himself wounded."

"Wounded? Badly?"

"Well, Shere Khan has sent a messenger who must have broken all records to let me know, and . . ."

"You are starting now?" interrupted the girl.

"Yes, my car and kit will follow me and be here in a few minutes, and I am going straight off. Shere Khan will have horses and escort waiting for me near Landhi Kotal."

"I'll come with you," said Sybil.

"What?"

"I'll come with you to Khairabad."

"Yes, I thought you would. You'll have to come as a boy. I sent Dost Mahommed down to the Bazaar to get the complete outfit of a Pathan youth. We'll take a *bourka* as well, and that'll change you from a Pathan lad into a woman, if necessary, in two seconds. Now, get together anything that you think will be useful for yourself or for him. Don't bother about lint, bandages, disinfectant, antiseptics, anything of that sort, because we'll stop at Kemp's and load up with that sort of thing and what we can get in the way of concentrated food stuff, chicken jelly, beef extract and so on."

"I suppose there's absolutely no possibility of

getting a European doctor at Khairabad."

"Ah, that's just what there is, my dear. By the mercy and grace of God, Bennell of Pannu is out on one of his preaching and healing rounds. Tommy Dodd got news only yesterday that he was on his way to the Afghan Border. I'll send Dost Mahommed after him, as soon as we get beyond the Khyber."

"Who is he?"

"One of the greatest of all medical missionaries; a great Christian, a great doctor, and a great hero. He's a saint. If we can get him to Wendover in time, and you will do the nursing . . ."

"Is he very badly hurt?"

"Well, badly enough for them to send an urgent message, and . . ."

"They wouldn't have sent for you if there hadn't been . . . if he had been . . ."

"No, my dear, they wouldn't have sent for me if he had been dead—or dying.

"Hullo," he added. "There's the car. Now you tell Charmian all about it, or what you think proper to tell her about it, and I'll leave a note for the General. You had best go as you are, till we leave the car. Tommy Dodd is going to drive us up to the end of the Pass, then it will be a long ride, and you'll have to wear a *bourka*."

§2

Richard Wendover, awake and conscious, stared idly at the door of his room as it opened to admit Shere Khan, a tall bearded man wearing the dress of a mendicant pilgrim, and a youth.

Wearily he closed his eyes. And then opened them again, as he realized that Shere Khan's companions were—different. The *sadhu* was wearing gold-rimmed glasses and he was fair as a European. The youth was fair also.

Again he closed his eyes, for the *sadhu* was an Englishman talking English, and the youth was Sybil Ffoulkes.

691

He hadn't realized that he was as far gone as that—even if he had had a sword-thrust through each lung.

Still, if one had to see things, what better than young Sybil? She had been rather on his conscience, and he would have liked to explain to her why he *had* to go that night. She'd forgive him when she knew the truth. Yes, being Sybil, she'd understand. She'd admit it was the only thing to do. Forgive him? Why, she would hardly have expected him to do otherwise. Good kid, Sybil. He had never appreciated her properly. And now it was too late.

And so, for some weeks, it indeed seemed to be, but the great skill of the famous doctor, handicapped though it was by lack of most of the things that he needed, began at length to prevail. During that time, Sybil Ffoulkes, as the doctor freely admitted, was literally indispensable. Without her nursing, the patient would have died; for weeks he hung between life and death, weeks which were the happiest and the most anxious through which she ever lived. At times hope was almost extinguished, and her soul was plunged in the depths of black despair. At times, as when in delirium he, unconscious of her presence, talked to her and about her, she was uplifted, happy in the knowledge that through the dark days of disgrace and exile, she had been in his mind; that the inarticulate undemonstrative man who had apparently never spoken of her (as Ganesh Hazelrigg admitted) and had never written to her, had thought of her.

"You know, my dear," babbled Wendover in delirium, "I felt pretty sure that you'd agree . . You see, it was no good coming home . . . It was no good coming back to India. Where could I go, except to Hell? . . . And it was no good writing letters telling you a lot of tripe, and that it was all a mistake and a 'wicked cruel shame'."

Silence broken only by laboured breathing.

"How could I possibly dream of dragging anybody else down into the depths that I was in? . . . A man thinks twice about going native himself. He thinks a long time before asking a woman to go native."

"We must get Breckinge's body in, somehow . . . We'll bury him inside the Fort, and later on, they can give him a fine tombstone with a proper inscription on it. You know. 'No man hath greater love,' sort of thing."

Wendover laughed. To the listening girl it was rather dreadful, the bitter-sounding laughter of an unconscious man, hovering between life and death.

"It was the right thing to do, wasn't it? Ganesh didn't think so, but I knew young Sybil would."

"What a mess.

"It must have been a bit of a shock for the General, and I really was sorry, but what else could I do? Let Shere Khan be hanged? They'd have hanged him all right, you know. He hadn't a leg to stand on. Plain wilful murder.

"It's a damn shame the way they hang these Pathans for doing what they think the right thing . . . Might just as well hang an Englishman for giving a burglar a black eye . . . Anyway, we got him out of it."

"It's no good your grousing, Ganesh. You'd have done the same yourself, and you've got to say as much to Sybil Ffoulkes. You just say that. Tell her you'd have done the same yourself. So would she, of course. She's a sportsman."

"*Don't!* . . . *Don't!* . . . Yes. Yes. Anything. It's whatever you say, Bailitzin. Are you a civilized man or a wild beast?"

A mumbled incoherent torrent of words.

"Yes, if it takes me the rest of my life and costs me my life, I'll wipe that out, Bailitzin."

"Sybil! . . . Good Lord! How on earth did you get here? Sorry I didn't write, but I didn't want to drag you into this mess . . . Why should I accept a pardon? Pardon for what? Still, one couldn't let a youngster face that. One knew too much about it, oneself. Had to come back. Major Richard Wendover, D.S.O., of Napier's Horse. Everyone looking and whispering. It's a damn difficult position, you know, with Shere Khan on the one hand and Vere-Vaughan on the other . . . If I stay by Shere Khan, Vere-Vaughan's Court-Martial may go wrong—and if I go back and leave Shere Khan . . . Can't be done. Neither thing can be done. And that's why my head is splitting. And to think that young Sybil . . ."

The doctor entered.

"The man I sent to Pannu has just arrived," said he to Sybil.

"Now we can go ahead. When we've got the temperature down and he has had some sleep, we shall see a lot of difference."

"He's going to live, Doctor?"

"That's in God's hands. I think he will—now. He's very strong, and he has led a perfectly healthy wholesome life up in these mountains. There's every hope."

"But only hope?"

"No, of course not. There's faith."

And Sybil Ffoulkes had hope and faith, which were justified.

§3

Slowly Richard Wendover returned from his long sojourn in the Valley of the Shadow of Death. Slowly he regained strength, until the day came when he was carried from the chamber in which he had lain for weeks, and taken out on to the battlements of the Fort whence he could see his beloved mountains and look down the great valley of Khairabad to the far rugged ranges of the hills of Khairastan.

To him came there daily the Khan Shere Khan Khudadad Khan Hassan Ali Khan of Khairastan, sitting in silence, a silence which occasionally he broke to praise Allah and to thank Him for his mercy and compassion in sparing the lives of his more-than-brother and himself. For he had sworn upon the Koran that should Gul Mahommed die, he would not survive him. Mounting his horse and accompanied by such as chose to follow him, he would ride into the country of Sufed Kot, and there meet his end, as quickly and bloodily as possible, among his enemies.

But Allah had willed otherwise. Praise be to Allah the Merciful, the Compassionate.

"All things work out for good," he observed sententiously, one evening as he spent his usual sunset hour with his friend.

"Without doubt, though the good is well concealed sometimes. Of what were you thinking?"

"Why, of that *dukandar* whom I slew in the Sudder Bazaar at Peshawar."

"That was evil enough, Shere Khan. What good has come from it?"

"Good? Why surely that is plain. Had I not slain the man, and had you not come to my rescue and fled with me, that Russian dog would be alive at this moment."

"True," agreed Wendover. "There's that to it."

It would be cruel and unworthy to stress the fact that the murder, the rescue and the flight had definitely, and once and for all, made Richard Wendover an outlaw and an exile, a potential gaol-bird, very badly wanted by the Police, and unable to return to his native land.

What a turn of Fortune's wheel! What a stroke of Fate! Just when circumstances had brought him back to his own again, and Sybil was . . .

"By the way, did I ever tell you about that man?" the voice of Shere Khan interrupted his melancholy musings.

"You did," he sighed. "He gave you some bazaar *gulli*, and then he spat at you, and so you murdered him."

"Ah, but I don't believe I ever told you who he was. That was why I struck at his neck with a dagger instead of giving him a crack on the head with my *lathi*."

"Never told me who he was? Why, who was he but a

dukandar?"

"No, I don't believe I ever told you," said Shere Khan. "I knew there was something interesting I . . ."

A sudden thought struck Wendover.

"Who was he?" he asked sharply.

"Why, that man Feodor the Monk. You know, up at Tashkent. The man who . . ."

Shere Khan turned his head sharply as his beloved friend groaned aloud.

"Oh, you thumb-footed ape, you bone-headed mule," said Wendover.

"Now, now, don't excite yourself, Gul Mahommed."

"You owl. You jungly son of a down-country jackal. You *bunnia* . . . Oh, my God!"

Wendover laughed feebly.

"What is it, Huzoor?"

"Why, in the name of Gehennum couldn't you have said so? You utter absolute . . ."

"But why? What does it matter, Sahib? What difference does it make?"

"Difference? The difference between a donation out of the Poor Box and a rope. A rope with a noose at the end of it. The difference between the magnificent public service of—er—*catching* the second most dangerous Russian spy in Asia, and just murdering a harmless and inoffensive shop-keeper."

"It was Feodor the Monk, Huzoor," said Shere Khan, a little puzzled. "He was disguised as a piece-goods seller. I went to buy a *lungi* for Bibi Jan. We had a bit of a wrangle, and just when I was going to hit him, I recognized him as the friend of the man who beat you. So I killed him."

"Yes, you killed him. And instead of telling me that you had qualified for the Order of Merit, you let me think it was for the gallows."

And again Wendover laughed.

"I don't want any Order of Merit," observed the mystified Shere Khan.

"No, and I don't think you'll get it now. It's a little bit late in the day."

"But not too late to give the authorities a new

version of the strange doings of Major Richard Wendover and the Battle of the Sudder Bazaar," he added.

"Huzoor?"

"Don't you see, you fool? The brainless, bone-
headed Police were butting in on a most delicate Secret
Service affair. There were we, quietly—*liquidating* I
think is the word—the most poisonous enemy of the
Sirkar, and the Police have to come and butt in and
make a public matter of it, a vulgar murder of it, a
common street brawl. Sickening."

"It is the way of the Police," observed Shere Khan
sententiously.

"Yes, entirely their fault, of course," smiled Wendover. . . .

"*Feodor the Monk!*" he groaned.

XVI

"Well, I suppose it is time I thought about the best way of getting back," said Sybil one evening, as she and the convalescent Wendover sat on the flat roof of his house in Khairabad Fort.

"Back? Back to what?"

"Peshawar."

"You are not going back to Peshawar."

"Why not?"

"Because I'm going to keep you here."

"You are going to keep me here, Dickie?"

"Yes."

"But . . . You are almost well now. I can't . . ."

"Oh, yes, you can, and oh, yes, you will, or I'll bring an action against you."

"An action for what?"

"Breach of promise. You promised to marry me."

"You don't want to marry me, Dickie," she said quietly, carefully controlling her voice.

"I didn't say I did."

"Do you?"

"No. I don't know that I want to marry you. But you get this quite clear in your young mind—you are not going back to Peshawar."

"What am I going to do then?"

"You are going to stay here."

"Stay with you always?"

"Always."

"All right, don't choke me," begged Wendover.

"Dickie, Dr. Bennell works other miracles besides those of healing."

"Eh?"

"He performs marriages as a side line."

"This seems to be your chance then. While I'm weak and defenceless."

"I asked you not to strangle me."

§2

"Do you love me, Dickie?"

"I don't know anything about that, but I like you about the place. I'm not going to let you out of my sight again, young Sybil."

§3

To the wedding came Ganesh Hazelrigg, with the intention of being best man, only to discover that Khan Shere Khan Khudadad Khan Hassan Ali Khan of Khairastan had no intention whatsoever of yielding that office to any man on earth. As he saw it, Khan or no Khan, he was Richard Wendover's man, his best man, his only man, and by his side he would stand at his wedding, as Wendover had stood at his.

"Why, of course," agreed Sybil. "Who's to give me away, if you are Dickie's best man?"

"I refuse to be married unless you give me away, Major Hazelrigg," she smiled, with greater earnestness and deeper feeling than she showed.

It was a genuine comfort to her that this solid stolid Englishman, so representative of all that was sane and normal and British, in spite of his fantastic and incredible way of life, should represent her father at this strange ceremony, this wedding held in the hall of a Border fortress; the parson dressed as a mendicant *sadhu*; her husband as a Pathan warrior; the best man, the Khan of Khairastan; her bridesmaids Pathan girls of the Khan's family, arrayed in purple and fine linen save for the satin trousers; everything so strange bizarre and dream-like.

And so with a radiant happiness and an ineffable gratitude to God who had brought this marvel about, she was married to Richard Wendover; and she knew that in his way, he loved her, loved her and wanted her.

His way might be different from the way of other men, but so was he different from other men—which was why she loved him so.

§4

The honeymoon was spent in Kashmir, in one of the loveliest spots in the whole world, a Paradise on earth; and to Sybil Ffoulkes was given the great reward of her great faithfulness.

EPILOGUE

And at the famous Durbar, when certain of the Great Ones journeyed to Khairastan, putting their trust in the good faith of Khan Shere Khan Khudadad Khan Hassan Ali Khan, it was finally and fully agreed that the Road should be driven through Khairastan, and that the Khan would guarantee the safety of the builders of the Road; and, after its completion, the safety of those who used it and passed along it upon their lawful occasions. Also, that the Khan of Khairabad would agree to the raising of a regiment to be known as the Khairastan Rifles, whose main business should be to guard the Road, in return for a handsome subsidy, much of which would necessarily go to their maintenance and up-keep.

All proposals made by His Excellency were readily and freely accepted by the Khan who, on his side, made one stipulation which the representative of the Government of His Majesty the King Emperor must accept, and to which he must agree, if the proceedings were to pass off without a hitch.

He must be allowed to nominate the officer commanding the Khairastan Rifles, and that officer must be allowed to choose his subordinates. In short, it must be a Pathan Regiment commanded by a Pathan and officered by Pathans.

To which His Excellency made reply that, provided the Khan's nominee were acceptable, the plan could certainly be given fair trial.

Whereupon Khan Shere Khan Khudadad Khan Hassan Ali Khan of Khairastan, rising to his feet, declared that the man he had in mind was his blood-brother and life-long friend, the Sirdar Gul Mahommed, who was at present the Wazir of Khairastan State.

And with no suggestion of a smile upon his sagacious face, the famous Major Bartholomew Hazelrigg

701

gave his strong support to the proposal, testifying that he had known the Sirdar Gul Mahommed for many years, that he was a soldier of great experience; and had, moreover, shown himself, in Khairastan State, to be a Wazir of marked ability.

Colonel Ormesby then, with serious mien, enquired whether such an appointment would be popular, and whether the body of Irregulars to be known as the Khairastan Rifles would welcome the appointment of the Sirdar Gul Mahommed to the post of Commandant.

"That point can be settled here and now," quoth the Khan, and advancing from his seat in the *shamiana*, he addressed the vast gathering of the tribesmen of Khairastan.

"Oh, men of Khairastan," boomed forth his great voice. "When our *pultan* is raised and we wear the uniform of the Khairastan Levies, receive our new rifles, occupy our new Forts above the Road, and are in all respects like a British Regiment, who shall be our Colonel?"

And with one heart and voice, with a roar that echoed from the hill-sides like the sound of the sea, came the answer:

"*Gul Mahommed!*"

THE END

Available P. C. Wren Titles
from
Riner Publishing Company

The Collected Short Stories

Volume One: ISBN 9780985032609
Volume Two: ISBN 9780985032616
Volume Three: ISBN 9780985032623
Volume Four: ISBN 9780985032630
Volume Five: ISBN 9780985032647

The Collected Novels

Volume One: *The Geste Novels*
   Part A: ISBN 9780985032678
   Part B: ISBN 9780985032685
Volume Two: *The Sinbad Novels*
   Part A: ISBN 9780692639382
   Part B: ISBN 9780692639429
Volume Three: *The Foreign Legion Novels*
   Part A: ISBN 9780999074909
   Part B: ISBN 9780999074916
Volume Four: *The Earlier India Novels*
   Part A: ISBN 9780999074923
   Part B: ISBN 9780999074930
Volume Five: *The Later India Novels*
   Part A: ISBN 9780999074947
   Part B: ISBN 9780999074954
Volume Six: *The English Novels*
   Part A: ISBN 9780999074961
   Part B: ISBN 9780999074978
Volume Seven: *A Mixed Bag of Novels*
   Part A: ISBN 9780999074985
   Part B: ISBN 9780999074992

Further information can be found at
rinerpublishing.wordpress.com